全新！NEW TOEIC

新多益閱讀題庫解析

All Fresh

新鮮直送
不添加
無效題

解答本

別擔心多益考題更新，我翻新、你放心！

Hackers Academia／著

目錄

本書特色

01 反映出新多益最新出題方向及難易度的實戰模擬書

完整地分析新多益的題目，以能夠反映出新多益出題方向及難易度的模擬問題所組成。透過練習比起模擬考試更具真實性的題目，學習者能夠自然且確實的累積實力，並於真實考試中完全發揮。

02 為了能夠完美地準備多益，收錄大量的豐富題型

10 回 1000 題的新多益閱讀測驗考卷，大量地收錄了在實際測驗中的所有題型，讓學習者能充分練習，並透過練習，實質上提升對於多益閱讀問題的解題能力。

03 最詳細明瞭的解題分析，提升成績如虎添翼！

詳盡清晰、簡單明瞭的解題分析，是提升成績的最佳幫手！本書提供完整試題分析，除了精準的中文翻譯，讓考生能夠輕鬆了解題意、掌握題目核心，也提供如考題類型說明、題目講解、換句話說、易考單字等詳細解析。

04 免費提供單字記憶 MP3

為了方便讀者記憶單字，本書將每一個題目列舉出的單字錄製成 MP3 光碟，MP3 以「美式腔調→英式／澳洲式腔調→中文意義」方式循環，讀者不但可以用聽的記單字，還能比較熟悉的美式腔調與其他腔調有甚麼不同之處，提升英文聽力的敏感度。

05 提供個別學習計畫

可以透過第一回的作題結果，選擇多樣的個別學習計畫。個別學習計畫是經過許多考生的經驗精密的安排，是極具參考價值與實踐性的學習計畫表，提供給想透過《全新！NEW TOEIEC 新多益閱讀題庫解析》加強實力的學習者能夠自由的利用。只要按照計畫表照表操課，絕對能大幅提升多益實力。

06 為達成高得分的自我檢測系統

超越單純的學習教科書，為了使學習者能夠自我設定目標並達成，本書建立一套自我檢測系統。請於教材首頁寫下目標得分，結束測試後檢測自我的解題方式，在該測試的最後一頁填寫自我檢測清單，使學習者直到最後一回也能謹記自己的目標。

07 準確的量化試算

沒有分數對照表的新多益模擬測驗卷，題目做了等於沒做，因為沒有辦法將答對題數量化成分數，是無法清楚地了解自己的實力所在，本書經由許多考生實測統計的分數對照表，可以清楚的標示您在實際多益考試上可能的成績。

08 自學、教課兩相宜的新多益教材

除了詳盡的解說方便自學者外，本書的雙書裝也十分方便老師授課，老師們可以用未附答案與詳解的題目本來實施課後的模擬測驗，另外在解說本未提到的部分進行補充。

頁面說明

2 題目的線索

Questions 157-159 refer to the following information.

157-159 根據下面的資訊回答問題。 ← **1 翻譯**

The ALL NEW Dockland Split Type Air Conditioner (BA501)

157-D Committed to producing energy-efficient products, Dockland Electronics has created the BA501, a new split type air conditioner with features designed to conserve power without compromising efficiency.

158-D Speed Cooling
This function allows the unit to reach preset temperatures in a short time.

158-A Temperature Equalizer
This function enables the unit to cool areas evenly by using dual-direction air vent technology.

158-C Sleep Mode
This function decreases the cooling temperature after the unit's first two hours of operation and maintains the room temperature for the next five hours before 158-C it automatically shuts off the unit.

The BA501 is equipped with a patented refrigerant and has a Seasonal Energy Efficiency Ratio (SEER) rating of 14. 159-D SEER measures the energy efficiency of air conditioners.

全新的 Dockland
分離式冷氣機（BA501） ← **1 翻譯**

157-D Dockland 電子致力於生產節約能源的產品，創造了 BA501 這種新式的分離式冷氣機，具有節省電力卻不影響效能的特殊設計。 ← **2 題目的線索**

158-D 快速降溫
這個功能讓冷氣機在短時間內就能達到預設的溫度。

158-A 溫度均勻
這項功能使用雙向出風口的技術讓冷氣機能夠使受冷範圍的溫度均勻。

158-C 睡眠模式
這個功能讓冷氣機運轉兩個小時後減少降溫，使冷氣機在五小時後 158-C 自動關機前能保持室內溫度。

BA501 配備專利冷卻劑，並獲得季節能源效率比（SEER）值 14，159-D SEER 是用來測量冷氣機的節能效果。

3 單字 — 單字
- commit v. 做，致力
- efficiency n. 效能，效率
- evenly ad. 均勻，平等地
- patented a. 專利的
- conserve v. 珍惜，保存
- allow v. 使可能
- maintain v. 維持
- rating n. 等級，排名
- compromise v. 連累，妥協
- enable v. 讓～能夠
- be equipped with phr. 配備，具有
- measure v. 測定，測量

157

What is mentioned about the Dockland Electronics product?
(A) It is powered by alternative energy.
(B) It obtains high market sales.
(C) It is made of durable materials.
(D) It consumes less electricity.

關於 Dockland 電器公司的產品文中提到了什麼？ ← **1 翻譯**
(A) 它是由替代能源供給電力的。
(B) 它擁有很高的市場銷售率。
(C) 它使用耐久的材料製造。
(D) 它消耗較少的電力。

4 題目分類 — Not/True True 問題

解答 (D) ← **7 簡答**

5 解析 — 本題是要在文章中找到與本問題的重點 the Dockland Electronics product 相關的內容後，比較選項與文章的 Not/True 問題。(A) (B) (C) 都是在文章中沒提到的內容。(D) Committed to producing energy-efficient products, Dockland Electronics has created the BA501 ~ with features designed to conserve power without compromising efficiency. 是指致力於開發高能源效率產品的 Dockland Electronics，設計出擁有不但不破壞效率，也節約電力等功能的 BA501。因此 (D) It consumes less electricity. 是正確答案。

6 換句話說 — 換句話說
energy-efficient 高能源效率 → consumes less electricity 消耗較少電力

3 單字 — 單字 alternative a. 替代的 obtain v. 保有，拿到 durable a. 耐久的 consume a. 消耗

1. 翻譯

為了幫助考生完整的理解題目以及與題目相關的文章，本書將所有的英文部分翻譯成中文，而在 Part 7 的部分，也將可以提示文章種類的問題說明也翻譯出來，因此可以一目瞭然的知道接下來所要看的文章屬於哪種類型。

2. 題目的線索

文章中與正確答案相關的重要線索的部分，以及這個部分的翻譯都會用另一種顏色來表示，讓讀者可以方便查詢。在閱讀解析前，請先看一遍這個部分，試著選出正確的選項，用這樣的方法再練習一次。

3. 單字

單字的列表可以讓讀者在閱讀問題及解析時省去大量翻閱字典的時間，請將文章與問題裡面出現的單字、片語它們的意義及詞性一併記憶下來。

4. 題目分類

將所有的問題全部細分為不同的種類，隨著問題的種類不同會有不一樣的慣性解題法，這些慣性的解法在《全新！NEW TOEIC 新多益閱讀題庫大全》都有詳盡的解說，想要針對特定種類的問題追加學習時，可以多加參考。

5. 解析

了解題目的種類後，會有基本解法的提示，並且針對正確答案及其他選項作說明，讓讀者徹底了解答案正確的理由及其他選項錯誤的理由，此外若有其他讀者需要知道的必要知識，也會詳加說明。

6. 換句話說

當文章的內容在題目當中以另外一種表達方式呈現時，會將這種「換句話說」的表現方式特別列出來。為了在下一次出現相似問題時能夠活用，讓相似問題可以迅速地獲得解答，每一題「換句話說」的表現方式煩請一一確認。

7. 簡答

每個問題簡單的正確答案就在「題目分類」的同一行，完成測驗對答案時，在確認了「簡答」跟「題目分類」後，立刻可以往下閱讀解析。

多益簡介及試場 Tips

什麼是多益？

TOEIC 是 Test Of English for International Communication 的縮寫，是針對非英語母語人士，著重於語言基本溝通能力的測驗，目的是評量日常生活與國際事務等方面的實用英語能力。因為是評量日常生活與商業環境中所需的英語能力，所以內容主要包括以下的實用主題。

- 合作開發：研究，產品開發
- 財務會計：借貸，投資，稅金，會計，銀行業務
- 一般事務：預約，協商，行銷，販賣
- 技術領域：電器，工業技術，電腦，實驗室
- 事務領域：會議，文書工作
- 物品採購：購物，產品訂購，費用支付

- 飲食：餐廳，聚餐，晚宴
- 文化：劇場，體育，郊遊
- 健康：醫療保險，醫院診療，牙科
- 製造：生產線，工廠經營
- 員工：錄用，退休，發薪，晉升，職缺
- 住宅：不動產，搬遷，企業用地

多益測驗的結構

領域	題型	題數	時間	配分
Listening Test 聽力測驗	Part 1 照片描述	10 題（1~10 題）	45 分鐘	495 分
	Part 2 應答問題	30 題（11~40 題）		
	Part 3 簡短對話	30 題（41~70 題）		
	Part 4 簡短獨白	30 題（71~100 題）		
Reading Test 閱讀測驗	Part 5 單句填空（文法 / 語彙）	40 題（101~140 題）	75 分鐘	495 分
	Part 6 短文填空（文法 / 語彙）	12 題（141~152 題）		
	Part 7 閱讀文章（理解）	單篇文章＝ 28 題（153~180 題） 雙篇文章＝ 20 題（181~200 題）		
總計	7 種題型	200 題	120 分鐘	990 分

1. 報名

- 測驗日期與報名期間，請參見官方網站 www.toeic.com.tw。
- 一般報名期間結束後，如果還有剩餘的名額，會開放追加報名。可追加報名的場次與追加報名期間，請參照官方網站公告。
- 網路報名是最方便的報名方式，只要登入網站，進入報名網頁並填寫資料即可。報名後，可以用信用卡、超商代收、ATM 轉帳等方式繳費。
- 請注意照片檔案必須符合網站中公告的標準，以 jpg 或 gif 格式上傳。

2. 考試當天應該準備的物品

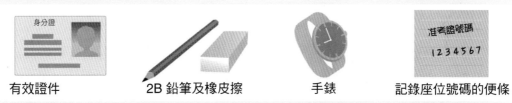

| 有效證件 | 2B 鉛筆及橡皮擦 | 手錶 | 記錄座位號碼的便條 |

*有效證件包括身分證正本或有效期限內的護照正本。未滿 14 歲者，可以用有照片的健保 IC 卡代替。因為不寄發准考證，所以要自己記錄座位號碼，依照號碼入座。

3. 測驗注意事項

- 測驗 15 分鐘前必須入場，遲到者不得入場應試，也不接受因為遲到而申請退費。
- 進入試場前，必須將行動電話、手錶等各類電子用品關閉（不得發出聲響）。在監試人員宣布可離開試場前，必須保持關機，否則以違規論，成績不予計分，且不得要求退費或延期。
- 測驗途中不休息。未經許可，不可中途離場或交卷。
- 台灣主辦單位規定，不可以在試題本或其他物品上抄寫題目、答案、劃線或作任何記號，否則視為違規，成績不予計分。

4. 成績查詢

- 測驗結束 19 天後，就可以在官方網站 www.toeic.com.tw 查詢成績。開放查詢成績的期間，請以網站公告為準。
- 紙本成績單大約會在測驗結束的 15 個工作天後寄出。
- 成績單寄發後，就可以在官方網站申請製作多益證書，或者補發成績單。多益證書大約需要 15 個工作天，補發成績單需要 10 個工作天。

各題型與解題策略

Part 5 單句填空（40 題）

- 在四個選項中選擇適合填入句內空格的題型，考驗考生的文法以及單字語彙能力。
- 理想解題時間：20 分鐘（每題約 25~30 秒）

題型

1. 文法

101. Carla Bourne is compiling a _____ list of people to invite to the opening ceremony.
  (A) completion   (B) complete   (C) completely   (D) completeness

解說 可以修飾名詞 list 的形容詞 (B) 是正確答案。

2. 語彙

102. S&W Limited regularly assess the market demand to stay ahead of the _____.
  (A) grade   (B) disagreement   (C) pursuit   (D) competition

解說 最適合「為了在___領先，S&W 公司定期性地評估市場需求」這個句意的單字是名詞 (D)。

解題策略

1. **先看選項掌握題目是文法問題或語彙問題。**
   看四個選項先掌握這題是要問文法、詞性，或是單字的意義。例如例題 101 的選項 completion, complete, completely, completeness 四個選項的詞性不盡相同，因此可以知道這是文法題。例題 102 則是 grade, disagreement, pursuit, competition 四個選項是相同的詞性，但意義不同的單字，因此可以知道這題是語彙題。

2. **隨著題型的不同，透過空格前後的文法構造或句意選擇正確答案。**
   文法題可以從空格前後的文法構造找出適合填在空格裡的答案。語彙題則是由句意來找出最適合填在空格裡的單字。

Part 6 短文填空（12 題）

- 在一篇短文內有 3 個空格需要被填入適合的文法詞性或單字。共有 4 篇短文填空。
- 理想解題時間：5 分鐘（每題約 20~25 秒）

題型

Questions 141-143 refer to the following e-mail.

I saw your advertisement for "get-to-know tours" in *Travel World* magazine, and I am interested in having your company arrange an _____ for me. I would like to visit

語彙 **141.** (A) agenda   (B) itinerary
                 (C) overnight   (D) outing

Europe again, but I must say that I was very _____ the first time I toured the continent.

語彙 **142.** (A) excited   (B) unprepared
               (C) disappointed   (D) refreshed

When my tour group traveled to eight cities in 14 days, there wasn't enough time to see the sights of the cities nor were we given personal time to go shopping or do individual sightseeing. For this reason, I would very much like to join a "get-to-know tour" for France and England. As I understand it, a tour package for these two countries _____ on only four cities. Can you give me more information on what the

文法 **143.** (A) to focus   (B) focusing
            (C) focus   (D) focuses

daily schedule will be like, and what spots will be visited? I look forward to hearing from you.

Annette Whitman

解說 141. 因為是邀請旅行社設計行程的內容，所以 (B) 是正確答案。

142. 在後面的文章提到第一次的歐洲旅行的觀光、購物時間不夠充分，可以看出作者對第一次旅行感到失望，所以要選 (C) 為正確答案。

143. 因為句子裡還缺乏動詞，可以知道正解應為 (C) 或 (D)。因為主詞是單數 a tour package，所以可以知道單數動詞 (D) 是正確答案。

解題策略

1. 先看選項掌握題目是文法問題或語彙問題。

與 Part 5 相同，可以先看四個選項掌握這題是要問文法、詞性，或是單字的意義。

2. 隨著問題的不同，可以透過空格該句、上下文，或是短文整體來選擇正確答案。

Part 6 不只會出只需透過與空格同句即能判斷答案的問題，也會出需要看完整篇短文的問題。因此當看完空格所在的句子還無法判斷出答案時，上下文，或看完整篇短文對於選擇正確答案也有幫助。

Part 7 閱讀文章（48 題）

- 閱讀文章並選出與題目最適當的選項為正確答案，考驗考生對文章的理解力。
- 構成：Single Passage 有 28 題，Double Passage 有 20 題。
- 理想解題時間：50 分鐘（每篇約 3 分 30 秒~4 分鐘）

題型

1. 單篇文章（Single Passage）

Questions 153-154 refer to the following advertisement.

DOWNTOWN OFFICE SPACE NOW AVAILABLE!

Everdeen Towers, located in the heart of Halifax's financial district, has office space currently for rent at $2800 per month. Details are below:

- 220 square meters
- Located on the eighth floor with elevator service
- Includes access to parking facility
- 24-hour guard service
- 12-hour daily reception service
- Includes one conference room, six private offices, and restroom facilities

Those interested in viewing the unit may call building administrator Denise Allen at (902) 555-8343.

---

153. What is NOT mentioned about the advertised unit?
(A) It has a room for meetings.
(B) It is accessible by elevator.
(C) It was recently renovated.
(D) It provides guard service.

154. How can potential tenants visit the space?
(A) By sending a message to Denise Allen
(B) By making a telephone call
(C) By going to the administrative office
(D) By contacting a real estate agency

解說 153. 因為文內沒有提及此商辦大樓最近修繕過，因此正確解答是 (C)。

154. 因為文中提及想參觀辦公室可以打電話聯絡（Those interested in viewing the unit may call），因此正確解答是 (B)。

2. 雙篇文章（Double passage）

Questions 181-185 refer to the following e-mails.

TO: Laurel Smith <laurith@geoforce.com>
FROM: Gloria Lopez <glopez@geoforce.com>
SUBJECT: Banquet Plans
DATE: June 9
Hi Laurel,
I've been working on the arrangements for the company's annual banquet taking place next month. I first called the hotel you recommended, but unfortunately they are fully booked on the date I requested. I did find three other possible venues, however. The new Italian restaurant Bellagio in Bayview has a large function hall and is available. Also, I contacted the Pemberton Hotel and they have an opening on that day. The third option is to take a dinner cruise on The Frisco Queen. The boat is large enough for everyone and they also provide entertainment.
All the establishments say they are willing to prepare vegetarian options and supply full bar service. However, Bellagio does not have its own parking facilities, so that could be problematic.
Anyway, let me know what you think of the options. But please give me your preferences as soon as possible, as the venues may not be available for long.
Gloria

TO: Gloria Lopez <glopez@geoforce.com>
FROM: Laurel Smith <laurith@geoforce.com>
SUBJECT: Re: Banquet Plans
DATE: June 10
Gloria,
Thanks for the information. It's a shame the Oroville Hotel wasn't available as they serve such excellent food. But I appreciate you finding other choices. I looked at all the venues online, and think the third option is best. It is a little pricier than the other choices, but I think it would be fun to do something different. Go ahead and make the reservation.
Laurel

181. Why did Ms. Lopez write the e-mail?
- (A) To reserve a facility for an event
- (B) To provide a selection of venue options
- (C) To inquire about attendance to a banquet
- (D) To request menu preferences

182. In the first e-mail, the word "opening" in paragraph 1, line 5 is closest in meaning to
- (A) entrance
- (B) vacancy
- (C) position
- (D) facility

183. Which facility did Ms. Lopez first contact?
- (A) Bellagio
- (B) Pemberton Hotel
- (C) The Frisco Queen
- (D) Oroville Hotel

184. What is NOT offered by Bellagio restaurant?
- (A) Beverage service
- (B) Meatless options
- (C) A parking facility
- (D) An event room

185. What is suggested about The Frisco Queen?
- (A) It is not available on the date requested.
- (B) It costs more than the other options.
- (C) It isn't large enough to accommodate the group.
- (D) It was recommended by Ms. Smith.

解說 181. 因為在第一封郵件中說了找到三個適合舉辦公司聚會的場所後，還對各場所作了說明，所以 (B) 是正確答案。

182. 在包含了 opening 的句子 the Pemberton Hotel ~ have an opening on that day 裡，opening 被拿來指沒有被預約的「空位」。因此要選擇有「空位」、「空席」等意思的 (B)。

183. 在第一封郵件中 Ms. Lopez 說第一家找到的飯店預約都滿了，第二封郵件中則說無法預約的那家飯店式 Orovile 飯店，因此要選擇 (D) 為正確答案。

184. 因為在第一封郵件中說到 Belagio 沒有停車服務，因此正確答案為 (C)。

185. 第一封郵件中提到 The Frisco Queen 是第三個選項，因為第二封郵件說第三個選項與其他選項比起來稍微貴一點，所以要選 (B) 為正確答案。

解題策略

1. 確認文章的主題，猜測文章大概的內容。

就像閱讀 Questions 153-154 refer to the following advertisement 後，可以猜測這是為了宣傳某種東西的文章，透過分析文章的種類或題目，可以猜測出這篇文章是在講述什麼內容。

2. 閱讀問題後找出問題的重點，並在文章裡找出關於正確答案的線索。

掌握了問題的重點後，在文章裡搜尋提到問題重點的部分，並詳讀此部分抓出線索。如果是 Double Passage，當無法在一篇文章裡馬上找到足夠的線索時，可以在另一篇文章裡尋找線索，再將兩個線索綜合並解答。

3. 選擇提到線索的選項或將線索用其他表達方式換句話說的選項。

選項中，如果提到了線索的部分，或是把線索的部分用「換句話說」的方式來表達，就有可能是正確的答案

個別學習計畫

完成第一回之後,可以選擇與自己的換算分數相對的學習計畫來學習。也可搭配參考書《全新！NEW TOICE 新多益閱讀題庫大全》來準備多益考試。

*閱讀分數換算表在題目本的第 289 頁。

2 週完成的學習計畫—400 分以上

2 週期間每天完成一回測驗的深入學習。

	Day 1	Day 2	Day 3	Day 4	Day 5
Week 1	完成第一回 深入學習	完成第二回 深入學習	完成第三回 深入學習	完成第四回 深入學習	完成第五回 深入學習
Week 2	完成第六回 深入學習	完成第七回 深入學習	完成第八回 深入學習	完成第九回 深入學習	完成第十回 深入學習

3 週完成的學習計畫—300~395 分

3 週期間第一天、第二天完成一回,並作深入理解學習,第三天則兩回一併複習。

	Day 1	Day 2	Day 3	Day 4	Day 5
Week 1	完成第一回 深入學習	完成第二回 深入學習	第一回& 第二回 復習	完成第三回 深入學習	完成第四回 深入學習
Week 2	第三回& 第四回 復習	完成第五回 深入學習	完成第六回 深入學習	第五回& 第六回 復習	完成第七回 深入學習
Week 3	完成第八回 深入學習	第七回& 第八回 復習	完成第九回 深入學習	完成第十回 深入學習	第九回& 第十回 復習

4 週完成的學習計畫—295 分以下

4 週期間，兩天完成一回測驗，並作深入的理解學習。

	Day 1	Day 2	Day 3	Day 4	Day 5
Week 1	完成第一回	第一回 深入學習	完成第二回	第二回 深入學習	完成第三回
Week 2	第三回 深入學習	完成第四回	第四回 深入學習	完成第四回	第五回 深入學習
Week 3	完成第六回	第六回 深入學習	完成第七回	第七回 深入學習	完成第八回
Week 4	第八回 深入學習	完成第九回	第九回 深入學習	完成第十回	第十回 深入學習

本書的其他活用法

1. 不須按照計畫，但要以實際考試的心態完成每一回。

2. 評分後，利用解析進行深入學習，老師也能做深入補充。
錯誤的問題或覺得較難的問題要透過解說再次仔細的確認。再以單字 MP3 來複習每回的單字。以此書為教材時，老師也可以做更深入的補充說明。

與《全新！NEW TOICE 新多益閱讀題庫大全》一起搭配的學習方法

1. 結束《全新！NEW TOICE 新多益閱讀題庫大全》「4 週學習計畫」中的第一週後，在兩天內完成本書的第一、第二回測驗，請好好利用時間較多的六日假期。

2. 結束測試後評分並進行深入學習。錯的問題或感到困難的問題可以參考解說，把握並理解正確的意義，再分析正確或錯誤的選項。一定要記住的內容要做筆記整理，利用 MP3 複習每回的單字內容。

3. 第二週的第三回、第四回，第三週的第五回、第六回也利用以上方法來學習。

4. 結束第四週的學習後，當作是要整理目前為止所學習的內容，用實際參加考試的心態來寫第七回至第十回。

5. 完成所有回數後，需要總整理答錯的問題，利用 MP3 複習所有回數的單字，為這次的學習做收尾的動作。

TEST 01

PART 5

101

Keynote speaker Melanie Allen will send the draft of _____ speech to the events committee on Thursday.
(A) she　　(B) hers　　(C) her　　(D) herself

特邀講員 Melanie Allen 將會在星期四把她演講的草稿寄給大會活動委員會。

■ 人稱代名詞　　　　　　　　　　　　　　　　　　　　　　　　　　解答 (C)

因為要選擇可以像形容詞一樣修飾名詞 speech 的人稱代名詞所有格，所以應該選 (C) her 為正確答案。人稱代名詞 (A)、所有格代名詞 (B)、反身代名詞 (D) 都無法修飾名詞。

單字 keynote speaker n. 特邀演講者　draft n. 草稿　committee n. 委員會

102

Should customers need additional _____ about the features of the company's appliances, they may call our toll-free number to speak to a technician.
(A) inform　　　　　　　　(B) informs
(C) information　　　　　　(D) informed

如果顧客需要更多關於公司家電產品特色的資訊，他們可以打免付費電話給技術人員。

■ 名詞的位置　　　　　　　　　　　　　　　　　　　　　　　　　　解答 (C)

因為受形容詞 additional 修飾的應該是名詞，所以 (C) information（資訊）才是正確答案。動詞 (A) 和 (B) 及動詞兼副詞的 (D) 則無法被形容詞修飾。另外，在此句中 Should customers need~ 是假設句，是從「If customers should + 動詞原形（need）」這句裡面，省略 if，把 customers 跟 should 倒裝的句型。

單字 additional a. 額外的　feature n. 特色　appliance n. 家電用品　toll-free a. 免費的

103

Please fill out the enclosed customer data sheet _____ we can let you know about our latest offerings and promotions.
(A) instead of　　　　　　(B) as much as
(C) so that　　　　　　　(D) as well as

請填寫隨信附上的顧客資料表，以便我們能讓您知道最新的產品與促銷訊息。

■ 副詞子句連接詞 目的　　　　　　　　　　　　　　　　　　　　　解答 (C)

因為本句的主要句子 Please fill out ~ sheet 已是完整的句子，可以把 ___ we can let ~ 視為附加資訊。因為此附加資訊裡有動詞 can let，可知為副詞子句，因此能引導副詞子句的連接詞 (B) 和 (C) 才是可能的答案。從「為了能夠傳送新產品的發行及促銷資訊，請填寫顧客資料表」的文意裡，可以知道 (C) so that（以便~）是正確答案。如果使用 (B) as much as（多到~）句意扭曲為「請填寫多到我們可以傳送新產品的發行和促銷資訊的顧客資料表」。介系詞 (A) instead of（~為了取代）無法帶領一個句子，如果是用對等連接詞 as well as（不只~也~）的話，會變成「不只傳送新產品的發行資訊和促銷活動，也請填寫顧客資料表」這樣奇怪的句子。

單字 enclosed a. 附上的　latest a. 最新的　offering n. 商品；供奉；貢獻　promotion n. 促銷，宣傳

104

Ms. Darcy is searching _____ office space with a capacity of at least 50 staff members.
(A) at　　(B) to　　(C) from　　(D) for

Darcy 小姐在尋找一個能容納五十名員工的辦公室空間。

■ 動詞片語　　　　　　　　　　　　　　　　　　　　　　　　　　　解答 (D)

空格前的動詞 search 是「找~」的意思，與其相對應的介系詞 (D) for 是正確答案。（search for：找~）。(A) at 意思是「在，處於」，表示視角或地點。(B) to 是「往~」的意思，(C) from 是「從~」的意思表示出發地或出處。也可以另外背下 look / seek for（找~）等片語。

單字 capacity n. 容量　staff n. 職員

105

Milkins Corporation will negotiate a two-year employment _____ with the former vice president of BG Holdings. (A) arrangement (B) arrangeable (C) arranged (D) arranger	Milkins 公司將要和 BG 控股公司的前副總裁商議一份為期兩年的工作合約。

■ 人物名詞 vs. 抽象名詞　　　　　　　　　　　　　　　　　　　　　　　　　　　解答 (A)

因為是可以同時接在「冠詞＋形容詞（a two-year）」的後面，並作為及物動詞 negotiate 受詞的名詞，所以 (A) 和 (D) 都可能是答案。在空格前面有 employment，所以抽象名詞 (A) arrangement（契約，協定）才是正確答案，表示「兩年雇用契約」。如果選擇人物名詞 (D) arranger（準備人員，編曲家）就會變成「商議一位兩年雇用的準備人員」這樣奇怪的句子。形容詞 (B) 和動詞 (C) 則無法出現在名詞的位置。如果把 (C) 視為可以修飾名詞 employment 的詞也會變成「與前副總裁一起協商的兩年雇用」這樣奇怪的句子。

單字 corporation n. 社團法人，公司　negotiate v. 商議，洽談　employment n. 雇用　former a. 前任的，之前的　vice president phr. 副總裁　arrangeable a. 可準備的

106

To apply for a library card, please proceed to the circulation desk _____ the second floor and present valid identification. (A) against (B) as (C) beside (D) on	要申請圖書證，請至二樓的流通櫃檯，並出示有效的身分證件。

■ 選擇介系詞 場所　　　　　　　　　　　　　　　　　　　　　　　　　　　　　解答 (D)

為了完成「在二樓的流通櫃檯」這個句子，可以放在 the second floor 前面的介系詞應該要表現出在表面上的意思，因此 (D) on 是正確答案。(A) against 是「在～對面，反抗」的意思，是表示意見或物品被放置的狀態，(B) as 是「當～」的意思表示身分或資格，(C) beside 則是「在～旁邊」的意思，表示方位。

單字 apply for phr. 申請　proceed to phr. 繼續下去，往　circulation desk phr. 流通櫃檯　present v. 展示，提交　valid a. 有效的　identification n. 身分證件，一體感，識別

107

As part of their _____ routine, the mechanical department conducts maintenance inspections on factory equipment. (A) normality (B) normally (C) normal (D) normalize	作為他們正常例行工作的一部分，機械部門對工廠的設備做了維修檢測。

■ 形容詞的位置　　　　　　　　　　　　　　　　　　　　　　　　　　　　　　　解答 (C)

因為要修飾在空格後的名詞 routine，所以形容詞 (C) normal（普通的）是正確答案。名詞 (A)、副詞 (B)、動詞 (D) 都無法修飾名詞。

單字 routine n. 日常，例行事務　conduct v. 實施　maintenance n. 維修，維持　inspection n. 檢測，調查　equipment n. 設備，裝備，用品

108

Organized by the Confectioners Society, the first Vale Confectionery Trade Fair will be _____ at the Anderson Assembly Hall from November 5 to 9. (A) grown (B) held (C) passed (D) appeared	由糕餅協會所組織的第一屆 Vale 糕餅貿易展將於 11 月 5 日至 9 日在 Anderson 大會堂舉行。

■ 動詞語彙　　　　　　　　　　　　　　　　　　　　　　　　　　　　　　　　　解答 (B)

因為文意是「展覽在 Anderson 大會堂舉行」，因此與空格前的 be 動詞連接成為被動式的動詞 hold（舉行，舉辦）的 p.p.形 (B) held 是正確答案。(A) 的 grow 是「長大」，(C) 的 pass 是「通過」，(D) 的 appear 是「出現」的意思。

單字 confectioner n. 糕餅，做糕餅的人

109

During the morning session of the program on well-being, a speaker will explain the benefits ＿＿＿＿ various teas.

(A) by　　　　(B) for　　　　(C) of　　　　(D) at

在健康研討會的早上時段中，講員將會說明各種茶對健康的益處。

■ 選擇介系詞 of　　　　　　　　　　　　　　　　　　　　　解答 (C)

因為要寫成「茶的益處」，所以在 benefits ＿＿ various teas 這裡 (C) of（～的）是正確答案。(A) by 是「到～」的意思，可以說明截止的時間點，或以「因為～，藉著～」的意思來說明方法或手段。(B) for 是「為了～」或「往～」的意思說明目標或方向，(D) at 是「在，處於」的意思，說明時間或場所。

110

Relations between Lune Hospital and Alma Healthcare have become ＿＿＿＿ ever since they organized a fundraiser together.

(A) friendlily　　　　　　(B) friendlier
(C) friendliness　　　　　(D) friendliest

自從 Lune 醫院與 Alma 醫療協會一起籌備了一場募款活動後，他們之間的關係變得更友好了。

■ 名詞補語 vs. 形容詞補語　　　　　　　　　　　　　　　解答 (B)

因為動詞 become 是需要主詞補語的動詞，因此可以當作補語使用的形容詞比較級 (B)、最高級 (D)、名詞 (C) 都可能是正確答案。因為本句意思為「Lune 醫院和 Alma Healthcare 醫療協會的關係變得更加友好」，因此形容詞 friendly（親近的）的比較級 (B) friendlier 是正確答案。如果要選擇形容詞的最高級 (D)，至少需要三個比較的對象才可以，但是此句中只有兩個比較的對象（募款活動前及募款活動後），因此無法選擇 (D)。如果選名詞 (C) friendliness（友情，親善）的話，主詞補語和主詞 Relations 同格，變成「關係變成友情」這種奇怪的句子。副詞 (A) 無法被放到補語的位置。

單字 organize v. 組織，準備　fundraiser n. 資金籌集人，募款活動

111

＿＿＿＿ newly hired technical support representatives are required to undergo a complete physical examination.

(A) All　　　　　　　　(B) Either
(C) Another　　　　　　(D) Much

所有新進的技術支援員工們都被要求接受全面的健康檢查。

■ 表示數量　　　　　　　　　　　　　　　　　　　　　　解答 (A)

因為複數可數名詞 representatives 前有空格，所以選可以放在複數可數名詞前的 (A) All（所有）為正確解答。(B) Either 意思是「兩者中的一個」，要作為限定詞使用時須使用單數可數名詞，和 or（～或）一起寫為相關連接詞 either A or B（A 或 B 中的一個）。(C) Another 要放在單數名詞前，(D) Much 則是放在不可數名詞前。

單字 representative n. 職員，代表　undergo v. 遭受，受到　complete physical examination phr. 全面身體檢查

112

The company has grown so much that it is running out of ＿＿＿＿ and will need to move to a bigger office.

(A) area　　　　　　　　(B) land
(C) room　　　　　　　　(D) location

該公司的成長已經大到空間不足的程度，而且需要搬到更大的辦公室。

■ 名詞語彙　　　　　　　　　　　　　　　　　　　　　　解答 (C)

是「空間不足且要搬到更大的辦公室」的句意，所以 (C) room（空間）是正確答案。(A) area 是「地域，區域」，(B) land 是「土地，地」，(D) location 是「位置」的意思。另外，run out 和介系詞 of 一起組成 run out of（～不足，～用完了）的形態是經常使用的片語。

113

| Ghyll Precision Industry's service department is known for finishing repairs _____ and in an efficient manner.
(A) noticeably　　　　(B) promptly
(C) indirectly　　　　(D) equally | Ghyll Precision 工業的服務部門以用高效率的方法迅速地完成維修而聞名。 |

■ 副詞語彙　　　　　　　　　　　　　　　　　　　　　　　　　　　　　　　解答 (B)

句意是「以迅速且有效率的方式完成維修」，因此副詞 (B) promptly（迅速地，即時地）是正確答案。(A) noticeably 是「顯眼地，顯著地」，(C) indirectly 是「間接性地」，(D) equally 是「一致地，相同地」的意思。

單字 be known for phr. 因為～而聞名　manner n. 方式

114

| The event staff will need to be at the conference venue an hour _____ everyone else to prepare.
(A) in between　　　　(B) provided
(C) until　　　　(D) ahead of | 活動人員必須要在其他人員準備前的一小時來到會場。 |

■ 修飾語「片語」與修飾語「子句」的不同　　　　　　　　　　　　　　　　　解答 (D)

本句內已有結構完整的主要子句 The event staff will need to be at the conference venue，因此我們要把 ____ everyone else to prepare 看作修飾語。因為此修飾語是沒有動詞的修飾語，因此可以領導一個修飾語片語的 (C) 和 (D) 都是可能的答案。依照「比其他人提早一個小時到達」的意思，(D) ahead of（比～先，比～提前）才是正確答案。如果選擇 (C) until（直到～），意思將會不完整。副詞 (A) in between（在中間，兩者之間）無法領導修飾語，從屬連接詞 (B) provided（如果～的話）不能領導「片語」，而是領導「子句」。

單字 conference n. 會議　venue n. 場所　prepare v. 準備

115

| The inexperienced accountant _____ recorded the CEO's personal trip to London as a company expense.
(A) mistaking　　　　(B) mistaken
(C) mistakenly　　　　(D) to mistake | 這個沒有經驗的會計師將公司執行長到倫敦的個人行程誤植為公司的一筆支出。 |

■ 副詞的位置　　　　　　　　　　　　　　　　　　　　　　　　　　　　　解答 (C)

因為要修飾動詞 recorded，所以應該選擇副詞 (C) mistakenly（不小心的）作為正確答案。現在分詞或動名詞 (A)，過去分詞 (B)，to 不定詞 (D) 都無法修飾動詞。

單字 inexperienced a. 缺少經驗的，不熟悉的　accountant n. 會計師　expense n. 費用，支出
　　mistaken a. 判斷錯誤的，做錯的

116

| Gift certificates will be given to those _____ complete Oriang Health Spa's service survey by July 18.
(A) who　　(B) they　　(C) what　　(D) theirs | 禮券將會發給在 7 月 18 日前完成 Oriang Health Spa 服務調查的人。 |

■ 關係子句的位置與寫法　　　　　　　　　　　　　　　　　　　　　　　　解答 (A)

本句的主要子句 Gift certificates will be given 已經是完整子句，因此要將 ____ complete ～ July 18 視為修飾語。因為此修飾語是在指示代名詞 those 之後的關係子句，因此正確答案為 (A) who。代名詞 (B)，名詞子句從屬連接詞 (C)，所有代格名詞 (D) 都無法被放到關係代名詞的位置。另外，those who 意為「那些～的人」，是很常使用的表現方式。

單字 gift certificate phr. 禮券　complete n. 完成　survey n. （問券）調查

117

Ms. Sofia Davis, president of Green Habitat Society, led an _____ lecture about the impact of global warming on the world's ecosystems. (A) instructs　　(B) instructionally (C) instruct　　(D) instructive	Green 棲息地協會主席 Sofia Davis 女士主導了一場有教育意義的演講，是關於全球暖化對於世界生態系統的影響。

■ 形容詞的位置　　　　　　　　　　　　　　　　　　　　　　　　　　　　解答 (D)

在不定冠詞 an 跟名詞 lecture 的中間應該要放入形容詞來修飾名詞，因此 (D) instructive（有教育意義的，有啟發性的）是正確答案。動詞 (A) 和 (C)，副詞 (B) 都無法修飾名詞。

單字 president n. 會長，主席，社長　lecture n. 講義，演講　impact n. 影響，效果　global warming phr. 全球暖化　ecosystem n. 生態系統　instruct v. 指示，教導

118

The objective of the Bogota International Forum is to help South American countries _____ better diplomatic ties. (A) advise　　(B) develop (C) happen　　(D) mention	Bogota 國際論壇的目的是為了幫助南美洲國家發展更佳的外交關係。

■ 動詞語彙　　　　　　　　　　　　　　　　　　　　　　　　　　　　　　解答 (B)

因為句意為「發展更佳的外交關係」，因此選擇 (B) develop（發展）。(A) advise 是「建議，忠告」，(C) happen 是「發生」，(D) mention 是「言及」的意思。

單字 objective n. 目標　diplomatic a. 外交的

119

Because of Mr. Doyle's busy schedule today, his meeting with the personnel director about organizing employee interviews was _____. (A) released　　(B) isolated (C) canceled　　(D) expired	因為 Doyle 先生今天的行程很忙，把原本要和人事主任討論安排員工訪談時間的會議取消了。

■ 動詞語彙　　　　　　　　　　　　　　　　　　　　　　　　　　　　　　解答 (C)

因為句意為「因為忙碌的行程取消了會議」的意思，因此應該要填入可以與空格前的 be 動詞 was 一起寫為被動式的動詞 cancel（取消）的 p.p 形 (C) canceled。(A) release 是「公開」，(B) isolate 是「孤立」，(D) expire 是「期滿，到期」。

單字 personnel n. 人事部；a. 人事的　organize v. 規畫，安排

120

Only journalists with relevant experience and writing skills will be _____ for the *Jatayu Business Journal*'s associate editor position. (A) estimated　　(B) published (C) promoted　　(D) considered	只有具備相關經驗和寫作技巧的記者，才會被考慮來擔任 *Jatayu* 商業報刊副編輯的職位。

■ 動詞語彙　　　　　　　　　　　　　　　　　　　　　　　　　　　　　　解答 (D)

因為句意為「只有具有相關經驗以及寫作技巧的記者會被考慮選為副編輯」的意思，因此可以與空格前的 be 動詞一起寫為被動式的動詞 consider（考慮）的 p.p 形 (D) considered 才是正確答案。

單字 relevant a. 有關係的　position n. 位置，職位

121

More than 50 young artists across the state will be participating in a painting _____ sponsored by the National Museum of Contemporary Art. (A) contestant　　　(B) contesting (C) contest　　　　(D) contested	州內有超過五十位的年輕藝術家將會參加由國家現代藝術博物館所贊助的作畫比賽。

■ 人物名詞與抽象名詞　　　　　　　　　　　　　　　　　　　　　　　　　　　　解答 (C)

因為只有名詞可以同時放在不定冠詞 a 的後面，並作為介系詞 in 的受詞，所以 (A) 和 (C) 為可能的答案。因為空格前有 painting，可以猜測是參加美術競賽，因此抽象名詞 (C) contest 是正確答案。若選擇人物名詞 (A) contestant（競爭者），則會出現「藝術家們參加美術競爭者」這種奇怪語意。

單字 state n. 州　participate in phr. 參與～　sponsor v. 贊助

122

Effective March 3, human resources director Arlene Rochester will _____ Dougal Seton in the role of vice president of Lawson Corporation. (A) inquire　　　　(B) suppose (C) replace　　　　(D) respond	人力資源部主任 Arlene Rochester 將取代 Dougal Seton 成為 Lawson 公司副董事長，從 3 月 3 日起生效。

■ 動詞語彙　　　　　　　　　　　　　　　　　　　　　　　　　　　　　　　　解答 (C)

因為句意為「Arlene Rochester 會取代 Dougal Seton 成為 Lawson 的副董事長」，因此動詞 (C) replace（取代）是正確答案。(A) inquire 是「提問」，(B) suppose 是「猜測」，(D) respond 是「回應」的意思。

單字 human resources director phr. 人力資源主任　vice president phr. 副董事長

123

The company's mobile phone plans are usually offered at _____ prices to new customers. (A) equivalent　　　(B) introductory (C) proportional　　　(D) dependent	這個公司的手機資費方案，通常提供新用戶入門價。

■ 形容詞語彙　　　　　　　　　　　　　　　　　　　　　　　　　　　　　　　解答 (B)

因為句意為「提供新用戶入門價」，因此選擇形容詞 (B) introductory（介紹的，入門的）為正確答案。(A) equivalent 是「同等的」，(C) proportional 是「按照比例的」，(D) dependent 是「依賴的」的意思。

124

Due to unforeseen circumstances, the organizer of the "1000 Megawatt" concert series suggested that the event _____ until further notice. (A) postponed　　　(B) postpones (C) be postponed　　　(D) has postponed	因為無法預測的情況，1000 Megawatt 系列音樂會的籌辦人建議在另行通知前，將活動延期舉辦。

■ 在提案、邀請、疑問類的主要子句後面，that 子句要使用原形動詞　　　　　　　解答 (C)

因為在主要子句出現動詞 suggested，因此在附屬子句應該要使用原形動詞，that 子句的主詞 the event 和動詞 postpone 是「活動被延期」的意思，所以要選擇 (C) be postponed 為正確答案。另外，在提案、邀請、疑問的句子通常會出現以下動詞：propose（提案），insist（主張要～），recommend（推薦），形容詞：essential（必要的），imperative（必須的）。

單字 unforeseen a. 無法預測的　circumstance n. 情況　suggest v. 建議
　　until further notice phr. 直到另行通知為止

125

During the Showroom Expo, more than 30 interior designers presented the _____ furniture pieces that attracted much attention. (A) redeemable　　　(B) innovative (C) proficient　　　(D) impressed	在 Showroom 展覽會期間,有超過三十位室內設計師展示他們備受注目的創新家具。

■ 形容詞語彙　　　　　　　　　　　　　　　　　　　　　　　　　　　解答 (B)

因為句意為「吸引許多注意的創新家具」,因此形容詞 (B) innovative(創新的)是正確答案。(A) redeemable 是「可贖回的」,(C) proficient 是「熟練的」,(D) impressed 是「印象深刻的」的意思。另外,(C) 和 (D) 都是只可以修飾人的形容詞。

單字 present v. 展示,呈現　furniture n. 家具　attract v. 吸引　attention n. 關注,注意

126

Mentor Technologies' _____ line of computers comes with faster processors and vastly improved storage capacity. (A) similar　　　(B) typical (C) optional　　　(D) newest	Mentor 科技公司最新的電腦系列產品將搭配更快的處理器與大大增加的儲存空間。

■ 形容詞語彙　　　　　　　　　　　　　　　　　　　　　　　　　　　解答 (D)

因為句意為「最新型電腦產品備有更快的處理器與更大的容量」,(D) newest(最新的)是正確答案。(A) similar 是「類似的」,(B) typical 是「典型的」,(C) optional 是「可選擇的」的意思。

單字 line n. 系列產品　processor n. 處理器　vastly ad. 龐大地,巨大地　improved a. 進步的　capacity n. 容量

127

Crimson Wellness Center continues to be the most popular fitness facility on the West Coast _____ the establishment of several local gyms in the past years. (A) meantime　　　(B) likewise (C) despite　　　(D) nevertheless	儘管在過去幾年有好幾家當地的健身房開張,Crimson Wellness Center 還是西岸最受歡迎的健身中心。

■ 修飾語「片語」與修飾語「子句」的不同　　　　　　　　　　　　　　解答 (C)

因為本句是具備主詞 Crimson Wellness Center,動詞 continues,受詞 to be the most popular fitness facility 的完整子句,因此我們要把 ____ the establishment ~ years 視為修飾語。因為這個修飾語沒有動詞,因此要選擇一個可以引領片語的介系詞 (C) despite(儘管)為正確答案。連接副詞 (A) meantime(與此同時),(B) likewise(同樣的),(D) nevertheless(即便如此還是~)無法帶領一個片語的修飾語。

單字 fitness n. 健身,健康　facility n. 設施　establishment n. 建立,建立的機構　local a. 當地的,本地的

128

Health Trails magazine featured an article last month on how and why staying inside an air-conditioned room for long periods can _____ illness. (A) produce　　　(B) producing (C) to produce　　　(D) has produced	*Health Trails* 雜誌在上個月特別報導了一篇文章,闡述在空調室內久待致病的原因與途徑。

■ 助動詞+動詞原形　　　　　　　　　　　　　　　　　　　　　　　　解答 (A)

因為助動詞 can 後面接動詞原形,因此 (A) produce(誘發)才是正確答案。副詞兼動名詞 (B),to 不定詞 (C),第三人稱單數形 (D) 都不能放在助動詞後面。

單字 feature v. 特別報導,以~為特色　article n. 文章,一則報導　period n. 期間

129

------ has been made to ensure that participants in this year's music festival will have sufficient parking.

(A) Accomplishment   (B) Amendment
(C) Accommodation   (D) Approval

已完成空間調整來確保今年音樂祭的參加者有充足的停車位。

■ 名詞語彙   解答 (C)

因為句意為「空間調整到讓每個人有充足的停車位」，因此 (C) Accommodation（調整空間、狀況以適應～，食宿）是正確答案。(A) Accomplishment 是「成就」，(B) Amendment 是「針對文字、憲法等的修正，改正」，所以不適合，(D) Approval 是「承認」的意思。

單字 ensure v. 保障，確保   sufficient a. 充足的

130

The Bloomfield Science Library in Texas is ------ equipped with security devices, such as surveillance cameras and door alarms, to monitor activities inside the building.

(A) completely   (B) complete
(C) completed   (D) completion

德州的 Bloomfield 科學圖書館以配備完備的保全裝置，如監視器攝影機和門上的警鈴等，來監控建築物內的活動。

■ 副詞的位置   解答 (A)

為了修飾動詞 is equipped 應該要選擇一個副詞，因此 (A) completely（完全地）是正確答案。動詞兼形容詞 (B)，動詞兼分詞 (C)，名詞 (D) 都無法修飾動詞。另外，be equipped with（裝備有～）是常用的慣用語。

單字 security n. 安全，保安   device n. 設備，裝置   surveillance n. 監視   monitor v. 監視
       complete v. 完成；a. 完整的

131

One of Vector Historical Foundation's focuses for next year is to put more ------ on establishing close partnerships with other similar institutions.

(A) emphasis   (B) emphasize
(C) emphasized   (D) emphatically

Vector 歷史基金會下年度的目標之一是加強與其他性質類似的機構建立緊密的合作關係。

■ 名詞的位置   解答 (A)

可以做為 to 不定詞 to put 受詞的是名詞，因此選擇 (A) emphasis（重點，強調）為正確答案。動詞 (B)，動詞兼分詞 (C)，副詞 (D) 都無法置於名詞的位置。另外，put emphasis on（強調～）是常用的慣用語。

單字 partnership n. 合作關係，合力，聯手

132

Many students at the institute have complained that they find it challenging ------ their tests within the given time limits.

(A) finishing   (B) finished
(C) to finish   (D) have finished

許多這所學院的學生曾抱怨要在給定的時間限制內完成他們的測驗很難。

■ 虛受詞 it 的句子 受詞的位置   解答 (C)

因為句中有動詞 find 的虛受詞 it，因此空格中應該填入真受詞。受詞形式可以是 to 不定詞或是 that 子句，因此 to 不定詞 (C) to finish 是正確答案。動名詞兼現在分詞 (A)，動詞兼過去分詞 (B)，動詞 (D) 在這裡都不能夠作為受詞。

單字 institute n. 學院，協會   complain v. 抱怨   challenging a. 困難的，具挑戰性的   time limit phr. 時間限制

133

The factory supervisor _____ instructed the workers to clean the plant and make certain that all equipment was in good working order before the inspector's visit.

(A) arguably   (B) invisibly

(C) forgetfully   (D) explicitly

廠長明確地指示工人在督察來訪前要清掃工廠，並確認所有的設備能良好運作。

■ 副詞語彙   解答 (D)

因為句意為「廠長對工人們明確的指示」，因此副詞 (D) explicitly（明確地）是正確答案。(A) arguably 是「可以說是～」，(B) invisibly 是「看不到」，(C) forgetfully 是「健忘地」的意思。

單字 instruct v. 指示   certain a. 明確的，特定的   in working order phr. 正常運作地   inspector n. 督察員

134

Because of the high cost of rent in the downtown area, Nelia Deluca is _____ as to whether or not she should open a copy center outlet in the city.

(A) incorrect   (B) relative   (C) arguable   (D) uncertain

因為在市中心的租金昂貴，Nelia Deluca 還不確定她是不是該在市區內開一家影印中心特賣店。

■ 形容詞語彙   解答 (D)

句意「因為高額的租金不確定該不該開設特賣店」，因此選擇 (D) uncertain（不能確定）為正確答案。(A) incorrect 是「不正確的」，(B) relative 是「相對的」，(C) arguable 是「能主張的，可爭辯的」的意思。

單字 downtown n. 市中心，都心   as to phr. 關於～   outlet n. 特賣店，排出口

135

The secretary informed Mr. Wallaby that the Merlin Restaurant _____ to provide a dining room that seats 100 people.

(A) to contract   (B) contracting

(C) contracts   (D) has been contracted

祕書告知 Wallaby 先生 Merlin 餐廳已經簽約，答應提供可容納一百人的用餐空間。

■ 動詞的單 / 複數，主 / 被動，時態   解答 (D)

因為 that 子句尚未有動詞，因此動詞 (C) 和 (D) 都是可能的答案。「餐廳已經簽約了」本句有被動的意思，又因為整句「餐廳已經簽了提供可容納一百人場地的約」的意思可以看出是以前已經先訂的契約對現在所造成的影響，因此現在完成被動式 (D) has been contracted 是正確答案。如果使用現在主動式的 (C) contracts 會變成「餐廳去簽約」的意思，但餐廳應為「被簽約以履行某事」的對象。to 不定詞 (A) 和分詞兼動名詞 (B) 則無法被放進動詞的位置。

單字 secretary n. 祕書   inform v. 通知   provide v. 提供   seat n. 座位

136

Chekwa Community Center often promotes free courses or activities to its long-term members in appreciation of their _____.

(A) performance   (B) loyalty

(C) application   (D) intention

Chekwa 社區中心常常提供免費的課程或活動給長期會員，以感謝他們的忠誠。

■ 名詞語彙   解答 (B)

因為句意為「因為感謝長期會員的忠誠而提供免費課程及活動」，因此選擇 (B) loyalty（忠誠）為正確答案。(A) performance 是「成果，演出」，(C) application 是「申請，適用」，(D) intention 是「意圖」的意思。另外，要記住 in appreciation of（對～感到感謝）是慣用語。

單字 long-term a. 長期的   appreciation n. 感謝，鑑賞

137

| Winners of this year's literary contest will be announced _____ in both the print and online versions of the publication *Literatura*.
(A) persuasively　　(B) officially
(C) truthfully　　(D) exceedingly | 今年文學比賽的得獎者將在 *Literatura* 實體與網路兩種出版品中被正式宣佈。 |

■ 副詞語彙　　　　　　　　　　　　　　　　　　　　　　　　　　　　解答 (B)

因為本句為「得獎人將在 Literatura 出版品中被正式宣佈」的意思，因此副詞 (B) officially（正式地）是正確答案。(A) persuasively 是「具說服力地」，(C) truthfully 是「真實地，正直地」，(D) exceedingly 是「非常，極度地」的意思。

單字　literary a. 文學的

138

| A Web developer _____ the social networking site 10 years ago to help people stay in touch with friends online.
(A) began　　(B) begins
(C) was begun　　(D) would begin | 網路開發者從十年前就開發社群網路來幫助人們在線上與朋友保持聯繫。 |

■ 動詞的單 / 複數，主 / 被動，時態　　　　　　　　　　　　　　　　　解答 (A)

因為有過去時間的表現 10 years ago，所以過去動詞 (A) 和 (C) 都可能是正確答案。因為「網路開發者開發社群網站」的意思具主動的意味，因此主動態動詞 (A) began 是正確答案。(D) 的 would 若是當過去的習慣所適用的助動詞，句意就會變成「網路開發者十年前重複開始社群網站」這種奇怪的意思。

單字　stay in touch phr. 保持聯繫

139

| Tourists who purchase a travel pass have _____ to ride any bus or subway within the city limits for a period of 24 hours.
(A) compliance　　(B) authorization
(C) determination　　(D) allocation | 購買旅遊通行卡的旅客可以在二十四小時內坐市區內任何的公車與地鐵。 |

■ 名詞語彙　　　　　　　　　　　　　　　　　　　　　　　　　　　　解答 (B)

因為句意為「旅客有搭乘任何公車或地鐵的權限」，因此名詞 (B) authorization（權限）是正確答案。(A) compliance 是「遵守」，(C) determination 是「決定，決心」，(D) allocation 是「配置」的意思。

單字　purchase v. 購買　　pass n. 搭乘券，通行證　　limit n. 限制，牽制

140

| The salon's supplier asked for payment of the hair products in full, _____ they cannot be shipped until next week.
(A) even though　　(B) apart from
(C) as soon as　　(D) due to | 儘管美髮店要的髮用產品要下星期才能送到，供應商還是要求要先付清貨款。 |

■ 副詞子句連接詞 讓步　　　　　　　　　　　　　　　　　　　　　　解答 (A)

主句是具有 The salon's supplier asked for payment 的完整子句，因此要把 ____ they cannot ~ next week 視為修飾語。而修飾語已具有動詞 cannot be shipped，故要選擇可以領導副詞子句的連接詞 (A) 或 (C)。因為本句為「儘管商品到下週才能完成配送，供應商依然要求支付款項」之意，所以 (A) even though（即使～也～）是正確答案。若選擇 (C) as soon as（一～就～）則變成「一但商品下週才能完成配送，供應商就要求支付款項」的奇怪語意。介系詞 (B) apart from（除～之外），(D) due to（由於～）都無法帶領一個子句。

單字　salon n. 美髮店，商店，接待室　　supplier n. 供應商　　in full phr. 完整的，全額　　ship v. 輸送，配送

PART 6

Questions 141-143 refer to the following announcement.　　141-143 根據下面的公告內容回答問題。

COME TO THE FIRST EVER DIOP TRADE SHOW!	請來參加史無前例的 DIOP 貿易展！
More than 200 Algerian manufacturers are scheduled to _____ their products at Maktub Convention Center in 141 (A) deliver　　(B) order 　　(C) reserve　　(D) showcase	141 11 月時，有超過兩百個阿爾及利亞製造商會在 Maktub 會議中心展示他們的產品。
November. A variety of Algerian-made merchandise will be featured at the trade show.	有各式各樣阿爾及利亞製造的商品將會在會場上展示。
Trade and Industry Minister Samir Klouchi _____ the 142 (A) opened　　　　(B) will open 　　　(C) was opening (D) has opened	142 貿易與工業部長 Samir Klouchi 在 11 月 5 日將會正式為貿易展開幕。
exhibition on November 5. The month-long event aims to support local businesses and to promote national pride among citizens.	為期一個月的展示旨在支持當地的產業，並向國人宣傳國家的驕傲。
It _____ on November 30 with a 15-minute fireworks display. 143 (A) concludes　(B) results 　　(C) stops　　　(D) fulfills	143 貿易展將在 11 月 30 日以一場 15 分鐘的煙火表演畫下句點。
For more information, please send an e-mail to diopshow @maktubevents.net.	欲知更多詳情，請寄電郵給 diopshow @maktubevents.net。

單字 **manufacturer** n. 製造商　**merchandise** n. 商品　**feature** v. 特別被收錄　**exhibition** n. 展覽（會）
　　aim v. 以～為目標　**firework** n. 煙火

141 ■ 動詞語彙 掌握上下文　　　　　　　　　　　　　　　　　　　　　　　　　　　　　解答 (D)

因為句意為「超過兩百個阿爾及利亞製造商預計＿＿他們的產品」，所以每個選項都有可能是正確答案。因為無法在有空格的句子裡馬上找到答案，所以要利用上下文把握文意。題目是貿易展，因為後面文章寫到本次貿易展中特別包含多樣的阿爾及利亞產品，所以可以知道他們將在貿易博覽會中展示產品。因此動詞 (D) showcase（展示）是正確答案。(A) deliver 是「配送」，(B) order 是「下單」，(C) reserve 是「預約」的意思。

142 ■ 未來式 掌握全文　　　　　　　　　　　　　　　　　　　　　　　　　　　　　　　解答 (B)

句意是「貿易與工業部長在 11 月 5 日為貿易展開幕」，但開幕的時間序沒辦法僅靠著有空格的句子判斷出正確答案，因此要掌握上下文或全文才能選出答案。因為在短文的前面部份說過預計要舉辦貿易展，因此可以知道長官們要開幕的時間應該是在未來。因此要選擇未來式 (B) will open 為正確答案。

143 ■ 動詞語彙　　　　　　　　　　　　　　　　　　　　　　　　　　　　　　　　　　　解答 (A)

因為「11 月 30 日落幕」這句話，得知動詞 conclude（結束）的第三人稱單數形 (A) concludes 是正確答案。(C) 的 stop 雖是「停止，停下」的意思，但比起「結束掉～」的意思，stop 有「正在做的事情再也不做，中斷」的語意，不適合用在此句。(B) 的 result 是「導致～的結果發生」，(D) 的 fulfill 是「實行義務、約定、職務」的意思。

144-146 根據下面的信件內容回答問題。

February 2	2 月 2 日
Ingrid Helgarson 43 Thompson Avenue Lansing, MI 48920	Ingrid Helgarson Thompson 大道 43 號 Lansing 市, 密西根州 48920
Dear Ms. Helgarson,	親愛的 Helgarson 小姐：
Our records indicate that you have been a regular visitor to Aberdeen Grocers for the past four years. We appreciate your _____. 144 (A) feedback (B) business (C) donation (D) understanding	我們的紀錄顯示您在過去四年一直都是 Aberdeen 雜貨店的常客，144 我們很感謝您的惠顧。
To help us enhance our products and services, we would like to request input from customers such as you.	為了幫助使我們的產品與服務更上層樓，我們要向您這樣的客戶尋求協助，我們請求您針對最近一次到離您最近的 Aberdeen 分店的經驗，145 上我們的網站 www.aberdeengrocers.com 填寫問卷。
Thus, we would like you to answer a _____ on our Web 145 (A) questionnaire(B) questionable (C) questions (D) questioning	
site, at www.aberdeengrocers.com, about your most recent visit to the Aberdeen branch nearest you.	
We assure our customers that any personal information collected during the survey will be kept confidential. The answers will be used _____ for monitoring our 146 (A) openly (B) externally (C) solely (D) roughly	我們向我們的客戶保證，這次調查所蒐集到的個人資料將會受到保密，146 您的回答只會用在我們品質監控與找出改進之處的用途上。
performance and identifying areas in need of improvement. Thank you in advance for your cooperation. Yours truly, Aberdeen Grocers Customer Service Team	在此先感謝您的合作。 Aberdeen 雜貨店客服務團隊 敬上

單字 **appreciate** v. 鑑賞，評價，感謝 **request** v. 邀請 **assure** v. 保障，肯定 **confidential** a. 祕密的，機密的 **identify** v. 找，確認 **cooperation** n. 協助

144 ■ 名詞語彙 掌握上下文　　　　　　　　　　　　　　　　　　　　　　　　　　解答 (B)

因為是「感謝您的____」的意思，所以所有選項都可能是答案。由於無法由一個句子看出正確答案，因此要掌握上下文，甚至全文。因為前文有提到在四年期間都是常客，所以可以知道是發信人要向收件人表示對於這期間所有商務交易的感謝之意。因此 (B) business（交易，惠顧）是正確答案。(A) feedback 是「反應，意見」，(C) donation 是「捐款」，(D) understanding 是「理解」的意思。

145 ■ 名詞的位置　　　　　　　　　　　　　　　　　　　　　　　　　　　　解答 (A)

可以做為及物動詞 answer 的受詞，又可以放在不定冠詞 a 和介系詞 on 中間的應該是單數可數名詞，因此單數可數名詞 (A) questionnaire（問卷）是正確答案。形容詞 (B) 無法放到名詞的位置。動詞的第三人稱單數或複數名詞 (C) questions（提問；問題）跟動名詞、分詞，且具有「質疑，審問」意味的不可數名詞 (D) questioning 則無法放在不定冠詞 a 的後面。

單字 **questionable** a. 可疑的，懷疑的

146 ■ 副詞詞彙 掌握上下文　　　　　　　　　　　　　　　　　　　　　　　　解答 (C)

選擇修飾「被用在品質監控與找出改進之處的用途上」的副詞，所以 (A) (B) (C) 都可能是答案。因無法從一個句子看出正確答案，所以要掌握上下文。前文提到在調查期間得到的個人資訊都會被保密，可以知道調查成果只有在該店為了尋求改善時才會使用，因此副詞 (C) solely（只有，惟）是正確答案。(A) openly 是「公開地，誠實地」，(B) externally 是「外部地」，(D) roughly 是「大略，粗糙地」的意思。

From: Larry Keith <l.keith@str.com> To: Norma Jennings <n_jennings@unitedmail.com> Date: January 5 Subject: Truck Rental Dear Ms. Jennings, Thank you for choosing Simons Truck Rental. The moving truck you requested for ＿＿＿＿ upcoming relocation to Los 　　147 (A) my　　　　(B) our 　　　　(C) your　　　　(D) their Angeles may be picked up for use. If you are unable to retrieve the truck yourself, you may send a representative who must present a valid identification card and a letter ＿＿＿＿ that you permit him or 　　148 (A) indicates　　(B) indicating 　　　　(C) indication　　(D) indicated her to claim the vehicle on your behalf. Should you need additional assistance with your transfer, please let us know. We provide services to help you unload and arrange your belongings quickly upon ＿＿＿＿. 　　149 (A) occupancy　(B) partnership 　　　　(C) purchase　　(D) operation Feel free to contact us if you are interested. Truly yours, Larry Keith Simons Truck Rental	寄件人: Larry Keith <l.keith@str.com> 收件人: Norma Jennings 　　　　　<n_jennings@unitedmail.com> 日期: 1 月 5 日 主題: 卡車租用 親愛的 Jennings 女士： 感謝您選擇 Simons 卡車出租公司。147 您為即將搬到洛杉磯所預定的搬家卡車現在已經備好等您來取車。 148 如果您無法親自前來取車，您可以請他人帶著有效的身分證件和您的授權書前來代您取車。 倘若您的搬遷需要額外的協助，請讓我們知道。149 我們能提供服務在您入住新居的第一天迅速地幫您卸貨與安置您的東西。 如果您有興趣，敬請與我們聯絡。 Larry Keith Simons 卡車出租公司 敬上

單字 **request** v. 邀請　**upcoming** a. 馬上，最近的　**relocation** n. 搬家，移轉　**retrieve** v. 找到～並帶來，回收
representative n. 代理人　**valid** a. 有效的　**permit** v. 許可　**belonging** n. 物件，私人物品，攜帶品
upon prep. 一～就～

147 ■ 人稱代名詞 掌握全文　　　　　　　　　　　　　　　　　　　　　　　　　　　解答 (C)

因為「最近＿＿＿的搬家」的意思，空格裡應該填入可以修飾名詞 relocation（搬家）的形容詞，跟形容詞一樣可以放置於名詞前修飾的所有格代名詞，也就是所有選項，都是可能的答案。由於無法由一個句子看出正確答案，因此要掌握上下文或全文的文意。收信人為 Ms. Jennings，且在後半段有提到「如果您需要搬家或相關的需求請聯絡我們」，所以可以知道要搬家的人是 Ms. Jennings，也就是收信人。因此可以指出收信人的第二人稱代名詞 (C) your 是正確答案。

148 ■ 現在分詞 vs. 過去分詞　　　　　　　　　　　　　　　　　　　　　　　　　解答 (B)

因為空格是在名詞 a letter 的後面，因此在可以放在名詞後修飾名詞的分詞 (B) 和 (D) 都有可能。被修飾的名詞 letter 跟分詞組合後的意思為「信件顯示得到許可」，因此是主動語態，要選擇現在分詞 (B) 為正確答案。過去分詞 (D) 是被動，動詞 (A) 和名詞 (C) 都無法修飾名詞。

149 ■ 名詞語彙　　　　　　　　　　　　　　　　　　　　　　　　　　　　　　　解答 (A)

因為這句的意思是「當您＿＿＿時立即幫您卸貨與安置您的東西」，選擇與介系詞 upon 放在一起時，可以變成「（到達搬家地點）馬上居住」的意思的 (A) occupancy（居住，佔領）為正確答案。(B) partnership 是「合夥關係」，(C) purchase 是「購買」，(D) operation 是「營運，手術」的意思。

Questions 150-152 refer to the following announcement.　　150-152 根據下面的公告內容回答問題。

Maincore Diving Center Au Cap, Seychelles	Maincore 潛水中心 Au Cap, Seychelles
Dear Students, Congratulations on _____ the three-day open water scuba 　　　150 (A) joining　　(B) completing 　　　　(C) developing (D) scoring diving course at Maincore Diving Center. As a final requirement for certification, you will perform your first deepwater dive tomorrow. Please be sure to follow the safety precautions you have learned from your instructors. This will help guarantee a _____ diving experience.　　151 (A) secure　　(B) moderate 　　　　　　　(C) partial　　(D) lengthy In addition, check whether your gear is in working order before getting on the boat. It is highly recommended that you wear gloves to shield your hands from sharp coral. The staff at the center _____ you in selecting and 　　152 (A) assisted　　　(B) is assisting 　　　　(C) has assisted　(D) will assist assembling your equipment. We hope you found this course to be a pleasant experience. Should you have any problem with our services, do not hesitate to send an inquiry to our office so that we can deal with your concern immediately. Thank you. Maincore Diving Center	親愛的學生們： 150 恭喜你們完成了在 Maincore 潛水中心為期三天的開放水域潛水課程。 明天你們將要進行第一次深海潛水，這是你們取得認證的最後一個要求，請確實遵守你們從教練那裏學到的安全措施，151 如此才能確保你們有個安全的潛水經驗。 此外，在上船前，檢查你們的裝備是否可用。強烈建議你們要戴手套以保護你們的手不因尖刺的珊瑚而受傷。152 潛水中心裡的員工會協助你們選擇並組裝你們的裝備。 我們希望你們認為這個課程是個愉快的經驗，如果對我們的服務有任何問題，不要猶豫，反應給我們的辦公室，以便我們能夠立即處理你們的疑慮。 謝謝。 Maincore 潛水中心

單字 **open water** phr. 開放水域　**requirement** n. 要素，必要　**certification** n. 資格證　**gear** n. 裝備　**highly** ad. 非常　**recommend** v. 建議　**shield** v. 保護　**coral** n. 珊瑚　**hesitate** v. 猶豫　**deal with** phr. 解決

150 　動詞語彙 掌握上下文　　　　　　　　　　　　　　　　　　　　　　　　　　　　　　　解答 (B)

因為是「恭喜_____潛水課程」的意思，所以 (A) (B) (C) 都可能是正確答案。由於無法由一個句子看出正確答案，因此要掌握上下文或全文的文意。在後面提到要取得資格證的最後一項條件就是深海潛水，因此可以知道這篇公告的對象正要準備結束潛水課程。因此動詞 complete（完成）的動名詞 (B) completing 是正確答案。(A) 的 join 是「加入」，(C) 的 develop 是「開發」，(D) 的 score 是「得分」的意思。

151 　形容詞語彙 掌握上下文　　　　　　　　　　　　　　　　　　　　　　　　　　　　　　解答 (A)

因為是「確保_____潛水經驗」的意思，所以 (A) (B) (D) 可能是答案。因無法由一個句子看出正確答案，故要掌握上下文或全文的文意。前文提到一定要跟著實行安全預防措施，因此句子中的 This（這個）應該是指安全預防措施，可知整句為「這個確保安全的潛水經驗」的意思。因此形容詞 (A) secure（安全的）是正確答案。(B) moderate 是「適當的」，(C) partial 是「部分的」，(D) lengthy 是「長的」的意思。

152 　未來時態 掌握上下文　　　　　　　　　　　　　　　　　　　　　　　　　　　　　　　解答 (D)

句子是「幫您選擇與組裝裝備」的意思，在這裡無法由一個句子看出正確答案，因此要掌握上下文或全文的文意。前文提到要在搭乘小船前確認裝備是否能正常運作，因此可以知道要選擇並組裝裝備的時間點應該是在未來。所以未來時態 (D) will assist 是正確答案。

PART 7

Questions 153-154 refer to the following notice.

153-154 根據下面的告示內容回答問題。

Green Valley High School	Green Valley 高中
You are entering a school zone. [153]Please observe the following guidelines to maintain orderly traffic inside the campus:	你現在正進入一個學校區域，[153] 請遵守下列的指示，以保持校園內的交通秩序：
· [154]Keep a speed limit of 15 miles per hour. · Give way to pedestrians. · Avoid honking vehicle horns during class hours. · Do not park in front of school building entrances. · Display a parking pass on the windshield.	· [154] 保持時速 15 英哩速限。 · 禮讓行人。 · 在上課時間避免鳴按喇叭。 · 不要在學校建築物出入口前停車。 · 請在擋風玻璃出示停車證。
Thank you and enjoy your visit.	謝謝你，並祝你來訪愉快！
Green Valley High School Security	Green Valley 高中警衛部門

單字 □observe v. 遵守，注意　□guideline n. 指示　□orderly a. 有秩序的，整頓的
□give way to phr. 讓路給～　□pedestrian n. 行人　□honk v. 按喇叭
□park v. 停車　□display v. 出示，展示　□windshield n. （汽車前面的）擋風玻璃

153

Why was the notice written?	為什麼會寫下這個告示？
(A) To notify students about class schedules	(A) 告知學生課程表
(B) To inform motorists of traffic rules	(B) 提醒駕駛交通規則
(C) To remind employees of new campus policies	(C) 提醒員工新的校園政策
(D) To announce the temporary closure of a parking lot	(D) 宣布停車場暫時關閉

■ 找出主題 寫文章的理由　　　　　　　　　　　　　　　　　　　　　　解答 (B)

因為是詢問發表這篇公告的理由，因此要特別注意文章前面的幾段。因為 Please observe the following guidelines to maintain orderly traffic inside the campus 是要求為了維持校內的交通秩序，請遵守以下指示的意思，並在後面寫出細部的規定，因此 (B) To inform motorists of traffic rules 是正確答案。

換句話說
guidelines 指示 → rules 規則

單字 notify v. 提醒，通知　inform v. 通知　motorist n. 駕駛　remind v. 提醒　policy n. 方針
temporary a. 暫時的，臨時的　closure n. 封閉，關閉

154

What are visitors asked to do?	訪客被要求做什麼？
(A) Register at the security office	(A) 在警衛室登記
(B) Sign up for a parking permit	(B) 申請停車證
(C) Drive slowly inside the campus	(C) 在校園內車子慢慢開
(D) Show an identification card	(D) 出示身分證證件

■ 六何原則 What　　　　　　　　　　　　　　　　　　　　　　　　　解答 (C)

是詢問校外人士被要求要做什麼的 What 問題，因為與問題的句子 visitors asked to do 有關聯，而且文中提到 Keep a speed limit of 15 miles per hour（要保持時速 15 英里的速限），因此 (C) Drive slowly inside the campus 是正確答案。

換句話說
keep a speed limit 維持速限 → Drive slowly 慢慢開

單字 register v. 登記，註冊　security office phr. 警衛室　sign up for phr. 申請，登記
identification card phr. 身分證件

Questions 155-156 refer to the following letter.

155-156 根據下面的信件內容回答問題。

Hernandez Construction Supplies
Guernsey Street
Dallas, TX 75209

December 1

Clifford Sparks
Credit Manager
Aero Door Handles
Evengrade Towers, Houston, TX 75101

Dear Mr. Sparks,

156-D It was a pleasure meeting you at the construction supplies fair last month. After learning about your wide range of door handles and comparing it with other manufacturers', 155 we have decided to carry your line in our hardware stores in Dallas. I was very impressed with both your products and presentation and feel that such an agreement could be mutually beneficial.

Therefore, 155 we would like to apply for consignment, preferably with a charge account ranging from $3,000 to $4,000 in value. As this is a rather large consignment, I was hoping you could offer us a higher rate of commission than the 18 percent you mentioned at the fair. May I suggest a commission of 20 percent? If that is agreeable to you, please let me know as soon as possible.

Enclosed is a copy of our company profile, business license, and the credit references you requested.

Thank you, and 155 we look forward to a successful business relationship with you and your company.

Truly yours,

Bryan Sims
Operations Manager
Hernandez Construction Supplies

Hernandez 建築材料公司
Guernsey 街
達拉斯，德州 75209

12 月 1 日

Clifford Sparks
信用部經理
Aero 門把公司
Evengrade 大樓，休士頓，德州 75101

親愛的 Sparks 先生：

156-D很榮幸在上個月建築材料展與您會面。在得知你們在門把的多樣選擇並與其他製造商比較之後，155我們已經決定在達拉斯的五金商店裡陳列販售你們的產品，我們對於你們的產品與呈現皆印象深刻，深覺這樣的合作能使雙方相為受益。

因此，155我們想要申請委託代售，希望賒帳的金額在三千至四千美元的範圍。因為這是一個頗大的委託代售，我希望您可以給我們比您在會展中提到 18% 更高的佣金。容我在此建議 20% 的傭金，好嗎？如果你同意，請盡快讓我知道。

隨函附上一份公司資料、營業執照與您要求的信貸資料。

在此感謝你，並155期待與您和貴公司建立成功的業務關係。

Bryan Sims
營運部經理
Hernandez 建築材料公司

單字　□a wide range of phr. 大範圍的，多樣的　□manufacturer n. 製造業，生產業　□carry v.（在商店中）陳列販售
　　　□impressed a. 印象深刻的　□mutually ad. 相互，彼此　□beneficial a. 有利益的，有利的
　　　□apply for phr. 申請　□consignment n. 代售　□preferably ad. 更好地，盡可能地
　　　□range from A to B phr. 範圍從 A 至 B　□commission n. 佣金　□agreeable a. 同意的，贊成的

Why did Mr. Sims write to Mr. Sparks?	為什麼 Sims 先生寫信給 Sparks 先生？
(A) To ask for a revision to an agreement	(A) 要求修改一份合約
(B) To propose a business partnership	(B) 提議商業上的合作關係
(C) To request information about construction supplies	(C) 要求與建築材料有關的資料
(D) To invite a supplier to an event	(D) 邀請一個供應商參加一場活動

■ **找出主題** 寫文章的理由　　　　　　　　　　　　　　　　　　　　　　解答 (B)

因為是在問 Sims 先生寫信給 Sparks 先生的理由，所以要注意文章的前段。 we have decided to carry your line in our hardware stores in Dallas 是在說 Sims 先生在達拉斯的五金行決定銷售 Sparks 先生公司的產品，並說 we would apply for consignment 表示要申請委託代售，信件的最後 we look forward to a successful business relationship with you and your company 指的是希望能跟您與您的公司有成功的業務往來。因此 (B) To propose a business partnership 為正確答案。

單字　propose v. 提議，提案　supplier n. 供應業者，供應商

What is mentioned about Mr. Sparks?	關於 Sparks 先生，何者正確？
(A) He only works on consignment.	(A) 他只從事委託代售工作。
(B) He already filled out an order form.	(B) 他已經填好了訂購單。
(C) He was sent a product catalog.	(C) 有一份產品目錄寄給他。
(D) He met Mr. Sims at a trade fair.	(D) 他和 Sims 先生在貿易展中見過面。

■ **Not/True** True 問題　　　　　　　　　　　　　　　　　　　　　　　解答 (D)

本題是要在文章中找到與本問題的重點 Mr. Sparks 相關的內容後，比較選項與文章的 Not/True 問題。(A) (B) (C) 都是在文章中沒有提到的內容。在 It was a pleasure meeting you at the construction supplies fair last month. 這句是說 Sims 先生很開心能夠在上個月的建築材料展上遇到 Sparks 先生，因此要選 (D) He met Mr. Sims at a trade fair. 為正確答案。

換句話說

the construction supplies fair 建築材料展 → a trade fair 貿易博覽會

單字　fill out v. 填寫　fair n. 博覽會

Questions 157-159 refer to the following information. 157-159 根據下面的資訊回答問題。

The ALL NEW Dockland Split Type Air Conditioner (BA501)

[157-D]Committed to producing energy-efficient products, Dockland Electronics has created the BA501, a new split type air conditioner with features designed to conserve power without compromising efficiency.

[158-D]Speed Cooling
This function allows the unit to reach preset temperatures in a short time.

[158-A]Temperature Equalizer
This function enables the unit to cool areas evenly by using dual-direction air vent technology.

[158-C]Sleep Mode
This function decreases the cooling temperature after the unit's first two hours of operation and maintains the room temperature for the next five hours before [158-C]it automatically shuts off the unit.

The BA501 is equipped with a patented refrigerant and has a Seasonal Energy Efficiency Ratio (SEER) rating of 14. [159-D]SEER measures the energy efficiency of air conditioners.

全新的 Dockland
分離式冷氣機（BA501）

[157-D]Dockland 電子致力於生產節約能源的產品，創造了 BA501 這種新式的分離式冷氣機，具有節省電力卻不影響效能的特殊設計。

[158-D]快速降溫
這個功能讓冷氣機在短時間內就能達到預設的溫度。

[158-A]溫度均勻
這項功能使用雙向出風口的技術讓冷氣機能夠使受冷範圍的溫度均勻。

[158-C]睡眠模式
這個功能讓冷氣機運轉兩個小時後減少降溫，使冷氣機在五小時後 [158-C]自動關機前能保持室內溫度。

BA501 配備專利冷卻劑，並獲得季節能源效率比（SEER）值 14，[159-D]SEER 是用來測量冷氣機的節能效果。

單字
- □commit v. 做，致力
- □efficiency n. 效能，效率
- □evenly ad. 均勻，平等地
- □patented a. 專利的
- □conserve v. 珍惜，保存
- □allow v. 使可能
- □maintain v. 維持
- □rating n. 等級，排名
- □compromise v. 連累，妥協
- □enable v. 讓～能夠
- □be equipped with phr. 配備，具有
- □measure v. 測定，測量

157

What is mentioned about the Dockland Electronics product?
(A) It is powered by alternative energy.
(B) It obtains high market sales.
(C) It is made of durable materials.
(D) It consumes less electricity.

關於 Dockland 電器公司的產品文中提到了什麼？
(A) 它是由替代能源供給電力的。
(B) 它擁有很高的市場銷售率。
(C) 它使用耐久的材料製造。
(D) 它消耗較少的電力。

Not/True True 問題　　　　　　　　　　　　　　　　　　　　　　　解答 (D)

本題是要在文章中找到與本問題的重點 the Dockland Electronics product 相關的內容後，比較選項與文章的 Not/True 問題。(A) (B) (C) 都是在文章中沒提到的內容。(D) Committed to producing energy-efficient products, Dockland Electronics has created the BA501 ~ with features designed to conserve power without compromising efficiency. 是指致力於開發高能源效率產品的 Dockland Electronics，設計出擁有不但不破壞效率，也節約電力等功能的 BA501。因此 (D) It consumes less electricity. 是正確答案。

換句話說
energy-efficient 高能源效率 → consumes less electricity 消耗較少電力

單字 alternative a. 替代的　obtain v. 保有，拿到　durable a. 耐久的　consume a. 消耗

What is NOT a feature of the air conditioner?	哪一項不是冷氣機的特色？
(A) Equalization of temperatures	(A) 溫度均勻
(B) Remote control	(B) 遙控操作
(C) Automatic shutdown	(C) 自動關機
(D) Fast cooling	(D) 快速降溫

■ Not/True True 問題　　　　　　　　　　　　　　　　　　　　　　　　　　　解答 (B)

本題是要在文章中找到與本問題的重點 a feature of the air conditioner 相關的內容後，比較選項與文章的 Not/True 問題。(A) 在文章中 Temperature Equalizer 項目的 This function enables the unit to cool areas evenly 講的就是能很平均的降低溫度，因此與文章內容一致。(B) 是文章內沒有提及的內容。因此 (B) Remote control 是正確答案。(C) 在 Sleep Model 的 it automatically shuts off the unit 提到睡眠模式狀態下冷氣有自動關機的功能，與文章內容一致。(D) 在 Speed Cooling 的 This function allows the unit to reach preset temperature in a short time. 提到快速冷卻的功能可以使冷氣短時間內達到設定的溫度，與文章內容一致。

單字 equalization n. 均等化

What is stated about the SEER rating system?	哪一項說明了關於季節能源效率比（SEER）系統？
(A) It is used by countries with limited fuel supplies.	(A) 用於燃料供給有限制的國家
(B) It was set by an international organization.	(B) 由一國際組織所制定
(C) It measures the durability of appliances.	(C) 用來測量電器產品的耐用度
(D) It calculates the energy performance of machines.	(D) 用來計算機器的能源表現

■ Not/True True 問題　　　　　　　　　　　　　　　　　　　　　　　　　　　解答 (D)

本題是要在文章中找到與本問題的重點 the SEER rating system 相關的內容後，比較選項與文章的 Not/True 問題。(A) (B) (C) 都是在文章中沒提到的內容。(D) 在文章中 SEER measures the energy efficiency of air conditioners 提到 SEER 會測量冷氣的能源效率，因此 (D) It calculates the energy performance of machines. 是正確答案。

換句話說

measures the energy efficiency of air conditioners 測量冷氣的能源效率
→ calculates the energy performance of machines 測量機器的能源表現

單字 fuel n. 燃料　durability n. 耐久性　appliance n. 家電製品　calculate n. 測量，計算

Questions 160-161 refer to the following catalog page.　　160-161 根據下面的目錄內容回答問題。

iConstruct www.iconstruct.com Find exactly the color you are looking with iConstruct for your next painting project! Painting your home is a major task, and deciding on which colors to use can be very tricky. To help you create a unique theme for your living space, 160-Acheck out the hundreds of colors from various manufacturers listed in this catalog. In addition to our extensive collection of hues and shades, 160-Cthis catalog includes photos showing different combinations that you may use for your bedrooms, living room, and dining area. You will be amazed at how many combinations you can make with our selection of paint. 160-BThe colors in the catalog may vary slightly from the actual shades, so we give customers free paint samples, which they may test on their walls. 160-D/161If you wish to get some samples, all you need to do is choose colors from our catalog and give us a call. Our customer service representatives will be happy to process your request. 161You may also order in person at our outlets. iConstruct	**iConstruct** www.iconstruct.com 在 iConstruct 找到你下一個粉刷計畫真正想要的顏色！ 粉刷你的家是一件大事，而決定你要選用什麼顏色可是件很麻煩的事。為了幫助你為你的居家環境創造一個獨特的主題，160-A看看這本目錄上多家廠牌的上百種顏色。 除了我們廣泛蒐集的色相與色度，160-C這本目錄包括了照片，告訴你能用在臥室、客廳和餐廳的不同組合，從我們的油漆中你能有這麼多種的組合，一定會讓你感到驚艷。 160-B目錄中的顏色可能會與實際上的色度有些許差異，所以我們會提供顧客免費的油漆樣品，讓他們實際在牆上測試，160-D/161假如你想要取得一些樣品，你所要做的就是打電話，告訴我們你從目錄中所選擇的顏色。我們的客戶服務人員會很樂意處理你的要求，161你也可以親自到我們的店裡訂購。 iConstruct

單字　□tricky a. 麻煩的，辛苦的　　□theme n. 主題，佈景　　□in addition to phr. 除了～，不只～
　　　□extensive a. 大範圍的　　□hue n. 顏色，色相　　□shade n. 色調，陰影
　　　□vary v. 不同，使多樣化　　□slightly ad. 有點，些微　　□representative n. 職員，代表
　　　□process v. 處理　　□request n. 邀請，要求　　□in person phr. 親自

160

What is NOT suggested about iConstruct? (A) It sells products made by other companies. (B) It guarantees the accuracy of paint colors in its catalog. (C) It provides customers with design ideas. (D) It offers to process orders over the phone.	關於 iConstruct，何者不正確？ (A) 銷售別家公司製造的產品。 (B) 保證目錄裡油漆顏色的準確度。 (C) 提供消費者設計上的靈感。 (D) 可以透過電話訂購。

■ **Not/True** Not 問題　　　　　　　　　　　　　　　　　　　　　　　　　　　解答 (B)

本題是要在文章中找到與本問題的重點 iConstruct 公司相關的內容後，比較選項與文章的 Not/True 問題。
(A) 在文章中 check out the hundreds of colors from various manufactures listed in this catalog 提到請顧客在目錄上確認多家廠牌的上百種顏色，與文章內容一致。(B) It guarantees the accuracy of paint colors in its catalog 跟文章中 The colors in the catalog may vary slightly from the actual shades （目錄中的顏色可能會與實際上的色度有些許差異）內容所提到的不一樣，因此 (B) 是正確答案。(C) 在文章中 this catalog includes photos showing different combinations that you may use 提到目錄裡也包含顧客可以使用的不同配色，跟文章內容一致。(D) 在 If you wish to get some samples, ~ give us a call 提到如果想要取得樣品請電話聯絡，也與文章內容一致。

單字　guarantee v. 保證　accuracy n. 準確度　offer v. 提供

How can customers receive product samples?	顧客如何能收到樣品？
(A) By calling an interior decorator	(A) 打電話給室內裝潢師
(B) By making an online request	(B) 從網路上提出要求
(C) By visiting an establishment	(C) 到店洽詢
(D) By coordinating with a manufacturer	(D) 和製造商協調

■ 六何原則 How　　　　　　　　　　　　　　　　　　　　　　　　　　　解答 (C)

是在問顧客們如何（How）取得樣品的問題，因此要與問題的重點 customers receive product samples 有關。文章中 If you wish to get some samples, ~ give us a call 提到如果想要取得樣品請電話聯絡，You may also order in person at our outlets 則是指也可以在賣場直接訂購，因此 (C) By visiting an establishment 是正確答案。

換句話說

outlets 賣場 → an establishment 店鋪，賣場

單字　interior decorator phr. 室內裝潢師　request n. 請求　establishment n. 賣場，店鋪
　　　coordinate v. 協議，協力　manufacture n. 製造業

Questions 162-164 refer to the following advertisement.   162-164 根據下面的廣告內容回答問題。

Rundin-Summers Business solutions for the modern world!	**Rundin-Summers 公司** 現代世界的企業諮詢！
[162]Chart your career and make your dreams a reality at Rundin-Summers!	[162]在 Rundin-Summers 公司裡，計畫你的生涯，讓你的夢想成真！
If you have talent and want to become part of a team determined to succeed at the highest level, then we need you.	如果你有天分，且希望成為成功的高層團隊的一分子，那你就是我們所需要的人。
Work at Rundin-Summers and take advantage of the career opportunities we have in store for you. [163-A]As a world leader in business solutions, Rundin-Summers provides exceptional human resource services for more than 500 companies internationally. **Our numerous clients require us to employ people from various industries. That is why** [164-B/C/D]our company is actively seeking qualified people from the healthcare, personnel management, finance, and publishing fields.	在 Rundin-Summers 公司工作，並善用我們為你預備的就業資源，[163-A] Rundin-Summers 公司在企業諮詢是全世界的領導者，提供獨一無二的人力資源服務給全球五百家以上的公司。我們為廣泛的客戶群招募來自各行各業的人才，這也是為什麼 [164-B/C/D] 我們公司一直積極地在醫療照護、人事管理、金融、出版業等領域尋找合適的人才。
In addition to ensuring our employees' career growth, we offer competitive salary and compensation packages as well as travel opportunities.	除了確保我們員工職業生涯的成長，我們提供了具有競爭性的薪水與福利，以及出差的機會。
Join our team now. To learn more about job openings at Rundin-Summers, please visit www.rundinsummers.com.	現在就加入我們的團隊！想知道更多 Rundin-Summers 公司的工作機會，請上我們的網站 www.rundinsummerscareers.com

單字　□chart v. 設立計畫，規畫　　□talent n. 才能　　□take advantage of phr. 利用～
　　　□opportunity n. 機會　　□in store phr. 準備，儲藏　　□exceptional a. 超群的，例外的
　　　□require v. 要求，需要　　□various a. 多樣的　　□field n. 領域
　　　□personnel a. 人事的，職員的　　□finance n. 金融，財政　　□in addition to phr. 除了～，不只～
　　　□ensure v. 保障　　□competitive a. 有競爭力的
　　　□compensation package phr.（包含薪水與福利的）總體薪酬　　□as well as phr. 不只～，也～

162

Why was the advertisement written?	為什麼有這則廣告？
(A) To introduce a service	(A) 要介紹一項服務
(B) To describe expansion plans	(B) 要描述擴張的計畫
(C) To promote a newly established company	(C) 要宣傳一家新公司
(D) To attract job applicants	(D) 要吸引工作應徵者

■ 找出主題 寫文章的理由　　　　　　　　　　　　　　　　　　　　　　　　　解答 (D)

因為是要找出寫這篇廣告的原因，所以要注意前半段 Chart your career and make your dreams a reality at Rundin-Summers! If you have talent and want to become part of a team determined to succeed at the highest level, than we need you. Work at Rundin-Summers and take advantage of the career opportunities we have in store for you. 提到 Rundin-Summers 需要有天分且想成為成功的高層團隊的一分子，先在 Rundin-Summers 公司工作累積經歷後，再善用公司提供的就業資源，移轉至其他工作。因此正確答案是 (D) To attract job applicants。

單字 expansion n. 擴張　attract v. 吸引　applicant n. 應徵者

What is indicated about Rundin-Summers?	文中指出關於 Rundin-Summers 公司的什麼？
(A) It is a global company.	(A) 它是一家全球性公司。
(B) It plans to operate additional branches.	(B) 它計畫要開分公司。
(C) It is involved with stock investment.	(C) 它跨足股票投資。
(D) It publishes medical material.	(D) 它出版醫療資訊。

■ **Not/True** True 問題 　　　　　　　　　　　　　　　　　　　　　　　　　　　　　　　　解答 (A)

本題是要在文章中找到與本問題的重點 Rundin-Summers 公司相關的內容後，比較選項與文章的 Not/True 問題。文章中 As a world leader in business solutions, Rundin-Summers provides exceptional human resource services for more than 500 companies internationally. 提到 Rundin-Summers 公司在企業諮詢界是全世界的領導者，提供獨一無二的人力資源服務給全球五百家以上的公司，因此要選擇 (A) It is a global company. 為正確答案。(B) (C) (D) 的內容都是文章中沒有提到的。

換句話說

provides ~ services ~ internationally 提供全球性的服務 → is a global company 全球化的企業

單字　stock investment phr. 股票投資　medical a. 醫學的，醫療的

Who most likely would NOT be considered for a position at Rundin-Summers?	誰最不可能被考慮成為 Rundin-Summers 的員工？
(A) Engineers	(A) 工程師
(B) Personnel officers	(B) 人事部職員
(C) Accountants	(C) 會計師
(D) Editors	(D) 編輯

■ **Not/True** Not 問題 　　　　　　　　　　　　　　　　　　　　　　　　　　　　　　　　解答 (A)

本題是要在文章中找到與本問題的重點 be considered for a position at Rundin-Summers 相關的內容後，比較選項與文章的 Not/True 問題。因此 (A) Engineers 是正確答案。文章中 our company is active seeking qualified people from the healthcare, personnel management, finance, and publishing fields 提到公司一直積極地在醫療照護、人事管理、金融、出版業等領域尋找合適的人才，而 (B) (C) (D) 都與本句有關，所以要選擇 (A) 為正確答案。

單字　accountant n. 會計師　editor n. 編輯

Questions 165-167 refer to the following announcement. 165-167 根據下面的告示內容回答問題。

The Discovery Center's Special Events	探索中心的特別活動
165The most-visited interactive science museum in Asia is celebrating its 20th birthday! Join us in commemorating the Discovery Center's two decades of educating the world about great scientific breakthroughs in fun and exciting ways.	165亞洲最多人參觀的互動式科學博物館正舉辦二十週年慶！和我們一起紀念探索中心二十年來透過趣味新奇的方式來教育世界偉大的科學突破發現。
During the entire month of June, we will conduct special exhibits related to technology, space exploration, environment, and biology. The schedule of events is as follows:	在整個六月份，我們會進行幾場和科技、太空探索與環境與生物相關的特別展覽，活動的時程如下：
June 1-8: Robots and Mechanical Devices June 9-14: Exploring Outer Space 166June 15-21: Ecosystems and Habitats June 22-30: Plants and Animals	6 月 1 日至 8 日: 機器人與機械裝置 6 月 9 日至 14 日: 外太空探險 1666 月 15 日至 21 日: 生態系統及保育地 6 月 22 日至 30 日: 植物與動物
167-DEntrance to the exhibits is included in the museum's regular admission fee. Take your family and friends to the Discovery Center and enjoy a new learning experience. For inquiries, call 555-8406.	167-D展覽的參觀包含在博物館的一般入場費裡面，帶你的家人和朋友來探索中心，好好享受一個全新的學習經驗，如有任何問題，請聯絡 558-8406。
DISCOVERY CENTER Canine Road, Great Heights www.discoverycenter.com	探索中心 Canine 路，Great Heights 市 www.discoverycenter.com

單字 □interactive a. 互動的　□commemorate v. 慶祝，紀念　□decade n. 十年
　　 □educate v. 教導，教育　□breakthrough n. 革新，突破　□exhibit n. （一場）展覽會，展示品
　　 □exploration n. 探查，探險　□admission n. 入場

165

What is the announcement about?	這個告示是關於什麼？
(A) An establishment's anniversary	(A) 一個機構建立的週年慶祝活動
(B) An upcoming lecture series	(B) 即將來到的一系列演講
(C) Changes to operation hours	(C) 營業時間的變動
(D) New admission rates	(D) 新的票價

■ 找出主題 主題　　　　　　　　　　　　　　　　　　　　　　　　　　　　　　　　　解答 (A)

因為是要找出寫這篇告示的原因，所以要注意前半段 The most-visited interactive science museum in Asia is celebrating its 20th birthday! 提到亞洲最多人參觀的互動式科學博物館正舉辦二十週年慶，而後面則附帶了慶祝活動的時程，因此要選 (A) An establishment's anniversary 為正確答案。

單字 upcoming a. 即將到來的，接近的　operation hour phr. 營業時間　rate n. 費用，價格

166

What will the event on June 20 most likely be about?	什麼樣的活動最有可能在 6 月 20 日舉行？
(A) Technology	(A) 科技
(B) Astronomy	(B) 天文
(C) Environment	(C) 環境
(D) Biology	(D) 生物

■ 六何原則 What   解答 (C)

這題是在問 6 月 20 日要舉辦什麼（What）活動的六何原則問題，因為問題的重點是 the event in June 20，在文章中與它相關的 June 15-21:Ecosystems and Habitats 提到 6 月 15 日至 6 月 21 日的活動與生態系統及保育地有關，因此 (C) Environment 是正確答案。

換句話說

Ecosystems and Habitats 生態系統及保育地 → Environment 環境

167

What is mentioned about the exhibits?	文中提到與展覽有關的事為何？
(A) They are exclusively for students.	(A) 這些展覽只針對學生。
(B) They will be conducted in two months.	(B) 這些展覽在兩個月後舉行。
(C) They will feature the work of local inventors.	(C) 展覽的特色是當地發明家的作品。
(D) They are covered by the admission fee.	(D) 展覽的參觀費包含在入場費裡面。

■ Not/True True 問題   解答 (D)

本題是要在文章中找到與本問題的重點 the exhibits 相關的內容後，比較選項與文章的 Not/True 問題。(A) (B) (C) 都是在文章中沒有出現過的內容。文章中 Entrance to the exhibits is included in the museum's regular admission fee 是在說明展覽的參觀費用已包含在一般入場費中，因此選擇 (D) They are covered by the admission fee. 為正確答案。

換句話說

include in the ~ admission fee 包含在入場費中 → covered by the admission fee 被入場費所包含

單字 exclusively ad. 只有，獨佔性地　local a. 當地的　inventor n. 發明家

Questions 168-171 refer to the following letter.

168-171 根據下面的信件內容回答問題。

Letters to the Editor

The article written by Vicky Mendel that appeared in last month's issue of *Metro Chic* was fascinating. It featured various types of safe and fast weight-loss treatments. [169-D] I work long hours and have no time to go to the gym, so learning about convenient ways to reduce weight really interests me.

[168]Convinced by the article, I tried the radio frequency treatment. It is a non-surgical technology that breaks down fat cells by using a machine that emits radio waves deep into the layers of a person's skin. At the same time, [171-C]it reduces the appearance of cellulite and makes the skin look smoother. According to Ms. Mendel, she had the procedure done on her abdominal area and lost four inches around her waist after just one session.

Last week, I had my appointment to receive radio frequency treatment at the same clinic Ms. Mendel visited. [170-C/171-A]The procedure was painless and took approximately 30 minutes, but [168]after measuring the results, I was disappointed to learn I had only lost one inch.

[171-B]The physician at the clinic then told me that results can vary greatly and depend on the number of times a person goes in for treatment. Also, in order to maintain my desired figure, I would need to return for additional sessions on a regular basis. [168/170-A]With each session costing $175, I find this treatment just isn't worth the money. Other readers may have a different point of view.

Marilyn Patterson
Chicago, IL

給編輯的信

Metro Chic 上個月那一期有一篇 Vicky Mendel 所寫的文章實在很吸引人。文中特別指出多種安全而快速的減重治療。[169-D]我的工作時數很長,沒有時間上健身房運動,所以對於學習便利的減重方式非常有興趣。

[168]我被這篇文章說服,於是嘗試了無線電波治療,這是一種非手術性的科技,利用機器發出無線電波深入皮膚內層來消除脂肪細胞,同時,[171-C]也減少了橘皮組織,讓皮膚看起來更光滑。根據 Mendel 女士,她在腹部做過這樣的治療,而且在一次治療後就減少了四吋的腰圍。

上個星期,我去了 Mendel 女士去的那家診所接受無線電波治療,[170-C/171-A]整個療程無痛,而且大概花了三十分鐘,不過 [168]在測量結果之後,我很失望我只減少了一吋。

[171-B]那家診所的醫生告訴我,治療後的成果差異很大,並取決於治療的次數,而且,為了維持我想要的身材,我必須定期回來接受額外的療程。[168/170-A] 一次療程要花費 175 美元,我覺得這樣的治療並不值得花這筆錢。其他的讀者可能會有不同的看法。

Marilyn Patterson
芝加哥,伊利諾州

單字 □fascinating a. 迷人的　□feature v.（文章等）特別指出,以～為特色
□treatment n. 手術,治療　□convince v. 說服　□break down phr. 瓦解
□emit v. 散發　□appearance n. 出現,冒出　□approximately ad. 大概,將近
□disappointed a. 感到失望的　□vary v. 差異　□maintain v. 維持
□desired a. 渴望的,希望的　□worth a. 有～價值的

168

What is the main purpose of the letter?
(A) To correct information in an article
(B) To congratulate the writer of a magazine
(C) To provide an opinion about a treatment
(D) To make a suggestion to an editor

這封信主要的目的為何?
(A) 指正文章中的資訊
(B) 恭喜一本雜誌中的作者
(C) 對一種治療方式提出意見
(D) 給編輯一個建議

■ 找出主題 目的　　　　　　　　　　　　　　　　　　　　　　　解答 (C)

這是一題需要找出寫信原因的問題。特別是需要瀏覽過整封信件再找出主題。文中 Convinced by the article, I tried the radio frequency treatment. 提到此封信的作者被文章說服,於是跑去嘗試無線電波治療之後,after measuring the results, I was disappointed to learn I only lost one inch 跟 With each session costing $175, I find this treatment just isn't worth the money. 則指出作者不滿意無線電波治療的結果,並認為沒有價值。因此要選 (C) To provide an opinion about a treatment 為正確答案。

What is mentioned about Ms. Patterson?	文中提到關於 Patterson 小姐的什麼？
(A) She contributes stories to *Metro Chic*.	(A) 她投稿給 Metro Chic 雜誌。
(B) She is trying to publish a new book.	(B) 她想要出版一本新書。
(C) She conducted an interview with Vicky Mendel.	(C) 她訪談了 Vicky Mendel。
(D) She cannot exercise due to a busy work schedule.	(D) 由於工作很忙，她無法運動。

■ **Not/True** True 問題　　　　　　　　　　　　　　　　　　　　　　　　解答 (D)

本題是要在文章中找到與本問題的重點 Ms. Patterson 相關的內容後，比較選項與文章的 Not/True 問題。(A) (B) (C) 都是在文章中沒有出現過的內容。(D) 在文章中 I work long hours and have no time to go to the gym 指出寫這封信的 Patterson 小姐因為長時間工作，沒有時間到健身房運動，因此要選 (D) She cannot exercise due to a busy work schedule. 為正確答案。

單字 contribute v. 貢獻，投稿　publish v. 出版　conduct v. 實施，進行

What does Ms. Patterson say about her experience at the clinic?	關於在診所中的經驗，Patterson 小姐說了什麼？
(A) It was not worth spending a lot of money on.	(A) 不值得花很多錢。
(B) Results became visible after one week.	(B) 成效在一週後顯現。
(C) The procedure caused some pain.	(C) 過程中會有點兒痛。
(D) The clinical staff was not very professional.	(D) 診所裡的員工不是很專業。

■ **Not/True** True 問題　　　　　　　　　　　　　　　　　　　　　　　　解答 (A)

本題是要在文章中找到與本問題的重點 Ms. Patterson 相關的內容後，比較選項與文章的 Not/True 問題。(A) 在文章中 With each session costing $175, I find this treatment just isn't worth the money. 指每次治療都要花 175 元，因此 Patterson 小姐認為沒有這個價值，所以 (A) It was not worth spending a lot of money on. 是正確答案。(B) 是文章中沒有提及的內容。(C) 文章中 The procedure was painless. 是指過程並不痛，與文章內容不符。(D) 也是文章中沒有提及的內容。

單字 visible a. 可見到的

What is NOT stated about radio frequency treatment?	關於無線電波治療，並沒有提到什麼？
(A) It lasts for about half an hour.	(A) 差不多要半個小時。
(B) It may require several sessions.	(B) 需要好幾次的療程。
(C) It improves the appearance of a person's skin.	(C) 能改善皮膚的外表。
(D) It involves regular visits to a local gym.	(D) 要定期去附近的健身房。

■ **Not/True** Not 問題　　　　　　　　　　　　　　　　　　　　　　　　解答 (D)

本題是要在文章中找到與本問題的重點 radio frequency treatment 相關的內容後，比較選項與文章的 Not/True 問題。選項 (A) 於文中 The procedure ~ took approximately 30 minutes 指整個療程大概花了三十分鐘，選項敘述與文章內容一致。選項 (B) 在 The physician at the clinic then told me that results ~ depend on the number of times a person goes in for treatment. Also, ~ I would need to return for additional sessions on a regular basis. 中說明醫生向作者解釋治療後的成果差異很大，且與治療的次數有關，要維持想要的身材，Patterson 小姐必須要定期再回來接受額外的療程，選項敘述與文章內容一致。選項 (C) 在 It reduces the appearance of cellulite and makes the skin look smoother. 中提到它可以減少橘皮組織，讓皮膚看起來更光滑，選項敘述與文章內容一致。(D) 則是文章內容中沒有提及的部分，所以 (D) It involves regular visits to a local gym. 是正確答案。

Questions 172-175 refer to the following letter.　　　172-175 根據下面的信件內容回答問題。

Percussion Unlimited 1214 Robson Street, Vancouver, BC V5Y-1V4	Percussion 公司 Robson 街 1214 號，溫哥華， 英屬哥倫比亞省 V5Y-1V4
April 6 Dear Mr. Howard, 172Thank you for inquiring about our sound equipment. We have been in the business for more than twenty years and have been providing music for weddings, business events, and music festivals. 173We would be happy to make arrangements for your company's upcoming anniversary party with a 1970s theme. In fact, 173we did something similar for Gentech Corporation just last month, which was attended by more than 500 guests. We can offer you a complete sound system package with a digital mixing console, amplifiers, loudspeakers, vocal microphones with stands, and disco lights. 174-DWe also have hundreds of 1970s tracks to keep your guests partying throughout the night. In addition, 174-A/Cour seasoned disc jockeys and technicians will ensure that our equipment provides high sound quality. 175We have a base rate for delivery to locations in the Vancouver area, including Victoria, Burnaby, and Surrey, but do charge more for events held in other locations within the province. For more information on our rental and delivery rates, see the enclosed brochure. If you are interested, please call me at 555-0606 so that we may reserve equipment for your event. Respectfully yours, Tanya Byers Manager Percussion Unlimited	4 月 6 日 親愛的 Howard 先生， 172謝謝您詢問我們的音響設備。我們從事這個行業已經超過二十年了，一直以來我們為婚禮、商業活動、音樂祭提供音樂，173我們很高興能安排貴公司即將到來，以七零年代為主題的年度派對。事實上，173上個月我們為 Gentech 公司安排了類似的活動，有超過五百位賓客參加。我們可以提供一整套的音響系統，有完整的數位混音控制台、擴音器、擴音喇叭、直立式麥克風和舞池燈光。174-D我們還有數百首七零年代的曲子，讓您的貴賓能玩個通宵，此外，174-A/C我們經驗豐富的 DJ 和技術人員會確保我們的設備提供高品質的音效。 175將設備運到溫哥華地區，含 Victoria、Burnaby 和 Surrey，有基本費用，但在該省其他地區舉辦活動，會收取更多費用。關於更多我們租借與運送的價格詳情，請參考隨函的小冊子，如果您有興趣，請撥打 555-0606 與我聯絡，我們可以為您的活動保留設備。 Tanya Byers 敬上 經理 Percussion 公司

單字　□inquire v. 提問　　　　　　□arrangement n. 準備，安排　　□amplifier n. 擴音器
　　　□loudspeaker n. 揚聲機，擴音喇叭　□seasoned a. 老練的，有經驗的　□ensure v. 保障
　　　□charge v. 收費　　　　　　　□province n. 州，省　　　　　□enclosed a. 封閉的，封入的
　　　□reserve v. 預約，保留

172

Why was the letter written?	為什麼寫這封信？
(A) To promote a new line of sound equipment	(A) 推銷新的音響設備
(B) To answer a question about services	(B) 答覆關於服務上的問題
(C) To inquire about a technical repair	(C) 詢問一項技術上的維修
(D) To decline a business offer	(D) 拒絕一項商業上的提議

■ 找出主題 寫文章的理由　　　　　　　　　　　　　　　　　　　　　　　　　　　解答 (B)

因為是在問寫這封信的理由，所以要注意前面段落。在 Thank you for inquiring about our sound equipment. 指出對於詢問音響設備表示感謝，接著針對 Percussion 提供的服務進行說明，因此 (B) To answer a question about services 是正確答案。

單字 promote v. 宣傳，推銷　decline v. 拒絕

What type of event was Percussion Unlimited previously involved in? (A) A musical concert (B) A trade show (C) A company celebration (D) A product launch	Percussion 公司之前辦的活動是什麼？ (A) 音樂會 (B) 貿易展 (C) 公司慶祝活動 (D) 新產品上市

■ 六何原則 What   解答 (C)

這題是在問 Percussion 公司之前參與的活動是哪種類型（What）的六何原則問題。要在文章中找出跟問題的重點 type of event ~ Percussion Unlimited previously involved in 有關係的內容。文章中 We would be happy to make arrangements for your company's upcoming anniversary 提到很高興能替貴公司安排即將到來的年度派對，之後也說到 we did something similar for Gentech Corporation just last month 表示上個月才替 Gentech 公司準備過類似的活動，因此 (C) A company celebration 是正確答案。

換句話說
company's ~ anniversary party 公司紀念日派對 → A company celebration 企業紀念活動

單字 launch n.（商品）發表

What does Ms. Byers NOT suggest about Percussion Unlimited? (A) It has a staff of technicians. (B) It has several branches. (C) It guarantees high sound quality. (D) It provides musical recordings.	Byers 小姐沒有提到 Percussion 公司的哪件事？ (A) 公司有技術人員。 (B) 有好幾個分公司。 (C) 保證高品質的音效。 (D) 提供音樂唱片。

■ Not/True Not 問題   解答 (B)

本題是要在文章中找到與本問題的重點 Percussion Unlimited 相關的內容後，比較選項與文章的 Not/True 問題。(A) 和 (C) 都與文章中的 our seasoned disc jockeys and technicians will ensure that our equipment provides high sound quality（我們經驗豐富的 DJ 和技術人員會確保我們的設備提供最高品質的音效）這句內容一致。(B) 則是在文章中沒有被提及的內容，因此 (B) It has several branches. 是正確答案。(D) 的內容跟 We also have hundreds of 1970s tracks（我們還有數百首七零年代的曲子）說法一致。

單字 branch n. 分店，分公司

What does Ms. Byers indicate? (A) The company offers services to locations throughout the province. (B) She met Mr. Howard at another event. (C) Discounts are offered in Vancouver. (D) She is unable to meet all of Mr. Howard's requirements.	Byers 小姐提到了什麼？ (A) 該公司在全省都可提供到府服務。 (B) 她和 Howard 先生在另一個場合見過面。 (C) 在溫哥華地區可享有折扣。 (D) 她無法滿足 Howard 先生所提的所有要求。

■ 推論 詳細內容   解答 (A)

這是需要藉著文章中關於寫信人 Ms. Byers 的線索推論出答案的題目。因為問題中沒有關於文章的重點，因此要由各選項的內容來找出答案。文章中 We have a base rate for delivery to locations in the Vancouver area, ~ but do charge more for events held in other locations within the province.（將設備運到溫哥華地區需要基本費用，而如果是在該省其他地方的話則需要更多的費用。）因此可以得知這項服務是可以提供全省服務的，所以 (A) The company offers services to locations throughout the province. 是正確答案。

單字 meet a requirement phr. 滿足需求

[176]**Furniture Maker Debuts on Morrow Stock Exchange**

[176]Jerome Furnishings made history yesterday by becoming the first-ever publicly listed furniture company on the Morrow Stock Exchange. **The firm floated 500,000 shares of stock at $20 apiece and collected $10 million equity capital in its initial public offering (IPO).**

[178]The capital obtained from the IPO is expected to allow the company to create new products and expand its range of services. Jerome Furnishings hopes to venture into customizing furniture for corporate centers, hotels, and recreational areas, in addition to creating new models of household furniture.

Theodore Campbell, Jerome Furnishings' managing director for East Asia, said the company is currently in talks with Ohana Bay Hotel over a proposal to renovate the establishment's rooms and facilities.

Founded in 1985, [177]the company has been famous for its stylish products and innovative interior design solutions. Since its initial launch, the company has seen many successful expansions, becoming one of the largest home furniture and décor manufacturers and retailers in the world with more than 30 branches all over Asia, Europe, and North America.

Nevertheless, [180]Jerome Furnishings was acquired by real estate developer Meredith Construction seven years ago when the furniture giant shut down some outlets due to alleged mismanagement of funds.

The successful stock auction, however, proves that Jerome Furnishings has regained its strength. "The event confirmed the public's confidence in the company and gave hope for the fulfillment of its future plans," Campbell said.

[176]家具製造商首次在 Morrow 股票交易市場上市

[176]Jerome 家具公司昨日創下新的歷史紀錄，是首家在 Morrow 股票交易市場公開上市的家具公司。這家公司釋出五十萬股，以每股 20 美元的價格，在首次公開募股（IPO）中募集到一千萬美元的主權資本。

[178]從公開募股中所得的資金將使公司能夠開發新產品，並擴展服務範圍。除了開發新樣式的居家家具，Jerome 家具公司希望能走向為企業中心、旅館、娛樂場所提供客製家具。

Jerome 家具公司的亞東區管理主任 Theodore Campbell 說該公司正在與 Ohana Bay 飯店商議一份裝修飯店房間與設施的提案。

這家公司建立於 1985 年，[177] 以具有流行風格的產品與創新室內設計方案聞名。自從創立以來，此公司已有多次成功的擴張，成為世界上最大的居家家具、裝潢製造商和零售商之一，在亞洲、歐洲、北美洲地區有超過三十家分公司。

不過，[180]七年前，當家具巨擘因為聲稱資金管理不當而關掉部分的暢貨中心時，Jerome 家具公司則由地產開發商 Meredith 建築公司取得經營權。

然而，這次成功的股票競價交易證明了 Jerome 家具公司已經重生，Campbell 先生說：「這個事件確定了大眾對公司的信心，並對於實現我們未來的計畫寄予厚望」。

單字 □list v.（將股票）列入目錄   □stock exchange phr. 股票交易市場 □float v. 發行（股票，公債等）

□equity capital phr. 主權資本   □initial public offering (IPO) phr. 首次公開募股

□venture into phr. 冒險進入，投注事業   □customize v. 客製化

□corporate a. 企業的，公司的   □renovate v. 更新，修繕   □found v. 設立

□innovative a. 創新的   □expansion n. 擴張   □décor n. 裝飾，裝飾物

□manufacturer n. 製造業   □retailer n. 零售業者，零售業   □acquire v. 買入，取得

□real estate phr. 不動產   □alleged a. 聲稱的，被斷言的   □auction n. 競標

□confirm v. 確認   □fulfillment n. 履行，實現

176

Where would this article most likely appear?	這篇文章最有可能在哪裡出現？
(A) In a furniture brochure	(A) 在家具的小冊子裡
(B) In a company's press release	(B) 在公司的新聞稿裡
(C) In an architecture magazine	(C) 在建築雜誌裡
(D) In a business newspaper	(D) 在商業報刊裡

■■ 推論 整體情報   解答 (D)

要透過在文章各處中所提供的線索來判斷這篇新聞可能刊載在哪個地方。新聞標題 Furniture Maker Debuts on Morrow Stock Exchange 以及 Jerome Furnishings made history yesterday by becoming the first-ever publicly listed furniture company on the Morrow Stock Exchange. 指出 Jerome 家具公司昨日創新歷史紀錄成為首家在 Morrow 股票交易市場公開上市的家具公司，之後的新聞大部份都是在說明 Jerome 家具公司的事業擴張及公開募股的報導。因此我們可以推論這篇報導應該刊登於經濟報紙。所以 (D) In a business newspaper 是正確答案。

單字 brochure n. 小冊子　press release phr. 新聞稿　architecture n. 建築

177

According to the article, why are Jerome Furnishings' products popular?	根據本文，為什麼 Jerome 家具公司的產品很受歡迎？
(A) They are custom-made.	(A) 他們的產品是客製化的。
(B) They last a long time.	(B) 他們的產品很耐久。
(C) They are fashionable.	(C) 他們的產品符合潮流。
(D) They are inexpensive.	(D) 他們的價格不貴。

■■ 六何原則 Why   解答 (C)

是詢問 Jerome 家具公司的產品為什麼（Why）會受到歡迎的六何原則問題。要在文章中找出跟問題的重點 Jerome Furnishing's products popular 有關係的內容。文章中 the company has been famous for its stylish products 說到 Jerome 家具公司以具有流行風格的產品而聞名。因此 (C) They are fashionable. 是正確答案。

換句話說
popular 受歡迎的 → famous for ~ 以～聞名
stylish 有風格的 → fashionable 流行的

單字 custom-made a. 客製的　last v. 維持，持續

178

Why did Jerome Furnishings raise capital?	為什麼 Jerome 家具公司要募集資金？
(A) It has to repay its loans.	(A) 為了要償還貸款。
(B) It needs to open new outlets.	(B) 為了要新開一間暢貨中心。
(C) It wants to broaden its offerings.	(C) 為了要擴展業務。
(D) It plans to renovate its office building.	(D) 為了要重新裝修他們的辦公大樓。

■■ 六何原則 Why   解答 (C)

是詢問 Jerome 家具公司為什麼（Why）要募集資金的六何原則問題。要在文章中找出跟問題的重點 raise capital 有關係的內容。文章中 The capital obtained from the IPO is expected to allow the company to create new products and expand its range of services. 指出從公開募股中所得之資金將使公司能夠開發新產品，並擴展服務範圍。因此 (C) It wants to broaden its offering. 是正確答案。

換句話說
create new products and expand its range of services 開發新產品，並擴展服務範圍
→ broaden its offering 擴大提供的服務

單字 repay v. 償還，還　loan n. 貸款，借出的東西　broaden v. 擴大　offering n. 提供的服務、商品

179

The word "alleged" in paragraph 5, line 2 is closest in meaning to (A) supposed (B) written (C) doubtful (D) warranted	在第五段第二行的「alleged」這個字的意思最接近哪個字？ (A) 料想的 (B) 書面的 (C) 懷疑的 (D) 保證的

■ 同義詞   解答 (A)

在包含 alleged 的句子 due to alleged mismanagement of funds 裡，alleged 的意思是「推論上的」的意思，因此有「推論」涵義的 (A) supposed 是正確答案。

180

What is implied about Meredith Construction? (A) It has several offices around the world. (B) It will construct a hotel. (C) It is seeking new investors. (D) It operates Jerome Furnishings.	關於 Meredith 建築公司，暗示著什麼？ (A) 在世界各地有好幾個辦公室。 (B) 要蓋一間飯店。 (C) 在尋找新的投資者。 (D) 經營 Jerome 家具公司。

■ 推論 詳細內容   解答 (D)

這是需要推論題目中提及的 Meredith Construction 的題目。文章中 Jerome Furnishings was acquired by real estate developer Meredith Construction seven years ago 在說 Jerome 家具公司在七年前由地產開發商 Meredith 建築公司取得經營權。因此我們可以推論 Jerome 家具公司目前是由 Meredith 建築公司在營運。所以 (D) It operates Jerome Furnishings. 是正確答案。

單字 seek v. 尋找，尋求　operate v. 營運

例文1

Cuddly Rascals' Fall Fever!

[181]This fall, we are offering our pet care services at reduced prices! Check out our discounted rates below:

Service	NORMAL RATE	DISCOUNTED RATE
Pet sitting	$25	$16/hour (daytime)
Pet boarding	$40	$35/24 hours
Pet grooming	$53	$45
Dog walking	$24	$18/30 minutes

Prices are on a per-pet basis.
Pets staying overnight are given
three daily meals and regular walks.
[185-A/D]Grooming consists of bathing, drying, brushing, and nail trimming.

[182-D]Take advantage of these low prices by booking a service for this fall. [184]Customers who book in August will receive a voucher for our fall prices. Don't delay, as [182-D]this promotion is valid only until the end of October. And if you are a first time customer, check out our excellent range of pet services.

Stop worrying about where to leave your dog or cat while you're busy at work or away on vacation. At Cuddly Rascals, we guarantee the best services for your pet - or you'll get your money back!

Please give us a call at 555-9312 for more information.

Cuddly Rascals 的秋季熱銷

[181]今年秋天，我們的寵物照顧服務要降價了！參考以下我們優惠的價格：

服務項目	平時價格	折扣價格
寵物保母服務	$25	$16 / 每小時（白天）
寵物住宿服務	$40	$35 / 每 24 小時
寵物清潔美容服務	$53	$45
遛狗服務	$24	$18 / 30 分鐘

以上價格為每一隻寵物計
過夜的寵物，給予一天三餐和
例行外出散步。
[185-A/D]清潔美容服務包括洗澡、吹乾、梳理和修剪指甲

[182-D]今年秋天預約我們的服務，好好利用這些優惠的價格。[184]在八月預約服務的客人，我們會送秋季優惠價的折價券。不要再等了，[182-D]這項優惠只到十月底止。如果你是第一次來店的顧客，好好看看我們提供的各種完善的寵物服務。

不要再擔心工作忙碌或外出度假時要把你的貓狗留在哪裡。在 Cuddly Rascals，我們保證為你的寵物提供最佳的服務，否則我們會把錢退還給你！

更多詳情，請來電 555-9312

例文2

To: Arthur Grady <arthurgrady@tymail.com>
From: appointments@cuddlyrascals.net

[184]Date: August 25
Subject: Re: About Services

Dear Mr. Grady,

[183/184]This is regarding your service request form that we received yesterday. Thanks for considering Cuddly Rascals for your pet care needs. We appreciate your interest in our services.

[183]You asked for two appointments on your form, one for this week and another for next week. Unfortunately, all our staff members are fully booked for this week and will not be able to provide you with [185-A/D]the grooming service you requested. However, the pet sitting and [185-B]dog walking services are available for next week. If you would like, we can schedule all three services together and perform the

收件人：Arthur Grady <arthurgrady@tymail.com>
寄件人：appointments@cuddlyrascals.net
[184]日期：8 月 25 日
主題：Re: 關於服務

親愛的 Grady 先生：

[183/184]關於我們昨天收到您寄來的洽詢表。謝謝您將 Cuddly Rascals 列入您寵物照顧需求的考慮。感謝您對我們的服務感到興趣。

[183]您在表格上問到的兩個預約時段，一個是這個星期，另一個是下個星期。很抱歉，我們的員工這個星期都被預約了，將無法為您提供 [185-A/D]您要求的寵物清潔美容服務。不過，[185-B]下星期可提供寵物保母及遛狗的服務。如果您想要，我們可以把這三項服

grooming service in your home. Feel free to contact us at your earliest convenience once you make a decision regarding our services. Also, if you do decide to use our services, we need some information about your dog to help us prepare for the appointments, such as its name, breed, and age. So please have this information on hand when you contact us.

Should there be other services that you would like to request for your dog, let us know so we can prepare for them right away.

Best regards,
Eloise Tyler
Cuddly Rascals Staff

務排在一起，就在您的府上進行寵物清潔美容服務。一旦您做了與我們的服務有關的決定，在您方便時儘早與我們聯絡。另外，如果您決定要我們的服務，我們需要一些關於您狗狗的資料，以幫助我們做準備，例如名字、品種和年齡。所以您在與我們聯絡時，請備好這些資料。

如果你想要為你的狗狗要求其他服務，請讓我們知道，好讓我們盡快為你安排。

Eloise Tyler 敬上
Cuddly Rascals 員工

例文 1 單字 □pet n. 寵物　　　　□board v. 用木板覆蓋，供膳宿　□groom v. 清潔（寵物等）
　　　　　□walk v. 遛（狗等寵物）　□basis n. 基準，基礎　　　□trim v. 修剪
　　　　　□voucher n. 折價券　　□guarantee v. 保證

例文 2 單字 □regarding prep. 關於～　□appointment n. 預約　　□perform v. 履行，實施
　　　　　□breed n. 品種　　　　□arrange v. 安排，處理（事情）

181

What is being advertised?	被廣告的是什麼？
(A) Services for domestic animals	(A) 居家寵物的服務
(B) A job at a pet store	(B) 寵物店的職缺
(C) Seasonal fashions	(C) 季節性的流行趨勢
(D) The opening of an establishment	(D) 新店開張

■ 找出主題 主題　　　　　　　　　　　　　　　　　　　　　　　　　　　　　解答 (A)

這一題需要找出為什麼要寫這篇廣告的原因，所以要在例文 1 裡找出相關的內容。This fall, we are offering our pet care services at reduced price! 這句說到今年秋天寵物照顧服務要降價，而後面的文章在說明提供的服務，因此 (A) Services for domestic animals 是正確答案。

換句話說

pet 寵物 → domestic animals 寵物

單字 domestic a. 馴養的，家庭的，國內的　establishment n. 設施，店鋪

182

What is indicated about Cuddly Rascals' promotional offer?	關於 Cuddly Rascals 的優惠文章指示了什麼？
(A) It is exclusively for current customers.	(A) 只針對現有的顧客。
(B) It is available on weekdays.	(B) 適用於星期一到星期五。
(C) It is limited to a particular branch.	(C) 僅限於一個特定的分店。
(D) It is a seasonal offer.	(D) 屬於季節性的優惠。

■ Not/True True 問題　　　　　　　　　　　　　　　　　　　　　　　　　解答 (D)

本題是要在文章中找到與本問題的重點 Cuddly Rascals's promotional offer 相關的內容後，比較選項與文章的 Not/True 問題。首先可以得知這是與例文 1 中 Cuddly Rascals 的促銷折扣有關的問題。(A) (B) (C) 都是文章沒有提及的內容。Take advantage of these low prices ~ for this fall 是說多利用這次秋天的低價服務，之後的 this promotion is valid only until the end of October 是說這次的促銷只有到十月，因此 (D) It is a seasonal offer. 是正確答案。

單字 particular a. 特定的　exclusively ad. 只為了～，獨家地

What is suggested about Cuddly Rascals?	關於 Cuddly Rascals 文章提到了什麼？
(A) It includes food with its pet sitting service.	(A) 寵物保母服務也會提供食物。
(B) It requires customers to fill out a form.	(B) 要求顧客填表。
(C) It takes in animals that have been abandoned.	(C) 收容被遺棄的動物。
(D) It offers coupons to those booking several services.	(D) 送折價券給預約多項服務的顧客。

■ 推論 詳細內容　　　　　　　　　　　　　　　　　　　　　　　　　　　解答 (B)

這是需要推論題目中提及的 Cuddly Rascals 的題目，由例文 2 中 Cuddly Rascals 寄出的信件內容進行推論。信件中的 This is regarding your service request form that we received yesterday. 指出這是關於昨天所收到的洽詢表的電子郵件，You asked for two appointments on your form 則是說在洽詢表中填寫了兩個預約時段，因此我們可以推論出 Cuddly Rascals 要求顧客要填寫洽詢表。所以 (B) It requires customers to fill out a form. 是正確答案。

單字 require v. 要求　　abandon v. 遺棄，拋棄

What is indicated about Mr. Grady?	關於 Grady 先生，文章指示了什麼？
(A) He qualifies for a special promotion.	(A) 他具備享有特別促銷活動的資格。
(B) He is a frequent customer of Cuddly Rascals.	(B) 他是 Cuddly Rascals 的常客。
(C) He has met Ms. Tyler in the past.	(C) 他見過 Tyler 小姐。
(D) He wants to work in the pet care industry.	(D) 他想在寵物照顧行業裡工作。

■ 推論 聯結問題　　　　　　　　　　　　　　　　　　　　　　　　　　　解答 (A)

這是綜合兩篇文章的內容之後，進行推論再解題的題型。首先從和問題中的重點 Mr. Grady 有較密切關係的例文 2 開始看起。

從例文 2 電子郵件的 Date: August 25 可判斷郵件是在 8 月 25 日寫的。This is regarding your service request form that we received yesterday. 指出這是關於昨天收到的洽詢表的回覆，因此可以得到第一個線索：Mr. Grady 是在 8 月時預約服務的。但是因為沒有說明 8 月預約的客人有什麼優惠，所以廣告 Customers who book in August will receive a voucher for our fall prices. 中所提到的 8 月預約服務的客人會收到秋季優惠價的優惠券是第二個線索。

綜合第一個線索：Mr. Grady 在 8 月時預約，跟第二個線索：8 月預約的客人會收到秋季優惠價的優惠券，我們可以推論出 Mr. Grady 的預約可以獲贈優惠券。因此 (A) He qualifies for a special promotion. 是正確答案。

單字 qualify for phr. 有資格　　promotion n. 促銷活動　　frequent customer phr. 常客　　industry n. 產業

What is NOT included in the services Mr. Grady requested?	Grady 先生要求的服務不包括何者？
(A) Brushing	(A) 毛髮梳理
(B) Walking	(B) 遛狗
(C) Feeding	(C) 餵食
(D) Bathing	(D) 洗澡

■ Not/True Not 問題　　　　　　　　　　　　　　　　　　　　　　　　　解答 (C)

本題是要在文章中找到與本問題的重點 the services Mr. Grady request 相關的內容後，比較選項與文章的 Not/True 問題。因為與 Mr. Grady 預約的服務有關，所以要從例文 2 中找出答案。grooming service you requested 提到了申請美容服務，再回到例文 1 的廣告中找出 Grooming consists of bathing, ~ brushing，可以知道美容服務包含了洗澡跟刷毛，由此一來 (A) 和 (D) 都符合文章內容。dog walking services are available for next week 是指下週可提供帶狗散步的服務，因此 (B) 也符合文章內容。(C) 則是與文章內容沒有相關，所以要選 (C) 為正確答案。

Questions 186-190 refer to the following e-mail and schedule.

186-190 根據下面的電郵和時程表內容回答問題。

例文1

To	Genevieve Javier <genevievejavier@shinodauniversity.edu>
From	Michael Eisenberg <michaeleisenberg@shinodauniversity.edu>
Date	May 20
Subject	Commencement Exercises
Attachment	1 file

Hello Genevieve,

I received a call this morning from Damien Sullivan's secretary, Kristy Cook. [186]She said that Mr. Sullivan will be arriving later than expected from a business conference in Kentucky at around 10 o'clock on June 3. [186]That will leave him with just enough time to get here before his scheduled speech at the graduation ceremony. She apologized for the inconvenience, but I told her we could make changes to the program prior to his speech so he can take time to prepare before he goes onstage. We also decided to include an activity right before the introduction of the guest speaker. [187-D]I have already e-mailed her a copy of the program schedule, and she said she would forward it to Mr. Sullivan right away.

[188]As with previous commencement exercises, you will be assigned to accompany our guest of honor. Make sure to be at the campus an hour before the program starts. Once Mr. Sullivan arrives, take him to the conference room in the faculty office, so he can rest a bit or prepare before his speech. I'll let you know when he can come onstage, since I'll be in charge of introducing him.

I have attached the revised schedule for your reference. If you have any questions, do not hesitate to call me at 555-9963.

Thank you.
Michael Eisenberg
Vice president, Shinoda University

收件人：Genevieve Javier <genevievejavier@shinodauniversity.edu>
寄件人：Michael Eisenberg <michaeleisenberg@shinodauniversity.edu>
日期：5 月 20 日
主旨：畢業典禮
附件：一個檔案

Genevieve 你好：

我今天早上接到一通 Damien Sullivan 的祕書 Kristy Cook 打來的電話，[186]她說 Sullivan 先生 6 月 3 日從 Kentucky 州的一個商業會議趕來，會比預計的時間晚到，大約十點左右，[186]如此一來，他只能剛好趕上畢業典禮上預訂的演講時間。她很抱歉造成這樣的不便，但是我告訴她我們可以調整在他演講前的節目，那麼他就能在上台前有些時間準備。我們還決定在介紹演講來賓之前安插一個活動。[187-D]我已經用 e-mail 寄給她一份節目表，她說她會馬上轉寄給 Sullivan 先生。

[188]如之前的畢業典禮，你被分配的工作是招呼我們請來的貴賓。務必在典禮開始前的一個小時到達校園，一旦 Sullivan 先生到了，帶他到教職員辦公室裡的會議間，讓他休息一會兒，或者在演講前稍作準備。我會讓你知道他什麼時候要上台，因為我會負責介紹他。

附件是調整後的節目表，讓你參考，如果你有任何問題，不要客氣，打電話給我，我的電話是 555-9963。

謝謝你。
Michael Eisenberg
副校長，Shinoda 大學

例文2

35TH COMMENCEMENT EXERCISES
SHINODA UNIVERSITY
Winchester Quadrangle■Friday, June 3■8 A.M. – 2:30 P.M.

TIME	ACTIVITY
8:00 – 8:30 A.M.	Processional
8:30 – 9:00 A.M.	Pledge to the Flag/National Anthem
9:30 – 9:50 A.M.	Opening Remarks (Constantino Tejero, President)
9:50 – 10:00 A.M.	Introduction of Student Speaker
10:00 – 10:30 A.M.	[190]Student Association President's Address (Alyssa Caronongan)

第三十五屆畢業典禮
SHINODA 大學
Winchester Quadrangle
6 月 3 日星期五上午八點至下午兩點半

時間	節目
上午 8:00-8:30	遊行
上午 8:30-9:00	向旗幟宣示 / 國歌
上午 9:30-9:50	開幕致詞（Constantino Tejero 校長）
上午 9:50-10:00	介紹學生致詞代表
上午 10:00-10:30	[190]學生會主席致詞（Alyssa Caronongan）

[189-C]10:30 – 10:45 A.M.	Intermission (Armstrong Choir performance)		[189-C]上午10:30-10:45	中場休息（Armstrong 合唱團表演）
10:45 – 11:00 A.M.	Introduction of Guest Speaker		上午10:45-11:00	介紹演講來賓
11:00 – 11:30 A.M.	Address (Damien Sullivan, Attorney, CEO, Sullivan and Associates)		上午11:00-11:30	致詞（Sullivan 聯合事務所執行長 Damien Sullivan 律師）
11:30 A.M. –12:00 P.M.	Presentation of Special Awards		上午11:30-12:00	頒發特別獎
12:00 – 1:30 P.M.	Awarding of Diplomas		下午12:00-1:30	頒發畢業證書
1:30 – 1:45 P.M.	Class Song		下午1:30-1:45	班級獻唱
1:45 – 2:00 P.M.	Closing Remarks (Michael Eisenberg, Vice president)		下午1:45-2:00	閉幕致詞（Michael Eisenberg 副校長）
2:00 – 2:30 P.M.	Recessional		下午2:00-2:30	退場

例文 1 單字 □inconvenience n. 不方便　□forward v. 遞送，轉寄　□commencement exercise phr. 畢業典禮
　　　　　□assign v. 指定，分配　□accompany v. 陪同，伴隨　□faculty n. 教職員，學系
　　　　　□in charge of phr. 負責　□hesitate v. 猶豫

例文 2 單字 □pledge n. 誓言　□national anthem phr. 國歌　□intermission n. 中場休息時間
　　　　　□address n. 演說，致詞　□diploma n. 畢業證書，學位

186

Why did Ms. Cook apologize to Mr. Eisenberg?	為何 Cook 小姐向 Eisenberg 先生道歉？
(A) A flight will be delayed.	(A) 班機會延誤。
(B) A meeting had to be postponed.	(B) 會議需要延期。
(C) An event venue has not been prepared.	(C) 會場尚未準備好。
(D) A schedule needed to be altered.	(D) 節目時間需要變動。

■ 六何原則 Why　　　　　　　　　　　　　　　　　　　　　　　　　　解答 (D)

這是在問 Ms. Cook 為什麼（Why）要跟 Mr. Eisenberg 道歉的六何原則問題。因此要從提到問題的重點 Ms. Cook apologize to Mr. Eisenberg 的例文 1 開始找答案。電子郵件中寫到 She said that Mr. Sullivan will be arriving later than expected from a business conference，當中 She，也就是 Ms. Cook 說 Mr. Sullivan 在商業會議後趕來時會比預計的時間晚到，接著 That will leave him with just enough time to get here before his scheduled speech ~ . She apologized for the inconvenience, but I told her we could make changes to the program 是 Ms. Cook 說 Mr. Sullivan 只能剛好趕上他的演講時間並感到抱歉，而 Mr. Eisenberg 則告訴 Ms. Cook 他可以調整節目表。因此 (D) A schedule needed to be altered 是正確答案。

單字 delay v. 延遲　postpone v. 延期　venue n. 場所　alter v. 變更

187

What is mentioned about Damien Sullivan?	關於 Damien Sullivan，提到了什麼？
(A) He is delivering a speech to a group of business professionals.	(A) 他對一群商務專業人士發表演講。
(B) He graduated from Shinoda University with top honors.	(B) 他以最高榮譽畢業於 Shinoda 大學。
(C) He is planning to donate some money to a school.	(C) 他打算捐錢給一所學校。
(D) He will receive a program schedule from his secretary.	(D) 他會從他祕書那裡收到一份節目表。

■ Not/True True 問題　　　　　　　　　　　　　　　　　　　　　　　解答 (D)

本題是要在文章中找到與問題的重點 Damien Sullivan 相關的內容後，比較選項與文章的 Not/True 問題。先從有言及 Damien Sullivan 的例文 1 中試著找出答案。(A) (B) (C) 都是文章中沒有提及的內容。I have already e-mailed her a copy of the program schedule, and she said she would forward it to Mr. Sullivan right away. 可以得知已經寄出一份節目表給 Ms. Cook，而 Ms. Cook 會即時轉寄給 Mr. Sullivan，因此 (D) He will receive a program schedule from his secretary. 是正確答案。

單字 top honor phr. 首席，最高榮耀　donate v. 捐贈

188

What is suggested about Genevieve Javier?	關於 Genevieve Javier，文章提到什麼？
(A) She has assisted important visitors at graduation ceremonies before.	(A) 她以前協助過畢業典禮上的重要來賓。
(B) She will receive an award for her outstanding service.	(B) 因為她提供的傑出服務而將獲獎。
(C) She is responsible for reviewing Mr. Sullivan's speech.	(C) 她負責審查 Sullivan 先生的演講。
(D) She will introduce the guest speaker this year.	(D) 她今年會介紹演講來賓。

■ 推論 詳細內容　　　　　　　　　　　　　　　　　　　　　　　　　　　解答 (A)

這是需要推論題目中提及的 Genevieve Javier 的題目，要由寄給 Genevieve Javier 的信件，也就是例文 1 的內容開始進行推論。As with previous commencement exercises, you will be assigned to accompany our guest of honor 指出根據以前畢業典禮的經驗，收件人 Genevieve Javier 被分配到招待貴賓的工作，因此我們可以推論收件人在前幾次的畢業典禮中也曾經招待貴賓。所以 (A) She has assisted important visitors at graduation ceremonies before. 是正確答案。

換句話說

guest of honor 貴賓 → important visitors 重要的來賓
commencement exercises 畢業典禮 → graduation ceremonies 畢業典禮

單字 assist v. 幫忙　outstanding a. 出眾的　review v. 檢討，審查

189

What is indicated about the program?	關於節目表，文章指示了什麼？
(A) Lunch will be served after the awarding of diplomas.	(A) 在頒發畢業證書後會供應午餐。
(B) The principal will be absent from the ceremonies.	(B) 校長不會出席典禮。
(C) A musical group will perform before a guest is introduced.	(C) 在介紹來賓之前會有一個音樂團體的表演。
(D) The closing remarks will be moved to a later time.	(D) 閉幕致詞的時間會往後延。

■ Not/True True 問題　　　　　　　　　　　　　　　　　　　　　　　　　解答 (C)

本題是要在文章中找到與問題的重點 the program 相關的內容後，比較選項與文章的 Not/True 問題。在例文 2 中附上的活動節目表找出相關的答案。(A) 和 (B) 都跟文章內容沒有相關。節目表中 10:30-10:45 A.M. Intermission (Armstrong Choir performance) 和 10:45-11:00 A.M. Introduction of Guest Speaker 表示 Armstrong 合唱團的表演比演講者介紹還要早進行，所以 (A) A musical group will perform before a guest is introduced. 是正確答案。(D) 則跟文章內容沒有關係，不可因節目表改變而推論閉幕致詞時間延後。

換句話說

Choir 合唱團 → a musical group 音樂團體

單字 absent a. 缺席，不參加　closing remarks phr. 閉幕致詞

190

Who is Alyssa Caronongan?	Alyssa Caronongan 是誰？
(A) A speech writer for an executive	(A) 為主管撰寫演講稿的人
(B) The leader of a student group	(B) 一個學生團體的領袖
(C) A secretary from a law firm	(C) 一家法律事務所的祕書
(D) The president of an academic institution	(D) 一家學術機構的會長

■ 六何原則 Who　　　　　　　　　　　　　　　　　　　　　　　　　　　解答 (B)

這是在問 Alyssa Caronongan 是誰（Who）的六何原則問題。因此從有提到 Alyssa Caronongan 的例文 2 開始尋找答案。與本問題的重點 Alyssa Caronongan 相關，而且在 Student Association President's Address (Alyssa Caronongan)（學生會長演說）的地方可以看出演說將由 Alyssa Caronongan 進行。所以選擇 (B) The leader of a student group 為正確答案。

換句話說

Student Association President 學生會長 → The leader of a student group 學生團體代表

單字 executive n. 主管，執行長　institution n. 機關，協會

例文1

Haven for Animals Clinic
　　　　Application period: November 1 – December 16

Job Opening for Veterinarians

Haven for Animals is a veterinary clinic accredited by the American Animal Hospital Organization and dedicated to providing quality healthcare to domesticated animals. [191-A/B]Since our establishment in San Diego 15 years ago, we have expanded into other cities such as Los Angeles and San Francisco. We are opening another facility in Sacramento and need five experienced veterinarians to join our team. [192-A/B/D]We offer new doctors a high starting salary and comprehensive compensation package, including retirement savings plans, professional liability packages, medical and dental health insurance, and continuing education allowance.

[194]**Qualifications:**

* A doctor of veterinary medicine degree
* A license to practice veterinary medicine
* [194]At least five years of work experience in a veterinary clinic or hospital
* Outstanding interpersonal skills and a positive, friendly attitude
* Ability to work alone or in a team

Responsibilities:

* Conduct physical examinations as well as medical, dental, and surgical procedures
* Explain examination results to clients and recommend treatments for illnesses as well as supplements for preventive healthcare
* Maintain records of animal patients
* Represent Haven for Animals Clinic at conventions and seminars

Interested applicants are advised to send their résumés and reference letters to our human resources department in San Diego. The deadline for submission of requirements is on December 16. Shortlisted candidates will be notified by phone or e-mail.

動物避風港診所
　　　　申請時間：11 月 1 日至 12 月 16 日

獸醫職缺

動物避風港是一家由美國動物醫院組織所認證的獸醫診所，致力於提供居家寵物高品質的醫療照顧。[191-A/B]從十五年前我們在聖地牙哥創立以來，到目前已擴張到其他城市，像是洛杉磯和舊金山。我們即將在沙加緬度再開一家診所，並需要五位有經驗的獸醫師加入我們的團隊，[192-A/B/D]我們提供新的醫生高額起薪，和綜合性的福利，包括退休儲蓄計畫、專業責任保險、醫療和牙醫保險、繼續進修補助等。

[194]資格：

* 擁有獸醫學位的博士
* 擁有獸醫執業執照
* [194]擁有至少五年在獸醫診所或獸醫院的工作經驗
* 絕佳的人際溝通技巧與正面友善的態度
* 獨立工作與團隊工作的能力

工作責任：

* 執行健康檢查，還有醫療、牙齒、手術等操作程序
* 向客戶解釋檢查結果、建議疾病的治療方式以及健康保養的補給品
* 維護動物病患的病歷資料
* 在會議與研討會中代表動物避風港診所

建議有興趣的應徵者將個人履歷與推薦信函寄給我們在聖地牙哥的人力資源部門，相關資料的繳交截止日期是 12 月 16 日，列入候選名單的應徵者會以電話或電郵通知。

例文2

November 3

Robert Rodriguez
Human resources director
Haven for Animals Clinic

Dear Sir or Madam,

I am writing in response to your job advertisement for veterinarians that appeared in *The Daily News* on November 1. I am a licensed veterinarian in California and am currently employed at St. Bernard Animal Hospital in Oakland. [194/195-C]I have been with the hospital since

11 月 3 日

Robert Rodriguez
人力資源主任
動物避風港診所

敬啟者：

我寫此信來應徵你們 11 月 1 日刊登在 The Daily News 上徵求獸醫師的廣告。我在加州擁有獸醫執照，目前在奧克蘭市的 St. Bernard 動物醫院任職，[194/195-C]從我兩年半前在聖地牙哥的 Riverbank

I finished my doctor of veterinary medicine degree at Riverbank University in San Diego two-and-a-half years ago.

I would like to apply for a position as [195-D]I wish to continue to practice my profession when I move to Sacramento next January. Although I have been in practice for only a short time, I have been highly trained in veterinary surgery and dentistry. Because of this, I am confident that my skills and professional experience will allow me to provide significant contributions to the development of your new clinic.

Enclosed are my résumé and reference letters. If you need more information about my credentials, please contact me at your convenience.

Thank you for your consideration.

Respectfully yours,

Natalie Marquez

大學取得獸醫學博士學位以後就一直在這家醫院工作。

[195-D]我希望在我明年 1 月份搬到沙加緬度後能繼續執行我的專業，因此我想應徵這個職缺。雖然我執業的時間不長，但是我在獸醫手術與牙科的領域受到很好的訓練。因為這個原因，我很有信心我的技術與專業經驗能讓我替你的新診所帶來重大的貢獻。

隨函附有我的個人履歷和推薦函，如你需要更多關於我專業認證的資料，請隨時與我聯絡。

感謝您的慎重考慮。

Natalie Marquez 敬上

例文 1 單字 □veterinary a. 獸醫的；n. 獸醫師
　　　　　□domesticated a. 馴化的
　　　　　□expand v. 擴張
　　　　　□compensation package phr. 福利，津貼
　　　　　□liability n. 責任
　　　　　□qualification n. 資格條件
　　　　　□interpersonal a. 待人處事的
　　　　　□physical examination phr. 健康診療
　　　　　□supplement n. （如維他命等）補充劑
　　　　　□résumé n. 履歷表
　　　　　□submission n. 提交
　　　　　□candidate n. 候補人選

□accredited a. 認可的，公認的
□establishment n. 設立
□comprehensive a. 綜合性的，包括性的
□retirement n. 退休
□allowance n. 補助
□outstanding a. 卓越的
□conduct v. 實施
□surgical a. 外科的，手術的
□preventive a. 預防的
□reference letter phr. 推薦信
□shortlist v. 把～列入最終挑選名單
□notify v. 通知

例文 2 單字 □apply v. 申請，應徵
　　　　　□significant a. 相當的，重要的

□profession n. 職業，專業
□contribution n. 貢獻

191

What is indicated about the Haven for Animals Clinic?
(A) It first opened in Los Angeles.
(B) It has several different locations.
(C) It is looking to hire veterinary assistants.
(D) It plans to renovate a facility.

關於動物避風港診所，文中指示什麼？
(A) 最早是開在洛杉磯。
(B) 有不同的分店。
(C) 正在徵求獸醫助理。
(D) 計畫要重新裝修診所。

Not/True True 問題
解答 (B)

是在文章中找到與本問題的重點 Haven for Animals Clinic 相關的內容後，比較選項與文章的 Not/True 問題。可以從提到 Haven for Animals Clinic 的部分，也就是例文 1 開始找出答案。針對選項 (A) Since our establishment in San Diego 15 years ago, we have expanded into other cities such as Los Angeles and San Francisco. 提到從十五年前他們在聖地牙哥創立以來，到目前已擴張到像是洛杉磯、舊金山等其他城市，所以 (A) 跟文章內容不符，而同樣這一句 Since our establishment in San Diego 15 years ago, we have expanded in to other cities such as Los Angeles and San Francisco. 提到許多不同的城市，因此 (B) It has several different locations. 是正確答案。(C) (D) 都是跟文章沒有相關的內容。

單字 renovate v. 整修

192

What benefit is NOT included in the compensation package? (A) A retirement plan (B) Financial aid for future studies (C) A housing allowance (D) Medical insurance coverage	哪一項沒有包含在福利裡？ (A) 退休計畫 (B) 對未來學習給予財務上的幫助 (C) 住房補助 (D) 醫療保險

■ Not/True Not 問題　　　　　　　　　　　　　　　　　　　　　解答 (C)

本題是要在文章中找到與本問題的重點 the compensation package 相關的內容後，比較選項與文章的 Not/True 問題。可以從提及 the compensation package 的廣告，也就是例文 1 開始探討。We offer ~ retirement savings plans, ~ medical and dental health insurance, and continuing education allowance. 指出提供高額的起薪，和綜合性的福利，包括退休儲蓄計畫、專業責任保險、醫療和牙醫保險、繼續進修補助，因此 (A) (B) (D) 都符合文章提及的內容。(C) 則是文章內沒有提到的內容，因此要選擇 (C) 為正確答案。

單字 financial a. 財政上的，財務上的

193

In the letter, the word "confident" in paragraph 2, line 4 is closest in meaning to (A) secretive　　(B) certain (C) satisfactory　　(D) communicative	在信件中的第二段第四行「confident」的意思最接近哪一個字？ (A) 遮遮掩掩的　　(B) 確定的 (C) 令人滿意的　　(D) 喜歡溝通的

■ 同義詞　　　　　　　　　　　　　　　　　　　　　　　　　解答 (B)

從例文 2 裡有包含到 confident 的句子 I am confident that my skills and professional experience will allow me to provide significant contributions to the development of your new clinic.（我很有信心我的技術與專業經驗能讓我替你的新診所帶來重大的貢獻。）可以知道 confident 在這裡是「確信」的意思，所以要選擇有「確信」涵義的 (B) certain 為正確答案。

194

Why might Dr. Marquez not be selected as a candidate for the job? (A) She has insufficient experience. (B) She does not perform surgical procedures. (C) She does not have a professional license. (D) She is unwilling to travel for work.	Marquez 醫生有可能因為什麼原因沒有通過甄選？ (A) 她的經驗不足。 (B) 她不會進行手術。 (C) 她沒有專業執照。 (D) 她不願意為工作出差。

■ 六何原則 聯結問題　　　　　　　　　　　　　　　　　　　　解答 (A)

這是綜合兩篇文章的內容之後，進行推論再解題的題型。除了要看問題的重點句 Dr. Marquez not be selected as a candidate for the job 以外，還要推論 Dr. Marques 為什麼（Why）沒有被選為候補的原因，所以要從有列出錄取資格及條件的例文 1 開始看起。

從例文 1 的 Qualifications: At least five years of work experience in a veterinary clinic or hospital 中，可以得到第一個線索為：錄取條件之一是至少要在獸醫診所或獸醫院服務五年。但是因為例文 1 中沒有顯示 Dr. Marquez 是否符合這個條件，所以要從例文 2 的信件內容來確認。在 I have been with the hospital since I finished my doctor of veterinary medicine degree ~ two-and-a-half years ago. 這句中，可以知道 Dr. Marquez 在兩年半前取得獸醫學博士學位後就一直在醫院工作，所以針對 Dr. Marquez 可以得到第二個線索為：Dr. Marquez 在醫院工作了兩年半。

綜合第一個線索：至少要在獸醫診所或獸醫院服務五年，和第二個線索：Dr. Marquez 在醫院工作了兩年半，可以得知 Dr. Marquez 是因為工作經驗不足，才無法成為候補的人選，因此 (A) She has insufficient experience. 是正確答案。

單字 insufficient a. 不充分的　perform v. 實行　be unwilling to phr. 不想做~

60 | 全新！NEW TOEIC 新多益閱讀題庫解析

195

What is mentioned about Dr. Marquez?	關於 Marquez 醫生，文中提到什麼？
(A) She has applied for a promotion.	(A) 她要申請升遷。
(B) She currently manages an animal clinic.	(B) 她目前管理一家動物診所。
(C) She is enrolled at a university in Sacramento.	(C) 她要去讀沙加緬度的一所大學。
(D) She plans to relocate to another city.	(D) 她計畫要搬到另一個城市。

■ **Not/True** True 問題   解答 (D)

本題是要在文章中找到與本問題的重點 Dr. Marquez 相關的內容後，比較選項與文章的 Not/True 問題。可以從 Dr. Marquez 寫的信，也就是例文 2 來找出相關內容。(A) 跟 (B) 都是文章沒有提及的內容。I have been with the hospital since I finished my doctor of veterinary medicine degree at Riverbank University in San Diego. 提到自從在聖地牙哥的 Riverbank 大學取得博士學位後就一直在這家醫院工作，因此選項 (C) 與文章內容不相符。I wish to continue to practice my profession when I move to Sacramento next January. 指出明年 1 月搬到沙加緬度後，希望能繼續在自己的領域工作，所以參加此次徵才。所以 (D) She plans to relocate to another city. 才是正確答案。

單字 promotion n. 升遷　 manage v. 管理，處理　 enroll v. 登錄，入學

例文1

To: Mathilda Bauwens <owner@wizobakeshop.be>

From: custserv@robbinsbakerysupplies.be

Date: September 7
Subject: Order No. 81692-07

Dear Ms. Bauwens,

196-C Robbins Bakery Supplies has been the preferred supplier of bakery shop owners all over Europe for nearly 50 years. With our extensive product knowledge and years of experience, you can be assured that we sell only the best baking ingredients and equipment.

We received your order on September 6 for the following products and are now preparing them for shipment. Please note that items may ship separately based on their availability.

199 PRODUCT NO.	199 DESCRIPTION	UNIT PRICE	QTY.	AMOUNT
EFS520	20-gal electronic flour sifter	€755.18	2	€1,510.36
RCP433	14" round cheesecake pan	€22.74	5	€113.70
SDC871	150-ml square dessert cup (set of 50)	€434.95	1	€434.95
EDC106	6-wheel expandable dough cutter	€98.60	2	€197.20

196-D Domestic deliveries are free of charge and will take one to two business days, depending on location. Your credit card will not reflect the payment for the costs of your order until the items are sent to the address you specified.

196-A You can follow up at any time by visiting our Web site at www.robbinsbakerysupplies.be. Just enter your order number in the appropriate box to see your purchase history. Once again, thank you and we hope for your continued business.

All the best,

Robbins Bakery Supplies
Customer Service

收件人: Mathilda Bauwens <owner@wizobakeshop.be>
寄件人: custserv@robbinsbakerysupplies.be
日期: 9 月 7 日
主題: 訂單號碼 81692-07

親愛的 Bauwens 女士：

196-C 近五十年來，Robbins 烘培材料公司一直都是全歐洲地區最受烘培店老闆青睞的烘培材料供應商。由於我們對產品的廣泛知識及多年的經驗，你可以安心我們只會販售最好的烘焙材料與設備。

我們在 9 月 6 日收到您訂購以下產品的訂單，現在已經在處理並準備出貨，請注意貨品會因為存貨數量的緣故而分開運送。

199 產品編號	199 產品說明	單價	數量	總價
EFS 520	20 加侖麵粉電動篩網	755.18 歐元	2	1510.36 歐元
RCP 433	14 吋圓形起士蛋糕烤盤	22.74 歐元	5	113.7 歐元
SDC 871	150 毫升方形點心杯（一組 50 個）	434.95 歐元	1	434.95 歐元
EDC 106	6 輪可擴大式麵糰切割器	98.6 歐元	2	197.2 歐元

196-D 國內免運費，依地點不同，需一到兩個工作天到貨。直到貨品運送到您指定的地點，您的信用卡才會被記帳扣除您訂貨的款項。

196-A 在 www.robbinsbakerysupplies.be 我們的網站 你可以隨時追蹤你的訂單，只要在適當的空格輸入你的訂單號碼，你就可以看到你的訂購紀錄。我們再一次感謝你，希望你能繼續來此消費。

Robbins 烘培材料公司敬上
客戶服務部

例文2

To: custserv@robbinsbakerysupplies.be

From: Mathilda Bauwens <owner@wizobakeshop.be>

Date: September 19
Subject: Re: Order No. 81692-07

To whom it may concern,

I received all the products I ordered, but [199]instead of 14" cheesecake pans, I got 10" ones. Unfortunately, I needed pans of the correct size to complete a job for a loyal and important client. In order to make the deadline, I was forced to take time away from my busy schedule, and pay substantially higher, to get the pans from another store. Needless to say, I am very disappointed, especially after [198]I'd heard so many good things about you from my business partner. Since I have no use for 10" pans, I am sending them back to you this week in exchange for a full refund. In addition, [200]I feel it is right to ask that you also reimburse me for the difference in price that I had to pay for the 14" ones. I hope to hear from you soon about this matter.

Mathilda Bauwens
Owner
Wizo Bakeshop

收件人:
custserv@robbinsbakerysupplies.be
寄件人: Mathilda Bauwens
<owner@wizobakeshop.be>
日期: 9 月 19 日
主題: Re: 訂單號碼 81692-07

敬啟者:

我所訂購的貨品皆已收到。不過，[199]我訂購的是 14 吋起士蛋糕烤盤，但是卻收到 10 吋的烤盤。很不巧地，我需要正確的尺寸來為一位重要的老客戶完成工作。為了要及時完成，我被迫在忙碌的行程中擠出時間，並且多付了許多錢從別家店裡取得這樣的烤盤。不用說也知道，我感到非常失望，尤其 [198]我從我的生意夥伴那裏聽到很多關於你們的好話。由於這些 10 吋的烤盤對我毫無用處，我這禮拜就寄還你，以換取全額的退款。此外，[200]我覺得應該要求你們補償我必須另買 14 吋烤盤的價差。關於此事，我希望能盡早得到你的回應。

Mathilda Bauwens
店長
Wizo 烘培屋

例文 1 單字 □prefer v. 偏好　□extensive a. 廣大的　□ingredient n. 材料
　　　　　□equipment n. 裝備　□shipment n. 配送，輸送　□separately ad. 個別地
　　　　　□base on phr. 根據，依據　□domestic a. 國內的，家庭的　□delivery n. 配送
　　　　　□depending on phr. 取決於～　□specify v. 具體指明

例文 2 單字 □deadline n. 期限　□be forced to phr. 被迫做～　□substantially ad. 相當大地
　　　　　□full refund phr. 全額退費　□reimburse v. 賠償，歸還

196

What is NOT mentioned about Robbins Bakery Supplies?
(A) It allows clients to view prior orders on a Web site.
(B) It has locations in several European cities.
(C) It has been in the supply business for several decades.
(D) It makes local deliveries at no extra charge.

關於 Robbins 烘培材料公司，文中沒有提到什麼？
(A) 顧客能在網站上看之前的訂單。
(B) 在好幾個歐洲城市有分店。
(C) 在材料供應業界已有幾十年。
(D) 對於本地的訂單無額外收費。

■ Not/True Not 問題　　　　　　　　　　　　　　　　　　　　　　　　解答 (B)

本題是要在文章中找到與本問題的重點 Robbins Bakery Supplies 相關的內容後，比較選項與文章的 Not/True 問題。可以從提及 Robbins Bakery Supplies 的電子郵件，也就是例文 1 開始探討。You can follow up at any time by visiting our Web site 指出無論何時都可進入網站確認訂單狀態，而之後 Just enter your order under ~ to see your purchase history. 則是說只要輸入訂單號碼就可以看到訂購紀錄，因此 (A) 與文章內容一致。因為 (B) 是文章中沒有提到的內容，所以 (B) It has locations in several European cities. 是正確答案。Robbins Bakery Supplies has been the preferred supplier of bakery shop owners ~ for nearly 50 years. 說到近五十年來，Robbins 烘培材料公司一直都是全歐洲地區最受烘培店老闆青睞的烘培材料供應商，與 (C) 選項一致。Domestic deliveries are free of charge 指本地的訂單免收運費，與 (D) 選項一致。

單字 prior a. 之前的　extra a. 額外的

197

In the first e-mail, the word "reflect" in paragraph 3, line 2 is closest in meaning to (A) show (B) copy (C) appear (D) think	在第一封電郵的第三段第二行，「reflect」的意思最接近哪一個字？ (A) 展示 (B) 複製 (C) 出現 (D) 思考

■ 同義詞　　　　　　　　　　　　　　　　　　　　　　　　　　　　　解答 (A)

在第一篇電子郵件中包含 reflect 的句子 Your credit card will not reflect the payment for the costs of your order 中，reflect 是「顯示」的意思。因此應該要選擇有「展現」意思的 (A) show 為正確答案。另外，因為 (C) appear（出現）是不接受詞的不及物動詞，要使用 (C) 的說法時，就會變成「信用卡不會出現」的意思。

198

What is suggested about Ms. Bauwens? (A) She wants to increase the quantity of her order. (B) She received separate shipments. (C) She missed a deadline for promotional offers. (D) She was referred to Robbins by a colleague.	關於 Bauwens 女士，談到了什麼？ (A) 她想要增加訂單的數量。 (B) 她收到分開的到貨。 (C) 她錯過了一個優惠方案的截止日期。 (D) 她的同事介紹她 Robbins 烘培材料公司。

■ 推論 詳細內容　　　　　　　　　　　　　　　　　　　　　　　　　解答 (D)

這是需要推論題目中提及的 Ms. Bauwens 這個人物的題目，由例文 2 中 Ms. Bauwens 寄出的信件內容進行推論。I'd heard so many good things about you from my business partner. 是說從事業夥伴那邊聽到很多關於 Robbins 公司的事，因此我們可以得知她是透過同僚得知 Robbins 的。所以 (D) She was referred to Robbins by colleague. 是正確答案。

單字 quantity n. 量　refer to phr. 提到，說

199

Which product is Ms. Bauwens referring to in her e-mail? (A) SDC871 (B) EDC106 (C) RCP433 (D) EFS520	Bauwens 小姐在電郵中提到關於哪一個產品？ (A) SDC871 (B) EDC106 (C) RCP433 (D) EFS520

■ 六何原則 聯結問題　　　　　　　　　　　　　　　　　　　　　　　解答 (C)

這是綜合兩篇文章的內容之後，進行推論再解題的題型。問題的重點句 product ～ Ms. Bauwens referring to in her e-mail 在問 Ms. Bauwens 在電子郵件中提到哪樣（Which）產品，所以要從 Ms. Bauwens 寫的電子郵件開始看。

第一個線索是在第二封信中寫到 instead of 14" cheesecake pans, I got 10" ones 意指拿到的不是 14 吋的起士蛋糕烤盤，而是 10 吋的。但是因為在這裡沒寫到這項產品的名稱，所以要回到第一封郵件來確認。第一封郵件的 PRODUCT NO., RCP433 跟 DESCRIPTION, 14" round cheesecake pan 可以得到第二個線索為：14 吋起士蛋糕烤盤的商品編號是「RCP433」。

結合第一個線索：Ms. Bauwens 拿到的不是 14 吋的起士蛋糕烤盤，而是 10 吋的。與第二個線索：起士蛋糕烤盤的商品編號是「RCP433」，我們可以知道 Ms. Bauwens 在郵件中提到的產品是「RCP433」，因此要選擇 (C) RCP433 為正確答案。

200

What does Ms. Bauwens ask Robbins Bakery Supplies to do?	Bauwens 小姐要求 Robbins 烘培材料公司做什麼？
(A) Compensate her for her purchase	(A) 補償她購買的價差。
(B) Mail her an updated catalog	(B) 寄給她新的目錄。
(C) Recommend her to some client	(C) 推薦她給一些客戶。
(D) Consider a business venture	(D) 考慮生意合作。

■ 六何原則 What   解答 (A)

因為是在問 Ms. Bauwens 要求 Robbins Bakery Supplies 要做什麼（What）的六何原則問題，所以先從 Ms. Bauwens 寫的郵件開始找答案。第二封郵件中寫道 I feel it is right to ask that you also reimburse me for the difference in price that I had to pay for the 14" ones 指出她認為要求 Robbins Bakery Supplies 補償必須另買 14 吋烤盤的價差是當然的、合理的。因此要選 (A) Compensate her for her purchase 為正確答案。

換句話說
reimburse 賠償 → compensate 補償

單字 compensate v. 補償 recommend v. 推薦

TEST 02

PART 5

101

The accountant _____ the expense reports of those who attended the Seville Conference by next Monday morning.
(A) will obtain
(B) has obtained
(C) obtaining
(D) obtainable

會計會在下個星期一早上前拿到那些參加 Seville 會議的人的費用報告。

■ 未來時態　　　　　　　　　　　　　　　　　　　　解答 (A)

因為句中沒有動詞，所以動詞 (A) 和 (B) 為可能的答案。而因為句中寫出時間是在未來（by next Monday morning），所以未來式 (A) will obtain 是正確答案。分詞兼動名詞 (C) 跟形容詞 (D) 都不是正確答案。另 those who 是「那些～的人們」的意思。

單字 attend v. 出席　obtain v. 獲取　obtainable a. 可取得的，可獲得的

102

Shunju Airways passengers may purchase their tickets online _____ make a phone reservation, and seats should be paid in full at the time of the booking.
(A) yet
(B) both
(C) because
(D) or

Shunju 航空的旅客不管是在網路上訂票或是用電話訂票，他們都需要在訂票時把所有機票費用付清。

■ 對等連接詞　　　　　　　　　　　　　　　　　　　解答 (D)

作為助動詞 may 後面的動詞片語，選出連結片語 purchase their tickets online 與片語 make a phone reservation 的連接詞是解題的重點。因為此句原意為「可以利用網路購票或以電話預約」，所以要使用對等連接詞 (D) or（或）為正確答案。(A) yet（尚未，但是）主要作為副詞來修飾動詞或連接詞來領導子句。(B) both（都）常與 and 一起出現，形成 both A and B（A 和 B 都）。(C) because 是「因為～」的意思，通常出現於副詞子句前。

單字 pay in full phr. 支付全額　booking n. 預約

103

The marketing strategies _____ want to use for our client's new product line were explained in detail in the document sent last week.
(A) we
(B) our
(C) ours
(D) us

我們想要用在客戶新產品上的行銷策略在上星期寄出的文件裡都已詳細說明了。

■ 人稱代名詞　　　　　　　　　　　　　　　　　　　解答 (A)

因為主句是已經有主詞 The marketing strategies，動詞 were explained 的完整句子，所以可以把 ___ want to use ~ product line 視為修飾語。這個修飾語本身有動詞 want 卻沒有主詞，所以可以知道空格內應該要填上可以做為主詞使用的人稱代名詞 (A) 或所有格代名詞 (C) 做為正確答案。從「我們想要使用的行銷策略」可以看出正確答案為人稱代名詞 (A) we。如果選擇所有格代名詞 (C) ours，意思會變為「我們的東西想使用的行銷策略」。另外，本句省略了空格前面的關係代名詞 which 或 that。人稱代名詞的所有格 (B) 是像形容詞一樣置於名詞前方修飾名詞，(D) 是人稱代名詞受格，要做為動詞或介系詞的受詞。

單字 strategy n. 策略　explain v. 解釋　in detail phr. 仔細地

104

Both the tenant and the owner share the responsibility of _____ the safety and cleanliness of the apartment. (A) assure　　(B) assuring　　(C) assured　　(D) assures	房客和房東雙方都有責任確保公寓的安全與清潔。

■ 名詞的位置　　　　　　　　　　　　　　　　　　　　　　　　　　　　　　解答 (B)

因為可以置於介系詞 of 後的應該是名詞，所以動詞 assure（確保）的動名詞 (B) assuring 是正確答案。動詞 (A) 和 (D) 及過去分詞 (C) 在這裡都無法作為介系詞的受詞。另外，the safety ~ apartment在此句中是作為動名詞 assuring 的受詞。

單字　tenant n. 承租人，房客　assure v. 保障，確保

105

Marcia Winters proved that she was the most _____ member of the staff when she secured the company several new clients. (A) products　　　　　　(B) productively (C) producing　　　　　(D) productive	當 Marcia Winters 為公司爭取到好幾名新客戶時，就證明了她是最有生產力的員工。

■ 形容詞的位置　　　　　　　　　　　　　　　　　　　　　　　　　　　　　解答 (D)

因為空格裡的字要修飾名詞 member 的關係，所以分詞 (C) 和形容詞 (D) 都可能是正確答案。因為本句意思是「那個女生證明了自己是最有生產力的員工」，所以選擇形容詞 (D) productive（有生產力的）為正確答案。如果選擇分詞 (C) producing（出產，生產）意思會變成「那個女生證明自己最會生產員工」。名詞 (A) 只有在做為複合名詞時可以修飾名詞，副詞 (B) 則無法修飾名詞。

單字　prove v. 證明，印證　secure v. 確保　productive a. 有生產力的

106

Based on the information collected in the survey, many office employees are _____ with a flexible schedule than one that is fixed. (A) busied　　(B) busier　　(C) busying　　(D) busily	根據在調查中所收集到的資料，很多彈性工時的辦公室員工比固定工時的更忙碌。

■ 比較級　　　　　　　　　　　　　　　　　　　　　　　　　　　　　　　　解答 (B)

因為空格在 be 動詞 are 之後，所以 p.p. 形態 (A) 和比較級 (B) 以及 -ing 形態 (C) 都可能為正確答案。而從空格後有 than 這一點，可以看出應該要選擇形容詞比較級 (B) busier 為正確答案。副詞 (D) 則無法被置於補語的位置。

單字　flexible a. 流動的，具彈性的　fixed a. 固定的

107

Due to a problem with production, the _____ of orders to clients will be delayed for up to two days. (A) delivers　　　　　　(B) deliverable (C) delivery　　　　　(D) deliver	因為生產上出了問題，客戶貨品的運送將會延誤兩天。

■ 名詞的位置　　　　　　　　　　　　　　　　　　　　　　　　　　　　　　解答 (C)

因為名詞可以被放在定冠詞 the 與介系詞 of 的中間，名詞 (B) 和 (C) 都是可能的答案。因為意思為「客戶貨品的運送將會延期」，所以 (C) delivery（配送，運送）是正確答案。如果選擇 (B) deliverable（待送貨物），就會變成「客戶貨品的待送貨品將會延期」的意思。而動詞 (A) 和 (D) 則不能作為名詞使用。

單字　due to phr. 由於～　order n.（訂購的）產品，訂單；v. 訂購　delay v. 延期，使延期

108

Pinnacle Company's digital camera is more expensive than other brands, but it produces high-quality pictures _____. (A) less effective (B) least effective (C) most effectively (D) more effective	Pinnacle 公司的數位相機比其他品牌的相機來得貴，但是卻能最有效果地照出高品質的照片。

■ 副詞的位置 解答 (C)

因為要修飾動詞 produces，所以應該要填入副詞，選項 (C) 副詞的最高級 most effectively（最具效果）為正確答案。形容詞 (A) (B) (D) 則無法修飾動詞。

單字 expensive a. 昂貴的

109

The new art center on Brentville Avenue, which was inaugurated on Friday, is _____ exhibiting the works of several local artists. (A) presented (B) present (C) presents (D) presently	在 Brentville 大道上的新藝術中心於星期五開幕了，那裏正在展示數名當地藝術家的作品。

■ 副詞的位置 解答 (D)

因為要修飾動詞 is exhibiting，所以要選擇副詞 (D) presently（現在）為正確答案。動詞兼分詞 (A) 與形容詞兼動詞兼名詞 (B)，動詞兼名詞 (C) 都沒辦法修飾動詞。另外，present 作為形容詞時意思是「現在的」，作為名詞時意思是「禮物，現在」，作為動詞時意思是「呈獻，展示」。

單字 inaugurate v. 舉行開幕式，使正式就任

110

Alessandro Fox _____ goes to the driving range at least three times a week to practice his golf swing. (A) always (B) softly (C) forever (D) sharply	Alessandro Fox 總是一星期至少到練習場三次去練習高爾夫球揮桿。

■ 副詞語彙 解答 (A)

因為動詞 goes 是現在式，句意又為「總是一星期至少到練習場三次」的關係，所以 (A) always（總是）是正確答案。(B) softly 是「柔軟的」，(C) forever 是「永遠的」，(D) sharply 是「銳利的，激烈的」的意思。另外，如果是在說明現在的狀態、反覆的動作或普遍事實的話都要使用現在式來表現。

單字 driving range phr. 高爾夫練習場

111

The third-level parking area is _____ to all residents at Arjuna Condominiums. (A) qualified (B) understandable (C) provable (D) accessible	三層樓的停車場是 Arjuna 大樓的所有住戶都可以使用的。

■ 形容詞片語 解答 (D)

因為空格前的 be 動詞 is 與空格後的介系詞 to 一起出現，因此可以合成片語「可以使用～」的形容詞 (D) accessible（可使用的）是正確答案。（be accessible to：可以使用～）。另外，accessible 的名詞形態 access（接近）也很常與介系詞 to 合用成 access to（往～接近）。(A) qualified 是「有資格的」的意思，與 be 動詞跟介系詞 for 合用、或與 to 不定詞合用成為「be qualified for / to 不定詞」，意思為「有～的資格」。(B) understanding 是「可以理解的」，(C) provable 是「可以認證的」的意思。

單字 level n. 層，水平，高度　 resident n. 居住者

112

| After concluding the negotiations, the CEOs from the two electronics manufacturers are expected to _____ their partnership at a press conference.
(A) inspire　　　　　(B) categorize
(C) require　　　　　(D) confirm | 在協商會議過後，兩位電器製造商的首席執行長預計在一場記者會中確認他們的合作關係。 |

■ 動詞語彙　　　　　　　　　　　　　　　　　　　　　　　　　　　　　　　解答 (D)

因為文意為「要確認兩家公司的合作關係」，所以要選擇動詞 (D) 為正確答案。(A) inspire 是「給予靈感」，(B) categorize 是「分類，分類為～」，(C) require 是「要求」的意思。另外，be expected to（被期待做～）是常被使用的慣用片語。

單字 negotiation n. 協商，交涉　partnership n. 夥伴，合作關係

113

| The memo reminds supervisors to _____ implement the new office dress code beginning next month.
(A) rigor　　　　　(B) rigorously
(C) rigorous　　　　(D) rigorousness | 備忘錄提醒主管們要嚴格執行下個月開始的新辦公室服裝規定。 |

■ 副詞的位置　　　　　　　　　　　　　　　　　　　　　　　　　　　　　　解答 (B)

為了修飾動詞 to implement，因此前面應該要填入副詞，所以選擇副詞 (B) rigorously（嚴格的）為正確答案。名詞 (A) 和 (D)，形容詞 (C) 都無法修飾動詞。另外，「beginning + 時間點」是「從～開始，從～」的意思。

單字 supervisor n. 監督員，管理者，主管　implement v. 實行

114

| Urban Textiles will not refund down payments to Ms. Smith _____ she cancel her order after the products have been shipped.
(A) should　　　　　(B) otherwise
(C) although　　　　(D) instead | 如果 Smith 女士在產品寄出後才取消訂單，Urban 紡織公司將不會把預付訂金退還給她。 |

■ 沒有 if 的假設法 假設法的倒裝　　　　　　　　　　　　　　　　　　　　　解答 (A)

主句已經是具有所有成分（Urban Textiles will not refund down payments）的完整子句，____ she ~ shipped 則只是修飾語。這個修飾語有動詞 cancel，所以要選擇可以帶領一個修飾語子句的助動詞 (A) 或是副詞子句連接詞 (C) 做為正確答案。除了因為修飾語子句中的主詞是第三人稱單數的 she，但使用動詞原形 cancel，我們可以知道要選擇助動詞 (A) should 為正確答案之外，也要能判斷出 Should she cancel ~ 是假設法 if she should cancel ~ 省略 if 後，並把主詞與助動詞倒裝的形態。如果要用連接詞 (C) although（即使）的話，主詞 she 的後面就不會使用原形動詞。副詞兼連接副詞 (B) otherwise（否則）和 (D) instead（做為替代）前面應該要使用分號（;）才能連接兩個句子。

單字 refund v. 退還，退款　ship v. 配送；n. 船

115

The Stymphal Library Web site provides detailed _____ on how interested individuals can apply for membership online. (A) directed (B) directing (C) directions (D) directly	Stymphal 圖書館的網站上為那些有興趣在線上申辦會員的人提供了詳細的說明。

■ 名詞的位置 解答 (C)

做為及物動詞 provides 的受詞且可以受到形容詞修飾的位置應該要填入名詞,所以名詞 (C) directions 是正確答案。如果把 (B) 視為動名詞,則雖可以做為動詞的受詞,但卻不能以形容詞,而是以副詞來修飾。動詞兼過去分詞 (A) 及副詞 (D) 都不能夠做為正確答案。

單字 detailed a. 詳細的   individual n. 個人

116

To promote seasonal vegetables, the sales staff _____ displays them at the main entrance of the supermarket. (A) intends (B) intentional (C) intentionally (D) intention	為了要推銷季節性的蔬菜,銷售人員刻意將這些蔬菜擺放在超級市場的主要入口。

■ 副詞的位置 解答 (C)

因為要修飾動詞 display,所以應該要選擇副詞 (C) intentionally(刻意地)做為正確答案。動詞 (A)、形容詞 (B)、名詞 (D) 都不能夠修飾動詞。

單字 promote v. 宣傳,升遷   seasonal a. 季節性的   display v. 陳列,展示

117

Sean Lucas was _____ by the International Symphony Society as one of the best composers of today for the stunning musical scores he has created for ballets. (A) compensated (B) discharged (C) recognized (D) enforced	Sean Lucas 因為替芭蕾舞創作出令人讚賞的音樂而被國際交響樂學會認定是現今最優秀的作曲家之一。

■ 動詞語彙 解答 (C)

因為句意為「Sean Lucas被認定為最優秀的作曲家之一」,空格前又有be動詞 was,所以要選擇被動的 recognize(認可)的 p.p. 形 (C) recognized 為正確答案。(A) 的 compensate 是「補償」,(B) 的 discharge 是「解僱」,(D) 的 enforce 是「執行,強制」的意思。

單字 composer n. 作曲家   stunning a. 驚艷的   score n. 樂譜

118

Because the human resources director was on leave, Ms. Hong was asked to interview candidates for the managerial position _____ herself. (A) to (B) by (C) from (D) near	因為人力資源部主任休假,洪小姐被要求獨自面試應徵管理職位的應徵者。

■ 反身代名詞 解答 (B)

因為句意為「獨自面試應徵者」的意思,所以要選擇可以跟反身代名詞 herself 一起表現「獨自,一個人」 by oneself 的選項,所以介系詞 (B) by 是正確答案。另外,除了 by oneself,還有 alone 跟 on one's own 都是表示「單獨、獨自」的意思。而句中的 on leave(休假中)則是慣用用法。

單字 human resources phr. 人力資源部   on leave phr. 休假中   candidate n. 應徵者

119

Elspeth Fanshaw is in charge of contacting all major banks _____ main headquarters are located in Northern Europe. (A) when　　　　(B) whom (C) whose　　　(D) which	Elspeth Fanshaw 負責聯絡所有總部在北歐的各大銀行。

■ 關係代名詞及選擇關係代名詞的方法　　　　　　　　　　　　　　　　　　　　　解答 (C)

主句已經是具有所有成分（Elspeth Fanshaw is in charge of contacting ~ banks）的完整子句，_____ main headquarters ~ Northern Europe 則是修飾語。因為本修飾語是在修飾空格前的名詞 all major banks，所以關係代名詞 (B) (C) (D) 都可能是答案。可以跟空格後的名詞 headquarters 一起當作主詞的所有格關係代名詞 (C) whose 是正確答案。(B) whom 則是在動詞或介系詞沒有受詞時做為受詞使用的受格關係代名詞，因為形容詞子句是被動式，不需要受詞，所以不能選 (B)。(D) which則是可以做為主格或受格的關係代名詞，但形容詞子句是已有 main headquarters are located 的完整子句，所以不能選 (C)。(A) 如果使用 when 做為連結兩個子句的話會出現「當總部座落於北歐時，Elspeth Fanshaw 負責聯絡所有各大銀行。」這種不太合邏輯的句子。

單字 be in charge of phr. 負責～，掌管～　headquarters n. 總部

120

Successful overseas workers not only support their families, but also bring _____ to their countries. (A) level　　　　(B) pride (C) population　(D) division	成功的海外工作者不僅能養家，還能為他們的國家帶來驕傲。

■ 名詞語彙　　　　　　　　　　　　　　　　　　　　　　　　　　　　　　　　　解答 (B)

因為句意為「成功的海外工作者為國家帶來驕傲」，因此名詞 (B) pride（驕傲）是正確答案。(A) level 是「程度，水準」，(C) population 是「人口，居民」，(D) division 是「分配，分裂」的意思。另外，連接動詞片語 support their family 和動詞片語 bring pride to their family 的是相關連接詞 not only A but (also) B（=B as well as A，不只 A 還有 B）。

單字 overseas a. 海外的

121

As indicated in the schedule, crisis management consultant Mimi Kim will conduct the _____ on labor disputes. (A) information　(B) incident (C) agenda　　　(D) discussion	如同行程表中所顯示的，危機管理顧問 Mimi Kim 將會進行關於勞動糾紛的討論。

■ 名詞語彙　　　　　　　　　　　　　　　　　　　　　　　　　　　　　　　　　解答 (D)

因為句意為「將進行與勞動糾紛相關的討論」，所以名詞 (D) discussion（討論，商討）是正確答案。另外，寫在 discussion 後面的介系詞 on 有「關於～，與～相關」的意思。(A) information 是「情報」，(B) incident 是「事情，事件」，(C) agenda 是「議程，案件」的意思。

單字 crisis n. 危機　management n. 管理　consultant n. 顧問　conduct v. 做（特定的事情），指揮，引導

122

_____ Baklase Pharmaceuticals shut down two factories last month, it still managed to meet its production target this year. (A) Although　　(B) Since (C) So　　(D) However	雖然 Baklase 製藥廠上個月關掉了兩間工廠，但是仍然設法達成他們今年的生產目標。

■ 副詞子句連接詞 讓步　　　　　　　　　　　　　　　　　　　　　解答 (A)

本句已經是具有所有成分（it still managed to meet its production target）的完整子句，_____ Baklase Pharmaceuticals ~ last month 則是修飾語。因為本修飾語有動詞 shut down，所以要選擇可以帶領它的副詞子句連接詞 (A) 或 (B) 做為正確答案。因為句意為「即使上個月關閉兩家工廠，依然設法達成今年的生產目標」，所以選擇 (A) Although（即使～也～）為正確答案。如果選擇 (B) Since（因為～）就會變成「因為上個月關閉兩家工廠，所以依然設法達成今年的生產目標」的奇怪語意。對等連接詞 (C) So（所以）跟連接副詞 (D) However（但是）則無法帶領當修飾語的副詞子句。

單字 **shut down** phr. 關門，停止　　**manage to** phr. 設法應付～　　**meet** v. 見面，達成　　**target** n. 目標

123

Due to the supplier's failure to deliver key ingredients, some pasta meals _____ in the menu are unavailable today. (A) pictured　　(B) guided (C) demonstrated　　(D) imitated	因為供應商沒能把主要的食材送到，好幾種印在菜單上的義大利麵餐點，今天都無法供應。

■ 動詞語彙　　　　　　　　　　　　　　　　　　　　　　　　　解答 (A)

因為句意為「幾種印在菜單上的義大利麵」，所以選擇動詞 picture（展示，描寫）的過去分詞 (A) pictured 為正確答案。(B) guide 是「引導，指導」的意思。(C) demonstrate 是「證明，說明」的意思，不是用圖畫或文字，而是以行動說明或示範來說明的意思。(D) imitate 是「模仿」的意思。

單字 **supplier** n. 供應業者，供應廠商

124

Alizarin Electronics began its foreign operations _____ the opening of a new factory in Seoul this year. (A) in　　(B) against (C) between　　(D) with	Alizarin 電子今年在首爾開了一家新工廠，開始展開海外營運。

■ 選擇介系詞 其他　　　　　　　　　　　　　　　　　　　　　　解答 (D)

因為句意為「透過開設新工廠開始展開海外事業」，表示同時發生的介系詞 (D) with（透過，與～一起）為正確答案。(A) in 主要與時間或場所有關，(B) against 是「反對，相對」的意思，(C) between 是在「兩者之間」的意思，常寫為 between A and B（A 和 B 之間），表示兩者的位置或關係。

單字 **foreign** a. 外國的　　**operation** n. 營運，手術

125

A property developer was dispatched to the _____ to determine whether it was feasible for a residential building project.

(A) scale　　　　　(B) layer
(C) extent　　　　　(D) area

一名地產開發人員被派到該區去決定住宅興建計畫在此是否可行。

■ 名詞語彙　　　　　　　　　　　　　　　　　　　　　　　　　解答 (D)

因為句意為「地產開發人員為了決定住宅興建計畫是否可行被派到該區」，所以名詞 (D) area（地區）是正確答案。(A) scale 是「規模，等級」，(B) layer 是「層、幕」，(C) extent 是「程度，大小」的意思。

單字 property developer phr. 地產開發員　dispatch v. 派遣　feasible a. 可實行的

126

For its fifth anniversary, Youngsters Sports released a new line of bicycles designed _____ for children aged five to seven.

(A) closely　　　　　(B) swiftly
(C) marginally　　　　(D) exclusively

Youngsters 運動用品為了五週年慶，推出了新一系列專門針對五至七歲兒童設計的腳踏車。

■ 副詞語彙　　　　　　　　　　　　　　　　　　　　　　　　　解答 (D)

因為句意為「專門為了五至七歲兒童設計的腳踏車」，所以要選副詞 (D) exclusively（專門）為正確答案。(A) closely 是「嚴密地，接近地」，(B) swiftly 是「迅速地，快速」，(C) marginally是「微小地，微不足道」的意思。另外，「人＋aged＋年紀」是指「～歲的人」的意思。

單字 anniversary n. 紀念日　release v. 釋放，公開

127

The organizers were _____ in their choice of the Quillen Hotel ballroom as the venue for the Advertising Awards event.

(A) total　　　　　(B) entire
(C) gathered　　　　(D) unanimous

策畫成員們一致同意選擇 Quillen 飯店的宴會廳作為舉行廣告頒獎活動的場所。。

■ 形容詞語彙　　　　　　　　　　　　　　　　　　　　　　　　解答 (D)

因為句意為「策畫成員們一致同意選擇 Quillen 飯店的宴會廳」，所以形容詞 (D) unanimous（一致同意的）是正確答案。要記得 be unanimous in（對～一致同意的）是慣用句。(A) total 是「總的，完整的」，(B) entire是「整體的，全部的」，(C) gathered是「聚集的」的意思。

單字 ballroom n. 宴會廳，供人跳舞的大廳　venue n. 場所

128

| _____ make articles as concise and clear as possible, most writers recommend using short and simple sentences.

(A) As if　　　　　(B) In reference to
(C) In order to　　(D) Owing to | 為了讓文章盡可能簡潔清楚，大多數的作家都建議要用簡短的句子。 |

■ to 不定詞的功能　　　　　　　　　　　　　　　　　　　　　　解答 (C)

因為句意為「為了讓文章盡可能簡潔清楚，建議要用簡短的句子。」，為了寫成可以表示目的的 to 不定詞形式，應該使用動詞原形 make。但是因為在選項中沒有 to，所以要選擇可以代替 to 來使用的 (C) In order to 做為正確答案。副詞子句連接詞 (A) As if（就像～一樣）後面要接子句，無法直接接動詞，介系詞 (B) In reference to（關於～）跟 (D) Owing to（因為～）之後應該要接名詞。另外，可以替代 to 不定詞的有 in order to 跟 so as to。

單字 concise a. 簡潔的　clear a. 分明的，亮的，清楚的

129

| Customer service representatives are trained to speak to shoppers _____ and work out the best solutions to a complaint or problem.

(A) generously　　(B) undeniably
(C) arguably　　　(D) politely | 客服部的職員們都接受過訓練來客氣地與消費者對話並針對抱怨與問題找出最佳的解決方式。 |

■ 副詞語彙　　　　　　　　　　　　　　　　　　　　　　　　　解答 (D)

因為句意為「客服部的職員們都接受過訓練來客氣地與消費者對話」的意思，所以要選副詞 (D) politely（客氣地）為正確答案。(A) generously 是「慷慨地，大方地」，(B) undeniably 是「不可否認地」，(C) arguably 是「可以認為，可以說是」的意思。

單字 representative n. 職員　train v. 訓練，養成　work out phr. 想出～，找出～

130

| Coles Press is in need of professional _____ to oversee the publication of a news magazine.

(A) editions　(B) editorials　(C) editors　(D) edits | Coles 出版社極需要專業的編輯來監督他們新聞雜誌的出版。 |

■ 人物名詞跟事物名詞　　　　　　　　　　　　　　　　　　　　解答 (C)

介系詞 of 後面的空格應該是接受形容詞 professional 修飾的名詞，所以名詞 (A) (B) (C) 都可能為正確答案。因為句意為「可以監督新聞雜誌出版的編輯」的關係，可以知道要選擇人物名詞 (C) editors（編輯）為正確答案。選擇事物名詞 (A) editions（版，號）或 (B) editorials（社論）都會使文意變得奇怪。動詞 (D) 則是無法當作名詞使用。另外，要記住 in need of（需要～）是慣用語。

單字 oversee v. 監督　publication n. 出版

131

| With the latest security devices installed throughout the museum, the curator is prepared for virtually any _____.

(A) availability　　(B) prohibition
(C) position　　　(D) contingency | 有了最新的保全裝置裝遍了博物館，館長已經差不多為任何突發狀況做好準備。 |

■ 名詞語彙　　　　　　　　　　　　　　　　　　　　　　　　　解答 (D)

因為句意為「館長已經對任何的突發狀況做好準備」，所以要選擇名詞 (D) contingency（突發狀況）做為正確答案。(A) availability 是「可利用性」，(B) prohibition 是「禁止」，(C) position 是「位置」的意思。

單字 install v. 設置，安裝　throughout ad. 遍布，從頭到尾　curator n. 館長　virtually ad. 實際上，差不多

132

Visitors to the special exhibition are asked to leave their bags at the counter _____ to protect the displays as to ensure a pleasant experience for all. (A) as well as (B) as much (C) so long (D) only if	特別展覽的參觀者被要求將他們的包包留在櫃檯，以保護展覽品，同時也確保所有人能愉快地參觀。

■ 原級   解答 (B)

因為空格後面有as，所以要選擇之後需要出現原級的「as + 形容詞 / 副詞 + as」句型 (B) as much 為正確答案。（as much as：跟～一樣）。在句中 as ~ as 是表現 to 不定詞片語 to protect the displays 跟另一個 to 不定詞片語 to ensure a pleasant experience 兩邊的同等位置。對等連接詞 (A) as well as 寫成 B as well as A 的形態表示「不只 A，B 也～」的意思。(B) so long 和 as 一起，成為副詞子句連接詞，表示「只做～的話，只要」的意思。另外，so long as 的 so 也可以用 as 來取代（so long as = as long as）。(D) only if 也是副詞子句連接詞，表示「只有～的話才～」

單字 display n. 展示品，展示，陳列   ensure v. 保障，一定要～

133

Anna Vertugi's accomplishments as a landscaper have been largely _____ on her unique abilities in design and innovation. (A) basis (B) based (C) basing (D) baseness	Anna Vertugi 能成為成功的景觀設計師主要是因為獨特的設計能力與創新。

■ 被動式（be + p.p.）   解答 (B)

因為空格在 be 動詞（have been）的後面，所以名詞 (A) 和 (D)、p.p. 形 (B)、-ing 形 (C) 都可能是答案。因為句意是說「Anna Vertugi 的成就是因為她獨特的能力」，從意義上來看 p.p. 形 (B) 是正確答案。（be based on：以～為基礎）。如果選擇名詞 (A) basis（基礎）或 (D) baseness（卑鄙），就會跟主詞（Anna Vertugi's accomplishments）同格變成「Anna Vertugi的成就是基礎」或「Anna Vertugi的成就是卑鄙」，所以 (A) 跟 (D) 不可能是正確答案。

單字 accomplishment n. 成就，才藝   landscaper n. 園藝師，造景師   largely ad. 主要地，巨大地
       innovation n. 創新

134

To increase rice output in agricultural areas, the local government _____ additional funds for the acquisition of farming tools and equipment. (A) anticipated (B) allocated (C) contained (D) surpassed	因為要在農業區增加稻米的產量，當地政府配發額外的資金來取得農耕工具與設備。

■ 動詞語彙   解答 (B)

因為句意為「當地政府配發額外的資金來取得農耕工具」，所以動詞 allocate（分派，分發）的過去式 (B) allocated 為正確答案。(A) anticipate 是「預測」，(C) contain 是「包含」，(D) surpass 是「優於」的意思。

單字 agriculture a. 農耕的   fund n. 基金，資金   acquisition n. 獲得

135

Since the concert hall renovations are still not finished, Kevin Ockham's upcoming concert _____ to next month.
(A) being postponed　　(B) was postponing
(C) to postpone　　(D) will be postponed

因為音樂廳的改建還沒有完成，Kevin Ockham 即將到來的音樂會將被延期到下個月。

■ 動詞要注意單複數、時制與語態　　　　　　　　　　解答 (D)

因為句子中還沒有動詞，所以動詞 (B) 跟 (D) 都可能會是答案。因為音樂會延期到下個月，可以得知是未來的狀況，所以應該使用未來式，又「音樂會將被延期」是被動的，所以要用未來被動語態 (D) will be postponed 為正確答案。

單字 **renovation** n. 修理，更新　**upcoming** a. 即將到來的，接近的　**postpone** v. 延期

136

Despite having warned motorists about the speed limits, the Transport Department _____ a high number of traffic violations on Honglin Boulevard this year.
(A) performed　　(B) offered
(C) recorded　　(D) infused

雖然已經警告駕駛人速限了，但是交通部門今年在Honglin大道還是記錄了多起交通違規事件。

■ 動詞語彙　　　　　　　　　　解答 (C)

因為句意為「雖然已經警告駕駛人速限了，但還是記錄了多起交通違規事件」，所以應該要選擇動詞 record 的過去式 (C) recorded 為正確答案。(A) perform 是「實施」，(B) offer 是「提供，提案」，(D) infuse 是「注入」的意思。

單字 **motorist** n. 駕駛　**speed limit** phr. 速限　**violation** n. 違反　**boulevard** n. 大路，寬廣的林蔭道

137

The city council will be accepting bid proposals for the Welby Library restoration project _____ the end of next month.
(A) onto　　(B) between　　(C) until　　(D) where

直到下個月月底為止，市議會將接受 Welby 圖書館整修計畫的投標提案。

■ 選擇介系詞 時間點　　　　　　　　　　解答 (C)

因為句意為「直到下個月月底為止，接受投標提案」，應該要選擇指出情況到一定時間為止的介系詞 (C) until（直到～為止）為正確答案。(A) onto 是「在～上面」的意思，表示位置。(B) between 是「兩者中間」的意思，表示兩者的關係或位置。疑問詞兼關係副詞 (D) 則應該要帶領子句。

單字 **council** n. 議會　**bid** n. 投標　**restoration** n. 整修，復原

138

All members of the Baja basketball team are required to commit to a high-protein and carbohydrate diet _____ training for the national games. (A) when　　　　　(B) that (C) by　　　　　　(D) at	所有 Baja 籃球隊的隊員都被要求在為全國比賽的訓練時，奉行高蛋白及碳水化合物的指定飲食。

■ 副詞子句連接詞　　　　　　　　　　　　　　　　　　　　　　　　　　　　　解答 (A)

主句已經是具有所有成分（All members ~ are required to commit）的完整子句，____ training for the national games 則是修飾語。因為句意為「在為了全國比賽訓練時要遵守飲食內容」，所以能夠表現出時間點的副詞子句連接詞 (A) when（～的時候）為正確答案。另外，在本句中，training for the national game 是把副詞子句 when they train for the national games 轉化為分詞構句的形態，而為了讓分詞構句的意思明白一些，所以不省略連接詞 when。關係代名詞兼連接詞 (B) that、介系詞 (C) by 和 (D) at 之後都不能使用分詞構句。如果把 training 視為動名詞而選擇 (C) by，「藉著訓練來遵守飲食內容」的意思較不恰當。

單字 require v. 要求，需要　commit v. 遵守，惹出　training n. 訓練

139

Kurd Corporation's 40 percent production rate improvement is an achievement that many _____ to the factory's streamlined assembly methods. (A) attribute　　　　(B) state (C) claim　　　　　(D) pass	Kurd 公司增加了 40% 的產能，這項成就多數歸功於工廠有效率的組裝方式。

■ 動詞相關句　　　　　　　　　　　　　　　　　　　　　　　　　　　　　　解答 (A)

選擇與其後的介系詞 to 一起，有「歸因於～」意思的 attribute to 的動詞 (A) attribute 為正確答案。（attribute to：歸因於）。(B) state 是「說，明示」。(C) claim 是「主張，要求」。(D) pass 是「通過，略過」的意思。

單字 achievement n. 成就　streamlined a. 有效率的　assembly n. 組裝，協會，集會

140

In order to extend a commercial license in the district, business owners are required to present their old _____ and pay a renewal fee of $1,000 to the Business Authorization Agency. (A) consent　　　　(B) patent (C) treaty　　　　　(D) permit	為了要延長這個地區的商業執照，公司負責人被要求出示他們舊有的許可證，並付美金一千元的換發費用給商業授權機構。

■ 名詞語彙　　　　　　　　　　　　　　　　　　　　　　　　　　　　　　　解答 (D)

因為句意為「出示他們舊有的許可證，並付美金一千元的換發費用」，所以要選擇名詞 (D) permit（許可證）為正確答案。(A) consent 是「同意」，(B) patent 是「專利」，(C) treaty 是「條約，協定」的意思。

單字 extend v. 延長，伸展　renewal n. 更新，重開　authorization n. 授權，認可　agency n. 機關，代理，經銷

PART 6

Questions 141-143 refer to the following announcement.　141-143 根據下面的備忘錄內容回答問題。

To: Staff Re: Attendance Policy Date: December 5 As discussed in the meeting, management will implement a stricter policy on _____. 　141 (A) tardiness　　(B) confidentiality 　　　(C) security　　　(D) breaks This is scheduled to go into effect on January 1 and applies to all office staff, except those who engage in field work. In this regard, employees who arrive late more than two times a month will be obligated to serve one day's suspension, _____ will be recorded in their employee evaluation.　142 (A) it　　　　(B) what 　　　　　　　　　(C) this　　　(D) which However, there are exceptions to this rule, _____ late 　　　143 (A) so that　　　(B) but also 　　　　　(C) such as　　(D) in addition arrivals due to emergencies or bad weather conditions. For questions and concerns regarding the new policy, please get in touch with the personnel department. Thank you.	收件者：員工 主旨：出席規定 日期：12 月 5 日 141 如同我們在會議中所討論的，管理團隊將會對遲到執行更嚴格的規定。 除了從事現場的工作人員外，這項新規定將適用於所有職員，並從 1 月 1 日起生效。在這件事情上，一個月遲到超過兩次的員工將要被罰停職一天，142 並且會紀錄在工作考勤上。 143 然而，這項規定也有例外，例如遲到是因為緊急事件或惡劣天氣所造成的。如果對於新規定有任何問題與疑慮者，請和人事部門聯絡，謝謝！

單字 discuss v. 討論　implement v. 施行　engage v. 使從事　in this regard phr. 從這一點看來
　　obligate v. 使遵行義務　suspension n. 停職　evaluation n. 評價　due to phr. 因為～
　　get in touch with phr. 與～聯絡　personnel department n. 人事部門

141 ■■ 名詞語彙 掌握全文　　　　　　　　　　　　　　　　　　　　　　　解答 (A)

因為文意為「對於___會實施更嚴格的規定」，所有的選項都有可能是正確答案。從有空格的句子裡無法直接找出答案，所以要從前後文或全文來判斷。這封回信的標題是「Attendance Policy（出席規定）」，而後面有提到一個月中遲到兩次以上的員工需要停職一天，所以可以知道是把遲到的政策變得更嚴格。因此，名詞 (A) tardiness（遲到）為正確答案。(B) confidentiality 是「祕密」，(C) security 是「安全」，(D) breaks 是「休息」的意思。

142 ■■ 關係子句的位置與寫法　　　　　　　　　　　　　　　　　　　　　解答 (D)

句子是已經有主詞 employees 和動詞 will be obligated 的完整子句，所以要把 ___ will be recorded in their employee evaluation 視為修飾語。因此，可以引導修飾語子句的關係代名詞 (D) which 是正確答案。代名詞 (A) 和 (C) 無法做為關係代名詞，名詞子句連接詞 (B) what 則無法置於有形容詞功用的修飾語子句句首。

143 ■■ 修飾用片語及修飾用子句的差別　　　　　　　　　　　　　　　　　解答 (C)

主句是已經有所有必須成分（there are exceptions）的完整子句，因此要把 ___ late arrivals ~ conditions 視為修飾語。由於這裡的修飾語沒有動詞，所以要選擇可以引導修飾語片語的介系詞 (C) such as（例如～）為正確答案。副詞子句連接詞 (A) so that 是「所以～，因此可以～」，主要是引導表示目標的子句，(B) bus also 是和 not only 一起使用，形成對等連接詞 not only A but also B（不只 A，B 也～）的意思。(D) in addition 是「此外」的意思，做為連接副詞，後面不能接名詞，而要接子句，不過 in addition to（除此之外還有～）則是介系詞片語，後面可以接名詞。

Questions 144-146 refer to the following letter.

144-146 根據下面的信件內容回答問題。

August 10	8 月 10 日
Jordan McLeod 451 N Garnet Drive Nashville, TN 37209	Jordan McLeod Garnet 北路 451 號 Nashville，田納西州 37209
Dear Mr. McLeod,	親愛的 McLeod 先生：
Thank you for your interest in _____ JointHands Foundation. 144 (A) expanding (B) incorporating (C) assisting (D) celebrating	144 謝謝你有興趣協助 JointHands 基金會。
We will have to match your time commitment and skills with our organization's needs. Please fill out the enclosed volunteer application form and return it to us no later than August 31.	我們必須針對你能服務的時間和技能與我們基金會的需求做配合。請填寫隨函的志工申請表，並於 8 月 31 日前寄回給我們。
Qualified applicants will be contacted for interviews. If you are accepted, you will go through an orientation session _____ starting your volunteer work. 145 (A) except (B) prior to (C) even though (D) whereas	我們會聯絡符合資格的申請者來面試。145 如果你被錄取了，你將會在開始志工工作前參加一個新人訓練。

At JointHands, volunteers are directly involved in the _____
                146 (A) organizing   (B) organizer
                   (C) organizes   (D) organize
phases of our outreach projects.
	146 在 JointHands，志工會直接參與我們到家關懷服務計畫的規劃階段。

If you have any further questions or concerns, please do not hesitate to call our office at 555-3719.	如果你有任何進一步的問題和疑慮，請不要客氣撥打 555-3719 與我們辦公室聯絡。
Best regards,	Vonda Barlow 敬上 活動策畫人 JointHands 基金會
Vonda Barlow Coordinator JointHands Foundation	

單字 commitment n. 投入，獻身   enclosed a. 附上的   no later than phr. 不要晚於～   contact v. 聯絡
undergo v. 接受，承受   involve v. 使參與   outreach n. 到家關懷服務   hesitate v. 猶豫

144 ■■ 動詞語彙 掌握全文   解答 (C)

因為文意為「謝謝你有興趣_____ JointHands 基金會」，所有的選項都有可能是正確答案。從有空格的句子裡無法直接找出答案，所以要從前後文或全文來判斷。後面有提到要填寫隨函的志工申請表，之後則是在說明志工工作的內容，可以知道收信者對於志工活動有興趣。因此，動詞 assist（幫忙）的 -ing 形 (C) assisting 為正確答案。(A) 的 expand 是「使擴張」，(B) 的 incorporate 是「合併」，(D) 的 celebrate 是「祝賀」的意思。

145 ■■ 選擇介系詞 時間點   解答 (B)

因為文意為「開始志工工作之前要先參加一個新人訓練」，所以要選擇有「在～之前，～之前」意思的 (B) prior to 為正確答案。如果選擇副詞子句連接詞兼介系詞 (A) except（除了～以外），就會變成「去參加新人訓練，除了開始志工工作外」的意思。副詞子句連接詞 (C) even though（雖然～），(D) whereas（～的相反），全都會讓文意變得奇怪。

146 ■■ 分詞的功能   解答 (A)

可以扮演形容詞角色修飾名詞 phases 的分詞 (A) organizing（計畫）是正確答案。(B) 只有變成複合名詞，才能夠修飾名詞。動詞 (C) (D) 都不能修飾名詞。

To: Letticia Lopez <letty_lopez@mailstream.com>

From: Norah Bailey <n.bailey@centennialhospital.org>

Subject: Seminar Speakers
Date: June 8

Dear Letticia,
We were informed of your intention to invite James Cortez to be a guest speaker at your _____ seminar in July.

147 (A) nutrition　　(B) health
(C) finance　　(D) literature

I'm sorry to say this, but he _____ unavailable during that

148 (A) was　　(B) has been
(C) will be　　(D) had been

month. He is scheduled to attend a medical conference from July 12 to 15 and will conduct clinical research after the event. If you have _____ other neurologists in mind,

149 (A) every　　(B) any
(C) all　　(D) no

give me their names, and I will personally request one of them to speak at the seminar. In fact, most of our neurologists at the hospital are colleagues of James Cortez in the Neuro Society, so I am confident that any one of them can provide an informative talk.

I will wait for your reply.

Sincerely,

Norah Bailey
Director of public relations

收件人：Letticia Lopez <letty_lopez@mailstream.com>

寄件人：Norah Bailey <n.bailey@centennialhospital.org>

主旨：研討會講員
日期：6 月 8 日

親愛的 Letticia：
147 我們得知你計畫要邀請 James Cortez 醫生在你們 7 月的健康研討會上演講。

148 很遺憾，他在那個月並沒有時間。他被安排在 7 月 12 至 15 日去參加一個醫學會議，而且在那個活動後會進行一個臨床研究。

149 如果你對其他任何神經科醫生有興趣，給我他們的名字，我會親自請他們其中一人去此研討會演講。實際上，我們醫院裡大多數的神經科醫生都是 Cortez 醫生在神經學會的同事，所以我有把握他們之中任何一個都可以提供一場具教育性的演說。

我會靜候你的消息。

Norah 敬上
公關主任

單字 clinical research phr. 臨床調查　neurologist n. 神經科醫師　colleague n. 同事　informative a. 資訊豐富的

147 ■■ 名詞語彙 掌握全文　　　　　　　　　　　　　　　　　　　　　　　　　　　解答 (B)

文意為「得知你計畫要邀請 James Cortez 參加_____研討會」，所有選項都有可能是答案。從有空格的句子裡無法直接找出答案，就要從前後文或全文來判斷。後面提到 James Cortez 預計參加醫學會議並有臨床研究，所以我們可以知道 James Cortez 被邀請參加的研討會是跟健康有關係的。因此，名詞 (B) health（健康）為正確答案。(A) nutrition 是「營養」，(C) finance 是「財務」，(D) literature 是「文學」的意思。

148 ■■ 未來時態 掌握前後文　　　　　　　　　　　　　　　　　　　　　　　　　解答 (C)

文意為「在那個月都沒有時間」，只看有空格的句子無法選出與時態符合的動詞，所以要從前後文或全文來做判斷。前文提到要邀請 James Cortez 參加 7 月的演說，所以可以知道「那個月」就是 7 月。因為 7 月是信件寄送日 6 月 8 日之後，可以知道時間是在未來。因此要選擇未來時態 (C) will be 為正確答案。

149 ■■ 否定形容詞 any　　　　　　　　　　　　　　　　　　　　　　　　　　　解答 (B)

空格後有複數可數名詞，所以可以寫在複數可數名詞前的 (B) (C) (D) 都可能是答案。因句意為「如果你對其他任何神經科醫生有興趣，告訴我他們的名字」，所以選擇 (B) any（任何）為正確答案。注意，any 主要用於否定句、疑問句、條件句。(C) all 是「全部」，(D) no 是「什麼都不」的意思，雖然可在可數、不可數名詞之前，若在本句中使用會造成奇怪的意思。(A) every 是「每一個」，和單數可數名詞一起使用。

Questions 150-152 refer to the following announcement.

150-152 根據下面的公告內容回答問題。

Creative Director Announced for Limelight Studios

Burbank - William York will become Limelight Studio's creative director starting next month, the company announced yesterday in a press release. The _____ of York

150 (A) resignation (B) investigation
(C) promotion (D) authorization

comes as no surprise to industry insiders, who predicted that York would take over the position, as current creative director Liza Michaels retires in May. Since Michaels announced her retirement, she has been _____ training York

151 (A) doubtfully (B) formerly
(C) infrequently (D) actively

for his new role at the studio.

In his new position, York will supervise the production of the studio's television series and films, as well as develop new ideas for future projects.

York has been a producer and director for Limelight Studios since 2003. Michaels comments that "_____

152 (A) Her (B) His
(C) Our (D) Their

knowledge of this company makes William York the perfect candidate for the job."

Limelight Studios 宣布新聘創意總監

Burbank 新聞。Limelight Studios 昨天在新聞稿中宣布，William York 將從下個月起成為該公司的創意總監。150 該行的圈內人早就預測 York 先生會取代今年 5 月退休的現任創意總監Liza Michaels，因次對York能晉升到這個職位並不意外。

151 自從 Michaels 女士宣布了她的退休，她就一直很積極地栽培York先生在這個電視台所擔任的新角色。

在 York 的新職位上，他要監督電視台的連續劇和影片的製作，同時也要為未來的計畫構思新的想法。

York 從 2003 年起就一路擔任 Limelight Studios 的製作人、總監。152 Michaels 女士對他的評語是「William York 對這間公司的認識，讓他成為這份工作的最佳人選。」

單字 announce v. 發表　press release phr. 新聞稿　supervise v. 監督

150 ■ 名詞語彙　　　　　　　　　　　　　　　　　　　　　　　　　　　　　　　　　　　　　　　解答 (C)

因為意思為「業界圈內人對於 York 的升遷並不意外，他們早就預測 York 會獲得這個職位」，所以名詞 (C) promotion（升遷）為正確答案。(A) resignation 是「辭職」，(B) investigation 是「調查」，(D) authorization 是「授權，許可」的意思。

151 ■ 副詞語彙　　　　　　　　　　　　　　　　　　　　　　　　　　　　　　　　　　　　　　　解答 (D)

因為意思為「自從 Michaels 女士宣布了她的退休，她就一直很積極地栽培 York 先生在這個電視台所擔任的新角色」，所以副詞 (D) actively（主動地，積極地）是正確答案。(A) doubtfully 是「疑惑地」，(B) formerly 是「以前」，(C) infrequently 是「很少」的意思。

152 ■ 名詞、代名詞須一致　　　　　　　　　　　　　　　　　　　　　　　　　　　　　　　　　解答 (B)

因為意思為「William York 對這個公司的____認識，讓他成為這份工作的最佳人選」的意思，空格裡填入的代名詞也就是 William York 本人。所以，應該要選與男性單數名詞 William York 一致的代名詞 (B) His 為正確答案。

PART 7

Questions 153-154 refer to the following notice.

153-154 根據下面的告示內容回答問題。

Brighten up your celebrations with Sky Sparks!

153-A Wuxi Sky Sparks produces a wide selection of safe and high quality fireworks that have earned us the Shoppers' Choice Award and the Global Excellence in Product Manufacturing Award. 153-D Our company has been recognized by the Asian Pyrotechnics Association as the number one fireworks brand **in the region**.

153-C We are also an official fireworks provider for world-class sports events, Independence Day celebrations in the United States, and other occasions that are held in amusement parks all over the world.

154 Present this advertisement from December 16 to 28 at any of our outlets in Sydney and get 25 percent off when you buy fireworks **from our aerial display line worth at least $100.**

Don't settle for an ordinary brand when you can have the best. Celebrate the New Year with a loud bang and light up the night with Wuxi Sky Sparks, a trusted name in fireworks.

Sky Sparks 點亮你的慶祝會！

153-A 無錫的 Sky Sparks 生產了一系列安全、高品質的煙火，讓我們贏得「消費者選擇獎」和「全球精品製造獎」。

153-D 我們公司已被「亞州煙火製造協會」認定是該地區首屈一指的煙火品牌。

153-C 我們還是世界級體育活動、美國獨立紀念日慶典，還有在全世界各地的遊樂園所舉辦的其他活動的官方指定煙火供應商。

154 從 12 月 16 日到 28 日，只要在我們雪梨的任何一家商店購買**價值至少一百元澳幣的空中展示系列**煙火，出示這張廣告，就可以得到七五折的優惠。

當你可以買到最好的，就不要屈就於一個普通的品牌。用巨響來慶祝新年，並讓無錫 Sky Sparks 這個值得信賴的煙火點亮夜空。

單字 □wide a. 寬廣的，多樣的　□selection n. 選擇　□earn v. 賺取，獲得
□pyrotechnics n. 煙火製造術　□association n. 協會，團體　□region n. 地區
□Independence Day phr. 獨立紀念日　□occasion n. 活動，盛典　□amusement park phr. 遊樂園
□present v. 發表，出示　□advertisement n. 廣告　□worth a. 有～的價值
□settle v. 定居，安頓，安於　□ordinary a. 平凡的

153

What is NOT stated about Wuxi Sky Sparks?
(A) It is a recipient of different kinds of awards.
(B) It is a sponsor of sports competitions.
(C) It is a brand used at prominent events.
(D) It is a recognized maker of quality products.

關於無錫 Sky Sparks，沒有提到什麼？
(A) 得到不同的獎項。
(B) 是運動賽事的贊助商。
(C) 是用在重要慶典的品牌。
(D) 是公認製造高品質產品的製造商。

■ **Not / True** Not 問題

解答 (B)

本題是要在文章中找到與本問題的重點 Wuxi Sky Sparks 相關的內容後，比較選項與文章的 Not/True 問題。(A) 在文中 Wuxi Sky Sparks ~ have earned us the Shoppers' Choice Award and the Global Excellence in Product Manufacturing Award 指出 Wuxi Sky Sparks 得到 Shoppers' Choice 跟 Global Excellence 兩個獎，與文章內容一致。(B) 則是文中沒有提到的內容，所以 (B) It is a sponsor of sports competitions. 為正確答案。(C) 在文中 We are ~ an official fireworks provider for world-class sports events, Independence Day celebrations in the United State, and other occasions that are held in amusement parks all over the world. 則提到他們是世界級體育活動、美國獨立紀念日慶典，還有在全世界各地的遊樂園所舉辦的其他活動的官方指定煙火供應商，與文章內容一致。(D) 在文中 Our company has been recognized ~ as the number one fireworks brand 是說他們被認定為世界首屈一指的煙火品牌，與文章內容一致。

單字 recipient n. 獲獎者，受頒者　award n. 獎　prominent a. 有名的

What will happen after December 28?	在 12 月 28 日以後會發生什麼事？
(A) A type of merchandise will be discontinued.	(A) 有一種商品不會再賣了。
(B) A fireworks display will be held in Sydney.	(B) 在雪梨會舉辦煙火展示。
(C) A business will open stores in different locations.	(C) 有一家公司會在不同地點開店。
(D) A promotional offer will no longer be valid.	(D) 一項優惠活動停止了。

■■ 六何原則 What 　　　　　　　　　　　　　　　　　　　　　　　　解答 (D)

這是在詢問 12 月 28 日之後會發生什麼（What）事情的六何原則問題。與問題的重點 happen after December 28 相關的句子 Present this advertisement from December 16 to 28 ~ and get 25 percent off when you buy fireworks 中可以看出「12 月 16 日開始到 28 日只要出示廣告單，就可以在結帳時得到七五折優惠」，並推論 12 月 28 日之後煙火優惠就無效了。所以 (D) A promotional offer will no longer be valid. 是正確答案。

單字 discontinue v.（生產）中斷　promotional a. 促銷的　valid a. 有效的

From: Now Mail <info@nowmail.com> To: Eloise Pendleton <eloise.pendleton@nowmail.com> Subject: Welcome! Date: December 18 Dear Ms. Pendleton, Thank you for signing up for a Now Mail Plus account. [155]Stay connected with your friends and family with the useful features of this e-mail account. With Now Mail Plus, you can see what e-mails you have received at a glance and decide which ones to read. This allows you to delete e-mails without having to click on them. You can save a lot of time with this feature. [156]We have also upgraded Now Mail Plus's attachment capacity! You can send up to 25 megabytes, which is twice as much as comparable services. Please use the following user ID and password every time you sign in to your account. User ID: eloise.pendleton Password: eloise501 We recommend that you change your password monthly for security reasons. To get started and learn about the features of your e-mail account, click here. If you have any questions please feel free to e-mail us at cuserve@nowmail.com. Best Regards, Now Mail Team	寄件者：Now Mail <info@nowmail.com> 收件者：Eloise Pendleton <eloise.pendleton@nowmail.com> 主旨：歡迎 日期：12 月 18 日 親愛的 Pendleton 小姐： 謝謝加入 Now Mail Plus 帳戶。[155]這個電郵帳戶有用的功能讓你和朋友與家人保持聯繫。有了 Now Mail Plus，你可以一眼就看到你收了什麼電郵，並決定要讀哪些，讓你不用點進去看就直接刪除，這個功能可以節省你許多時間，[156]我們還升級了 Now Mail Plus 的附件容量！你可以寄送容量至 25M，這是其他同級服務的兩倍。 請每次都使用以下的用戶帳號和密碼來登入你的帳戶。 用戶帳號：eloise.pendleton 密碼：eloise501 為了安全考量，我們建議你每個月改變你的密碼，要開始認識你電郵帳戶的功能，請點這裡。如果你有任何問題，請不要客氣寄電郵給我們：cuserve@nowmail.com。 Now Mail 團隊敬上

單字 □sign up phr. 登錄   □feature n. 特色   □at a glance phr. 一眼認出，馬上
　　 □attachment n. 附件   □capacity n. 容量   □comparable a. 比得上的，可比較的
　　 □sign in phr. 登入   □security n. 保安，安全

155

What is the main purpose of the e-mail? (A) To inform a client that an account has been renewed (B) To offer free online data storage (C) To provide information on a service's features (D) To clarify privacy terms and conditions	這封電郵的目的為何？ (A) 通知一位顧客帳戶已經更新了 (B) 提供免費的線上資料儲存空間 (C) 針對一項服務的功能提供資訊 (D) 釐清隱私條款

■ 找出主題 目的   解答 (C)

因為是要確認寄送電子郵件目的的問題，所以要特別注意文章的前半部分。Stay connected with your friends and family with the useful features of this e-mail account. 提到利用這個電郵帳戶有用的功能，讓自己和朋友與家人保持聯繫，說明了提供服務的特徵，所以 (C) To provide information on a service's features 為正確答案。

單字 storage n. 倉庫，儲存空間，庫存量　clarify v. 澄清，闡明　term n. 條款　condition n. 條件

156

What can Ms. Pendleton do with Now Mail Plus?
(A) Transfer a large amount of information
(B) Sign in without typing a password
(C) Store up to 25 megabytes of e-mails
(D) Upload pictures in seconds

Pendleton 小姐可以用 Now Mail Plus
做什麼？
(A) 傳輸大量的資料
(B) 登入時不需要輸入密碼
(C) 可以儲存 25M 的電郵容量
(D) 幾秒鐘內就能上傳照片

■ 六何原則 What   解答 (A)

本題是在問 Ms. Pendleton 可以利用 Now Mail Plus 做什麼（What）的六何原則問題。跟問題重點 do with
Now Mail Plus 相關的句子 We have also upgraded Now Mail Plus's attachment capacity! You can send up to 25
megabytes, which is twice as much as comparable services. 指出 Now Mail Plus 的寄送容量升級到 25M，與其
他公司提供的服務相較是兩倍，(A) Transfer a large amount of information 為正確答案。

單字 store v. 儲存

A Niche for the Classic and Beautiful

By Hanna Crowell

PARIS, June 5 - After seeing the beautiful collection of home furnishings and decorative items at The Nostalgia Corner in Place d'Aligre, visitors agree that it is a necessary stop for anyone interested in antiques.

[157]Established two years ago by Parisian antique collectors Jeremy Almary and Sandra Baude, the shop features European pieces dating back to the 17th century. [158]What is fascinating about this shop is the effort it puts into displays. [158]Items are arranged according to which part of the world they come from. Each vintage piece is also tagged with information about its composition, style, and the period in which it was made, **thus allowing customers to appreciate the item even more.**

"We would like people who visit our shop to be delighted by the beauty and artistic worth of our collection," Baude **said. Because of this,** [157]The Nostalgia Corner has become not only a store, but also a must-see attraction for travelers to Paris.

With the business doing well, the proprietors plan to expand their collection by offering antique pieces from East Asian countries. "[159]Within the next 10 years, we hope to provide our customers with a larger selection of antiques by including items from China and South Korea," Baude added.

一個古典與美麗的空間

Hanna Crowell

巴黎，6 月5 日 – 在 Place d'Aligre 的 Nostalgia Corner 看過美輪美奐的居家家具與裝潢產品後，參觀者都同意對骨董有興趣的人都應該來此駐足。

[157]兩年前由巴黎的骨董收集家 Jeremy Almary 和 Sandra Baude 所成立，這家店的特色是擁有追溯至十七世紀歐洲的骨董。[158]這家店最吸引人的地方在於他們對展示商品付出的努力。[158]商品的安排都依據它們來自於世界上哪些地方，每一件珍藏品都標示著它的組成成分、風格以及在哪個時期製造的，因此讓顧客們更能夠去欣賞每一件商品。

Baude 説：「我想要所有來我們店裡參觀的人都能讚賞我們收藏品的美麗與藝術價值。」正因為如此，[157]Nostalgia Corner 不僅僅是一家商店，還是來到巴黎的遊客必到的一個景點。

由於生意不錯，店主人還計畫要擴展他們的收藏，提供來自東亞國家的骨董。Baude 補充説到：「[159]在未來十年內，我們希望能以包括來自中國和南韓的物品，提供顧客更多的骨董選擇。」

單字 ☐ furnishing n. 家具   ☐ decorative a. 裝飾的   ☐ antique n. 骨董
      ☐ established a. 被建立的   ☐ feature v. 以～為特徵   ☐ fascinating a. 令人驚奇的
      ☐ effort n. 努力   ☐ arrange v. 陳列，排列   ☐ according to phr. 根據～
      ☐ tag v. 做記號，附著   ☐ composition n. 構成，作曲   ☐ appreciate v. 欣賞
      ☐ delighted a. 高興的，快樂的   ☐ artistic a. 藝術式的，藝術的   ☐ worth n. 價值
      ☐ attraction n. 景點   ☐ proprietor n. 經營者

157

Why was the article written?
(A) To introduce a new trend in interior decoration
(B) To explain the history of antique collecting
(C) To guide consumers in appraising items
(D) To describe a successful business venture

為什麼寫這篇文章？
(A) 介紹一種室內裝潢的新趨勢
(B) 解釋骨董收集的歷史
(C) 指導消費者鑑賞物品
(D) 介紹一個成功的創業

◼ 找出主題 寫文章的理由   解答 (D)

這是在問寫這篇新聞的理由。要透過整篇文章才能看出主題。Established ~ by Parisian antique collectors ~, the shop features European pieces dating back to 17th century. 指出這家店是由巴黎的骨董收集家 Jeremy Almary 和 Sandra Baude 所成立，並以擁有追溯至十七世紀歐洲的骨董為特色，之後的 The Nostalgia Corner has become not only a store, but also a must-see attraction 則是說 Nostalgia Corner 不僅僅是一家商店，還是來到巴黎的遊客必到的一個景點，因此 (D) To describe a successful business venture 為正確答案。

單字 appraise v. 鑑賞，評價

158

What does the article suggest about The Nostalgia Corner?	關於 Nostalgia Corner 這篇文章暗示了什麼？
(A) It recently sold a famous piece of artwork.	(A) 最近賣了一件有名的藝術品。
(B) It regularly conducts sales on furniture.	(B) 定期舉辦家具特賣。
(C) It was inherited from one of the owners' relatives.	(C) 從店主人的一位親戚那裏繼承而來的。
(D) It carefully plans the presentation of its merchandise.	(D) 很精心地規劃商品的陳列。

■ 推論 詳細內容 　　　　　　　　　　　　　　　　　　　　　　　　　　　　　　解答 (D)

這是需要推論問題中提及的重點 The Nostalgia Corner 的題目。What is fascinating about this shop is the effort it puts into displays. 是說這家店最吸引人的地方在於他們對展示品所付出的努力，之後 Items are arranged according to which part of the world they come from. Each vintage piece is also tagged with information about its composition, style, and the period in which it was made 則是說所有展示商品的陳列依據它們來自於世界上哪些地方，每一件珍藏品都標示著它的組成成分、風格以及在哪個時期製造的，所以我們可以推論 The Nostalgia Corner 對於商品的陳列非常謹慎講究，因此 (D) It carefully plans the presentation of its merchandise. 為正確答案。

單字 conduct v. 實施，施行　inherit v. 遺傳，繼承　presentation n. 陳列，說明，發表

159

What do the proprietors want to do within a decade?	店主人在十年內想做什麼？
(A) Seek additional investors	(A) 尋找更多的投資者
(B) Offer pieces from other global regions	(B) 提供世界其他地區的物件
(C) Establish a branch in another European country	(C) 在歐洲另一個國家成立一間分店
(D) Build a warehouse for fragile collections	(D) 為易碎的收藏品蓋一間倉庫

■ 六何原則 What 　　　　　　　　　　　　　　　　　　　　　　　　　　　　　　解答 (B)

因為是在問經營者們十年內想要做什麼（What）的六何原則問題，跟問題重點 the proprietors want to do within a decade 相關的句子 Within the next 10 years, we hope to provide our customers with a larger selection of antiques by including items from China and South Korea 指出未來十年內，該店希望能以包括來自中國和南韓的物品，提供顧客更多的骨董選擇，所以 (B) Offers pieces from other global regions 為正確答案。

單字 warehouse n. 倉庫　fragile a. 易碎的

MEMORANDUM	備忘錄
To: Food safety inspectors From: Director Raymond Jensen, Rockford Food Department Date: March 3 Re: Training	收件者：食品安全稽查員 寄件者：Rockford 食品部主任 Raymond Jensen 日期：3 月 3 日 關於：訓練

160The Bureau of Food and Drugs and the Health Department will hold a state-wide training seminar on food safety inspection at the Health Department conference hall in Springfield on March 15. The seminar has been arranged to ensure proper evaluation of food handling procedures in restaurants and fast-food outlets. The Bureau will also introduce new inspection guidelines during the event. These will include new policies from the bureau that must be implemented by the end of this year. Therefore, all Rockford Food safety officers are required to attend. 161Theresa Lloyd, our new administrative assistant, is responsible for reserving seats at the seminar and making transportation arrangements. All attendees will also be booked to stay at the Printemps Hotel. 161Please contact her to confirm your attendance before the end of the week so that she can make all the necessary bookings and reservations.

160 食品藥物局和健康部門將於 3 月 15 日在春田市健康部門的會議廳舉辦一個關於食品安全檢查的全州研討會，安排這個研討會是為了要確保餐廳和速食店適當評估處理食物的過程。食品藥物局將會在研討會上介紹新的檢查綱要，包括了食品藥物局必須在今年底前實施的新政策，因此所有 Rockford 食品的安檢人員都一定要參加。161 我們新來的行政助理 Theresa Lloyd 負責研討會的座位保留和交通安排，所有參加者都會安排住在 Printemps 飯店。161 請於本週結束前和 Theresa 聯絡，確認你的出席，讓她可以處理所有必要的訂位與訂房。

單字
□inspector n. 督導	□bureau n.（美國的）政府部門	□state-wide a. 整州的，全國的
□inspection n. 檢查	□arrange v. 安排	□ensure v. 確保
□proper a. 正確的，適切的	□evaluation n. 評價，評估	□handling n. 處理
□procedure n. 過程	□outlet n. 賣場	□guideline n. 指導
□administrative a. 行政上的，管理上的		□assistant n. 助理，祕書
□transportation n. 交通	□arrangement n. 準備，安排	□booking n. 預約

160

What is the memo mainly about?	這個備忘錄主要是關於什麼？
(A) Inspection instructions	(A) 檢查的教學
(B) Employee responsibilities	(B) 員工的工作權責
(C) Scheduling corrections	(C) 行程的修正
(D) Event information	(D) 活動資訊

找出主題 主題　　　　　　　　　　　　　　　　　　　　　　　　　　　解答 (D)

因為是在詢問備忘錄是與什麼東西相關的題目，所以要特別注意備忘錄的前半部分。The Bureau of Food and Drugs and the Health Department will hold a state-wide training seminar on food safety inspection 指出食品藥物局和衛生部門將會舉辦一個關於食品安全檢查的全州研討會，所以可以知道這是在簡介研討會內容並邀請人員與會的相關資訊，因此要選 (D) Event information 為正確答案。

單字 instruction n. 指示，教學　correction n. 修正，更改

161

What is suggested about Ms. Lloyd?	關於 Lloyd 小姐，提示了什麼？
(A) She is Mr. Jensen's personal assistant.	(A) 她是 Jensen 先生的個人助理。
(B) She will compile an attendance list for an event.	(B) 她會整理出一份活動參加者名單。
(C) She is organizing an upcoming seminar.	(C) 她在籌備即將舉辦的研討會。
(D) She was recently transferred to the Health Department.	(D) 她最近才轉到健康部門。

■ 推論 詳細內容   解答 (B)

這是要推論問題的重點 Ms. Lloyd 的問題。Theresa Lloyd ~ is responsible for reserving seats at the seminar and making transportation arrangements. 是說 Theresa Lloyd 負責研討會的座位保留和交通安排，之後又寫到 Please contact her to confirm your attendance ~ so that she can make all the necessary bookings and reservations. ，說明請和 Theresa 確認參加與否，讓她可以處理所有必要的訂位與訂房，所以可以推論 Ms. Lloyd 日後需要統計參加人員的名單，因此 (B) She will compile an attendance list for an event. 為正確答案。

單字 compile v. 編輯，彙編，統計

The Garden Fields	The Garden Fields	花園地	花園地
Where dreams do come true!		夢想實現的地方！	
Celebrate life's special moments at The Garden Fields. With our enchanting gardens and Spanish-inspired courtyards, [162]you can plan an occasion that will definitely be a unique experience for your clients and their guests. If you want to organize a formal garden wedding or birthday party, we can help you. [163-A]The Garden Fields has different reception venues for anniversaries, corporate events, and other functions. In addition, we have affiliated catering companies ready to arrange extravagant meals for different occasions. We provide tables, seating, serving dishes, and floral arrangements. If you have any other requirements or additional requests for decorations, our expert event planners will do their best to accommodate you. Contact us today and let us help you create the celebration of a lifetime!	20 Cluny Drive Singapore To make a booking or [164]for further information, please contact The Garden Fields office at 555-4144 Or visit www.thegardenfields.com.	在花園地慶祝生命特別的時刻，在我們夢幻的花園以及仿西班牙式的庭院，[162] 你可以籌畫一個絕對讓客戶及賓客們難以忘懷的活動。假如你要籌畫一個正式的花園婚禮或生日派對，我們可以幫助你。[163-A] 花園地有針對週年慶、公司活動及其他功能的不同會場。此外，我們有合作的外燴公司來安排各式場合的盛大餐會。我們提供桌椅、餐具及花卉擺設。如果你有任何其他追加的裝飾要求，我們專業的活動企畫人員會盡心盡力的滿足你的需求。今天就和我們聯絡，讓我們幫助你舉辦一個永生難忘的慶祝活動！	Cluny 路 20 號，新加坡 預約與[164] 洽詢請聯絡花園地辦公室 555-4144 或上官網 www. thegardenfields. com。

單字　□enchanting a. 魅惑的，使人著迷的　□courtyard n. 庭院，後院　　□occasion n. 活動，時刻
　　　　□organize v. 準備，籌畫　　　　□formal a. 官方的，正式的　　□reception n. 接待，宴會
　　　　□venue n. 場所　　　　　　　　□affiliate v. 使隸屬於，使緊密聯繫　□catering a. 承辦宴會的，提供外燴的
　　　　□arrange v. 安排，排列　　　　□extravagant a. 奢華的，放肆的

162

For whom is the brochure most likely intended?	這本小冊子最有可能是給誰看？
(A) Wedding photographers	(A) 婚禮攝影師
(B) Event planners	(B) 活動企畫人員
(C) Landscape architects	(C) 景觀設計建築師
(D) Flower shop owners	(D) 花店老闆

■ 推論 整體情報　　　　　　　　　　　　　　　　　　　　　　　解答 (B)

這是要綜合例文中所有分散的線索的題目。you can plan an occasion that will definitely be a unique experience for your clients and their guests 是說「你可以籌畫一個絕對讓客戶及賓客們難以忘懷的活動」，之後說明 The Garden Fields 提供的活動規劃相關服務，因此可以知道這是以活動企畫人員為對象製作的資料，所以 (B) Event planners 是正確答案。

單字 landscape n. 風景，地景

163

What feature of The Garden Fields is mentioned?	本文提到了花園地的什麼特色？
(A) It has a variety of event facilities.	(A) 有多樣的活動設施。
(B) It offers vegetarian menu options.	(B) 有素食餐點的選擇。
(C) It has on-site kitchen facilities.	(C) 花園地本身有廚房設備。
(D) It is famous for its collection of exotic plants.	(D) 以異國植物而著名。

■ Not / True True 問題　　　　　　　　　　　　　　　　　　　解答 (A)

本題是要在文章中找到與本問題的重點 feature of The Garden Fields 相關的內容後，比較選項與文章的 Not/True 問題。 The Garden Fields has different reception venues for anniversaries, corporate events, and other functions. 提到花園地有針對週年慶、公司活動及其他功能的不同會場，所以 (A) It has a variety of event facilities. 為正確答案。(B) (C) (D) 都是文中沒有提及的部分。

換句話說

different reception venues 多樣的宴會場所 → a variety of event facilities 多樣的活動設施

單字 vegetarian a. 素食主義者的，吃素的 n. 素食者　exotic a. 異國情調的，外來的

164

What should clients do to learn more about The Garden Fields?	顧客們如何得知更多關於花園地的資訊？
(A) Visit the venue	(A) 親自來訪
(B) Send an e-mail	(B) 寄電郵
(C) View a Web site	(C) 上官網
(D) Call an affiliated hotel	(D) 打電話詢問合作的飯店

■ 六何原則 What　　　　　　　　　　　　　　　　　　　　　　解答 (C)

這是在問顧客們為了更了解 The Garden Fields，要做什麼（What）才可以的六何原則問題。與問題的重點 to learn more about The Garden Fields 相關的 for further information, please ~ visit www.thegardenfields.com 是說想了解更多，請上官網 www.thegardenfields.com 的意思，所以 (C) View a website 為正確答案。

換句話說

to learn more 為了解更多 → for further information 為了更多的資訊

Mangrove Resort
Special Packages

Bask in clear beach waters at Mangrove Resort and enjoy five-star treatment in our luxurious rooms, restaurants, and sports facilities! Everyone can find something to take part in with Mangrove's variety of tours, diving excursions, and recreational activities. Mangrove Resort is the perfect place for a vacation with your friends and families. And as a special promotion, [165]from July 20 to August 20, we will offer vacation packages at 15 percent off peak rates. Take advantage of this chance for incredible savings and enjoy the beach with your loved ones.

[166-A/B/C]**Day Tour Package**

Adult: $40   Children: $30

Includes:

- Buffet lunch
- Airport transfers by land and sea
- [166-B]Speed boat trips to snorkeling sites
- [166-A]Use of water sports equipment, including kayaks and full snorkeling gear
- [166-C]Use of resort facilities, basketball courts, beach volleyball courts, **and music room**

[166-D]**Overnight Package**

Bay Cottages and Beach Villas

Single: $130 per person, per night

Double: $110 per person, per night

Includes:

- Airport transfers by land and sea
- Speed boat trips to snorkeling sites
- Room-service breakfast, lunch, and dinner buffet
- [167]Lunch on Alligator Island*
- [166-D]A choice of an introductory scuba diving course* or free spa services
- Use of water sports equipment, including kayaks and full diving gear
- Use of resort facilities, basketball courts, beach volleyball courts, and music room

[167]*Only available to guests staying more than two nights.

All packages include service charges and applicable government tax.

Mangrove 渡假村
特惠方案

在 Mangrove 渡假村清澈沙灘海水裡享受陽光的溫暖，在我們豪華的房間、餐廳、運動設施裡享受五星級的待遇！在 Mangrove 渡假村裡，每個人都可以在各式的旅遊、潛水行程和娛樂活動中找到事情做，Mangrove 渡假村是你和家人好友渡假的最佳去處。[165]從 7 月 20 日至 8 月 20 日止，我們將提供旺季價格八五折的渡假方案，以作為特別促銷。好好利用這個難得的折扣機會，和你所愛的人盡情享受海灘。

[166-A/B/C] 一日遊方案
成人：四十元美金   兒童：三十元美金
包括：

- 自助午餐
- 機場海陸運接送
- [166-B] 快速遊艇往返浮潛地點
- [166-A] 使用水上運動設備，包括小船和整套的浮潛裝備
- [166-C] 使用渡假村設施、籃球場、海灘排球場和視聽室

[166-D] 過夜方案
海灣小木屋和沙灘別墅
單人房：每人每晚一百三十元美金
雙人房：每人每晚一百一十元美金
包括：

- 機場海陸運接送
- 快速遊艇往返浮潛地點
- 客房服務早餐、午餐和自助晚餐
- [167] 在鱷魚島上享用午餐*
- [166-D] 一堂初級潛水課程*或免費水療服務，二選一
- 使用水上運動設備，包括小船和整套的潛水裝備
- 使用渡假村設施、籃球場、海灘排球場和視聽室

[167]*只提供給停留超過兩晚以上的客人。
所有的方案都以包括服務費和相關的政府稅金

單字 □bask v. 享受陽光　　□peak rate phr. 旺季費用　　□airport transfer phr. 機場接送
　　□equipment n. 設備　　□bay n. 灣　　□cottage n. 小屋，農舍
　　□introductory n. 初級　　□charge n. 費用

165

What will most likely take place after August 20? (A) New recreational activities will be offered. (B) Regular prices will apply. (C) Travel package options will be changed. (D) Tax will be excluded from the package.	在 8 月 20 日後可能發生什麼情況？ (A) 會提供新的娛樂活動。 (B) 原價收費。 (C) 旅遊方案內容會改變。 (D) 稅金將不包含在旅遊方案內。

🔲 推論 詳細內容　　　　　　　　　　　　　　　　　　　　　　　　　　　解答 (B)

這是要推論什麼會 take place after August 20 的問題，from July 20 to August 20, we will offer vacation package at 15 percent off peak rates 提到從 7 月 20 日至 8 月 20 日止，將提供旺季價格八五折的渡假方案，所以可以推論 8 月 20 日之後會回復為正常價格，因此 (B) Regular prices will apply. 為正確答案。

單字 apply v. 適用　exclude v. 除外

166

What is NOT included in the day tour travel package? (A) Snorkeling equipment usage (B) Boat tours to nearby locations (C) Use of sports facilities (D) Beginner diving classes	什麼沒有包含在一日遊方案內？ (A) 浮潛設備的使用 (B) 鄰近區域的乘船行程 (C) 使用運動設施 (D) 初級潛水課程

🔲 Not / True Not 問題　　　　　　　　　　　　　　　　　　　　　　　　　解答 (D)

本題是要在文章中找到與本問題的重點 the day tour travel package 相關的內容後，比較選項與文章的 Not/True 問題。文中 Day Tour Package 的 Use of water sports equipment, including ~ full snorkeling gear 提到使用水上運動設備，包括小船和整套的浮潛裝備，所以 (A) 與文章內容一致。Day Tour Package 的 Speed boat trips to snorkeling sites 提到快速遊艇往返浮潛地點，所以 (B) 與文章內容一致。Day Tour Package 的 Use of ~ basketball courts, beach, volleyball courts 提到使用渡假村設施、籃球場、海灘排球場，(C) 也與文章內容一致。A choice of an introductory scuba diving course（初級潛水課程）是在 Overnight package 才有的選項，因此 (D) 與文章內容不一致，答案為 (D)。

單字 usage n. 使用　nearby a. 鄰近的

167

What is offered exclusively to guests staying two nights or more? (A) Tickets to sporting events (B) A meal at a special site (C) Scuba diving excursions (D) A room upgrade	有什麼是特別提供給停留兩晚以上的遊客？ (A) 體育活動的門票 (B) 在特別地方用餐 (C) 潛水之旅 (D) 房間升級

🔲 六何原則 What　　　　　　　　　　　　　　　　　　　　　　　　　　　解答 (B)

這是在問針對停留兩天以上的旅客提供什麼（What）服務的六何原則問題。與問題重點 guest staying two nights or more 相關的 Lunch on Alligator Island*（在鱷魚島上享用午餐*），公告下方提到 Only available to guests staying more than two nights.，表示有標示 * 記號的服務只提供給停留兩晚以上的旅客。所以正確答案是 (B) A meal at a special site。

單字 excursion n. 旅行

Trade Explorer Magazine 1030 Newbury Street, Philadelphia, PA March 12 Lance Hughes Marketing Manager E-book Station Dear Mr. Hughes, [169]Our records show that you haven't published an advertisement with *Trade Explorer Magazine* for the past six months. We sincerely value the business of customers like yourself and [168]would like to offer you a special promotion. [169/170]In the past, you have taken out several full-page advertisements in our monthly publication. [168/170/171]We would like to offer you the chance to post a full-page advertisement at half the standard rate for our next four issues. If you accept our proposal, we will also provide you with a free button advertisement on our Web site. [171]To place an advertisement, please fill out the enclosed form and mail it back to us. Should you need any assistance with the layout or design of your advertisement, we are also willing to accommodate you in that regard. You may contact our business representative, Juliet Abbot, at 555-0306 for additional information. We hope you will find our offer beneficial and cost-effective. Sincerely yours, Liza Huntington Managing Editor *Trade Explorer Magazine*	貿易探險家雜誌 Newbury 街 1030 號，費城，賓州 3 月 12 日 Lance Hughes 行銷經理 電子書站 親愛的 Hughes 先生： [169]我們的紀錄顯示您在過去六個月都沒有在貿易探險家雜誌刊登廣告，我們就如同你自己一般，真心看重顧客們的事業，[168]因此想要提供你一個特別優惠。[169/170]之前，您在我們的月刊中刊登數個整頁廣告，[168/170/171]我們想要提供機會，讓您在我們下四期的刊物中以半價刊登一個整頁廣告。如果你接受我們的提案，我們還會在我們的官網上提供您免費的按鈕廣告。 [171]若要刊登廣告，請把信封內的表格填好後寄回來給我們。如果您在廣告的排版與設計上需要任何協助，我們也願意在這方面配合您，您可以撥打555-0306和我們的業務代表 Juliet Abbot 聯絡，以獲取更多的資訊。 我們希望您會認為我們所提供的優惠有幫助且經濟實惠。 Lisa Huntington 敬上 雜誌編輯 貿易探險家雜誌

單字 □record n. 紀錄　　□value v. 看重，珍視　　□full-page a. 整面的
　　　□standard n. 標準　　□rate n. 費用　　□proposal n. 提案
　　　□accommodate v. 協助，配合　　□representative n. 職員

168

Why was the letter written? (A) To update a subscription (B) To revise a mailing list (C) To offer services to a client (D) To advertise a local business	為什麼寫這封信？ (A) 續訂刊物 (B) 修訂郵寄名單 (C) 提供服務給顧客 (D) 推銷一個當地的公司

■ 找出主題 寫文章的理由　　　　　　　　　　　　　　　　　　　　　　　　　　解答 (C)

這是在問為什麼要寫這封郵件的問題。這問題特別要從文章的中間開始找出相關的內容。在 would like to offer you a special promotion 跟 We would like to offer you the chance to post a full-page advertisement at half the standard rate 中先提到想要提供一個特別的促銷機會，再說到內部細節是提供以半價刊登一個整頁廣告的優惠，所以 (C) To offer services to a client 是正確答案。

單字 subscription n. 訂閱　revise v. 修正　mailing list phr. 郵寄名單

169

What is suggested about Lance Hughes?	關於 Lance Hughes 提示了什麼？
(A) He owns a business journal.	(A) 他擁有一家商業刊物。
(B) He works for an advertising agency.	(B) 他替一個廣告代理商工作。
(C) He requires assistance with layout.	(C) 他要求排版上的協助。
(D) He is a former client of the magazine.	(D) 他是這家雜誌社以前的客戶。

■ 推論 詳細內容　　　　　　　　　　　　　　　　　　　　　　　　　　解答 (D)

這是要推論問題中 Lance Hughes 角色的問題。Our records show that you haven't published an advertisement with *Trade Explorer Magazine* for the past six months 提到紀錄顯示收件人 Lance Hughes 在過去六個月都沒有在貿易探險家雜誌刊登廣告，之後 In the past, you have taken out several full-page advertisements in our monthly publication. 則是說之前 Lance Hughes 在月刊中刊登數個整頁的廣告，因此可以推測 Lance Hughes 以前是這個雜誌社的客戶，所以正確答案應為 (D) He is a former client of the magazine.。

單字 journal n. 新聞，雜誌，期刊　agency n. 代理商　former a. 以前的

170

How long will the promotion be available?	這項優惠持續多久？
(A) Two months	(A) 兩個月
(B) Four months	(B) 四個月
(C) Six months	(C) 六個月
(D) Seven months	(D) 七個月

■ 六何原則 How Long　　　　　　　　　　　　　　　　　　　　　　　解答 (B)

這是在詢問促銷期間有多久（How Long）的六何原則問題。跟問題的核心 the promotion be available 相關的 In the past, you have taken out several ~ advertisements in our monthly publication 指出之前在月刊中刊登過幾次廣告，之後 We would like to offer you the chance to post a full-page advertisement at half the standard rate for our next four issues. 則是說提供下四期的刊物中以半價刊登一個整頁廣告的機會，可以知道這次促銷在四個月期間都可以使用，所以 (B) Four months 為正確答案。

171

How can Mr. Hughes receive a reduced rate?	Hughes 先生如何能得到折扣價？
(A) By renewing a membership	(A) 更新會員
(B) By placing a large order	(B) 下一大筆訂單
(C) By sending a completed form	(C) 寄回填好的表格
(D) By extending his subscription	(D) 繼續訂購雜誌

■ 六何原則 How　　　　　　　　　　　　　　　　　　　　　　　　　　解答 (C)

因為是詢問 Mr. Hughes 如何（How）獲得優惠的六何原則問題，所以要找與問題重點 receive a reduced rate 相關的內容。We would like to offer you the chance to post a full-page advertisement at the half the standard rate 是「提供下四期的刊物中以半價刊登一個整頁廣告的機會」的意思，而 To place an advertisement, please fill out the enclosed form and mail it back to us. 則是說「如果要刊登廣告，請填寫以下的表格並寄回來給我們」，因此可以知道 (C) By sending a completed form 為正確答案。

單字 membership n. 會員

Questions 172-175 refer to the following letter.

172-175 根據下面的信件內容回答問題。

MEMO

To: All staff members
From: Matilde Montagna, Chairperson, Turini Film Festival

Date: October 5
Subject: Film Festival Schedule

I have finalized the timetable of activities for the film festival. Since we are currently understaffed, [172]I want you to start on the necessary preparations as soon as possible to ensure that the schedule is strictly followed. Below is the timetable for the event:

Date	Activity	Venue(s)	Time
Friday, February 16	Film Festival Launch	Giovanni Boccaccio Theatre	7 P.M. - 8 P.M.
Saturday, February 17	Feature Films	Arthur Place Cinemas 1-7	9 A.M. - 12 P.M.
Sunday, February 18	Short Films	Arthur Place Cinemas 1-5	9 A.M. - 9 P.M.
Monday, February 19	Documentaries	Arthur Place Cinemas 1-5	9 A.M. - 5 P.M.
[173]Tuesday, February 20	Awards Presentation	Tasso Dome	8 P.M. - onwards

As discussed at the meeting, the film and the documentary committees are responsible for arranging show times for all entries. [174]The list containing each entry's screening time should be finalized by October 20 to give enough time for the preparation of invitations, advertisements, and press releases for the festival.

Moreover, I want to inform you that [173]a dinner party will be held following the awards presentation. [173/175]Ms. Belle is currently looking for restaurants and bars that might be interested in providing food and beverages. If you want to recommend a business, please coordinate with her.

備忘錄

收件人：所有員工
寄件人：都靈影展主席 Matilde Montagna
日期：10 月 5 日
主題：影展時程表

影展的活動時程表已經定稿了，由於我們目前人手不足，[172] 我希望你們盡早開始必要的準備，以確保能嚴格遵行這個時程表。以下是活動的時程表：

日期	活動	地點	時間
2 月 16 日 星期五	影展開幕	Giovanni Boccaccio 劇院	晚上七點至八點
2 月 17 日 星期六	劇情片	Arthur Place 電影院1-7	早上九點至中午十二點
2 月 18 日 星期日	短片	Arthur Place 電影院1-5	早上九點至晚上九點
2 月 19 日 星期一	記錄片	Arthur Place 電影院1-5	早上九點至下午五點
[173]2 月 20 日 星期二	頒獎典禮	Tasso 巨蛋	晚上八點起

如同在會議中討論的，影片和紀錄片委員會負責安排所有參展作品的播放時間。[174] 每件作品的播放時間列表應該在 10 月 20 日前定稿，以便有足夠的時間來準備影展的邀請、廣告和新聞稿等。

此外，我想要通知你們，[173] 頒獎典禮後會接著舉行一個晚宴。[173/175] Belle 小姐目前正在找有意願供應食物和飲料的餐廳和酒吧。如果你們有任何想推薦的店家，請和她協調。

單字 ☐understaffed a. 人員不足的　☐timetable n. 時間表，日程　☐committee n. 委員會
　　 ☐entry n. 參加作品　☐press release phr. 新聞稿　☐recommend v. 推薦
　　 ☐coordinate v. 協調

172

What is the purpose of the memo?	這個備忘錄的目的為何？
(A) To report recent management changes	(A) 報告管理團隊最近的變動
(B) To confirm the opening of an establishment	(B) 確認一個機構的開幕
(C) To gather suggestions for a print advertisement	(C) 收集一個平面廣告的建議
(D) To provide additional information on event preparations	(D) 提供活動準備的更多資訊

■ 找出主題 目的 　　　　　　　　　　　　　　　　　　　　　　　　　　　解答 (D)

這是在詢問本備忘錄主題的問題，要特別注意文章前面的部分。I want you to start on the necessary preparations ~ to ensure that the schedule is strictly followed 是說「希望你們盡早開始必要的準備，以確保能嚴格遵行這個時程表」，並附上時程表，所以 (D) To provide additional information on event preparations 為正確答案。

單字 confirm v. 確認，通知

173

What will happen on the last day of the festival?	在活動的最後一天會發生什麼？
(A) Food will be served.	(A) 會供應食物。
(B) Film production will begin.	(B) 會開始製作影片。
(C) The committee meeting will be held.	(C) 會舉辦委員會議。
(D) Short movies will be shown.	(D) 會播放短片。

■ 六何原則 What 　　　　　　　　　　　　　　　　　　　　　　　　　　　解答 (A)

這是在問活動最後一天有什麼（What）事情的六何原則問題。與問題的重點 the last day of the festival 相關的時程表最後一項 Tuesday, February 20 – Award Presentation 跟 a dinner party will be held following the awards presentation 是表示活動最後一天 2 月 20 日舉辦的頒獎典禮之後有晚宴，之後 Ms. Belle is ~ looking for restaurants and bars ~ interested in providing food and beverages. 則提到 Belle 小姐目前正在找有意願供應食物和飲料的餐廳和酒吧，可以知道晚宴會提供飲食。所以 (A) Food will be served. 為正確答案。

單字 serve v. 提供

174

What needs to be submitted on October 20?	什麼需要在 10 月 20 日交出？
(A) Responses to invitations	(A) 邀請回函
(B) A list of screening times	(B) 影片播放時間的列表
(C) Press releases	(C) 新聞稿
(D) Drafts of advertisements	(D) 廣告草稿

■ 六何原則 What 　　　　　　　　　　　　　　　　　　　　　　　　　　　解答 (B)

這是在問 10 月 20 日前需要提交什麼東西（What）的六何原則問題。和問題的重點 be submitted on October 20 有關聯的 The list containing each entry's screening time should be finalized by October 20 是說包含著每個作品播放時間的清單要在 10 月 20 日之前定稿，所以 (B) A list of screening times 為正確答案。

單字 submit v. 提交　draft n. 草稿

175

What is Ms. Belle responsible for?	Belle 小姐負責什麼？
(A) Adjusting event schedules	(A) 調整活動時程表
(B) Catering service arrangements	(B) 外燴服務的安排
(C) Invitation distribution	(C) 邀請卡的發放
(D) Organizing the awards ceremony	(D) 籌畫頒獎典禮

■ 六何原則 What   解答 (B)

這是在問 Ms. Belle 負責什麼（What）事務的六何原則問題。與問題的重點 Ms. Belle responsible for 相關的 Ms. Belle is ~ looking for restaurants and bars ~ interested in providing food and beverages. 指出 Belle 小姐目前正在找有意願供應食物和飲料的餐廳和酒吧，所以 (B) Catering service arrangement 是正確答案。

換句話說

providing food and beverages 提供食物與飲料 → Catering 提供飲食

單字 adjust v. 調整　distribution n. 分配

Questions 176-180 refer to the following article.

176-180 根據下面的文章內容回答問題。

From: Josie Roberts <j.roberts@brentontradehall.com>

To: Kurt Bowman <k_bowman@expressmail.com>

Date: July 24
Subject: Re: Booth Reservation
Attachment: Services and Facilities

Dear Mr. Bowman,

[176]I received your e-mail this morning regarding the Great Homes Fair at Benton Trade Hall from August 20 to 22. I appreciate your interest, and [176]I hope my reply will provide you with sufficient information.

The facility is located in downtown Seattle. As the largest real estate fair in the Northwest, [178-A/D]the event attracts more than 300 property developers, broker firms, and financial companies every year. Real estate firms will sell various properties, ranging from residential apartments and office spaces to industrial facilities. Last year more than 12,000 people attended the event, and [178-C]a grand total of 720 buildings, homes, and properties were sold.

We highly recommend that your company arrange for a booth at the fair, as the vast majority of companies that do so report successful sales. Arrangements can be made to accommodate your staff, and a variety of types and sizes of booths are available. [177/179-D]We also suggest that you and your sales agents attend the free real estate seminar on the last day of the event. Summerset Development Corporation vice president [177/179-D]Anita Cooper will deliver a talk on client relations, which we are certain that brokers like you will benefit from.

Attached to this message is a list of services and facilities offered by Benton Trade Hall. This includes detailed descriptions of booths and a list of fees. [180]To view images of our event halls, booths, and facilities, visit our Web site at www.bentontradehall.com.

Josie Roberts, Events Coordinator, Brenton Trade Hall

寄件人：Josie Roberts <j.roberts@ brentontradehall.com>
收件人：Kurt Bowman <k_bowman@ expressmail.com>
日期：7 月 24 日
主題：回覆：攤位預訂
附件：服務與設施

親愛的 Bowman 先生：

176 我今天早上收到你的電郵，是關於 8 月 20 日至 22 日在 Benton 貿易會議廳所舉辦的 Great Homes 展覽會，感謝您的洽詢，176 希望我的回答將提供你足夠的資訊。

活動場地位在西雅圖市區。作為西北地區最大型的不動產展覽會，178-A/D 每年這個活動都吸引了超過三百個地產開發商、仲介公司和財務公司。不動產公司會銷售各式的房地產，從住家公寓和辦公室空間到工業用場所。去年有超過一萬兩千人來參加這個活動，178-C 總計賣掉七百二十件大樓、住家和地產。

我們極力建議貴公司在這個展覽會中安排一個攤位，絕大多數這麼作的公司都回報說賣得很好。我們可以根據你的員工安排，同時有各種樣式及大小的攤位可供選擇。177/179-D 我們還建議你和你的銷售代表參加活動最後一天的免費房地產座談會。Summerset 開發公司的副總裁 177/179-D Anita Cooper 會針對顧客關係作演講，相信像你這樣的仲介商將從中獲益。

附件是一份 Benton 貿易會議廳提供的服務和設施清單，包括了攤位詳細的說明和費用列表。180 要看我們活動大廳、攤位和設施的照片，請上我們的網站 www.bentontradehall.com。

Josie Roberts 敬上，活動策畫人，Brenton 貿易會議廳

單字 □reply n. 回應　　　　□sufficient a. 充足的　　　　□real estate phr. 不動產

　　□property n. 房地產　　□broker n. 仲介　　　　　□firm n. 公司，企業

　　□residential a. 居住的　□deliver v. 演說、演講　　□relation n. 關係

　　□benefit v. 獲得幫助，獲利

Why did Ms. Roberts send the e-mail to Mr. Bowman? (A) To promote a new property development (B) To reply to an inquiry about an event (C) To request attendance at a meeting (D) To answer a question about a product	為什麼 Roberts 小姐寄這封電郵給 Bowman 先生？ (A) 推銷一個新的地產開發 (B) 回覆關於活動的詢問 (C) 要求參加一場會議 (D) 回答關於產品的問題

■ 找出主題 寫文章的理由　　　　　　　　　　　　　　　　　　　　　　解答 (B)

這是在問 Ms. Roberts 為什麼要寄電子郵件給 Mr. Bowman 的問題，要特別注意文章的前半部分。I received your e-mail ~ regarding the Great Homes Fair 跟 I hope my reply will provide you with sufficient information 指出收到關於 Great Homes 展覽會的洽詢，並希望回答能提供足夠的資訊，之後則是附上與展覽會相關的細節，所以 (B) To reply to an inquiry about an event 為正確答案。

單字 inquiry n. 提問，發問

What does Ms. Roberts recommend Mr. Bowman do? (A) Attend a lecture given by Anita Cooper (B) Take advantage of a promotional offer (C) Reserve an exhibition hall for a fair (D) Submit the forms as soon as possible	Roberts 小姐建議 Bowman 先生做什麼？ (A) 參加 Anita Cooper 的演講 (B) 好好利用促銷活動 (C) 為展覽會預定展示場地 (D) 盡早繳交表格

■ 六何原則 What　　　　　　　　　　　　　　　　　　　　　　　　解答 (A)

這是在問 Ms. Roberts 向 Mr. Bowman 推薦了什麼（What）的六何原則問題。與問題重點 Ms. Roberts recommend Mr. Bowman do 有關的 We ~ suggest that you ~ attend the free real estate seminar 跟 Anita Cooper will deliver a talk ~ you will benefit from 提到向郵件的收件者 Mr. Bowman 推薦去參加 Anita Cooper 的演講，而且將從中獲益。所以 (A) Attend a lecture given by Anita Cooper 為正確答案。

單字 lecture n. 演講　exhibition n. 展覽

What is NOT mentioned about the Great Homes Fair? (A) It attracts a large number of attendees. (B) It is the most advertised real estate fair in the country. (C) It yields a significant amount of sales. (D) It is held on an annual basis.	關於 Great Homes 展覽會，沒有提到什麼？ (A) 吸引了很多人參加。 (B) 是該國最被宣傳的不動產展覽會。 (C) 衍生大量的交易。 (D) 每年舉辦一次的活動。

■ Not / True Not 問題　　　　　　　　　　　　　　　　　　　　　　解答 (B)

這題是要在文章中找到與問題的重點 the Great Home Fair 相關的內容後，比較選項與文章的 Not/True 問題。the event attracts more than 300 property developers, broker firms, and financial companies every year 是說年這個活動都吸引了超過三百個地產開發商、仲介公司和財務公司，所以 (A) 和 (D) 都跟文章內容一致。(B) 是文章中沒有提及的內容。a grand total of 720 buildings, homes, and properties were sold 則是說總計賣掉七百二十件大樓、住家和地產，所以 (C) 也跟文章內容一致。

換句話說

every year 每年 → on an annual basis 每年

單字 attendee n. 參加者　significant a. 重大的，顯著的

179

What is indicated about Mr. Bowman?	關於 Bowman 先生暗示了什麼？
(A) He is in charge of setting up trade shows.	(A) 他負責組織貿易展。
(B) He previously rented a booth at an event.	(B) 他之前在一場活動中租了一個攤位。
(C) He registered for the fair already.	(C) 他報名了這個展覽會。
(D) He works as a real estate broker.	(D) 他是一個不動產仲介商。

■ **Not / True** True 問題   解答 (D)

本題是要在文章中找到與問題的重點 Mr. Bowman 相關的內容後，比較選項與文章的 Not/True 問題。(A)
(B) (C) 都是在文章中沒提到的內容。We also suggest that you ~ attend the free real estate seminar 是建議 Mr.
Bowman 參加免費房地產座談會，之後的 a talk on client relations, which ~ brokers like you will benefit from
則是說因為這場演講談到顧客關係，對於向 Mr. Bowman 這樣的仲介商會有幫助，與文章內容一致，因此
(D) He works as a real estate broker. 是正確答案。

單字 **previously** ad. 先前地　**register** v. 登錄，報名

180

According to the e-mail, what can Mr. Bowman do on the company's Web site?	根據這封電郵，Bowman 先生能在公司的網站上做什麼？
(A) Register for an event	(A) 登記參加這次活動
(B) Review facility rental fees	(B) 檢閱場地租借費用
(C) See pictures of Benton Trade Hall	(C) 瀏覽 Benton 貿易會議廳的照片
(D) Make arrangements for a booth	(D) 安排一個攤位

■ **六何原則** What   解答 (C)

這是在詢問 Mr. Bowman 能在公司的網站上做什麼（What）的六何原則問題。與問題的重點 Mr. Bowman
do on the company's Web site 相關的 To view images of our event halls, booths, and facilities, visit our Web site at
www.bentontradehall.com 是要看活動場地、攤位和設施的照片，請上官網的意思，所以 (C) See pictures of
Benton Trade Hall 為正確答案。

單字 **review** v. 檢閱，回顧　**make arrangement for** phr. 準備～

例文1

Robertson's
Your Neighbourhood Superstore

Sign in | Register | Search all departments

OTHER DEPARTMENTS ▼	You are shopping in > Indoor Appliances > Vacuum Cleaners

Shop by Category
Upright Vacuums
Canister Vacuums
Sticks & Handhelds
Robotic Vacuums
Parts & Accessories

Shop by Brand
Baronial
Irona
Jiffy
Lutschen
Macdougal
Samuelson

181-D Related sections
Warranties
Return policy
181-D Repairs

SPECIAL OFFER
185 Register for an account before September 1 to enjoy single-click transactions; free shipping on orders worth $100 or more, and discounts on select online purchases. Terms and conditions apply. Click for details.

181-B Need more assistance?
Click here to contact a live operator, 24 hours a day, 7 days a week, or call 555-0101.

VACUUM CLEANERS
Click on the links below to view models from each category.
181-A/C Robertson's carries all the leading brands at the best prices. In fact, if you find one of our products advertised for less on other retailers' Web sites, send us a link to their page and we will match their price—guaranteed!*

UPRIGHT VACUUM CLEANERS
Ideal for cleaning carpets, upright vacuum cleaners provide a wide cleaning swath to remove dirt buried deep within floor coverings. They include a variety of attachments and special features. 184 This month only, all Baronial upright vacuums come with an extended two-year manufacturer's warranty.**

CANISTER VACUUM CLEANERS
Canister vacuum cleaners are convenient to use and easy to operate. They are recommended for cleaning bare floors, upholstery, stairs, and difficult-to-reach places. Get a 5 percent rebate when you buy a Lutschen TK50.

STICK & HANDHELD VACUUM CLEANERS
Stick and handheld vacuum cleaners are perfect for cleaning up spills and getting in between tight spaces. They come in both corded and cordless varieties. Take advantage of a buy-one-get-one-free offer on Jiffy handheld car vacuums (select models only).

ROBOTIC VACUUMS
182 Robotic vacuums are becoming one of our best-sellers, as they take all the work out of cleaning floors. Simply charge the robot, input a few settings, and the machine takes care of the rest. Best for maintaining the overall cleanliness of floors in common areas. Buy an Irona and

---

Robertson's
你家附近的超級商店

登入 | 註冊 | 搜索所有的部門

其他部門	你正在購買>室內家電>吸塵器

依分類購物
直立式吸塵器
筒狀式吸塵器
杖式 & 手握式
機器人吸塵器
零件與配件

依品牌購物
Baronial
Irona
Jiffy
Lutschen
Macdougal
Samuelson

181-D 相關資訊
保固
退貨規定
181-D 維修

特別優惠
185 在 9 月 1 日前註冊一個帳號享受點擊立即購物、購物滿一百元美金以上免運費、線上限定商品折扣。須符合細則與條款之規定。
詳情請點此

181-B 需要更多的協助？
點此來聯絡一位在線服務人員，一週七日，一日二十四小時，或撥打 555-0101。

吸塵器
點選以下的連結來瀏覽每個分類下的機型。
181-A/C Robertson's 以最好的價格銷售所有主要品牌。事實上，如果找到其他零售商的網站廣告以較低價格銷售我們任何的產品，把網頁連結寄給我們，我們保證配合他們的價格*。

直立式吸塵器
適合清理地毯，直立式吸塵器提供大片的吸塵面寬度來去除深藏在地板覆蓋物的灰塵，包括各式各樣的附件和特殊功能。184 只有這個月，所有 Baronial 直立式吸塵器附贈兩年製造商延長保固**。

筒狀式吸塵器
筒狀式吸塵器方便使用也容易操作，推薦用於沒有鋪地毯的地板、各式襯套、階梯和不易接觸到的地方。買 Lutschen TK50 可以獲得 5% 的現金回饋。

杖式 & 手握式吸塵器
杖式及手握式吸塵器適合清理溢出物和狹小空間的髒污，有有線與無線兩種類型。Jiffy 手握式車裝吸塵器（特定機種）現在買一送一。

機器人吸塵器
182 機器人吸塵器已經漸漸成為我們最暢銷的類型之一，因為它們能把地板清理的工作全都做完。只要幫機器人充電、輸入一些設定，機器就會把其他工作做完。最適合用來維持公共區域的整體清潔工作。現在買 Irona 吸塵器，就能免費得到一組替換的電池。

181-A *不適用於二手貨
184 **只有把掃描的完整製造商保固卡寄到 customerservice@robertsons.com 才有效

get a free set of replacement batteries.

181-A* Does not apply to items sold second-hand

184** Valid only when you send a scanned copy of the completed manufacturer's warranty card to customerservice@robertsons.com

About Us	Contact Us	Privacy Policy	Terms and Conditions	Site Map

關於我們	聯絡我們	隱私條款	細則與條款	網站地圖

例文2

To: customerservice@robertsons.com

From: Francis Tordesillas
        <francistordesillas@happymail.net>
Date: September 7
Subject: Some Concerns
Attachment: Warranty Card

To whom it may concern,
I ordered a vacuum cleaner from your online store last week and it was just delivered this morning. 184As per the instructions on your Web site, I have attached a scanned copy of the manufacturer's product warranty card. I trust that I still qualify for the extended two-year warranty since 185I completed my purchase in August.

In addition, I am enclosing a link to the Web site of an appliance retailer in Florida. According to their advertisement, 185they are selling the Goldline compact refrigerator for just $156, versus $172 on your Web site. I would prefer to order the appliance from you since I have already registered for an account, but I'd like to confirm that you are able to match this competitor's price.

Here is the link: http://www.plotkinappliance.com/refrigeration/goldline.html

Best regards,

Francis Tordesillas

收件人：customerservice@robertsons.com
寄件人：Francis Tordesillas <francis-tordesillas@happymail.net>
日期：9 月 7 日
主旨：一些問題
附件：保固卡

敬啟者：
我上星期從你們網路商店訂購了一台吸塵器，今天早上剛收到。184 根據你們網站上的說明，我把製造商的保固卡掃描並附在這封電郵一起寄給你，我相信我仍然符合兩年延長保固的資格，因為 185 我是在 8 月完成購買的。

此外，我附上一個在佛羅里達州某家電零售網站的連結，根據他們的廣告，185 他們賣的 Goldline 小型冰箱只要美金一百五十六元，而你們賣美金一百七十二元。因為我已經註冊你們的帳號，所以想跟你們買，但是我想確認你們能夠配合這個競爭對手的價格。

網站的連結在此：http://www.plotkin-appliance.com/refrigeration/goldline.html

Francis Tordesillas 敬上

例文 1 單字 □carry v. 帶，運送
□remove v. 去除
□extended a. 被延長的
□upholstery n. 沙發等的襯套
□take advantage of phr. 利用～
□overall a. 整體的

□match v. 配合
□bury v. 埋藏，埋葬
□warranty n. 保固
□rebate n. 折現，折扣
□charge v. 充電
□common a. 普通的，共同的

□ideal a. 理想的
□feature n. 特徵，特色
□canister n. 金屬罐，筒狀容器
□tight a. 緊的
□ input v. 輸入，提供
□second-hand a. 二手的，間接的

例文 2 單字 □attach v. 附加
□appliance n. 家電
□account n. 帳戶

□qualify v. 具有～資格
□compact a. 小型的
□confirm v. 確認

□enclose v. 隨信附上
□register v. 註冊
□competitor n. 競爭者

What is NOT indicated about Robertson's?	關於 Robertson's 並未指出什麼？
(A) It sells second-hand items for less than its competitors.	(A) 賣二手貨的價格比競爭者較低。
(B) It provides services any time of the day.	(B) 一天的任何時刻都提供服務。
(C) It does not manufacture its own line of products.	(C) 沒有製造自己的產品。
(D) It offers customers information about repairs.	(D) 提供消費者關於維修的資訊。

■ **Not / True** True 問題　　　　　　　　　　　　　　　　　　　　　　　　　解答 (A)

本題是要在文章中找到與本問題的重點 Robertson's 相關的內容後，比較選項與文章的 Not/True 問題。從提到 Robertson's 的例題 1 網頁中先找線索。Robertson's carries all the leading brands at the best prices. ~ if you find one of our products advertised for less on other retailers' Web sites ~ we will match their price – guaranteed!* 是說 Robertson's 以最好的價格銷售所有主要品牌。如果找到其他的網站以較低價格銷售任何產品，保證配合他們的價格。之後 *Does not apply to items sold second-hands 則提到二手商品不適用於此規定，因此 (A) It sells second-hand items for less than its competitors. 與文章內容不一致，是正確答案。Need more assistance?, Click here to contact a live operator, 24 hours a day, 7 days a week 是指如果需要更多協助，可以隨時向在線服務人員聯絡，所以 (B) 與文章內容一致。Robertson's carries all the leading brands 指出 Robertson's 有所有的品牌，也就是主要負責販賣，因此 (C) 也與文章內容一致。Related sections, Repairs 則是說他們有維修的相關資訊，因此 (D) 與文章內容一致。

According to the Web page, which category of vacuum cleaners is in high demand?	根據網頁，哪一種類型的吸塵器有高需求？
(A) Stick	(A) 杖式
(B) Canister	(B) 筒狀式
(C) Upright	(C) 直立式
(D) Robotic	(D) 機器人

■ 六何原則 Which　　　　　　　　　　　　　　　　　　　　　　　　　　　解答 (D)

根據網站詢問目前有高需求的吸塵器是哪一種（Which）類型的六何原則問題。先從提到問題重點 category of vacuum cleaners ~ in high demand 的例文 1 開始確認答案。例文 1 的 Robotic vacuums are becoming one of our best-sellers 提到機器人吸塵器漸漸成為最暢銷的類型之一，所以要選 (D) Robotic 為正確答案。

單字 demand n. 需求

In the e-mail, the word "trust" in paragraph 1, line 3 is closest in meaning to	在電郵中，第一段第三行的 trust 的意思最接近哪一個字？
(A) acknowledge	(A) 承認
(B) rely	(B) 依賴
(C) expect	(C) 期待
(D) commit	(D) 交付

■ 同義詞　　　　　　　　　　　　　　　　　　　　　　　　　　　　　　　解答 (C)

在例文 2 中包含 trust 的句子 I trust that I still qualify for the extended two-year warranty 裡 trust 是「相信」的意思。整句意思是「我相信我仍然符合兩年延長保固的資格」，所以要選擇有「期待，認為會有～」的 (C) expect 為正確答案。

單字 acknowledge v. 承認　expect v. 期待　rely v. 依賴　commit v. 把～委託給，交付

184

Which brand of vacuum cleaner did Mr. Tordesillas most likely buy? (A) Jiffy (B) Lutschen (C) Baronial (D) Irona	Tordesillas 先生最有可能買哪一品牌的吸塵器？ (A) Jiffy (B) Lutschen (C) Baronial (D) Irona

■ 推論 連結問題   解答 (C)

這是要綜合兩篇例文才能解題的連結問題。問題的重點 brand of vacuum cleaner ~ Mr. Tordesillas most likely buy 是在問 Mr. Tordesillas 最有可能是買哪一個牌子的吸塵器，所以要從 Mr. Tordesillas 寫的電子郵件開始找線索。

例文 2 電子郵件中 As per the instructions on your Web site, I have attached a scanned copy of the manufacturer's product warranty card. I trust that I still qualify for the extended two-year warranty 提到因為 Mr. Tordesillas 依照網站的說明掃描了製造商的保固卡，所以他認為具有兩年延長保固的資格，這是第一個線索。但是例文 2 對於掃描保固卡後寄回檔案的話，可以延長為兩年的產品是什麼並沒有多加解釋，所以要回到例文 1 確認網站內容。例文 1 中提到 This month only, all Baronial upright vacuums come with an extended two-year manufacturer's warranty.** 指出所有 Baronial 的直立式吸塵器都提供兩年的延長保固，另外，網站下方 ** Valid only when you sent a scanned copy of the completed manufacturer's warranty card 表示只有寄出掃描的完整製造商保固卡才有效，而這個是第二個線索。

透過綜合線索一：Mr. Tordesillas 掃描了製造商的保固卡因此有兩年延長保固與線索二：Baronial 的直立式吸塵器都提供兩年的延長保固，但只有寄出掃描的完整製造商保固卡才有效，可以推論出 Mr. Tordesillas 的吸塵器品牌是 Baronial。因此，應該選 (C) Baronial 為正確答案。

185

What is suggested about Mr. Tordesillas? (A) He resides in the state of Florida. (B) He missed the deadline for a promotion. (C) He wants a refund for a recent purchase. (D) He will get free shipping for his next order.	關於 Tordesillas 先生，提示了什麼？ (A) 他住在佛羅里達州。 (B) 他錯過了促銷的期限。 (C) 他想退回最近買的一個商品並拿回退款。 (D) 他下次購物可以免運費。

■ 推論 連結問題   解答 (D)

這是要綜合兩篇例文才能解題的連結問題。所以要從問題重點 Mr. Tordesillas 寫的電子郵件開始找線索。

例文 2 電子郵件中寫道 I completed my purchase in August. 可以知道 Mr. Tordesillas 在 8 月時已經有了帳號，they are selling the Goldline compact refrigerator for just $156, versus $172 on your Web site 跟 I would prefer to order the appliance from you since I have already registered for an account 是指其他網站的 Goldline 小型冰箱只要美金一百五十六元，比 Robertson's 賣的還要便宜，但是 Mr. Tordesillas 已經註冊了 Robertson's 的帳號，所以想在 Robertson's 買那台冰箱，這是第一個線索。但是，因為沒有顯示如果註冊帳號有什麼優惠，所以要再到例文 1 的網頁中找尋相關線索。例文 1 網頁中顯示 Register for an account before September 1 to enjoy ~ free shipping on orders worth $100 or more 表示 9 月 1 日之前只要註冊帳號且消費滿 100 美元即可獲得免運費的優惠，這是這二個線索。

綜合第一個線索：因為 Mr. Tordesillas 已經在 8 月買吸塵器前註冊了 Robertson's 的帳號，所以想在 Robertson's 買那台超過 100 美元的冰箱，第二個線索：9 月 1 日之前只要註冊帳號且消費滿 100 美元即可獲得免運費的優惠，可以看出 Mr. Tordesillas 的下一筆訂單將會免除運費，因此應該要選 (D) He will get free shipping for his next order. 為正確答案。

單字 reside v. 居住，住   refund v. 退貨退款   deadline n. 期限   promotion n. 促銷

例文1

April 2

To our new accountants,

Welcome to Yagit Consulting! We are delighted that you are joining our team and look forward to a long and mutually rewarding work relationship with you. I am sure you will all have a lot of questions about the company's systems, structure and organization, so please don't hesitate to ask. You can reach me by e-mail at amno@yagit.org or give me a call at extension #402.

However, I hope many of your questions will be answered during your new employee orientation. To help you all make smooth transitions into your new roles, [186-A/187]an orientation will be held on your first day of work. You will see in the enclosed schedule that [188]the orientation begins with a speech from Yagit's vice president of finance. Then talks from some of our senior-level executives will follow. They will include a presentation about our company and its goals, and [189]one more from the accounting director before lunch. [186-D]After my closing remarks, there will be a reception on the second floor of our office building to provide you with an opportunity to meet your new coworkers.

Finally, I would like to remind all of you to [186-C]submit the results of your medical examinations on or before April 10. Please e-mail them or bring them in person to the human resources department on the fifth floor. Thank you.

Best regards,

Amber Norris
Human Resources Director
Yagit Consulting

4 月 2 日

敬致我們新的會計師們：

歡迎來到 Yagit 顧問公司！我們很高興你們加入團隊，期待與你們有長久及互利的工作關係。我相信你們對於公司的系統、結構和組織一定有很多問題，所以不要客氣來問我，你們可以電郵給我：amno@yagit.org 或打電話給我：分機 402。

然而，我希望你們大部分的問題可以在新進員工座談會中得到答案，為了幫助你們能夠順利融入這個新角色中，[186-A/187]座談會會在你們上班的第一天舉行，隨信附件是座談會的時程表，[188]以 Yagit 財務部副總裁的演講拉開序幕。接著是一些我們高階主管的談話，其中包括一個關於公司介紹和公司目標的報告，[189]另一個是午餐前會計主任的報告。[186-D]在我做總結報告後，我們在辦公大樓二樓有一個接待茶會，讓你們有機會認識新的工作夥伴。

最後，我想要提醒各位 [186-C]要在 4 月 10 日之前或當天繳交你們健康檢查的報告。請以電郵寄來或親自送到五樓的人力資源部，謝謝！

Amber Norris 敬上
人力部主任
Yagit 顧問公司

例文2

YAGIT CONSULTING
[187]Accounting Orientation
April 18, 7:30 A.M. - 5:30 P.M.

SCHEDULE OF EVENTS		
7:30 A.M.	[188]Welcome Remarks	Roger Pate
8:00 A.M.	Introduction to Yagit and its Mission and Vision	Brenda Clements
[189]10:00 A.M.	Presentation: The Yagit Style to Creative Financial Planning	Todd Whitley
12:00 P.M.	LUNCH	
[190]1:00 P.M.	Creating and Analyzing Budgets	Kelly Irwin
3:00 P.M.	Financial Modeling and Forecasting	Danny O'Hara
5:00 P.M.	Closing Speech	Amber Norris
5:30 P.M.	COCKTAIL PARTY	

Yagit 顧問公司
[187]會計部新進員工座談會
4 月 18 日上午 7:30 至下午 5:30

時程表		
7:30 A.M.	[188]歡迎致詞	Roger Pate
8:00 A.M.	介紹 Yagit 及其任務與理念	Brenda Clements
[189]10:00 A.M.	口頭報告：Yagit 風格的創意財務規劃	Todd Whitley
12:00 P.M.	午餐	
[190]1:00 P.M.	建立與分析預算	Kelly Irwin
3:00 P.M.	財務模式與預測	Danny O'Hara
5:00 P.M.	閉幕致詞	Amber Norris
5:30 P.M.	雞尾酒晚宴	

例文 1 單字 □accountant n. 會計師　　□delighted a. 快樂的　　□mutually ad. 彼此

□rewarding a. 有益的，有報酬的　□transition n. 變化，轉移　□senior-level a. 高層的，固有的

□executive n. 主管　　□remark n. 演說　　□medical examination phr. 醫療檢查

例文 2 單字 □analyze v. 分析　　□budget n. 預算　　□forecast v. 預測，預想

186

| What is indicated about the new accountants at Yagit?
(A) They recently completed a series of orientation sessions.
(B) They will have flexible work hours after the training period.
(C) They must have a health check-up on April 10.
(D) They will have a chance to socialize immediately after Ms. Norris' speech. | 關於 Yagit 公司的會計師，何者正確？
(A) 他們最近完成了一連串的新進員工座談。
(B) 在訓練階段過後，他們會有彈性的工作時間。
(C) 他們必須要在四月十日接受健康檢查。
(D) 他們在 Norris 小姐的致詞後，有機會立即和人閒聊互動。 |

■ 六何原則 Why　　　　　　　　　　　　　　　　　　　　　　　　　　　　　　　　解答 (D)

本題是要在文章中找到與本問題的重點 the new accountants at Yagit 相關的內容後，比較選項與文章的 Not/True 問題。an orientation will be held on your first day of work 是說座談會會在上班的第一天舉行，因此 (A) 與文章內容不一致。(B) 則是文中沒有提到的部分。submit the results of your medical examinations on or before April 10 表示要在 4 月 10 日之前或當天繳交健康檢查的報告，因此 (C) 與文章內容不一致。After my closing remarks, there will be a reception ~ to provide you with an opportunity to meet your new coworkers 指出寄件者 Ms. Norris 總結報告後會有機會認識新的工作夥伴，因此 (D) They will have a chance to socialize immediately after Ms. Norris' speech. 跟文章內容一致，是正確答案。

換句話說

an opportunity to meet ~ new coworkers 認識新同事的機會 → a chance to socialize 參與交際的機會

單字 a series of phr. 一系列的，一連串的　socialize v. 參與交際，社交　immediately ad. 立即

187

| When are the new accountants expected to report to the office?
(A) On April 2
(B) On April 10
(C) On April 18
(D) On April 26 | 這些新的會計師什麼時候要報到？
(A) 4 月 2 日
(B) 4 月 10 日
(C) 4 月 18 日
(D) 4 月 26 日 |

■ 六何原則 連結問題　　　　　　　　　　　　　　　　　　　　　　　　　　　　　　解答 (C)

這是要綜合兩篇例文才能解題的連結問題。問題的重點 the new accountants expected to report to the office 是問新來的員工什麼時候（When）要到公司報到，所以要從有提到上班的例文 1 開始找尋線索。

例文 1 信件內提到 an orientation will be held on your first day of work，可以看出上班第一天有座談會，這是第一個線索。例文 2 中的行程表有寫到 Accounting Orientation, April 18 指出會計部的座談會在 4 月 18 日舉行，這是第二個線索。

綜合線索一：上班第一天有座談會，與線索二：會計部座談會在 4 月 18 日舉行，可以推斷出新的會計師們上班的日期是 4 月 18 日。因此 (C) On April 18 是正確答案。

單字 report v. （會議或工作中的）報到

Who is the vice president of finance for Yagit Consulting?	誰是 Yagit 顧問公司的財務部副總裁？
(A) Brenda Clements	(A) Brenda Clements
(B) Danny O'Hara	(B) Danny O'Hara
(C) Kelly Irwin	(C) Kelly Irwin
(D) Roger Pate	(D) Roger Pate

■ 六何原則 連結問題   解答 (D)

這是綜合兩篇例文才能解題的連結問題。問題的重點 the vice president of finance for Yagit Consulting 是問 Yagit 顧問公司的財務部副總裁是誰（Who）的問題，所以要從提到財務部副總裁的例文 1 開始尋找線索。

例文 1 信件中寫道 the orientation begins with a speech from Yagit's vice president of finance 指出座談會以 Yagit 財務部副總裁的演講拉開序幕，這是第一個線索。但是沒有說誰是財務部的副總裁，所以要看例文 2 的時程表來確認是誰。例文 2 時程表中寫道 Welcome Remarks, Roger Pate 表示座談會一開始是由 Roger Pate 所進行的，這次第二個線索。

綜合第一個線索：座談會以 Yagit 財務部副總裁的演講，與第二個線索：座談會一開始是 Roger Pate 所進行的，可以知道 Yagit 顧問公司的財務部副總裁是 Roger Pate，因此正確答案是 (D) Roger Pate。

Which talk will be given by Yagit's head of accounting?	Yagit 的會計部主任的演講題目是什麼？
(A) Financial Modeling and Forecasting	(A) 財務模式與預測
(B) The Yagit Style to Creative Financial Planning	(B) 具 Yagit 風格的創意財務
(C) Creating and Analyzing Budgets	(C) 建立與分析預算
(D) Introduction to Yagit and its Mission and Vision	(D) 介紹 Yagit 及其任務與理念

■ 六何原則 連結問題   解答 (B)

這是要綜合兩篇例文才能解題的連結問題。問題的重點 talk ~ given by Yagit's head of accounting 是問 Yagit 的會計主任會報告哪一種（Which）內容，所以要從有提到 Yagit 會計主任的例文 1 開始尋找線索。

例文 1 信件中提到 one more from accounting director before lunch 是在說午餐前會有會計主任的報告，這是第一個線索。由於沒有提到會計主任的報告內容，所以要由例文 2 的時程表中尋找線索。時程表中的 10:00 A.M., Presentation: The Yagit Style to Creative Financial Planning 跟 12:00 P.M., LUNCH 可以看出在午餐前的報告是關於 Yagit 公司創意性的財務規劃方法，這是第二個線索。

綜合第一個線索：午餐前會有會計主任的報告，與第二個線索：午餐前的報告是關於 Yagit 公司創意性的財務規劃方法，可以知道 Yagit 的會計主任會報告關於 Yagit 公司創意性的財務規劃方法，因此 (B) The Yagit Style to Creative Financial Planning 是正確答案。

What time will the new accountants learn about estimating expenses?	這些會計師在幾點會學到如何預估經費？
(A) At 8 A.M.	(A) 早上八點
(B) At 10 A.M.	(B) 早上十點
(C) At 1 P.M.	(C) 下午一點
(D) At 3 P.M.	(D) 下午三點

■ 六何原則 What time   解答 (C)

這是在問新進員工們幾點（What time）開始學習預估經費的六何原則問題，先從與問題重點 the new accountants learn about estimating expenses 相關的時程表尋找線索。例文 2 時程表中 1:00 P.M., Creating and Analyzing Budgets 提到下午一點有跟建立預算與分析相關的演說，因此，(C) At 1 P.M. 是正確答案。

換句話說

estimating expenses 預估經費 → Creating and Analyzing Budgets 建立與分析預算

單字 estimate v. 預估，估算

Questions 191-195 refer to the following e-mails.

191-195 根據下面的電郵內容回答問題。

例文1

To: Lauren Crawford <Lcraw@double.net>

From: Anthony Dixon <dixony@leeland.com>

Date: October 14
Subject: A favor

Hi Lauren,

How are things going in Madagascar? I expect you are very busy working on the Faritany project, and hope everything is coming along smoothly. Actually, [191]the reason why I'm writing to you is because I need your expert guidance with a project I am currently planning. [193]I'll be going to Belize next year, not as a member of the archaeological crew but as its project administrator. Since [193]I've never held a position like this before, I'd really appreciate it if you could assist me regarding the preparations that my staff and I have to make before the excavation in January. I know you have led many such expeditions, and I am hoping you may be able to provide some insight concerning the planning stages of my project.

[192]I'm attaching a tentative schedule for the project and a brief outline of our goals and what we hope to accomplish during the given time. Please have a look at them and let me know if you think we've scheduled enough time to meet our goals. Any suggestions you could give me would be very welcome. Also, I am interested in knowing what particular supplies we will need to bring, especially in regard to equipment.

Thanks in advance, and I'll be waiting for your reply.

Anthony

收件人：Lauren Crawford <Lcraw@double.net>
寄件人：Anthony Dixon <dixony@leeland.com>
日期：10 月 14 日
主題：幫一個忙

Lauren 你好：

在馬達加斯加島的一切如何？我想你一定忙於 Faritany 專案，希望一切都很順利。事實上，[191] 我寫信給你是因為我正在籌畫的專案需要你這個專家的建議，[193] 我明年會去貝里斯，並不是以考古人員的身分前往，而是一個專案經理。因為 [193] 我之前從來沒有擔任過這樣的職務，如果你能就我跟我的人員們在一月開挖前的準備事項上協助我，我會非常感謝。我知道你曾經帶領過很多這樣的考察隊，我希望你能夠針對我這個尚在籌劃階段的專案，給我些專業的意見。

[192] 附件是這個專案暫定的時程表，和一份含有目標及希望在一定時間內完成事項的簡短大綱。請幫我看一下，讓我知道你是否認為我們安排了足夠的時間來達成目標，如果你能給我任何建議，那就太好了。我還想知道有什麼特定的東西是我們需要帶去的，尤其是設備。

在此先向你說聲謝謝，我會等你的回覆。

Anthony

例文2

To: Anthony Dixon <dixony@leeland.com>

From: Lauren Crawford <Lcraw@double.net>

Date: October 16
Subject: Re: A favor

Hello Anthony,

So far, everything's been going smoothly here in Madagascar and we're ahead of schedule with the Faritany project. It's a lot of hard work, but the results we've seen so far are promising.

Anyway, I'm sure you'll do a great job as a project administrator. It can be challenging at first, but I think your knowledge of archaeological sites will really help you with the project. But [195-B]before you begin your excavation in Belize, make sure you have all the required permits from

收件人：Anthony Dixon <dixony@leeland.com>
寄件人：Lauren Crawford <Lcraw@double.net>
日期：10 月 16 日
主題：回覆：幫一個忙

Anthony 你好：

到目前為止，在馬達加斯加島的一切都進行地很順利，我們 Faritany 專案的進度還超前，工作很辛苦，但是我們所得到的結果目前看起來都很有希望。

總之，我知道你會是一位出色的專案經理，剛開始的時候會很有挑戰性，但是你對考古場地的知識會對你的專案有很大的幫助，[195-B] 在你在貝里斯開挖之前，確定你取得當地政府所有相關的許

the local government. I've had some difficulties with this before, so make certain that all your documents are in order before you proceed with anything.

Also, [195-C]you and your staff will need on-site access to both shelter and toilet facilities for convenience purposes. It will definitely make your work on the site more comfortable, and I would make arrangements for those facilities before leaving for Belize. You will need Internet access, but don't expect 24-hour service as the connections aren't very reliable. And make sure to bring a couple of small power generators for recharging mobile phones, computers, and other equipment. Of course [195-A]you will also need to develop safe working procedures for your team to reduce the risk of accidents and injuries.

I had a look at the schedule and outline you sent me, and it seems like you've allotted the perfect amount of time to finish the project.

Good luck and keep me updated on your project.

Lauren

可證。關於這種事，我以前遇過一些麻煩，所以在你開始進行任何事情之前，確定你準備了所有的文件。

還有，為了方便起見，[195-C]你和你的隊友會需要在工作現場有休息和上廁所的地方，這絕對會讓你們在現場工作比較舒適，而且在我離開前往貝里斯之前，我會安排那些設施。你會需要用到網際網路，但是不要期待整天都有網路可用，因為連線不是很穩定，還有，記得帶幾個小型的發電機來給手機、電腦和其他設備充電，當然，[195-A]你要為你的團隊做一些安全工作流程，以減少意外與受傷的危險。

我看過了你寄給我的時程表與大綱，看起來你對專案完成的時間做了最佳的規劃。

祝你好運，也讓我知道你的專案進度。

Lauren

例文 1 單字	smoothly ad. 順利	expert a. 專業的	archaeological a. 考古學的
	crew n. 成員，工作人員	appreciate v. 感謝，欣賞	excavation n. 開挖
	expedition n. 考察，考察團	tentative a. 暫定的	outline n. 提綱，概要
例文 2 單字	promising a. 有希望的	on-site a. 工作現場的	shelter n. 休憩場所
	generator n. 發電機	procedure n. 流程，程序	allot v. 分配

191

Why did Mr. Dixon write the e-mail?
(A) To provide information on an archaeological discovery
(B) To give suggestions about a research proposal
(C) To ask for recommendations about an upcoming project
(D) To invite participants to an international conference

為什麼 Dixon 先生寫這封電郵？
(A) 針對一項考古發現提供資訊
(B) 對一個研究提案提供建議
(C) 對一個即將進行的專案詢問意見
(D) 邀請參與一個國際會議

■ 找出主題 寫文章的理由　　　　　　　　　　　　　　　　　　　　　　　　　　　　　　　　　解答 (C)

因為是在問 Mr. Dixon 寫電子郵件的理由，因此要從 Mr. Dixon 寫的電子郵件開始找線索。電子郵件中寫道 the reason why I'm writing to you is because I need your expert guidance with a project I am currently planning，是希望對目前計畫中的專案提供建言的意思，因此 (C) To ask for recommendations about an upcoming project 為正確答案。

192

What is attached to Mr. Dixon's e-mail?
(A) A map of his destination
(B) A flight schedule
(C) An archeological report
(D) A list of objectives

Dixon 先生的電郵加了什麼附件？
(A) 他的目的地的地圖
(B) 飛機時刻表
(C) 一份考古報告
(D) 目標清單

■ 六何原則 What　　　　　　　　　　　　　　　　　　　　　　　　　　　　　　　　　　　　　解答 (D)

因為是在問 Mr. Dixon 的電子郵件中附有什麼（What）附件的六何原則問題，因此在例文 1 Mr. Dixon 寫的電子郵件中尋找與問題的重點 attached 有關係的部分。郵件中寫道 I'm attaching ~ a brief outline of our goals and what we hope to accomplish during the given time. 表示附件是專案暫定的時程表，和含有目標及希望在一定時間內完成事項的簡短大綱，因此 (D) A list of objectives 為正確答案。

換句話說

a brief outline of ~ goals 目標的簡短大綱 → A list of objectives 目標清單

193

What is indicated about Mr. Dixon?	關於 Dixon 先生，暗示了什麼？
(A) He wants to work with Ms. Crawford.	(A) 他想要和 Crawford 小姐一起工作。
(B) He is currently in Belize for business.	(B) 他現在在貝里斯出差。
(C) He has never led a team before.	(C) 他從沒有帶領過一個團隊。
(D) He is having difficulty with his current project.	(D) 他目前手上的專案遇到困難。

■ 推論 詳細內容　　　　　　　　　　　　　　　　　　　　　　　　　解答 (C)

這是需要推論題目中提及的 Mr. Dixon 的題目，首先從 Mr. Dixon 寫的電子郵件來找相關的內容。例文 1 電子郵件中寫到 I'll be going to Belize next year ~ as its project administrator. 跟 I've never held a position like this before 指出明年 Mr. Dixon 要做為專案經理前往貝里斯，因為沒有相關的經驗，所以可以推論 Mr. Dixon 沒有帶領一個團隊的經驗。因此 (C) He has never led a team before. 為正確答案。

194

In the second e-mail, the phrase "in order" in paragraph 2, line 5 is closest in meaning to	在第二封電郵的第二段第五行中，「in order」的意思最接近哪一個字？
(A) aligned	(A) 排成一列
(B) prepared	(B) 準備
(C) shipped	(C) 運送
(D) packed	(D) 包裝

■ 同義詞　　　　　　　　　　　　　　　　　　　　　　　　　　　　解答 (B)

第二封電子郵件中包含了 in order 的句子 make certain that all your documents are in order before you proceed with anything 中，in order 是「有條不紊」的意思，是說所有文件都準備的有條不紊。因此有「準備」意思的 (B) prepare 是正確答案。

單字 align v. 排成一列　pack v. 包裝　ship v. 配送

195

What is NOT a suggestion given by Ms. Crawford to Mr. Dixon?	Crawford 小姐沒有建議 Dixon 先生做什麼？
(A) Implement safety measures	(A) 實施安全措施
(B) Gather essential documents for field operations	(B) 取得現場作業重要文件
(C) Ensure ready access to sanitation facilities	(C) 確認有衛生設備可以使用
(D) Minimize the use of electrical devices	(D) 對電子設備的使用降到最低

■ **Not/True** Not 問題　　　　　　　　　　　　　　　　　　　　　解答 (D)

本題是要在文章中找到與本問題的重點 a suggestion given by Ms. Crawford to Mr. Crawford to Mr. Dixon 相關的內容後，比較選項與文章的 Not/True 問題。

所以從例文 2 Ms. Crawford 寫的郵件中找相關的內容。you will also need to develop safe working procedures 是說「你需要為你的團隊做一些安全工作流程」，所以 (A) 與文章內容一致。before you begin your excavation ~ make sure you have all the required permits from the local government 則指出在貝里斯開挖之前，要確定有取得當地政府所有相關的許可證，(B) 也與文章內容一致。you and your staff will need on-site access to ~ toilet facilities 是說「你和你的隊友會需要在工作現場有休息和上廁所的地方」，與文章內容一致。(D) 則是文中沒有提及的內容。因此 (D) Minimize the use of electrical devices 是正確答案。

單字 implement v. 施行　minimize v. 最低化　ensure v. 確認　access n. 使用　sanitation n. 衛生
　　gather v. 聚集　essential a. 需要的　operation n. 作業，運營

例文1

Jamadevi: Job openings

196-A/C Jamadevi has provided excellent service in Thailand's tourism industry for the past 15 years. We've developed a strong reputation among visitors to Thailand and are proud to have a lot of repeat business. Due to popular demand for our tours and charters, we at Jamadevi have immediate job openings for experienced tour guides.

197 Applicants must possess a certificate from a reputable tour guide training academy and should be energetic, reliable, and adventurous. In addition, 198 they must possess a valid driver's license as it will be necessary to operate a vehicle from time to time. Proficiency in other languages besides Thai and English is an advantage, as well as an extensive knowledge of local geography and history.

Interested individuals are encouraged to call +66-23-555-7119 and ask for Chariya Kasem for application instructions. Ms. Kasem can be reached from Tuesday to Sunday between the hours of 8:00 A.M. and 7:00 P.M.

Jamadevi 公司：工作職缺

196-A/C 在過去十五年，Jamadevi 公司為泰國的旅遊業提供了優良的服務，我們在前往泰國旅遊的遊客中建立了口碑，對於眾多回流的顧客，我們感到很自豪。由於我們旅遊和包機的廣大需求，Jamadevi 公司立即需要有經驗的導遊。

197 這個職缺的申請者必須取得知名導遊訓練學校的證書，而且要精力旺盛、可靠、富冒險精神。此外，還有 198 擁有有效的駕駛執照，因為有時候會需要開車。如果精通泰語和英語以外的語言，還有對當地地理歷史有豐富的知識，將會是一項優勢。

有興趣者請撥打+66-23-555-7119，向 Chariya Kasem 洽詢應徵辦法。Kasem 小姐的服務時間為週二至週日，早上八點到晚上七點。

例文2

To: ckasem@jamadevi.th
From: sujit_khongmalai@lamphunmail.th
Date: March 25
Subject: Tour Guide Application

Dear Ms. Kasem,

Based on your instructions for applying for the tour guide position, I am sending you my qualifications and employment history. Unfortunately, 198 I was not able to attach a copy of my driver's license as I am still in the process of obtaining one.

Name	Sujit Khongmalai
Address	3541 Chao Street, Pomprab, Bangkok 101008
Contact Number	(00662) 555-6280
Goal	To work as a tour guide for an established firm that will help enhance my skills and experience in this field
Experience	199 Tour Guide, Nakorn Travel (Present) • Lead tour groups, give talks about the culture, language, and history of Thailand, and 200-B make tour itineraries Promotions Officer, Mahayana Tours (3 years) • Oversaw the creation, promotion, delivery, monitoring, and evaluation day tours Travel Agent, Banchee Vacations (2 years) • Processed ticketing transactions and coordinated the details of travel packages

收件人：ckasem@jamadevi.th
寄件人：sujit_khongmalai@lamphunmail.th
日期：3 月 25 日
主旨：導遊應徵

親愛的 Kasem 小姐：

根據你對導遊一職所提供的應徵方式，我把我的資格認證和工作經驗寄給你，不過，198 我無法把我的駕駛執照影本附加上去，因為我還在設法取得駕照當中。

姓名	Sujit Khongmalai
地址	Chao 街 3541 號，Pomprab 區，曼谷市 101008
聯絡電話	（00662）555-6280
目地	在一家有規模的公司擔任導遊有助於提升我在這個領域的技術與經驗
經驗	199 Nakorn旅遊公司的導遊（目前） ・帶團，講解泰國的文化、語言和歷史，並 200-B 設計旅遊行程 Mahayana 旅遊公司的推廣人員（三年） ・監督一日遊的創造、推廣、執行、監控和評估 Banchee 假期的旅行代辦人（兩年） ・處理票務，協調套裝旅遊的細節

Education	Bachelor's degree in sociology, Bangkok National University
Skills and Certifications	• Tourism Licensure Certificate, Thai Academy of Licensed Tour Guides • 200-C Competent in all computer programs, especially word processing, spreadsheets, and image and video editing software • 200-A Proficient in Thai, English, and Chinese
References available upon request.	

Thank you for your time and consideration. I look forward to hearing from you soon.

Sincerely,

Sujit Khongmalai

教育程度	曼谷國立大學社會學學士
技能與 證書	• 泰國執業導遊協會，觀光執照認證 • 200-C 會使用所有電腦軟體，特別是文書處理、試算表和圖像影片編輯軟體 • 200-A 泰語、英語、中文流利
如應要求，可提供推薦信函	

謝謝您的時間與考慮，期待很快得到您的回音。

Sujit Khongmalai 敬上

例文 1 單字 □ reputation n. 評判，名望
□ certificate n. 證書，結業證書
□ proficiency n. 精通，熟練
例文 2 單字 □ qualification n. 資格認證
□ delivery n. 施行，傳達
□ transaction n. 交易

□ demand n. 要求，需求；v. 要求
□ reputable a. 有名望的
□ extensive a. 寬廣的
□ itinerary n. 旅行計畫
□ monitor v. 觀察，監控
□ coordinate n. 調整

□ charter n.（交通工具的）租賃
□ reliable a. 可信賴的
□ geography n. 地理
□ oversee v. 監督
□ evaluation n. 評價
□ look forward to phr. 期待～

196

What is mentioned about Jamadevi?
(A) It has been operating for over a decade.
(B) It advertises its services overseas.
(C) It offers tours throughout Southeast Asia.
(D) It was recognized with an award.

關於 Jamadevi 公司，何者正確？
(A) 已經經營超過十年了。
(B) 在海外廣告他們提供的服務。
(C) 提供東南亞的旅遊行程。
(D) 獲獎受到肯定。

■ Not / True True 問題   解答 (A)

本題是要在文章中找到與本問題的重點 Jamadevi 相關的內容後，比較選項與文章的 Not/True 問題。要從提到 Jamadevi 的例文 1 工作職缺廣告中尋找線索。Jamadevi has provided ~ service ~ for the past 15 years. 表示過去 15 年間長久提供服務，所以 (A) It has been operating for over a decade. 是正確答案。(B) 則是文中未提及的內容。選項 (C) 與文中提及的內容 Jamadevi has provided ~ service in Thailand's tourism industry（在泰國的觀光產業中持續提供服務）不一致。(D) 則是文中未提及的內容。

換句話說

has provided services 長久提供服務 → has been operating 長久經營

for the past 15 years 過去 15 年間 → for over a decade 十年以上

What is a requirement for the advertised position? (A) A history degree (B) Knowledge of local geography (C) A professional certificate (D) Travel agency experience	這個職缺的要求是什麼？ (A) 有歷史學位 (B) 了解當地的地理 (C) 有專業的證照 (D) 有旅行代辦公司的經驗

■ 六何原則 What　　　　　　　　　　　　　　　　　　　　　　　　　　解答 (C)

這是在問廣告中職缺的條件是什麼（What）的六何原則問題，所以從與問題重點 a requirement for the advertised position 相關的廣告開始解題。例文 1 的職缺廣告 Applicants must possess a certificate from a reputable tour guide training academy 表示應徵者們需要有知名導遊訓練學校發給的證書，所以 (C) A professional certificate 為正確答案。

換句話說

a certificate from a reputable tour guide training academy 著名導遊訓練學校發給的執照
→ A professional certificate 專業證書

單字 requirement n. 需要條件，要求條件

Why might Mr. Khongmalai not be considered for the position? (A) He cannot speak Chinese. (B) He has an expired passport. (C) He has no driver's license. (D) He is not a Thai resident.	為什麼 Khongmalai 可能不會被考慮？ (A) 他不會說中文。 (B) 他的護照過期了。 (C) 他沒有駕照。 (D) 他不是泰國居民。

■ 六何原則 連結問題　　　　　　　　　　　　　　　　　　　　　　　　解答 (C)

這是要綜合兩篇例文才能解題的連結問題。問題的重點 Mr. Khongmalai not be considered for the position 在問 Mr. Khongmalai 為什麼（Why）不會被考慮的原因，所以要從 Mr. Khongmalai 寫的電子郵件開始看。
例文 2 的電子郵件中 I was not able to attach a copy of my driver's license as I am still in the process of obtaining one 指出 Mr. Khongmalai 正在設法取得駕照，所以無法提供駕照影本，這是第一個線索。但是這裡沒有提到應徵的職位需不需要駕照，所以要回到例文 1 確認關於駕照的內容。例文 1 中提到 they must possess a valid driver's license as it will be necessary to operate a vehicle from time to time 表示因為偶爾會需要開車，所以應徵者須要有有效期間內的駕照，這則是第二個線索。綜合第一個線索：Mr. Khongmalai 現在還沒有駕照，無法附上駕照影本，與第二個線索：應徵者需要有有效期限內的駕照，可以知道因為 Mr. Khongmalai 無法提交駕照影本，所以可能不會被考慮。因此 (C) He has no driver's license. 為正確答案。

單字 expired a. 期滿的

199

At which company is Mr. Khongmalai employed?	Khongmalai 目前在哪家公司工作？
(A) Banchee Vacations	(A) Banchee 假期
(B) Nakorn Travel	(B) Nakorn 旅遊公司
(C) Mahayana Tours	(C) Mahayana 旅遊公司
(D) Thai Academy	(D) 泰國協會

■ 六何原則問題 Which 　　　　　　　　　　　　　　　　　　　　　　　　　　解答 (B)

這是在問 Mr. Khongmalai 被哪一個（Which）公司雇用的六何原則問題，所以要在提到本問題重點句 company ~ Mr. Khongmalai employed 的電子郵件中找到線索。例文 2 的電子郵件中提到 Tour Guide, Nakorn Travel (Present) 表示 Mr. Khongmalai 現在在 Nakorn 旅行社中擔任導遊，所以 (B) Nakorn Travel 是正確答案。

單字 employ v. 雇用

200

What is NOT indicated about Mr. Khongmalai?	關於 Khongmalai 先生，並未提示什麼？
(A) He speaks three languages.	(A) 他會說三種語言。
(B) He organizes tour schedules.	(B) 他安排旅遊行程。
(C) He is knowledgeable in computers.	(C) 他會用電腦。
(D) He manages a travel agency.	(D) 他管理一家旅行社。

■ Not / True Not 問題 　　　　　　　　　　　　　　　　　　　　　　　　　　解答 (D)

本題是要在文章中找到與本問題的重點 Mr. Khongmalai 相關的內容後，比較選項與文章的 Not/True 問題，這是與例文 2 相關的問題。文中提及 Proficient in Thai, English, and Chinese 是說泰語、英語及中文都很流利，所以 (A) 是與文章內容一致的。make tour itineraries 則提到設計旅遊行程，所以 (B) 與文章內容一致。因為 Competent in all computer programs 指出熟悉所有電腦應用程式，所以 (C) 與文章內容一致。(D) 則是文章沒有提及的部分，所以 (D) He manages a travel agency. 為正確答案。

單字 organize v. 計畫，組織

TEST 03

PART 5

101

All visitors to the Kentworth Plant are asked to sign in at the security office _____ pick up a guest pass.
(A) and
(B) yet
(C) in
(D) which

所有到 Kentworth 工廠的訪客都被要求在警衛室登記並領取訪客證。

■ 對等連接詞　　　　　　　　　　　　　　解答 (A)

因為需要可以讓動詞子句 sign in at the security office 和動詞子句 pick up a guest pass 連結的對等連接詞，所以 (A) 和 (B) 都可能是正確答案。而句意應該是「警衛室要求客人必須登記並領取訪客證」的意思，所以要選 (A) and（還有）為正確答案。(B) yet 是「但是」的意思，會使句意變成相反的意思。(C) in 是表時間或場所的介系詞，(D) which 則是有「哪個」意思的疑問詞，也可作為關係代名詞。

單字 sign in phr. 簽名　security office phr. 警衛室　pick up phr. 撿起～，獲得　pass n. 通行證

102

Lara Karowski's chances of winning last year's badminton finals _____ when she sustained a major knee injury.
(A) diminish
(B) diminished
(C) diminishingly
(D) diminutive

Lara Karowski 贏得去年羽毛球決賽的機會在她膝蓋嚴重受傷時就減少了。

■ 過去式　　　　　　　　　　　　　　　解答 (B)

因為句子裡缺少動詞，所以動詞 (A) 和 (B) 都是可能的答案。而因為有表示過去的時間 last year，所以應該選過去式的 (B) diminished 為正確答案。副詞 (C) 跟形容詞 (D) 都無法作為動詞使用。(A) 則是現在式，不能與有表示過去的表現一起使用。

單字 finals n. 決賽　sustain v. 忍受（傷害），使～維持　injury n. 受傷　diminish v. 縮減，減少
　　diminutive a. 非常小的

103

Marina practiced some ballet steps by _____ while waiting for the instructor to show up and class to begin.
(A) she
(B) her
(C) herself
(D) hers

Marina 在等待老師出現開始上課前，就自己先練習一些芭蕾的舞步。

■ 反身代名詞　　　　　　　　　　　　　解答 (C)

可以做為介系詞 by 受詞的人稱代名詞受格 (B)，反身代名詞 (C)，所有格代名詞 (D) 都是可能的答案。因為句意為「獨自練習一些芭蕾舞步」的意思，所以要找與介系詞 by 共同使用時會有「獨自，以一個人的力量」等意思，也就是 by oneself 的反身代名詞。如果選擇 (B) 和 (D) 則變成「因為她練習」和「因為她的東西練習」的意思，而人稱代名詞主格則無法置於介系詞後。

單字 practice v. 練習　instructor n. 講師，指導員

104

We suggest you look around the computer store for a while, and one of our staff will attend to you _____.
(A) moment
(B) momentum
(C) momentarily
(D) momentary

我們建議你先在電腦店逛一下，我們的店員很快就會來招呼你。

■ 副詞的位置　　　　　　　　　　　　　解答 (C)

可以修飾動詞 attend 的是副詞，因此副詞 (C) momentarily（馬上）為正確答案。名詞 (A) 和 (B)，形容詞 (D) 都無法作為副詞使用。另外，要記得 look around（環顧四周）是常用的片語。

單字 for a while phr. 暫時　attend to phr. 應對，照顧　moment n. 瞬間，時刻　momentary a. 瞬間的，短暫的

105

Drivers leaving their vehicles unattended in front of the terminal may have to pay a fine or risk the _____ of their car by a towing service.
(A) removal   (B) communication
(C) damage   (D) transit

把空車停在航站前的駕駛人可能會被罰款或有車子被拖吊的風險。

■ 名詞語彙   解答 (A)

因為句意為「把車子停放在航站前的駕駛會有車子被拖吊的風險」的意思，所以名詞 (A) removal（移動，去除）是正確答案。(B) communication 是「溝通，傳達」，(C) damage 是「損害」，(D) transit 是「運送，變化」的意思。

單字 unattended a. 沒人照料的　pay a fine phr. 支付罰金　risk v. 冒…的風險　tow v. 牽引，拖

106

Neither the restaurant manager _____ the supervisor was notified about the fire safety inspection scheduled for tomorrow.
(A) of   (B) both
(C) while   (D) nor

餐廳經理與主管都沒有被告知表定明天的火災安全稽查。

■ 相關連接詞   解答 (D)

可與相關連接詞 neither 一起使用的 (D) nor 為正確答案。（Neither A nor B：A 和 B 都不是）(A) of 「也～」的的意思，是表示所有關係的介系詞，(B) both 是「兩者（的）」的意思，常常以作為相關連接詞 both A and B（A 和 B 兩者都）的形態出現，(C) while 是「在～期間」的意思，是表示時間的副詞子句連接詞。

單字 manager n. 經理　supervisor n. 管理者，監督者　notify v. 通報，通知　inspection n. 檢查，審視

107

Because Eye Specialists will move to a new location, management has decided to _____ the hospital's operations for a week.
(A) provide   (B) advertise
(C) distribute   (D) suspend

因為眼科醫生要搬到新的地方去，管理階層決定醫院暫停營業一週。

■ 動詞語彙   解答 (D)

因為句意為「由於要搬到新地方，所以醫院暫時歇業一週」的意思，所以動詞 (D) suspend（中斷）為正確答案。(A) provide 是「提供」，(B) advertise 是「廣告」，(C) distribute 是「分配」的意思。

單字 location n. 場所，位置　management n. 管理　operation n. 營運

108

If you have questions or problems with your security equipment, please call our 24-hour customer service hotline to receive prompt _____.
(A) attend   (B) attention
(C) attendance   (D) attentive

如果你對你的安全設備有疑問，請撥打我們二十四小時客戶服務熱線，以得到立即的回應。

■ 名詞的位置   解答 (B)

因為名詞可以做為 to 不定詞 to receive 的受詞，所以 (B) 和 (C) 都可能為正確答案。而文意為「為了得到立即的回應」的意思，所以 (B) attention（注意，照顧）為正確答案。如果選 (C) attendance（出席），則文意會變為「接受立即的出席」的意思。動詞 (A) 和形容詞 (D) 則無法作為名詞使用。

單字 prompt a. 即刻的　attend v. 出席　attentive a. 留意的

109

Grant applications submitted after the _____ of October 1 will not be considered for this year's funding.
(A) rule
(B) deadline
(C) limit
(D) grade

在十月一日截止日期以後遞交的補助申請書，將不會被認定為今年度的資金。

■ 名詞語彙　　　　　　　　　　　　　　　　　　　解答 (B)

因為文意為「不會認定在 10 月 1 日之後繳交的補助申請書」的意思，所以名詞 (B) deadline（截止日，期限）為正確答案。(A) rule 是「規則」，(C) limit 是「限制，界線」，(D) grade 是「品質，成績」的意思。

單字 grant n. 補助金　application n. 申請書

110

The supervisor was _____ with the performance of most of the trainees and recommended that all but one be given permanent employment.
(A) satisfying
(B) satisfied
(C) satisfies
(D) satisfy

主管很滿意大部分的受訓人員的表現，且建議除了一人以外，其他所有人皆可獲聘正職。

■ 區分情感動詞的主動態/被動態　　　　　　　　　解答 (B)

因為空格是在 be 動詞 was 之後，可接在 be 動詞後 -ing 形 (A) 和 p.p. 形 (B) 都是可能的答案。欲填入空格的動詞 satisfy 是表示情感的動詞，因文意為「主管很滿意」，所以是被主詞所感受到的感情，應該要使用被動態。因此可與 be 動詞一起且有被動意義的 p.p.形 (B) satisfied 為正確答案。

單字 performance n. 成果　trainee n. 受訓者　but prep. 除了～以外　permanent a. 正職的，永遠的

111

Thank-you letters will be sent to _____ the benefactors to express the community's appreciation for their donations.
(A) all
(B) much
(C) whose
(D) what

感謝函會寄送給所有捐助者，以表達社區對他們的捐贈的謝意。

■ 表現數量　　　　　　　　　　　　　　　　　　　解答 (A)

因為空格在複數可數名詞 benefactors 之前，所以要選擇可以置於複數名詞前的 (A) all（全部）為正確答案。另外，all 可以以「all the + 名詞」或「all of the + 名詞」的形態使用。(B) much（多的）須放在不可數名詞前，(C) whose 是所有關係代名詞，無法直接接定冠詞 the，(D) what 是名詞子句連接詞，所以一定要連接有動詞的子句。

單字 benefactor n. 捐助人　express v. 表現　appreciation n. 感謝　donation n. 捐獻

112

Some inconsistencies in the report convinced the accounting manager to go back and double-check the _____ records.
(A) future
(B) narrow
(C) leading
(D) previous

報告中一些矛盾的內容讓會計主管回過頭來再次查核之前的紀錄。

■ 形容詞語彙　　　　　　　　　　　　　　　　　　解答 (D)

因為句意為「報告中部份矛盾的內容讓會計主管再次查核之前的紀錄」的意思，因此形容詞 (D) previous（之前的）為正確答案。(A) future 是「未來的」，(B) narrow 是「窄的」，(C) leading 是「最重要的，領頭的」的意思。

單字 inconsistency n. 不一致，前後矛盾　convince v. 說服某人做某事，確信　double-check v. 再次檢查

113

Sales of luxury vehicles fell _____ during the fourth quarter of last year due to the reduction in consumer spending. (A) signifying　　　　　(B) signifies (C) significant　　　　　(D) significantly	因為消費者支出的量縮，豪華汽車的銷售在去年第四季一落千丈。

■ 副詞的位置　　　　　　　　　　　　　　　　　　　　　　　　　　　　　　　　解答 (D)

因為要修飾動詞 fell，所以應該要選擇副詞 (D) significantly（相當地）為正確答案。分詞兼動名詞 (A)，動詞 (B)，形容詞 (C) 都無法修飾動詞。另外，常與 fall（墜落）和 rise（上升）一起使用的副詞為：dramatically（戲劇性地）和 gradually（漸漸地）。

單字 vehicle v. 汽車　quarter n. 季度　reduction n. 減少

114

It is crucial _____ all employees comply with the dress code to create a unified, professional image for the company. (A) among　　(B) why　　(C) that　　(D) with	所有員工遵從穿著規定對於創造一個統一、專業的公司形象是很重要的。

■ 虛主詞 it　　　　　　　　　　　　　　　　　　　　　　　　　　　　　　　　　解答 (C)

因為文意為「所有員工遵從服裝規定是很重要的」，所以可以知道 It 是虛主詞，而空格後的子句為主詞。因此與虛主詞 it 相關可以做為主詞領導名詞子句的 (C) that 為正確答案。(A) among 是「在～之間」的意思，表位置，(B) why 是疑問詞或是可帶領名詞子句的疑問副詞，(D) with 是有「與～一起」意思的介系詞。

單字 crucial a. 重要的　comply with phr. 依據，遵守　dress code phr. 服裝規則　unified a. 統一的

115

The opinions given by Mr. Tolentino differed from _____ of the accounting department's other staff. (A) those　　(B) they　　(C) this　　(D) them	Tolentino 先生給的意見不同於會計部門其他員工的意見。

■ 指示代名詞　　　　　　　　　　　　　　　　　　　　　　　　　　　　　　　　解答 (A)

因為文意為「Tolentino 先生給的意見不同於會計部門其他員工的意見」，可做為代表句中出現的 opinions 的指示代名詞 (A) those 為正確答案。另外，若要以指示代名詞 that/those 取代前面曾經出現的名詞，則在 that/those 後面一定要接上修飾語（介系詞子句，關係子句，副詞）。(B) they 是人稱代名詞，應該作為主詞。(C) this 是在單數名詞之前使用的指示形容詞，有「這～」的意思，也可作為代替單數名詞的指示代名詞。(D) them 是人稱代名詞受格，要作為受詞使用。

單字 opinion n. 意見　differ from phr. 與～不同

116

Customers who already own a licensed software are automatically _____ to upgrade to the latest one for free. (A) qualify　　　　　　(B) qualifies (C) qualification　　　　(D) qualified	已經擁有授權軟體的客戶自動符合免費升級到最新版本的資格。

■ 動詞的單複數、時態都要一樣　　　　　　　　　　　　　　　　　　　　　　　　解答 (D)

因為文意為「客戶可符合升級到最新版本的資格」，有被動的意思，所以要選擇可以置於 be 動詞 are 之後形成被動語態的動詞 qualify 的 p.p.形 (D) qualified 為正確答案。動詞原形 (A) 和單數動詞 (B) 無法置於 be 動詞 are 後，名詞 (C) 與主詞 customers 在語意上無法成為同位語的關係，所以不是正確答案。

單字 licensed a. 獲得許可的　automatically ad. 自動地　latest a. 最新的

117

Mr. Roberts was named _____ the new head of IVN Bank following the former CEO's resignation. (A) at　　　　　　　(B) as (C) along　　　　　　(D) around	在前任執行長辭職後，Roberts 先生被指名接任 IVN 銀行的新任總裁。

■ 選擇介系詞　　　　　　　　　　　　　　　　　　　　　　　　　　　解答 (B)

可以與 name （任命）一同使用，有「任命為～」的意思的介系詞 (B) as（作為～）為正確答案。另外，本句是 name A as B （任命 A 為 B）的被動式。(A) at 是「在～」的意思，表示時間或場所，(C) along 是「隨著～」的意思，是表示方向的介系詞，(D) around 是「周圍的」的意思，表示位置和時間的介系詞。

單字 former a. 先前的　resignation n. 辭職書

118

Briseis Bakery in downtown Manhattan is known for using only ingredients of the freshest _____ in its baked goods. (A) property　　　　　　(B) quality (C) feature　　　　　　(D) manner	位在曼哈頓市中心的 Briseis 烘培店以只使用最新鮮的食材為產品原料而聞名。

■ 名詞語彙　　　　　　　　　　　　　　　　　　　　　　　　　　　　解答 (B)

因為句意為「Briseis 烘培店以只使用最新鮮的食材為產品原料而聞名」，所以應該要選擇名詞 (B) quality（品質，特徵）為正確答案。(A) property 是「財產，所有權」，(C) feature 是「特色」，(D) manner 是「方式，態度」的意思。

單字 be known for phr. 以～而聞名　ingredient n. 材料

119

The tour guide _____ prepared to give the guests a tour of the island resort after they check in. (A) was being　　　　　(B) have been (C) would have　　　　(D) will be	在遊客入住後，導遊將會準備為他們做一個島上觀光景點的導覽。

■ 未來式　　　　　　　　　　　　　　　　　　　　　　　　　　　　　解答 (D)

因為文意「導遊準備好導覽」具有被動的意義，所以能和動詞 prepare（準備）的 p.p. 形態（prepared）一起，並有被動意義的 (A)，(B)，(D) 都可能是正確答案。在表示時間的 after 子句中使用現在式 check in，所以可以知道主要子句要使用未來式，因此 (D) will be 是正確答案。

單字 prepare v. 準備

120

Because of the high demand, office spaces in the city's financial district _____ cost more than anywhere else. (A) type (B) typing (C) typically (D) typical	因為需求高，市區金融商圈裡的辦公空間一般來説比其他任何地方都來得貴。

🔲 副詞的位置   解答 (C)

因為要用副詞才能夠修飾動詞 cost，所以要選擇副詞 (C) typically（一般地，典型地）為正確答案。名詞兼動詞 (A)，分詞兼動名詞 (B)，形容詞 (D) 都無法修飾動詞。

單字 high a.（量比平常）多   district n. 區

121

Some of the attendees at the technology convention were charged a _____ fee, as they were able to register as a group. (A) final (B) total (C) reduced (D) costly	有些在科技大會的參加者以團體身分來登記參加，因此而被收取較低的費用。

🔲 形容詞語彙   解答 (C)

因為文意為「因他們以團體身分登記，而被收取較低的費用」的意思，所以形容詞 (C) reduced（減少的）為正確答案。(A) final 是「最後的，決定性的」，(B) total 是「整體的」，(D) costly 是「貴的」的意思。

單字 attendee n. 出席者   convention n. 會議   charge v. 收費   register v. 登錄

122

Charity foundations and educational institutions are _____ from paying income tax to the government as they are considered nonprofit organizations. (A) contented (B) guaranteed (C) exempt (D) isolated	慈善基金會和教育機構不用繳納所得税給政府，因為他們被視為非營利性組織。

🔲 形容詞語彙   解答 (C)

因為文意為「慈善基金會和教育機構是非營利性組織，不用繳納所得税」的意思，所以形容詞 (C) exempt（免除）的意思。(A) contented 是「滿足的」，(B) guaranteed 是「保證的，有保障的」，(D) isolated 是「孤立的，隔離」的意思。

單字 charity n. 慈善   institution n. 機關   income tax phr. 所得税   nonprofit a. 非營利性的

123

Those who are attending the economic forum should pay the registration fee in full _____ a week of signing up for the event. (A) within (B) besides (C) over (D) behind	參加經濟論壇的人應該要在報名該活動後的一周內繳清報名費。

■ 選擇介系詞   解答 (A)

因為句意為「要在報名該活動後的一周內繳清報名費」，所以要選擇可以表示特定期限內的介系詞 (A) within（～以內）為正確答案。(B) besides 是「除了～」，有附加的意思，(C) over 是「～期間，～以來」的意思，還能以「～上面」的意思來表示位置。(D) behind 是「～的後面」的意思，表示場所或之後的時間點。

單字 registration n. 登錄

124

Use of the penthouse and conference rooms for special occasions requires the _____ of the building administrator. (A) permissive (B) permitted (C) permission (D) permissible	因特殊場合要使用頂樓或會議室必須取得大樓行政主管的許可。

■ 名詞的位置   解答 (C)

可以在定冠詞 the 和介系詞 of 中間，作為動詞 requires 的受詞的應該是名詞，所以名詞 (C) permission（承認，許可）為正確答案。形容詞 (A) 和 (D)，動詞兼分詞 (B) 無法作為名詞使用。

單字 conference n. 會議　require v. 要求　administrator n. 管理者　permissive a. 寬容的，自由放任式的　permit v. 允許　permissible a. 可允許的

125

Benoic Bikes encourages its first-time customers to buy helmets with their bicycle purchase, but it is completely _____. (A) wide (B) solitary (C) optional (D) reachable	Benoic 自行車行鼓勵首次購買自行車的顧客一併購買安全帽，但購買與否由客人自行決定。

■ 形容詞語彙   解答 (C)

句意為「購買安全帽是自行決定的」的意思，所以形容詞 (C) optional（可以自由選擇的）為正確答案。(A) wide 是「寬廣的」，(B) solitary 是「獨自的，分離的」，(D) reachable 是「可觸及的」的意思。另外，要記得「encourage + 受詞 + to 不定詞」（鼓勵～做～）是慣用句之一。

單字 encourage v. 鼓勵，慫恿　purchase n. 購買　completely ad. 完全地

126

All short-term rental apartments at Thompson Suites are equipped with stoves, refrigerators, and other necessary household _____. (A) materials (B) appliances (C) belongings (D) souvenirs	所有在 Thompson 套房的短期出租公寓都配有爐子、冰箱和其他必要的家電用品。

■ 名詞語彙   解答 (B)

因為文意為「所有短期出租公寓都配有爐子、冰箱和其他必要的家電用品」，所以名詞 (B) appliances（家電用品）為正確答案。(A) material 是「材料」，(C) belonging 是「財產」，(D) souvenir 是「紀念品」的意思。

單字 short-term a. 短期的   rental a. 租的   be equipped with phr. 具備～   household a. 家用的

127

The members of the tour group decided that they would rather visit the city's shopping district _____ the history museum as planned. (A) up to (B) instead of (C) apart from (D) farther than	旅遊團的成員決定他們要去城市裡的購物區，而不要去原來計畫參觀的歷史博物館。

■ 選擇介系詞 除外   解答 (B)

因為這句是「以參觀市區的購物區取代博物館」的意思，所以要選擇介系詞 (B) instead of（取代～）為正確答案。(A) up to 是「直到～」的意思，(C) apart from 是「除了～，在～之外」的意思，(D) farther than 是「比起～遠」的意思。

單字 rather ad. 還不如，寧願

128

Government officials attending the trade summit hope to increase _____ within the region's sizable business community. (A) collaboration (B) collaborative (C) collaborator (D) collaborate	政府官員參加貿易高峰會議是希望能增加區域內大型商業區的合作。

■ 人物名詞 vs. 抽象名詞   解答 (A)

因為缺少動詞 increase 的受詞，所以要選擇可以作為受詞的名詞 (A) 或 (C) 為正確答案。因為句意為「希望增加區域內大型商業區的合作」，所以抽象名詞 (A) collaboration（合作）為正確答案。如果使用人物名詞 (C) collaborator（合夥人），會變成「希望增加區域內大型商業區合夥人的合作」，且應為複數。形容詞 (B) 和動詞 (D) 都無法作為受詞使用。

單字 official n. 公務員，管理   summit n. 高峰會   sizable a. 具相當規模的   collaborative a. 協作的，聯名的

129

By the end of the writing workshop, participants will have gained a thorough _____ of the rules of grammar.
(A) understand　　　　　(B) understanding
(C) understandably　　　(D) understands

在寫作工作坊結束的時候，參加者將會對文法規則有通盤的了解。

■ 名詞的位置　　　　　　　　　　　　　　　　　　　　　　　　　　解答 (B)

因為可以放在動詞 have gained 的受詞的位置，又可以被形容詞 thorough 修飾的是名詞，所以名詞 (B) understanding（理解）為正確答案。動詞 (A) 和 (D)，副詞 (C) 都無法被形容詞修飾

單字 participant n. 參加者　thorough a. 完全的，徹底的　understandably ad. 可以理解地，理所當然地

130

Drivers waiting in the loading zone must switch off the engines of their delivery vans and avoid leaving them _____.
(A) idle　　　　　　　　(B) valid
(C) blank　　　　　　　(D) empty

在裝卸載貨區等待的司機必須要將他們貨車的引擎熄火，且避免讓車子空轉。

■ 形容詞語彙　　　　　　　　　　　　　　　　　　　　　　　　　　解答 (A)

因為句意為「司機需要把引擎熄火，避免讓車子空轉」，所以要選形容 (A) idle（空轉的，懶惰的）為正確答案。(B) valid 是「有效的」，(C) blank 是「空的，空白的」，(D) empty 是「空的」的意思。另外，「leave + 受詞 + 受詞補語」是指「讓～在～的狀態」的意思。另外，若是車上沒有人或是沒有人看管的話，可以使用 unattended（沒有人注意）。

單字 load v. 裝載（行李）　switch off phr. 關閉～

131

Starting in September, use of the parking spaces located at the back of Winklevoss Tower will be _____ to tenants from the first to fifth floors of the building only.
(A) automatic　　　　　(B) matched
(C) precise　　　　　　(D) limited

從九月開始，在 Winklevoss 大樓後方停車場將僅限於大樓內一樓至五樓的住戶使用。

■ 形容詞語彙　　　　　　　　　　　　　　　　　　　　　　　　　　解答 (D)

因為句意為「停車場的使用將僅限於大樓內一樓至五樓的住戶」，所以形容詞 (D) limited（限定的，限制的）為正確答案。(A) automatic 是「自動的」，(B) matched 是「適合的，貼切的」，(C) precise 是「精確的」的意思。

單字 tenant n. 住戶

132

Business entrepreneur Todd Mallory is known not only for his various _____ ventures, but also for his generous contributions to charity.

(A) profited   (B) profitable
(C) profitably   (D) profiteer

企業家 Todd Mallory 眾所周知的不僅是他多樣獲利的產業，還有他對慈善活動的慷慨奉獻。

■ 形容詞的位置   解答 (B)

因為要用形容詞修飾名詞 ventures，所以形容詞 (B) profitable（有收益的）為正確答案。動詞兼分詞 (A)，副詞 (C) 都無法修飾名詞。名詞 (D) 因為不是複合名詞，所以不能修飾名詞。另外，be known for~（藉著～而有名）, not only A but (also) B（不只 A，B 也），都是慣用句。

單字 entrepreneur n. 事業家，企業家   venture v.（投機）活動，冒險   generous a. 慷慨的   contribution n. 捐獻   charity n. 慈善（機構）

133

All expenses incurred during the company outing have been _____ for in a report submitted by the branch supervisor to the head office in Jakarta.

(A) account   (B) accountant
(C) accounting   (D) accounted

所有在公司旅遊期間的花費都已經在報告裡說明，由分公司的主管交給在雅加達的總公司。

■ 區分主動語態與被動語態   解答 (D)

因為空格是在 be 動詞的後面，所以名詞 (A) 和 (B)，-ing 形 (C)，p.p. 形 (D) 都可能是正確答案。因為動詞後面沒接受詞，文意為「所有花費都會被說明」的意思，所以要選擇接在 be 動詞後面可以有被動意義的動詞 account（說明）的 p.p.形 (D) accounted 為正確答案。另外，要記得 account for（說明～）是慣用句。如果選擇名詞 (A) account（帳戶）和 (B) accountant（會計師），就會變得跟主詞 all expenses 形成同位語，變成有兩個主詞，不合文法。

單字 expense n. 費用   incur v. 使發生，招惹   outing n. 短途旅遊

134

It is widely recognized that adults who engage in sports _____ social activities experience less stress.

(A) within   (B) as well as
(C) as long as   (D) ever

普遍認為，參與運動與社交活動的成人承受較少的壓力。

■ 對等連接詞   解答 (B)

因為要連接介系詞 in 前後的名詞 sport, social activities，所以要選擇有「不只 A，B 也」意思的 (B) as well as 為正確答案。(A) within 是「在～以內」的意思，是表示時間的介系詞，(C) as long as 是「只要」的意思，是表示條件的副詞子句連接詞，(D) ever 是否定詞，放在疑問句內或有 if 的句子內，便成為副詞「無論何時，任何時候」的意思。

單字 recognize v. 辨識   engage in phr. 參與～

135

Owner Sylvia Aspen decided to hire more servers for her café _____ the increasing number of customers. (A) whereas (B) if only (C) due to (D) besides	因為來客數的增加，店主人 Sylvia Aspen 決定要為她的咖啡廳聘僱更多服務人員。

■ 選擇介系詞 理由　　　　　　　　　　　　　　　　　　　　　　　　　解答 (C)

因為本句 Owner Sylvia Aspen decided to hire more servers 已經是內容完整的完整子句。 _____ the increasing ~ customer 則要視為修飾用的子句。而因為修飾句中沒有動詞，所以要選擇可以領導修飾子句的介系詞，所以 (C) 和 (D) 都是可能的答案。句意為「因為來客數增加」的意思，所以要選擇 (C) due to（因為～）為正確答案。(D) besides 作為介系詞時則有「除了～」的意思，作為連接副詞時則有「甚至」的意思。副詞子句連接詞 (A) whereas（反之，而）和 (B) if only（只要是～的話）都可以領導副詞子句。

單字 hire v. 雇用　server n. 侍者，員工

136

_____ the expansion plan was not authorized by the board, the company will no longer be accepting bids from construction firms. (A) Apart from (B) Given that (C) As if (D) Which	考慮到董事會並沒有授權擴建計畫，公司將不再接受建築公司的投標。

■ 副詞子句連接詞 條件　　　　　　　　　　　　　　　　　　　　　　　解答 (B)

因為 the company will ~ be accepting bids 已經是內容完整的完整子句。 _____ the expansion ~ the board 則可以視為修飾用的子句。因為此修飾子句有動詞 was not authorized，所以要選擇可以帶領此子句的副詞子句連接詞 (B) 或 (C) 為正確答案。句意為「考慮到董事會並沒有授權擴建計畫，公司將決定不再接受投標」的意思，所以要選 (B) Given that（考慮到～）為正確答案。如果選擇 (C) As if（假如，好像～）則句意會變成奇怪的：「好像董事會不授權擴建計畫，公司將不會再接受建設公司的投標。」 (A) Apart from 是有「除此之外」意義的介系詞，無法引導副詞子句，而關係代名詞 (D) Which 的前面應該要有先行詞，所以不會是正確答案。

單字 expansion n. 擴張　authorize v. 授權　bid n. 出價

137

To mark Lukering Technologies' 50th _____, the company will launch its first-ever charity foundation benefiting science scholars. (A) intention (B) initiation (C) anniversary (D) command	為了要慶祝 Lukering 科技公司的五十周年慶，公司決定要創辦公司裡第一個慈善基金會來造福科學家們。

■ 名詞語彙　　　　　　　　　　　　　　　　　　　　　　　　　　　　　解答 (C)

因為句意為「為了紀念 Lukering 科技公司的五十周年」，所以要選名詞 (C) anniversary（紀念日）為正確答案。(A) intention 是「意圖，目的」，(B) initiation 是「加入，創始」，(D) command 是「命令，指揮」的意思。

單字 mark v. 紀念，標記　launch v. 開始，出動　first-ever a. 史上最初的　foundation n. 財團，地基，基礎

138

------- a ship maker canceled its contract with Asia Steelworks, the value of the steel manufacturer's shares on the stock market dropped.

(A) Yet　　　　　　　(B) Unless
(C) Along　　　　　　(D) Since

因為一個造船廠取消了和 Asia Steelworks 的合約，進而使這家鋼鐵製造廠的股價下跌。

■ 副詞子句連接詞 理由　　　　　　　　　　　　　　　　　　　　　　　　解答 (D)

本句是有主詞 the value 和動詞 dropped 的完整句子，所以要把 _____ a ship ~ Asia Steelworks 視為修飾語句。因為此修飾語句有動詞 canceled，所以要選擇可以領導此修飾語句的副詞子句連接詞 (B) 或 (D) 為正確答案。句意為「因為造船廠取消合約，所以股價下跌了」的意思，所以要選 (D) Since（因為～）為正確答案。如果選擇 (B) Unless（除非），則會不符句意。(A) Yet 是「但是」的意思，作為對等連接詞連接同等的子句，(C) Along 是有「沿著～」意義的介系詞，無法領導子句。

單字 ship n. 船舶　steel n. 鋼鐵　manufacturer n. 製造商　share n. 股票　stock market phr. 股票市場

139

Fast Mail returns packages and documents to senders ------- it fails to deliver the items to their intended recipients.

(A) still　　　　　　　(B) where
(C) or　　　　　　　　(D) when

當包裹和文件無法遞送到指定的收件者手上，Fast Mail 公司會將郵件退回給寄件者。

■ 副詞子句連接詞 時間　　　　　　　　　　　　　　　　　　　　　　　　解答 (D)

因為在空格前包含主詞 Fast mail 和動詞 returns 的子句，空格後則有包含主詞 it 和動詞 fails 的子句，所以要選擇可以連結兩子句的對等連接詞 (C) 或副詞子句連接詞 (D) 為正確答案。因為句意為「無法將包裹或文書配送給收件人時，則將退回給寄件人」的意思，所以要選 (D) when（～時）為正確答案。如果選 (C) or（或）就會與句意不相符。(A) still 是「仍然，還是」的意思，是表時間的副詞。(B) where 是與場所相關而且要有先行詞的關係副詞。

單字 document n. 文件　intended a. 預期的，故意的　recipient n. 接收者，收件人

140

The factory's production ------- has been relatively low this month because of recurring problems with the equipment.

(A) study　　　　　　(B) output
(C) designation　　　(D) establishment

因為設備一直反覆發生問題，這個月工廠的產出相對較低。

■ 名詞語彙　　　　　　　　　　　　　　　　　　　　　　　　　　　　　　解答 (B)

句意為「因為設備問題，工廠的生產量相對減少」的意思，所以要選擇名詞 (B) output（生產量）為正確答案。(A) study 是「讀書，研究」，(C) designation 是「指定，指名」，(D) establishment 是「機關，設施」的意思。

單字 relatively ad. 相對性地　recurring a. 再發的，循環的　equipment n. 裝備

PART 6

Questions 141-143 refer to the following letter.　　　　141-143 根據下面的信件內容回答問題。

December 9

Winston Wheeler
Manager
ATA Electronics

Dear Mr. Wheeler,

This is in response to the letter you sent me regarding the information about the overhead projectors I requested on behalf of Northshire University. I appreciate your taking the time to recommend some of the brands _____ in your

141 (A) avails　　　　(B) availability
　　 (C) availably　　　(D) available

shop. However, the ones suggested are too expensive. In addition, I have found a different _____ that can provide

142 (A) courier　　　(B) vendor
　　 (C) developer　　(D) advisor

the university with what it needs. Nevertheless, I would like to know more about the speaker system you suggested for the university's multimedia classrooms. _____ you present a demonstration in my office on Monday?

143 (A) Do　　　　(B) Could
　　 (C) Why will　　(D) How should

Please let me know if you are free on that day as soon as possible. Thank you.

Matt Nicholson
IT Department Head
Northshire University

---

12 月 9 日

Winston Wheeler
經理
ATA 電器行

親愛的 Wheeler 先生：

關於我代表 Northshire 大學向您詢問投影機的訊息，根據您所寄來的資訊，我在此回覆。141 我很感謝您花時間介紹您店裡有的一些品牌給我，然而，您建議的都太貴了。

此外，142 我找到另一個賣家可以提供 Northshire 大學所需要的東西。

然而我想要知道更多關於您建議給大學多媒體教室的擴音系統，143 您能在星期一時在我辦公室展示一下嗎？

請您盡快讓我知道您那一天是否有空，謝謝。

Matt Nicholson
資訊科技部門主任
Northshire 大學

單字 **projector** n. 設計者，投影機　**appreciate** v. 感謝　**present** v. 展現，出示　**demonstration** n. 實地示範，說明

141. ■ 形容詞的位置　　　　　　　　　　　　　　　　　　　　　　　　　　　　　　　解答 (D)

因為文意為「您店裡可以買到的一些品牌」，所以要選形容詞 (D) available（可買到的）為正確答案。另外，_____ in your shop 是在修飾前面的名詞 some of the brands 的關係子句，名詞跟關係子句間省略了「關係代名詞＋be 動詞」（which are）。這時，如果之後再加上名詞則會與先行詞同位語，如果之後加上形容詞則有說明先行詞的意義。因為名詞 (B) availability（有效性）跟先行詞 some of the brands 在意義上無法成為同位語，所以不能作為答案。而且，要記得省略「關係代名詞＋be 動詞」之後，比較常出現的是形容詞，而不是名詞。

單字 **avail** v. 有幫助，有用處　**availably** ad. 有效用地，有幫助地

142. ■ 名詞語彙 掌握全文　　　　　　　　　　　　　　　　　　　　　　　　　　　　　解答 (B)

句意為：「我找到另一個 _____ 可以提供 Northshire 大學所需要的東西。」，空白處應填進名詞，四個選項皆可能是正確答案。因此必須透過掌握全文文意理解來判斷答案。從上文可以看出建議的投影機都太貴，且已經找到新的賣家提供投影機。因此答案 (B) vendor（賣家）為正確答案。(A) courier 是「信差，嚮導」，(C) developer 是「開發者」，(D) advisor 是「顧問」的意思。

143. ■ 助動詞 掌握上下文　　　　　　　　　　　　　　　　　　　　　　　　　　　　　解答 (B)

這是選擇疑問句句首應該要使用哪個助動詞的問題，所有選項都可能是正確答案。因為無法單靠有空格的句子判斷出答案，所以要掌握前後文。因為前一句是說即便如此也想更了解您所介紹的擴音系統，所以可以知道是在詢問關於產品的內容，因此可以表示請求的助動詞 (B) Could 是正確答案。

Questions 144-146 refer to the following information.

144-146 根據下面的資訊回答問題。

Replacing printer ink cartridges is expensive. Moreover, disposing of them is _____ to the environment. Most cartridges

144 (A) beneficial   (B) harmful
      (C) trivial   (D) wasteful

still work after their first use. Recycling them is better than throwing them away because it not only saves money but also reduces pollution.

If you do not know how to _____ your cartridges, Office

145 (A) reuse   (B) exchange
      (C) clean   (D) resell

Center is here to help.

Illinois' largest office supplies store has ink-refilling stations in its outlets. All you need to do is drop them off at a service counter and have them _____. Once we find that

146 (A) tested   (B) to test
      (C) testing   (D) tests

the cartridges are still in good condition, we will refill them with ink at half the price of a brand new cartridge. You can save money and assist in conserving nature.

Log on to www.officecenter.com now to learn more about this service.

Note: Office Center supports the government's Clean and Save campaign by selling brands of biodegradable office materials.

換印表機墨水匣很貴，144 而且丟棄墨水匣會對環境造成傷害。

大部分的墨水匣在使用第一輪後仍然可再次使用，回收它們比丟棄來得更好，因為這不僅省錢，而且降低汙染。

145 假如你不知道如何再利用墨水匣，Office Center 能幫助你。伊利諾州最大的辦公室耗材店的賣場裡有墨水補充站，

146 你所要做的就是把墨水匣交給一個服務櫃台來檢測。只要我們發現墨水匣狀況仍然很好，我們就會將墨水匣補充墨水，只要新的墨水匣的一半價錢。你可以省錢，同時幫助保育自然環境。

現在就登入 www.officecenter.com 了解這項服務的更多資訊。

注意：Office Center 以銷售可生物分解的辦公室耗材品牌來支持政府的淨化節能運動。

單字 replace v. 交換，取代 dispose v. 丟棄，處理 pollution n. 汙染 outlet n. 賣場 conserve v. 愛惜，保存 biodegradable a. 可生物分解的

144. 形容詞語彙 掌握上下文   解答 (B)

因為句意為「丟棄印表機墨水匣會對環境造成 _____」，所以 (A) 和 (B) 都可能是正確答案。因為無法單靠有空格的句子判斷出答案，所以要掌握前後文。後一句有提到回收可以降低汙染，所以可以推斷出把墨水匣丟棄會造成汙染。因此，形容詞 (B) harmful（有害的）為正確答案。(A) beneficial 是「有利的」，(C) trivial 是「微小的」，(D) wasteful 是「浪費的」的意思。

145. 動詞語彙 掌握上下文   解答 (A)

因為句意為「假如你不知道墨水匣 _____ 的方法，Office Center 能幫助你」，所以所有選項都可能為答案。因為無法單靠有空格的句子判斷出答案，所以要掌握前後文。後文有提到在耗材店裡有墨水補充站，所以可以得知在 Office Center 能夠幫助補充墨水並再利用墨水匣。因此，動詞 (A) reuse（再使用）為正確答案。(B) exchange 是「交換」，(C) clean 是「清掃」，(D) resell 是「再次販賣」的意思。

146. 以原形不定詞取代 to 不定詞成為受詞補語   解答 (A)

使役動詞 have 的受詞 them 與受詞補語的關係是「墨水匣接受測試」的被動關係，所以 p.p.形 (A) tested 才是正確答案。另外，雖然使役動詞 make, let, have 的受詞補語裡要加入原形不定詞而不是 to 不定詞，但如果解釋成受詞是「受詞補語」的被動意義的話，就要使用 p.p. 形態。例如本句中的墨水匣是「被人測試」的，所以 test 的 p.p. 形 tested 才正確，若使用原形不定詞變成 have them test，意思就會變成「墨水匣去測試」，造成錯亂的語意。

Dear Ms. Sunders,

Edildburgh Technologies has been in the media lately for _____ reasons. It is now being reported that we are the

147 (A) commercial　　(B) good
　　(C) social　　　　　(D) misunderstood

fastest-growing technology company in the region.Without the support of shareholders, we would not have become one of the top _____ companies in Western Europe

148 (A) finance　　　　(B) electronics
　　(C) insurance　　　(D) furnishing

that we are today. In this regard, we would like to show our appreciation of your valuable support of Edildburgh Technologies at a dinner party that _____ the company's

149 (A) will commemorate　　　(B) commemorating
　　(C) commemorated　　　　(D) commemorative

achievements over the past two and a half decades.

Enclosed is an invitation to the event. To confirm your attendance, please contact our public relations department and ask for Ruth Mendez. Thank you.

Respectfully yours,

Jasper Diaz
President
Edildburgh Technologies

親愛的 Sunders 女士：

147 Edildburgh 科技公司最近因為諸多好事在媒體上曝光。媒體報導我們是在該區域的一家快速成長的科技公司。

沒有股東們的支持，148 我們是無法成為西歐地區現今頂尖的電器公司之一。

對此，149 我們想要舉辦一個晚宴慶祝公司過去二十五年的成功，同時也對您珍貴的支持表達感謝之意。

隨函是晚宴的邀請函。如果您能前來參加，請和我們公關部門的 Ruth Mendez 聯絡，謝謝您！

Jasper Diaz 敬上
總裁
Edildburgh 科技公司

單字 shareholder n. 股東　in this regard phr. 關於這一點　appreciation n. 感謝，鑑賞　achievement n. 成就　decade n. 十年　public relations phr. 公關

147. ■ 形容詞語彙 掌握全文　　　　　　　　　　　　　　　　　　　　　　　　　　解答 (B)

因為句意為「最近因為 _____ 常在媒體上曝光」，所以所有選項都可能為正確答案。因為無法單靠有空格的句子判斷出答案，所以要掌握全文文意。後文提到被報導為成長得最快速的科技公司，所以可以知道這公司是因為好的理由被報導。所以，形容詞 (B) good（好的）為正確答案。(A) commercial 是「商業性的」，(C) social 是「社會性的」，(D) misunderstood 是「誤會的」的意思。

148. ■ 名詞語彙 掌握上下文　　　　　　　　　　　　　　　　　　　　　　　　　　解答 (B)

因為句意為「成為西歐最頂尖的 _____ 公司」，所以所有選項都可能為正確答案。因為無法單靠有空格的句子判斷出答案，所以要掌握前後文。前文提到他們是成長得最快速的科技公司，所以可以知道 Edildburgh Technologies 是跟科技有關的公司。因此，名詞 (B) electronics（電子儀器）為正確答案。(A) finance 是「財務，財經」，(C) insurance 是「保險」，(D) furnishing 是「裝備，家具」的意思。

149. ■ 未來式　　　　　　　　　　　　　　　　　　　　　　　　　　　　　　　　解答 (A)

因為主格關係子句 that ~ decades 沒有動詞，所以動詞 (A) 和 (C) 都是可能的答案。因為文意為「舉辦一個慶祝公司過去二十五年的成功，同時也能對您珍貴的支持表達感謝之意的晚宴」，所以可以知道晚宴是在未來舉行的，因此要選未來式 (A) will commemorate 為正確答案。

單字 commemorate v. 紀念

Questions 150-152 refer to the following memo. | 150-152 根據下面的備忘錄內容回答問題。

To: Security guards
From: Michael Reni, Building Security Head
Subject: Security Inspections

There have been several instances when staff members working overtime have forgotten to lock their offices, leaving the building vulnerable to burglary. _____ this,

150 (A) Apart from   (B) On account of
    (C) In addition to (D) In spite of

management wants guards on the night shift to conduct their security checks immediately after all office workers have left the building.

Conference rooms and offices on every floor _____.

151 (A) must be inspected   (B) were inspected
    (C) had inspected   (D) could be inspected

Moreover, please make sure all fluorescent lights are switched off, except in the hallways and stairwells. Air conditioning units and other office equipment should also be turned off.

This new _____ takes effect tonight. Feel free to contact

152 (A) routine   (B) proposal
    (C) recommendation (D) appointment

me if you have questions.

收件人：保全人員
寄件者：大樓保全主任 Michael Reni
主旨：安全檢查

因為加班的員工忘了將辦公室鎖上，使得大樓讓小偷有機可趁，而導致好幾起事件發生。150 對此，管理團隊要求晚班的保全人員在所有辦公室員工離開後，立即進行安全檢查。

151 每層樓的會議室和辦公室都必須檢查。此外，請確定除了在走道和樓梯的日光燈之外，其他所有的日光燈都要關掉。空調和其他辦公室設備也要關掉。

152 這個新的例行性工作從今晚開始，如有任何問題，請與我聯絡。

單字 instance n. 情況，實例　overtime n. 超時　vulnerable a. 易受傷害的　burglary n. 竊盜　night shift phr. 夜班　conduct v. 實施，指揮　security n. 保安，安全　immediately ad. 立即　inspect v. 檢查，調查　fluorescent light phr. 日光燈　hallway n. 走廊　stairwell n. 樓梯間，有樓梯的地方　take effect phr. 施行，生效

150. ■ 選擇介系詞 掌握上下文　　　　　　　　　　　　　　　　　　　　　　　解答 (B)

因為空格與之後的代名詞 this 跟逗號一起在句子的開頭作為連接副詞，所以要把握前句與本句的因果關係之後再從介系詞 (A) (B) (C) (D) 中選擇正確答案。前句提到因為忘了將辦公室鎖上，使得大樓讓小偷有機可趁，而本句是說管理團隊要求晚班的保全人員進行安全檢查，所以要選擇可以表示因果關係的介係詞 (B) On account of（因為～）為正確答案。(A) Apart from 是「把～除外，除了～」，(C) In addition 是「除了～」，(D) In spite of 是「儘管～」的意思。

151. ■ 助動詞 掌握前後文　　　　　　　　　　　　　　　　　　　　　　　　解答 (A)

句意為「檢查每層樓的會議室與辦公室」，而此句無法單靠有空格的句子判斷出答案，所以要掌握前後句。後文提到要關掉日光燈與空調設備的內容，所以可以知道這是在轉達要檢查會議室的命令。因此，要選擇包含可以表示命令、邀請的助動詞 must 的 (A) must be inspected 為正確答案。

152. ■ 名詞語彙 掌握全文　　　　　　　　　　　　　　　　　　　　　　　　解答 (A)

因為句意為「這項新的_____今晚開始實施」，所以所有的選項都可能為正確答案。因為無法單靠有空格的此句判斷出答案，所以要掌握前後文或者全文。從例文整體看來，可以知道為了強化安全，夜間保全每天晚上要固定檢查建築物，所以要選擇名詞 (A) routine（固定行程）為正確答案。(B) propose 是「提案」，(C) recommendation 是「推薦」，(D) appointment 是「約定，約會」的意思。

PART 7

Questions 153-154 refer to the following announcement.　　153-154 根據下面的公告內容回答問題。

[154] Broughester University Drama Guild and *The Scholar* present *Anita* [153] Join us for this season's production of the English musical *Anita* from June 2 to 4 at the Valdez Auditorium. The show features award-winning actress Bernadette Summers and actor George Fair, star of the popular TV series Best Friends. The rest of the cast is made up of members of the drama guild. Show times: June 2, Friday - 5 P.M. June 3, Saturday - 8 P.M. June 4, Sunday - 6 P.M. Tickets are available at *The Scholar* press office.	[154] Broughester 大學戲劇社與 *The Scholar* 公演 *Anita* [153] 歡迎參加我們本季從 6 月 2 日到 4 日在 Valdez 表演廳演出的英語音樂劇 *Anita*。這齣戲由得獎女演員 Bernadette Summers 和廣受歡迎的電視影集 Best Friends 男演員 George Fair 主演。其他的陣容則由戲劇社社員所組成。 演出時間： 6 月 2 日星期五 – 下午 5 點 6 月 3 日星期六 – 下午 8 點 6 月 4 日星期日 – 下午 6 點 購票請洽 *The Scholar* 新聞處

單字 □feature v. 由～主演，以此為特徵　□be made up of phr. 以～而組成　□available a. 可取得的

153

What is being announced? (A) An awards ceremony (B) A movie premiere (C) A theatrical performance (D) A news conference	公布了什麼消息？ (A) 一場頒獎典禮 (B) 一部電影首映 (C) 一齣戲劇表演 (D) 一場記者會

■■ 找出主題 主題　　　　　　　　　　　　　　　　　　　　　　　　解答 (C)

因為是在問公告內容的尋找主題的題目，所以要特別注意公告前部分。前面提到 Join us for this season's production of the English musical Anita 是指本季將演出的英語音樂劇 Anita，後面則是在說明音樂劇的細部內容，因此 (C) A theatrical performance 為正確答案。

換句話說

musical 音樂劇 → A theatrical performance 劇場演出

單字 movie premiere phr. 電影首映會　news conference phr. 記者會

154

Where would the announcement most likely be found? (A) At a science museum (B) On a school campus (C) At a country club (D) In a research center	這個公告最有可能在哪裡被發現？ (A) 在科學博物館裡 (B) 在學校校園裡 (C) 在鄉村俱樂部裡 (D) 在研究中心裡

■■ 推論 整體情報　　　　　　　　　　　　　　　　　　　　　　　　解答 (B)

要找出在例文裡的所有線索，綜合起來再推論此公告可能貼在那些地方。文中提到 Broughester University Drama Guild，另外例文內容主要是講大學戲劇社的演出內容，所以可以推論這是在校園裡可以看到的公告。因此 (B) On a school campus 為正確答案。

單字 school campus phr. 校園

Questions 155-156 refer to the following e-mail.

155-156 根據下面的電郵內容回答問題。

To: ADT Bank finance managers
    <managersgroup@adt.com>
From: Peter Honorat <p.honorat@adt.com>
Subject: Annual Budget Proposal

Date: December 1

Hello everyone,

The finance department is completing a budget proposal for next year. The proposal will be discussed at ADT Bank's yearly planning meeting in January. In connection with this, [155]we request that you submit the budget estimates for your respective branches within the week.

In particular, we need your recommended salary adjustments as well as your estimated expenses for supplies and equipment. As agreed in the last meeting, [156]your budget proposals should meet the standards provided by the finance department. [155]Please turn in the documents no later than December 8.

Sincerely,

Peter Honorat
Administrative Assistant
Finance Department

收件人：ADT 銀行財務經理
    <managersgroup@adt.com>
寄件人：Peter Honorat
    <p.honorat@adt.com>
主旨：年度預算提案
日期：12 月 1 日

各位好：

財務部門正在進行下年度的預算提案，這個提案會在一月的 ADT 銀行年度計畫會議中討論。為了這件事，[155] 我們要求在本週內提交你們各分部的預算預估。

特別注意，我們需要你們對於薪資調整的建議，以及耗材及設備的預估費用。如同上次會議裡所決議的，[156] 你們的預算提案應該要符合財務部門提出的標準。[155] 請於 12 月 8 日前提交應繳之文件。

Peter Honorat 敬上
行政助理
財務部門

單字 □budget n. 預算　　　　　　□proposal n. 案子，提案　　　□in connect with phr. 與～相關
    □estimate n. 估價單，估計數；v. 估計，推算　　　　　　　　□respective a. 分別的，各自的
    □salary n. 薪水　　　　　　□adjustment n. 調整　　　　□meet v. 滿足，符合
    □standard n. 基準　　　　　□turn in phr. 繳交

155

What is the e-mail mainly about?
(A) A proposed project
(B) A submission deadline
(C) The schedule of conference activities
(D) The promotion of an employee

這封電郵主要是關於什麼？
(A) 一個建議的計畫
(B) 繳交截止的最後期限
(C) 會議活動的行程
(D) 員工的升遷

■ 找出主題 主題　　　　　　　　　　　　　　　　　　　　　　　　　　　　　　　　　　　解答 (B)

這是在詢問電子郵件主要關於什麼的問題。而這問題要特別透過全文來找出答案。we request that you submit the budget estimates for your respective branches within the week 是指要求要在一週內提出各分部的預算預估，之後 Please turn in the documents no later than December 8. 是說希望最晚要在 12 月 8 日之前提出資料的意思，因此 (B) A submission deadline 為正確答案。

According to the e-mail, what is the finance department's role in budget planning?	根據這封電郵，財務部門在預算計畫扮演什麼角色？
(A) Assigning accounting consultants to branches	(A) 指派會計顧問給各分部
(B) Updating the shareholders on company income	(B) 跟股東報告公司最新的收入
(C) Soliciting price quotations from suppliers	(C) 向供應商詢價
(D) Setting guidelines for estimating expenses	(D) 制定估算費用的指導方針

■ 六何原則 What   解答 (D)

這是在詢問在預算計畫裡財務部門擔任什麼角色的六何原則問題。要先找出與問題的重點 the finance department's role in budget planning 有關聯的地方，your budget proposals should meet the standards provided by the finance department 是指預算案應該要符合財務部門提出的標準，所以要選擇 (D) Setting guidelines for estimating expenses 為正確答案。

單字 assign v. 配置，分配 update v. 告知（最近的情報） shareholder n. 股東 solicit v. 徵求，徵集 quotation n. 估價單，引用

Questions 157-159 refer to the following information.

157-159 根據下面的資訊回答問題。

Savor a good cup of brewed coffee the easy way!

The Coffee Bits French Press

Try our recommended method of brewing with the Coffee Bits French Press and enjoy quality coffee in your own home.

Suggested mix:

10 grams or 2 tablespoons of ground Coffee Bits coffee = 180 milliliters of water*
*Use hot filtered water.

157-D Brewing instructions:

158-D Remove the plunger, add ground coffee, and 159 pour in hot water based on the recommended proportion. 157-A If you find the suggested mix too strong, fill the French Press with water up to about 1.25 centimeters below the rim. 159 Then stir the mixture and 158-D put the plunger on top of the container. 157-B Allow the coffee to steep for about three minutes. Press the plunger and pour the coffee into a cup. Enjoy

輕鬆就能享受一杯好喝的現煮咖啡

Coffee Bits 法式濾壓壺

試試我們推薦的方法使用 Coffee Bits 法式濾壓壺沖泡，你在家也可以享受香醇的咖啡。

建議調配份量：

10 克或 2 湯匙 Coffee Bits 研磨咖啡 = 180 毫升水*
*使用熱過濾水。

157-D 沖製方法：

158-D 將塞蓋取出，加入研磨咖啡，159 倒進建議份量的熱水。157-A 假如你覺得這個調配份量太濃，你可以加水到法式濾壓壺裡，大約加至壺緣下方 1.25 公分處。159 攪拌咖啡和水，158-D 將塞蓋放回去。157-B 讓咖啡浸泡約三分鐘，將塞蓋壓下，把咖啡倒進杯子裡，然後好好享用咖啡。

單字 □savor v. 享受～，感受～　□brew v. 泡（茶、咖啡），煮　□method n. 方法
□quality a. 品質好的；n. 品質　□ground a. 磨碎的，磨平的　□plunger n.（水壓機，抽水機的）栓塞
□rim n. 邊框　□stir v. 攪拌　□mixture n. 混合物
□steep v. 浸泡

157

What is NOT stated in the information?
(A) The method of adjusting coffee strength
(B) The steeping process duration
(C) The steps for cleaning the press
(D) The way to operate the equipment

哪一項沒有被提到？
(A) 調整咖啡濃度的方法
(B) 浸泡過程的時間
(C) 清理濾壓壺的步驟
(D) 操作器材的方法

■ **Not/True** Not 問題　　解答 (C)

這是在詢問說明書內未提及部分的 Not/True 問題。因為問題本身並沒有具體指出重點，所以要透過例文來尋找與各選項相關的內容。If you find the suggested mix too strong, fill the French Press with water up to about 1.25 centimeters below the rim. 是指如果覺得這個調配份量太濃，加水到法式濾壓壺裡，大約加至壺緣下方 1.25 公分處，所以 (A) 與例文內容一致。Allow the coffee to steep for about three minutes 是指讓咖啡浸泡約三分鐘，所以 (B) 與例文內容一致。(C) 是例文沒有提及的內容。因為是在 Brewing instruction 裡先提到泡製方法後，再說明如何使用 French Press 泡製咖啡，所以 (D) 也與例文內容一致。

單字 adjust v. 調節，調整

158

What is mentioned as a characteristic of the French Press? (A) It comes in a variety of sizes. (B) It is simple to store. (C) It is made of strong materials. (D) It consists of several components.	文中提到的法式濾壓壺特色是什麼？ (A) 有各種大小尺寸。 (B) 很容易收納。 (C) 用堅固的材料製成。 (D) 有好幾個組件組成。

■ **Not/True** True 問題

解答 (D)

這是要先在例文中找出與問題的重點 a characteristic of the French Press 相關的部分，並與選項進行對照的 Not/True 問題。(A) (B) (C) 都是在例文中沒有提及的內容。因為 Remove the plunger 和 put the plunger on top of the container 是指「取出塞蓋」與「將塞蓋蓋回容器上方」，所以可以知道 French Press 有分為塞蓋跟容器，所以 (D) 與例文內容一致。因此要選 (D) It consists of several components. 為正確答案。

單字 component n. 構成要素，零件

159

What should users do after pouring water into the French Press? (A) Stir the mixture (B) Add hot milk (C) Filter the ground coffee (D) Put some sugar	使用者在倒水進法式濾壓壺後要做什麼？ (A) 攪拌咖啡和水 (B) 加熱牛奶 (C) 過濾研磨咖啡 (D) 加點糖

■ 六何原則 What

解答 (A)

這是問使用者在把水倒入 French Press 之後要做什麼（What）的六何原則問題。要找出與問題重點 after pouring water 有關聯的部分，pour in hot water 是說把水倒進去，之後 Then stir the mixture 是指攪拌咖啡和水，所以要選 (A) Stir the mixture 為正確答案。

單字 filter v. 過濾

Questions 160-163 refer to the following article.　　　　160-163 根據下面的文章內容回答問題。

Decoding the Happiness Formula

[160]Happiness is not only found but also created. This is the message of celebrated psychiatrist Jonathan Hammond in his new book, *The Happiness Formula*, which unravels the secrets of leading a happy and contented life.

According to Hammond, [161-C]happy people are healthier, have better relationships with their families and friends, and are more productive at work. Although it is true that much of people's happiness is influenced by their genes and other factors such as income and socioeconomic status, happiness is also heavily influenced by the activities people do in their everyday lives. Based on this, Hammond studied how people find joy in life. [163]He found out that those who are active and positive experience lasting contentment, compared with people who live more passively and have a more negative outlook on life.

[163]He said people can motivate themselves to be happy by engaging in sports and participating in activities that help them find meaning in life. Doing simple things, such as dancing, singing, smiling, or laughing out loud also stimulates positive energy. Hammond stressed that the key to long-lived happiness is making the decision to stay optimistic.

[162-B]Hammond, who is also a respected professor at Southcane University, has authored different books about personality enhancement and developmental psychology. *The Happiness Formula* was launched two weeks ago by Leehorn Publishing House and is currently number one on the *Fortnightly Informant's* best-seller list.

解碼快樂方程式

[160] 快樂不僅可以被發掘，還可以被創造。聞名遐邇的精神科醫師 Jonathan Hammond 在他的新書 *The Happiness Formula* 中告訴我們這個訊息，這本書闡明了走向快樂知足人生的祕密。

Hammond 表示，[161-C] 快樂的人比較健康，也和他們的家人朋友保持較好的關係，同時在工作上也更有生產力。雖然人們的快樂絕大多數的確受到基因，以及像是收入、社經地位等其他因素的影響，但是快樂也大大受到人們每日的活動影響。根據這個理論，Hammond 研究人們如何在生活中找到樂趣。[163] 和那些活得較消極的、對生命的看法較負面的人比較起來，他發現積極正面的人能有較持久的滿足感。

[163] 他說人們可以藉由做運動和參與幫助他們找到生命意義的活動來促進快樂，做一些簡單的事，例如跳舞、唱歌、微笑、大笑都可以刺激正面的能量。Hammond 強調長久快樂的關鍵在於下定決心要保持樂觀。

[162-B] Hammond 也是 Southcane 大學受人愛戴的教授，寫過關於人格提升和發展心理學等不同的書籍，*The Happiness Formula* 兩週前由 Leehorn 出版社出版銷售，已經榮登 *Fortnightly Informant* 暢銷書排行榜的寶座。

單字　□decode v. 解讀，解碼　□celebrated a. 有名的　□unravel v. 解開
　　　□lead v. 使過（某種生活）　□contented a. 心滿意足的　□productive a. 生產性的
　　　□influence v. 給予影響　□lasting a. 持續的，永遠的　□contentment n. 滿足
　　　□passively ad. 被動地　□outlook n. 視野，觀點　□motivate v. 給予動機，激發
　　　□stimulate v. 刺激　□optimistic a. 樂觀的　□author v. 開創，編寫
　　　□enhancement n. 提升

160

What is the article mainly about?
(A) Ideas featured in a publication
(B) Secrets of successful people
(C) Tips on time management
(D) Stories reviewed in a journal

這篇文章主要在講什麼？
(A) 一本出版品的核心概念
(B) 成功人士的祕密
(C) 時間管理的祕訣
(D) 期刊裡的報導評論

📖 找出主題 主題　　　　　　　　　　　　　　　　　　　　　　　　　　解答 (A)

這是找出此文章主題的提問，所以要多留意例文的前面部分。Happiness is not only found but also created. 是指快樂不僅能發掘，也能創造，之後 This is the message of celebrated psychiatrist Jonathan Hammond in his new book, *The Happiness Formula* 是指這是知名精神科醫師 Jonathan Hammond 在新書 *The Happiness Formula* 裡傳達的訊息。由此可知是在介紹書的內容，因此 (A) Ideas featured in a publication 為正確答案。

單字 **feature** v. 以～為特點　**review** v. 評論

161

What does the article mention about happy people?	關於快樂的人，文章中提到什麼？
(A) They are more popular.	(A) 他們比較受歡迎。
(B) They have more money.	(B) 他們比較有錢。
(C) They are healthier.	(C) 他們比較健康。
(D) They have more friends.	(D) 他們有比較多朋友。

■ **Not/True** True 問題　　　　　　　　　　　　　　　　　　　　　　　　　解答 (C)

這是要先在例文中找出與問題的重點 happy people 相關的部分，並與選項進行對照的 Not/True 問題。(A) (B) (D) 是例文中沒有提及的內容。happy people are healthier 是指快樂的人比較健康的意思，因為 (C) 與例文的內容一致，所以 (C) They are healthier. 為正確答案。

單字 popular a. 受歡迎的

162

What is stated about Dr. Hammond?	關於 Hammond 博士，提到了什麼？
(A) He publishes his own work.	(A) 他出版自己的書。
(B) He has written previous publications.	(B) 他之前就出過書。
(C) He is a career adviser.	(C) 他是一位生涯顧問。
(D) He heads a university department.	(D) 他是一大學系所的主任。

■ **Not/True** True 問題　　　　　　　　　　　　　　　　　　　　　　　　　解答 (B)

這是要先在例文中找出與問題的重點 Dr. Hammond 相關的部分，並與選項進行對照的 Not/True 問題。(A) (C) (D) 是例文中沒有提及的內容。Hammond ~ has authored different books 是指 Hammond 寫過不同的書，所以 (B) 與例文內容一致。因此要選 (B) He has written previous publications. 為正確答案。

換句話說

has authored ~ books 寫過這些書 → has written ~ publications 寫過這些出版物

單字 publish v. 出版　career n. 職業　head v. 帶領～　department n. 系，科

163

According to Dr. Hammond, how can a person stay happy?	根據 Hammond 博士，一個人要如何維持快樂？
(A) By being more physically active	(A) 讓體能上更加活躍
(B) By having a stable job	(B) 有一份穩定的工作
(C) By being independent	(C) 能獨立自主
(D) By setting reasonable goals	(D) 設定合理的目標

■ 六何原則 How　　　　　　　　　　　　　　　　　　　　　　　　　　　解答 (A)

這是在詢問人們如何過得快樂的六何原則問題。要先在例文中找出與問題的重點 stay happy 相關的部分，He found out that those who are active and positive experience lasting contentment, compared with people who live more passively and have a more negative outlook on life. 是指他發現積極正面的人與活得消極、對生命看法較負面的人比較起來能有較持久的滿足感，之後 He said people can motivate themselves to be happy by engaging in sports and participating in activities that help them find meaning in life. 則是指他說人們可以藉由做運動和參與幫助他們找到生命意義的活動來促進快樂，因此 (A) By being more physically active 為正確答案。

單字 stable a. 穩定的　independent a. 獨立的　reasonable a. 合理的

Questions 166-165 refer to the following flyer.

160-163 根據下面的廣告單內容回答問題。

Don't let another year go by!
Get in shape today at Phoenix Fitness

Come to the Phoenix Fitness gym and see all of our improvements for yourself! Visit us on Ballard Street in Elmwood, between Pita Wraps and Gilbert's Cycles to see our enlarged exercise facilities and [165-D]newly renovated locker rooms and lobby! To celebrate the completion of renovations, present this flyer to [165-A]get a 50 percent discount on a one-year membership! In addition, all new members [165-C]get a trial session with one of our professional trainers.

[164]This promotion is valid until February 15 at the Elmwood branch exclusively.

Phoenix Fitness
18 Ballard Street, Elmwood
Tel. 555-3243

別再讓一年就這樣過去了！
今天就到 Phoenix 健身中心變健康

來 Phoenix 健身中心，親眼看看我們的進步！我們位在 Elmwood 市的 Ballard 街，就在 Pita Wraps 和 Gilbert's Cycles 的中間，來參觀我們擴增的運動設施及 [165-D]重新整修的更衣室與大廳！為了要慶祝重新整修的完工，出示這張傳單，[165-A]就可以得到一年會費的五折優待！此外，所有的新會員可以 [165-C]得到一次與專業教練進行的體驗課程。

[164]這項優惠僅限於 Elmwood 分店，到 2 月 15 日截止。

Phoenix 健身中心
Elmwood 市 Ballard 街 18 號
電話：555-3243

單字 □go by phr. 送走～，經過　　□get in shape phr. 使變得健康，鍛鍊體力
　　□improvement n. 改善，進步　　□enlarged a. 擴大的　　□trial n. 試用
　　□valid a. 有效的　　□exclusively ad. 只有

164

What is suggested about Phoenix Fitness?
(A) It sells athletic equipment.
(B) It plans to renovate its lobby.
(C) It has several locations.
(D) It is looking to hire trainers.

關於 Phoenix 健身中心，提示了什麼？
(A) 在販賣運動設備。
(B) 計畫要重新整修大廳。
(C) 有數個分店。
(D) 在招聘新的健身教練。

■ 推論 詳細內容　　　　　　　　　　　　　　　　　　　　　　　　　　　解答 (C)

這是需要推論與問題的重點 Phoenix Fitness 相關內容的問題。This promotion is valid ~ at the Elwood branch exclusively. 是指此特價活動只有在 Elwood 分店才有效，所以可以推測出 Phoenix Fitness 有很多的分店。因此 (C) It has several locations. 為正確答案。

165

What will NOT be offered to customers?
(A) A 12 month membership
(B) Discounts on bicycles
(C) A free training session
(D) Usage of a locker room facility

下列哪一項不會提供給顧客？
(A) 十二個月的會員資格
(B) 自行車的優惠
(C) 一次免費的訓練課程
(D) 使用更衣室

■ Not/True Not 問題　　　　　　　　　　　　　　　　　　　　　　　　　解答 (B)

這是要先在例文中找出與問題的重點 offered to customers 相關的部分，並與選項進行對照的 Not/True 問題。get a 50 percent discount on a one-year membership 是指一年的會費可以得到五折優待，所以 (A) 與例文一致。(B) 是例文中沒有提及的內容，所以 (B) Discounts on bicycle 是正確答案。get a trial session with one of our professional trainers 是指可以與專業教練進行免費體驗課程，所以 (C) 與例文內容一致。newly renovated locker rooms 是指重新整修的更衣室，因此 (D) 也與例文一致。

換句話說
a trial session with ~ trainers 與專業教練一起的體驗課程 → A free training session 免費訓練課程

單字 usage n. 使用

TO: Taxi Drivers
FROM: Mike Holt, Transpoway Chief Operator
SUBJECT: Some Things to Keep in Mind

It has come to my attention that [167-D]many passengers have complained about the rude behavior of some Transpoway taxi drivers. Please remember that many of our passengers are tourists, and transportation is a significant part of their experience. As such, [168]it is our duty to give them the utmost respect and our best service. [166]Here are some basic guidelines on treating passengers properly.

(A) [168]Be polite. Always smile and let passengers feel that you are happy to serve them. Don't forget to say "please" and "thank you" whenever necessary.

(B) Be honest. If passengers do not know how to get to a destination, take the fastest route. Do not take advantage of passengers by taking long routes to keep your meter running.

(C) Do not be choosy about passengers. Many people have said Transpoway drivers refused to take them to locations outside the city. Except for security reasons, no driver is allowed to reject passengers.

These are simple points that, if remembered and put into action, will allow us to win back the loyalty of our clients. Please note that the company will continue to solicit comments and suggestions from passengers through its hotline.

收件人：計程車司機
寄件人：Transpoway 營運主任 Mike Holt
主旨：注意事項

我注意到 [167-D] 有很多乘客在抱怨一些 Transpoway 計程車司機不好的行為。請記住，我們很多乘客都是觀光客，而交通是他們旅行經驗很重要的一部分，因此，[168] 讓他們感受到備受尊重及提供最佳的服務是我們的職責。[166] 這裡有一些基本要點，讓你們知道如何適當地接待乘客。

(A) [168] 要有禮貌。要總是面帶微笑，讓乘客感受到你很高興能接待他們。別忘了在必要的時候說「請」和「謝謝」。

(B) 要誠實。假如乘客不知道要如何到達目的地，走最近的路，不要占乘客的便宜，用繞路的方式多收錢。

(C) 不要拒載乘客。很多人說 Transpoway 司機拒絕載他們到市郊的地點。除了安全的考量之外，任何司機都不能拒載乘客。

這些簡單的原則，如果你能記得並付諸行動，就能夠贏回乘客的心。請注意，公司將會繼續透過熱線徵求乘客的意見與建議。

單字
□ **attention** n. 注意
□ **significant** a. 重要的
□ **destination** n. 目的地
□ **solicit** v. 要求，尋找
□ **behavior** n. 行為，舉止
□ **utmost** a. 最大的
□ **choosy** a. 挑剔的，挑三揀四的
□ **comment** n. 意見
□ **transportation** n. 交通方式
□ **guideline** n. 指南
□ **loyalty** n. 信賴，忠誠
□ **hotline** n. 諮詢熱線

166

What is the memo mainly about?
(A) Traffic regulations
(B) Customer relations guidelines
(C) License renewal
(D) Revised company policies

這個備忘錄主要是關於什麼？
(A) 交通規則
(B) 顧客關係守則
(C) 駕照換新
(D) 新修正的公司政策

■ 找出主題 主題　　　　　　　　　　　　　　　　　　　　　　　　　　　　　　　　解答 (B)

這是在詢問此備忘錄主題的問題。因為例文中間部分提到關於主題的內容，所以要特別注意。Here are some basic guidelines on treating passengers properly. 是指這裡有些能適當接待乘客的基本要點，所以可以知道這是在說明基本要點，因此要選 (B) Customer relations guidelines 為正確答案。

單字 **renewal** n. 更新　**revised** a. 修正的　**policy** n. 政策

167

What did Mr. Holt mention about the passengers?	Holt 先生提到關於乘客什麼事？
(A) They are particular about taxis.	(A) 他們挑剔計程車。
(B) They often lose their valuables.	(B) 他們常常弄丟貴重物品。
(C) Some feel that the rates are too expensive.	(C) 有些人覺得車資太貴。
(D) Some have complained about drivers.	(D) 有些人抱怨過司機。

■ **Not/True** True 問題　　　　　　　　　　　　　　　　　　　　　　　　　　　解答 (D)

這是要先在例文中找出與問題的重點 the passengers 相關的部分，並與選項進行對照的 Not/True 問題。(A) (B) (C) 是例文中沒有提及的內容。many passengers have complained about the rude behavior of some Transpoway taxi drivers 是指有很多乘客在抱怨 Transpoway 計程車司機的不良行為，所以 (D) 與例文內容一致。因此 (D) Some have complained about drivers. 為正確答案。

單字 **particular** a. 特定的，挑剔的　　**valuables** n. 貴重物品

168

What are drivers expected to do?	司機被期望要做什麼？
(A) Find alternative routes	(A) 找一條替代路線
(B) Give directions to tourists	(B) 指引觀光客方向
(C) Practice defensive driving	(C) 練習防禦性的駕駛方式
(D) Treat passengers with respect	(D) 對待乘客要尊重

■ **六何原則** What　　　　　　　　　　　　　　　　　　　　　　　　　　　　解答 (D)

這是在詢問期待司機們做什麼（What）的六何原則問題。與問題的重點 drivers expected to do 相關的部分是 it is our duty to give them the utmost respect and our best service 是指司機要讓他們（也就是乘客）感受到備受尊重及提供最佳的服務，之後也提到 Be polite. Always smile and let passengers feels that you are happy to serve them. 意思是「要有禮貌，總是面帶微笑，讓乘客感受到你很高興能接待他們。」所以 (D) Treat passengers with respect 為正確答案。

單字 **alternative route** phr. 替代路線　　**defensive** a. 防禦性的

[169]**Nashville Eagles Bowling League**
"We Produce Champions!"

[169]We are Southern Tennessee's oldest surviving bowling club, with hundreds of members from every age group and skill level.

[172-A]Club meetings are held every Thursday, from 4 P.M. to 6 P.M., at Global Bowl in downtown Nashville.

[172-D]League Tournaments
Wednesdays and Saturdays
Open Tournaments
Second and third Sunday of the month
Juniors
Saturday mornings only
Seniors
Tuesday and Friday afternoons

[172-C]The Nashville Eagles thanks its sponsor, Global Bowl: Supporting Fair Play and Family Fun for All!

Global Bowl is located at 98 Hamlet Avenue, Nashville, TN
Tel. 555-2382

[171-A/D]**Lane Hours**
Monday to Thursday
　10 A.M. to 10 A.M.
Friday10 A.M. to 12 A.M.

[171-A]Saturday 8 A.M. to 2 A.M.
Sunday　9 A.M. to 7 P.M.
([171-D]Closed every other Wednesday)

Office Hours
Weekdays
10 A.M. to 4 P.M.

[170]**Extensions**
104 Lane Reservations
105 Brownie's Café
[170]106 League Administrator
107 League Updates

[170]Teams may register for league play by calling or visiting the administrator anytime during office hours.

Global Bowl is wheelchair-friendly.
[171-C]No pets allowed!

[169]Nashville 老鷹保齡球聯盟
「我們出產冠軍！」

169 我們是南田納西州現存歷史最久遠的保齡球社團，有來自各年齡層和各種程度的上百個會員！

172-A 社團聚會的時間是每星期四下午四點到六點，在 Nashville 市區的 Global Bowl。

172-D 聯盟比賽
星期三和星期六
公開比賽
每個月的第二和第三個星期日
青少年組
僅星期六早上
長青組
星期二和星期五下午

172-C Nashville 老鷹保齡球謝謝贊助商 Global Bowl：支持公平競賽和闔家同樂！

Global Bowl 位在田納西州 Nashville 市 Hamlet 大道 98 號
電話: 555-2382

171-A/D 球道時間
星期一至星期四
上午十點到晚上十點
星期五
上午十點到凌晨十二點

171-A 星期六
上午八點到凌晨兩點
星期日
上午九點到晚上七點
（171-D 隔週三公休）

上班時間
星期一至星期五
上午十點到下午四點

170 分機號碼
104 球道預約
105 Brownie 咖啡廳
170 106 聯盟行政人員
107 聯盟最新消息

170 球隊可報名參加聯盟比賽，請在上班時間來電或臨櫃洽詢行政人員。

Global Bowl 歡迎輪椅使用者。
171-C 寵物禁入！

單字 □extension n. 內線，分機　　□reservation n. 預約　　□administrator n. 管理者
　　 □register for phr. 登錄～　　□league play phr. 聯盟比賽

169

Where would this brochure most likely be found?	這本小手冊最有可能在哪裡找到？
(A) At a recreational facility	(A) 在一個休閒娛樂設施
(B) At a community library	(B) 在一個社區圖書館
(C) At a sports arena	(C) 在一個運動場
(D) At a university clubhouse	(D) 在一個大學社團中心

■ 推論 整體細節 　　　　　　　　　　　　　　　　　　　　　　　　　　解答 (A)

要找出例文裡的所有線索，綜合起來再推論可能在哪裡看到小冊子。透過小冊子上端的 Nashville Eagles Bowling League 可以知道這是關於 Nashville Eagles 保齡球聯盟的內容。We are Southern Tennessee's oldest surviving bowling club 是在介紹南田納西州歷史最久遠的保齡球社團，之後說明球道時間、辦公時間及分機號碼等，可以推測這是在休閒娛樂場所看到的小冊子。因此 (A) At a recreational facility 為正確答案。

單字 arena n. 競技場

170

Which number should people dial to arrange for league play?	要安排聯盟比賽應該要打哪個分機號碼？
(A) 104	(A) 104
(B) 105	(B) 105
(C) 106	(C) 106
(D) 107	(D) 107

■ 六何原則 Which 　　　　　　　　　　　　　　　　　　　　　　　　　解答 (C)

這是在詢問如果要聯絡聯盟比賽應該要打哪一個（Which）分機號碼的六何原則問題。與問題的重點 dial to arrange for league play 相關的部分是 Extensions 裡寫到 106 League Administrator 聯盟行政人員的分機號碼，以及 Teams may register for league play by calling or visiting the administrator anytime during office hours. 表示參賽的隊伍要在辦公時間內打電話或臨櫃洽詢聯盟行政人員，所以 (C) 106 為正確答案。

171

What is stated about Global Bowl?	關於 Global Bowl，提示了什麼？
(A) It doesn't operate after midnight.	(A) 午夜之後不營業。
(B) It is the venue for a national competition.	(B) 是全國比賽的場地。
(C) Pets are allowed inside the premises.	(C) 寵物可以進入。
(D) Lanes are closed on some Wednesdays.	(D) 有些星期三球道會關閉。

■ Not/True True 問題 　　　　　　　　　　　　　　　　　　　　　　　解答 (D)

這是要先在例文中找出與問題的重點 Global Bowl 相關的部分，並與選項進行對照的 Not/True 問題。因為 Lane Hours 裡 Saturday 8 A.M. to 2 A.M. 是指星期六時球道從早上 8 點開到凌晨 2 點，所以 (A) 與例文內容不一致。(B) 是例文中沒有提及的內容。No pets allowed! 是指寵物不能進場，所以 (C) 也與例文內容不一致。Lane Hours 裡 Closed every other Wednesday 是指球道隔週三公休，所以 (D) 與例文內容一致。因此 (D) Lanes are closed on some Wednesday. 為正確答案。

單字 operate v. 營業，運營　national a. 全國性的，國家的　premises n. 營業場所，用地

172

What is NOT indicated about the bowling league?	關於保齡球聯盟，並未暗示什麼？
(A) It holds weekly meetings.	(A) 每週都有聚會。
(B) Children can play for free on weekends.	(B) 小孩在週末可以免費打球。
(C) It is sponsored by Global Bowl.	(C) 由 Global Bowl 贊助。
(D) Regular tournaments are held.	(D) 會定期舉辦比賽。

■ Not/True Not 問題 　　　　　　　　　　　　　　　　　　　　　　　解答 (B)

這是要先在例文中找出與問題的重點 Global Bowl 相關的部分，並與選項進行對照的 Not/True 問題。Club meetings are held every Thursday 是指社團聚會是在每週四舉行，因此 (A) 跟例文內容一致。(B) 是例文中沒有提到的內容，因此 (B) Children can play for free on weekends. 為正確答案。The Nashville Eagles thanks its sponsor, Global Bowl 是指對 Nashville Eagles 的贊助者 Global Bowl 表示感謝，所以 (C) 也與例文內容一致。League Tournaments, Wednesdays and Saturdays 跟 Open Tournaments, Second and third Sunday of the month 分別是說「每週三、六有聯盟比賽」、「每個月的第二和第三個星期日有公開比賽」，所以 (D) 也與例文內容一致。

Questions 173-175 refer to the following announcement.

173-175 根據下面的公告內容回答問題。

East Scholastic Institute

[173]East Scholastic Institute is inviting its graduates to the Grand Alumni Homecoming on Saturday, February 4, at 7 P.M., at the Marina Bay Hotel. The event will mark the anniversary of the founding of East Scholastic Institute and the establishment of East Scholastic Foundation.

Reunite with your classmates, friends, and professors while remembering old times. This is also the perfect opportunity to renew your commitment to your alma mater. [174]Support the plan to increase the institute's annual scholarship grants. East Scholastic Foundation will be sponsoring the education of at least 15 students every year through the help of the alumni association and other benefactors.

[175]The registration fee for the event is $250 and may be paid at the East Scholastic Institute Alumni Office. The funds raised at the event will serve as the foundation's startup fund. For more information, call the office at 555-7444 and ask for Melissa.

East Scholastic Institute

[173]East Scholastic Institute 邀請畢業生在 2 月 4 日星期六下午 7 點到 Marina Bay 飯店來參加盛大校友回校活動。這個活動除了慶祝 East Scholastic Institute 成立的週年，也要慶祝 East Scholastic Foundation 的成立。

和你的同窗同學、朋友和教授重聚，回首過去，這也是一個絕佳的機會讓你重溫對母校的承諾。[174]支持我們增加年度獎學金的計畫。East Scholastic Foundation 將會透過校友會和其他贊助者的幫助，每年至少提供獎學金給十五個學生。

[175]參加這次活動的報名費是美金 250 元，可以在 East Scholastic Institute 的校友辦公室付款。這個活動所募得的錢將會用於創建基金會的基金。更多詳情，請撥打 555-7444，洽 Melissa。

單字　□alumnus n. 校友（pl. alumni）　□mark v. 恭賀，紀念　□establishment n. 設立
　　　□foundation n. 基金會　□reunite v. 再次相遇　□commitment n. 承諾
　　　□alma mater phr. 母校　□annual a. 每年的，一年一次的　□scholarship n. 獎學金
　　　□sponsor v. 贊助，支援　□benefactor n. 贊助者　□raise v. 募集（人力或資金）
　　　□startup a. 著手的，開始的

173

For whom is the announcement intended?	這個公告的對象是誰？
(A) Faculty members	(A) 教職員
(B) Former students	(B) 以前的學生
(C) Administrative employees	(C) 行政職員
(D) Previous donors	(D) 以前的贊助者

■ 推論 整體細節　　　　　　　　　　　　　　　　　　　　　　　　　　　　　　解答 (B)

這是要推論公告對象的問題。East Scholastic Institute is inviting its graduates to the Grand Alumni Homecoming 是說 East Scholastic 學校邀請畢業生參加校友活動，所以可以推測這是以之前畢業的學生們做為對象所發布的公告，因此要選 (B) Former Students 為正確答案。

換句話說
graduates 畢業生 → Former student 以前的學生

單字 administrative a. 行政上的，管理上的　donor n. 捐款人

174

What is the goal of the foundation?	這個基金會的目標為何？
(A) To award scholarships	(A) 提供獎學金
(B) To train professors	(B) 訓練教授
(C) To keep alumni connected	(C) 讓校友保持聯絡
(D) To fund the institute's operations	(D) 為學校的運轉提供經費

■ 六何原則 What　　　　　　　　　　　　　　　　　　　　　　　　　　　解答 (A)

這是在詢問基金會的目標是什麼（What）的六何原則問題。要先在例文中找出與問題的重點 the goal of the foundation 相關的部分。Support the plan to increase the institute's annual scholarship grants. 是指透過這個計畫來支援學校每年的獎學金計畫，之後的 East Scholastic Foundation will be sponsoring the education of at least 15 students every year 是指 East Scholastic 基金會每年至少提供獎學金給 15 名學生，所以要選 (A) To awards students 為正確答案。

單字 award v. 給予，授予　fund v. 提供資金　operation n. 運營

175

How can readers register for the event?	閱讀公告的人如何報名這個活動？
(A) By sending a check payment	(A) 寄支票付款
(B) By contacting the alumni office	(B) 聯絡校友辦公室
(C) By coming by the institute	(C) 來學校
(D) By writing to Melissa	(D) 寫信給 Melissa

■ 六何原則 How　　　　　　　　　　　　　　　　　　　　　　　　　　　解答 (C)

這是在詢問看到公告的人如何（How）報名此活動的六何原則問題。在例文中找出與問題的重點 register for the event 相關的部分 The registration fee ~ may be paid at the East Scholastic Institute Alumni Office 是在說報名費要在 East Scholastic Institute 的校友會辦公室付款，所以要選 (C) By coming by the institute 為正確答案。

單字 register v. 登錄　check payment phr. 支票付款　come by phr. 訪問，進入

Antoinette Ricks, Manager, Fiesta Catering
78 Park Avenue, Detroit, MI 48206

Dear Ms. Ricks,

I am sending this letter to contest the billing charges for the catering service you provided for Zaider Corporation last Saturday night. During the occasion, my staff noticed that the buffet menu differed from the one included in the package we had selected. In particular, [176-A]the entrées were dishes included in Package B and not Package A, which is the more expensive menu. In spite of the error, your staff charged us the full price for Package A.

In addition, my guests were served only one round of soft drinks, even though [178-D]our contract states that drinks would be unlimited at no extra charge. If my memory serves me right, [177]you even told me that the upgrade was complimentary for regular clients, such as Zaider Corporation. [179]I mentioned this to your head waiter, but he indicated that he was not told to provide bottomless drinks. As a result, the additional soft drinks consumed that night were charged to my running total.

I am seriously disappointed with what happened. I request that you personally look into the matter, as [180]I will not submit my payment until [176-A]the excess costs of the entrées and extra charges for the drinks have been deducted from the total. A copy of our contract is enclosed for your reference.

I look forward to your immediate action on the matter.

Katherine Bailey, Sales Manager, Zaider Corporation

Fiesta 外燴公司經理 Antoinette Ricks
48206 密西根州底特律市 Park 大道 78 號

親愛的 Ricks 小姐：

我寄這封信來討論上星期六晚上你們為 Zaider 公司提供外燴服務的收費問題。在當天的活動裡，我的員工注意到自助餐的菜單和我們所選擇的套餐不一樣。特別是[176-A] 主菜是屬於 B 套餐，而不是價格較高的 A 套餐，儘管發生了這個錯誤，你們還是收取我們 A 套餐的全額價錢。

此外，你們只提供我的客人一次不含酒精的飲料，而[178-D] 我們的合約上註明飲料是無限制供應，也不會另外收費。如果我沒有記錯，[177] 你甚至告訴我這是給像是 Zaider 公司這種常客的禮遇。[179] 我告訴你們的服務生領班，但是他卻告訴我他沒有被告知要提供免費暢飲。因此，那晚多喝的不含酒精飲料全都被記在帳單上。

我很失望會發生這樣的事情。我要求你親自查辦這件事情，[176-A] 在多出來的主菜和飲料的費用沒有從帳單扣除之前，[180] 我是不會付款的。隨函附上我們的合約，以供你參考。

期待你立即處理這件事情。

Zaider 公司銷售經理 Katherine Bailey

單字　□contest v. 對～提出質疑　□catering n. 外燴服務　□occasion n. 活動
　　　□notice v. 注意　□differ v. 區別　□entrée n. 主餐
　　　□soft drink n. 無酒精飲料　□unlimited a. 無限制的　□complimentary a. 贈送的
　　　□bottomless a. 無限制的　□running total phr. 合計　□deduct v. 扣除
　　　□reference n. 參考，參照　□immediate a. 即時的

176

What does Ms. Bailey say about the services she was provided? (A) The charges are excessive. (B) The food selection was limited. (C) The catering staff was rude. (D) The guests were served late.	根據 Baily 小姐所説的，關於她得到的服務何者正確？ (A) 她被超收費用。 (B) 食物的選擇很有限。 (C) 外燴的員工很沒有禮貌。 (D) 客人很晚才被招待。

■ **Not/True** True 問題　　　　　　　　　　　　　　　　　　　　　　　　　　解答 (A)

這是要先在例文中找出與問題的重點 the service she was provided 相關，而且是寄件者 Ms. Bailey 所言及的內容，並與選項進行對照的 Not/True 問題。the entrées were dishes included in Package B and not Package A, which is the more expensive menu. In spite of the error, your staff charged us the full price for Package A. 是說主菜是屬於 B 套餐，而不是比較貴的 A 套餐，儘管發生了這個錯誤，員工還是收了 A 套餐的全額，之後的 the excess costs of the entrees and extra charges for the drinks 則提到多出來的主菜與飲料費用，所以 (A) 與例文的內容一致，因此要選 (A) The charges are excessive. 為正確答案。(B) (C) (D) 都是例文中沒有提及的內容。

單字 excessive a. 過度的

177

What is indicated about Zaider Corporation? (A) It violated the terms of its contract. (B) It will hold its next event at a restaurant. (C) It has hired Fiesta Catering before. (D) It chose few main courses for the party.	關於 Zaider 公司，暗示了什麼？ (A) 違反了合約上的條款。 (B) 下一個活動會在一家餐廳舉辦。 (C) 以前雇用過 Fiesta 外燴公司。 (D) 為派對選擇極少的主菜。

■ **推論** 詳細內容　　　　　　　　　　　　　　　　　　　　　　　　　　　　解答 (C)

這是要針對問題中的重點 Zaider Corporation 進行推論的問題。you even told me that the upgrade was complimentary for regular clients, such as Zaider Corporation 是指 Fiesta Catering 公司曾提到這是給像是 Zaider Corporation 這種常客的免費優待，所以可以推論出 Zaider Corporation 在之前也曾經找過 Fiesta Catering 公司辦理類似服務。因此 (C) It has hired Fiesta Catering before. 為正確答案。

單字 violate v. 違反　　term n. 條件

178

According to Ms. Bailey, what did Ms. Ricks mention about the drinks? (A) They would be served in small quantities. (B) They are not included in the package. (C) They are limited to juices and other non-alcoholic beverages. (D) They would be available throughout the event at no extra cost.	根據 Baily 小姐所説，Ricks 小姐對飲料一事説過什麼？ (A) 可以用小份量的方式來提供給客人。 (B) 沒有包括在套餐中。 (C) 僅限於果汁和其他不含酒精的飲料。 (D) 可以在活動中暢飲而不多收費用。

■ **Not/True** True 問題　　　　　　　　　　　　　　　　　　　　　　　　　解答 (D)

這是要先在例文中找出與問題的重點 Ms. Ricks 相關的部分，並與選項進行對照的 Not/True 問題。(A) (B) (C) 是例文中沒有提及的內容。our contract states that drinks would be unlimited at no extra charge 是指 Ms. Bailey 與 Ms. Ricks 所簽的合約中提到飲料是無限制供應也不另外收費的，所以要選 (D) They would be available throughout the event at no extra cost. 為正確答案。

單字 quantity n. 量　　limit v. 限制　　beverage n. 飲料

Why did the waiter refuse to recognize the agreement between Ms. Ricks and Ms. Bailey?	為什麼服務生拒絕履行 Ricks 小姐和 Baily 小姐間的合約？
(A) The catering service does not normally serve complimentary drinks.	(A) 外燴服務通常不提供免費招待的飲料。
(B) He was not given specific instructions to do so.	(B) 他沒有被特別告知要這麼做。
(C) He failed to contact Ms. Ricks and verify the contract.	(C) 他無法聯絡到 Ricks 小姐來確認合約內容。
(D) There was an inadequate supply of beverages.	(D) 飲料不夠供應。

■ 六何原則 Why   解答 (B)

這是在詢問為什麼（Why）服務生拒絕履行 Ms. Ricks 和 Ms. Baily 間合約的六何原則問題。要先在例文中找出與問題的重點 the waiter refuse to recognize the agreement 相關的部分。I mentioned this to your head waiter, but he indicate that he was not told to provide bottomless drinks. 是說 Ms. Baily 詢問服務生領班提到飲料供應的問題，但服務生領班卻說沒有被告知要提供免費暢飲，所以要選 (B) He was not given specific instructions to do so. 為正確答案。

單字 recognize v. 承認　agreement n. 協議　inadequate a. 不充足的

What does Ms. Bailey plan to do?	Baily 小姐打算要怎麼做？
(A) Meet Ms. Ricks	(A) 和 Ricks 小姐會面
(B) Withhold payment	(B) 暫不付款
(C) Demand an apology	(C) 要求一個道歉
(D) Submit a legal complaint	(D) 提出一個法律的申訴

■ 六何原則 What   解答 (B)

這是在詢問 Ms. Baily 接下來計畫做什麼（What）事的六何原則問題。要先在例文中找出與問題的重點 Ms. Baily plan to do 相關的部分。I will not submit my payment until excess costs of the entrées and extra charges for the drinks have been deducted from the total 是指在多出來的主菜跟飲料費用沒有被扣除之前，她不會付款。所以可以知道 (B) Withhold payment 為正確答案。

換句話說
not submit ~ payment 沒有支付費用 →Withhold payment 費用保留

單字 withhold v. 保留，不給～　demand v. 要求　submit v. 提交　legal a. 合法的，法律的

Questions 181-185 refer to the following article and e-mail.

Cuelebre Business Journal   Page 12

PERCHTA APPOINTS NEW CHIEF OPERATING OFFICER

VIENNA, February 4 - Perchta Incorporated, one of Austria's largest department store chains, recently named former vice president for operations Leonie Gruber as its new chief operating officer. Ms. Gruber replaced Johann Müller, who retired on January 28 after 35 years of service to the company.

In her new post, Ms. Gruber will be responsible for all of Perchta's day-to-day sales, marketing, and service operations. She will also play a key role in developing strategic retailer-supplier relationships, which will ensure Perchta's flexibility in the constantly changing marketplace.

Ms. Gruber has more than 20 years of experience in operations management and strategic communications. Since [183-C]she joined Perchta as a marketing supervisor 12 years ago, she has been instrumental in securing the company's position as an industry leader.

"I believe Perchta has the potential to become one of Europe's premier retail chains." [181]Ms. Gruber said during a telephone interview. "As [182-A/184]we open our first overseas branch in Argentina in June, I look forward to contributing to our company's continued success."

[181]Reported by Franz Heideck

To: Franz Heideck <heideck@cuelebrebizjourn.at>
From: Esther Schwarz <esther158@bibelotphotography.at>
Date: February 5
Subject: Leonie Gruber article

Hi Franz,

As you know, I've been organizing a portrait photo exhibit of some of the country's most successful business executives. I read your article yesterday about Leonie Gruber's recent promotion at Perchta Incorporated, and [185]I was wondering if you could give me her phone number and e-mail address. I'm interested in featuring her as a subject in [184]my exhibit, which will be launched in the same month that Perchta's Argentine branch opens.

Thanks, and I hope you can accommodate my request.

Esther Schwarz

Cuelebre 商業雜誌   第十二頁

PERCHTA 公司任命新的首席營運長

維也納，2 月 4 日 – Perchta 公司是奧地利最大的連鎖百貨公司之一，最近任命前任營運副總裁 Leonie Gruber 為新任的首席營運長。Gruber 女士接替在該公司服務三十五年，於 1 月 28 日退休的 Johann Müller。

在這一新的職位上，Gruber 女士將負責所有 Perchta 公司的每日銷售、行銷和服務運作。她還會在零售商與供應商之間的策略發展關係扮演關鍵角色，以確保 Perchta 公司在不斷變化的市場上能靈活運作。

Gruber 女士在營運管理和策略性溝通上有超過二十年的經驗，自從[183-C]她十二年前加入 Perchta 公司擔任行銷主管以來，她對確保公司在此行業的龍頭寶座貢獻良多。

[181]Gruber 女士在一次電話訪問中提到：「我相信 Perchta 公司有潛力成為歐洲首屈一指的零售連鎖店，隨著[182-A/184]我們六月在阿根廷成立第一家海外分店，我期盼為公司持續的成功奉獻心力。」

[181]Franz Heideck 報導

收件人：Franz Heideck <helideck@cuelebrebizjour.at>
寄件人：Esther Schwarz <esther158@bibelotphotography.at>
日期：2 月 5 日
主旨：Leonie Gruber 的文章

Franz 你好：

如同你所知道的，我一直在籌備一個關於國內一些頂尖企業家的攝影展。昨天讀了你關於最近 Leonie Gruber 在 Perchta 公司受到擢升的文章後，[185]我想知道你是否可以給我她的電話號碼和電郵地址。我有興趣將她納為我展覽的主題之一，[184]我這個展覽會在他們阿根廷分店開幕的同一個月開始。

謝謝你，我希望你能答應我的請求。

Esther Schwarz

例文 1 單字 □appoint v. 指名，任命　□name v. 指名，任命　□replace v. 取代
　　　　　　□retire v. 退休，退隱　□post n. 職位，職責　□strategic a. 策略性的
　　　　　　□ensure v. 保障　　　　□flexibility n. 柔軟性，靈活性　□constantly ad. 無止盡地
　　　　　　□instrumental a. 有幫助的　□secure v. 把～弄牢，確保　□potential n. 潛能
　　　　　　□premier a. 最好的　　□overseas a. 海外的　□contribute v. 捐獻

例文 2 單字 □portrait n. 人物照，肖像畫　□exhibit n. 展覽　□executive n. 管理人，執行者
　　　　　　□promotion n. 升遷　　□launch v. 開始　□accommodate v. 聽從，接納

181

What is suggested about Mr. Heideck?	關於 Heideck 先生，提示了什麼？
(A) He works for a daily newspaper.	(A) 他在一家日報工作。
(B) He interviewed Ms. Gruber for an article.	(B) 他為了一篇文章訪談 Gruber 女士。
(C) He has met Ms. Schwarz before.	(C) 他和 Schwarz 小姐從前見過面。
(D) He is unable to provide some contact information.	(D) 他無法提供一些聯絡資訊。

■ 推論 詳細內容　　　　　　　　　　　　　　　　　　　　　　　　　　　　　解答 (B)

這是要針對問題的重點 Mr. Heideck 進行推論的問題。所以要先從 Mr. Heideck 親自寫的例文 1 中尋找線索。透過 Reported by Franz Heideck 可以知道 Mr. Heideck 寫了這篇新聞。Ms. Gruber said during a telephone interview 是指 Ms. Gruber 在電話訪問裡說了些事情的意思，所以我們可以推論 Mr. Heideck 訪問了 Ms. Gruber，因此正確答案是 (B) He interviewed Ms. Gruber for an article.。

182

What is mentioned about Perchta Incorporated?	關於 Perchta 公司，提到了什麼？
(A) It plans to open a new store abroad.	(A) 計畫在海外成立一家新分店。
(B) It is renovating its headquarters.	(B) 正在重新整修總部。
(C) It will offer more product lines in all its stores.	(C) 將會在所有店裡提供更多的產品。
(D) It has temporarily stopped hiring new personnel.	(D) 目前暫停招聘新人。

■ Not/True True 問題　　　　　　　　　　　　　　　　　　　　　　　　　解答 (A)

這是要先在例文中找出與問題的重點 Perchta Incorporated 相關的部分，並與選項進行對照的 Not/True 問題，所以要透過例文 1 尋找與 Perchta 公司相關的內容。we open our first overseas branch in Argentina in June 是指 Perchta 公司六月在阿根廷開設第一個海外分店，因此 (A) 與例文內容一致，所以要選 (A) It plans to open a new store abroad. 為正確答案。

換句話說

open ~ overseas branch 開設海外分店 → open a new store abroad 在國外開設新分店

單字 renovate v. 修理，改造　headquarters n. 總公司，總部　temporarily ad. 短暫地　personnel n. 職員

183

What is stated about Ms. Gruber?	關於 Gruber 女士，提到了什麼？
(A) She organized a retirement party for Mr. Müller.	(A) 她為 Müller 先生辦了一個退休派對。
(B) She will be stationed at a branch in Argentina.	(B) 她將會被派駐在阿根廷的分店。
(C) She first held a marketing position at Perchta.	(C) 她最早在 Perchta 公司擔任市場行銷的工作。
(D) She has agreed to meet with Ms. Schwarz.	(D) 她答應要和 Schwarz 小姐會面。

■ Not/True True 問題　　　　　　　　　　　　　　　　　　　　　　　　　解答 (C)

這是要先在例文中找出與問題的重點 Ms. Gruber 相關的部分，並與選項進行對照的 Not/True 問題。(A) (B) (D) 是例文中沒有提及的內容。she joined Perchta as a marketing supervisor 12 years ago 是指 Ms. Gruber 十二年前加入 Perchta 公司擔任行銷主管，因為 (C) 與例文內容一致，所以要選 (C) She first held a marketing position at Perchta. 為正確答案。

單字 organize v. 準備，組織　retirement n. 退休，隱退　station v. 配置，部署　hold v. 承擔，主辦

184	
When will Ms. Schwarz launch her photo exhibit? (A) In January (B) In February (C) In May (D) In June	Schwarz 小姐何時要開始她的展覽？ (A) 一月 (B) 二月 (C) 五月 (D) 六月

■ 六何原則 連結問題　　　　　　　　　　　　　　　　　　　　　　　　　　　　解答 (D)

這是要綜合兩篇例文才能解題的連結問題。問題的重點 Ms. Schwarz launch her photo exhibit 是要問 Ms. Schwarz 什麼時候（When）要舉行攝影展，所以要 Ms. Schwarz 所寫的例文 2 中尋找線索。

例文 2 中提到 my exhibit, which will be launched in the same month that Perchta's Argentina branch opens，是說 Ms. Schwarz 的展覽會與 Perchta 公司的阿根廷分公司開幕在同個月分舉辦，所以可以把這當作第一個線索。但是由於例文 2 中沒有說明 Perchta 公司阿根廷分公司在何時開幕，所以要透過例文 1 新聞才會知道。例文 1 中提到 we open our first overseas branch in Argentina in June 指出 Perchta 公司阿根廷分公司將在六月開幕，而這便是第二個線索。

線索一：在 Perchta 公司阿根廷分公司開幕的月份，會舉行 Ms. Schwarz 的攝影展、線索二：Perchta 公司阿根廷分公司將在六月開幕。透過綜合兩個線索，我們可以知道 Ms. Schwarz 的攝影展將在六月舉辦，因此要選 (D) In June 為正確答案。

185	
What does Ms. Schwarz request from Mr. Heideck? (A) Perchta's mailing address (B) Ms. Gruber's contact information (C) A copy of his article (D) Details on the Argentine branch	Schwarz 小姐對 Heideck 先生的請求為何？ (A) Perchta 公司的郵寄地址 (B) Gruber 女士的聯絡資訊 (C) 他文章的一份複本 (D) 阿根廷分店的詳細資料

■ 六何原則 What　　　　　　　　　　　　　　　　　　　　　　　　　　　　　解答 (B)

這是在問 Ms. Schwarz 向 Mr. Heideck 詢問什麼（What）的六何原則問題。所以要從問題的重點 Ms. Schwarz 所寫的例文 2 尋找線索。例文 2 中寫到 I was wondering if you could give me her phone number and e-mail address 是 Ms. Schwarz 向 Mr. Heideck 詢問她，也就是 Ms. Gruber 的電話號碼及電子郵件地址，所以 (B) Ms. Gruber's contact information 為正確答案。

換句話說
phone number and e-mail address 電話號碼與電子郵件地址 → contact information 聯絡方法

Questions **186-190** refer to the following itinerary and e-mail.

186-190 根據下面的文章和電郵內容回答問題。

例文 1

PRAHA EXPRESS
Your No. 1 Express Train Across Czech Republic!

Customer Name: Jakob Ginsberg
Reservation No.: 20385446
186-BType of Ticket: Round-trip
Date of Booking: July 21

Train No.	Departure			189Arrival		
	Station	Date	Time	Station	Date	Time
JW 8121	Prague	August 16	5:50 A.M.	Ekaterinburg	August 17	8:10 A.M.
186-CStopover Time: 1 hour						
JW 0993	Ekaterinburg	August 17	9:10 A.M.	189Kiev	August 17	7:40 P.M.
JW 1476	Kiev	August 23	4:30 P.M.	Ekaterinburg	August 24	3:00 A.M.
Stopover Time: 1 hour						
JW 5074	Ekaterinburg	August 24	4:00 A.M.	Prague	August 25	6:20 A.M.

186-APlease present a copy of this document to the ticketing desk at the station. Customers are advised to check in at least 40 minutes prior to their scheduled departure. 186-DShould you wish to make a change to your itinerary, please contact our customer service department no later than 10 days before your departure date. 187-AA fee of €45 must be paid for changes or cancellations.

Starting September 1, 187-BPraha Express' free luggage allowance for each passenger will change from three to two bags. A flat rate of €25 per bag will be applied to any additional luggage.

PRAHA 快車
遍遊捷克共和國的快車首選

乘客姓名：Jakob Ginsberg
預約號碼：20385446
186-B 車票類形：來回票
訂票日期：7 月 21 日

班次	出發			189 抵達		
	站名	日期	時間	站名	日期	時間
JW 8121	Prague	8 月 16日	上午 5:50	Ekaterinburg	8 月 17日	上午 8:10
180-C 中途停留時間：一小時						
JW 0993	Ekaterinburg	8 月 17日	上午 9:10	189Kiev	8 月 17日	下午 7:40
JW 1476	Kiev	8 月 23日	下午 4:30	Ekaterinburg	8 月 24日	上午 3:00
中途停留時間：一小時						
JW 5074	Ekaterinburg	8 月 24日	上午 4:00	Prague	8 月 25日	上午 6:20

186-A 請在車站的票務台出示這份文件，建議乘客在列車出發時間前至少四十分鐘報到。186-D 如果你想要改變行程，請於出發日期前十天與我們的客戶服務部門聯絡。187-A 取消或改票會收取四十五歐元的費用。

從 9 月 1 日起，187-BPraha 快車允許每位乘客攜帶的免付費行李從三件改為兩件。多出來的每一件行李一律收取二十五歐元的費用。

例文 2

To: Jakob Ginsberg <jakobg@checkmail.com>
From: Barbora Kodetova <b.kodetova@prahaex.cz>
Date: August 3
Subject: Itinerary Update

Dear Mr. Ginsberg,

188/189We would like to let you know that your train to Kiev will arrive at its destination an hour early on August 17. This is because there will no longer be a stopover at the Ekaterinburg station contrary to what was shown in your original itinerary. So, the train departing from Prague will travel nonstop to Kiev. The schedule for your return trip to Prague, on the other hand, will remain the same.

收件人：Jakob Ginsberg
　　　　<jakobg@checkmail.com>
寄件人：Barbora Kodetova
　　　　<b.kodetova@prahaex.cz>
日期：8 月 3 日
主旨：行程更新

親愛的 Ginsberg 先生：

188/189我們想讓你知道你到 Kiev 的火車將會在八月十七日提早一小時抵達目的地。這是因為這班列車不會如行程表上所顯示的在 Ekaterinburg 站停留。所以，從 Prague 出發的火車會直接開往 Kiev 而不會中途停留。不過，回程到 Prague 的火車行程則沒有改變。

[Left column] [190]Please respond to this e-mail to confirm receipt of this information. Once we hear back from you, we will send you another e-mail with your finalized itinerary. Thanks for your cooperation.

Barbora Kodetova
Customer Service
Praha Express

[Right column] [190] 請回覆這封電郵，讓我們知道你已經收到這個訊息。一旦我們得到你的確認，我們會寄給你確認後的行程，謝謝你的合作。

Barbora Kodetova
客戶服務
Praha 快車

例文 1 單字
□reservation n. 預約　　□booking n. 預約　　□itinerary n. 旅行行程
□departure n. 出發　　□arrival n. 抵達　　□stopover n. 滯留，中途停留
□present v. 出示　　□document n. 文件　　□advise v. 建議，勸導
□check in phr. 辦理搭乘手續　　□prior to phr. 在～之前，～前　　□no later than phr. 不能夠晚於～
□luggage n. 行李　　□allowance n. 限額　　□flat rate phr. 固定費率
□additional a. 額外的

例文 2 單字
□destination n. 目的地　　□contrary to phr. 與～不同　　□nonstop ad. 中途未停靠，直達
□receipt n. 收信，收件　　□cooperation n. 協助，協力

186

What is NOT indicated about the itinerary?
(A) It must be shown to an agent when checking in.
(B) It contains details for a two-way journey.
(C) It includes an overnight stopover.
(D) It may be changed up to ten days before departure.

關於這份行程，並未暗示什麼？
(A) 報到時一定要向員工出示這份行程。
(B) 包括了去程與回程的詳細資料。
(C) 包括過夜的中途停留。
(D) 在出發十天前可做改變。

Not/True Not 問題　　　　　　　　　　　　　　　　　　解答 (C)

這是在例文中找到與問題的重點 the itinerary 相關的內容後，比較選項與例文的 Not/True 問題，先從例文 1 開始尋找線索。Please present a copy of this document to ticketing desk at the station 是請在車站票務台出示這份文件，因此 (A) 與例文內容一致。Type of Ticket: Round-trip 可以看出旅程是來回的，而後文也提到接下來的旅行計畫，所以 (B) 也與例文內容一致。Stopover Time: 1 hour 是指中途停留 1 小時，所以可以知道 (C) It includes an overnight stopover. 與例文內容不符，因此要選 (C) 為正確答案。Should you wish to make a change to your itinerary, please contact our customer service department no later than 10 days before your departure date. 是指如果想要改變行程，請於出發日期前十天與客戶服務部門聯絡，因此 (D) 也與例文內容相符。

換句話說
Round-trip 往返 → a two-way journey 來回旅行

單字 agent n. 職員　contain v. 包含　two-way a. 來回的，雙方的　overnight a. 一夜的，一夜之間的

187

What is indicated about Praha Express?
(A) It allows passengers to make changes for free.
(B) It will reduce its free luggage allowance.
(C) It plans to expand its list of destinations.
(D) It sells tickets on a Web site.

關於 Praha 快車，暗示了什麼？
(A) 乘客可以免費改票。
(B) 將減少免付費的行李件數。
(C) 將擴增列車到達的目的地。
(D) 在網路上賣票。

Not/True True 問題　　　　　　　　　　　　　　　　　解答 (B)

這是在例文中找到與問題的重點 Praha Express 相關的內容後，比較選項與例文的 Not/True 問題，先從例文 1，Praha Express 公司發行的行程表開始尋找線索。A fee of €45 must be paid for changes or cancellations. 是指取消或更改車票都會收取四十五歐元的費用，所以 (A) 與例文內容並不一致。Praha Express' free luggage allowance for each passenger will change from three to two bags 是指 Praha Express 的免付費行李從三件改為兩件，所以 (B) It will reduce its free luggage allowance 為正確答案。(C) 跟 (D) 都是例文中沒有提及的內容。

單字 reduce v. 減少　expand v. 擴大，擴張

188		
Why did Ms. Kodetova write to Mr. Ginsberg?		為什麼 Kodetova 小姐寫信給 Ginsberg 先生？
(A) To recommend a travel agency		(A) 建議一家旅行社
(B) To verify his flight information		(B) 確認班機資訊
(C) To inform him of a modification		(C) 通知他一項改變
(D) To notify him of new ticket prices		(D) 告知新的票價

■ 找出主題 寫文章的理由　　　　　　　　　　　　　　　　　　　　　　　　　　解答 (C)

這是找出主題的問題，詢問 Ms. Kodetova 寫電子郵件給 Mr. Ginsberg 的理由。因此先透過例文 2，Ms. Kodetova 寫的郵件尋找相關內容。郵件中提到 We would like to let you know that your train to Kiev will arrive at its destination an hour early on August 17. 是指往 Kiev 的火車將會在 8 月 17 日提早一小時抵達目的地，所以要選 (C) To inform him of a modification 為正確答案。

單字 recommend v. 推薦　travel agency phr. 旅行社　verify v. 確認　modification n. 變更

189		
When will Mr. Ginsberg arrive in Kiev?		Ginsberg 先生何時會抵達 Kiev？
(A) At 4:30 P.M.		(A) 下午四點半
(B) At 6:40 P.M.		(B) 下午六點四十分
(C) At 7:40 P.M.		(C) 下午七點四十分
(D) At 8:10 P.M.		(D) 下午八點十分

■ 六何原則 連結問題　　　　　　　　　　　　　　　　　　　　　　　　　　　　解答 (B)

這是要綜合兩篇例文才能解題的連結問題。問題的重點 Mr. Ginsberg arrive in Kiev 是問 Mr. Ginsberg 什麼時候（When）會到達 Kiev，所以要從例文 2，Mr. Ginsberg 寫的電子郵件開始看。

例文 2 的郵件中寫到 We would like to let you know that your train to Kiev will arrive at its destination an hour early on August 17. 是指往 Kiev 的火車將會在 8 月 17 日提早一小時抵達目的地，這是第一個線索。但是由於例文 2 中沒有提到原本預計的到達時間，所以要到例文 1 中找相關內容。例文 1 行程表中寫到 Arrival: Kiev, August 17, 7:40 P.M. 是指列車預計到達時間為晚間 7 點 40 分，這是第二個線索。

綜合第一個線索：往 Kiev 的火車將會在 8 月 17 日提早一小時抵達目的地，與第二個線索：列車原本預計到達時間為晚間 7 點 40 分，我們可以推算出 Mr. Ginsberg 會在晚間 6 點 40 分到達 Kiev。因此 (B) At 6:40 P.M. 為正確答案。

190		
What will Mr. Ginsberg most likely do?		Ginsberg 先生最有可能做什麼？
(A) Make a phone call		(A) 打一通電話
(B) Contact the Kiev station		(B) 和 Kiev 站聯絡
(C) Post an office notice		(C) 張貼辦公室告示
(D) Reply to an e-mail		(D) 回覆電郵

■ 推論 詳細內容　　　　　　　　　　　　　　　　　　　　　　　　　　　　　　解答 (D)

這是要針對問題的重點 Mr. Ginsberg 進行推論的問題，因此從例文 2，Mr. Ginsberg 所寫的郵件開始尋找相關內容。Please respond to this e-mail to confirm receipt of this information. 是指「請回覆這封電郵，讓我們知道你已經收到這個訊息。」所以我們可以推論接下來 Mr. Ginsberg 將回覆此郵件，因此要選 (D) Reply to an e-mail 為正確答案。

單字 post v. 公告，發布

Questions 191-195 refer to the following e-mails.

例文1

To: evan.bearden@avesmail.com
From: sales@raptorconstructionsupplies.com

Date: August 8
Subject: Purchase Confirmation No. 10039

Dear Mr. Bearden,

[191]Thank you for using Raptor Construction Supplies' online order form. [195]Below is the list of items you ordered on August 7.

PRODUCT NO.	DETAILS	UNIT PRICE	QTY.	AMOUNT
CT6311	Condor all-weather clay tile	$3.10/ sq. ft.	2,000	$6,200.00
BG4570	Falcon black utility pipe (16")	$54.75/ piece	4	$219.00
[194]RN1907	Eagle stainless steel roofing nails (5-lb box)	$35.49/ box	5	$177.45
GM7496	Vulture extra-strength stain remover	$73.99/ gallon	2	$147.98
SP3884	Osprey aluminum siding attachments (box of 8)	$6.82/ box	10	$68.20

Sub-total	$6,812.63
Tax	$681.26
[192-B] Shipping and Handling	$340.63
TOTAL	**$7,834.52**

Based on our records, you paid 30 percent of the total amount with your credit card. Please be reminded that your outstanding balance must be paid in full before we can ship your order. Deliveries will arrive 3 to 5 days after payment has been received. In addition to credit cards, other acceptable payment methods are cash, check, money order, and bank transfer.

Please do not hesitate to call our customer service hotline if you have any questions or concerns. Once again, thank you for your purchase.

191-195 根據下面的電郵內容回答問題。

收件人：evan.bearden@avesmail.com
寄件人：sales@raptorconstructionsupplies.com
日期：8 月 8 日
主旨：購買確認號碼 10039

親愛的 Bearden 先生：

[191] 謝謝你採用 Raptor 建築材料公司的線上訂購單，[195] 以下是你 8 月 7 日訂購的品項。

產品號碼	說明	單價	數量	總價
CT6311	Condor 四季陶瓦	$3.10/ 平方呎	2000	$6200.00
BG4570	Falcon 黑色輸水管（16 吋）	$54.75/ 件	4	$219.00
[194]RN1907	Eagle 不鏽鋼屋頂釘（五磅盒裝）	$35.49/ 盒	5	$177.45
GM7496	Vulture 加強型污漬去除劑	$73.99/ 加侖	2	$147.98
SP3884	Osprey 鋁製滑動附件（八件盒裝）	$6.82/ 盒	10	$68.20

小計	$6812.63
稅金	$681.26
[192-B] 物流處理費	$340.63
總計	**$7834.52**

根據我們的紀錄，你用信用卡付了百分之三十的金額，請注意，尚未付清的餘額必須在我們運送你的訂單之前全額付清，在收到貨款後的三到五天，你就能收到貨品。除了信用卡之外，我們也接受現金、支票、匯票和銀行轉帳。

如果你有任何問題，不要客氣，請與我們的客戶服務熱線聯絡。再一次感謝您的光顧。

例文 2

To: sales@raptorconstructionsupplies.com
From: evan.bearden@avesmail.com
Date: August 9
Subject: Re: Purchase Confirmation No. 10039

Thank you for sending me the purchase confirmation. All the details are accurate, but [194]I would like to request three more boxes of product number RN1907. In addition, I want to inquire whether your shipment of the Hawk fiber cement siding cutters has already arrived. [195]The cutters were sold out on the day I made the order online for the other items, so I called your customer service department and was informed that the shipment was scheduled for today. If it has been received, please include two of the cutters in my order and send me a revised invoice. That way, I can pay the balance by bank transfer as soon as possible.

Evan Bearden

收件人：sales@raptorconstructionsupplies.com
寄件人：evan.bearden@avesmail.com
日期：8 月 9 日
主旨：回覆：購買確認號碼 10039

謝謝你寄來的購買確認信。所有的細節都正確無誤，[194] 但是我想要多買三盒編號 RN1907 的產品。此外，我想詢問 Hawk 水泥纖維板切割器是否已經到貨，[195] 我那天在線上訂購其他商品時，這個切割器缺貨，所以我電洽你們的客戶服務部門，被告知今天會到貨，如果已經到貨了，請你在我的訂單上加上兩個切割器，然後寄給我新的發貨單，如此一來，我可以盡速用銀行轉帳來付款。

Evan Bearden

例文 1 單字
- □ purchase n. 購買
- □ clay n. 黏土
- □ stain n. 瑕疵
- □ outstanding a. 未償付的
- □ acceptable a. 可以接受的，值得接受的
- □ bank transfer phr. 銀行轉帳
- □ confirmation n. 確認
- □ utility pipe phr. 水管
- □ siding n. 牆板
- □ balance n. 餘額
- □ hesitate v. 猶豫
- □ all-weather a. 全天候的
- □ stainless a. 無瑕疵的，不銹的
- □ attachment n. 附屬物
- □ ship v. 配送
- □ money order phr. 郵政匯票
- □ concern n. 關心，問題

例文 2 單字
- □ accurate a. 正確的
- □ revise v. 修正
- □ inquire v. 提問，問
- □ shipment n. 配送，輸送

191

Why was the first e-mail written?
(A) To provide feedback on a report
(B) To verify changes to an account
(C) To confirm an online purchase
(D) To give service recommendations

為什麼寫第一封電郵？
(A) 提供對一份報告的回饋
(B) 確認一個帳戶的變更
(C) 確認一次線上的購物
(D) 提供服務建議

■ 找出主題 寫文章的理由   解答 (C)

因為這是問寫例文 1 的理由，所以要從例文 1 開始確認相關內容。Thank you for using Raptor Construction Supplies' online order form. Below is the list of items you ordered on August 7. 是指「謝謝你採用 Raptor 建築材料公司的線上訂購單，以下是你 8 月 7 日訂購的品項。」所以要選 (C) To confirm an online purchase 為正確答案。

單字 provide v. 提供，給 feedback n. 回饋 account n. 帳號，帳戶 confirm v. 確認

192

What is indicated about Raptor Construction Supplies?
(A) It manufactures its own products.
(B) It charges extra for shipping fees.
(C) It has several branches around the state.
(D) It provides discounts for large orders.

關於 Raptor 建築材料供應公司，暗示了什麼？
(A) 製造自己的產品。
(B) 收取額外的運費。
(C) 在該州有多個分店。
(D) 給大訂單折扣。

■ **Not/True** True 問題   解答 (B)

本題是要在例文中找到與本問題的重點 Raptor Construction Supplies 相關的內容後，比較選項與例文的 Not/True 問題，所以要先從例文 1，有提到 Raptor Construction Supplies 的電子郵件中尋找線索。(A) (C) (D) 都是例文中沒有提及的內容。Shipping and Handling $340.63 是指物流處理費為$340.63 美元，所以 (B) 與例文內容一致，要選 (B) It charges extra for shipping fees. 為正確答案。

單字 manufacture v. 製造　charge extra (for) phr. 額外收費

193

In the first e-mail, the word "outstanding" in paragraph 2, line 2 is closest in meaning to (A) unpaid (B) incredible (C) complete (D) separated	在第一封電郵中，第二段第二行 outstanding 這個字的意思，最接近哪一個字？ (A) 尚未付款 (B) 難以置信 (C) 完整的 (D) 分開的

■ 同義詞   解答 (A)

在例文 1 中有包含 outstanding 的句子 outstanding balance must be paid in full 裡，outstanding 的意思是「尚未付清的」的意思，因此，要選擇同樣有「尚未付清的」的意思的 (A) unpaid 為正確答案。

194

Which item does Mr. Bearden want to increase the quantity of? (A) Clay tiles (B) Aluminum siding (C) Roofing nails (D) Utility pipe	Bearden 先生想要增購哪一項產品？ (A) 陶瓦 (B) 鋁製牆板 (C) 屋頂釘 (D) 水管

■ 六何原則 連結問題   解答 (C)

這是要綜合兩篇例文才能解題的連結問題。問題的重點 item ~ Mr. Bearden want to increase the quantity of 是問 Mr. Bearden 想要增加訂購數量的是哪一項（Which）產品，所以要從例文 2，Mr. Bearden 寫的電子郵件開始看。

例文 2 的郵件中寫到 I would like to request three more boxes of product number RN1907 是指要多訂購三箱編號 RN1907 的產品，這是第一個線索。因為在例文 2 裡沒有提到編號 RN1907 是什麼產品，所以要到例文 1 中尋找相關的內容。例文 1 中提到 RN1907, Eagles stainless steel roofing nails 是指 Eagle 不鏽鋼屋頂釘，這是第二個線索。

綜合第一個線索：要多訂購三箱編號 RN1907 的產品，與第二個線索：RN1907 是指 Eagle 不鏽鋼屋頂釘，我們可以知道 Mr. Bearden 想要增加訂購數量的是 Eagle 不鏽鋼屋頂釘，所以要選 (C) Roof nails 為正確答案。

單字 quantity n. 數量，量

What is suggested about Mr. Bearden?	關於 Bearden 先生，提示了什麼？
(A) He wants the items delivered at an earlier time.	(A) 他想要貨品早一點運到。
(B) He was unable to buy some items on August 7.	(B) 他在 8 月 7 日無法買到一些商品。
(C) He is asking for a discount on his total purchase.	(C) 他要求給他的訂單一些折扣。
(D) He paid the full amount by credit card.	(D) 他用信用卡全額付款。

■ 推論 連結問題　　　　　　　　　　　　　　　　　　　　　　　解答 (B)

這是要綜合兩篇例文才能開始推論的連結問題。問題的重點是 Mr. Bearden，所以要從例文 2，Mr. Bearden 寫的電子郵件開始看。

例文 2 的郵件中寫到 The cutters were sold out on the day I made the order online for the other items 是指那天在線上訂購其他商品時，切割器缺貨，這是第一個線索。但是例文 2 中沒有提到線上訂購其他商品的日期，所以可以在例文 1 中尋找相關的內容。例文 1 的郵件中寫到 Below is the list of items you ordered on August 7. 是指以下是在 8 月 7 日訂購的品項，所以可以知道線上訂購商品的日期是 8 月 7 日，這是第二個線索。

綜合第一個線索：那天在線上訂購其他商品時，切割器缺貨，與第二個線索：線上訂購商品的日期是 8 月 7 日，我們可以得知 Mr. Bearden 在 8 月 7 日時無法購買某物品，所以正確答案是 (B) He was unable to buy some items on August 7.。

Questions 196-200 refer to the following advertisement and e-mail. 196-200 根據下面的廣告和電郵內容回答問題。

例文 1

Explore the Scottish Highlands with Baketbah Travel and Tours!

196If you're looking for a fun and educational tour of Scotland for your history students, Baketbah has just the right tour package for your class! Our affordable three-day, two-night Highland Tour Package is ideal for a group of 30 travelers.* 197-A/BThe package includes hotel accommodations with breakfast and lunch buffets. 197-DOn board our spacious minivans, our expert local guides will engage you and your students with their animated storytelling as you go along each point of your itinerary.

For price quotes and other inquiries, please e-mail Audrey Boggs at aboggs@baketbah.com.

*199Discount rates available for groups of 30 or more

隨著 Baketbah 旅遊公司探索蘇格蘭高地

196 假如你在為你的歷史課學生尋找一個有趣而富教育意義的蘇格蘭之旅，Baketbah 旅遊公司有一個行程正好符合你的班級！我們這個划算的三天兩夜高地套裝行程對三十人的團體來說是很理想的*。197-A/B 這個套裝行程包括含早餐、自助式午餐的旅館住宿。197-D 坐上我們空間寬敞的箱型車，我們專業的當地導遊將以生動無比的故事帶你和你的學生走遍行程中的每個景點。

如要詢價或其他問題，請寄電郵給 Audrey Boggs: aboggs@baketbah.com

*199 三十人以上有團體優惠

例文 2

To: Erwin McGhee <ermc@emailing.com>
From: Audrey Boggs <aboggs@baketbah.com>
Date: February 8
Subject: Highland Package

Dear Mr. McGhee,

Thanks for contacting us about our Highland Tour Package. 199The regular rate per person is £290, but because of our special group rate, you will only have to pay £220 per person. In addition, if you pay on or before February 20, your class will be entitled to a further 10 percent discount as part of our ongoing promotion.

198Regarding your question about the payment methods, we cannot accept bank transfer transactions at the moment. I am sorry for the inconvenience. However, you can still pay by cash, check, or money order. 200You also asked whether or not we can arrange for round-trip flights to Scotland for your group. For that, you can directly call our booking agent, Gladys Kessler, at 555-4144. Ms. Kessler will be more than happy to contact our affiliate airline companies on your behalf and reserve tickets for you.

I have attached the itinerary of the Highland Tour Package and some pictures of the local scenery. If there is anything else I can help you with, please do not hesitate to contact me. Once again, thank you for your business and we look forward to serving you again in the future.

Yours truly,

Audrey Boggs
Customer service manager
Baketbah Travel and Tours

收件人：Erwin McGhee <ermc@emailing.com>
寄件人：Audrey Boggs <aboggs@baketbah.com>
日期：2 月 8 日
主旨：高地套裝行程

親愛的 McGhee 先生：

謝謝你跟我們聯絡關於高地旅遊套裝行程，199一般的價格是每人二百九十英鎊，但是因為我們特別的團體價格，你只要付每人二百二十英鎊即可。此外，如果你在二月二十日以前付款，你的班級還可以再享有九折的優惠，這是我們目前進行的一項優惠。

198關於你詢問的付款方式，我們此時無法接受銀行轉帳。造成你的不便，我很抱歉。不過，你仍然可以以現金、支票或匯票來付款。200你還問到是否可以為你們的團體安排蘇格蘭的來回機票，對此，你可以直接打電話給我們的訂票專員 Gladys Kessler，電話是 555-4144，Kessler 小姐會很樂意向我們合作的航空公司為你訂票。

附件是高地旅遊套裝行程和一些當地景點的照片，如果還有任何我可以協助的地方，請不要客氣與我聯絡。再一次感謝你的惠顧，我們很期待在未來還能為你提供服務。

Audrey Boggs 敬上
客戶服務經理
Baketbah 旅遊公司

例文 1 單字　☐explore v. 探險　　　☐highland n. 高地　　　☐educational a. 教育性的
　　　　　　☐affordable a.（價格）合理的，可負擔的　　☐ideal a. 適切的，理想的
　　　　　　☐spacious a. 寬闊的，寬廣的 ☐expert a. 專家　☐engage v. 沉溺
　　　　　　☐animated a. 有活力的，活潑的　　　　　　☐quote n. 引述
　　　　　　☐inquiry n. 疑問　　　☐available a. 可使用的

例文 2 單字　☐entitle v. 賦予資格　　　☐ongoing a. 進行中的　　☐transaction n. 交易，處理
　　　　　　☐inconvenience n. 不方便　☐round-trip a. 往返的　☐affiliate n. 子公司，附屬公司
　　　　　　☐on one's behalf phr. 代替～ ☐attach v. 使依附　　☐scenery n. 風景，背景

196

Where would the advertisement most likely be found?	這個廣告最有可能在哪裡出現？
(A) In a hotel brochure	(A) 在飯店的小冊子裡
(B) In a teachers journal	(B) 在教師的雜誌裡
(C) In a business publication	(C) 在商業出版品中
(D) In an airline magazine	(D) 在航空公司的雜誌裡

■ 推論 整體細節　　　　　　　　　　　　　　　　　　　　　　　　　　解答 (B)

因為這是在詢問廣告應該刊登在哪裡，所以要先透過例文了解相關內容。例文 1 廣告中 If you're looking for a fun and educational tour of Scotland for your history students, Baketbah has just the right tour package for your class! 是指如果想為歷史課學生們尋找一個有趣而富教育意義的蘇格蘭之旅，Baketbah 旅遊公司有一個行程正好符合該班級，所以可以推論這個廣告是以老師為對象，而且可能在雜誌中看到，因此要選 (B) In a teachers journal 為正確答案。

197

What is NOT included in the Highland Tour Package?	什麼沒有包含在高地旅遊的套裝行程裡？
(A) Food	(A) 食物
(B) Lodgings	(B) 住宿
(C) Tourist guidebooks	(C) 遊客導覽書籍
(D) Ground transportation	(D) 陸地上的交通

■ Not/True True 問題　　　　　　　　　　　　　　　　　　　　　　　解答 (C)

本題是要在例文中找到與本問題的重點 the Highland Tour Package 相關的內容後，比較選項與例文的 Not/True 問題，要先從例文 1 中與高地旅遊行程相關的內容開始確認。The package includes hotels accommodations with breakfast and lunch buffets. 是指套裝行程含有附早餐和自助式午餐的旅館住宿，所以 (A) 和 (B) 都與例文內容一致。(C) 是例文中沒有提及的內容。因此 (C) Tourist guidebook 是正確答案。On board our spacious minivans 是指會搭乘空間寬敞的箱型車，所以 (D) 也與例文內容一致。

單字 lodging n. 食宿，投宿　ground a. 陸地的，地上的　transportation n. 交通

198

What is suggested about Mr. McGhee?	關於 McGhee 先生，提示了什麼？
(A) He teaches a geography class in secondary school.	(A) 他在中學裡教地理。
(B) He has been to Scotland more than once.	(B) 他去過蘇格蘭不只一次。
(C) He has experience doing business with Ms. Boggs.	(C) 他曾和 Boggs 小姐有生意往來的經驗。
(D) He wanted to pay through bank transfer.	(D) 他想要用銀行轉帳的方式付款。

■ 推論 詳細內容　　　　　　　　　　　　　　　　　　　　　　　　　　　　　　　　　　　解答 (D)

這是要針對問題的重點 Mr. McGhee 進行推論的問題，因此從例文 2，Mr. McGhee 所寫的郵件開始尋找相關內容。電子郵件寫到 Regarding your question about payment methods, we cannot accept bank transfer transactions at the moment. 是指 Mr. McGhee 詢問了付款方式，而得到此時無法接受銀行轉帳的回覆，因此可以推論 Mr. McGhee 想要以銀行轉帳的方式支付款項，所以要選 (D) He wanted to pay through bank transfer. 為正確答案。

單字 geography n. 地理　do business with phr. 與～做生意

199

What is indicated about the students in Mr. McGhee's class?	關於 McGhee 先生班上的學生，暗示了什麼？
(A) They are studying in Scotland.	(A) 他們在蘇格蘭上學。
(B) They cannot pay the fees by February 20.	(B) 他們無法在二月二十日之前付款。
(C) They total more than 30 in number.	(C) 總數多於三十人。
(D) They want to reschedule the tour to an earlier date.	(D) 他們想要把行程安排在早一點的時候。

■ 推論 連結問題　　　　　　　　　　　　　　　　　　　　　　　　　　　　　　　　　　　解答 (C)

這是要綜合兩篇例文才能開始推論的連結問題。要從有提及問題的重點是 the students in Mr. McGhee's class 的例文 2 開始尋找相關內容。

例文 2 中寫到 The regular rate per person is £290, but because of our special group rate, you will only have to pay £220 per person. 是指一般的價格，每人是兩百九十英鎊，但是因為 Mr. McGhee 的學生可享有特別團體價，所以每人只要兩百二十英鎊，這是第一個線索。但是這裡沒寫為什麼 Mr. McGhee 會有特別團體價，所以要到例文 1 找出相關的內容。例文 1 廣告下端有寫 Discount rates available for groups of 30 or more 是說三十人或以上的團體有團體優惠，這是第二個線索。

綜合第一個線索：Mr. McGhee 的學生可享有特別團體價，所以每人只要兩百二十英鎊，與第二個線索：三十人或以上的團體有團體優惠，我們可以推論 Mr. McGhee 的班級學生數多於 30 人，所以正確答案是 (C) They total more than 30 in number.。

單字 reschedule v. 更改（日程）

200

What will Mr. McGhee probably request Ms. Kessler to do?	McGhee 先生可能會要求 Kessler 小姐做什麼？
(A) Make changes in an itinerary	(A) 變更行程
(B) Take photographs of the tour	(B) 在旅遊中照相
(C) Deliver a message to a colleague	(C) 傳一個訊息給同事
(D) Book plane tickets to Scotland	(D) 訂購前往蘇格蘭的機票

■ 推論 詳細內容　　　　　　　　　　　　　　　　　　　　　　　　　　　　　　　　　　　解答 (D)

這是要針對問題的重點 Mr. McGhee ~ request Ms. Kessler 進行推論的問題，因此從例文 2，Mr. McGhee 所寫的，提起 Ms. Kessler 的郵件中尋找相關內容。郵件中寫到 You ~ asked whether or not we can arrange for round-trip flights to Scotland for your group. For that, you can directly call our booking agent, Gladys Kessler 是說「你還問到是否可以為你們的團體安排蘇格蘭的來回機票，對此，你可以直接打電話給我們的訂票專員 Gladys Kessler」，之後還提到 Ms. Kessler will be more than happy to ~ reserve tickets for you.，說明 Kessler 小姐會很樂意替 McGhee 先生向合作的航空公司訂票。所以我們可以推論接下來 Mr. McGhee 會請 Ms. Kessler 幫忙訂購飛往蘇格蘭的機票，因此要選 (D) Book plane tickets to Scotland 為正確答案。

單字 colleague n. 同僚

TEST 04

Part 5 翻譯・解說

Part 6 翻譯・解說

Part 7 翻譯・解說

101

To indicate that Mr. Drake had been refunded for the broken items, the invoice was _____ by the accountant. (A) modifies　　(B) modified (C) modifying　　(D) modificatory	為了表示 Drake 先生已經取得瑕疵品的退款，會計在發票上做了更正。

■ 區分主動態與被動態　　　　　　　　　　　　　　　　　　　　　　　　　　　　　　解答 (B)

因為空格前有 be 動詞 was，所以 p.p. 形 (B)，-ing 形 (C) 與形容詞 (D) 都可能是正確答案。因為句意為「會計在發票上做了更正」，有被動的意義，而且動詞後沒有受詞，所以要選擇可以和 be 動詞 was 一起表示被動的動詞 modify（修正）的 p.p. 形 (B) modified 為正確答案。單數動詞 (A) modifies 不能放在 be 動詞後面，(C) modifying 是要放在 be 動詞後面會變成主動態，因此無法做為答案。形容詞 (D) modificatory 是「修正的」，會讓句意變得奇怪。另外，主動態的主詞若出現在被動態的句子中，則要以「by + 主詞」的形態出現。

單字 indicate v. 指名　refund v. 退還　broken a. 破損的　invoice n. 發票　accountant n. 會計師

102

Ms. Lee saw the delivery person _____ through the window, and went to the front doors. (A) arrived　　(B) arriving (C) has arrived　　(D) to arrive	Lee 女士透過窗戶看到了貨運人員抵達後，她走到了前門。

■ 以原形不定詞取代 to 不定詞成為受詞補語　　　　　　　　　　　　　　　　　　　　解答 (B)

做為感官動詞 see (saw) 的受詞補語不能使用 to 不定詞，而是要使用原形不定詞或現在分詞。所以現在分詞 (B) arriving 為正確答案。另外，受詞補語的位置如果寫成現在分詞，就會變成一直強調進行的動作。如果選 p.p. 形 (A) arrived 的話，會變成受詞 the delivery person 與受詞補語 arrived 變成「配送員被到達」的奇怪句意，動詞 (C) 不能做為受詞補語使用，to 不定詞 (D) 則不能做為感官動詞的受詞補語。

103

The tourists were very _____ to learn that the Palm Hotel was as beautiful in real life as it was in the advertisement. (A) pleases　　(B) pleasing (C) pleased　　(D) pleasingly	遊客很高興知道 Palm 飯店實際上就像廣告中介紹的一樣漂亮。

■ 區分情感動詞的主動態/被動態　　　　　　　　　　　　　　　　　　　　　　　　　解答 (C)

因為空格出現在 be 動詞 were 之後，-ing 形 (B) 跟 p.p. 形 (C) 都可能是正確答案。please（開心）是表示情感的動詞，而句意為「遊客很高興」，所以可以知道要把主詞的感情以「be 動詞 were + 一起可以做為被動態的 p.p. 形 pleased」為正確答案。

104

A chemist from the Science Bureau was given extra funding for _____ study on herbal medicines and its effects on blood pressure.

(A) she (B) herself
(C) hers (D) her

從科學局來的化學家得到了一筆額外的資金來資助她研究草藥醫學以及它對血壓的影響。

■ 人稱代名詞　　　　　　　　　　　　　　　　　　　　　　解答 (D)

可以像形容詞一樣寫在名詞 study 前面的是人稱代名詞所有格，所以 (D) her 是正確答案。要注意不要看到空格前面的 for 之後，想起 for oneself 而選擇反身代名詞 (B) herself。

單字 chemist n. 化學家　funding n. 資金　blood pressure phr. 血壓

105

Spec Glass _____ with Iron Spark and is now able to sell glass windows in both local and international markets.

(A) will merge (B) merging
(C) has merged (D) to merge

Spec 玻璃公司和 Iron Spark 公司合併之後，現在能夠在當地與國際市場上賣玻璃窗。

■ 現在完成式　　　　　　　　　　　　　　　　　　　　　　解答 (C)

對等連接詞 and 後面有包含動詞的子句，所以前面的子句也有包含動詞。因此動詞 (A) 和 (C) 都是可能的答案。因為句意為「公司合併之後，現在能夠在當地與國際市場上賣玻璃窗」，所以要寫過去發生的事情直到現在還在發揮影響的現在完成式 (C) has merged 為正確答案。

單字 glass window phr. 玻璃窗　local a. 國內的；地區的　international a. 國際性的

106

Kerb Holdings is _____ conducting negotiations with some private investors regarding the company's expansion plans in Asia.

(A) currently (B) hardly
(C) anyhow (D) far

Kerb Holdings 目前正在和一些私人投資者進行在亞洲地區公司擴張計畫的協商談判。

■ 副詞語彙　　　　　　　　　　　　　　　　　　　　　　解答 (A)

因為使用現在進行式 is conducting 且句意為「正在進行協商談判」，所以副詞 (A) currently（現在）是正確答案。(B) hardly 是「幾乎不」，(C) anyhow 是「無論如何，隨便」的意思，(D) far 是「遠」的意思，可以做為副詞或形容詞使用，如果做為副詞修飾形容詞或比較級的話，有「大大，遠大於」的意思。

單字 negotiation n. 協商　private a. 私人的；個人持有的　regarding prep. 關於～

107

| The Vernon Medical Center administration is considering adjusting the _____ it charges for laboratory tests and outpatient treatments.

(A) amounts   (B) duties
(C) taxes   (D) damages | Vernon 醫學中心的行政團隊正考慮調整實驗室檢驗與門診治療的費用。 |

■ 名詞語彙   解答 (A)

因為句意為「調整實驗室檢驗與門診治療的費用」，所以 (A) amount（額數，量）為正確答案。(B) duty 是「職務，職責」，(C) tax 是（州，政府收取的）稅金，(D) damage 是「損害賠償金」的意思。另外，跟錢有關係的名詞還有 fine（罰金），fare（交通費）。

單字 administration n. 行政部門   consider v. 考慮   adjust v. 調整   outpatient n. 門診病人

108

| Since its establishment 10 years ago, Klapius Foundation has been _____ college scholarships to deserving students.

(A) moving   (B) deciding
(C) providing   (D) asking | Klapius Foundation 自從十年前建立以來，一直都提供大學獎學金給應該得到援助的學生。 |

■ 動詞語彙   解答 (C)

因為句意為「提供大學獎學金給學生」，所以動詞 provide（提供）的 -ing 形 (C) providing 是正確答案。(A) move 是「移動」，(B) decide 是「決定」，(D) ask 是「邀請，問」的意思。另外，provide B to A（提供 B 給 A）跟 provide A with B（提供 B 給 A）兩個要分清楚。

單字 establishment n. 設立   scholarship n. 獎學金

109

| The marketing team had to _____ study all the information gathered during the recently conducted consumer surveys.

(A) comprehend   (B) comprehensively
(C) comprehension   (D) comprehending | 行銷團隊必須徹底地研究所有他們從最近進行的消費者調查得到的資訊。 |

■ 副詞的位置   解答 (B)

為了修飾動詞 study，要選擇副詞 (B) comprehensively（徹底地）為正確答案。動詞 (A)，名詞 (C)，動名詞 (D) 都無法修飾動詞。

單字 recently ad. 最近地

110

Louise Simms wants workshop participants to be in the art room _____ she begins her lecture so as to avoid any interruptions. (A) before　　　　　　(B) off (C) except　　　　　　(D) on	Louise Simms 想要工作坊的參加者在她開始上課前就進入美術教室，以避免有任何干擾。

■ 副詞子句連接詞 時間　　　　　　　　　　　　　　　　　　　　　　　　　　　　解答 (A)

本句是以具備必要成分 Louise Simms wants workshop participants to be in the art room 的完整句，_____ she begins ~ interruption 是修飾語句，因為此修飾語句是有動詞 begins 的修飾語句，所以要找可以帶領修飾語句的副詞子句連接詞 (A) 或 (B) 為正確答案。因為句意為「在上課前就進入美術教室，以避免有任何干擾」，所以 (A) before（～之前）為正確答案。如果寫 (C) except（以外，除外），句意會變成「除了開始上課之外就進入美術教室」這種奇怪的句子。(B) off 跟 (D) on（在～）都無法領導一個副詞子句，而且之後應該接名詞。

單字 participant n. 參加者　interruption n. 妨礙

111

Building administrators must carry out _____ maintenance checks on electrical wiring to reduce the risk of fire. (A) contrary　　　　　　(B) routine (C) absent　　　　　　(D) former	大樓行政管理人員必須執行電子線路的例行維護檢查，以減少火災的風險。

■ 形容詞語彙　　　　　　　　　　　　　　　　　　　　　　　　　　　　　　解答 (B)

因為句意為「必須執行電子線路的例行維護檢查，以減少火災的風險」，所以形容詞 (B) routine（例行性的）為正確答案。(A) contrary 是「相反的」，(C) absent 是「不在的，缺席的」，(D) former 是「先前的」的意思。

單字 administrator n. 管理者　electrical a. 電器的　wiring n. 線路

112

Peter Delara said that he would like _____ a different venue for the annual stockholders meeting scheduled for next month. (A) suggests　　　　　　(B) suggested (C) to suggest　　　　　　(D) is suggested	Peter Delara 說他想要針對下個月舉辦的年度股東會議建議一個不一樣的地點。

■ 助動詞 + 動詞原形　　　　　　　　　　　　　　　　　　　　　　　　　　　解答 (C)

因為句意為「想要建議一個不一樣的地點」，所以要選擇可以跟空格前的 would like 一起組合表示「想做～」意義，類似助動詞的 would like to 的 (C) to suggest 為正確答案。第三人稱單數形 (A) 和 (D)，過去式 (B) 都無法置於 would like to 後面。另外，和 would like to 一樣性質類似助動詞的還有 have to（必須），had better（最好～），used to（習慣～），be able to（可以～）。

單字 venue n. 場所　stockholder n. 股東

113

Keeping with its expansion plans, United Oil established a new fuel processing plant _____ Indonesia early this year. (A) in (B) over (C) by (D) out	United Oil 油氣公司繼續進行擴張計畫，今年初在印尼成立了一個新的燃油處理工廠。

■ 選擇介系詞 in   解答 (A)

因為要寫成「在印尼」的意思，所以可以表示場所的介系詞 (A) in 為正確答案。(B) over 以「～期間」的意思表示時間，以「～之上」的意思表現位置。(C) by 是以「為止」的意思表示截止日，「～旁邊」的意思表現位置。(D) out 主要以 out of 的形態表示「在～外面」的意思。

單字 establish v. 設立   plant n. 工廠

114

The plant species that Dr. Kinghorn discovered in Puerto Rico proved to be _____ to his medical research. (A) joint (B) useful (C) precise (D) competent	Kinghorn 博士在波多黎各所發現的植物品種被證實對他的醫學研究有幫助。

■ 形容詞語彙   解答 (B)

因為句意為「被證實對他的醫學研究有幫助」，所以形容詞 (B) useful（有用的）為正確答案。(A) joint 是「共同的，協同的」，(C) precise 是「精確的」，(D) competent 是「有能力的」的意思。

單字 species n. 種類   discover v. 發現

115

The increasing demand for Rubber Barter's merchandise enabled the company to grow faster than _____ projected. (A) finally (B) accidentally (C) previously (D) physically	對 Rubber Barter 公司的商品需求增加，使得該公司成長的比預期還快速。

■ 副詞語彙   解答 (C)

因為句意為「成長的比預期還快速」，所以副詞 (C) previously（以前地）為正確答案。另外，previously 是比提到的時間還早時所使用的詞。(A) finally 是「終於」，(B) accidentally 是「偶然地」，(D) physically 是「身體上地」的意思。

單字 merchandise n. 商品   enable v. 使可以～；讓～變得可能

116

Gastown Corporation will give discounts on _____ automobile parts at the trade show this week. (A) much (B) little (C) all (D) every	Gastown 公司在本週的貿易展中，所有的汽車零件都有折扣。

■ 限定詞與名詞   解答 (C)

可以修飾複數可數名詞 parts 的限定詞 (C) all（所有）為正確答案。(A) much 是「多的」，(B) little 是「幾乎沒有的」，只可修飾不可數名詞，(D) every 是「每一個」，只可修飾單數可數名詞。

單字 discount n. 折扣   automobile a. 汽車的；n. 汽車

117

The editorial board of *Business and Industry* magazine apologized for a factual error in last month's cover story in an _____ released to the press.

(A) announce　　　　(B) announcing
(C) announces　　　(D) announcement

在一份新聞聲明中，*Business and Industry* 雜誌的編輯委員會對上個月封面故事的一個事實陳述錯誤道歉。

■ 名詞的位置　　　　　　　　　　　　解答 (D)

可以做為介系詞 in 的受詞也可以接在不定冠詞 an 後面的單數名詞 (D) announcement（聲明）為正確答案。另外，released to the press 是在名詞 announcement 後面補充的分詞構句。動詞 (A) 和 (C)，分詞 (B) 都無法置於名詞的位置，即使把 (B) 視為動名詞，因為空格前有不定冠詞 an 的關係，無法做為正確答案。

單字 editorial board n. 編輯委員會　apologize v. 道歉　press n. 媒體

118

Please be reminded that the finance department only _____ expense reports that have been signed by an immediate supervisor.

(A) obtains　　　　(B) accepts
(C) limits　　　　(D) sponsors

請注意財務室僅接受由直屬長官簽名的開銷報告表。

■ 動詞語彙　　　　　　　　　　　　解答 (B)

因為句意為「僅接受由直屬長官簽名的開銷報告表」，所以動詞 accept（接受，認證）的第三人稱單數形 (B) accepts 為正確答案。(A) obtain 是「（經過努力後）獲得」，(C) limit 是「（量的）限制」，(D) sponsor 是「贊助」的意思。

單字 immediate a. 即刻的；直接的　supervisor n. 管理者

119

To ensure that its customers' complaints are processed _____, Haula Shipping upgraded its Web site to include an online feedback form.

(A) directly　　　　(B) directed
(C) directing　　　(D) directness

為了確保顧客的申訴直接受到處理，Haula 貨運將網站升級，提供線上回饋表。

■ 副詞的位置　　　　　　　　　　　解答 (A)

因為要修飾動詞 are processed，所以要選擇副詞 (A) directly（直接地）為正確答案。過去分詞兼動詞 (B)，現在分詞兼動名詞 (C)，名詞 (D) 都無法修飾動詞。

單字 ensure v. 保障　process v. 處理　include v. 包含

120

It takes only five minutes for vehicles to pass _____ the tunnel that was built on the highway leading to the country's largest province. (A) over　　　　　　(B) onto (C) down　　　　　　(D) through	車輛只要花五分鐘就可以通過高速公路上通往該國最大省分的隧道。

■ 選擇介系詞 方向　　　　　　　　　　　　　　　　　　　　　　　　　　　　　　　　　　　解答 (D)

因為句意為「車輛通過隧道」，所以介系詞 through（通過）為正確答案。要記得 pass through（通過，貫通）是慣用語句。(A) over 以「～期間」的意思表示時間，以「～之上」的意思表現位置。(B) onto 是「上面」的意思，表示場所或位置。(C) down 是「（場所，位置，數值等）下面」的意思。其中，如果與 pass 一起寫的話，會有「傳給（後代）」的意思。

單字 vehicle n. 汽車　highway n. 高速公路　province n. 州，鄉間

121

For exceptionally difficult cases, Mr. Hallis makes it a habit to _____ his associates in the firm to make certain he takes the correct approach. (A) appeal　　　　　　(B) consult (C) support　　　　　　(D) assure	對於特別困難的案子，Hallis 先生很習慣向公司裡其他同事請教以確定他採取的是正確的方法。

■ 動詞語彙　　　　　　　　　　　　　　　　　　　　　　　　　　　　　　　　　　　　　解答 (B)

因為句意為「習慣向公司裡其他同事請教以確定他採取的是正確的方法」，所以動詞 (B) 是正確答案。(A) appeal 是「上訴」，(C) support 是「支持」，(D) assure 是「確認，保證」的意思。另外，appeal 可以跟介系詞 to 一起寫，有「上訴，引起興趣」的意思。

單字 exceptionally ad. 特殊地　habit n. 習慣　associate n. 同僚　approach n. 方法

122

_____ poor weather conditions resulting from a coming hurricane, all Cailleach Airway flights have been postponed until further notice. (A) Regardless of　　　(B) But that (C) As though　　　　(D) Because of	因為即將到來的颶風造成天候不佳，所有 Cailleach 航空公司的飛機都要延遲起飛，並靜待通知。

■ 選擇介系詞 理由　　　　　　　　　　　　　　　　　　　　　　　　　　　　　　　　　　解答 (D)

本句是有主詞 all ~ flights 與動詞 have been postponed 的完整句，_____ poor weather ~ hurricane 是修飾語句，此修飾語句是沒有動詞的修飾語句，所以可以領導修飾語句的介系詞 (A) 或 (D) 都是可能的答案。因為句意為「因為天候不佳」，所以 (D) Because of（因為～）為正確答案。如果選擇 (A) Regardless of（無論～）則句意會變成「不論是否天候不佳，所有飛機都要延遲起飛」，文意將變得很奇怪。(B) But that（要不是～的話，沒有～的話）跟 (C) As through（就像～一樣）是副詞子句連接詞，之後要接著子句才可以。另外，but that 與 unless（除非）的意義相近。

單字 postpone v. 使～延期

123

The _____ of the surveys on laundry soaps reveal that Jobert is still the most popular brand on the market.

(A) impacts
(B) methods
(C) results
(D) effects

調查結果顯示 Jobert 仍是市場上最受歡迎的洗衣肥皂品牌。

■ 名詞語彙 　　　　　　　　　　　　　　　　　解答 (C)

因為句意為「調查結果顯示 Jobert 仍是市場上最受歡迎的品牌」，所以 (C) result（結果）是正確答案。(A) impact 是「影響」，(B) method 是「方法」，(D) effect 是「效果」的意思。

單字 survey n. 調查 　laundry n. 洗衣房；洗好的衣服 　reveal v. 展現，呈現

124

For your convenience, a list of authorized repair centers in all major cities is _____ on Cornelius Appliances' Web site.

(A) capable
(B) suitable
(C) possible
(D) available

在 Cornelius 家電的網站上有所有位在主要城市的授權維修中心名單，以方便您查詢。

■ 形容詞語彙 　　　　　　　　　　　　　　　　解答 (D)

因為句意為「為方便您查詢，可使用網站查詢」，所以形容詞 (D) available（可以使用）為正確答案。(A) capable 是「有～的能力」，(B) suitable 是「適合的」，(C) possible 是「可能的」的意思。另外，要記得 capable of，suitable for，possible to 這些形態。

單字 convenience n. 方便 　authorized a. 授權的

125

A tour of showroom houses _____ at Sunrise Court, the newest residential property in the state.

(A) is holding
(B) held
(C) is being held
(D) holds

在全州最新的住宅區 Sunrise Court 舉辦了展示屋之旅。

■ 區分主動態與被動態 　　　　　　　　　　　　解答 (C)

因為句意為「舉辦展示屋之旅」有被動的意義，而空格後沒有受詞，所以被動式 (C) is being held 為正確答案。主動式 (A) (B) (D) 都無法做為答案。

單字 showroom n. 展示間 　residential a. 居住的

126

At the psychology forum, Dr. Dukes explained what can lead to _____ in a child's speech and language development.

(A) reversely
(B) reversed
(C) reversals
(D) reversible

在心理學論壇上，Dukes 博士解釋可能導致兒童說話與語言發展逆轉的原因。

■ 名詞的位置 　　　　　　　　　　　　　　　　解答 (C)

因為可以放在介系詞 to 受詞位置的是名詞，所以 (C) reversals（失敗，逆轉）為正確答案。副詞 (A)，動詞兼分詞 (B)，形容詞 (D) 都無法置於名詞的位置。另外，lead to（帶到某處，導致）為慣用語。

單字 psychology n. 心理學

127

Software manufacturers expressed concerns about the _____ development of a current programming language that developers consider very complicated. (A) puzzled (B) ongoing (C) rotating (D) silenced	軟體製造商對於現在一款開發者認為相當複雜的程式語言的持續發展表達關切。

■ 形容詞語彙   解答 (B)

因為句意為「軟體製造商對目前持續發展的程式語言表達關切」，所以要選擇 (B) ongoing（進行中的）為正確答案。(A) puzzled 為「暈頭轉向的」，(C) rotating 是「旋轉」，(D) silenced 是「使沉默」的意思。

單字 manufacture n. 製造業　concern n. 關心；掛念　complicated a. 複雜的

128

Not once did the supervisor _____ during the staff dispute, hoping the employees involved would find a solution for themselves. (A) intervene (B) to intervene (C) intervening (D) intervened	主管一次也沒有介入員工間的糾紛，希望員工們能為他們自己找出一個解決方案。

■ 倒裝句   解答 (A)

這是把否定詞 Not 置於句首，主詞、動詞倒裝的句子。句子前若出現 do 助動詞 did，則動詞需要使用原形動詞，因此 (A) intervene 為正確答案。

單字 intervene v. 介入　dispute n. 爭論　involved a. 關聯的

129

A _____ of the local government in the region is providing residents with efficient, speedy, and adequate public transportation. (A) magnitude (B) contract (C) profession (D) responsibility	當地政府在該地區有責任提供居民有效率、快速及足夠的公共交通工具。

■ 名詞語彙   解答 (D)

因為句意為「當地政府在該地區有責任提供居民有效率、快速及足夠的公共交通工具」，因此名詞 (D) responsibility（責任）為正確答案。(A) magnitude 是「大小」，(B) contract 是「合約」，(C) profession 是「職業」的意思。

單字 local a. 鄉村的，當地的　region n. 地區　adequate a. 足夠的

130

After the leadership training, the organizing committee will meet _____ to discuss the event. (A) lately (B) oppositely (C) reliably (D) briefly	在領導力訓練結束後，組織委員會短暫地集合以討論這項訓練活動。

■ 副詞語彙   解答 (D)

因為句意為「短暫的集合以討論這項訓練活動」，因此要選擇副詞 (D) briefly（短暫地）為正確答案。另外，briefly 可以使用在強調某事在短時間內實現的時候。(A) lately 是「最近地，不久前」，(B) oppositely 是「對面地，相對地」，(C) reliably 是「不得不信地，確信地」的意思。

單字 committee n. 委員會

131

As he was not aware that the shirt was on sale, the cashier _____ charged Ms. Adams the full cost of the item.
(A) wronged
(B) wronging
(C) wrongs
(D) wrongly

因為沒有注意到襯衫正在促銷，收銀員誤向 Adams 小姐收取全額的價錢。

■ 副詞的位置　　　　　　　　　　　　　　　　　　　　　解答 (D)

因為要修飾動詞 charged，所以要選擇副詞 (D) wrongly 為正確答案。動詞兼過去分詞 (A)，動名詞兼現在分詞 (B)，名詞 (C) 都無法作為副詞使用。另外，be aware that 之後要接子句，be aware of 之後則接由單字組成的短語。

單字 on sale phr. 促銷中的　cashier n. 收銀員

132

The attorneys of Lawfield Associates are adept at _____ professional lectures for lawyers and state prosecutors.
(A) organizing
(B) organized
(C) organizes
(D) organizations

Lawfield 法律事務所的律師們都很擅長為律師和州檢察官安排專業的課程。

■ 動名詞 vs. 名詞　　　　　　　　　　　　　　　　　　　解答 (A)

可以做為介系詞 at 受詞的動名詞 (A) 或 (D) 都可能是答案。其中，後面可以加上受詞 professional lectures 的是動名詞，所以 (A) organizing 為正確答案。如果要使用名詞 (D)，則名詞 organizations 和名詞 professional lectures 中間需要有特別的連結才可以，不能直接使用。另外，be adept at（熟練～）為慣用句。

單字 attorney n. 律師　adept a. 熟練的　lecture n. 課程　prosecutor n. 檢察官

133

Award-winning director Marion Poole's new film drew _____ acclaim from viewers who attended the special screening.
(A) inventive
(B) enthusiastic
(C) purposeful
(D) anxious

獲獎導演 Marion Poole 的新電影得到參加特展的觀眾的熱烈反應。

■ 形容詞語彙　　　　　　　　　　　　　　　　　　　　　解答 (B)

因為句意為「新電影得到參加特展的觀眾的熱烈反應」，所以形容詞 (B) enthusiastic（熱情的）為正確答案。(A) inventive 是「創意性的，獨創性的」，(C) purposeful 是「有目的性的，有決斷力的」，(D) anxious 是「焦躁的」的意思。

單字 acclaim n. 歡呼　attend v. 出席

134

The feasibility research _____ that the corner lot on Siam Avenue is a strategic location for the supermarket.
(A) centers
(B) changes
(C) indicates
(D) measures

可行性研究指出 Siam 大道角落的那一塊空地是蓋超級市場的策略地點。

■ 動詞語彙　　　　　　　　　　　　　　　　　　　　　　解答 (C)

因為句意為「報告顯示 Siam 大道角落的地是蓋超級市場的策略地點」，所以要以動詞 indicate（指出）的第三人稱單數形 (C) indicates 為正確答案。(A) center 是「中心」，(B) change 是「改變，使改變」，(D) measure 是「測量」的意思。

單字 feasibility n. 可行性　strategic a. 策略性的

135

The Habana General Hospital is in need of doctors willing to deliver healthcare _____ to the residents of rural communities.

(A) services
(B) worries
(C) prospects
(D) collections

Habana 綜合醫院需要願意為農村社區的民眾提供醫療服務的醫生。

■ 名詞語彙   解答 (A)

因為句意為「醫院需要願意為農村社區民眾提供醫療服務的醫生」，所以名詞 (A) service（服務）為正確答案。(B) worry 是「擔心，考慮」，(C) prospect 是「展望」，(D) collection 是「收藏品，收集，募集的錢」的意思。另外，deliver service（提供服務）與 be in need of（需要）都是慣用句。

單字 be in need of phr. 需要～　rural a. 鄉村的

136

The city council requires blueprints of the old buildings so that the original designs can be _____ before the owners begin restoration work.

(A) monitored
(B) summarized
(C) preserved
(D) resisted

市議會要求屋主在開始整修前，提供老建築的藍圖以保留原本的設計。

■ 動詞語彙   解答 (C)

因為句意為「要求提供老建築的藍圖以保留原本的設計」，空格前有 be 動詞，所以可以形成被動式的 preserve（保存）的 p.p. 形 (C) preserved 為正確答案。(A) monitor 是「監視」，(B) summarize 是「總結」，(D) resist 是「抗拒」的意思。

單字 city council phr. 市議會　blueprint n. 藍圖，計畫　restoration n. 修復

137

Mr. Stevens ordered full-color brochures _____ the black-and-white ones he previously handed out at the trade fair.

(A) instead of
(B) even if
(C) as of
(D) owing to

Stevens 先生訂購全彩的小冊子，來取代之前在貿易展發放的黑白小冊子。

■ 選擇介系詞 除外   解答 (A)

本句是有主詞 Mr. Stevens，動詞 ordered，受詞 brochures 的完整句，_____ the black-and-white ~ trade fair 則可視為修飾語句。此修飾語句是沒有動詞的修飾語句，可引領修飾句的介系詞 (A) (C) (D) 都可能是正確答案。因為句意為「取代黑白小冊子而訂購全彩小冊子」，所以 (A) instead of（取代～）為正確答案。(C) as of 是「現在，從～開始」的意思，用來表示時間，(D) owing to 是「因為」的意思，表示理由或原因，(B) even if（即使～）是表示「讓步」的意思，可帶領副詞子句連接詞。另外，he previously ~ fair 是修飾先行詞 ones 的修飾關係子句，所以完全不影響答案的選擇。

138

Management has decided to shut down the factory in Pennsylvania on account of _____ malfunctioning equipment, which raised the company's overhead expenses last quarter. (A) its　　　　　　　(B) his (C) any　　　　　　　(D) whose	管理階層基於無法正常運作的設備造成公司上一季營運支出的增加，因此決定要關閉在賓州的工廠。

■ 名詞 – 代名詞要一致　　　　　　　　　　　　　　　　　　　　　　　　　　解答 (A)

因為意義為「（工廠的）設備故障」，所以可以知道要填入空格中的代名詞是代表 the factory 的意思。因此要與單數事物名詞 factory 有相同意義，又像形容詞一樣可寫在名詞 equipment 前的所有格代名詞 (A) its 為正確答案。(C) any（任何，哪種）在已經有指稱的對象時不能使用。所有格關係代名詞 (D) whose 不能跟介系詞 of 一起使用。另外，account of（因為～）是慣用句。

單字 malfunction v. 發生故障；n. 故障　overhead a. 經常的，管理的

139

Had the publishing firm sent the manuscript to the printer earlier, the advertising team _____ to issue an announcement on a change of date in the book's release. (A) did not need　　　　　(B) could not have needed (C) would not have needed　(D) is not needing	假如出版社早一點將手稿付印，廣告團隊就不用發佈改變出書日期的聲明。

■ 沒有 if 的假設法 倒裝句　　　　　　　　　　　　　　　　　　　　　　　　解答 (C)

句子以 Had 開頭，主詞 the publishing firm 後面接 p.p. 形 sent 可以看出假設法過去完成式的 if 子句中省略 if 把主詞跟動詞倒裝的句型。因此，可以跟 if 子句裡的 Had sent 一起的 (B) 和 (C) 為可能的答案。因為句意為「假如早一點將手稿付印，廣告團隊就不用發佈改變出書日期的聲明」，所以要選 (C) would not have needed 為正確答案。如果選擇 (B) could not have needed 就會變成「假如提早將手稿付印，就不能需要發佈改變出書日期的聲明」這樣奇怪的句子。

140

It was declared that Carla Meyers would temporarily take over as Pennington Bank's chief financial officer after Joshua Greenberg _____ submitted his resignation. (A) reasonably　　　　　(B) primarily (C) impossibly　　　　　(D) unexpectedly	在 Joshua Greenberg 無預警的遞交辭呈之後，Pennington 銀行已經宣布 Carla Meyers 會暫時接任首席財務長。

■ 副詞語彙　　　　　　　　　　　　　　　　　　　　　　　　　　　　　　　解答 (D)

因為句意為「Joshua Greenberg 無預警的遞交辭呈」，所以副詞 (D) unexpectedly（無預警的）是正確答案。另外，unexpectedly 是強調沒有想到會發生的事發生時使用的副詞。(A) reasonably 是「合理的，適可的」，(B) primarily 是「主要」，(C) impossibly 是「不可能的」的意思。

PART 6

Questions 141-143 refer to the following letter.　　　　141-143 根據下面信件的內容回答問題。

Dear Editor,

I read an editorial regarding the influx of foreign language schools in the country. I could not have agreed more when you mentioned that most of them are highly business-driven and offer poor-quality courses. _____,

141 (A) With this in mind (B) However
(C) Therefore　　　　(D) As such

I beg to differ with your comments on the quality of education given by Lingua Universal.

I took an advanced Spanish course at the school. I can say that its instructors are experts in teaching foreign languages to nonnative speakers, providing clear translations, and directly _____ to inquiries about grammar

142 (A) discussing　(B) rejecting
(C) transporting(D) responding

and word usage. After studying at Lingua Universal, I was able to acquire a full-time job as an interpreter in a Spanish-owned corporation.

Because of this experience, I would have no reservations about endorsing Lingua Universal for professionals who seek career _____ in the field of foreign languages.

143 (A) search　　(B) extension
(C) aspiration　(D) growth

Thank you for taking the time to read my letter.

Best regards,

Janice Ong

親愛的編輯：

我讀了你寫的關於外語學校大舉湧入的社論，對於內容提到大部分的學校極為商業導向，且提供的課程品質低下，我非常同意你的看法。141 然而，我無法認同你對 Lingua Universal 的教育品質的意見。

我在那家學校上過進階西班牙語，我可以說那裡的老師在教導非母語學生學習外國語言這方面是專家，他們提供明確的翻譯，142 直接回應關於文法與用字的問題。在 Lingua Universal 學習後，我得到了一份在西班牙公司做全職翻譯的工作。

因為這個經驗，143 我極度推薦 Lingua Universal 給想要在外語方面職涯成長的專業人士。

感謝你抽出時間讀我這封信。

Janice Ong 敬上

單字 editorial n. 社論　influx n. 湧入　instructor n. 講師　expert n. 專家　nonnative a. 非本國的
acquire v. 尋找，取得　interpreter n. 翻譯人員　corporation n. 企業　reservation n. 保留
endorse v. 推薦，背書

141 ■ 連接副詞 掌握上下文　　　　　　　　　　　　　　　　　　　　　解答 (B)

因為空格與逗號同時在句首的連接副詞位置，所以要掌握前一句與本句的關聯性，再選擇正確答案。前文提到同意大部分學校極為商業導向，提供品質低下的課程的看法，但是在空格句裡提到不同意對於 Lingua Universal 提供的教育品質的看法，因此要選擇可以用來對照前後句的 (B) However（然而）為正確答案。(A) With this in mind 是「考慮到這一點」，(C) Therefore 是「因此，所以」，(D) As such 是「確切而言」的意思，如果放到空格中則句意會變得奇怪。另外，「could not + 動詞 + 比較級」是利用比較級寫出最高級的意義，因此有「非常～」的意思。例文中寫到的 could not agree more（感到非常同意）跟 could not be better（非常好）都是慣用句型。

142 ■ 動詞語彙　　　　　　　　　　　　　　　　　　　　　　　　　　　解答 (D)

因為句意為「直接回應關於文法與用字的問題」所以要選擇動詞 respond（回答）的動名詞 (D) responding 為正確答案。(A) discuss 是「討論」，(B) reject 是「拒絕」，(C) transport 是「輸送」的意思。

143 ■ 名詞語彙　　　　　　　　　　　　　　　　　　　　　　　　　　　解答 (D)

因為句意為「極度推薦 Lingua Universal 學校給想要在外語方面職涯成長的專業人士」，所以名詞 (D) growth（成長）為正確答案。(A) search 是「搜索」，(B) extension 是「延長」，(C) aspiration 是「志向」的意思。

Questions 144-146 refer to the following letter.

144-146 根據下面信件的內容回答問題。

Carmen Francisco President Francisco Skin and Body Clinic	Carmen Francisco 院長 Francisco 皮膚與身體診所

Dear Dr. Francisco,

I am writing in response to your proposal to _____ me as

144 (A) promote　　(B) interview
　　 (C) petition　　(D) employ

an associate at your clinic. I looked through the details of your offer and found it very interesting, but _____ a

145 (A) after　　(B) into
　　 (C) although　　(D) while

thorough reflection on the advantages and disadvantages of accepting the position, I have decided to pass up the opportunity. Accepting the job would require my family and me to move to Manhattan. It is the middle of the school year now, and my children would definitely have a hard time adjusting to a new school if we were _____.

146 (A) relocating　　(B) to relocate
　　 (C) relocate　　(D) relocation

I am optimistic that we will find the chance to collaborate in the future. Thank you for considering me for the position.

Sincerely,

Greta Castro

親愛的 Francisco 醫生：

144 我寫這封信回覆您提議僱用我在您的診所任職一事。我仔細地研究了您提供的條件，且對此相當有興趣。

145 但是在完整分析接受這份工作的優缺點之後，我決定放棄這個機會，因為接受這份工作需要我和我的家人搬到曼哈頓。

而現在正是學期中，146 如果我們搬家的話，我的孩子們在新學校裡絕對會適應困難。

我認為我們未來一定有機會可以一起共事。謝謝你考慮讓我擔任這個職位。

Greta Castro 敬上

單字 **proposal** n. 提案　**associate** n. 同僚　**reflection** n. 深思　**pass up** phr. 放棄　**definitely** ad. 絕對地
　　adjust v. 適應　**optimistic** a. 肯定性的，樂觀的　**collaborate** v. 合作

144　動詞語彙 掌握全文　　　　　　　　　　　　　　　　　　　　　　　　　　　　　　　　解答 (D)

因為句意為「回覆您要_____我在您的診所任職」，(A) 和 (D) 都可能是正確答案。因為單靠有空格的句子無法選出正確答案，所以要透過前後文或全文來找出答案。因為有提到如果接受這個職位就需要搬家，感謝考慮我來擔任這個職位，所以可以知道寫信的人收到了雇用邀請，因此要選擇 (D) employ（雇用）為正確答案。(A) promote 是「使升遷」，(B) interview 是「面試」，(C) petition 是「請願」的意思。

145　副詞子句連接詞 vs. 介系詞　　　　　　　　　　　　　　　　　　　　　　　　　　　解答 (A)

but 之後是有主詞 I 和動詞 have decided 的完整子句，_____ a thorough reflection ~ the position 則要視為修飾語才可以。因為此修飾語沒有動詞，所以要選擇可以帶領修飾語的介系詞 (A) 或 (B) 為正確答案。因為句意是「在完整的分析過後」，所以 (A) after（～之後）為正確答案。副詞子句連接詞 (C) 和 (D) 都無法放在介系詞的位置。

146　假設法過去式　　　　　　　　　　　　　　　　　　　　　　　　　　　　　　　　　　解答 (B)

因為空格前面有 be 動詞 were，可以置於 be 動詞後面的 -ing 形 (A)，to 不定詞 (B)，名詞 (D) 都可能是正確答案。有空格的句子 if we were 是假設法的過去式，句意為「如果搬家的話，孩子們會適應困難」，所以可以知道這件事情未來發生的機率較低，因此可以形成假設法過去式中表現出希望較微弱的 were to 的 to 不定詞 (B) to relocate 為正確答案。如果選擇 -ing 形 (A) relocating 則會變成過去進行式，因為名詞 (D) relocation（搬家）與主詞 we 在意義上不能作為同位語，無法作為答案。

單字 **relocate** v. 搬家，移動

From: Tristan Beach <t_beach@breadcrumbs.com>

To: Brian Craft <b.craft@jetway.com>

Subject: Bread and cupcake orders
Date: April 1

Dear Mr. Craft,

We have received the follow-up letter about your orders for next week. I sent an e-mail to our main branch to inform them about the _____ you made. They will supply

147 (A) policies　　　　(B) requests
　　(C) improvements　　(D) presentations

you with all the baked items you require for your business. The main branch verified your orders on Sunday and notified us that they _____ them on Monday morning.

148 (A) delivered　　(B) has delivered
　　(C) will deliver　(D) was delivering

We are confident _____ your customers will be more than

149 (A) what　　　(B) which
　　(C) them　　　(D) that

satisfied once they sample our products. We look forward to continuing to serve you.

Sincerely,

Tristan Beach

寄件人：Tristan Beach
　　　　<t_beach@breadcrumbs.com>

收件人：Brian Craft
　　　　<b.craft@jetway.com>

主旨：麵包與杯子蛋糕的訂購

日期：4 月 1 日

親愛的 Craft 先生：

我們收到您對下週訂單的追蹤信件。我已經聯絡我們的總店，147 並知會他們您的訂單，他們會提供所有您為您的生意所訂購的烘焙品。

總店已經在週日確認您的訂單，148 並且通知將會在週一上午送貨過去。

149 我們確信只要您的顧客品嘗我們的產品，他們將會十分滿意。期待繼續為您服務。

Tristan Beach 敬上

單字 follow-up a. 後續的　verify v. 確認　notify v. 提醒　satisfied a. 滿足的　sample v. 品嘗

147 　名詞語彙 掌握上下文　　　　　　　　　　　　　　　　　　　　解答 (B)

句意為「我們已經聯絡本店並知會他們您的_____」，所有的選項都可能為正確答案。因為單靠有空格的句子無法選出正確答案，所以要透過前後文判斷。前文中提到收到對下週訂單的追蹤信件，後面則寫到總店會提供所有烘焙品，所以可以知道寫信的人已經轉告總店 Mr. Craft 先生的訂單，所以要選名詞 (B) request（需求）為正確答案。(A) policy 是「政策」，(C) improvement 是「改善」，(D) presentation 是「發表」的意思。

148 　未來時態 掌握上下文　　　　　　　　　　　　　　　　　　　　解答 (C)

因為句意為「週一上午送貨過去」，而在此句中無法單靠有空格的句子選出正確時態的動詞，因此要掌握前後文來解答。因為前文有提到總店將會提供所有烘焙品，所以可以看出產品配送的時間比起寄出電子郵件的時間晚，所以可以知道是在未來，因此要選未來式 (C) will deliver 為正確答案。

149 　名詞子句連接詞 that　　　　　　　　　　　　　　　　　　　　解答 (D)

形容詞 confident 與子句 your customers ~ products 之間要有名詞子句連接詞才行，所以名詞子句連接詞 (A) (B) (D) 都是可能的答案。confident 在 that 子句中作為形容詞使用，所以 (D) that 是正確答案。(A) what 跟關係代名詞 (B) which 後面要加不完全子句，人稱代名詞 (C) them 則無法名詞子句連接詞。

Questions 150-152 refer to the following notice.　　　　150-152 根據下面公告的內容回答問題。

NOTICE TO VALUEMART SHOPPERS

Valuemart management would like to announce that the city has _____ a request to convert the empty lot adjacent

　150 (A) denied　　　(B) submitted
　　　(C) encouraged(D) approved

to the store into a parking space.

The lot has to be paved and fenced off and undergo other light construction. However, this has already been arranged and work _____ to commence very soon.

　151 (A) expects　　　(B) is expecting
　　　(C) is expected (D) expectancy

The parking lot should be usable before the end of the month. During this time, we ask that customers avoid parking in front of the lot in order to allow the passage of construction personnel and equipment. _____, additional

　152 (A) Instead　　　(B) Nonetheless
　　　(C) In short　　　(D) Provided that

spaces are available at a parking facility on Boer Road, one block west of the store.

Please bear with us as we work toward making your Valuemart shopping experience a more convenient and enjoyable one. Thank you.

Petra Magno
Branch Manager
Valuemart Retail

致 VALUEMART 的購物者

150 Valuemart 的管理階層想要宣布該市已經同意將一塊靠近商店的空地變更為停車場。

這塊空地需要整地、架設籬笆，並進行其他簡單的工程，151 不過這一切都已經安排好了，將在近期展開工作。

停車場在月底前應該就能夠使用，在這段期間，我們要求顧客避免在這塊空地前停車，如此工程人員和設備才能通行，152 作為替代，在商店往西一個街區之外的 Boer 路上的停車場，有更多的停車位可供使用。

請體諒我們目前的施工，這是為了讓你們在 Valuemart 的購物更為方便與愉悅，謝謝！

Peter Mango
分店經理
Valuemart 零售店

單字 convert v. 轉換，換　adjacent a. 鄰接的　pave v. 鋪設　commence v. 開始　passage n. 通過
　　 bear with phr. 忍耐～；撐　convenient a. 方便的

---

150 ■ 動詞語彙 掌握上下文　　　　　　　　　　　　　　　　　　　　　　　　　解答 (D)

因為句意為「管理階層想要宣布該市已經_____將一塊靠近商店的空地變更為停車空間。」所以所有選項都可能是正確答案。因為只靠有空格的句子無法選出正確答案，所以要掌握前後文或全文。在之後文章中提到停車場在本月底前就能使用，所以可以知道這是把空地變更為停車空間的許可及同意，因此，approve（同意）的 p.p. 形 (D) approved 為正確答案。(A) deny 是「拒絕，否認」，(B) submit 是「提交」，(C) encourage 是「鼓勵」的意思。

151 ■ 被動式動詞片語　　　　　　　　　　　　　　　　　　　　　　　　　　　解答 (C)

「期待做某件事」是以 be expected to 來表現，所以 (C) is expected 為正確答案。

152 ■ 連接副詞 掌握上下文　　　　　　　　　　　　　　　　　　　　　　　　　解答 (A)

因為空格與逗號同時在句首的連接副詞位置，所以要掌握前一句與本句的關聯性，再選擇正確答案。前一句有提到要求顧客避免在空地前停車，因此本句可能是進一步提醒在此商店往西的街區之外有停車設施能夠利用，所以要選擇可以對前文增加說明的 (A) Instead（作為替代）為正確答案。如果選擇 (B) Nonetheless（仍然）或 (C) In short（簡而言之）都會使句意變得奇怪，而 (D) Provide that（萬一～的話）不能放在逗號前面。

PART 7

Questions 153-154 refer to the following notice.

153-154 根據下面告示的內容回答問題。

	Jones Gas Company		
Account Name	Christy Winston	Date	July 1
Account Number	000521-141-011	[153]Amount Overdue	$156.25
Service Address	5555 West 6th Street, Los Angeles, CA 90036	Final Payment Date	July 31

Notice of Disconnection

Our records show that as of July 1, your account has exceeded the credit limit. [154]To avoid service disconnection, please pay the amount overdue in full at any of our branch offices before July 31.

If it becomes necessary to suspend the service, reactivation will require a fee of $50. However, the standard $70 installation charge applies when a reconnection request is made more than 10 days after the final payment date.

For questions and concerns regarding this notice, please call our customer service hotline at 555-2368. Thank you.

	Jones 瓦斯公司		
帳戶名稱	Christy Winston	日期	7 月 1 日
帳戶號碼	000521-141-011	[153] 逾期金額	美金 156.25
服務地址	90036 加州洛杉磯市西六街 5555 號	付款期限	7 月 31 日

斷線通知

我們的紀錄顯示在 7 月 1 日，你的帳戶已經超過了信用額度，[154] 為了避免服務中斷，請在 7 月 31 日前在我們任何一個分行將逾期金額全數繳納。

如果有暫停服務的必要，重新啟動服務將須繳納美金 50 元，在付款期限過後 10 天以上要求要重新啟動服務，將有標準安裝費美金 70 元須繳納。

關於此通知，如有任何問題與疑慮，請撥打我們客戶服務熱線 555-2368，謝謝！

單字 □as of phr. 以～　□exceed v. 超過　□limit n. 限度
□disconnection n. 中斷　□overdue a. 過期的　□branch n. 分店
□suspend v. 中止　□reactivation n. 再啟動　□require v. 要求
□standard a. 標準的　□installation n. 設置

153

What is suggested about Ms. Winston?	關於 Winston 小姐，何者正確？
(A) She has missed a deadline for a payment.	(A) 她錯過了付款的期限
(B) She made a service deactivation request.	(B) 她要求中斷服務
(C) She charged an installation fee to her credit card.	(C) 她用信用卡支付安裝費
(D) She complained about incorrect account details.	(D) 她抱怨錯誤的帳戶資料

■ 推論 詳細內容　　　　　　　　　　　　　　　　　　　　　　　解答 (A)

這是要針對問題的重點 Ms. Winston 進行推論的重要答案。帳單中寫到 Amount Overdue: $156.25 是指 Ms. Winston 的逾期金額為 156.25 美金，因此可以推論 Ms. Winston 因為錯過繳費期限，而產生逾期金額，所以要選 (A) She has missed a deadline for a payment 為正確答案。

單字 deactivation n. 停用　account n. 帳號，結算，算數

What should Ms. Winston do to avoid paying reactivation fee?	Winston 小姐要怎麼做才能避免支付重新啟動的費用？
(A) Submit a request form to a department	(A) 給部門寄出一份申請表
(B) Confirm some of her personal information	(B) 確認部分個人資料
(C) Settle an account before the end of the month	(C) 在月底前付清帳款
(D) Schedule an installation within the next ten days	(D) 在十天內安排安裝的時間

■ 六何原則 What   解答 (C)

這是在詢問 Ms. Winston 要做什麼（What）才能避免支付重新啟動的費用的六何原則問題。與問題的重點 to avoid paying reactivation fee 相關的 To avoid service disconnection, please pay the amount overdue in full ~ before July 31. If becomes necessary to suspend the service, reactivation will require a fee of $50 指出為了避免服務中斷，請在 7 月 31 日前將逾期的金額全數繳納，如果中斷服務，重新啟動服務須繳納美金五十元。因此可以知道為了避免支付重新啟動的費用，要在 7 月 31 日前繳納應付的金額。所以要選擇 (C) Settle an account before the end of the month 為正確答案。

換句話說

pay the amount overdue 支付應繳納的金額 → Settle an account 支付結算額

單字　settle v. 支付，付（債，金額）

Cooper Memorial High School	Cooper 紀念高中
September 10	9 月 10 日
Dear Families,	親愛的家長們：
As part of our curriculum, [157]we are taking our students on an educational trip to Meadows Farm in Bodmin, Cornwall, on October 15. The purpose of this tour is to expose students to practical activities for science learning and introduce the concept of countryside conservation.	作為我們課程的一環，[157] 我們在 10 月 15 日要帶學生到 Cornwall 郡 Bodmin 鎮的 Meadows 農場去校外教學。這趟旅程的目的在於讓學生能參與科學學習和介紹鄉村保育概念的實踐活動。
[156]If you wish for your children to attend, please note the following information about the trip:	[156] 如果你希望你的孩子能夠參加，請注意以下關於校外教學的資訊：
Date: October 15	**日期**：10 月 15 日
Time: [155] 8 A.M. – Departure time from school 7 P.M. – Expected time of arrival from the trip **What to bring**: Packed lunch and refreshments **What to wear**: Comfortable and casual clothing and athletic shoes	**時間**：[155] 上午 8 點 - 從學校出發 晚上 7 點 - 預計返抵時間 **帶什麼東西**：午餐便當和點心 **穿什麼**：舒適輕便的衣服和運動鞋
[155]Students are required to be at school at least 30 minutes before departure. [156]To notify the school about your decision, please complete the permission slip **below** and return it to us no later than September 25. Thank you.	[155] 學生需要在出發前 30 分鐘到到達學校。[156] 請填寫並交回以下的回條告知是否參加，並於 9 月 25 日之前交回，謝謝！
Sincerely,	
Russel Hibbard Year 4 level coordinator	Russel Hibbard 敬上 四年級活動負責人
---	---
[157]Student's name: <u>Cassandra Fuentes</u>	[157] 學生姓名：<u>Cassandra Fuentes</u>
Date: <u>September 20</u>	日期：<u>9 月 20 日</u>
[156/157] __X__ Yes, my child will join the school trip.	[156/157] __X__ 是，我的孩子會參加校外教學
_____No, my child will not join the school trip. Signature of parent or guardian over printed name : *Ronaldo Fuentes* Ronaldo Fuentes	_____不，我的孩子不會參加校外教學 家長或監護人在鉛印姓名上簽名 : *Ronaldo Fuentes* Ronaldo Fuentes

單字 ☐curriculum n. 課程，教程　☐purpose n. 目的　☐expose v. 使露出
☐practical a. 實際性的，實用性的　☐conservation n. 保存　☐refreshment n. 零食，茶果
☐comfortable a. 舒服的　☐athletic a. 運動的，體育的　☐complete v. 完成，使完整
☐permission slip phr. （父母親同意讓學生能夠參加學校活動的）同意書，許可單
☐guardian n. 監護人

155

What time should students arrive at school for the trip? (A) 7:00 A.M. (B) 7:30 A.M. (C) 8:00 A.M. (D) 8:30 A.M.	學生幾點應該到校去參加校外教學？ (A) 早上 7 點 (B) 早上 7 點 30 分 (C) 早上 8 點 (D) 早上 8 點 30 分

■ 六何原則 What time 　　　　　　　　　　　　　　　　　　　　　　　　　　解答 (B)

這是在詢問學生們幾點（What time）要到學校的六何原則問題。與問題重點 students arrive at school 相關的 8 A.M. – Departure time from school 是指在學校出發的時間是早上 8 點，Students are required to be at school at least 30 minutes before departure 則是指學生要至少要比出發時間早 30 分鐘到學校，因此要選 (B) 7:30 A.M. 為正確答案。

156

Why did Mr. Fuentes fill out the slip? (A) To express support for an environmental project (B) To approve of an institution's dress code policy (C) To provide formal consent for an activity (D) To confirm attendance to a parents meeting	為什麼 Fuentes 先生要填寫回條？ (A) 表達對環境計畫的支持 (B) 同意一個機構的服裝規定政策 (C) 對一項活動提出正式的同意 (D) 確認參加家長座談會

■ 六何原則 Why 　　　　　　　　　　　　　　　　　　　　　　　　　　　　解答 (C)

這是在詢問 Mr. Fuentes 為什麼（Why）要填寫回條的六何原則問題。與問題的重點 fill out the slip 相關的 If you wish for your children to attend, please note the following information about the trip 首先提到如果同意子女參加校外教學，要先注意底下的訊息，接著 To notify the school about your decision, please complete the permission slip 是說為了告知學校參加與否，要填寫回條，X Yes, my child will join the school trip. 是說 Mr. Fuentes 的小孩會參加學校的旅行，所以要選 (C) To provide formal consent for an activity 為正確答案。

單字 formal a. 正式的　consent n. 同意，許可　approve v. 承認　express v. 表現　support n. 支持

157

What is suggested about Cassandra Fuentes? (A) She will be visiting a farm with her classmates. (B) She needs to pay extra for an educational tour. (C) She has to purchase a new set of uniforms soon. (D) She will be taking a science exam in advance.	關於 Cassandra Fuentes 何者正確？ (A) 她會和她的同學一起去參觀農場 (B) 她需要額外付費來參加校外教學 (C) 她很快必須買一套新的制服 (D) 她會提前參加自然科考試

■ 推論 詳細內容 　　　　　　　　　　　　　　　　　　　　　　　　　　　　解答 (A)

這是要針對問題的重點 Cassandra Fuentes 進行推論的問題。首先 we are taking our students on an education trip to Meadows Farm 是說學校要帶學生到 Meadows 農場去校外教學，接著在回條上的 Student's name: Cassandra Fuentes、X Yes, my child will join the school trip. 是說 Cassandra Fuentes 會參加學校舉辦的校外教學，所以可以推論 Cassandra Fuentes 會和同學們一起到農場進行校外教學，所以要選 (A) She will be visiting a farm with her classmates 為正確答案。

單字 extra a. 增加的，額外的　purchase v. 購買　in advance phr. 提前

Questions 158-159 refer to the following article.

158-159 根據下面文章的內容回答問題。

October 25	*The Informant Page*	10

Hotel Giant Halts Jumeirah Project

DUBAI – [158-D]France's largest hospitality chain, [159]Arnaud Hotels, has decided to postpone the construction of a one-billion-dollar hotel complex in Palm Jumeirah due to recent global economic problems. "[159]The decision was made in an effort to secure the company's funds since the crisis has been adversely affecting Dubai's tourism industry," Arnaud Hotels spokesperson Sebastian Lefebvre said. Tourism in the Arab city has suffered heavy losses after several companies slashed jobs and real estate prices tumbled. Lefebvre said [158-C]Arnaud Hotels will resume the construction once Dubai's economic condition becomes stable. [158-B]The spokesman, however, dismissed rumors about the suspension of ongoing renovation projects in London, Rome, and Madrid.

10 月 25 日	通報者	第十頁

飯店巨擘暫停 Jumeirah 計畫

杜拜 — 受到近來全球經濟問題的影響，[158-D] 法國最大的飯店連鎖集團 [159] Arnaud 飯店已經決定推遲在 Palm Jumeirah 建造一個高達十億美金的飯店區。Arnaud 飯店的發言人 Sebastian Lefebvre 說：「[159] 這個決策是為了要確保公司的資金，因為這次的經濟危機已經對杜拜的觀光產業造成了不利的影響了」。在幾個公司裁員、房地產崩盤之後，阿拉伯城市的觀光產業遭受到嚴重的損失，Lefebvre 表示 [158-C] 一旦杜拜的經濟情況變得穩定，Arnaud 飯店就會再繼續建築工程。不過，[158-B] 發言人否認了在倫敦、羅馬和馬德里正在進行的整修案會暫停的謠言。

單字
- □ hospitality n. 旅館，接待，款待
- □ secure v. 保護
- □ affect v. 影響
- □ loss n. 損失
- □ tumble v. 暴跌，大幅度下滑
- □ stable a. 安定的
- □ renovation n. 翻新，修理
- □ postpone v. 延期
- □ crisis n. 危機
- □ spokesperson n. 發言人
- □ slash v. 大幅減少
- □ resume v. 繼續
- □ dismiss v. 解散，否認
- □ complex n. 社區，複合住宅
- □ adversely ad. 不利地
- □ suffer v. 承受，受苦
- □ real estate phr. 不動產
- □ condition n. 狀況
- □ suspension n. 暫停，中止

158

What is NOT indicated about Arnaud Hotels?
(A) It experienced great financial losses.
(B) It has branches in several global cities.
(C) It will resume a project in the future.
(D) It is the largest chain in a country.

關於 Arnaud 飯店，何者錯誤？
(A) 遭逢重大的經濟損失。
(B) 在全球幾個城市有分店。
(C) 未來會重啟建案。
(D) 是一國內最大的連鎖飯店。

■ **Not/True** Not 問題

解答 (A)

這是要先在例文中找出與問題的重點 Arnaud Hotel 相關的部分，並與選項進行對照的 Not/True 問題。(A) 是例文中沒有提及的內容。因此 (A) It experienced great financial losses. 為正確答案。The spokesman ~ dismissed rumors about the suspension of ongoing renovation projects in London, Rome, and Madrid 是指飯店發言人否認了在倫敦、羅馬和馬德里的整修案會停止的謠言，因此 (B) 與例文內容一致。而 Arnaud Hotels will resume the construction once Dubai's economic condition becomes stable 是指等杜拜的經濟情況穩定，工程便會繼續，因此 (C) 也與例文內容相符。France's largest hospitality chain, Arnaud Hotels 是指 Arnaud Hotels 是法國最大的飯店連鎖集團，因此 (D) 也與例文內容一致。

單字 experience v. 經驗，經歷　loss n. 損失，遺失　resume v. 繼續

Why did Arnaud Hotels delay the construction plans?	為什麼 Arnaud 飯店要推遲建築計畫？
(A) It could not find a suitable location.	(A) 無法找到合適的地點。
(B) It wants to conserve capital.	(B) 想要保留資金。
(C) It is reducing its overseas workforce.	(C) 要減少海外的勞動力。
(D) It was unable to get a building permit.	(D) 無法取得建築許可。

■ 六何原則 Why   解答 (B)

這是在詢問 Arnaud 飯店為什麼（Why）把建設計畫推遲的六何原則問題。與問題的重點 delay the construction plans 相關的 Arnaud Hotels, has decided to postpone the construction of a one-billion-dollar hotel complex 跟 The decision was made in an effort to secure the company's funds 是說 Arnaud 飯店決定要推遲一個十億元的飯店建設案，這個決策是為了保護公司的資金，所以要選 (B) It wants to conserve capital. 為正確答案。

單字 suitable a. 適當的，合適的　conserve v. 維持，保存　capital n. 資本　overseas a. 海外的
workforce n. 人力　permit n. 許可

Questions 160-161 refer to the following e-mail.

160-161 根據下面電郵的內容回答問題。

From: Suzanne Gilmore <sgilmore@united-steel.com>

To: Matthew Nelson <mnelson@beaverton-builders.com>

Date: January 22

[160]Subject: Meeting

Dear Mr. Nelson,

I am sorry to inform you that I will not be able to meet with you on Tuesday, January 27. I know that [161]we planned to discuss the materials we will be supplying for your upcoming building project then, but I have mixed up the dates on my calendar. My director asked me to attend a trade fair in New York at the last minute, and my return flight does not arrive until late Tuesday evening. Therefore, [160]I would like to request that we move the date to Wednesday, the 28th instead, at around 1 P.M. Please let me know if this time is OK with you by calling me at 555-3812 anytime during office hours.

Thank you very much.

Sincerely,

Suzanne Gilmore
Sales representative
United Steel Corporation

寄件人：Suzanne Gilmore
　　　　<sgilmore@united-steel.com>
收件人：Matthew Nelson
　　　　<mnelson@beaverton-builders.com>
日期：1 月 22 日
[160]主旨：會議

親愛的 Nelson 先生：

我很抱歉通知你 1 月 27 日星期二我無法與你會面，我知道 [161] 我們計畫討論那些提供給你們即將開始的建案的建材，但是我在行事曆上把日期給搞混了，我們主管臨時要求我參加一個在紐約的貿易展，而我回程的飛機要到星期二深夜才會抵達，因此，[160] 我想要求把會面的時間改到 28 日星期三下午 1 點左右，如果時間上沒有問題，請在上班時間任何時候打電話給我，我的電話是 555-3812。

非常感謝你！

Suzanne Gilmore 敬上
業務代表
United 鋼鐵公司

單字 □inform v. 通知　　　　　　　□material n. 素材　　　　　　□mix up phr. 混合
　　　□at the last minute phr. 在最後關頭，最後
　　　□representative n. 員工，職員，代表

160

What does Ms. Gilmore want Mr. Nelson to do?
(A) Modify a flight itinerary
(B) Participate in a convention
(C) Delay the start of a project
(D) Reschedule a meeting

Gilmore 小姐想要 Nelson 先生做什麼？
(A) 改變一個航班的行程
(B) 參加一個會議
(C) 延期計畫的開工
(D) 重新安排會面時間

■ 六何原則 What

解答 (D)

這是在詢問 Ms. Gilmore 想要 Mr. Nelson 做什麼（What）的六何原則問題。與問題的重點 Ms. Gilmore want Mr. Nelson to do 相關的 Subject: Meeting 與 I would like to request that we move the date to Wednesday, the 28th instead, at around 1 P.M. 是說想把會面的時間改到 28 日星期三下午 1 點左右，因此要選 (D) Reschedule a meeting 為正確答案。

換句話說
move the date 移動日期 → Reschedule 變更日程

161

What is suggested about United Steel?	關於 United 鋼鐵公司，提示了什麼？
(A) Its offices are open every day.	(A) 辦公室每天都營業。
(B) It distributes building materials.	(B) 分派建築材料。
(C) Its management will fund a project.	(C) 管理階層會提供資金給一個計畫。
(D) It will merge with another company.	(D) 會和另一家公司合併。

■ 推論 詳細內容 　　　　　　　　　　　　　　　　　　　　　　　　　　　　　　　　　　解答 (B)

這是要針對問題的重點 United Steel 進行推論的問題。we planned to discuss the materials we will be supplying for your upcoming building project 是指我們計劃要討論我們（也就是 United Steel 公司）提供建材給你們（也就是 Mr. Nelson）即將開始的建案，因此可以推論 United Steel 公司是供給建築材料的公司，所以要選 (B) It distributes building materials. 為正確答案。

單字 distribute v. 分派　management n. 經營　merge v. 合併

162-164 根據下面廣告的內容回答問題。

Pacific Boltmaster

345 Richwell Drive
Daly City, CA 94017
www.pacificboltmaster.com

[162]Have you ever locked yourself outside your house or office and just couldn't figure out what to do? [162]The next time it happens, don't delay and call Pacific Boltmaster!

With 15 years of professional experience in the field, [164]Pacific Boltmaster provides emergency services for residential and commercial clients 24 hours a day, seven days a week. [163-C]We offer key duplication, broken key removal, provision of master keys, and [163-A]the installation of knob locks and deadbolt locks, which can also be purchased at our shop.

Locked out of your car? Not a problem! We provide emergency vehicle lockout services as well. Our services are available to customers in the counties of San Mateo, Santa Clara, and San Francisco only. [163-B]For inquiries or service requests, you may call 555-8080.

Pacific Boltmaster

94917 加州 Daly 市 Richwell 路 345 號
www.pacificboltmaster.com

[162] 你曾經把自己鎖在家裡或辦公室的門外而無計可施嗎？[162] 下一次再發生這樣的事，別遲疑，打電話給 Pacific Boltmaster！

秉持著十五年在這個領域的專業經驗，[164]Pacific Boltmaster 為住家與公司行號客戶提供一週七天、一天二十四小時的緊急服務。[163-C] 我們提供鑰匙的複製、移除損壞的鑰匙、萬能鑰匙的製造，還有 [163-A] 喇叭鎖和門閂鎖的安裝，這兩者也都可以在我們店裡購買。

被鎖在車外？沒問題！我們也提供緊急汽車解鎖服務，不過我們的服務僅提供給住在 San Mateo、Santa Clara 和 San Francisco 的顧客。[163-B] 如需諮詢或申請服務，請撥打 555-8080。

單字 □lock somebody / oneself out phr. 把某人鎖在門外　　□figure out phr. 發現，想出
□field n. 領域，現場　　□emergency n. 緊急　　□residential a. 居住的
□commercial a. 商業的　　□duplication n. 複製，影印　　□provision n. 提供
□deadbolt n. 門栓

162

What is the advertisement mainly about?	這則廣告是關於什麼？
(A) A package delivery company	(A) 包裹遞送公司
(B) A variety of lock services	(B) 各式鎖具服務
(C) A surveillance equipment supplier	(C) 監視設備的供應商
(D) A residential security system	(D) 住宅保全系統

■ 找出主題 主題　　　　　　　　　　　　　　　　　　　　　　　　　　　　　　　　　　解答 (B)

這是在詢問此廣告主要是關於什麼，所以要特別注意廣告的前部分。Have you ever locked yourself outside your house or office 先問是不是曾經把自己鎖在家裡或辦公室外之後，The next time it happens, don't delay and call Pacific Boltmaster! 是指下次在發生相同情況時，不要遲疑，打電話給 Pacific Boltmaster，接下來介紹與鑰匙相關的服務，所以要選 (B) A variety of lock services 為正確答案。

單字 surveillance n. 監視，監督

163

What is NOT offered by Pacific Boltmaster?	Pacific Boltmaster 不提供什麼服務？
(A) Distribution of door knobs	(A) 販售門把
(B) Consultation over the phone	(B) 透過電話洽詢
(C) The replication of different kinds of keys	(C) 複製不同的鑰匙
(D) The shipping of items to multiple locations	(D) 將貨品運到多處地點

■ **Not/True** Not 問題　　　　　　　　　　　　　　　　　　　　　　　　　　　　　　　　解答 (D)

這是要先在例文中找出與問題的重點 offered by Pacific Boltmaster 相關的部分，並與選項進行對照的 Not/True 問題。the installation of knob locks ~, which can also be purchased at our shop 是說喇叭鎖和門閂鎖的安裝，都可以在店裡選購，因此 (A) 與例文內容一致。For inquiries ~ you may call 555-8080. 是說欲知更多詳情，請撥打電話，因此 (B) 與例文內容一致。we offer key duplication 是說提供鑰匙的複製，因此 (C) 也與例文內容一致。(D) 是例文中沒有提及的內容，因此要選 (D) The shipping of items to multiple locations 為正確答案。

單字 distribution n. 供給，配給　consultation n. 諮詢　replication n. 複製　multiple a. 多樣的

164

What is suggested about Pacific Boltmaster?	關於 Pacific Boltmaster，提示了什麼？
(A) It responds promptly to customers.	(A) 很快回應顧客的詢問。
(B) It transferred its headquarters to San Francisco.	(B) 總部要移到 San Francisco。
(C) It produces a range of surveillance devices.	(C) 生產一系列的監視器材。
(D) It has partnered with a vehicle manufacturer.	(D) 和汽車製造商合作。

■ 推論 詳細內容　　　　　　　　　　　　　　　　　　　　　　　　　　　　　　　　　　解答 (A)

這是要針對問題的重點 Pacific Boltmaster 進行推論的問題。Pacific Boltmaster provides emergency services ~ 24 hours a day, seven days a week 是指 Pacific Boltmaster 的緊急服務是一天二十四小時、一週七天提供的，因此可以推論出 Pacific Boltmaster 公司對於客戶的任何邀請都能夠迅速的反應並回復，因此要選 (A) It responds promptly to customers. 為正確答案。

單字 promptly ad. 立即地　transfer v. 移轉　headquarters n. 總部

NOTICE: Tenants of Rosenmore Place	公告：Rosenmore 社區的住戶
[165]FIRE DRILL Monday, August 15, 8 A.M.	[165] 火災演習 8 月 15 日星期一 早上 8 點
[167]In accordance with state laws, [165]Rosenmore Place will hold a fire drill on Monday next week. All tenants are required to participate. The exercise is meant to familiarize residents with the building's alarm system and emergency exit points. It also aims to educate them on how to evacuate the building safely in case of a fire.	[167] 按照州的法律，[165]Rosenmore 社區將在下週一舉辦一場火災演習。所有的住戶都要參加。這個演習的目的在於讓所有住戶都熟悉大樓的警報系統和緊急逃生門，另外也著重於教育住戶要如何在火災時安全地從大樓中疏散。
A complete set of instructions on the drill has been distributed to all units. Tenants are advised to read the exit procedure thoroughly to avoid accidents during the exercise. [166]It will start with the ringing of the alarm, which will signal everyone to leave the building and proceed to the open parking area. After that, security personnel will inspect all floors to make sure that the building is vacant. Please note that no one will be allowed to return to their units until the alarm has been shut off.	演習的完整說明已經全部發送給所有的住戶，建議住戶要仔細地閱讀逃生程序，避免在演習中發生意外。[166] 最先會聽到警鈴，這是要每個人都離開大樓並前往開放的停車區域的信號。接著，保全人員會檢查所有的樓層以確定所有人都離開了大樓，請注意，沒有人可以在警鈴解除前回到他們的家。
The drill is expected to last for about 15 minutes provided that everyone vacates the building as instructed. Management looks forward to tenants' full cooperation and hopes that this exercise will make them more knowledgeable about fire safety procedures.	火災演習大約會持續 15 分鐘，讓所有人能依指示從大樓中撤離。管理委員會希望住戶全力配合，讓這一次的火災演習能讓大家更知道火災安全逃生的程序。

單字　□tenant n. 住戶，承租人　　□fire drill phr. 火災演習　　□in accordance with phr. 按照～
　　　□familiarize v. 使熟悉　　　□emergency n. 緊急（狀況）　□point n. 位置
　　　□aim v. 目標　　　　　　　□evacuate v. 逃出，躲避　　□in case of phr. 萬一～
　　　□instruction n. 指導，說明　□distribute v. 分配，配給　　□unit n. 單位
　　　□procedure n. 程序　　　　□thoroughly ad. 仔細地，有步驟地　□signal v. 通知
　　　□proceed to phr. 往～前進　□personnel n. 職員，人員　　□inspect v. 檢查
　　　□vacant a. 空的　　　　　　□note v. 注意　　　　　　　□vacate v. 使變空，離開
　　　□cooperation n. 合作　　　□knowledgeable a. 有知識的，廣博的

165

What is the notice mainly about? (A) Emergency tips (B) New apartment units (C) A procedural change (D) A safety exercise	這個公告主要關於什麼？ (A) 緊急狀況的提示 (B) 新的公寓 (C) 宣布程序上的一項改變 (D) 宣布一項安全演習

■ 找出主題 主題　　　　　　　　　　　　　　　　　　　　　　　　　　　　　解答 (D)

這是在問此公告是關於什麼的找出主題問題，所以要特別注意公告的前部分。公告上端的 FIRE DRILL 與 Rosenmore Place will hold a fire drill 是先說 Rosenmore Place 會舉行火災演習後，再說明與火災演習相關的細節，因此要選 (D) A safety exercise 為正確答案。

換句話說
a fire drill 火災演習 → A safety exercise 安全訓練

166

According to the notice, what should residents do upon hearing the alarm?	根據這個告示，住戶聽到警鈴後，應該做什麼？
(A) Proceed to a designated location	(A) 前往一個指定的地點
(B) Look for a security guard	(B) 找一個警衛
(C) Read the drill instructions	(C) 閱讀火災演習的資料
(D) Contact the building management	(D) 聯絡大樓的管理委員會

■ 六何原則 What   解答 (A)

這是在詢問住戶聽到警鈴後，應該做什麼（What）的六何原則問題。與問題的重點 residents do upon hearing the alarm 相關的 It will start with the ringing of the alarm, which will signal everyone to leave the building and proceed to the open parking area 是說會先聽到警鈴，這是要每個人都離開大樓並前往開放的停車區域的信號，所以要選 (A) Proceed to a designated location 為正確答案。

單字 designated a. 指定的

167

What is suggested about Rosenmore Place?	關於 Rosenmore 社區，提示了什麼？
(A) It acquired new equipment.	(A) 取得新的設備。
(B) It has many fire hazards.	(B) 有很多火災的隱患。
(C) It adheres to government policies.	(C) 遵守政府的政策。
(D) It has hidden exit points.	(D) 有隱藏的逃生點。

■ 推論 詳細內容   解答 (C)

這是要針對問題的重點 Rosenmore Place 進行推論的問題。因為 In accordance with state laws, Rosenmore Place will hold a fire drill 是說根據州政府的規定，Rosenmore Place 將舉辦火災演習，所以可以推論 Rosenmore Place 是遵守政府政策的，因此 (C) It adheres to government policies. 為正確答案。

換句話說
In accordance with state laws 按照州的法律 → adheres to government policies 遵守政府政策

單字 acquire v. 尋求，獲得 hazard n. 危險源 adhere to phr. 根據～，遵守 hidden a. 隱藏的

From: Brent Watson <bwatson@dixon-solutions.com>	寄件人：Brent Watson <bwatson@dixon-solutions.com>
[169]To: Marketing Staff <marketingstaff@dixon-solutions. com>	[169]收件人：行銷人員 <marketingstaff@dixon-solutions.com>
[171-D]Date: October 12 Subject: New Office	[171-D]日期：10 月 12 日 主旨：新辦公室
To all staff members,	致所有同仁：
You may have observed that [169]the demand for our department's services has increased substantially over the last two quarters. As a result, we have had to double our workforce. Unfortunately, the addition of staff has not produced the expected increase in productivity. [168-A]After studying the problem, I have found the cause to be a lack of adequate facilities.	你們可能已經注意到 [169] 在 過去兩季裡，對我們部門服務的需求大幅增加，因此，我們必須要將人手增加一倍。然而，新進人員所增加的產值並不如預期。[168-A] 在我們探討了這個問題之後，我發現原因出在缺乏合適的設施。
I raised the issue with upper management and am happy to announce that [170/171-A]during last week's meeting, the board approved a proposal to move our offices to a larger space on the eighth floor of the building. [171-C]The new office will come with fully equipped workstations for everyone, as well as several rooms for holding meetings and training seminars.	我已將這個問題告訴高層，[170/171-A] 並很高興能在上週的會議中宣布，董事會同意了一項提案，要將我們的辦公室搬到這棟大樓八樓一個更大的空間，[171-C] 在新的辦公室裡，為每個人提供了配備完整的工作站，同時還會有好幾個空間作為會議與訓練課程之用。
[171-D]Renovations on the eighth floor are expected to begin at the end of this month and last through November. In the meantime, some of us will begin working out of a temporary office space on the third floor.	[171-D] 八樓的整修預計在本月底開始，持續到 11 月，同時，我們其中一些人將會開始在三樓的臨時辦公空間工作。
I appreciate your understanding. Please let me know if you have any questions.	我很感謝你們的諒解，如果有任何問題，請讓我知道。
Sincerely,	
Brent Watson Marketing director	Brent Watson 敬上 行銷部主任

單字 □observe v. 目擊，觀察　□substantially ad. 相當地　□workforce n. 勞動力
　　 □unfortunately ad. 可惜地，不幸地　□productivity n. 生產率，生產力　□adequate a. 適切的，充分的
　　 □raise v. 舉起　□approve v. 承認　□temporary a. 臨時的

168

What problem does Mr. Watson mention?	Watson 先生提到什麼問題？
(A) Employees do not have a suitable work environment.	(A) 員工沒有合適的工作環境。
(B) The company cannot increase wages as planned.	(B) 公司不能依計畫增加薪資。
(C) Customers have been complaining about the staff.	(C) 顧客對員工有所抱怨。
(D) Management is unhappy with the quality of its products.	(D) 管理階層對於公司的產品品質不滿意。

■ **Not/True** True 問題　　　　　　　　　　　　　　　　　　　　　　　　　解答 (A)

這是要先在例文中找出與問題的重點 problem 相關的部分，並與選項進行對照的 Not/True 問題。After studying the problem, I have found the cause to be a lack of adequate facilities. 是指探討問題後發現原因出在缺乏合適的設施，因此 (A) 與例文內容一致，要選擇 (A) Employees do not have a suitable work environment. 為正確答案，(B) (C) (D) 則是例文中沒有提及的內容。

換句話說

a lack of adequate facilities 缺乏適切的設施 → do not have a suitable work environment 沒有適合的工作環境

單字 suitable a. 適合的　wage n. 工資，薪水

169

What is suggested about the marketing department?	關於行銷部門，提示了什麼？
(A) It has moved to another location.	(A) 已經搬到別的地點。
(B) It plans to hire more staff members.	(B) 計畫聘僱更多的人員。
(C) It is located at the company's headquarters.	(C) 位在公司的總部。
(D) It experienced a period of growth.	(D) 經歷了一段成長期。

推論 詳細內容　　　　　　　　　　　　　　　　　　　　　　　　　　　　解答 (D)

這是要針對問題的重點 the marketing department 進行推論的問題。透過電子郵件上端的 To Marketing Staff 可以知道這封信件是以行銷部職員為對象寄出，the demand for our department's services has increased substantially over the last two quarters. As a result, we have had to double our workforce 是說在過去兩季裡對於本部門服務的需求大幅增加，因此將部門人手增加一倍，所以可以推論出行銷部在特定時間內迅速成長，因此要選 (D) It experienced a period of growth. 為正確答案。

單字 growth n. 成長

170

According to Mr. Watson, what happened last week?	根據 Mr. Watson，上週發生了什麼事？
(A) A training seminar was held.	(A) 舉行了一場訓練研習。
(B) An order of furniture arrived.	(B) 訂購的家具送到了。
(C) An organizational meeting took place.	(C) 召開一個組織的會議。
(D) A board member was introduced.	(D) 介紹一位董事會成員。

六何原則 What　　　　　　　　　　　　　　　　　　　　　　　　　　　　　解答 (C)

這是在詢問上周發生什麼（What）事情的六何原則問題。與問題重點 happened last week 相關的 during last week's meeting, the board approved a proposal 是說上週的會議中宣布董事會同意一項提案，所以要選 (C) An organizational meeting took place. 為正確答案。

單字 introduce v. 介紹

171

What is NOT stated about the proposal?	關於提案，並沒有提到什麼？
(A) It was approved only recently.	(A) 最近才剛通過。
(B) It will be included in next year's budget.	(B) 包括在下年度的預算中。
(C) It contained a provision for new equipment.	(C) 包含提供新設備。
(D) It will go into effect at the end of October.	(D) 在十月底生效。

Not/True Not 問題　　　　　　　　　　　　　　　　　　　　　　　　　　　解答 (B)

這是要先在例文中找出與問題的重點 the proposal 相關的部分，並與選項進行對照的 Not/True 問題。during last week's meeting, the board approved a proposal 是指上週的會議中宣布董事會同意一項提案，因此 (A) 與例文的內容一致。(B) 是例文中沒有提及的內容，所以 (B) It will be included in next year's budget. 為正確答案。The new office will come with fully equipped workstations 是說新的辦公室中有完善的設備，因此 (C) 也與例文內容一致。在電子郵件上端的 Date: October 12 與 Renovations on the eighth floor are expected to begin at the end of this month 可以知道電子郵件是在 10 月時寄出，八樓的整修則在本月底，也就是 10 月底開始，因此 (D) 與例文內容一致。

單字 recently ad. 最近地　budget n. 預算　contain v. 包含　go into effect phr. 生效

Business Today

In the spotlight: Heyworth Industries

[172]A known producer of high performance protective equipment, Heyworth Industries ensures the safety of workers in the chemical, healthcare, and automotive industries, as well as other sectors that involve the handling of hazardous materials. [174-C]Founded 30 years ago in Syracuse, New York, it began by designing and manufacturing a broad array of protective garments such as fireproof clothing, chemical resistant clothing, and limited-use and disposable clothing. Over the years, these products became widely known and used by companies not only within the United States but all over the world. [172]As a result, Heyworth Industries developed from a small local business into a multinational corporation.

To meet rising client demand, [173]Heyworth Industries established its first overseas headquarters in Toronto, Canada.

Two years after that, it opened a factory in Guadalajara, Mexico, to increase its production capacity. Last year, another facility began operations in Shanghai, China, which helped in the manufacturing process while at the same time lowering costs. Heyworth Industries also boosted its logistics system by building a warehouse in Birmingham, Alabama. Finally, a shipping and distribution center was opened in Chicago, Illinois, to handle the shipment of products to various locations in the United States.

In addition to the continuous improvement of its facilities, Heyworth Industries has made the placement of orders easier for customers. [175]Orders are now received through its toll-free hotline at 1-800-555-2948, by fax at (315) 555-2950, and through its Web site at www.heyworth.com.

今日商業

焦點故事：Heyworth Industries

[172]Heyworth Industries 是一個以生產高性能保護裝置的著名製造商，以確保在化學、醫療保健、汽車產業，及其他處理危險物質產業的員工的安全。[174-C]三十年前在紐約州雪城成立，剛開始是以設計並製造各種安全保護衣著裝備起家，像是防火衣、抗化學腐蝕性衣著、限制性用途或拋棄式衣物。這麼多年以來，這些產品已經廣為人知，而且不僅廣泛用於美國國內的公司，還遍及世界各地。[172]因此，Heyworth Industries 從一個區域性的小公司發展成一個跨國公司。

為了配合成長的顧客需求，[173]Heyworth Industries 在加拿大的多倫多成立第一個海外總部。

兩年後，在墨西哥的 Guadalajara 設立了一家工廠，以增加生產量。去年，另一個工廠在中國的上海開始營運，除了幫助製程，同時也降低成本。為了強化其物流系統，Heyworth Industries 還在阿拉巴馬州的伯明罕建立了一個倉庫。最後，在伊利諾州的芝加哥建立一個物流中心來處理美國境內多處的產品運送。

除了持續改善其設備，Heyworth Industries 也讓顧客訂貨變得更簡易。[175]顧客可以透過免付費專線 1-800-555-2948、傳真 (315)555-2950 和網站 www.heyworth.com 來下訂單。

單字　□high performance phr. 高性能　□protective a. 保護的　□ensure v. 保障

□hazardous a. 危險的　□an array of phr. 一系列的　□garment n. 衣服

□fireproof clothing phr. 防火裝　□disposable a. 拋棄式的　□multinational a. 多國籍的

□demand n. 需求　□establish v. 設立　□overseas ad. 海外地

□capacity n. 能力，容量　□boost v. 強化，使增加　□logistics n. 物流

□warehouse n. 倉庫　□toll-free phr. 免費的　□hotline n. 諮詢專線

172

Why was the article written?	為什麼寫這篇文章？
(A) To highlight the development of a company	(A) 強調一家公司的發展
(B) To outline the achievements of an individual	(B) 列出一個人的成就
(C) To discuss the uses of protective equipment	(C) 討論保護裝置的使用
(D) To introduce a new line of merchandise	(D) 介紹一種新的系列商品

找出主題 寫文章的理由   解答 (A)

這是在詢問寫出此報導的理由。本問題要注意例文的整體內容才能夠找出主題。A known producer of high performance protective equipment, Heyworth Industries 是在介紹 Heyworth 公司是生產高性能保護裝置的著名製造商，As a result, Heyworth Industries developed from a small local business into a multinational corporation 則是說 Heyworth 公司從一個區域性的小公司發展為跨國公司，因此要選 (A) To highlight the development of a company 為正確答案。

單字 outline v. 講述～的概要　individual n. 個人　introduce v. 介紹，引進

173

Where did Heyworth Industries open its first foreign headquarters?	Heyworth Industries 在哪裡成立第一個海外總部？
(A) In Shanghai	(A) 上海
(B) In Chicago	(B) 芝加哥
(C) In Syracuse	(C) 雪城
(D) In Toronto	(D) 多倫多

六何原則 Where   解答 (D)

這是在詢問 Heyworth 公司首次在海外的哪裡（Where）設立總部的六何原則問題。與問題的重點 first foreign headquarters 相關的 Heyworth Industries established its first overseas headquarters in Toronto, Canada 是指 Heyworth 公司在加拿大多倫多成立第一個海外總部，所以要選擇 (D) In Toronto 為正確答案。

換句話說

open ~ foreign headquarters 開設海外總部 → established overseas headquarters 設立海外總部

174

What is stated about Heyworth Industries?	關於 Heyworth Industries，提到了什麼？
(A) It will relocate its logistics division to Asia.	(A) 將把物流部門移至亞州。
(B) It plans to establish more facilities overseas.	(B) 打算在海外成立更多的據點。
(C) It has been operating for three decades.	(C) 已經成立有三十年了。
(D) It needs to improve its sales performance.	(D) 需要改進銷售業績。

Not/True True 問題   解答 (C)

本題是要在文章中找到與本問題的重點 Heyworth Industries 相關的內容後，比較選項與文章的 Not/True 問題。(A) (B) (D) 都是例文中沒有提及的內容。而 Founded 30 years ago in Syracuse, New York 是指三十年前在紐約州雪城成立，所以 (C) 與例文內容一致，因此要選 (C) It has been operating for three decades. 為正確答案。

單字 division n. 部門　establish v. 設立　decade n. 十年

What is suggested about Heyworth Industries' ordering system?
(A) It presents a selection of different shipping services.
(B) It allows clients to make requests through various methods.
(C) It was designed to help the company save on operational costs.
(D) It requires that all payments be made through a Web site.

關於 Heyworth Industries 的訂單系統，提示了什麼？
(A) 提供不同的運送服務。
(B) 讓顧客透過不同的方式下訂單。
(C) 設計來幫助公司節省營運成本。
(D) 要求所有的付款都要透過網站。

■ 推論 詳細內容　　　　　　　　　　　　　　　　　　　　　　　解答 (B)

這是要針對問題的重點 Heyworth Industries' ordering system 進行推論的問題。Orders are now received through its toll-free hotline ~, by fax~, and through its Web site 是指可以透過免付費專線、傳真及網站來下訂單，因此要選 (B) It allows clients to make requests through various methods. 為正確答案。

單字 operational a. 營運上的　allow v. 同意

Questions 176-180 refer to the following memo.

176-180 根據下面備忘錄的內容回答問題。

Delta Technologies

To: Sales department employees
From: Pete Springer, director
     Alice Lee, assistant director
Date: February 15
Subject: Wholesale Operations

[177]The board is pleased with the sales department's performance last year. By forming agreements with distributors across the country, Delta Technologies increased retail sales of desktop and laptop computers by 20 percent. [178-B]This year, the board wants us to intensify wholesale operations by bidding for supply contracts with public and private companies.

In connection with this, [176]we have decided to create a standard procedure for preparing bids:

* **Research your client.** Find out the nature of the client's business to identify its equipment needs.
* [179]**Define the client's bid evaluation criteria.** Read quotation requests thoroughly to learn the client's decision-making process and preferences for selecting equipment.
* [180]**Identify price trends.** To make a competitive offer, learn the standard wholesale packages, discounts, and special services provided by competitors.
* **Create a strategy for product endorsement and pricing.** [180]Once you have identified the client's needs and the most probable offers from competitors, determine the best bid you can give without compromising the transaction's profitability.
* **Prepare a bid presentation.** Create a presentation discussing your offer. Highlight product features and their benefits to the client's operations.

If you have questions or comments regarding the procedure, please contact us.

Delta 科技公司

收件人：業務部門職員
寄件人：Pete Springer 主任
     Alice Lee 助理主任
日期：2 月 15 日
主旨：批發業務

[177] 董事會非常滿意業務部門去年的表現，藉由和全國的經銷商達成共識，Delta 科技公司在桌上型電腦和筆記型電腦的零售上增加了 20%。[178-B] 今年，董事會要我們藉由參與公家單位和私人企業的設備合約競標來加強批發業務。

為了要達到目標，[176] 我們制定了一套準備競標的標準程序：

* **認識你的客戶**：去研究客戶是做什麼的，並找出他們對設備的需求。
* [179] **定義客戶對競標的評估條件**：詳讀報價的要求，來了解客戶選擇設備的決策過程與偏好。
* [180] **確認價錢的趨勢**：為了要提出一個具有競爭力的報價，必須要知道標準的批發內容、折扣，還有我們競爭對手所提出的特別服務。
* **為產品的背書與定價制定一個策略**：[180] 一旦你已經確認了客戶的需求，以及競爭對手最可能的報價，接著就決定你能提出的最好而不會影響利潤的報價。
* **準備競標的口頭報告**：做一份口頭報告來討論你的報價，強調產品的特色和產品對客戶營運的好處。

如果你對這個程序有問題或意見，請和我們聯絡。

單字
□ wholesale a. 批發的，大量販賣的
□ operation n. 營運，經營
□ board n. 董事會
□ performance n. 表現，成果
□ agreement n. 協議
□ distributor n. 物流業者，批發商
□ retail a. 零售的
□ intensify v. 強化
□ bid v. （在拍賣中）喊價
□ in connection with phr. 與～有關聯
□ procedure n. 過程
□ identify v. 確認，認證
□ evaluation n. 評價
□ criterion n. 基準（pl. criteria）
□ quotation n. 報價
□ competitive n. 有競爭力的
□ endorsement n. 背書
□ probable a. 很可能發生的，可信的
□ determine v. 決定，確定
□ compromise v. 妥協，危及
□ transaction n. 交易
□ profitability n. 獲利性
□ highlight v. 強調
□ feature n. 特徵

Why was the memo written?	為什麼寫這個備忘錄？
(A) To outline a project plan	(A) 列出專案計畫的大綱
(B) To schedule a meeting	(B) 安排一個會議的時間
(C) To detail an office policy	(C) 詳述一個辦公室的政策
(D) To explain a set of procedures	(D) 解釋一套程序

■ **找出主題** 寫文章的理由　　　　　　　　　　　　　　　　　　　　　解答 (D)

這個問題是在詢問發布此備忘錄的理由。在這問題中要特別注意在例文中間提及的相關內容。we have decided to create a standard procedure for preparing bids 是指為了達到目標而制定了一套投標的標準程序，因此要選 (D) To explain a set of procedure 為正確答案。

單字　detail v. 告知細節

Why are members of the board pleased?	為什麼董事會的成員很滿意？
(A) Production rates rose.	(A) 生產率提升
(B) Brand awareness improved.	(B) 品牌能見度改善
(C) Sales levels increased.	(C) 銷售成果增加
(D) New clients have been found.	(D) 找到新客戶

■ **六何原則** Why　　　　　　　　　　　　　　　　　　　　　　　　解答 (C)

這是在詢問董事會的成員為什麼（Why）開心的六何原則問題。與問題的重點 members of the board pleased 有關聯的 The board is pleased with the sales department's performance last year. 是指董事會非常滿意業務部門去年的表現，之後提到 Delta Technologies increased retail sales of desktop and laptop computers by 20 percent 是指 Delta Technologies 公司在桌上型電腦和筆記型電腦的零售上增加了 20%，所以可以知道董事會成員們因為販賣量增加而感到開心，所以要選擇 (C) Sales levels increase 為正確答案。

換句話說

increased retail sales 零售販賣額增加 → Sales levels increased 販賣量增加

單字　awareness n. 認知度，認知

What is mentioned about Delta Technologies?	關於 Delta 科技公司，何者正確？
(A) It has several outlets around the world.	(A) 在世界各地有好幾個據點。
(B) It sells items in large quantities.	(B) 產品大量銷售。
(C) It is owned by public investors.	(C) 由大眾投資者擁有這家公司。
(D) It has elected a new board member.	(D) 已選出一位新的董事會成員。

■ **Not/True** True 問題　　　　　　　　　　　　　　　　　　　　　　解答 (B)

這是要先在例文中找出與 Delta Technologies 問題的重點相關的部分，並與選項進行對照的 Not/True 問題。(A) (C) (D) 都是例文中沒有提及的部分。This year, the board wants us to intensify wholesale operations 是指董事會想要加強批發業務，因此要選與內容一致的 (B) It sells items in large quantities. 為正確答案。

換句話說

wholesale operations 批發販賣 → sells items in large quantities 大量販賣商品

單字　outlet n. 店鋪，量販店　elect v. 選出，抽選

179

What do employees need to know about prospective clients to prepare bids?	員工需要知道潛在客戶的什麼，以準備投標？
(A) Their shipping and handling preferences	(A) 他們對運送與管理的偏好
(B) The budget for their advertising campaigns	(B) 他們廣告活動的預算
(C) Their equipment purchasing habits	(C) 設備購買的習慣
(D) The status of their current assets	(D) 他們目前資產的狀態

■ 六何原則 What   解答 (C)

這是在詢問員工需要知道潛在客戶們需要什麼（What）以準備投標的六何原則問題。與問題重點 employees need to know about prospective clients to prepare bids 相關的 Define the client's bid evaluation criteria 是說要先定義客戶對競標的條件，之後的 Read quotation requests thoroughly to learn the client's decision-making process and preferences for selecting equipment. 則是指要詳讀報價的要求，來了解客戶選擇設備的決策過程與偏好，因此要選擇 (C) Their equipment purchasing habits 為正確答案。

換句話說
decision-making process and preferences for selecting equipment 選擇設備的決策過程與偏好
→ equipment purchasing habits 採購習慣

單字 prospective a. 將來的，有希望的 budget n. 預算，預算案 status n. 狀態 asset n. 資產，財產

180

What is indicated about Delta Technologies' bidding strategy?	關於 Delta 科技公司的競標策略為何？
(A) It will guarantee large profits from transactions.	(A) 確保交易獲得很大的利潤。
(B) It was designed by a consultant.	(B) 由顧問來設計。
(C) It compares prices to those of competitors.	(C) 和競爭對手的價格做比較。
(D) It is primarily for private clients.	(D) 主要針對私人企業的客戶。

■ 推論 詳細內容   解答 (C)

這是要針對問題中的重點 Delta Technologies 進行推論的問題。Identify price trends. To make a competitive offer, learn the standard wholesale packages, discounts, and special services provided by competitors. 是指要找出價錢的趨勢，為了要提出一個具有競爭力的報價，標準的批發內容、折扣、還有我們競爭對手所提出的特別服務都要知道，這樣才能確認價格走向，Once you have identified ~ the most probable offers from competitors, determine the best bid 則是說一旦確認過競爭者可能的報價，接著就要決定最佳的價格，所以可以知道 Delta Technologies 公司會比較過競爭者的價格後再決定競標價，因此要選 (C) It compares prices to those of competitors. 為正確答案。

單字 guarantee v. 保障 compare v. 比較 primarily ad. 主要地

例文1

Asgardheim Incorporated
Where Your Dreams Reign Supreme
Giallanghorn 89, SE-102 29 Stockholm, Sweden

To: Customer Service team
From: Georgina Lindberg, Customer Service Director

Date: March 15
Subject: New Assignments

Finally, our new offices in Reykjavik, Oslo, and Helsinki will open next month. [182]As our business expands into other European countries for the first time, we expect a significant increase in the number of client inquiries. That is why the management has decided to rearrange our client service system. Starting April 1, the following people will be in charge of addressing all questions and concerns that fall under their respective fields of responsibility:

Britta Ostergard	Membership changes and terminations
David Gronholm	Membership upgrades and renewals
Eva Andersen	Membership suspensions and transfers
[181/184]Hans Birkeland	General inquiries about Asgardheim insurance plans

We trust that everyone will continue their outstanding performance in the new assignments. If you have any questions, you may contact me directly at extension number 188.

例文2

To: cs@asgardheimincorporated.co
From: Astrid Jakobsson <astrid.jakobsson@odinsmail. com>
Date: April 8
Subject: Membership

To whom it may concern,

[185-D]I moved here from Copenhagen last March 31 and heard from one of my new colleagues that your company provides excellent homeowners' insurance plans. [185-B]I am currently living in a one-bedroom apartment unit in Helsinki at Freyja Towers, and [185-C]I would like to have my personal property insured, particularly those items that are not covered by the building association's policy.

[184]I would really appreciate it if you could get back to me with information about your available insurance plans. Thank you for your time.

Astrid Jakobsson

Asgardheim 公司
在這裡，你的夢想是至高無上的
瑞典 Stockholm 市 Giallanghorn 路 89
號，SE102 29

收件人：客戶服務團隊
寄件人：Georgina Lindberg，客戶服務
主任
日期：3 月 15 日
主旨：新的工作分配

我們在 Reykjavik 市、Oslo 市和 Helsinki 市的新辦公室終於在下個月要開幕了，[182] 隨著我們的業務第一次擴展到歐洲其他國家，我們可以預期客戶詢問的量會顯著地增加，這也是為什麼管理階層決定要重新安排我們的客戶服務系統。從 4 月 1 日起，以下這些人會負責處理落在他們負責領域裡的所有問題與疑慮。

Britta Ostergard	會員更改與終止
David Gronholm	會員升級與續約
Eva Andersen	會員中止與移轉
[181/184]Hans Birkeland	關於 Asgardheim 保險計畫的一般詢問

我們相信每個人會在新的工作分配上繼續有突出的表現。如果你有任何問題，可以撥打分機 188 與我直接連絡。

收件人：cs@asgardheimincorporated.co
寄件人：astrid.jakobsson@odinsmail.com
日期：4 月 8 日
主旨：會員

敬啟者：

[185-D] 我上個月 3 月 31 日從哥本哈根搬到這裡，我聽我一個新同事說你們提供的屋主保險計畫很棒，[185-B] 我現在住在 Helsinki 市的 Freyja 大樓中的一房公寓，[185-C] 我想要針對我個人的財產投保，尤其是那些大樓保單沒有涵蓋的項目。

[184] 如果你能提供我你目前有的保險計畫，那就太感謝了，在此謝謝你撥冗處理。

Astrid Jakobsson

例文 1 單字 □supreme a. 最佳的，最大的 □expand v. 擴張　　　　□inquiry n. 疑問
　　　　　　□rearrange v. 重新配置　　□in charge of phr. 負責～，交辦　□address v. 處理，回應
　　　　　　□respective a. 各自的，分別的　　　　　　　　　　　□termination n. 終止
　　　　　　□renewal n. 更新　　　□suspension n. 中止，保留，暫緩　□outstanding a. 傑出的，顯著的
　　　　　　□assignment n. 工作，任務
例文 2 單字 □colleague n. 同僚　　　□personal property phr. 個人財產　□cover v. 保障

181

What is most likely Asgardheim Incorporated?	Asgardheim 公司最有可能是做什麼的？
(A) A travel agency	(A) 旅行社
(B) A marketing firm	(B) 行銷公司
(C) An insurance company	(C) 保險公司
(D) A shipping corporation	(D) 運輸公司

■ 推論 整體內容　　　　　　　　　　　　　　　　　　　　　　　解答 (C)

因為是要推論與問題重點 Asgardheim Incorporated 的問題，所以要從有提到 Asgardheim 公司的表格中開始尋找相關的內容。表格中 Hans Birkeland, General inquiries about Asgardheim insurance plans 指出 Asgardheim 公司有專門負責保險計畫諮詢的職員，因此可以推論出 Asgardheim 是保險公司，所以要選 (C) An insurance company 為正確答案。

單字 agency n. 代辦處　shipping n. 海運，運輸

182

What is suggested in the memo about Asgardheim Incorporated?	在備忘錄中，關於 Asgardheim 公司，提示了什麼？
(A) It already has offices in Europe.	(A) 在歐洲已經有辦公室了。
(B) It plans to launch a service in April.	(B) 在四月份要開始一項新的服務。
(C) It needs to downsize its workforce.	(C) 需要減少員工數。
(D) It will reorganize its management structure.	(D) 管理階層會重新組織。

■ 推論 詳細內容　　　　　　　　　　　　　　　　　　　　　　　解答 (A)

這是要推論在表格內與問題重點 Asgardheim Incorporate 相關的問題，因此要由例文 1 的表格中尋找與 Asgardheim 相關的內容。表格中的 As our business expands into other European countries for the first time 是指業務第一次擴展到歐洲其他國家，因此可以推論在歐洲已經有一個辦公室，所以要選 (A) It already has offices in Europe. 為正確答案。

單字 launch v. 開始，發行　downsize v. 減少　reorganize v. 重新編制，重新組織　structure n. 構造，體制

183

In the memo, the word "addressing" in paragraph 1, line 4 is closest in meaning to	在備忘錄裡的第一段第四行，「addressing」的意思與哪個字最接近？
(A) revising	(A) 修改
(B) forwarding	(B) 轉寄
(C) answering	(C) 回答
(D) directing	(D) 引導

■ 同義詞　　　　　　　　　　　　　　　　　　　　　　　　　　　解答 (C)

例文 1 的表格中提到 addressing 的句子 the following people will be in charge of addressing all questions and concerns 中的 address 是「操作，處理（問題）」，也就是「回應（問題）」的意思，因此要選擇同樣有「回應」意思的 (C) answering 為正確答案。

單字 revise v. 修正　forward v. 傳送　direct v. 指示

184

Who will probably attend to Ms. Jakobsson's inquiry? (A) Britta Ostergard (B) Hans Birkeland (C) Eva Andersen (D) David Gronholm	誰有可能處理 Jakobsson 小姐的問題？ (A) Britta Ostergard (B) Hans Birkeland (C) Eva Andersen (D) David Gronholm

■ 推論 連結問題　　　　　　　　　　　　　　　　　　　　　　　　　　　　解答 (B)

這是要綜合兩篇例文才能解題的連結問題。所以要從有提及問題重點 Ms. Jakobsson's inquiry 的例文 2 電子郵件中開始確認相關內容。

例文 2 電子郵件中 I would really appreciate it if you could get back to me with information about your available insurance plans 是說 Ms. Jakobsson 要求提供保險計畫，這是第一個線索。但是這邊並沒有提到是誰負責關於保險計畫的業務，所以要透過例文 1 尋找相關內容。例文 1 的表格中有寫到 Hans Birkeland, General inquiries about Asgardheim insurance plans 是指 Hans Birkeland 是 Asgardheim 公司中負責關於保險計畫疑問的職員，這是第二個線索。

綜合第一個線索：Ms. Jakobsson 要求提供保險計畫，與第二個線索：Hans Birkeland 是 Asgardheim 公司中負責關於保險計畫疑問的職員，可以推論出 Ms. Jakobsson 的問題將會交由 Hans Birkeland 來處理，因此要選 (B) Hans Birkeland 為正確答案。

單字 attend to phr. 處理～，實行

185

What is mentioned about Ms. Jakobsson? (A) She was recently offered a promotion. (B) She will move into an apartment soon. (C) She wants to cancel a policy. (D) She previously lived in Copenhagen.	關於 Jakobsson 小姐，何者正確？ (A) 她最近升遷了。 (B) 她很快會搬進一間公寓。 (C) 她想要取消保單。 (D) 她之前住在哥本哈根。

■ Not/True True 問題　　　　　　　　　　　　　　　　　　　　　　　　　解答 (D)

本題是要在文章中找到與本問題的重點 Ms. Jakobsson 相關的內容後，比較選項與文章的 Not/True 問題，因此要從例文 2 Ms. Jakobsson 寫的電子郵件開始確認相關的內容。(A) 是例文中沒有提及的內容。I am currently living in a ~ apartment unit 是指現在住在公寓中，因此 (B) 與例文內容不符合。I would like to have my personal property insured 是指希望能有個人財產保險，因此 (C) 也與例文內容不符合。I moved here from Copenhagen last March 31 是說 3 月 31 日從哥本哈根搬到這裡，因此要選與例文內容一致的 (D) She previously live in Copenhagen. 為正確答案。

單字 promotion n. 升遷

Questions 186-190 refer to the following application and e-mail.   186-190 根據下面申請書和電郵的內容回答問題。

例文1

City of Paphos   Permit No.: 849410
Cyprus   Date: August 20

186SIGN PERMIT REQUEST FORM

Type of Sign: ____ Industrial ____ Residential
       X Temporary (includes promotional
       materials for events, such as banners,
       posters, etc.)

187-BOrganization / Company Name : Victrix Travel Agency
Contact Person   : Ophelia Persakis
Phone No. / E-mail Address   : (+35726) 555-2189 /
       ophie23@victrixtravels.com
187-BEvent Title   : Pygmalion Travel Festival
187-DEvent Location   : Galatea Heritage Park
187-AEvent Date(s) / Time(s)   : September 22 to 25 /
       10 A.M. to 10 P.M.
Setup / Cleanup Dates   : September 21 /
       September 26

189Completed permit applications should be submitted directly to the City Planning and Development Office (CPD). Please note that promotional materials must first be inspected by a CPD official at least three weeks prior to the event. Requests for inspection may be sent to cpd_argyros @paphos.gov. Applicants whose signs do not meet the ordinance requirements will be notified within two working days following the inspection.

例文2

To: Basil Argyros <cpd_argyros@paphos.gov>
From: Ophelia Persakis <ophie23@victrixtravels.com>
Date: August 23
Subject: Sign Permit Application

189Dear Mr. Argyros,

I am writing on behalf of my company, Victrix Travel Agency, about the sign permit application that we submitted to your office on August 20. We are planning to have a booth at the Pygmalion Travel Festival to promote some of our new package tours. 190The two banners that we intend to use at the festival have just been delivered to our office from the printer. 188Could you please dispatch one of your representatives to our agency to inspect the material as soon as possible? I would bring them to your offices myself, but they are too large to transport easily. We need the banners to be approved by the city's deadline on September 1. Please call me directly at the number indicated in our application to let me know when someone will be available. Thank you for your assistance in this matter.

Sincerely,
Ophelia Persakis

Paphos 市   許可證號碼：849410
賽普勒斯   日期：8 月 20 日

186招牌許可證申請

路標種類： ___工業區用 ___住宅區用
       X 臨時性（包括活動宣
       傳物，例如布條、海
       報等等）

187-B 組織/公司行號： Victrix 旅行社
聯絡人：Ophelia Persakis
電話號碼/電郵：(+35726)555-2189/
       ophie23@victrixtravels.com
187-B 活動名稱：Pygmalion 旅遊節
187-D 活動地點：Galatea 遺址公園
187-A 活動日期/時間：9月22日至25日
       /上午10點至晚上10點
佈置/清理日期：9月21日/9月26日

189填寫完畢的許可證申請書要直接遞交給城市規劃與發展辦公室，請注意，宣傳物必須在活動的三個星期前先由城市規劃與發展辦公室的人員檢查，請電郵至 cpd_argyros@paphos.gov 申請檢查，招牌不符合法令規定的申請者，將會在檢查後的兩個工作天內接到通知。

收件人：Basil Argyros
       <cpd_argyros@paphos.gov>
寄件人：Ophelia Persakis
       <ophie23@victrixtravels.com>
日期：8 月 23 日
主旨：招牌許可證申請

189親愛的 Argyros 先生：

我以我們公司 Victrix 旅行社的名義寫這封信給你，是關於在 8 月 20 日遞交到你辦公室的招牌許可證申請。我們計畫在 Pygmalion 旅遊節搭設一個攤位來促銷一些我們新的套裝旅遊，190 我們想要用的兩個布條已經由印刷廠商那裡送到我們的辦公室，188 你可以儘快派一個代表到我們的旅行社來檢查嗎？我很想親自把這兩個布條送到你的辦公室，但是太大了，並不容易搬運，這兩個布條需要在 9 月 1 日前獲得市政府的許可，請撥打我們申請書上的電話與我直接聯絡，讓我知道什麼時候能有人來檢查，謝謝你在這件事上的協助。

Ophelia Persakis 敬上

例文 1 單字　□sign n. 看板，招牌　　□permit n. 許可　　　　□industrial a. 工業用的
　　　　　　□temporary a. 臨時的　　□banner n. 布條　　　　□setup n. 設置，組成
　　　　　　□cleanup n. 拆除，清掃　□submit v. 提交　　　　□directly ad. 直接
　　　　　　□inspect v. 檢查　　　　□ordinance n. 規定，法令，條例　□notify v. 通知，告知
　　　　　　□working day phr. 工作日，平日

例文 2 單字　□on behalf of phr. 代表～　□dispatch v. 派遣　　　□transport v. 運送
　　　　　　□assistance n. 幫助，支援

186

For whom is the form most likely intended?	這個申請書最有可能是給誰的？
(A) Residents wanting a business license	(A) 想取得商業執照的居民
(B) Businesses hoping to host events	(B) 希望舉辦活動的公司行號
(C) People wishing to post signs	(C) 希望張貼招牌的人
(D) Organizations applying for sponsorship	(D) 申請贊助的機關團體

■ 推論 整體內容　　　　　　　　　　　　　　　　　　　　　　　　　　　　解答 (C)

這是要推論這個申請書針對的對象的問題，所以要從與申請書有關聯的例文 1 開始尋找相關內容。申請書上端寫著 SIGN PREMIT REQUEST FORM，所以可以知道這個申請書是招牌許可申請書，而之後也寫到許多詳細申請內容，所以可以推論本申請書的對象是想要申請設立招牌的人或單位。因此，(C) People wishing to post signs 為正確答案。

單字　host v. 主辦　post v. 投寄　sponsorship n. 贊助

187

What is NOT indicated about the event?	關於這個活動，並未提示什麼？
(A) It will begin on September 22.	(A) 在 9 月 22 日開始。
(B) It will involve tourism and travel.	(B) 是關於觀光旅行。
(C) It will be free to the public.	(C) 大眾免費參加。
(D) It will be held in a park.	(D) 會在一個公園裡舉行。

■ Not/True Not 問題　　　　　　　　　　　　　　　　　　　　　　　　　解答 (C)

本題是要在文章中找到與本活動相關的內容後，比較選項與文章的 Not/True 問題，因此要從有提及問題的重點 the event 的例文 1 申請書開始確認相關內容。Event Date(s)/ Time(s):September 22 to 25 是說明活動日期為 9 月 22 日到 9 月 25 日，因此 (A) 與例文內容一致。Event Title: Pygmalion Travel Festival 是指活動名稱為 Pygmalion 旅遊節，而 Organization/Company Name: Victrix Travel Agency 指出申請活動的公司為旅行社，因此可以知道這是與觀光及旅行有關的活動，因此 (B) 也與例文內容一致。(C) 則是例文沒有提及的內容。Event Location: Galatea Heritage Park 指出活動場所將於 Galatea Heritage 公園，因此 (D) 也符合例文內容。

單字　involve v. 關聯

188

What does Ms. Persakis ask Mr. Argyros to do?	Persakis 小姐要求 Argyros 先生做什麼？
(A) Follow up on a report	(A) 追蹤一個報告
(B) Send an inspector	(B) 派一個檢查員
(C) Provide an update on a project	(C) 提供一個計畫的最新情形
(D) Pick up an event application	(D) 拿一份活動申請表

■ 六何原則 What   解答 (B)

這是在詢問 Ms. Persakis 要求 Mr. Argyros 做什麼（What）要求的六何原則問題。因此要由有提及問題重點 Ms. Persakis ask Mr. Argyros to do 的電子郵件開始確認相關內容。例文 2 電子郵件中寫到 Could you please dispatch one of your representatives to our agency to inspect the material 要求為了檢查布條，請 Mr. Argyros 派遣一位職員到旅行社的意思，因此要選 (B) Send an inspector 為正確答案。

單字 follow up phr. 採取進一步行動　pick up phr. 拿來

189

Who most likely is Mr. Argyros?	Argyros 先生最有可能是誰？
(A) A travel agent	(A) 旅行社代辦
(B) A city official	(B) 市政府員工
(C) An event organizer	(C) 活動企畫人員
(D) An advertising executive	(D) 廣告公司經理

■ 推論 連結問題   解答 (B)

這是要綜合兩篇例文才能解題的連結問題，要從有提及問題的重點 Mr. Argyros 例文 2 開始尋找相關的內容。

透過例文 2 電子郵件中此句 Dear Mr. Argyros, I am writing ~ about the sign permit application that we submit to your office 可以知道寫信的人向 Mr. Argyros 的辦公室繳交了一份招牌許可申請書，這是第一個線索。但是這裡並未提到繳交招牌申請書的場所為何，所以透過例文 1 尋找相關內容。例文 1 申請書中提到 Completed permit applications should be submitted directly to the City Planning and Development Office (CPD) 是指要將填寫完畢的申請書繳交至城市規劃與發展辦公室，這是第二個線索。

綜合第一個線索：寫信的人向 Mr. Argyros 的辦公室繳交了一份招牌許可申請書，與第二個線索：填寫完畢的申請書要繳交至都市計畫開發部門，我們可以推論出 Mr. Argyros 是在城市規劃與發展辦公室（CPD）工作，因此 (B) A city official 為正確答案。

單字 official n. 公務員　organizer n. 發起人，計畫者　executive n. 執行者，經理

190

Where are Victrix Travel Agency's banners now?	Victrix 旅行社的布條現在在哪裡？
(A) At a travel agency	(A) 在旅行社
(B) At a printing shop	(B) 在印刷店
(C) At an event venue	(C) 在活動會場
(D) At a city office	(D) 在市政辦公室

■ 六何原則 Where   解答 (A)

這是在詢問 Victrix 旅行社的布條現在在哪裡（Where）的六何原則問題。要透過有提及問題重點 Victrix Travel Agency's banners 的例文 2 電子郵件來確認相關的內容。電子郵件中的 The two banners that we intend to use at the festival has just been delivered to our office from the printer 是指將於活動中將使用的兩條布條已經從印刷廠送到公司，所以要選 (A) At a travel agency 為正確答案。

例文1

Volledig Incorporated: For those with a sweet tooth!

Special New Year Offer!

For more than 50 years, [191]Volledig Incorporated has been one of the leading providers of chocolates, caramels, toffees, and other confectionery products in Europe. Whether your company is looking for top quality finished products or ingredients to manufacture your own sweets, Volledig Incorporated has the perfect items to suit your needs. Based in Antwerp, Belgium, [192-D]our business is built on providing individualized attention to customers and manufacturers alike. Our product diversity and numerous locations make us capable of catering to businesses of all sizes, from small candy stores to large chocolate corporations.

[192-B/C]Starting January 1, [195]our new clients can take advantage of a 20 percent discount on their domestic and international shipment totaling a weight of 10 tons or more. Additional information on this offer are available on our Web site at www.vollediginc.com. You can also contact our sales director, Hendrik Bushnell, at henbush@vollediginc. com should you have any questions.

例文2

To: Hendrik Bushnell <henbush@vollediginc.com>
From: Liesbeth Weidman <weidlies@zoet.net>
Date: February 8
Subject: Promotional Offer

Dear Mr. Bushnell,

I am the sales manager of Zoet Bonbon Company, a chocolate manufacturer specializing in hand-finished chocolates and other cocoa-based products like chocolate drinks, brownies, and cookies. You can find our products sold in malls and supermarkets in Belgium, France, the UK, and the Netherlands.

We are pleased to say that [193]this year we are expanding our operations into the Asian market, starting in Japan and South Korea. However, we are concerned that our current supplier, [194]Ganesvoort Distributors, does not offer a large enough variety of items. That was why we were pleased to find out that your company has such a huge selection. We also know that you offer a special promotion to new clients. While [195]Zoet Bonbon only requires 9 tons of products for this year, we are hoping that you will provide us a 20 percent discount if we sign a five-year contract. Let me know if this is possible.

I would appreciate it very much if you could provide us with more information about your services. Please contact me directly at (+32) 555-8169 as soon as possible. Thank you.

Liesbeth Weidman

Volledig 公司：給那些喜歡甜食的人

新年特別優惠

[191]Volledig 公司超過五十年來一直都是歐洲地區巧克力、焦糖、太妃糖和其他糕點產品的主要供應商之一，不管你的公司在尋找高品質的製成品或用來製造甜點的材料，Volledig 公司有最好的產品來滿足你的需求。我們公司位在比利時的 Antwerp 市，[192-D] 我們的生意是建立在提供顧客和製造商的個別需求，我們的產品多樣化，而且有多個據點，使得我們能夠提供食品給大大小小的公司，從小型的糖果店到大型的巧克力公司。

[192-B/C] 從 1 月 1 日起，[195] 我們的新客戶購買總重量 10 噸以上運往國內國外的產品，可享有 8 折優惠。其他相關這項優惠的資訊，請上網 www.vollediginc. com 瀏覽。如果有任何問題，也可以寫電郵到 henbush@vollediginc.com 聯絡我們的行銷經理 Hendrik Bushnell。

收件人：Hendrik Bushnell
　　　　<henbush@vollediginc.com>
寄件人：Liesbeth Weidman
　　　　<weidlies@zoet.net>
日期：2 月 8 日
主旨：特價優惠

親愛的 Bushnell 先生：

我是 Zoet Bonbon 公司的業務經理，Zoet Bonbon 是一家巧克力公司，專門做手工巧克力和其他像巧克力飲料、布朗尼蛋糕和餅乾等可可產品。在比利時、法國、英國和荷蘭等地的大型商場和超級市場，都有銷售我們的產品。

我們很高興地宣布 [193]今年我們將生意擴展到亞洲的市場，日本和南韓是第一站。不過，我們擔心我們目前的供應商 [194]Ganesvoort 經銷商無法供應我們夠大量的各種產品。所以我們很高興能發現你們公司能提供這麼多的選擇。我們還知道你們提供新客戶特別優惠，雖然 [195] Zoet Bonbon 今年只需要 9 噸的產品，我們希望在簽訂一份 5 年合約的情況下，你們能給我們 8 折優惠。

我們會很感謝你們提供我們更多關於你們的服務資訊。請儘快撥打 (+32)555-8169 直接與我聯絡。謝謝！

Liesbeth Weidman

例文 1 單字 ☐leading a. 領頭的　　　☐provider n. 供應商　　　☐toffee n. 太妃糖
　　　　　☐confectionery n. 糕點糖果　☐ingredient n. 材料　　☐individualized a. 個別的
　　　　　☐diversity n. 多樣性　　　☐cater v. 提供飲食　　　☐domestic a. 國內的

例文 2 單字 ☐specialize in phr. 專門研究～
　　　　　☐hand-finished a. 手製的，以手工收尾的

191

What is being advertised?	這是在廣告甚麼？
(A) A manufacturing plant	(A) 一個製造工廠
(B) A department store chain	(B) 一個連鎖百貨公司
(C) A shipping service	(C) 貨運服務
(D) A product supplier	(D) 產品供應商

■ 找出主題 主題　　　　　　　　　　　　　　　　　　　　　　　　　　　　解答 (D)

這是在詢問被刊登在廣告上的東西是什麼的找出主題問題。因此從例文 1 著手確認廣告內容。廣告裡 Volledig Incorporated has been one of the leading providers of chocolates, caramels, toffees, and other confectionery products 是指 Volledig 公司一直都是巧克力、焦糖、太妃糖和其他糕餅產品的主要供應商，因此要選 (D) A product supplier 為正確答案。

192

What is NOT indicated about Volledig Incorporated?	關於 Volledig 公司，並未提示什麼？
(A) It has won many prestigious awards.	(A) 已經獲得許多知名的獎項。
(B) It will start a special promotion from the first day of the year.	(B) 從 1 月 1 日起有特別優惠。
(C) It deals with overseas orders.	(C) 接受海外訂單。
(D) It provides customized service to its clients.	(D) 提供客製化的服務給客戶。

■ Not/True Not 問題　　　　　　　　　　　　　　　　　　　　　　　　　解答 (A)

本題是要在文章中找到與本問題的重點 Volledig 相關的內容後，比較選項與文章的 Not/True 問題，所以要先從有提及問題重點 Volledig Incorporated 的例文一開始尋找線索。(A) 是例文中沒有提的內容，因此 (A) It has won many prestigious award. 為正確答案。Starting January 1, our new clients can take advantage of a 20 percent discount on their domestic and international shipment totaling weight of 10 tons or more 是指從 1 月 1 日開始，Volledig 公司的新客戶購買總重量十噸以上運往國內及國外的產品，可享有八折優惠，因此 (B) 和 (C) 都與例文內容一致。our business is built on providing individualized attention to customers and manufactures alike 是說 Volledig 公司的生意建立在提供顧客與製造商的個別需求，因此 (D) 也與例文內容一致。

單字 deal with phr. 處理　customized a. 客製化的

193

What is implied about Zoet Bonbon Company's products?	關於 Zoet Bonbon 公司的產品，何者正確？
(A) They will be offered in regional hotels.	(A) 供應給地區性的飯店。
(B) They are manufactured in Belgium.	(B) 在比利時製造。
(C) They will be sold in Korea this year.	(C) 今年會在韓國販賣。
(D) They are made with imported ingredients.	(D) 用進口的材料製造。

■ 推論 詳細內容　　　　　　　　　　　　　　　　　　　　　　　　　　　解答 (C)

這是要針對問題的重點 Zoet Bonbon Company's products 進行推論的問題，所以要從有提及 Zoet Bonbon 公司的產品的例文 2 開始尋找相關的內容。電子郵件中寫到 this year we are expanding our operations into the Asia market, starting in Japan and South Korea 指出今年公司（也就是 Zoet Bonbon 公司）將以日本及南韓作為進軍亞洲市場的第一站，因此我們可以推論 Zoet Bonbon 公司的產品會於今年開始在南韓販賣，所以要選 (C) They will be sold in Korea the year. 為正確答案。

單字 manufacture v. 生產，製造　import v. 輸入

194

What is suggested about Ganesvoort Distributors?	關於 Ganesvoort 經銷商，提示了什麼？
(A) It is a subsidiary of Zoet Bonbon Company.	(A) 是 Zoet Bonbon 公司的子公司。
(B) It will relocate to an office in Antwerp.	(B) 會搬到 Antwerp 市的一個辦公室。
(C) It will stop its business operations next year.	(C) 明年會停止營運。
(D) It has a limited selection of products.	(D) 產品的選擇有限。

■ 推論 詳細內容   解答 (D)

這是要針對問題的重點 Ganesvoort Distributors 進行推論的問題，所以要從有提及 Ganesvoort Distributors 的例文 2 開始尋找相關的內容。電子郵件中寫到 Ganesvoort Distributors, does not offer a large enough variety of items 說明了 Ganesvoort Distributors 沒有辦法供應多種品項的大量需求，所以可以推論選擇 Ganesvoort Distributors 公司的產品時會遇到一定的限制，因此要選擇 (D) It has limited selection of products. 為正確答案。

單字 subsidiary n. 子公司　relocate v. 重新安置，重新移動　limited a. 有限制的，限定的

195

Why might Zoet Bonbon be ineligible for the special discount?	Zoet Bonbon 公司為什麼可能無法得到優惠價格？
(A) It will not order enough to qualify.	(A) 訂購量不足。
(B) It cannot sign a long-term contract.	(B) 無法簽訂長期的合約。
(C) It is not a first-time customer.	(C) 不是首次訂購的顧客。
(D) It will not ship the items within Europe.	(D) 訂購的產品不會在歐洲運送。

■ 推論 連結問題   解答 (A)

這是要綜合兩篇例文才能解題的連結問題。要先從有提及問題的重點 the special Discount 的廣告，也就是例文 1 開始看。

例文 1 中提到 our new clients can take advantage of a 20 percent discount on ~ shipment totaling weight of 10 tons or more 指出新客戶購買總重 10 噸以上的產品，可享有 8 折優惠，這是第一個線索。但是因為廣告中未提及 Zoet Bonbon 公司是否有達到優惠資格，因此要由例文 2 中尋找線索。例文 2 電子郵件中寫到 Zoet Bonbon only requires 9 tons of products for this year 所以我們得知 Zoet Bonbon 公司今年只需要九噸的產品，這是第二個線索。

綜合第一個線索：新客戶購買總重 10 噸以上的產品，可享有 8 折優惠，與第二個線索：Zoet Bonbon 公司今年只需要 9 噸的產品，我們可以推論出因為 Zoet Bonbon 公司的訂單未達到享有優惠的量，因此要選 (A) It will not order enough to qualify. 為正確答案。

單字 ineligible a. 沒有資格的　long-term a. 長期的

Questions 196-200 refer to the following e-mails.

196-200 根據下面電郵的內容回答問題。

例文1

To: Bertram Kiersted <bertkiersted@laufeypoolcleaners.dk>

From: Adriana Handsel <handsel@forsetibandb.dk>

Date: March 16
Subject: Price Inquiry

Dear Mr. Kiersted,

My name is Adriana Handsel and 196-B/D am the owner of Forseti Bed-and-Breakfast, located at 8261 Jostein Road. 197 Your business was recommended to me by my associate, Damian Jantzen, who runs a small inn close to your office in Roskilde. He vouched for your reasonable prices and competent staff.

196-C I would appreciate it if you could send me a quote for the weekly cleaning of the 50-meter pool at my establishment. 200 Is it possible for the first cleaning to be scheduled next week, specifically on March 25? I would like to personally meet the crew in charge and introduce them to my assistant, who will be overseeing their work in April while I am away on a business trip.

Thank you, and I hope to receive a response soon.

Adriana Handsel

例文2

To: Adriana Handsel <handsel@forsetibandb.dk>

From: Bertram Kiersted <bertkiersted@laufeypoolcleaners.dk>
Date: March 17
Subject: Re: Price Inquiry
Attachment: Brochure

Dear Ms. Handsel,

We appreciate your choosing Laufey Pool Cleaners! We have been the leading pool cleaning service provider in the city for more than seven years, thanks to a steadily growing client base and hardworking staff. We pride ourselves on using only the most advanced equipment to ensure that we can provide results of the highest quality. 199 I also encourage you to look through the attached brochure for additional details on our services.

200 My staff is free on the day you requested. Just let me know what time you want the cleaning done so the crew can prepare ahead of time. 197 Please note that there is a €60 surcharge for establishments that are outside of the city limits, so we will have to charge you for that. The full service cleaning of your pool will cost €170 and will take three to four hours to complete.

收件人：Bertram Kiersted <bertkiersted@laufeypoolcleaners.dk>
寄件人：Adriana Handsel <handsel@forsetibandb.dk>
日期：3 月 16 日
主旨：詢價

親愛的 Kiersted 先生：

我的名字是 Adriana Handsel，196-B/D 我是位於 Jostein 路 8261 號 Forseti 住宿早餐酒店的老闆，197 我的合作夥伴 Damian Jantzen 向我推薦你的公司，他在 Roskilde 靠近你辦公室的地方經營一家小旅館。他向我保證你們有合理的價格和能幹的員工。

196-C 我想要請你針對我酒店裡 50 公尺游泳池每週清潔工作的報價。200 下星期的 3 月 25 日可以做第一次的清潔工作嗎？我想要親自和負責的人員見面，並向他們介紹我的助理，在我 4 月份出差時，我的助理會監督他們的清潔工作。

謝謝你，希望很快聽到你的回音。

Adriana Handsel

收件人：Adriana Handsel <handsel@forsetibandb.dk>
寄件人：Bertram Kiersted <bertkiersted@laufeypoolcleaners.dk>
日期：3 月 17 日
主旨：回覆：詢價
附件：小冊子

親愛的 Handsel 小姐：

謝謝你選擇 Laufey 泳池清潔公司！我們成為 Roskilde 市游泳池清潔服務的領導品牌已超過七年了，相當感謝穩定成長的客戶群和辛苦工作的員工。我們很自豪的只使用最先進的設備，以確保我們能夠提供最高品質的成果。199 我建議你看看附件的小冊子，以了解更多我們服務的細節。

200 在你指定的那一天，我們的員工有空。請讓我知道你想要他們幾點把清潔工作做完，好讓他們能事前準備。197 請注意，如果地點不在市區內，我們會向你索取一筆 60 歐元的費用。清潔游泳池的費用為 170 歐元，大概會花 3 到 4 個小時完成。

Please respond to this e-mail if you find the quote acceptable so I can confirm the schedule. Once again, thank you, and I look forward to doing business with you.

Yours truly,
Bertram Kiersted
Manager
Laufey Pool Cleaners

如果你可以接受這的報價，請回覆這封電郵，好讓我定下時間，再一次感謝你，期待你能成為我們的客戶。	

Bertram Kiersted 敬上
經理
Laufey 泳池清潔公司

例文 1 單字　□recommend v. 推薦　　□associate n. 同僚　　□vouch v. 保障，斷言
　　　　　　　□reasonable a. 合理的　□competent a. 有能力的　□quote n. 報價
　　　　　　　□specifically ad. 具體地　□business trip phr. 出差

例文 2 單字　□steadily ad. 平穩地　　□encourage v. 鼓勵，激勵　□surcharge n. 額外金額
　　　　　　　□confirm v. 確定，確認

196

What does Ms. Handsel NOT mention in her e-mail?	在 Handsel 小姐寫給 Kiersted 先生的電郵中，沒有寫到什麼？
(A) The name of her assistant	(A) 她助理的名字
(B) The location of her business	(B) 她公司的地址
(C) The size of her swimming pool	(C) 游泳池的尺寸
(D) The type of establishment she owns	(D) 她的公司的類型

Not/True Not 問題　　　　　　　　　　　　　　　　　　　　　　　　　　解答 (A)

本題是要在文章中找到與本問題的重點 Ms. Handsel 相關的內容後，比較選項與文章的 Not/True 問題，所以要先從 Ms. Handsel 寫的電子郵件，也就是例文 1 開始尋找線索。(A) 是例文中沒有提及的內容。因此 (A) The name of her assistant 為正確答案。I am the owner of Forseti Bed-and-Breakfast, located at 8261 Jostein Road 是說寫信的 Ms. Handsel 是位於 Jostein 路 8261 號 Forseti 住宿早餐酒店的老闆，所以 (B) 和 (D) 都與例文內容一致。I would appreciate it if you could send me a quote for the weekly cleaning of the 50-meter pool at my establishment. 是說「想要請你針對我酒店裡五十米的游泳池做每周清潔工作的報價」，所以 (C) 也與例文內容一致。

單字 assistant n. 祕書，助手

197

What is indicated about Forseti Bed-and-Breakfast?	關於 Forseti 住宿早餐酒店，暗示了什麼？
(A) It is currently undergoing some renovations.	(A) 目前正在進行整修。
(B) It will come under new management in April.	(B) 在 4 月份時會由一批新的人來管理。
(C) It is located outside the city limits of Roskilde.	(C) 位在 Roskilde 市區的範圍外。
(D) It will hire more personnel to accommodate its expansion plans.	(D) 會雇用更多的人來配合擴展的計畫。

推論 連結問題　　　　　　　　　　　　　　　　　　　　　　　　　　　　解答 (C)

這是要綜合兩篇例文才能解題的連結問題。要先從有提及問題的重點 Forseti 住宿早餐酒店的例文 2 電子郵件開始看。

電子郵件中寫到 Please note that there is €60 surcharge for establishment that are outside of the city limits, so we will have to charge you for that. 是指「如果地點不在市區內，會有一筆 60 歐元的額外收費，所以我們會向你索取這筆費用」，因此，我們可以知道 Forseti 住宿早餐酒店需要此服務，這是第一個線索。但由於例文 2 沒有指出 Laufey 泳池清潔公司在哪個市區，所以要在例文 1 中尋找相關內容，第一封電子郵件寫到 Your business was recommended to me by my associate ~ who runs a small inn close to your office in Roskilde. 因此我們可以得到 Laufey 泳池清潔公司位在 Roskilde 市的第二個線索。

綜合第一個線索：Forseti 住宿早餐酒店不在市內，所以會有額外費用，以及第二個線索：Laufey 泳池清潔公司位在 Roskilde 市，我們可以推論出 Forseti 住宿早餐酒店位於 Roskilde 市外，因此 (C) It is located outside the city limits of Roskilde. 為正確答案。

單字 undergo v. 經歷 come under phr. 被包括在～之下 management n. 經營團隊
accommodate v. 能容納，使相符 expansion n. 擴張

198

In the second e-mail, the word "encourage" in paragraph 1, line 4 is closest in meaning to (A) support (B) recommend (C) assist (D) relieve	在第二封電郵的第一段第四行中，「encourage」 一字的意思最接近哪一個字？ (A) 支持 (B) 推薦 (C) 協助 (D) 減輕

■ 同義詞　　　　　　　　　　　　　　　　　　　　　　　　　　　　　　　解答 (B)

在有包含 encourage 的例文 2 電子郵件中提到 I also encourage you to look through the attached brochure for additional details on our services. 在此句中，encourage 是「建議」的意思，因此，要選擇有「建議，推薦」意思的 (B) recommend 為正確答案。

單字 support v. 支援，支持 assist v. 幫助 relieve v. 緩和

199

What information is included in the attachment? (A) A list of branch locations (B) A complete work schedule (C) Information on pool cleaning services (D) Fees for home repairs	什麼資訊包含在附件中？ (A) 一份分店位址的清單 (B) 一份完整的工作時程表 (C) 泳池清潔服務的資訊 (D) 住家修繕的費用

■ 六何原則 What　　　　　　　　　　　　　　　　　　　　　　　　　　　　解答 (C)

因為這是在詢問信箱附件的內容是什麼（What）的六何原則問題，所以要從有提及問題重點 the attachment 的第二封電子郵件開始尋找相關內容。I also encourage you to look through the attached brochure for additional details on our services. 是指「我建議你看看附件的小冊子，以了解更多我們服務的細節」，因此我們可以知道 (C) Information on pool cleansing services 為正確答案。

200

When will Mr. Kiersted's staff most likely clean Ms. Handsel's pool? (A) On March 16 (B) On March 17 (C) On March 24 (D) On March 25	Kiersted 先生的員工最有可能在什麼時候清潔 Handsel 小姐酒店裡的游泳池？ (A) 3 月 16 日 (B) 3 月 17 日 (C) 3 月 24 日 (D) 3 月 25 日

■ 推論 連結問題　　　　　　　　　　　　　　　　　　　　　　　　　　　　解答 (D)

這是要綜合兩篇例文才能解題的連結問題。因為是問 Mr. Kiersted 的職員什麼時候（When）會清掃游泳池，所以要從有提及問題重點 Mr. Kiersted's staff ~ clean Ms. Handsel's pool 的例文 2 電子郵件中開始確認相關內容。

第二封電子郵件中寫到 My staff is free on the day you requested，可以得到 Ms. Handsel 要求的日子裡 Mr. Kiersted 的職員可以為她工作，這是第一個線索。但是因為這裡沒有提到 Ms. Handsel 要求的日子是哪一天，所以要透過例文 1 電子郵件來尋找相關內容。第一封電子郵件寫到 Is it possible for the first cleaning to be scheduled next week, specifically on March 25?，透過此句我們可以得知 Ms. Handsel 想要把第一次清掃安排在 3 月 25 日，這是第二個線索。

綜合第一個線索：Ms. Handsel 要求的日子裡 Mr. Kiersted 的職員可以為她工作，以及第二個線索：Ms. Handsel 想要把第一次清掃安排在 3 月 25 日，我們可以推論出 Ms. Kiersted 的職員們將於 3 月 25 日進行游泳池清掃，因此 (D) On March 25 為正確答案。

TEST 05

PART 5

101

| After the members of the volleyball team attended the awards ceremony, all of _____ went to Daphne's Grill to celebrate the victory.
(A) they　　(B) them　　(C) their　　(D) theirs | 在所有的排球員參加完頒獎典禮後，他們全部前往 Daphne Grill 來慶祝勝利。 |

■ 人稱代名詞　　　　　　　　　　　　　　　　　　　　　　　　　　　解答 (B)

能當作介系詞 of 受詞的受格人稱代名詞 (B) 與所有格代名詞 (D) 可能為正確答案。由「他們前往 Daphne's Grill」的句意看來，受格人稱代名詞 (B) them 是正確的。如果填入 (D) theirs 的話，意思會變成「他們的東西都前往 Daphne's Grill」。而人稱代名詞 (A) 與人稱代名詞所有格 (C) 則不能當作介系詞的受格。

單字 volley ball phr. 排球　attend v. 參加　awards ceremony phr. 頒獎典禮　celebrate v. 慶祝

102

| Coeval Museum of History recently opened a new _____ as part of its summer calendar of events.
(A) exhibitory　　　　　(B) exhibitor
(C) exhibit　　　　　　(D) exhibited | Coeval 歷史博物館最近開放了一個新的展覽，作為夏日活動日程的一部份。 |

■ 人物名詞 vs. 抽象名詞　　　　　　　　　　　　　　　　　　　　　解答 (C)

空格為及物動詞 opened 的受詞，且受形容詞 new 的修飾，應為名詞，因此應考慮名詞 (B) 與 (C) 可能為正確答案。句意應為「最近開放了一個新的展覽，作為夏日活動日程的一部份」，因此抽象名詞 (C) exhibit（展覽）為正確答案。人物名詞 (B) exhibitor（展覽者）會讓句意變為「開放了一個新的展覽者」，因此並非正確答案。形容詞 (A) 與動詞或分詞 (D) 則不能當作受詞使用。

單字 recently ad. 最近

103

| The workers _____ about the modified work schedule, as notices were put up on bulletin boards yesterday.
(A) know　　　　　　(B) are knowing
(C) will have known　　(D) knows | 因為通知昨天被貼到佈告欄上，工人們都知道修改後的工作時程。 |

■ 動詞 / 的單 / 複數，主 / 被動，時態　　　　　　　　　　　　　　解答 (A)

句意為「因為通知昨天被貼到佈告欄上，工人們都知道修改後的工作時程」表示現在工人的狀態，因此現在簡單式的 (A) 跟 (D) 都有可能是正確答案。因為主詞 The workers 是複數，所以複數動詞的選項 (A) know 是正確答案。狀態動詞 know（知道）不能夠寫成進行式，所以 (B) 不能當作答案，未來完成式 (C) 用在未來某個時間點之前發生了某件事情，影響到未來的該時間點，因此也不能夠當作答案。

單字 modify v. 更改，修改　put up phr. 張貼，告示

104

| A representative called to notify the manager that the office's fire insurance policy _____ on May 30.
(A) expires　　　　　(B) extracts
(C) transfers　　　　(D) leaves | 有一位業務員打電話來通知經理說，辦公室的火災保險在 5 月 30 號到期。 |

■ 動詞語彙　　　　　　　　　　　　　　　　　　　　　　　　　　　解答 (A)

由「火災保險到期」的句意看來，動詞 expire（到期）的第三人稱單數形 (A) expires 為正確答案。(B) extract 為「抽出」，(C) transfer 為「移動」，(D) leave 則是「離開」的意思。

單字 representative n. 職員，代表　notify v. 通知

105

The Easy-Update system _____ Heritage cardholders to change their personal information on the company's Web site. (A) permission　　　(B) permissible (C) permitting　　　(D) permits	Easy-Update 系統讓使用 Heritage 卡的持有者可以在公司網頁修改他們的個人資料。

■ 動詞的位置　　　　　　　　　　　　　　　　　　　　　　　　　　　　　解答 (D)

句中沒有動詞,因此動詞 permit(准許)的第三人稱單數形 (D) permits 是正確答案。要注意 permit 常見的句型用法為「permit + 受詞 + to 不定詞」(允許受詞做〜)。名詞 (A)、形容詞 (B)、分詞 (C) 皆不是動詞。

單字 cardholder n. 卡片持有人

106

Ella Santiago had to overcome a variety of _____ when she decided to open her own travel agency a few years ago. (A) difficulty　　　(B) difficulties (C) difficult　　　(D) most difficult	當 Ella Santiago 在幾年前決定自己開一家旅行社時,她需要克服種種的困難。

■ 表示數量　　　　　　　　　　　　　　　　　　　　　　　　　　　　　解答 (B)

空格前有搭配複數名詞且表示數量的 a variety of(各式各樣的),因此複數名詞 (B) difficulties(困難)為正確答案。單數名詞 (A) 無法與 a variety of 一起使用,形容詞 (C) 與形容詞最高級 (D) 則不能當作名詞使用。

單字 overcome v. 克服　a variety of phr. 各式各樣的

107

Neglecting to clean the filter of the air conditioner regularly will cause the unit to work less _____. (A) effective　　　(B) effectiveness (C) effectively　　　(D) effect	疏於定期清潔冷氣的濾網,會降低機器的功效。

■ 副詞的位置　　　　　　　　　　　　　　　　　　　　　　　　　　　　解答 (C)

因為要修飾與比較級表現 less 一起使用的 to 不定詞(to work),答案應為副詞,因此副詞 (C) effectively(有效地)為正確答案。形容詞 (A)、名詞 (B)、可當動詞與名詞的 (D) 皆無法修飾由動詞所形成的不定詞。

單字 neglect v. 疏忽、無視　regularly ad. 規律地

108

The well-known saxophone player Thomas Winthrop is currently busy rehearsing for his _____ concert in Guam at the end of the month. (A) upcoming　　　(B) late (C) rising　　　(D) replayed	有名的薩克斯風演奏家 Thomas Winthrop 目前正忙著排練他本月月底即將在關島的音樂會。

■ 形容詞語彙　　　　　　　　　　　　　　　　　　　　　　　　　　　　解答 (A)

由「Thomas Winthrop 目前正忙著排練他本月月底即將在關島的音樂會」的句意看來,形容詞 (A) upcoming(即將來臨的)為正確答案。(B) late 是「晚的」、(C) rising 是「升起的」、(D) replayed 是「再現的」。另外,請記住「be busy +-ing」表示「因〜而忙碌」是經常出現的句型。

單字 currently ad. 現在　rehearse v. 排練

109

Clover Cosmetics decided to modify its advertising campaign _____ suffering a significant decline in sales last year. (A) next (B) after (C) yet (D) except	Clover 化妝品公司在經歷去年銷售量明顯下滑後，決定修改它的廣告計畫。

■ 副詞子句連接詞 時序　　　　　　　　　　　　　　　　　　　　　　　　　　　　解答 (B)

主句為由主詞 Clover Cosmetics 與動詞 decided 所組成的完整句子，_____ suffering ~ year 應為修飾的分詞構句。因為修飾的分詞構句包含了 suffering a significant decline ~，因此副詞子句連接詞 (B) 與 (D) 有可能為正確答案。句意應為「經歷去年銷售量明顯下滑後，決定修改它的廣告計畫」，所以 (B) after（之後）為正確答案。(D) except（除～之外）則與句意不相符，因此並非答案。suffering 是動名詞，與介系詞 (A) next（～的旁邊）搭配的話句意也不相符。對等連接詞 (C) yet（儘管，但是），不能搭配副詞子句。

單字 suffer v. 經歷、承受　sale n. 銷售

110

According to a recent census, suburban residents today have become _____ more diverse in cultural background than they were in the 1960s. (A) remarkable (B) remarkably (C) remarks (D) remarked	根據一份最近的人口普查，今日住在郊區的居民，其文化背景明顯變得較 1960 年代更多元。

■ 副詞的位置　　　　　　　　　　　　　　　　　　　　　　　　　　　　　　　　解答 (B)

空格應為修飾比較級形容詞 more diverse 的副詞，因此副詞 (B) remarkably（引人注目地，明顯地）為正確答案。形容詞 (A)，可當動詞與名詞的 (C)，可當分詞與動詞的 (D) 皆無法用來修飾形容詞。

單字 census n. 人口調查　suburban a. 郊外的　diverse a. 多元的　remark v. 提及 n. 評論

111

Due to some problems with the lease, Mr. Jackson has postponed his ------- move to the new apartment by two weeks. (A) anticipate (B) anticipates (C) anticipated (D) anticipating	因為租約有些問題，所以 Jackson 先生需將事先搬遷新公寓的安排順延兩週。

■ 現在分詞 vs. 過去分詞　　　　　　　　　　　　　　　　　　　　　　　　　　　解答 (C)

所有格人稱代名詞 his 與名詞 move 之間的空格應為修飾名詞的形容詞或帶有形容詞作用的分詞，因此過去分詞 (C) 與現在分詞 (D) 可能為正確答案。受修飾的名詞 move 與分詞結合為「預定搬遷」之意，因此過去分詞 (C) anticipated（被預定的，受期望的）為正確答案。使用現在分詞 (D) anticipating（預定的，期望的）會出現「搬遷這件事期望～」這種奇怪的句意。動詞 (A) 與 (B) 則不能修飾名詞。

單字 lease n. 租賃契約　postpone v. 延期　anticipate v. 預想、期待

112

With the new contract, the monthly rate of Agate Corporate Tower's office rental space now _____ all utility charges except electricity costs. (A) reveals　　　　　(B) covers (C) finishes　　　　　(D) reaches	在新的合約下，現在 Agate Corporate Tower 的辦公室租用空間將包含所有的公用設施費，除了電費以外。

■ 動詞語彙　　　　　　　　　　　　　　　　　　　　　　　　　　　　解答 (B)

由「辦公室租用空間將包含所有的公用設施費，除了電費以外」的句意看來，動詞 cover（包含）的第三人稱單數形 (B) covers 為正確答案。(A) reveal 是「揭開，揭露」，(C) finish 是「結束」，(D) reach 是「到達」的意思。

單字 contract n. 合約　utility a. 公共的，實用的　charge n. 費用

113

The company director announced that Coleen Reyes will be overseeing the branch _____ a couple of months while our manager is away on vacation. (A) to　　　　　　　(B) for (C) with　　　　　　(D) along	公司董事宣佈在我們經理休假的兩個月中，將由 Coleen Reyes 來管理我們這間分公司。

■ 選擇介系詞 期間　　　　　　　　　　　　　　　　　　　　　　　解答 (B)

因為有表示期間的片語 a couple of months，因此同樣可以表示期間的介系詞 (B) for（～期間）為正確答案。(A) to（到～）與 (D) along（跟著～）是表示方向的介系詞。(C) with（與～一起，帶著～）也與句意不相符，因此並非答案。

單字 oversee v. 監督、管理

114

The supervisor wants to know Mr. Brown's e-mail address so that she can inform _____ about changes in work assignments. (A) he　　　　　　　(B) him (C) himself　　　　　(D) his	主管想要知道 Brown 先生的電子郵件地址，以便通知他有關工作任務的變更。

■ 人稱代名詞　　　　　　　　　　　　　　　　　　　　　　　　　　解答 (B)

可以當作及物動詞 inform 受詞的受格人稱代名詞 (B)、反身代名詞 (C) 與所有格代名詞 (D) 可能為正確答案。由「主管～以便通知他有關工作任務的變更」的句意看來，受格人稱代名詞 (B) him 為正確答案。反身代名詞的動詞受格應與主詞相同，(C) himself 則與主詞 she 不同，因此並非答案。所有格代名詞代替的是「人稱代名詞的所有格 + 名詞」，為避免名詞反覆出現而使用，若填入 (D) his 則句意會變為「通知他的東西（電郵地址）」，變成通知東西而不是通知人，產生奇怪語意。

115

With some advance _____, Pamela will surely save a lot of time and money on her trip to Asia in December. (A) plan　　　　　　　(B) planners (C) planned　　　　　(D) planning	由於事先的規畫，Pamela 必定可以在她 12 月的亞洲之旅中，節省很多的時間與金錢。

■ 人物名詞 vs. 抽象名詞　　　　　　　　　　　　　　　　　　　　　解答 (D)

空格是介系詞 with 的受詞，並受修飾複數可數名詞與不可數名詞的限定詞 some 的修飾，因此複數可數名詞 (B) 與不可數名詞 (D) 有可能為正確答案。由「由於事先的規畫，可以節省很多的時間與金錢」的句意看來，抽象名詞 (D) planning（計畫）為正確答案。若填入人物名詞 (B) planners（計畫者）的話，則句意會變為「由於事先的計劃者們，可以節省很多的時間與金錢」，因此並非正確答案。

116

Article drafts should _____ be reviewed thoroughly to ensure that they follow the rules in the style manual.

(A) quite　　(B) almost　　(C) always　　(D) hardly

文章的草稿應該總是要徹底的檢視校閱，以確保符合格式手冊的規定。

■ 選擇副詞 頻率　　　　　　　　　　　　　　　　　　　　　解答 (C)

由句意應為「文章的草稿應該總是要仔細的檢視校閱」看來，頻率副詞 (C) always（總是）為正確答案。應記住 always 適用於無論發生什麼特定狀況仍反覆發生的事情。(A) quite 的中文翻譯雖為「相當地」但英文原意有「相當～但不完全是」的語意，使用會變成「草稿應該相當（而不完全的）徹底檢查校閱」，語意不合邏輯。用 (B) almost（幾乎）則會出現「幾乎（但沒有徹底）」與「徹底」兩種語意的衝突。 (D) hardly（幾乎不～）則會讓句意變為「文章的草稿幾乎不被仔細的檢視校閱，以確保符合格式手冊的規定」也不合邏輯，因此並非答案。要注意，強調副詞 quite 置於「a/an + 名詞」之前，表示強調之意，或是與形容詞和副詞的最高級一起搭配使用。頻率副詞 hardly 有「幾乎不」的否定意味，並不與 not 或 never 等其他否定詞一起使用。應與被當作形容詞與副詞使用的 hard（困難的，努力的）區分清楚。

單字 draft n. 草案　ensure v. 確保　thoroughly ad. 徹底地

117

Attendants on the train treated all the passengers _____ and made sure they were comfortable during the trip.

(A) courted　　　　　　　(B) courteous
(C) courteously　　　　　(D) courting

火車上的服務員應有禮貌地對待所有的乘客，並確保旅客在旅程中是舒適的。

■ 副詞的位置　　　　　　　　　　　　　　　　　　　　　　解答 (C)

空格應為修飾動詞 treated 的副詞，因此副詞 (C) courteously（有禮貌地）為正確答案。可當作過去分詞與動詞的 (A)、可當作現在分詞與動名詞的 (D) 與形容詞 (B) 皆無法修飾動詞。

單字 attendant n. 交通運輸服務員　court v. 追求　courting a. 戀愛中的

118

Mr. Mitchell had to _____ his car alarm after it accidentally went off, to avoid disturbing his neighbors.

(A) silent　　　　　　　(B) silence
(C) silently　　　　　　(D) silenced

在 Mitchell 先生的車子警報器不小心響起後，他須讓警報器消音，以免打擾到鄰居。

■ 助動詞 + 動詞原形　　　　　　　　　　　　　　　　　　解答 (B)

與助動詞使用方法相同的 had to 後面應接動詞原形，因此動詞原形 (B) silence（使安靜）為正確答案。形容詞 (A)、副詞 (C)、可當作分詞與過去動詞的 (D)，皆無法接在助動詞之後。要注意，與 have to 一樣和助動詞有相同使用方法的片語有：had better（最好～）、would like to（想做～）、used to（過去曾經～）。

單字 accidentally ad. 意外地、偶然　go off v. （警報器等）響起　disturb v. 妨礙

119

One of the highlights of the seminar was Mr. Choi's talk on how to deal with _____ difficult tasks.

(A) firmly　　　　　　　(B) particularly
(C) carefully　　　　　　(D) quickly

此專題研討會中最精彩的一個部份，就是 Choi 先生演說如何處理特別困難的任務。

■ 副詞語彙　　　　　　　　　　　　　　　　　　　　　　　解答 (B)

由「如何處理特別困難的任務」的句意看來，副詞 (B) particularly（特別地）是正確答案。要注意，應記住 particularly 適用於提到特定事物的情況。(A) firmly 是「堅固地，斷然地」，(C) carefully 是「小心地」，(D) quickly 是「快速地」。並應記住慣用語 deal with（處理）。

120

Provided that the laboratory results arrive on time, Ms. Yap is _____ that she will finish the analysis of the drug sample by Tuesday. (A) rapid　　　　　(B) useful (C) confident　　　(D) evident	在實驗室結果可以準時送達的前提下，Yap 小姐有信心可以在星期二完成藥物樣品的分析。

■ 形容詞語彙　　　　　　　　　　　　　　　　　　　　　　　　　　　　解答 (C)

句意應為「在結果可以準時送達的前提下，有信心可以在星期二完成藥物樣品的分析」，因此形容詞 (C) confident（有信心的）為正確答案。(A) rapid 是「迅速的」，(B) useful 是「有用的」，(D) evident 是「明顯的」的意思。要注意，應記住 provided that（若是～）被當作副詞子句連接詞使用，並記住慣用語 on time（準時）與 be confident that（確信～）。

單字 provided that phr. 若是～　analysis n. 分析

121

The submission deadline for financial aid _____ for international students at Ostlere University has been put off until June 28. (A) methods　　　　　(B) contestants (C) notices　　　　　(D) applications	Ostlere 大學的國際學生助學貸款的申請送件截止日，已延至 6 月 28 日。

■ 名詞語彙　　　　　　　　　　　　　　　　　　　　　　　　　　　　解答 (D)

由句意應為「國際學生助學貸款的申請送件截止日，已延至 6 月 28 日」看來，名詞 (D) applications（申請書）為正確答案。(A) method 是「方法」，(B) contestant 是「參加者」，(C) notice 是「公告」的意思。

單字 submission n. 繳交　deadline n. 期限　put off phr. 延期

122

Arab Energies _____ to announce its merger with petroleum supplier Kuwait Petrochemical at a joint press conference. (A) would like　　　(B) is liking (C) is liked　　　　(D) was liked	阿拉伯能源公司將在聯合新聞發表會上，宣布與石油供應廠商科威特石化公司合併。

■ 助動詞 + 動詞原形　　　　　　　　　　　　　　　　　　　　　　　　解答 (A)

本題是要填入動詞的問題，由句意應為「宣布合併」看來，能搭配空格後的 to 當作助動詞使用的 would like to（想要做～）為正確答案。要注意，應記住 like 是表示感情與心理狀態的動詞，沒有進行式與被動語態。

單字 announce v. 宣布　merger n. 合併　petroleum n. 石油　supplier n. 供應商　joint a. 共同的

123

| It is _____ for all construction workers to wear protective gear when they are at the project site.
(A) mandator   (B) mandate
(C) mandatorily   (D) mandatory | 工人在工地工作時，須強制配戴保護器具。 |

■ 補語的位置   解答 (D)

空格是接於 be 動詞 is 之後的補語，因此名詞 (A) 與 (B)、形容詞 (D) 可能為正確答案。在本句中 It 為假主詞，to wear ~ project site 為真主詞，for all construction workers 則為實際意義上要去做動作的主詞。由句意應為「工人須強制配戴保護器具」看來，說明真主詞 to wear protective gear 的形容詞 (D) mandatory（義務的，強制的）為正確答案。若填入名詞 (A) 與 (B) 的話，則會與真主詞形成同格關係，使句意變為「配戴保護器具為強制者」、「配戴保護器具為強制」，與原本語意不符，因此並非正確答案。要注意，應記住 (B) mandate 是表示「命令」之意的動詞。

單字 construction n. 建設、工程   protective a. 保護的   site n. 現場

124

| Ms. Hilburn will teach the accounting course for new employees _____ the financial manager attends the conference.
(A) in   (B) while
(C) due to   (D) without | 在財務經理去參加會議時，Hilburn 女士將替新進員工上會計課。 |

■ 副詞子句連接詞 時間   解答 (B)

由於主要子句 Ms. Hilburn will teach the accounting course 具有句子的必須成分，所以 ___ the financial manager ~ the conference 應視為修飾語。因為修飾語具有動詞 attends，所以空格需填入能夠引導副詞子句的連接詞 (B) while（～期間）為正確答案。介系詞 (A) in（～裡面）、(C) due to（因為～）、(D) without（沒有～）無法連接子句，後面必須接名詞。

單字 accounting n. 會計   financial manager phr. 財務經理   conference n. 會議

125

| Because of all the conventions and special events taking place in the city, not a _____ hotel room is available this weekend.
(A) solitary   (B) remote
(C) reserved   (D) hidden | 因為市區內正在舉行各種會議及特別活動，這個週末飯店旅館連一間空房都沒有。 |

■ 形容詞語彙   解答 (A)

由句意應為「因為市區內正在舉行的會議及活動，這個週末飯店旅館連一間空房都沒有」看來，形容詞 (A) solitary（僅有的，單獨的）為正確答案。(B) remote 是「偏僻的，遙遠的」，(C) reserved 是「已預約的」，(D) hidden 是「藏起來的」的意思。要注意，應記住慣用語「not a + solitary / single + 名詞」（連一個都～不，沒有）。

126

| A Veldspar Phone Service representative can help you determine _____ calling plan is perfect for your budget.
(A) when　　　　　　(B) whom
(C) which　　　　　　(D) who | Veldspar 電話公司業務員可幫您決定哪一個通話方案是最符合您的預算。 |

■ 名詞子句連接詞 which　　　　　　　　　　　　　　　　　　　　　解答 (C)

本題是要填入動詞 determine 與受詞名詞子句 calling plan ~ budget 的連接詞，因此所有的選項皆可能是答案。修飾後面出現的名詞 calling plan 且能帶出名詞子句的疑問形容詞 (C) which 為正確答案。要注意，疑問副詞 (A) when 會讓語意變為「可幫您決定什麼時候的通話方案是最符合您的預算」，因此並非正確答案，受格疑問代名詞 (B) whom 因為名詞子句已經有介系詞 for 的受詞 your budget，因此不是答案。疑問代名詞 (D) who 必須為名詞子句的主詞，所以也不是答案。

單字 calling plan phr. 通話方案

127

| In preparation for her new position at the Montreal branch, Ms. Thatcher chose to _____ for an intensive French course to improve her language skills.
(A) register　　　　　　(B) access
(C) attend　　　　　　(D) submit | 為了準備她在蒙特婁分公司的新職位，Thatcher 女士選擇報名一個密集的法語課程來改善她的語言能力。 |

■ 動詞相關語句　　　　　　　　　　　　　　　　　　　　　　　　　解答 (A)

由句意應為「報名一個密集的法語課程來改善她的語言能力」看來，能與空格後介系詞 for 一起使用表示「報名～」之意的 register for，也就是動詞 (A) register（報名）為正確答案。(B) access 是「接近」，(C) attend 是「參加」，(D) submit 是「繳交」，因為全部都是及物動詞，因此不能和介系詞 for 一起使用，後面必須接可以當作受詞的名詞。

單字 in preparation for phr. 準備～　intensive a. 集中的

128

| One of Maxwell Distributor's _____ as a supplier of raw materials for industrial plants is to deliver needed goods in a timely and efficient manner.
(A) obligatory　　　　　　(B) obligation
(C) obligations　　　　　　(D) obligator | 作為工廠原料的供應商，Maxwell Distributor 其中一項責任就是將所需的貨物以及時且有效率的方式送達。 |

■ 限定詞與名詞　　　　　　　　　　　　　　　　　　　　　　　　　解答 (C)

空格為介系詞 of 的受詞，所有格 Maxwell Distributor's 後面接名詞，因此名詞 (B) (C) (D) 皆有可能為正確答案。因為有置於複數可數名詞前的數量表現用法 One of（～之一），因此複數名詞 (C) obligations（責任）為正確答案。

單字 supplier n. 供應商　raw material phr. 原料　timely a. 及時的、適時的

129

------ Dulce Country Club is already fully booked for May, suggestions on a suitable venue for the sports festival are urgently needed.
(A) Because
(B) Whereas
(C) During
(D) Nevertheless

因為 Dulce 鄉村俱樂部 5 月已全部被預訂，我們急切地需要有人建議另一個適合辦體育節的場地。

■ 副詞子句連接詞 理由

解答 (A)

本題是由主詞 suggestions 與動詞 are needed 所組成的主要子句和修飾語 ___ Dulce Country Club ~ for May 所組成的，修飾語有動詞 is booked，因此可以帶出副詞子句的連接詞 (A) 與 (B) 有可能為正確答案。因句意應為「預約都客滿了所以需要有人建議另一個適合體育節的場地」，因此表示理由的副詞子句連接詞 (A) Because（因為～）為正確答案。(B) Whereas（反之～）則會變為「預約都客滿了，反之需要有人建議另一個適合體育節的場地」的奇怪句意，因此並非正確答案。介系詞 (C) During（～期間）與連接副詞 (D) Nevertheless（然而）無法連接從屬子句。

單字 booked a. 已預約的　suggestion n. 建議　suitable a. 適合的　urgently ad. 緊急地

130

The wait staff has gotten used to the rotating shift system designed by the manager, and the executive chef has found that the setup is _____.
(A) reflective
(B) resistant
(C) productive
(D) decreasing

餐廳服務生已經適應由經理設計的輪班制，且行政主廚發覺這樣的制度很有效果。

■ 形容詞語彙

解答 (C)

由句意應為「服務生已適應輪班制，而且行政主廚發覺制度很有效果」看來，形容詞 (C) productive（有效果的，有產能的）為正確答案。(A) reflective 是「思考的」，(B) resistant 是「抵抗的，有抵抗力的」，(D) decreasing 是「減少的」的意思。要注意，應記住慣用語「get used to 名詞」（適應～）。

單字 wait staff phr. 服務員　rotating shift phr. 輪班　setup n. 構造，方案

131

Defective _____ should be returned to the store together with the official receipt within seven days from the date of purchase.
(A) option
(B) wholesaler
(C) merchandise
(D) reimbursement

瑕疵商品應在購買後七日內帶著正式的收據到商店退貨。

■ 名詞語彙

解答 (C)

由句意應為「瑕疵商品應帶著收據退還」看來，名詞 (C) merchandise（商品，產品）為正確答案。(A) option 是「選擇，選擇權」，(B) wholesaler 是「批發商」，(D) reimbursement 是「償還，退款」，要注意，應記住 merchandise 是集合名詞故沒有複數形，總是以單數形態做使用。

單字 defective a. 有缺陷的　purchase n. 購買

132

Global Patent Association is _____ to supporting the production of vehicles fueled by renewable energy. (A) dedicate　　　　(B) dedicated (C) dedicatory　　　(D) dedication	全球專利協會致力於支持使用再生能源的車輛生產。

■ 被動語態動詞常用表現　　　　　　　　　　　　　　　　　　　　　　　　　　解答 (B)

片語 be dedicated to 表示「致力於～」，因此動詞 dedicate 的 p.p. 形 (B) dedicated 為正確答案。

單字 vehicle n. 車子　fuel v. 以～為燃料　renewable a. 可再生的

133

Upon checkout, hotel guests can drop their feedback forms in the brown box located _____ the reception desk. (A) through　　　　(B) among (C) beside　　　　(D) into	退房時，飯店旅客可以將他們的意見單放進接待處旁邊的咖啡色箱子。

■ 選擇介系詞 場所　　　　　　　　　　　　　　　　　　　　　　　　　　　　解答 (C)

由於是在說明用來放置意見單的箱子位置，因此用來描述位置的介系詞 (B) 與 (C) 有可能為正確答案。置於單數名詞 reception desk 前，表示「接待處旁邊的咖啡色箱子」的介系詞 (C) beside（～旁邊）為正確答案。(B) among（在～之中）通常是用於有三者以上的人或物之前，後面接複數名詞，因此並非答案。(A) through（穿過～，歷經～期間）用來描述方向、方法、手段與時間，(D) into（到～裡）是用來表示方向的介系詞，所以也不是答案。

單字 drop v. 丟入，扔下　reception desk phr. 接待處

134

According to a news bulletin, Dido Megatrade Hall was _____ with job seekers during the career fair last weekend. (A) pack　　　　(B) packs (C) packed　　　(D) packing	根據一份新聞快報，上週末的就業博覽會中，Dido Megatrade 大廳擠滿了求職者。

■ 被動語態動詞常用表現　　　　　　　　　　　　　　　　　　　　　　　　　　解答 (C)

片語 be packed with 表示「充滿了～」，因此 (C) packed 為正確答案。要注意，be crowded with（擠滿了～）與 be filled with（充滿了～）也是常使用被動語態的慣用語。

單字 bulletin n. 公告，快報　job seeker phr. 求職者　fair n. 博覽會

135

Following lengthy discussions, the board agreed to _____ the workers' dispute by offering them a modest increase in pay.

(A) achieve　　　　　(B) implement
(C) resolve　　　　　(D) determine

經過冗長的討論，董事會同意微幅調整工人的薪水，以解決工人們的紛爭。

■ 動詞語彙　　　　　　　　　　　　　　　　　　　　　　　　　　解答 (C)

由句意應為「調整工人的薪水，以解決工人們的紛爭」看來，動詞 (C) resolve（解決）為正確答案。(A) achieve 是「達成」，(B) implement 是「實施」，(D) determine 是「決心，決定」的意思。

單字 lengthy a. 冗長的　board n. 董事會，理事會　dispute n. 紛爭　modest a. 適度的，謙虛的

136

Students _____ careers in journalism are recommended to apply for internships at publishing companies for which they would actually want to work.

(A) describing　　　　(B) revising
(C) pursuing　　　　　(D) attracting

建議想要往新聞界發展的學生們，去申請他們實際想要進入的出版公司的實習機會。

■ 動詞語彙　　　　　　　　　　　　　　　　　　　　　　　　　　解答 (C)

由句意應為「想要往新聞界發展的學生們」看來，動詞 pursue（追求）的現在分詞 (C) pursuing 為正確答案。(A) describe 是「描述」，(B) revise 是「修正」，(D) attract 是「吸引」的意思。

單字 journalism n. 新聞業，新聞工作　recommend v. 推薦，建議

137

Like other dining establishments in the city, Shadow Restaurant uses tableware made of recycled material _____ environmental conservation efforts.

(A) to support　　　　(B) as supporting
(C) in support　　　　(D) for the supported

如同城市中其他的餐飲機構，Shadow 餐廳使用由回收原料所製成的餐具，以支持環境保育工作。

■ to 不定詞的用法　　　　　　　　　　　　　　　　　　　　　　解答 (A)

主句含有主詞 Shadow Restaurant、動詞 uses、受詞 tableware 的完整子句，因此 ___ environmental conservation efforts 應視為修飾語。此修飾語，會使空格後面的名詞成為受詞，意思應為「以支持環保工作」，因此表示目的的 to 不定詞 (A) to support 為正確答案。分詞構句 (B) as supporting 讓句意變成「使用由回收原料所製成的餐具，如同支持環保工作」，介系詞片語 (D) for the supported 則讓句意變成「為了被支持的環保工作，使用由回收原料所製成的餐具」，兩個句意都很奇怪。(C) in support（支持）的 support 為介系詞 in 受詞的名詞，後面沒有再接介系詞的話無法直接接名詞。

單字 tableware n. 餐具　conservation n. 保護、保存

138

Participants at yesterday's meeting were convinced by Benjamin York, who spoke _____ on expanding the range of Bateman Firm's charitable sponsorships. (A) seemingly　　　(B) consequently (C) eloquently　　　(D) mutually	昨日會議的參加者被 Benjamin York 說服了，他極具說服力地要求擴大 Bateman 公司慈善贊助的範圍。

■ 副詞語彙　　　　　　　　　　　　　　　　　　　　　　　　　　　　　　　解答 (C)

由句意應為「他極具說服力地要求擴大 Bateman 公司慈善贊助的範圍」看來，副詞 (C) eloquently（具說服力地）為正確答案。要注意，應記住 eloquently 是用於表示有效地說服他人。(A) seemingly 是「表面上」，(B) consequently 是「結果」，(D) mutually 是「彼此，互相之間」的意思。

單字　expand v. 擴張　charitable a. 慈善的

139

Fionnad Telecom's recently launched broadband service promises to be faster and more _____ compared to those of the company's competitors. (A) relies　　　　　(B) reliable (C) reliability　　　(D) relying	Fionnad 電信最近投入寬頻服務，保證提供比其他業界競爭者更快更可靠的服務。

■ 對等關係構句　　　　　　　　　　　　　　　　　　　　　　　　　　　　　解答 (B)

對等連接詞 and 前有形容詞比較級 faster，因此 and 後也應有形容詞比較級。所以形容詞 (B) 與可當作形容詞使用的分詞 (D) 有可能為正確答案。空格後搭配 more，句意應為「保證提供比其他業界競爭者更快更可靠的服務」，因此形容詞 (B) reliable（可靠的，值得信賴的）為正確答案。如果填入現在分詞 (D) relying（去相信的，去依賴的）的話，則會變為「保證服務比其他業界競爭者更快更依賴」這種奇怪語意，因此並非正確答案。動詞 (A) 與名詞 (C) 則無法當作形容詞比較級使用。

單字　broadband a. 寬頻的　rely v. 倚靠，相信

140

According to analysts, the steady decline in Oregon's unemployment rate over the last three years is a positive _____ of the state's economic growth. (A) indicator　　　(B) collector (C) regulator　　　(D) messenger	根據分析師表示，奧勒岡州三年來失業率穩定的下降，是本州經濟成長的一項正向指標。

■ 名詞語彙　　　　　　　　　　　　　　　　　　　　　　　　　　　　　　　解答 (A)

由句意應為「失業率下降是正向指標」看來，(A) indicator（指標）為正確答案。(B) collector 是「收藏家」，(C) regulator 是「管理機關，管理者」，(D) messenger 是「傳遞者，送信人」的意思。

單字　analyst n. 分析師　decline n. 減少　unemployment rate phr. 失業率

Questions 141-143 refer to the following announcement.　　141-143 根據下面職缺廣告的內容回答問題。

Exodus Manpower Services Wanted: Cashiers The Mandarin Sports Club is _____ need of two cashiers 　　141 (A) on　　　　　　(B) in 　　　　(C) within　　　　 (D) by for its new restaurant. Candidates should have at least a year of experience working in a restaurant, resort, or retail environment. _____ university degrees are not required for this position, 142 (A) Only if　　　(B) Furthermore 　　 (C) Even though (D) Whichever priority will be given to applicants who have some applicable education. To apply, please e-mail your résumé and references to req@mandarinpersonnel.com on or before May 6. Those who qualify will receive a reply containing the date of their _____ with the manager of the sports club. 143 (A) entry　　　(B) cooperation 　　 (C) interview　 (D) admission	Exodus 人力公司 徵求：出納員 141 Mandarin 運動俱樂部新的餐廳需要兩名出納員，應徵者至少應有一年在餐廳、度假中心或零售業工作的經驗。 142 雖然此職缺不需要大學學歷，但有相關學歷者具優先權。 申請者請將履歷表及參考文件在 5 月 6 日前，電郵到 req@mandarinpersonnel. com。143 合格者會收到一封回函，內含與運動俱樂部經理面談的時間。

單字 **cashier** n. 出納員　**at least** phr. 至少　**retail** a. 零售的　**degree** n. 學位　**priority** n. 優先權
applicable a. 合適的，相關的　**reference** n. 推薦函

141 ■ 與動詞、形容詞、名詞一起使用的介系詞　　　　　　　　　　　　　　　　　　　　　　解答 (B)

句意應為「新的餐廳需要兩名出納員」，介系詞 (B) in 可與空格後的 need of 搭配。表示「需要～」，因此為正確答案。

142 ■ 副詞子句連接詞 讓步　　　　　　　　　　　　　　　　　　　　　　　　　　　　　　　解答 (C)

這句是由含 priority will be given 的主要子句與 ___ university degrees ~ this position 的修飾語所組成，因為修飾語有動詞 are not required，因此能連接副詞子句的連接詞 (A) (C) 與複合關係代名詞 (D) 可能為正確答案。因句意應為「不需要大學學歷，但有相關學歷者具優先權」，因此表示讓步語氣的 (C) Even though（雖然～）為正確答案。表示條件的副詞子句連接詞 (A) Only if（唯有在～情況下）會讓語意變為「唯有不需要大學學歷，具有相關學歷者有優先權」。複合關係代名詞 (D) Whichever（無論是～）雖然可以連接名詞子句與副詞子句，但會讓語意變為「無論哪一所大學學歷都不需要，具有相關學歷者有優先權」。(B) Furthermore（再加上）則不能當作副詞子句連接詞。

143 ■ 名詞語彙　　　　　　　　　　　　　　　　　　　　　　　　　　　　　　　　　　　　解答 (C)

由句意應為「合格者會收到一封回函，內含與運動俱樂部經理面談的時間」看來，名詞 (C) interview（面試）為正確答案。(A) entry 是「入場，加入」，(B) cooperation 是「合作」(D) admission 是「進入許可，入場券」的意思。

Questions 144-146 refer to the following letter. 　　144-146 根據下面信件的內容回答問題。

November 31	11 月 31 日
Dear Mr. Terence Collins,	親愛的 Terence Collins 先生：
Thank you for choosing to _____ the services of Bali	144 感謝您選擇使用 Bali 租車公司的服務！按照您的要求，此次服務費用已由您的信用卡支付。145 您可以從明天到星期日，也就是 12 月 1 日到 12 月 7 日，駕駛 Rivelette Beam 512（車牌：DK 1025）。
144 (A) use 　　(B) improve	
(C) expand 　(D) fund	
Transport! As you requested, the payment for this service has been charged to your credit card. You may drive our Rivelette Beam 512 (plate number: DK 1025) _____	
145 (A) starts 　　(B) started	
(C) starter 　(D) starting	
tomorrow, December 1, until Sunday, December 7.	
Enclosed are your receipt and a copy of the car's registration certificate. Please remember to take these documents and your driver's license with you when driving. In case of mechanical problems, do not hesitate to contact us for assistance.	附上的是您的收據及車輛登記證書的複本。開車時，請記得攜帶這些文件及您的駕照。若遇到操作上的問題，請不要猶豫與我們聯絡尋求協助。
We hope that _____ one of Bali Transport's vehicles will	146 我們希望租了一台 Bali 租車公司的車子，會讓您的旅程更加舒適。
146 (A) purchasing 　(B) renting	
(C) testing 　(D) personalizing	
make your travels more comfortable.	
Respectfully yours,	
Bali Transport	Bali 租車公司 敬上

單字 request v. 要求　charge v. 索費　registration certificate phr. 登記證，登記證明書
driver's license phr. 駕照　mechanical a. 機械的，操作上的　hesitate v. 猶豫

144 ■ 動詞語彙 掌握上下文 　　　　　　　　　　　　　　　　　　　　　　　　　　　　解答 (A)

句意應為「感謝您選擇 ___ Bali 租車公司的服務」，因此所有的選項皆有可能為正確答案。無法單以空格所在的該句選擇答案的話，就要參考前後的文意。後面寫到服務費用已由信用卡支付，因此可以知道是收信人為了使用 Bali Transport 的服務所付的款項，所以動詞 (A) use（使用）為正確答案。(B) improve 是「改善」，(C) expand 是「擴張」，(D) fund 是「資助」的意思。

145 ■ 分詞構句 　　　　　　　　　　　　　　　　　　　　　　　　　　　　　　　　　解答 (D)

主句是由含有主詞 You、動詞 may drive、受格 our Rivelette Beam 512 的完整句子，因此 ___ tomorrow 為修飾語，而且修飾語中並沒有動詞，可以知道並非子句。選項當中可以用來修飾主要句子的為過去分詞 (B) 與現在分詞 (D)。空格與其後的 tomorrow 是表示「從明天開始」的分詞構句，因此現在分詞 (D) starting 為正確答案。動詞 (A) 與名詞 (C) 則不符合文法。

146 ■ 動詞語彙 掌握全文 　　　　　　　　　　　　　　　　　　　　　　　　　　　　　解答 (B)

由句意「我們希望 ___ 一台 Bali 租車公司的車子，會讓您的旅程更加舒適」看來，(A) 與 (B) 有可能為正確答案。無法單以空格所在的該句選擇答案的話，就要參考前後與全文的文意。前面提到收信人從 12 月 1 號開始到 7 號為止都可以駕駛 Bali Transport 的車子，因此可以知道是客人租了 Bali Transport 的車，所以動詞 rent（租）的 -ing 形 (B) renting 是正確答案。(A) 的 purchase 是「購買」，(C) 的 test 是「測試」，(D) 的 personalize 是「個人化」的意思。

Questions 147-149 refer to the following e-mail.

All newly hired tour guides _____ the first part of their

147 (A) will begin   (B) have begun
     (C) will have begun   (D) were beginning

hospitality management training with a seminar on customer service and public relations. Attendance is required, as it is part of your orientation for the position.

On June 5, instructors from the East Tourism Institute in Singapore, which has produced top travel administrators, will deliver _____ lectures at Charten Cruise Lines' main

148 (A) weekly   (B) recorded
    (C) public   (D) separate

office from 2 P.M. to 4 P.M. in the conference room on the second floor. Class materials will be handed out on the days each lecture is held.

Note that the _____ will consist of a one-hour talk on a

149 (A) researches (B) sessions
    (C) tests   (D) trials

given topic followed by a 40-minute group activity. The group activities will provide participants with the opportunity to test their learning in a fun and social environment. The final 20 minutes will be used to recap discussions and allow participants to ask the speaker questions.

For inquiries, please contact the personnel department at 555-8963.

147 所有新聘導遊的第一階段接待管理訓練，將由一場以客服及公關為主題的研討會展開序幕，您必須出席，這是您新進人員訓練的一部份。

在 6 月 5 日下午兩點到四點，148 新加坡東方旅遊協會的講師們會在 Charten Cruise Lines 主要辦事處的二樓會議室，進行各別的課程，這協會訓練出很多頂尖的旅遊界管理者。上課教材將於每堂課當日被發放。

149 請注意研討課程的程序如下，先有一小時的主題式演講，接著是四十分鐘的小組活動。小組活動會讓參與者有機會在趣味中及聯誼性的情境下，檢視自己所學，最後二十分鐘將會複習討論的重點，並可以讓參與者向講師提問。

若需諮詢，請洽人事部 555-8963。

單字 hospitality n. 接待，款待　management n. 管理，經營　public relations phr. 公關　attendance n. 參加
administrator n. 管理者　recap v. 重述要點

147 ■ 未來式 掌握全文　　　　　　　　　　　　　　　　　　　　　　　　　　　　解答 (A)

由「所有新聘導遊的管理訓練」句意看來，無法選出正確時態的動詞，因此要參考上下文與整篇的文意來選擇正確答案。題目中間部分提到在 6 月 5 日講師會進行授課，因此可以知道訓練的時間應為未來式，所以 (A) will begin 為正確答案。

148 ■ 形容詞語彙 掌握上下文　　　　　　　　　　　　　　　　　　　　　　　　　解答 (D)

由「6 月 5 日講師會進行_____課程」的文意看來 (C) 與 (D) 有可能為正確答案，無法單以空格所在的該句選擇答案的話，就要參考前後的文意。後面提到上課教材將於每堂課當日發放，因此形容詞 (D) separate（各別的）為正確答案。在題目一開始提到這是為了新雇用的導遊們所舉行的，因此 (C) public（大眾的，公開的）並不是答案。(A) weekly 是「每週的」，(B) recorded 是「被錄音的，記錄下來的」的意思。

149 ■ 名詞語彙 掌握全文　　　　　　　　　　　　　　　　　　　　　　　　　　　解答 (B)

由「____ 先有一小時的主題式演講，接著是四十分鐘的小組活動」的句意看來，所有的選項都有可能，無法單以空格所在的該句選擇答案的話，就要參考前後或全文的文意。文章的前半提到因為新進導遊的訓練，開始了研討會，然後詳細的說明跟教育訓練相關的研討課程執行方式，因此名詞 (B) sessions（研討課程）為正確答案。(A) researches 是「研究，調查」，(C) tests 是「考試，實驗」，(D) trials 是「審判，試驗」的意思。

232 | 全新！NEW TOEIC 新多益閱讀題庫解析

Questions 150-152 refer to the following announcement.　150-152 根據下面電郵的內容回答問題。

From: Harold Merritt <h.merritt@eventsmaster.com>
To: Beatriz Lester <b.lester@eventsmaster.com>
Date: June 2
Re: Museum Event

Dear Beatriz,

I'm sorry for the delayed response to your e-mail. I've been busy all day making arrangements for the inauguration of the Natural Science Museum.

The guest list for the event _____. I took care of that this

150 (A) will be revised　(B) has been revised
(C) had been revised (D) is being revised

morning and also sent invitations to major broadcasting companies and newspapers to ensure full media coverage of our event. Although we are done with the guest list, there are still some changes _____ in the program.

151 (A) to be making　(B) have been made
(C) to be made　(D) are being made

I spoke with the museum's chief curator this morning to finalize the details of the performances, and she asked that we make a shorter line-up for the _____ ceremony so

152 (A) awards　(B) graduation
(C) opening　(D) signing

that the guests will have more time to enjoy the sights at the museum. In addition, she wants us to purchase some small souvenir items that can be given away to those in attendance. Perhaps we should meet with the team to revise the program and discuss the souvenir items. Please reply to this e-mail as soon as possible so that we can post an announcement for the staff tomorrow. Thanks.

Best regards,

Harold

寄件人：Harold Merritt
　　　　〈h.merritt@eventsmaster.com〉
收件人：Beatriz Lester
　　　　〈b.lester@eventsmaster.com〉
主旨：6 月 2 日
日期：博物館活動

親愛的 Beatriz：

我很抱歉這麼晚才回應您的電郵。我整天都在忙著安排自然科學博物館的開幕儀式。

150 本次開幕的嘉賓名單已修正完成，我今早已處理完畢，並已將邀請函發送至各個主要的廣播公司及報社，以確保媒體完整報導我們的活動。

151 雖然我們已經確定了嘉賓名單，但是節目表還是有需要修改的地方。

我今早已跟博物館的館長敲定了表演節目的細節，152 她要求我們縮短開幕式的流程，讓嘉賓們能有更多的時間來欣賞博物館的景物。此外，她希望我們購買一些小紀念品來贈送給出席者。

或許我們應該與團隊開個會來修正節目表，並討論有關紀念品的事。請盡速回覆此郵件，以便讓我們能將此公告在明天向員工宣布。感謝您。

Harold 上

單字　arrangement n. 安排　inauguration n. 開幕式　broadcasting n. 廣播　media coverage phr. 媒體報導
　　line-up n. 行程，流程

150　■ 現在完成式 掌握上下文　　　　　　　　　　　　　　　　　　　　　　　　　　解答 (B)

單就「修正本次開幕的嘉賓名單」的句意看來，並無法選出正確時態的動詞，因此應參考前後文意來選擇正確答案。後面提到已處理完畢，可判斷應是通知對方處理結果，過去發生的事直到現在仍有影響，因此現在完成式 (B) has been revised 為正確答案。

151　■ to 不定詞的用法　　　　　　　　　　　　　　　　　　　　　　　　　　　　　解答 (C)

主句是含有 there are still some changes 的完整句子，___ in the program 是用來修飾空格前名詞 changes，具形容詞功用的修飾語，因此 to 不定詞 (A) 與 (C) 為可能的答案。受修飾的名詞 changes 與 to 不定詞結合成為「需要被修改」的被動關係，因此 (C) to be made 為正確答案。

152　■ 名詞語彙 掌握全文　　　　　　　　　　　　　　　　　　　　　　　　　　　　解答 (C)

單由「她要求我們縮短 _____ 儀式的流程」的句意看來並無法選出正確答案，因此要參考前後及全文的文意。題目前段提到都在忙自然科學博物館的開幕儀式，後面則對開幕儀式做了較仔細的說明，因此名詞 (C) opening（開館，開幕）為正確答案。(A) award 是「頒獎、判決」，(B) graduation 是「畢業」，(D) signing 是「簽署」的意思。

PART 7

Questions 153-154 refer to the following notice.　　　　　153-154 根據下面備忘錄的內容回答問題。

MEMO	備忘錄
To: Joseph Pruitt, Marketing Manager From: Carl Scallot, Marketing Director Date: January 12 Re: Proposal	寄件人：Joseph Pruitt, 行銷經理 收件人：Carl Scallot, 行銷主任 主旨：1 月 12 日 日期：提案
[153]I reviewed your proposal this morning. Overall, you have some excellent ideas, but you will need to confirm your financial projections with Katherine. In addition, [153]I have made some other recommendations, which you will find in an e-mail I have sent you.	[153] 我今早已檢閱你的提案。整體來說，你有一些很棒的想法，但是你需要跟 Katherine 確認你的財務預測。此外，[153] 我也在我寄給你的電郵中提供了一些建議。
After you have revised your proposal, [154]please contact me on my mobile phone at 555-1324. I will be out of the office until 2:30 P.M., but we can meet sometime later in the afternoon.	在你修改你的提案後，[154] 請打手機給我 555-1324。我下午兩點半前不會在辦公室，但我們可以約下午晚一點的時間。
Thanks.	謝謝。
Carl	Carl

單字 □review v. 檢閱　　　□proposal n. 提案書　　　□overall ad. 全面地、全部

　　　□confirm v. 確認　　　□financial a. 財務的，金融的　　□projection n. 計畫，預想，推測

　　　□recommendation n. 意見、建議　□revise v. 修正，改正

153

Why was the memo written? (A) To discuss a product (B) To provide feedback (C) To introduce a client (D) To schedule a seminar	為什麼需要寫這個備忘錄？ (A) 討論一個產品 (B) 提供回饋 (C) 介紹一位客戶 (D) 安排一個研討會

■ **找出主題** 寫文章的理由　　　　　　　　　　　　　　　　　　　　　　　　　　　　解答 (B)

因為是問寫這份備忘錄的理由的主題搜尋問題，因此要特別注意文章前面的幾段。I reviewed your proposal this morning. 提到看過提案書後 I have made some other recommendations, which you will find in an e-mail I have sent you. 表示提供了一些建議，因此 (B) To provide feedback 是正確答案。

換句話說

recommendations 建議，提案 → feedback 建議，回饋

單字 discuss v. 討論，商談　client n. 顧客，委託

154

What does Mr. Scallot ask Mr. Pruitt to do?	Scallot 先生要求 Pruitt 先生做什麼？
(A) Call him on the telephone	(A) 打電話給他
(B) Meet him at a restaurant	(B) 與他在一家餐廳見面
(C) Prepare a video presentation	(C) 準備一個影片報告
(D) Collect money from a customer	(D) 向一位客戶收錢

■ 六何原則 What   解答 (A)

本題是問 Mr. Scallot 要求 Mr. Pruitt 做什麼（What）的六何原則問題。由與本問題重點 Mr. Scallot ask Mr. Pruitt to do 相關的內文 please contact me on my mobile phone at 555-1324 看來，寫備忘錄的 Mr. Scallot 是叫收信者 Mr. Pruitt 打電話給他，因此 (A) Call him on the telephone 為正確答案。

單字 prepare v. 準備   collect v. 收款，募捐

TRANSATLANTIC IMPORTS INCORPORATED	Transatlantic 進口公司
Demos Nikolaidis Jolly Greek Grocer 82 Armistice Avenue, Glendale, CA	Demos Nikolaidis 先生 Jolly Greek 食品雜貨店 加州，Glendale 郡，Armistice 街 82 號
July 15	7 月 15 日
Dear sir,	先生您好：
155/156-D This is a second reminder that your account with us is past due (please see the enclosed copy of the invoice). A payment of $320 was due two months ago on May 15. 155Please settle your account before August 1. Otherwise, we will have to turn the matter over to a collection agency. Should you wish to explore other payment options, you may call our accounts department at 555-0392. 156-AOur office is open from Monday to Friday, 9 A.M. to 5 P.M., and on Saturday from 9 A.M. to 12 P.M. Please ignore this letter if payment has already been sent.	155/156-D 這是第二封催繳通知，您的帳單已經逾期（請參看附上的請款單），有一筆 320 元美金的款項已在 5 月 15 日到期，請您在 8 月 1 日前處理您的帳單。否則，我們不得不將此事移交給討債公司。如果您希望了解其他的付款方式，您可以電話 555-0392 洽詢我們的會計部門 。156-A 我們辦公室的營業時間從星期一到星期五，早上九點到下午五點，以及星期六的早上九點到中午十二點。請忽略此信如果您已將款項送出。
Thank you.	謝謝您。
Susan Crane Chief Accountant Transatlantic Imports	Susan Crane 總會計師 Transatlantic 進口公司

單字 ☐ reminder n. 催繳通知　☐ account n. 帳單，帳戶　☐ due n. 期限；a. 應支付的
　　 ☐ enclosed a. 隨信附上的　☐ invoice n. 發票，請款單　☐ settle v. 結帳，支付，處理
　　 ☐ turn over phr. 移交，翻轉　☐ collection agency phr. 討債公司
　　 ☐ ignore v. 忽略

155

What is the purpose of the letter? (A) To ask for a billing statement (B) To apologize for overcharging (C) To request a payment (D) To place an order	此信件的目的為何？ (A) 要求帳單 (B) 對多收錢道歉 (C) 要求付款 (D) 下訂單

■ 找出主題 目的　　　　　　　　　　　　　　　　　　　　　　　　　　　　　　　　解答 (C)

本題是問寫這封信的目的的主題搜尋問題，應注意文章的前段部分。This is a second reminder that your account with us is past due 指出這是第二封催款通知，而 Please settle your account before August 1. 則是要對方在 8 月 1 日前處理帳單，因此 (C) To request a payment 為正確答案。

單字 billing statement phr. 帳單　overcharge v. 索價過高　request v. 要求　place an order phr. 下訂單

156

What is indicated in the letter?	這封信指出了什麼？
(A) Transatlantic Imports is open seven days a week.	(A) Transatlantic 進口公司一週七天都營業。
(B) Mr. Nikolaidis has already mailed in his payment.	(B) Nikolaidis 先生已經把款項郵寄出去。
(C) Transatlantic Imports operates a collection agency.	(C) Transatlantic 進口公司經營一家討債公司。
(D) Mr. Nikolaidis has been previously contacted.	(D) 之前已經連絡過 Nikolaidis 先生。

■ **Not/True** True 問題   解答 (D)

這題是將題目內容與原文對照的 Not/True 問題。這類的問題無從得知重點在哪一個部分，因此要對照文章內容才能找到答案。Our office is open from Monday to Friday ~ and on Saturday 提到 Transatlantic Imports 公司從禮拜一開到禮拜六，與 (A) 的敘述不相符。(B) 與 (C) 的內容在文中並未被提及。This is a second reminder that your account with us is past due 提到這是第二封逾期繳款催款通知，可以知道 Mr. Nikolaidis 已經收過一封。所以 (D) Mr. Nikolaidis has been previously contacted. 為正確答案。

Questions 157-159 refer to the following information.

157-159 根據下面公告的內容回答問題。

Pacific Shots

March 5 and 6
From 9 A.M. to 5 P.M.
Location: The Landien Tower Exhibit Center

157/159-C The Omega Scuba Club invites you to a two-day photo exhibit featuring the Pacific Ocean's natural wonders at the Landien Tower exhibit center. Explore the rich marine life of the world's largest ocean through the lenses of our very own underwater photographers. The show will also feature the works of more than 20 renowned photographers, and is an event not to be missed!

158-C Omega chairperson and *Wild Voyager* photographer Allen Crowley will open the event with a short presentation on underwater photography. This will be followed by a guided tour of the exhibition area. Many of the photographers will be on hand to discuss their photographs and answer your questions. 159-A Admission is free and open to the public. For more information, please visit Omega Scuba Club's Web site at www.omegadive.com.

太平洋攝影展

3 月 5 日及 6 日
早上九點到下午五點
地點：Landien Tower 展覽中心

157/157-C Omega 潛水俱樂部邀請您參加一個為期兩天的攝影展，主題是太平洋海中的自然奇觀，地點在 Landien Tower 展覽中心塔。藉由我們特派的水中攝影師來帶您探索全世界最大海洋中豐富的海洋生物，此次展覽也會同時展出二十多位著名攝影師的作品。是一個不容錯過的活動！

158-C Omega 的主席，也是 *Wild Voyager* 的攝影師，Allen Crowley 會以一場水中攝影主題的簡報揭開活動序幕，緊接著會有展場的導覽，許多攝影師會在場與您討論他們的作品及回答您的問題。159-A 此次活動是免費入場並對外公開的。若您需要更多資訊，請上 Omega Scuba 俱樂部的官網：www.omegadive.com。

單字 □exhibit n. 展示，展覽
□explore v. 探險，探索
□underwater a. 水中的
□admission n. 入場

□feature v. 以～為特徵
□rich a. 豐富的，富有～的
□renowned a. 有名的
□public n. 大眾； a. 大眾的

□natural wonder phr. 自然奇觀
□marine life phr. 海洋生物
□guided a. 導覽的

157

What is the announcement mainly about?
(A) A diving lesson
(B) A photography display
(C) A leadership seminar
(D) A sea exploration

此公告主要與什麼有關？
(A) 一堂潛水課
(B) 一場攝影展
(C) 一場領導力研討會
(D) 一場海洋探勘

■ 找出主題 主題

解答 (B)

要找出文章主旨應注意內容的前段部分。The Omega Scuba Club invites you to a two-day photo exhibit featuring the Pacific Ocean's natural wonders 此句中提到 Omega Scuba 俱樂部邀請參加一個為期兩天的攝影展，後文並繼續進行細部的說明，因此 (B) A photography display 為正確答案。

換句話說
a ~ photo exhibit 攝影展覽會 → A photography display 攝影展

單字 exploration n. 探險，探索

158

What is mentioned about Allen Crowley?	文中提到有關 Allen Crowley 的什麼事？
(A) He will conduct a guided tour.	(A) 他會進行一場導覽。
(B) He is the owner of a magazine.	(B) 他是一家雜誌的老闆。
(C) He is the leader of an organization.	(C) 他是一個組織的領導者。
(D) He will give a series of lectures.	(D) 他會做一系列的演講。

■ Not/True True 問題　　　　　　　　　　　　　　　　　　　　　　　　　解答 (C)

本題是找尋和關鍵字 Allen Crowley 有關的內容並與選項相互對照的 Not/True 問題。(A) 與 (B) 的內容在文章當中並沒有提到。在 Omega chairperson ~ Allen Crowley 一句當中提到 Allen Crowley 是 Omega 的主席，與 (C) 相符，因此 (C) He is the leader of an organization. 是正確答案。(D) 在題目中也未被提及。

換句話說
chairperson 老闆 → the leader 領導者

單字 **conduct** v. 帶領，指揮　**a series of** phr. 一系列的　**lecture** n. 講座，演講

159

What is stated about the event?	文中指出活動的哪一件事？
(A) It is open to everyone.	(A) 它是對外公開的。
(B) It is held once every year.	(B) 它一年舉辦一次。
(C) It is organized by a travel agency.	(C) 它是由一個旅行社所主辦的。
(D) It is sponsored by *Wild Voyager*.	(D) 它由 *Wild Voyager* 贊助。

■ Not/True True 問題　　　　　　　　　　　　　　　　　　　　　　　　　解答 (A)

本題是找尋和關鍵字 the event 有關的內容並與選項相互對照的 Not/True 問題。在 Admission is free and open to the public. 一句當中提到入場免費且對大眾開放，與 (A) 的敘述相符。因此 (A) It is open to everyone. 為正確答案。(B) 的部分在文中並未提及。文中提到 The Omega Scuba Club invites you to a two-day photo exhibit 為「Omega Scuba 俱樂部邀請您參加一個為期兩天的攝影展」之意，與 (C) 的敘述並不一致。(D) 的內容在文中則未被提及。

單字 **sponsor** v. 贊助；n. 贊助

The Bond Street Journal folds, to Reemerge Online

[160]Hornbull Corporation has announced it will cease publication of *The Bond Street Journal*, effective January 1, ending the newspaper's 60-year run as the nation's leading source of financial news. On the company's Web site, CEO Jack Diamond explains that the newspaper will continue to exist, but only in cyberspace. "[160]With the excessively high cost of printing daily, the board of directors wisely decided to pursue an Internet-only strategy first proposed two years ago," he said. It was further revealed that [161-A]*The Bond Street Journal*'s 200,000 subscribers would automatically receive free subscriptions to the online version of *The Bond Street Journal*.

[161-B]Hornbull will still publish its most popular monthly titles, *Observer, Magnate,* and *Livret,* which continue to enjoy significant newsstand sales. Among the remaining industry players, Deep Blue's *Oracle* is expected to emerge as *The Bond Street Journal's* successor, although [161-D]most observers believe it is only a matter of time before all print publications make the transition online.

The Bond Street 停刊但於網路重現

[160] Hornbull 股份有限公司宣佈它即將從 1 月 1 日起停止發行 *The Bond Street* 日報，結束它連續六十年為全國經濟新聞的主要來源。在公司的官網上，首席執行長 Jack Diamond 解釋報紙會繼續存在，但是只存在於網路上。他表示：「[160] 因為每日印刷過高的成本，董事會明智的決定施行僅發行網路版的政策，此方案在兩年前首次被提出。」他進一步的表示，[161-A] *The Bond Street* 的二十萬紙本訂戶會自動收到免費線上版的電子報。

[161-B] Hornbull 會繼續發行它每月最受歡迎的月刊 *Observer*、*Magnate* 及 *Livret*，它在報攤的銷售量持續保持佳績。至於剩下的業者，大家預測 Deep Blue 的 *Oracle* 將成為 *The Bond Street* 日報的繼承者，雖然大部分的觀察者相信所有的印刷出版品轉變成為線上版只是時間上的問題。

單字
- □fold v. 停刊，褶疊
- □effective a. 有效的，生效的
- □wisely ad. 明智地，聰明地
- □further ad. 進一步
- □newsstand n. 書報亭
- □successor n. 後人，繼承者
- □reemerge v. 再躍上，再出現
- □leading a. 領導的，很重要的
- □pursue v. 追求，追尋
- □reveal v. 揭開，揭露
- □remain v. 留下，殘存
- □observer n. 觀察者，奉行者
- □cease v. 中斷，停止
- □excessively ad. 超過地，過度地
- □strategy n. 戰略
- □title n. 出版品，書籍
- □emerge v. 浮現，顯露
- □transition n. 變化，移動

160

Why did Hornbull Corporation decide to stop printing *The Bond Street Journal*?
(A) Readership had gone down.
(B) Consumers found it uninteresting.
(C) The owner chose to retire.
(D) Publishing it was too expensive.

為什麼 Hornbull 公司會決定停止出版 *The Bond Street* 日報？
(A) 讀者群下降。
(B) 消費者覺得它無趣。
(C) 老闆決定退休。
(D) 印刷太過昂貴。

■ 六何原則 Why　　　　　　　　　　　　　　　　　　　　　　　解答 (D)

這是在問為什麼 Hornbull 公司會決定停止出版 *The Bond Street* 日報的六何原則問題。應找出與題目關鍵字 stop printing *The Bond Street Journal* 有關的部分，Hornbull Corporation has announced it will cease publication of *The Bond Street Journal* 一句中提到 Hornbull 公司宣佈它即將從 1 月 1 日起停止發行 *The Bond Street Journal*，之後再提到 With the excessively high cost of printing daily, the board of directors wisely decided to pursue an Internet-only strategy，即每日印刷過高的成本，董事會明智的決定施行僅發行網路版的政策，因此 (D) Publishing it was too expensive. 為正確答案。

換句話說
excessively high cost 過高的費用 → too expensive 太貴

單字 readership n. 讀者群

161

What is NOT indicated in the article?	文中沒有指出下列哪個項目？
(A) Free memberships to a site will be given.	(A) 將給予一個網站的免費會員資格。
(B) Hornbull will continue to publish other titles.	(B) Hornbull 會繼續出版其他的刊物。
(C) Competitors are experiencing rising sales.	(C) 競爭者感受到銷售量的上揚。
(D) Experts believe printed materials will become obsolete.	(D) 專家相信印刷出版品將會被淘汰。

■ **Not/True** Not 問題   解答 (C)

這是要將題目選項與文章內容對照的 Not/True 問題。因為問題本身沒有關鍵字，因此必須尋找與各選項中的關鍵字有關的內容。*The Bond Street Journal*'s 200,000 subscribers would automatically receive free subscriptions to the online version of *The Bond Street Journal* 中提到日報的二十萬訂戶會自動收到免費的線上版電子報，與 (A) 的敘述相符。 Hornbull will still publish its most popular monthly titles 中提到 Hornbull 會繼續發行它每月最受歡迎的出版品，與 (B) 的敘述相符。(C) 的部分在文中則未提及。因此 (C) Competitors are experiencing rising sales. 為正確答案。most observers believe it is only a matter of time before all print publications make the transition online 中提到大部分的觀察者相信所有的印刷出版品轉變成為線上版只是時間上的問題，與 (D) 的敘述一致。

單字 competitor n. 競爭公司，競爭者　obsolete a. 淘汰的

Sportswear Manufacturers Association of America (SMAA)
SIXTH ANNUAL TRADERS CONVENTION
Plebeian Center, 39 Larkspur Way,
Jericho Springs, IL
Thursday, June 4 - Sunday, June 7

EVENT HIGHLIGHTS

DAY ONE

9 A.M. to 1 P.M.	165-AIntroductory remarks and 165-Cpress conference with SMAA by outgoing president Dean Caldwell (Dorset Hotel)
1 P.M. to 4 P.M.	165-BNetworking event (Dorset Hotel) Trade show opens (Main Hall)

162DAY TWO

9 A.M. to 7 P.M.	Closed-door exhibit for industry professionals (Main Hall)

DAY THREE

9 A.M. to 12 P.M.	Trade show opens to the public 163Special appearance by hockey hall-of-fame inductee Greg Hellman (Main Hall)
12 P.M. to 4 P.M.	164Free basketball youth clinic hosted by legendary Iowa coach Tim Waterson (Activity Center)
4 P.M. to 8 P.M.	Raffle draw for all trade show participants and guests; prizes include autographed sports memorabilia, athletic wear, instructional videos, and more (Main Hall)

DAY FOUR

10 A.M. to 2 P.M.	Autograph signing sessions and photo opportunities with visiting gold medalists (Activity Center)
2 P.M. to 5 P.M.	Final remarks, cocktail party and farewell banquet (Dorset Hotel)

美國運動服製造商協會（SMAA）
第六屆年度商人會議
伊利諾州 傑里科泉
Larkspur 路 39 號 Plebeian 中心
6 月 4 日星期四至 6 月 7 日星期日
重點活動

第一天 上午九點至下午一點	165-A 開場及 SMAA 165-C 記者會，由即將卸任的主席 Dean Caldwell 主持（在 Dorset 飯店）
下午一點至下午四點	165-B 聯誼交流（在 Dorset 飯店）貿易展開始（在大廳）
162 第二天 早上九點至下午七點	業界專家的非公開展覽（在大廳）
第三天 上午九點至中午十二點	貿易展對外開放 163 由進入曲棍球名人堂的 Greg Hellman 做特別演出（在大廳）
中午十二點至下午四點	164 由愛荷華隊傳奇性教練 Tim Waterson 所主持的免費青年籃球講授課（在活動中心）
下午四點至晚上八點	所有參與貿易展的成員及嘉賓的摸彩；獎品包含親筆簽名的體育紀念用品、運動服、教學錄影帶等等（在大廳）
第四天 早上十點至下午兩點 下午兩點至下午五點	來訪的金牌選手親筆簽名會及拍照時間（活動中心）最後致詞、雞尾酒會及告別宴會（在 Dorset 飯店）

單字 □outgoing a. 卸任的，直率的　　□closed-door a. 非公開的　　□appearance n. 演出，外貌
　　□inductee n. 入會者　　　　　　□host v. 主辦，進行　　　　□autograph v. 簽名，署名 n. 簽名
　　□memorabilia n. 紀念品，收藏品　□instructional a. 教學用的　　□farewell a. 告別的

162

What is suggested about the event?
(A) Some activities are limited to sportswear manufacturers.
(B) There will be a farewell party for the president.
(C) It is organized for sports athletes.
(D) It will offer products at reduced prices to the public.

關於這個活動提示了什麼？
(A) 有些活動只限於運動服製造者參加。
(B) 會有一個替協會會長辦的告別宴會。
(C) 此活動是為運動員所安排的。
(D) 產品會以較低的價格提供給民眾。

■ 推論 詳細內容　　　　　　　　　　　　　　　　　　　　　　　　　　　　解答 (A)

這題是依題目關鍵字 the event 來進行推論的問題。DAY TWO: Closed-door exhibit for industry professionals 中提到第二天有提供給業界專家的非公開展覽，因此可以推論部分活動是專以運動服製造者為對象所舉行的。因此 (A) Some activities are limited to sportswear manufacturers 為正確答案。

163

Why would hockey fans probably be interested in attending the event?	為什麼曲棍球迷可能會對此活動有興趣？
(A) To obtain product samples	(A) 為了得到產品的試用品
(B) To bid on auctioned memorabilia	(B) 為了在紀念物拍賣會上投標
(C) To see Mr. Hellman in person	(C) 為了見 Hellman 先生本人
(D) To get Mr. Waterson's autograph	(D) 為了得到 Waterson 先生的親筆簽名

■ 推論 詳細內容　　　　　　　　　　　　　　　　　　　　　　　　　　　　解答 (C)

這題是依題目關鍵字 hockey fans ~ be interested in attending the even 來進行推論的問題。Special appearance by hockey hall-of-fame inductee Greg Hellman 中提到進入曲棍球名人堂的 Greg Hellman 有特別演出，因此可推論曲棍球迷為了見到 Hellman 先生本人會對此活動產生興趣，因此 (C) To see Mr. Hellman in person 為正確答案。

單字 auctioned a. 拍賣　in person phr. 親自，本人

164

What will take place in the activity center?	什麼活動會在活動中心舉行？
(A) A product demonstration	(A) 產品展示會
(B) Sports classes	(B) 運動課
(C) Career seminars	(C) 職業生涯研討會
(D) Team trials	(D) 隊伍選拔

■ 六何原則 What　　　　　　　　　　　　　　　　　　　　　　　　　　　　解答 (B)

這是問在活動中心會舉行什麼（What）的六何原則問題。題目關鍵字為 the activity center，在 Free basketball youth clinic ~ (Activity Center) 中提到在活動中心會有免費的籃球授課，因此 (B) Sports classes 為正確答案。

換句話說
Free basketball youth clinic 免費青少年籃球教室 → Sports classes 體育課程

單字 demonstration n. 展示會，示威　trial n. 考驗，選拔

165

What will NOT be held at the hotel?	何者活動不會在飯店舉行？
(A) A speech by the association's president	(A) 協會主席的演講
(B) A social gathering for attendees	(B) 出席者的社交聚會
(C) A meeting with press members	(C) 與媒體的記者會
(D) Announcement of prize winners	(D) 獲獎者的宣布

■ Not/True Not 問題　　　　　　　　　　　　　　　　　　　　　　　　　　解答 (D)

這是尋找與題目關鍵字 the hotel 有相關的內容並對照比較的 Not/True 題目。Introductory remarks ~ by outgoing president Dean Caldwell (Dorset Hotel) 中提到開場及 SMAA 記者會，由即將卸任的主席 Dean Caldwell 在 Dorset 飯店主持，因此與 (A) 的敘述一致。Networking event (Dorset Hotel) 中提到聯誼交流的活動在 Dorset Hotel 舉行，因此與 (B) 的內容一致。press conference ~ (Dorset Hotel) 中提到記者會會在飯店舉行，與 (C) 的內容一致。(D) 的內容在文中則未被提及。因此 (D) Announcement of prize winners 為正確答案。

單字 association n. 協會　press n. 記者，報紙媒體

To: mildred.barrie@hostmost.com From: anthony.steadman@spotplan.com Re: Last Weekend Date: May 20 Dear Ms. Barrie, On behalf of our CEO, Mr. Jenkins, and everyone else at SpotPlan, [167]thank you for putting together such a stunning event for us last weekend in Redmond. We received many compliments from visitors who were visibly impressed with our booth exhibit. [167]You really made our products stand out and your colorful displays attracted a lot of attendees. We had a 12 percent increase in orders, which we believe was partially thanks to your company's incredible work. Due to our success, [166]I'd like to offer your company the chance to assemble another exhibit for us at our next event in Atlanta this July. It will once again be for a trade fair, and although the venue will be smaller than the one in Redmond, we consider the event to be no less important. We will need you to make a few changes to the exhibits you did before, as we have some additional products to show. [168]I will be flying up to New York in the next two weeks to attend a conference. Could I stop by your office to discuss the event with you? I hope to hear from you soon. Sincerely, Anthony Steadman Marketing Director SpotPlan	收件人：mildred.barrie@hostmost.com 寄件人：Anthony.steadman@spotplan.com 主題：上週末 日期：5 月 20 日 親愛的 Barrie 女士： 謹代表我們的執行長 Jenkins 先生及 SpotPlan 的所有人向您 [167] 致上感謝，上週末為我們在 Redmond 組織了一個這麼令人驚嘆的活動，我們接到很多對我們展覽攤位印象深刻參觀者的讚美，[167] 你真的令我們的產品脫穎而出，而你多采多姿的陳列方式吸引了很多的參與者。我們的訂單增加了 12%，而我們相信有一部份是歸功於貴公司了不起的成果。 因為我們的成功，[166] 我想提出一個機會給貴公司，幫我們組織下一個在這個七月份於亞特蘭大舉行的活動，它一樣也是個貿易展，儘管這次的展場會比 Redmond 那次小，但我們並不會覺得這個活動比較不重要。因為我們這次展覽會增加一些新的產品，所以我們需要你將之前所做的再做些修改。[168] 我下兩週將會飛去紐約參加一個會議，我可以去您的辦公室與您討論這個活動嗎？我希望可以盡快得到您的答覆。 Anthony Steadman 敬上 行銷總監 SpotPlan 公司

單字 □on behalf of phr. 代表～　　□put together phr. 組織，安排　　□stunning a. 令人驚嘆的
□compliment n. 稱讚，讚美　　□visibly ad. 醒目地
□be impressed with phr. 對～印象深刻　　□stand out phr. 突出
□incredible a. 驚人的　　□assemble v. 組織，組成　　□venue n. 場所
□stop by phr. 拜訪

166

Why was the e-mail written? (A) To find a sponsor for a trade show (B) To schedule a product presentation (C) To thank a client for attending an event (D) To offer additional business	為什麼會寫這封電郵？ (A) 為了尋找貿易展的贊助者 (B) 為了安排一個展品展示的時間 (C) 為了謝謝一位客戶參加活動 (D) 為了提供另一個生意

■ 找出主題 寫文章的理由　　　　　　　　　　　　　　　　　　　　　　　　　　解答 (D)

這題是問為什麼要寫這封電郵，為找出文章主旨的問題。特別要注意題目中段部分有提及的相關的內容。I'd like to offer your company the chance to assemble another exhibit for us at our next event 中提到想要提供一個機會來舉辦下一個活動，因此 (D) To offer additional business 為正確答案。第一段的內容雖然是在寫感謝的理由，但是是因為感謝所以提出了另一項交易，因此感謝並非整封信的真正的主旨。

單字 sponsor　n. 贊助者　offer　v. 提案，提議

167

What does Mr. Steadman thank Ms. Barrie for? (A) Organizing a trade fair (B) Creating a product display (C) Speaking at an event (D) Assembling some equipment	Steadman 先生為了什麼事向 Barrie 女士致謝？ (A) 安排一個貿易展 (B) 設計一個產品展示 (C) 替一個活動致詞 (D) 組裝一些設備

🔲 六何原則 What 　　　　　　　　　　　　　　　　　　　　　　　　　　　　解答 (B)

這題是問 Mr. Steadman 感謝 Ms. Barrie 什麼（What）的六何原則問題。應找出與題目關鍵字 Mr. Steadman thank Ms. Barrie for 有關的部分，thank you for putting together such a stunning event 中感謝對方準備如此令人驚嘆的活動，後面又提到 You really made our products stand out and your colorful displays attracted a lot of attendees.，即 Ms. Barrie 令產品脫穎而出，且她多采多姿的陳列方式吸引了很多的參與者，因此 (B) Creating a product display 為正確答案。

單字 equipment n. 裝備

168

What is suggested about Ms. Barrie? (A) She has a busy schedule. (B) She is unable to attend the fair. (C) She was recommended by an associate. (D) She works in New York.	關於 Barrie 女士，暗示了什麼？ (A) 她有一個忙碌的行程。 (B) 她無法參加展覽。 (C) 她被一個合夥人推薦。 (D) 她在紐約工作。

🔲 推論 詳細內容 　　　　　　　　　　　　　　　　　　　　　　　　　　　　解答 (D)

這是依題目關鍵字 Ms. Barrie 的相關內容來進行推論的問題。I will be flying up to New York in the next two weeks to attend a conference. 中提到未來兩週會待在紐約，後又提到 Could I stop by your office，即在詢問可否拜訪 Ms. Barrie 的辦公室，因此可推論 Ms. Barrie 的辦公室在紐約，所以 (D) She works in New York. 為正確答案。

單字 associate n. 同事，職員

Noah's Full Service Carwash in Geyserville
Welcomes you to the neighborhood!

For over 20 years, [169-D]Noah's has established itself as the leading chain of full-service car wash facilities in Pasadena County. We use state-of-the-art equipment, nonabrasive cleaners, and environmentally conscious methods.

We do hope you will try us for your vehicle maintenance needs! To welcome you to the area, [171]we are attaching a coupon for a markdown on any one of the following car wash packages, which you will need to present upon receiving the services:

[170-A/C]**BASIC**

Regular Price: $29.99
Special Introductory Price: $19.99
[170-A]Foam wash, Hand dry, Glass cleaner, [170-C]Tire polish

[170-A/B/C/D]**PREMIUM**

Regular Price: $39.99
Special Introductory Price: $29.99

[170-A/C]Same as basic plus: Interior vacuum, [170-B/D]Blow dry, Air-freshener

ULTIMATE

Regular price: $49.99
Special Introductory Price: $34.99
Same as premium plus: Rainbow wash, Interior shampoo, Exterior wax

[169-B]*We take all forms of payment with the exception of personal checks.*

在 Geyserville 鎮 Noahs's 的全方位洗車服務歡迎你來到這個鄰里

在過去的二十年中，[169-D] 在 Pasadena 郡 Noah's 已成為全方位洗車連鎖店的領導者。我們使用最先進的設備、非侵蝕性的洗劑以及具環保意識的洗車方式。

我們真心希望當您的車子需要維修時，您可以讓我們試試。為了歡迎您來到這個地區，[171] 我們附上下列任何一樣洗車套組減價的優待券，當您來接受服務時，您需要出示此優待券：

[170-A/C] 基本套組
原價：$29.99
特別推薦價：$19.99
[170-A] 泡沫洗車、用手擦乾、玻璃清潔、[170-C] 輪胎擦亮

[170-A/B/C/D] 優質套組
原價：$39.99
特別推薦價：$29.99
[170-A/C] 基本套組加上內部吸塵、[170-B/D] 吹乾、空氣清新劑

超級套組
原價：$49.99
特別推薦價：$39.99
優質套組加上彩虹洗、內部清洗、外部上蠟

[169-B] *我們接受除了個人支票外的任何付款方式*

單字
☐ neighborhood n. 區域，鄰居
☐ county n. 郡，縣
☐ conscious a. 思考的，有意識的
☐ vacuum v. 用吸塵器清潔
☐ exterior n. 外部

☐ leading a. 領導的
☐ state-of-the-art a. 最先進的
☐ introductory a. 前言的，介紹的
☐ air-freshener n. 空氣清新劑

☐ facility n. 設施
☐ nonabrasive a. 非侵蝕的
☐ polish n. 打磨，擦亮
☐ ultimate a. 最終的，究極的

169

What is mentioned about Noah's?
(A) It has just opened in Geyserville.
(B) It does not accept credit cards.
(C) It offers basic car repair services.
(D) It has several branches in Pasadena.

文中提到有關 Noah's 的什麼？
(A) 它最近才在 Geyserville 開張。
(B) 它不接受信用卡。
(C) 它提供基本的車子維修服務。
(D) 它在 Pasadena 有幾家分店。

■ **Not/True** True 問題 　　　　　　　　　　　　　　　　　　　　　　　　　解答 (D)

這是尋找與題目關鍵字 Noah's 的有關內容與選項相互對照的 Not/True 問題。 (A) 的部分在題目中並未提及。廣告單後段有提到 We take all forms of payment with the exception of personal checks. ，即指接受除了個人支票外的任何付款方式，因此與 (B) 的敘述不相符。(C) 的內容在文中則未被提及。Noah's has established itself as the leading chain in full-service car wash facilities in Pasadena County 中提到在 Pasadena 郡 Noah's 已成為全方位洗車連鎖店的領導者，與 (D) 的敘述相符，因此 (D) It has several branches in Pasadena. 為正確答案。

170

What is NOT a part of the premium service? (A) Rainbow wash (B) Air-freshener (C) Tire polish (D) Blow dry	優質套組中不包含哪一個部份？ (A) 彩虹洗 (B) 空氣清新劑 (C) 輪胎擦亮 (D) 吹乾

■ **Not/True** True 問題 　　　　　　　　　　　　　　　　　　　　　　　　　解答 (A)

這是尋找與題目關鍵字 the premium service 的相關內容並與選項相互對照的 Not/True 問題。BASIC 提供 Foam wash, Hand dry, Glass cleaner, Tire polish，即泡沫洗車、用手擦乾、玻璃清潔、輪胎擦亮等服務，PREMIUM 則提供 Same as basic plus: Interior vacuum, Blow dry, Air-freshener，即基本套組加內部吸塵、吹乾、空氣清新劑，但卻沒有包含彩虹洗車，因此與 (A) 的敘述不相符。因此 (A) Rainbow wash 為正確答案。PREMIUM 提供 Blow dry, Air-freshener，即吹乾、空氣清新劑，因此與 (B) (D) 敘述一致。BASIC 提供 Tire polish，即提供輪胎擦亮， PREMIUM 中也提到 Same as basic plus，即含基本套組，因此與 (C) 的敘述一致。

171

How can customers receive the special introductory price? (A) By paying in cash (B) By submitting a coupon (C) By purchasing a package offer (D) By trying out a new service	顧客如何得到特別推薦價？ (A) 付現金 (B) 繳交優待卷 (C) 購買所提供的套組 (D) 嘗試新的服務項目

■ 六何原則 How 　　　　　　　　　　　　　　　　　　　　　　　　　解答 (B)

這是在問顧客要如何（How） 得到特別推薦價的六何原則問題。題目關鍵字為 the special introductory price，文章中 we are attaching a coupon for a markdown ~, which you will need to present upon receiving the services 表示來接受服務時，需要出示此優待券，因此 (B) By submitting a coupon 為正確答案。

單字 purchase v. 購買 try out phr. 嘗試

Arthur to Boost Asia Presence

Arthur Holdings has just revealed that it will be building three new shopping malls in Thailand, Vietnam, and Cambodia this year. [172-A]The largest shopping mall developer in Southeast Asia has reserved $4 billion in capital for the project.

During a press conference for the company's upcoming stock offering, Arthur Holdings president Francis Brewster said the new malls are part of the firm's two-year development plans. [172-A]Last year, the firm opened malls in Myanmar and Taiwan despite the gloomy economy.

Each of the three shopping malls will have an approximate area of 20,000 square meters. [173-A/C/D]The malls to be established in Thailand and Vietnam will have convention halls and activity centers equipped with conference rooms, gymnasiums, bowling alleys, and movie theaters.

According to Brewster, funding will be derived from recently sold bonds amounting to $3 billion, foreign loans, and proceeds of the upcoming stock offering.

The president believes that [175]Arthur's notable achievements in the past year will help the company collect more capital when it auctions off new shares on Monday.

According to financial figures released by Arthur Holdings last year, revenues from its Singapore operations grew 15 percent, to $250 million. Moreover, profits went up 20 percent, to $175 million.

"Arthur Holdings has proven itself to be a strong company in Asia. Because of this, we are expecting more people to invest in our rapidly growing business," Brewster said.

Arthur 欲增加在亞洲的市場

Arthur Holdings 公司剛剛透露，他們今年將會蓋三棟新的大型購物中心，分別位於泰國、越南及柬埔寨。[172-A]這個東南亞最大的大型購物中心開發商將為此計畫儲備四十億的資金。

在一個即將上市的股市發行記者會上，Arthur Holdings 的主席 Francis Brewster 表示，新的購物中心是公司兩年發展計畫中的一部份，[172-A] 去年，儘管經濟低迷，此公司在緬甸及台灣仍開了購物中心。

這三棟大型購物中心，大約各佔地兩萬平方公尺，[173-A/C/D] 在泰國及越南的購物中心將會有會議廳及配有會議室、健身房、保齡球道及電影院的活動中心。

據 Brewster 表示，資金會來自於最近賣掉的三十億債卷、外國貸款以及即將發行的股票所得。

主席相信，[175] Arthur 去年亮眼的成績，會在星期一拍賣新股份時，幫助公司募得更多的資金。

根據去年由 Arthur Holding's 釋出的財務報告，新加坡的營運收入增加了15%，達到兩億五千萬。此外，利潤增加20%，達到一億七千五百萬。

「Arthur Holdings 證明自己在亞洲是一個實力雄厚的公司，也因此，我們期待有更多人投資我們快速成長的生意。」Brewster表示。

單字　□reserve v. 貯存，保留　　　□capital n. 資本（額），資產　　　□gloomy a. 停滯的，沉悶的
　　　□approximate a. 大約，大略的　□equipped with phr. 具備～　　　□derive from phr. 由～產生
　　　□amount to phr. 達～　　　　　□proceeds n. 收益　　　　　　　　□notable a. 值得注意的
　　　□auction off phr. 拍賣掉　　　　□revenue n. 收益　　　　　　　　□profit n. 利潤

172

What is mentioned about Arthur Holdings?
(A) It owns a chain of shopping centers.
(B) It is in need of foreign capital.
(C) It is seeking investment opportunities.
(D) It operates corporate buildings.

文中提到有關 Arthur Holdings 的什麼？
(A) 它擁有連鎖的購物中心。
(B) 它需要外國資金。
(C) 它正在尋找投資的機會。
(D) 它經營企業建設。

🔳 Not/True True 問題　　　　　　　　　　　　　　　　　　　　　　　　　　解答 (A)

這是尋找與題目關鍵字 Arthur Holdings 有關的內容並與選項相互對照的 Not/True 問題。The largest shopping mall developer in Southeast Asia 中提到 Arthur Holdings 公司是東南亞最大的購物中心開發商，Last year, the firm opened malls in Myanmar and Taiwan despite the gloomy economy. 中提到儘管經濟低迷，此公司仍在緬甸及台灣開了購物中心，因此 (A) It owns a chain of shopping centers. 為正確答案。(B) (C) (D) 的內容在文中則未被提及。

173

What will NOT be included in Arthur's Vietnam facility? (A) Conference areas (B) Museums (C) Theaters (D) Sports venues	Arthur 設在越南的購物中心不會包含哪項設施？ (A) 會議區 (B) 博物館 (C) 電影院 (D) 運動場

🔳 Not/True Not 問題　　　　　　　　　　　　　　　　　　　　　　　　　　解答 (B)

這是尋找與題目關鍵字 Arthur's Vietnam facility 有相關的內容並與選項相互對照的 Not/True 問題。The malls to be established in Thailand and Vietnam will have ~ activity centers equipped with conference rooms, gymnasiums, bowling alleys, and movie theaters. 中提到在泰國及越南的購物中心將會有會議廳及配有會議室、健身房、保齡球道及電影院的活動中心，與 (A) (C) (D) 選項相符。(B) 的部分在文中則未被提及。因此 (B) Museums 為正確答案。

174

The word " derived " in paragraph 4, line 1 is closest in meaning to (A) originated (B) generated (C) destined (D) departed	在第四段的第一行中，「derived」這個字最接近的意思是 (A) 引起 (B) 產生 (C) 注定 (D) 離開

🔳 同義詞　　　　　　　　　　　　　　　　　　　　　　　　　　　　　　　　解答 (B)

提到 derived 的句子為 funding will be derived from recently sold bonds，其中的 derived 是「由～產生」的意思，因此帶有相同意思的 (B) generated 為正確答案。

單字 **originate** v. 來自　**destine** v. 預定（用於某種目的、用途）

175

What does the company expect on Monday? (A) A loan approval (B) Additional funds (C) A growth in profits (D) Business proposals	此公司預期星期一會發生什麼事？ (A) 貸款的批准 (B) 額外的資金 (C) 利潤的成長 (D) 生意的提案

🔳 六何原則 What　　　　　　　　　　　　　　　　　　　　　　　　　　　　解答 (B)

這是在問公司預期星期一會發生什麼（What）的六何原則問題。與題目關鍵字 on Monday 相關的句子為 Arthur's notable achievements in the past year will help the company collect more capital when it auctions off new shares on Monday，其中提到主席相信，Arthur 去年亮眼的成績，會在星期一拍賣新股份時，幫助公司募得更多的資金，因此 (B) Additional funds 為正確答案。

TO: Events Staff
FROM: Marinella Garnet, Project Manager
SUBJECT: Upcoming Seminar
DATE: September 23

As announced at the recent meeting, [176]our company is organizing a three-day business seminar on e-commerce. The seminar, to be held six months from now, will be attended by small and medium business owners wishing to learn how to sell their products and services on the Internet.

In line with this, I have posted a list of seminar committees and their members on the bulletin board. The committees are as follows:

Speakers Committee, Venue Committee, Food Committee, Marketing Committee, Registration Committee

You will notice that, except for the marketing committee, all committees are composed of new members. [178]The marketing committee must coordinate with Mr. Donaldson, our marketing director, so that they will be familiar with the company's new sponsorship packages. Since the seminar is free, [177-C/199]I would like the marketing committee to look for many sponsors so that majority of the seminar's costs may be assumed by income from advertisers. Make sure that sponsors are aware of the benefits they will receive in return for their assistance, including the use of their logos in promotional materials for the seminar.

Furthermore, [177-C/180]I also want the speakers committee to present a list of potential guest speakers. If possible, invite executives from online books, arts and crafts, computers, and clothing retailers.

收件人：活動人員
寄件人： Marinella Garnet, 專案經理
主旨： 即將到來的研討會
日期： 九月二十三日

如同在最近一次開會上所宣布的，[176] 我們公司正在安排一個為期三天，以電子商務為主題的業務研討會，此次研討會將在六個月後舉行，由希望學習如何在網路上販賣他們的產品及服務的中小型企業老闆來參加。

本著這一精神，我在佈告欄上張貼了研討會委員會及其成員的名單，委員會如下：

講座委員會、場地委員會、食物委員會、行銷委員會、報名委員會

你將會發現，除了行銷委員會外，所有的委員會的成員都是新的。[178] 行銷委員會需要與我們的行銷主任Donaldson 先生協力合作，如此一來他們才能熟悉公司新的贊助方案。因為研討會是免費的，[177-C/199] 所以我希望行銷委員會可以尋找許多的贊助商，如此一來，研討會大部分的費用可以從廣告商那邊的收入取得。請確認贊助商知道他們的協助會得到的利益回報，包含在研討會宣傳品上使用他們的商標。

此外，[177-C/180] 我也希望講座委員會提報可能的客座講者清單，如果可能的話，邀請線上書店、藝術手工藝品店、電腦店以及服飾零售商的業務主管。

單字
□organize v. 安排
□bulletin board phr. 公佈欄
□coordinate with phr. 與～合作
□in return for phr. 作為～回禮
□craft n. 工藝品

□in line with phr. 與～符合
□except for phr. 除了～
□be familiar with phr. 對～熟悉
□potential a. 潛在的，有可能的

□post v. 公告
□be composed of phr. 由～構成
□sponsorship n. 贊助
□executive n. 執行部門，業務主管

176

What is the topic of the seminar?
(A) Employee management
(B) Brand development
(C) Online marketing
(D) Event planning

研討會的主題為何？
(A) 員工管理
(B) 品牌發展
(C) 網路行銷
(D) 活動規劃

■ 找出主題 主題 解答 (C)

這題要找出研討會的主題，應注意文章的前半部分。our company is organizing a three-day business seminar on e-commerce 中提到公司將安排一個為期三天，以電子商務為主題的業務研討會，後面又提到 The seminar ~ will be attended by ~ business owners wishing to learn how to sell their products and services on the Internet.，即由希望學習如何在網路上販賣他們的產品及服務的老闆來參加，因此 (C) Online marketing 為正確答案。

177

What is mentioned about the committees?	文中提到有關委員會的是？
(A) They have yet to select team leaders.	(A) 他們尚未選出團隊的領導人。
(B) They are composed of temporary employees.	(B) 他們由臨時雇員所組成。
(C) They have been given different assignments.	(C) 他們被指派不同的任務。
(D) They have limited budgets.	(D) 他們的經費有限。

■ Not/True True 問題 解答 (C)

這是尋找與題目關鍵字 the committees 的相關內容，再與選項互相對照的 Not/True 問題。 (A) 與 (B) 在文中並未被提及。I would like the marketing committee to look for many sponsors 中提到希望行銷委員會可以尋找許多的贊助商，之後又提到 I ~ want the speakers committee to present a list of potential guest speakers，即也希望講座委員會提報可能的客座講者清單，與 (C) 的內容一致，因此 (C) They have been given different assignments. 為正確答案。(D) 的內容在文中也未被提及。

單字 temporary employee phr. 約聘制，臨時職員

178

What are members of the marketing committee asked to do?	行銷委員會的成員被要求做什麼？
(A) Consult a colleague	(A) 請教同事
(B) Send solicitation letters	(B) 發送招攬函
(C) Create client directories	(C) 建立客戶目錄
(D) Hire catering companies	(D) 聘請外燴公司

■ 六何原則 What 解答 (A)

這題是問行銷委員會的成員被要求做什麼（What）的六何原則問題。題目關鍵字為members of the marketing committee asked to do，在文中 The marketing committee must coordinate with Mr. Donaldson, our marketing director, so that they will be familiar with the company's new sponsorship packages. 提到行銷委員會需要與行銷主任 Donaldson 先生進行協調，如此一來他們才能熟悉公司新的贊助方案，因此 (A) Consult a colleague 為正確答案。

單字 solicitation n. 誘惑，懇請 directory n. 名單，工商名錄 catering n. 提供飲食

179

What is suggested about the seminar?	從文中可推論此次研討會的什麼？
(A) It will cost less than previous events.	(A) 它會比上次活動花費更少。
(B) It will take place over six days.	(B) 它會為期六天。
(C) It will be sponsored by businesses.	(C) 它會由廠商贊助。
(D) It will be held at a marketing firm.	(D) 它會由一個行銷公司舉辦。

■ 推論 詳細內容 解答 (C)

這是利用題目關鍵字 the seminar 的相關內容來進行推論的問題。I would like the marketing committee to look for many sponsors so that majority of the seminar's costs may be assumed by income from advertisers 中提到希望行銷委員會可以尋找許多的贊助商，如此一來研討會大部分的費用可以從廣告商那邊的收入取得，因此可以推論研討會將由企業贊助，所以 (C) It will be sponsored by businesses. 為正確答案。

單字 business n. 企業 take place phr. 展開，舉辦 firm n. 公司

What will the speakers committee most likely do?	講座委員會最有可能需要做什麼？
(A) Contact resource personnel	(A) 與資源管理人員接洽
(B) Survey online stores	(B) 調查網路商店
(C) Interview businessmen	(C) 訪問商人
(D) Invite industry professionals	(D) 邀請此行業的專家

■ 推論 詳細內容　　　　　　　　　　　　　　　　　　　　　　　　　　　　　解答 (D)

這是利用題目關鍵字 the speakers committee 的相關內容來進行推論的問題。I also want the speakers committee to present a list of potential guest speakers. If possible, invite executives from online books, arts and crafts, computers, and clothing retailers. 中提到也希望講座委員會提報可能的客座講者清單，如果可能的話，邀請線上書店、藝術手工藝品店、電腦店以及服飾零售商的業務主管，因此可以推論講座委員會將會招待業界的專家，所以 (D) Invite industry professionals 為正確答案。

單字　resource　n.　資源　personnel　n. 職員

Questions 181-185 refer to the following advertisement and e-mail. 181-185 根據下面發票和電郵的內容回答問題。

例文1

The Glass House

880 Cottage Grove Road,
Bloomfield, CT 06002

INVOICE	
180-B Issue Date	Reference Number
May 3	200-367777

Client	Address	Date Shipped	Payment Method
Abigail Hoffman	Studio Bar and Restaurant 752 Post Road East, Westport, CT 06880	May 5	Check

Item#	Description	182 Unit Price	Quantity	Amount
BC507	Lily sherry glass (3 ¾ oz)	$ 79.50	1 case (36 pieces)	$79.50
OT289	185 Rosetta champagne glass (6 ½ oz)	$ 38.00	4 cases (12 pieces)	$152.00
BP203	Thunder hi-ball glass (10 oz)	$ 86.90	1 case (35 pieces)	$86.90
PL033	Alexandria all-purpose water goblet (11 ½ oz)	$146.99	3 cases (24 pieces)	$440.97
WT230	Anchor Collins glass (10 oz)	$ 57.25	2 cases (24 pieces)	$114.50
			Subtotal	$873.87
			Discount	- $87.39
			181-D Shipping	$25.00
			Total	$811.48

*181-A All prices are inclusive of sales tax.
182-B From May 1 to 31, customers will be given a 10 percent discount on total purchases.

Please make all checks payable to The Glass House.

To report any problem, contact the sales representative who took your order by e-mail or by calling 555-9773.

Thank you for your business!

玻璃房子公司

06002 康乃迪克州
Cottage Grove 路 880 號

發票	
180-B 發行日期	訂單編號
5 月 3 日	200-367777

客戶	地址	送貨日	付款方式
Abigail Hoffman	Studio 酒吧餐廳: 06880 康乃迪克州 Westport 市 Post 路東 752 號	5 月 5 日	支票

產品編號	產品說明	185 單價	數量	總價
BC 507	百合雪莉酒杯 （3 3/4 盎司）	79.50 美元	1箱 （36件）	79.50 美元
OT 289	185 羅塞塔香檳酒杯 （6 1/2 盎司）	38.00 美元	4箱 （12件）	152.00 美元
BP 203	雷聲球玻璃杯 （10 盎司）	86.90 美元	1箱 （35件）	86.90 美元
PL 033	亞歷山大萬用高腳水杯 （11 1/2 盎司）	146.99 美元	3箱 （24件）	440.97 美元
WT 230	Anchor Collins玻璃杯 （10 盎司）	57.25 美元	2箱 （24件）	114.50 美元
		小計		873.87 美元
		折扣		-87.39 美元
		181-D 運費		25.00 美元
		總計*		811.48 美元

*181-A 所有的價錢已含營業稅
181-D 從 5 月 1 日到 31 日，客戶可享有總購買金額 10% 的折扣。

所有的支票抬頭請寫「The Glass House」。

有任何問題，請用電郵與當初接單的業務連絡，或撥打 555-9773。
感謝您的惠顧

例文2

To: Robert Smith <r.smith@theglasshouse.com>

From: Abigail Hoffman <a.hoffman@studio.com>

Date: May 6
Subject: Order
Attachment(s): Glass order e-mail

Dear Mr. Smith,

收件者：Robert Smith
　　　　<r.smith@theglasshouse.com>
寄件者：Abigail Hoffman
　　　　<a.hoffman@studio.com>
日期：5 月 6 日
主旨：訂單
附件：玻璃杯訂單電郵

親愛的 Smith 先生：

[182]I would like to report an error in my latest glassware order with the reference number 200-367777. [182/183-C/185]I specifically requested three cases of Rosetta champagne glasses in the previous e-mail I sent you. However, when my delivery arrived at the restaurant yesterday, [182/185]I noticed that you gave me four cases, which was also incorrectly specified on the invoice that came with the delivery. In addition, when I opened the other boxes, [182]I found that a couple of sherry glasses had broken stems.

[185]I will be returning the extra case, along with the sherry glasses, and expect that you will cover the cost of shipping. In addition, [184]I ask that you replace the damaged items as soon as possible. My assistant manager, Catherine Simmons, will call you this afternoon to make any necessary arrangements.

I have attached a copy of my last e-mail for your reference. I hope you will address my concerns immediately and take measures to prevent this from happening again.

Sincerely,

Abigail Hoffman
Proprietor, Studio Bar and Restaurant

---

[182] 我想要告訴您，在我最後一次的玻璃杯訂單中有一個錯誤，訂單編號是 200-367777。在我寄給你的上一封電郵中，[182/183-C/185] 我特別明確地要求三箱的羅塞塔香檳酒杯，但當我的貨品昨天抵達餐廳時，[182/185] 我發現你給我四箱，連同收據上也是相同的錯誤，此外，當我打開其他的箱子時，[182] 我發現有兩個雪莉酒杯的杯腳有破損。

[185] 我將會退回多的那一箱，連同雪莉酒杯，而我希望你會負擔運費。此外，[184] 我請求你盡快將損壞的品項補上，我的協理 Catherine Simmons 今天下午會打電話給您以做出適當的安排。

我附上我上封信的副本供您參考，我希望您會馬上解決我所關切的這件事，並採取必要的措施來防止這樣的事情再度發生。

Abigail Hoffman 敬上
Studio 酒吧餐廳老闆

例文 1 單字 □invoice n. 發票　　□issue n. 發行　　□unit price phr. 單價
　　　　　　□inclusive a. 包含的　　□sales representative phr. 銷售人員，業務

例文 2 單字 □specifically ad. 明確地，仔細地　　□specify v. 具體說明
　　　　　　□replace v. 替代　　□take measures phr. 採取措施

181

What is indicated about the glasses ordered by Ms. Hoffman?
(A) They are sold exclusive of taxes.
(B) They were ordered within a promotional period.
(C) They are popular brands on the market.
(D) They were shipped to the client for free.

文中關於 Hoffman 小姐所訂的玻璃杯何者正確？
(A) 它們是不含稅的。
(B) 它們是在促銷期間訂的。
(C) 它們是市場上受歡迎的品牌。
(D) 它們免費運送給客戶。

■ Not/True True 問題　　　　　　　　　　　　　　　　　　　　　　解答 (B)

這是尋找與題目關鍵字 the glasses ordered by Ms. Hoffman 相關內容並與選項相互對照的 Not/True 問題，因此要看第一篇文章 Ms. Hoffman 的訂購明細與發票的詳細內容。All prices are inclusive of sales tax. 中提到所有的價錢已含營業稅，因此與 (A) 選項不符。　(B) 在文章中 From May 1 to 31, customers will be given a 10 percent discount on total purchases. 提到從 5 月 1 日到 30 日，客戶可享有總購買金額 10% 的折扣，Issue Date: May 3 也代表發票發行日為 5 月 3 日，可以知道 Ms. Hoffman 是在促銷期間進行訂購的。因此 (B) They were ordered within a promotional period 為正確答案。(C) 的部分在文中則未提及。shipping: $25.00 表示運送費為 25 美元，因此與 (D) 選項不符。

單字 exclusive a. 除了～，獨佔的

182

What is the e-mail mainly about?	電郵中最主要與什麼有關？
(A) An additional order	(A) 額外的訂單
(B) An inquiry about payment	(B) 有關付款的諮詢
(C) Problems with a delivery	(C) 送貨的問題
(D) Price details of products	(D) 產品的詳細價格

■ 找出主題 主題　　　　　　　　　　　　　　　　　　　　　　　　　　　　　　　　解答 (C)

這題是找出電郵中的主旨，因此要看第二篇的信件內容。I would like to report an error in my latest glassware order 中寫道「我想要告訴您，在我最後一次的玻璃杯訂單中有一個錯誤」，後來又提到 I specifically requested three cases of Rosetta champagne glasses 與 I noticed that you gave me four cases，即「我特別明確地要求三箱的羅塞塔香檳酒杯」與「我發現你給我四箱」，最後 I found that a couple of sherry glasses had broken stems 表示發現有兩個雪莉酒杯的杯腳有破損，因此 (C) Problems with a delivery 為正確答案。

單字 inquiry n. 諮詢

183

What does Ms. Hoffman mention about her order?	Hoffman 小姐提到她的訂單怎麼了？
(A) She asked a sales agent for a discount.	(A) 她要求一個銷售代理給她折扣。
(B) She sent photographs of some glassware she requested.	(B) 她發送了她所訂購的玻璃品的一些照片。
(C) She was specific about the quantity of products she wanted.	(C) 她對於她所需要的商品數量很明確。
(D) She gave special instructions regarding the packaging of merchandise.	(D) 她對商品包裝有特別的指令。

■ Not/True True 問題　　　　　　　　　　　　　　　　　　　　　　　　　　　　　　解答 (C)

這題是尋找題目關鍵字 her order 的相關內容，再與選項互相對照的 Not/True 問題，因此要看第二篇 Ms. Hoffman 所寫的電子郵件。(A) 與 (B) 的內容在文中未被提及。I specifically requested three cases of Rosetta champagne glasses 中提到特別具體地要求三箱的羅塞塔香檳酒杯，與 (C) 選項相符。因此 (C) She was specific about the quantity of products she wanted 為正確答案。 (D) 的內容在文中則未被提及。

單字 sales agent phr. 銷售代理

184

What is Mr. Smith being asked to do?	Smith 先生被要求做什麼事？
(A) Make further arrangements with Ms. Simmons	(A) 與 Simmons 女士作進一步的安排
(B) Deliver an extra case of sherry glasses	(B) 運送另一箱的雪莉酒杯
(C) Request a full refund from the restaurant	(C) 要求餐廳全額退費
(D) Contact The Glass House's warehouse	(D) 連絡 The Glass House 的倉庫

■ 六何原則 What　　　　　　　　　　　　　　　　　　　　　　　　　　　　　　　　解答 (A)

這題是問 Smith 先生被要求做什麼（What）的六何原則問題，因此要尋找題目關鍵字 Mr. Smith ~ asked to do 的相關內容。電子郵件中寫道 I ask that you replace the damaged items as soon as possible. My assistant manager, Catherine Simmons, will call you this afternoon to make any necessary arrangements. 表示請求對方盡快將損壞的品項補上，協理 Catherine Simmons 今天下午會打電話，因此 (A) Make further arrangements with Ms. Simmons 為正確答案。

How much should be subtracted from Ms. Hoffman's bill?	Hoffman 女士的帳單應該扣除多少錢？
(A) $87.39	(A) 87.39 美金
(B) $86.90	(B) 86.90 美金
(C) $57.25	(C) 57.25 美金
(D) $38.00	(D) 38.00 美金

■ **六何原則** 的整合問題　　　　　　　　　　　　　　　　　　　　　　　　　　解答 (D)

這題是綜合兩篇文章的整合問題，題目關鍵字為 subtracted from Ms. Hoffman's bill，是在問 Ms. Hoffman 的帳單應該扣除多少錢（How much），因此應先確認第二封 Ms. Hoffman 所寫的電子郵件。應先注意電子郵件當中提到 I specifically requested three cases of Rosetta champagne glasses 與 I noticed that you gave me four cases，即 Ms. Hoffman 向 Rosetta 訂購三箱的羅塞塔香檳酒杯，但是對方卻給了四箱，第二段寫到 I will be returning the extra case，表示會退還多的一箱，但因為這裡並沒有提到一箱是多少錢，因此必須看第一篇文章。第一篇的內容寫道 Rosetta champagne glass, Unit price, $38.00，在第二段可以知道一箱羅塞塔香檳酒杯為 38 美元。綜合會退還多的一箱與一箱羅塞塔香檳酒杯為 38 美元這兩點，可以知道 Hoffman 女士的帳單應該扣除 38 美元，因此 (D) $38.00 為正確答案。

單字 **subtract** v. 扣除

Questions 186-190 refer to the following e-mail and schedule.

186-190 根據下面廣告和電郵的內容回答問題。

例文1

Vitruvian Gym

186-C As part of our 10th anniversary celebration, **we are giving new members the chance to try out any of our fitness classes for free.** 187-D If you sign up for membership anytime between June 1 and June 15, you will be eligible for one free session of the class of your choice. 186-A/187-B You will also receive a voucher that entitles you to a full body massage at our affiliate establishment, Triquetra Health Spa. **Lastly,** 187-A new members will get to choose a free gym bag from the two designs available.

Below is the schedule of our classes:

CLASS	186-D DAY	TIME	FEE
Aerobics	Monday	5:30-6:30 P.M.	Member: $15/session
	Wednesday	3:00-4:00 P.M.	Non-member: $18/session
188 Yoga	Tuesday	7:00-8:00 P.M.	Special rates are available for those registering for three sessions or more.
	Thursday	6:15-7:15 P.M.	
Kickboxing	Wednesday	4:30-5:30 P.M.	
	Friday	6:00-7:00 P.M.	
Dance	Saturday	3:45-4:45 P.M.	

HURRY! Take advantage of this opportunity and become a Vitruvian Gym member today!

Vitruvian 健身房

186-C 作為十週年慶活動之一，我們提供新會員免費試上我們任何一堂健身課的機會，187-D 如果您在 6 月 1 日到 6 月 15 日的任何時間中加入會員，您將免費獲得一堂您任選的課。186-A/187-B 你也會收到一張全身按摩券，讓您可在我們的關係企業 Triquetra 健康水療中心使用。最後，187-A 新會員可以選擇一個免費的運動包，有兩種款式可供選擇。

以下是我們課程的時間表：

課程	186-D 星期	時間	費用
有氧課	星期一	下午 5:30~6:30	會員：$15/節
	星期三	下午 3:00~4:00	非會員：$18/節
188 瑜珈	星期二	下午 7:00~8:00	報名三堂課以上者，可再享優惠。
	星期四	下午 6:15~7:15	
拳擊	星期三	下午 4:30~5:30	
有氧	星期五	下午 6:00~7:00	
舞蹈	星期六	下午 3:45~4:45	

趕快！利用這樣的機會，今天就變成 Vitruvian 健身房的會員吧！

例文2

To: custserv@vitruviangym.com
From: Sarah Leone <sarah@jocondemail.com>

Date: June 25
Subject: Special Rates

188 I went to my complimentary class last Tuesday, **June 20** and found the exercises to be enjoyable and extremely relaxing. Your instructor Melinda Yale was also very professional and accommodating. Given my positive experience, I would like to continue attending the class. 189 Your advertisement indicated that special rates are available for those who register for a certain number of sessions. I am interested in registering for four. **Can you please let me know what the rates are?**

Also, I brought my free gym bag to work the other day and received some compliments for it from my colleagues. As we were talking, I told them about signing up at your gym and some of them are now interested in joining. I understand your promotion has ended, but they would like to know whether there is some other enticement they could be offered to become a member. 190 One of them was curious about the possibility of a group discount. Could you let me know whether such a thing is being offered at your gym?

收件人：custserv@ritruviangym.com
寄件人：Sarah Leone
　　　　<sarah@jocondemail.com>
日期：6 月 25 日
主旨：特價

188 我上週二，也就是 6 月 20 日，去參加了我的免費課程，我發現運動是愉快的而且也很放鬆，你們的教練 Melinda Yale 也很專業且親切，由於此次有好的經驗，我想要繼續來上課。189 你們的廣告指出，對於報名一定堂數的人會有特價，我有興趣登記四堂課。你可以讓我知道價格為何嗎？

此外，我有天帶著我免費的運動包去工作時，我得到同事的一些稱讚，當我們在聊天時，我告訴他們有關於去你們健身房報名的事，他們有些人現在有興趣加入，我知道你們的促銷活動已經截止，但是他們想要知道是否還可以提供其他的優惠，以吸引他們成為會員？190 他們其中有一位想知道是否團體折扣的可能性，您可否讓我知道您的健身房有沒有提供這樣的服務？

Thanks for your help, and I look forward to my classes at your facility. Sarah Leone	謝謝您的協助並期待去您的健身房上課。 Sarah Leone

例文 1 單字 □gym n. 健身房　□celebration n. 慶祝活動　□eligible a. 有資格的
　　　　　　□voucher n. 折價券　□entitle v. 給～資格　□affiliate n. 同盟，關係企業
　　　　　　□establishment n. 機關　□lastly ad. 最後地　□take advantage of phr. 利用～

例文 2 單字 □complimentary a. 免費的　□relaxing a. 放鬆的　□instructor n. 講師
　　　　　　□accommodating a. 親切的，樂於助人的　□rate n. 價格
　　　　　　□the other day phr. 之前某一天　□compliment n. 稱讚
　　　　　　□colleague n. 同事　□enticement n. 誘因　□possibility n. 可能性

186

What is mentioned about Vitruvian Gym? (A) It is partnered with a spa. (B) It is launching a new branch in June. (C) It is celebrating 20 years of business. (D) It is open seven days a week.	文中提到關於 Vitruvian 健身房的什麼事？ (A) 它與一個水療中心合夥。 (B) 它將在 6 月開一家新的分店。 (C) 它正舉辦二十週年慶。 (D) 它一週營業七天。

■ **Not/True** True 問題　　　　　　　　　　　　　　　　　　　　　　解答 (A)

這題是尋找與題目關鍵字 Vitruvian Gym 相關的內容並與選項相互對照的 Not/True 問題。應看第一篇提及 Vitruvian 健身房的廣告文章。You will also receive a voucher that entitles you to a full body massage at our affiliate establishment, Triquetra Health Spa. 中提到會收到一張全身按摩券，可在關係企業 Triquetra 健康水療中心使用，與 (A) 的敘述一致。因此 (A) It is partnered with a spa. 為正確答案。(B) 的內容在文中則未被提及。As part of our 10th anniversary celebration 中提到這是十週年慶的活動之一，與 (C) 選項不相符。由課程時間表可知只有 Monday, Tuesday, Wednesday, Thursday, Friday, Saturday，一週六天有課程，因此與 (D) 選項也不相符。

換句話說
affiliate establishment 關係企業 → is partnered with 與～合作

單字 partner v. 合作，結夥

187

What is NOT a benefit for new members? (A) A sports bag (B) A free massage (C) A yoga mat (D) A trial class	成為新會員沒有下列哪一項福利？ (A) 一個運動包包 (B) 一次免費的按摩 (C) 一張瑜珈墊 (D) 一堂體驗課程

■ **Not/True** Not 問題　　　　　　　　　　　　　　　　　　　　　　解答 (C)

這題是尋找與題目關鍵字 a benefit for new members 的相關內容，再與選項互相對照的 Not/True 問題，看第一篇提及會員優惠的廣告文章。new members will get to choose a free gym bag from the two designs available 中提到新會員可以選擇一個免費的運動包，與 (A) 選項相符，You will also receive a voucher that entitles you to a full body massage at our affiliate establishment, Triquetra Health Spa. 中提到也會收到一張全身按摩券，可在 Triquetra 健康水療中心使用，與 (B) 的敘述相符。(C) 的內容在文中則未被提及。因此 (C) yoga mat 為正確答案。If you sign up for membership ~ you will be eligible for one free session of the class of your choice. 即如果加入會員，將免費獲得一堂任選課程，與 (D) 的內容相符。

單字 trial n. 體驗，試驗

188

What class did Ms. Leone most likely try out? (A) Yoga (B) Dance (C) Aerobics (D) Kickboxing	哪一堂課是 Leone 女士最有可能體驗的？ (A) 瑜伽 (B) 舞蹈 (C) 有氧課 (D) 拳擊有氧

■ 推論 聯結問題　　　　　　　　　　　　　　　　　　　　　　　　　　　　解答 (A)

這題是綜合兩篇文章內容進行推論才能解決的問題，由題目關鍵字 class ~ Ms. Leone ~ try out 來看應先看第二篇的電子郵件，第一個線索當中提到 I went to my complimentary class last Tuesday，表示 Ms. Leone 上個禮拜二去上免費課程，然而禮拜二的課程是什麼，必須看第一篇的廣告才能知道。第一篇廣告當中提到 Yoga: Tuesday，即禮拜二為瑜珈課。由第一個線索：Ms. Leone 上個禮拜二去上免費課程。和第二個線索：禮拜二為瑜珈課，可以推論出 Ms. Leone 體驗的課程為瑜珈課，因此 (A) Yoga 為正確答案。

189

What is indicated about Ms. Leone in the e-mail? (A) She lives close to the sports facility. (B) She has been a member for a long time. (C) She may qualify for a special rate. (D) She cannot attend a scheduled session.	電郵中指出有關 Leone 女士的哪一件事？ (A) 她住在健身房附近。 (B) 她已經成為會員很久。 (C) 她可能有資格享有特價。 (D) 她無法參加一個預定的課程。

■ 推論 詳細內容　　　　　　　　　　　　　　　　　　　　　　　　　　　　解答 (C)

這題是依題目關鍵字 Ms. Leone 的相關內容的推測問題，應看提到 Ms. Leone 的第二篇文章。Your advertisement indicated that special rates are available for those who register for a certain number of sessions. 提到對於報名一定堂數的人會有特價，之後又提到 I am interested in registering for four.，即「我有興趣登記四堂課」，因此可以推論 Ms. Leone 可能可以享有特價，所以 (C) She may qualify for a special rate. 為正確答案。

單字 qualify v. 有資格的

190

What does Ms. Leone inquire about? (A) Where to buy a gym bag for a friend (B) Whether rates are reduced for groups (C) How to refer new members to the gym (D) When the next promotion event will be held	Leone 女士詢問關於什麼的事情？ (A) 在哪裡可以替她朋友買到運動包 (B) 團體是否享有折扣 (C) 如何介紹新的會員進入健身房 (D) 下次的優惠活動將在什麼時候舉行

■ 六何原則 What　　　　　　　　　　　　　　　　　　　　　　　　　　　　解答 (B)

這題是問 Leone 女士詢問什麼（What）的六何原則問題。應看有提到題目關鍵字 Ms. Leone inquire about 相關內容的第二封電子郵件文章。電子郵件中寫道 One of them was curious about the possibility of a group discount. 與 Could you let me know whether such a thing is being offered at your gym?，即「他們其中有一位想知道團體折扣的可能性，您可否讓我知道您的健身房有沒有提供這樣的服務？」，因此 (B) Whether rates are reduced for groups 為正確答案。

單字 inquire v. 詢問　refer to phr. 交付給～，提交給～

例文1

VOLARE GIFT SHOP

343 Hedge Street, Hickory Hills, IL 60457
www.volaregifts.com
March 28

Francesca Balaguer
3376 Bruce Avenue
Maryland Heights, MO 63141

Dear Ms. Balaguer,

It was great meeting you at the trade fair in Belgrade last week. As we discussed, [191]I'm interested in purchasing some of your souvenir products for my gift shop in Rockford, Illinois.

We haven't been very pleased lately with the quality of merchandise from our current supplier. In fact, many of our customers have complained about the substandard items. I think that this is one of the reasons why our sales have recently declined.

Viewing your exhibit at the trade fair, [192]I was impressed not only with the quality of the materials that you use, but also with the intricate detail in each design.

Enclosed with this letter is an order form that I downloaded from your Web site. Please let me know if you can produce the requested items for us. [194]We are thinking of introducing your merchandise in time for the summer tourist season, when we get twice as many visitors to our location. If successful, we would be interested in developing a long-term business relationship with you.

If you have any questions, do not hesitate to send me an e-mail at octavio.guzman@volaregifts.com. Thank you and we look forward to hearing from you soon.

Sincerely yours,

Octavio Guzman
Co-owner
Volare Gift Shop

例文2

To: Octavio Guzman <octavio.guzman@volaregifts.com>

From: Francesca Balaguer
　　　 <f.balaguer@terrestrialcrafts.com>
Date: April 15
Subject: Order
Attachment(s): Sales invoice
　　　　　　　 Contract
Dear Mr. Guzman,

I appreciate your interest in Terrestrial Crafts. I'm very

VOLARE 禮品店
60457　伊利諾州　Hickory Hills 市
Hedge 街 343 號
www.volaregifts.com
3 月 28 日

Francesca Balaguer
60457 密蘇里州 Maryland Heights 市
Bruce 街 3376 號
親愛的 Balaguer 女士：

很高興在上週於 Belgrade 的展銷會中遇見您，如同我們討論到的，[191] 我有興趣幫我在伊利諾州 Rockford 市的禮品店購買一些您的紀念商品。

最近，我們對於我們目前供應商的商品品質並不是特別滿意，事實上，很多我們的顧客抱怨商品未達標準，我想這是我們最近銷售量下滑的原因之一。

觀賞您在展銷會上的展示時，[192] 不僅是您所使用的材料品質，亦或是每樣設計中精細複雜的細節，都令我印象深刻。

與本信件一同附上的是我從你的網站上所下載的訂貨單，請讓我知道您是否可以生產出我們所要求的品項，[194] 我們正在考慮在夏季旅遊旺季時及時推出您的商品，屆時會有兩倍的旅客到我們的景點，如果成功的話，我們將有興趣與您建立長期的業務合作關係。

如果您有任何問題，請不要猶豫寄電郵到 octavio.guzman@volaregifts.com。謝謝您並期待能很快得到您的回音。

Octavio Guzman 敬上

Volare 禮品店共有人

收件人：Octavio Guzman
　　　　 <octavio.guzman@volaregifts.com>
寄件人：Francesca Balaguer
　　　　 <f.balaguer@terrestrialcrafts.com>
日期：4 月 15 日
主旨：訂貨
附件：銷售發票
　　　 合約
親愛的 Guzman 先生：
感謝您對 Terrestrial 工藝品的喜愛，我

grateful for your order considering that [195-B]I started this business just a few months ago. [195-D]My exhibit at the trade fair was a success, and I received proposals from several companies during the event.

Since you ordered more than 50 different types of items from our catalog, [194]it may take me longer than usual to finish making all of the items. However, I've recently hired five assistants to help me out with production, so I am confident we can send the items to you at the start of your busy season.

Attached is a scanned copy of the signed contract, as well as the invoice for your order. For any inquiries, please give me a call at 555-0099. [195-C]You may also check out our Web site for information on new products at www. terrestrialcrafts. com for any future orders. Thank you very much.

Yours,

Francesca Balaguer

很謝謝您的訂單，因為 [195-B] 我幾個月前才開始從事這項生意。[195-D] 我在展銷會上的展示很成功，我在那個活動上接到幾個公司的提案。

因為您從我們的目錄上訂購超過 50 件不同的商品，[194] 我可能會需要比平常更久的時間來完成所有的商品。不過，我最近雇用了五位助手來協助生產，所以我有信心我們可以在您旺季開始時將貨品寄出。

附上的是一份已簽名合約的掃描副本及您訂單的發票，如要詢問任何事，請電洽 555-0099。關於未來的訂購，[195-C]您也可以上我們的網站查看我們的新產品：www.terrestrialcrafts.com。非常感謝您。

Francesca Balaguer 上

例文 1 單字 □souvenir n. 紀念品
□current a. 現在的
□substandard a. 水準以下的，低於標準的
□exhibit n. 展示品，展覽
□intricate a. 精細的，巧妙的
□hesitate v. 猶豫
例文 2 單字 □terrestrial a. 地上的，地球的
□considering prep. 考慮到～
□assistant n. 助理，助手
□contract n. 合約書，契約

□quality n. 品質
□In fact phr. 事實上
□decline v. 減少，消退
□impressed a. 印象深刻的
□introduce v. 介紹，導入
□look forward phr. 期待
□craft n. 工藝品
□proposal n. 提案
□confident a. 確信的，有自信的
□invoice n. 發票

191

What is the main purpose of the letter?
(A) To register for a trade fair
(B) To ask about an upcoming tour
(C) To change a product purchase
(D) To inquire about ordering merchandise

此信件的主要目的是什麼？
(A) 報名一場展銷會
(B) 詢問一個即將到來的巡演
(C) 修改一個產品購買
(D) 詢問有關訂購商品

🔳 尋找文章主旨 目的　　　　　　　　　　　　　　　　　　　　　　　　解答 (D)

因為是在問信件主旨，所以應看第一篇的信件內容。I'm interested in purchasing some of your souvenir products for my gift shop 中提到為了禮品店，有興趣購買對方的紀念品，因此 (D) To inquire about ordering merchandise 為正確答案。

單字 register v. 登記，報名　upcoming a. 即將來臨的　merchandise n. 商品，物品

Why is Mr. Guzman interested in Ms. Balaguer's items?	為什麼 Guzman 先生會對 Balaguer 女士的產品感興趣？
(A) They are being sold at reasonable prices.	(A) 它們的售價很合理。
(B) They have been featured in a renowned magazine.	(B) 它們曾在一個著名雜誌被特別介紹。
(C) They have particularly detailed designs.	(C) 它們有特別精細的設計。
(D) They have been recommended by his colleagues.	(D) 它們被他的同事所推薦。

■■ 六何原則 Why   解答 (C)

這是問 Guzman 先生為什麼（Why）會對 Balaguer 女士的產品感興趣的六何原則問題，因此應看提及題目關鍵字 Mr. Guzman interested in Ms. Balaguer's items 相關內容的第二封信。信中寫到 I was impressed not only with the quality of the materials that you use, but also with the intricate detail in each design，即不僅是 Mr. Guzman 對 Ms. Balaguer 所使用材料的品質，亦或是每樣設計中精細複雜的細節都印象深刻，因此 (C) They have particularly detailed designs 為正確答案。

單字 reasonable a. 合理的　feature v. 特別報導，以～為特徵

In the letter, the word "substandard" in paragraph 2, line 2 is closest in meaning to	在信的第二段第二行中，「substandard」這個字最接近的意思是
(A) inexpensive	(A) 不昂貴的
(B) satisfactory	(B) 滿意的
(C) average	(C) 普通的
(D) inferior	(D) 次級的

■■ 同義詞   解答 (D)

第一封信提到 substandard 的句子為「many of our customers have complained about the substandard items」，當中的 substandard 為「低於標準的」的意思。因此表示「次級的」的 (D) inferior 為正確答案。

單字 satisfactory a. 滿意的　inferior a. 次級的　average a. 平均的

What will most likely happen in the summer?	暑假最有可能發生什麼事？
(A) Some items will be delivered to a store.	(A) 有些物品會送到店中。
(B) Terrestrial Crafts will open a new branch in Illinois.	(B) Terrestrial 工藝品店會在伊利諾州開一家新的分店。
(C) Volare Gift Shop will celebrate its first anniversary.	(C) Volare 禮品店將慶祝它的第一個周年慶。
(D) Some staff members will be given an orientation.	(D) 有些員工會接受一個新進訓練。

■■ 推論 聯結問題   解答 (A)

這題是將兩篇文章綜合比對後進行推測的問題。先看提到題目關鍵字 happen in the summer 相關內容的第一封信，第一封信中寫道 We are thinking of introducing your merchandise in time for the summer tourist season，表示正考慮在夏季旅遊旺季推出商品，但是不確定是否來得及製作。第二篇電子郵件寫到 it may take me longer than usual to finish making all of the items. However, ~ I am confident we can send the items to you at the start of your busy season.，即 Ms. Balaguer 可能會需要比平常更久的時間來完成所有的商品。不過有信心可以在您旺季開始時將貨品寄出。由第一個線索：夏季旅遊旺季推出商品，和第二個線索：在您旺季開始時可以將貨品寄出，可以推論在夏天時會有商品寄到店中，因此 (A) Some items will be delivered to a store. 為正確答案。

What is NOT suggested about Terrestrial Crafts? (A) It is a small family-run business. (B) It is a relatively new company. (C) It has a list of its merchandise for sale on a Web site. (D) It displayed its products at a recent event.	文中沒有提到哪項與 Terrestrial 工藝品店有關的事？ (A) 它是一家小型的家族生意。 (B) 它是一家較新的公司。 (C) 它在網站上有商品清單。 (D) 它有在最近的一個活動中展示它的商品。

■ Not/True Not 問題　　　　　　　　　　　　　　　　　　　　　　　　　　　　　　　解答 (A)

這是尋找題目關鍵字 Terrestrial Crafts 的相關內容，再與選項互相對照的 Not/True 問題，應先看有提到 Terrestrial Crafts 的第二篇電子郵件。(A) 的內容在文中未被提及，因此 (A) It is a small family-run business 為正確答案。I started this business just a few months ago 表示 Terrestrial Crafts 是幾個月前才開始營運的，與 (B) 選項一致。You may also check out our Web site for information on new products 提到可以在 Terrestrial Crafts 的網站上看到新商品的資訊，與 (C) 的敘述一致。My exhibit at the trade fair was a success 表示在博覽會 Terrestrial Crafts 的展覽是成功的，與 (D) 選項相符。

單字　relatively ad. 相對地，比較地

例文1

VYPERIAS COMPUTERS
254 Leviath Drive, Green Point, NSW 2251

(+612) 555-9634

Dear Ms. Dempsey,

On behalf of Vyperias Computers, thank you for your business! We hope that you are completely satisfied with your purchase and that you will rely on us for all your computer needs. At Vyperias, we take steps to provide only the highest quality products and services, which is why we have had so many repeat customers over the last 15 years.

We understand that our success relies upon our commitment to our customers, so we are always happy to hear your comments and suggestions on areas you feel need improvement. 196We would greatly appreciate it if you could take the time to fill out the enclosed feedback form and let us know about your experience using our products and services. 200One of our supervisors will get in touch with you regarding any concerns you might have:

200Sales	Glenn Sinclair
Advertising	Crystal Werner
Customer Service	Marcela Galvan
Technical Support	Oliver Kimball

Once again, thank you, and we are looking forward to hearing from you.

Best regards,
Jimmy Cuevas
Director, Research and Development

VYPERIAS 電腦公司
2251 新南威爾士州 Green Point 市
Leviath 道 254 號
(+612) 555-9634

親愛的 Dempsey 女士：

謹代表 Vyperias 電腦公司感謝您的惠顧！我們希望您對您所購買的商品非常滿意，而且你會將你所有電腦上的需求都交給我們，在 Vyperias，我們設法使我們只提供最高品質的商品及服務，這就是為什麼我們在過去十五年中有很多回頭客。

我們了解我們的成功依靠我們對於客戶的承諾，所以在您覺得需要改進的地方，我們總是很高興能聽到您的意見及建議，196 我們將會很感謝您花時間填寫附上的回饋單，讓我們知道你對於使用我們產品及服務的經驗，如果您有任何的問題，200 我們其中一位主管將會與您聯絡：

200 銷售	Glenn Sinclair
廣告	Crystal Werner
客服	Marcela Galvan
技術服務	Oliver Kimball

再一次感謝您，我們期待聽到您的回音。

Jimmy Cuevas 敬上
研發部主管

例文2

VYPERIAS COMPUTERS Customer Feedback Form				
198-BName	Bethany Dempsey			
Address	14-C Hobbes Apartments, 573 Whaler Street, Green Point NSW 2251			
Telephone Number	555-6032			
Business Purpose	Bought a Zylogo F1000H Laptop			
Your responses will be used to enhance our capacity to better address your future requests and concerns.				
Please evaluate us on a scale of 1 to 4, with 1 being excellent and 4 being poor:	1	2	3	4
Professionalism and courtesy	X			
Thoroughness and attention to detail		X		
Knowledge and expertise	X			
Punctuality of service		X		

Vyperias 電腦公司 客戶回饋表				
198-B名字	Bethany Dempsey			
住址	2251 新南威爾士州 Whaler 街 573號 14-C Hobbes公寓			
電話號碼	555-6023			
商業目的	購買一個 Zylogo F1000H 筆記型電腦			
您的答覆將會用來提升我們的專業，以便更妥善的處理您未來的需求及問題。				
請以 1 到 4 的等級來評估我們，1是優等，4是劣等	1	2	3	4

Pricing of products			X	
Overall satisfaction with Vyperias Computers		X		

198-C **Comments**: I was very impressed with the service I received from your staff. The store representative who attended to me was friendly and patient when I was asking about the features of each laptop. His knowledge of computers really helped me in choosing a unit that is perfect for my lifestyle. However, 199/200 I think your prices are a little more expensive than others. I was walking around the mall last weekend and learned that some stores are selling the laptop I bought from you at 10 percent less than what I paid for mine. Although I have no complaints about your services, your company might want to look into this matter more closely.

198-D **How did you hear about us?** I saw your advertisement in a newspaper.

Could a Vyperias supervisor get in touch with you regarding your response? Sure, that is not a problem.

專業度及禮貌	X			
徹底性和對細節的關注		X		
知識及專業技能	X			
準時的服務		X		
產品的價格			X	
對Vyperias電腦的整體滿意度		X		

198-C 意見：我對於你們員工的服務印象深刻，當我詢問有關每台筆記型電腦的特色時，接待我的客服人員很友善也很有耐心，他的電腦知識真的幫我選到一台很符合我生活習慣的電腦，但是，199/200 我想你們的價格比其他店貴一點，我上週在一個購物中心逛街時，得知有些店以少 10% 的價格賣我跟你們買的那一台筆記型電腦。雖然我對你們的服務沒有怨言，但是你們公司可能會想要更深入探究這個問題。

198-D 你如何知道我們的？我在一份報紙上看到你們的廣告

關於您的回應 Vyperias 的主管可以與您聯絡嗎？ 當然，沒有問題。

例文 1 單字 □on behalf of phr. 代表～ □completely ad. 完美地，完全地 □take steps phr. 採取行動
□rely upon phr. 出於～，依靠～ □commitment n. 承諾，奉獻 □comment n. 評論
□suggestion n. 提案 □improvement n. 改善 □appreciate v. 感激
□supervisor n. 管理者 □get in touch with phr. 與～聯絡
例文 2 單字 □response n. 回答 □enhance v. 提升，強化 □capacity n. 能力
□address v. 處理 □evaluate v. 評價 □professionalism n. 專業性
□courtesy n. 有禮 □thoroughness n. 徹底 □expertise n. 專業技術
□punctuality n. 嚴守時間 □overall a. 全面的 □satisfaction n. 滿意度
□representative n. 職員，代表 □patient a. 有耐心的 □complaint n. 抱怨

196

Why was the letter written?
(A) To give details about a transaction
(B) To verify the cancellation of an order
(C) To solicit information from a client
(D) To announce the promotion of an employee

為什麼要寫這封信？
(A) 提供一個交易的細節
(B) 確認一個訂單的取消
(C) 請求一個客戶提供資訊
(D) 宣佈一個員工的升遷

■ 找出主題 寫文章的理由　　　　　　　　　　　　　　　　　　　　　　　　　解答 (C)

要找出寫這封信的理由，所以要先看第一篇文章的信件部分，尤其要注意文章中段提到的相關內容。We would greatly appreciate it if you could take the time to fill out the enclosed feedback form and let us know about your experience using our products and services. 提到希望對方能花時間填寫附上的回饋單，以了解對於使用產品及服務的經驗，因此 (C) To solicit information from a client 為正確答案。另外，這封信的前段部分為感謝顧客的購買與對公司的信心。

單字 transaction n. 交易　verify v. 確認　solicit v. 請求　promotion n. 升遷，宣傳

197

| In the letter, the word "regarding" in paragraph 2, line 5 is closest in meaning to
(A) accepting
(B) observing
(C) applying
(D) concerning | 在信的第二段第五行中，「regarding」這個字最接近的意思是？
(A) 接受
(B) 觀察
(C) 申請
(D) 涉及 |

■ 同義詞 　　　　　　　　　　　　　　　　　　　　　　　　　　　　　　　　解答 (D)

在第一篇的電子郵件中包含 regarding 的文句為 One of our supervisors will get in touch with you regarding any concerns you might have，其中的 regarding 表示「與～有關」，因此表示「涉及～」的 (D) concerning 為正確答案。

單字 accept v. 接受　observe v. 觀察，遵守　apply v. 申請　concern v. 與～有關

198

| What is NOT included in the survey Ms. Dempsey answered?
(A) What she paid for her purchase
(B) Her personal information
(C) Her opinions about a store
(D) How she learned about Vyperias | 在 Dempsey 女士所回答的調查表中沒有包含哪一項？
(A) 他付了多少
(B) 她的個人資料
(C) 她對商店的看法
(D) 她如何得知Vyperias |

■ Not/True Not 問題 　　　　　　　　　　　　　　　　　　　　　　　　　　解答 (A)

這是對照文章內容與選項的 Not/True 問題。由於在問題當中沒有關鍵字，所以必須確認各個選項與其相關內容。(A) 的內容在文中未被提及，因此 (A) What she paid for her purchase 為正確答案。Name、Address、Telephone number 中提到了 Ms. Dempsey 的姓名、住址、電話號碼等，與 (B) 選項相符。Comments 中提到了 Ms. Dempsey 對商店的建議，與 (C) 選項一致。How did you hear about us? I saw your advertisement in a newspaper. 中提到 Ms. Dempsey 是由報紙廣告知道 Vyperias，與 (D) 選項相符。

199

| What did Ms. Dempsey complain about?
(A) The staff's communication skills
(B) The speed of delivery
(C) The manager's lack of expertise
(D) The pricing of products | Dempsey 女士抱怨哪件事？
(A) 員工的溝通技巧
(B) 送貨的速度
(C) 經理缺乏專業技能
(D) 產品的價格 |

■ 六何原則 What 　　　　　　　　　　　　　　　　　　　　　　　　　　　　解答 (D)

這題是問 Ms. Dempsey 抱怨什麼（What）的六何原則問題，因此要注意題目關鍵字 Ms. Dempsey complain 的相關內容，由第二篇表格尋找答案。I think your prices are a little more expensive the others 中提到覺得 Vyperias 的價格比起其他店還來的貴，後面又寫到 I was walking around the mall ~ and learned that some stores are selling the laptop I bought from you at 10 percent less than what I paid for mine. 表示 Ms. Dempsey 在一些店看到她跟 Vyperias Computers 買的那一台筆記型電腦，但價格便宜 10%，因此可以知道 (D) The pricing of products 為正確答案。

Which supervisor will most likely contact Ms. Dempsey?	哪一位主管最有可能和 Dempsey 女士連絡？
(A) Oliver Kimball (B) Marcela Galvan (C) Glenn Sinclair (D) Crystal Werner	(A) Oliver Kimball (B) Marcela Galvan (C) Glenn Sinclair (D) Crystal Werner

■ 推論 聯結問題　　　　　　　　　　　　　　　　　　　　　　　　　解答 (C)

這是將兩篇文章內容相互對照後進行推測的整合推測問題。應從含有題目關鍵字 Ms. Dempsey 的第二篇表格看起。

第二篇格中寫到 I think your prices are a little more expensive than others，及 Ms. Dempsey 對商品價格表示不滿，此為第一個線索。但是對商品價格不滿是由哪位主管負責的則要看第一封電子郵件，當中寫到 One of our supervisors will get in touch with you regarding any concerns you might have 與 Sales: Glenn Sinclair，即與銷售有關的抱怨由 Glen Sinclair 負責聯絡，此為第二個線索。

綜合第一個線索：Ms. Dempsey 對商品價格表示不滿，與第二個線索：與銷售有關的抱怨由 Glen Sinclair 負責聯絡，可以推論出會跟 Ms. Dempsey 聯絡的應為 Glenn Sinclair，所以 (C) Glenn Sinclair 為正確答案。

單字　contact v. 聯絡

TEST 06

PART 5

101

Due to the region's low levels of rainfall, Arizona maintains the lowest _____ of plant and animal life in the country. (A) affiliation　　(B) concentration (C) alteration　　(D) formation	因為這個區域的低降雨量，亞利桑那州在全國維持著最低密度的動植物分布。

■ 名詞語彙　　　　　　　　　　　　　　　　　　　　　　　　　　　解答 (B)

由「因為低降雨量所以維持著最低密度的動植物分布」的句意看來，名詞 (B) concentration（密集）為正確答案。(A) affiliation 是「加入，聯合」，(C) alteration 是「變化，改造」，(D) formation 是「形成」的意思。

102

Every morning, Levi makes sure to replenish the selection of daily newspapers _____ the coffee table in the staff's lounge area. (A) between　(B) on　　(C) toward　　(D) within	每天早上，Levi 確認補足職員休息室茶几上的各種日報。

■ 選擇介系詞 場所　　　　　　　　　　　　　　　　　　　　　　　解答 (B)

句意應為「補足職員休息室茶几上的各種日報」，因此表示物體上面的介系詞 (B) on（～上）為正確答案。(A) between（～之間）是指兩個物體之間，(C) toward（向～）是表示方向，(D) within（～內）是表示特定的距離、時間內。

單字 make sure phr. 確認，確保　replenish v. 補充，再填滿　lounge n. 休息室

103

With the higher grade requirements for admission, it has become _____ more difficult for high school students to be accepted to Madison University. (A) progress　　(B) progressively (C) progresses　　(D) progressed	對於入學要求更高的分數，高中生要進入 Madison 大學漸漸地變得更困難了。

■ 副詞的位置　　　　　　　　　　　　　　　　　　　　　　　　　　解答 (B)

答案應是可以修飾空格後副詞 more 的副詞，因此 (B) progressively（日益增加地）為正確答案。可當動詞與名詞的 (A)、動詞 (C)、可當動詞與分詞的 (D) 皆無法修飾副詞。

單字 grade n. 分數　requirement n. 要件，必須條件　admission n. 入學

104

The ticketing clerk reminded the passengers of how _____ it is for them to arrive at the train station at least two hours before their scheduled departure time. (A) important　　(B) importance (C) importantly　　(D) import	售票員提醒乘客至少在火車預定出發前兩小時抵達火車站的重要性。

■ 形容詞的位置　　　　　　　　　　　　　　　　　　　　　　　　　解答 (A)

名詞子句 how ~ time 為介系詞 of 的受詞，受疑問副詞 how 的修飾而成為「至少在火車預定出發前兩小時抵達火車站的重要性」的意思，因此形容詞 (A) important（重要的）為正確答案。空格是名詞子句 how ~ time 的假主詞 it 和真主詞 to arrive ~ 的補語，名詞 (B) importance（重要性）與 (D) import（輸入）雖然可以當作補語使用，但是無法受疑問副詞 how（多少）修飾，副詞 (C) importantly（重要地）則不能當作補語。要注意，for them 是 to 不定詞意義上的主詞。

單字 clerk n. 店員，職員　remind v. 提醒　departure n. 出發

105

The ticket prices of Penfold Airlines are _____ to change without prior notice depending on the season and fuel prices. (A) satisfied (B) located (C) invaluable (D) subject	Penfold 航空公司的票價容易根據季節與油價無預警地變動。

■ 形容詞 片語   解答 (D)

由「票價容易根據季節與油價無預警地變動」的句意看來,空格與前面的 are 搭配空格後的介系詞 to,應為「易於~」的意思,因此形容詞 (D) subject(易於~)為正確答案。(A) satisfied 是「滿意的」,(B) located 是「位於~」,(C) invaluable 是「貴重的」的意思。要注意,應一併記住慣用語 be subjective to(依~改變)。

單字 depending on phr. 依據~   fuel n. 燃料

106

All audio-visual presentations have already been prepared by the staff _____ the seminar, including the video advertisements. (A) by (B) as (C) to (D) for	工作人員已經為研習會準備好所有視聽簡報,包括影像廣告。

■ 選擇介系詞 目的   解答 (D)

句意應為「已經為研習會準備好所有視聽簡報」,因此介系詞 (D) for(為了~)為正確答案。(A) by 表示位子時為「旁邊~」,表示時間為「到~為止」。(B) as 表示資格為「作為~」,用作比較時為「像~」的意思。(C) to 表示方向為「往~」的意思。要注意,應記住慣用表現「be prepared to + 動詞原形」(準備~)。

107

Out of all her charitable projects, the _____ of the town library is what Fatima McCoy is best known for. (A) establishes (B) established (C) establishment (D) establisher	市鎮圖書館的建立是 Fatima McCoy 所有慈善計畫中,最為人所知的。

■ 人物名詞 vs. 抽象名詞   解答 (C)

定冠詞 the 與介系詞 of 之間應為名詞,因此名詞 (C) 與 (D) 有可能為正確答案。由句意「市鎮圖書館的建立是所有慈善計畫中,最為人所知的」看來,抽象名詞 (C) establishment(建立)為正確答案。如果代入人物名詞 (D) establisher(建立者)的話,意思會變為不合邏輯的「市鎮圖書館的建立者是所有慈善計畫中,最為人所知的」。動詞 (A) 與可當分詞和動詞 (B) 不能放在名詞的位置。要注意,應記住慣用語 be known for(以~知名)。

108

Despite the economic crisis, Blixen Finance _____ generates a return on its investments well above analysts' expectations. (A) far (B) still (C) then (D) however	儘管面臨經濟危機,Blixen 金融公司仍然在投資上有著高於分析師預期的收益。

■ 選擇副詞 時間   解答 (B)

句意應為「雖然面臨經濟危機仍有收益」,因此副詞 (B) still(仍然)為正確答案。(A) far(更,遠)表示程度或距離,(C) then 表示「那時」與「然後」,(D) however 是「但是」的意思,為副詞,如果用於句中,前後應有逗點。

單字 analyst n. 分析師   expectation n. 期待,預想

109

After the musical performance yesterday evening, the cast came out from backstage and _____ audience members. (A) greet　　　　　　(B) greeted (C) will greet　　　　(D) are greeting	在昨晚的音樂表演之後，表演人員從後台出來向觀眾致意。

■ 對等關係構句　　　　　　　　　　　　　　　　　　　　　　　　　　解答 (B)

由「表演人員從後台出來向觀眾致意」的句意看來，對等連接詞 and 是連接動詞 came out 和另一個動詞。前面的動詞為過去式 came，所以動詞 greet（致意）的過去式 (B) greeted 為正確答案。要注意，表示過去的時間 yesterday evening，也是線索之一。

單字 performance n. 表演　cast n. 卡司

110

Subsidiary companies are advised to _____ for the trade show by January 12 to receive a 15 percent discount on fees. (A) take off　　　　　(B) show through (C) put away　　　　(D) sign up	建議子公司在 1 月 12 日之前報名貿易展，以取得報名費用的八五折優惠。

■ 動詞語彙　　　　　　　　　　　　　　　　　　　　　　　　　　　　解答 (D)

由「建議在 1 月 12 日之前報名貿易展，以取得優惠」的句意看來，空格搭配後面的介系詞 for 應為「報名～」的意思，因此能變成 sign up for 的動詞 (D) sign up（報名）為正確答案。(A) take off 是「脫掉（衣帽）、（飛機）起飛」，(B) show through 是「（透過）展示」，(C) put away 是「歸位，儲蓄」的意思。

單字 subsidiary company phr. 子公司

111

The company president talked to Mr. Blant about his request and asked him to consider _____ carefully. (A) he　　　　　　　(B) it (C) himself　　　　　(D) itself	公司的總裁和 Blant 先生談論他的請求，並要求他認真地考慮。

■ 人稱代名詞　　　　　　　　　　　　　　　　　　　　　　　　　　　解答 (B)

可以當作及物動詞 consider 受詞的受格人稱代名詞 (B)、反身代名詞 (C) 與 (D) 皆有可能是答案。句意應為「要求他認真地考慮他的請求」，因此可以代稱他的請求事項（his request）的 (B) it 為正確答案。如果用 (C) himself 的話，語意會變為「要求他認真考慮公司總裁本人」，因此並不正確。用 (D) itself 的話主詞應為 it。反身代名詞在主詞與受詞一樣時可以使用。主格人稱代名詞 (A) 則不能當作受詞。

單字 president n. 總裁，總統（President）　request n. 要求事項

112

Ms. Grabowski was assigned to _____ the conference speakers from the entrance to the convention hall. (A) maintain　　　　(B) circulate (C) expedite　　　　(D) escort	Grabowski 女士被指派去護送會議講員從入口到會議廳。

■ 動詞語彙　　　　　　　　　　　　　　　　　　　　　　　　　　　　解答 (D)

由「被指派去護送會議講員從入口到會議廳」的句意看來，動詞 (D) escort（陪同，護送）為正確答案。(A) maintain 是「維持」，(B) circulate 是「流傳」，(C) expedite 是「促進」的意思。要注意，記住慣用語 be assigned to（被指派～）。

單字 assign v. 分派，賦予

113

| Ms. Glass asked each of the _____ about their previous work experience in the advertising and Internet publishing industries.
(A) applicants　　　(B) applicable
(C) applying　　　　(D) applications | Glass 女士詢問每一個申請者關於他們之前在廣告業與網路出版業的工作經驗。 |

■ 人物名詞 vs. 事物名詞　　　　　　　　　　　　　　　　　　　　　　　　　　　　　解答 (A)

放在定冠詞 the 與介系詞 about 之間的應為名詞，因此名詞 (A) 與 (D) 有可能為正確答案。句意應為「詢問了每一位申請者有關工作經驗的問題」，因此人物名詞 (A) applicants（申請者）為正確答案。如果填入事物名詞 (D) applications（申請書）的話，語意會變為「詢問了每一個申請書有關工作經驗的問題」，因此並不正確。形容詞 (B) 不能放在名詞的位置，(C) applying 雖然可以當作動名詞，但是後面沒有受詞，因此無法和定冠詞 the 一起使用，故也非正確答案。

單字 publishing n. 出版　applicable a. 適用的，合適的

114

| Customers can download a _____ of Mithras Cosmetics' latest catalog from its Web site.
(A) copy　　(B) reminder　　(C) schedule　　(D) record | 消費者可以從網站上下載一份 Mithras 化妝品公司最新的目錄。 |

■ 名詞語彙　　　　　　　　　　　　　　　　　　　　　　　　　　　　　　　　　　　解答 (A)

由「可以從網站上下載一份目錄」的句意看來。(A) copy（份，副本）為正確答案。(B) reminder 是「催單，提醒物」(C) schedule 是「行程」，(D) record 是「紀錄」的意思。要注意，記住 (C) schedule 常考的題目為 behind schedule（比預定晚地）。

單字 latest a. 最新的　reminder n. 催單，提醒物

115

| During the investment seminar, participants were urged to provide examples of their own experiences in _____ stock.
(A) lifting　　　　　(B) placing
(C) delegating　　　(D) trading | 在投資研習會上，參加者被鼓勵提供他們在買賣股票上的親身經歷。 |

■ 動詞語彙　　　　　　　　　　　　　　　　　　　　　　　　　　　　　　　　　　　解答 (D)

由「參加者被鼓勵提供他們在買賣股票上的親身經歷」的句意看來，動詞 trade（交易）的 -ing 形 (D) trading 為正確答案。(A) 的 lift 是「舉起」，(B) 的 place 是「放，設置」，(C) 的 delegate 是「委任」的意思。要注意，應記住「be urged to + 動詞原形」（被要求做，鼓勵做～）的慣用句型。

單字 urge v. 力勸，慫恿　stock n. 股票，庫存品

116

| The first-place winner at the Annual Geo-Science Fair built a machine to demonstrate _____ earthquakes are caused.
(A) about　　(B) how　　(C) which　　(D) over | 在年度地理科學展上的首獎得主建了一個機器來說明地震是如何造成的。 |

■ 名詞子句 連接詞 how　　　　　　　　　　　　　　　　　　　　　　　　　　　　　解答 (B)

空格後連接了含主詞 earthquakes 與動詞 are caused 的子句，因此可以連接子句的連接詞 (B) 與 (C) 有可能為正確答案。包含空格的子句 _____ earthquakes are caused 是動詞 demonstrate（說明，示範）的受格名詞子句，句意應為「來說明地震是如何造成的」，因此名詞子句連接詞 (B) how（如何～）為正確答案。填入疑問詞 (C) which 的話，語意會變成不合邏輯的「說明是哪個地震發生」，所以不正確。介系詞 (A) 與 (D) 無法連接子句，後面也不能加名詞。

單字 draft n. 草案　ensure v. 確保　thoroughly ad. 徹底地

117

If the elevator _____, press this button and someone from the maintenance department will respond to the emergency as soon as possible. (A) breaks down (B) stays in (C) turns out (D) calls up	假如電梯故障，請按這個按鈕，維修部門會有人盡快回應緊急狀況。

■ 動詞片語　　　　　　　　　　　　　　　　　　　　　　　　　　　　　解答 (A)

句意應為「假如電梯故障，按這個按鈕會有人回應」，因此表示「故障」的動詞片語 (A) breaks down 為正確答案。（break down：發生故障）。(B) stay in 是「留下」，(C) turn out 是「展露」，(D) call up 是「叫醒」的意思。

單字 press v. 按　maintenance n. 維持　emergency n. 緊急事項　as soon as possible phr. 盡快

118

Your order of printer paper has already been shipped from our warehouse _____ will most likely arrive late due to poor weather conditions. (A) but (B) until (C) even (D) since	你訂購的影印紙已經從我們的倉庫送出，不過很可能會因為惡劣的天氣狀況而延遲送達。

■ 對等連接詞　　　　　　　　　　　　　　　　　　　　　　　　　　　　解答 (A)

空格應是擁有共同主詞 Your order 的兩個動詞 has already been shipped 和 will most likely arrive 的對等連接詞，句意應為「已經送出但可能會延遲抵達」，所以對等連接詞 (A) but（但是）為正確答案。but 連接意思相反的句子。可當副詞子句連接詞與介系詞的 (B) 與 (D)，以及強調副詞 (C)，皆無法連接兩個動詞。

單字 warehouse n. 倉庫　likely ad. 很可能　even ad. 更，就連～　since conj. 自從～，因為 ～

119

For a minimal fee, customers of Umbria Travels can personally _____ their itineraries online or add options to their bookings. (A) differ (B) board (C) change (D) look	僅需極少的費用，Umbria 旅遊公司的客戶就能親自在線上更改他們的行程，或替他們預定的行程追加選項。

■ 動詞語彙　　　　　　　　　　　　　　　　　　　　　　　　　　　　　解答 (C)

句意應為「用很少的費用線上更改行程」，因此動詞 (C) change（變更）為正確答案。(A) differ 與 from 搭配時表示「與～不同」，即片語 differ from，(B) board 有「登（機、船）」的意思，(D) look 雖是「看，檢討」的意思，但後面要有介系詞 at、into、over 才能接名詞，

單字 minimal a. 最小的　itinerary n. 旅行行程

120

Most outsourcing companies operate on _____ shift schedules to adequately accommodate their clients' needs. (A) alternation (B) alternates (C) alternate (D) alternately	大多數外包公司都以輪班的方式來運作,以適度地配合他們顧客的需求。

■ 形容詞的位置   解答 (C)

能放在名詞 shift schedules 前修飾的即為形容詞,因此形容詞 (C) alternate(交替的)為正確答案。名詞 (A)、動詞 (B)、副詞 (D) 無法修飾名詞。

單字 adequately ad. 適當地　accommodate v. 使相符,容納

121

Session Television is planning to broadcast a primetime comedy series for a mature _____ this upcoming season. (A) portion (B) audience (C) fraction (D) selection	Session 電視台計畫在新的一季針對成人觀眾播放黃金時段的喜劇影集。

■ 名詞語彙   解答 (B)

句意應為「針對成人觀眾播放的喜劇影集」,因此名詞 (B) audience(觀眾)為正確答案。(A) portion 是「份,分配」,(C) fraction 是「片段,一部分」,(D) selection 是「收藏品,蒐藏」的意思。

單字 broadcast v. 放映,廣播　primetime n. 黃金時段　mature a. 成熟的

122

Dr. Lillian Stern is trying to _____ which area of the city would best suit the needs of the clinic she plans to open next year. (A) maintain (B) develop (C) launch (D) decide	Lillian Stern 醫生正試著決定城市裡的哪個區域最符合她明年開張的診所的需求。

■ 動詞語彙   解答 (D)

由「正決定城市裡的哪個區域最符合她的診所需求」的句意看來,動詞 (D) decide(決定)為正確答案。(A) maintain 是「維持」,(B) develop 是「使發展」,(C) launch 是「著手,從事」的意思。

單字 suit v. 與～符合

123

Merov Technologies, one of Russia's _____ providers of telecommunication services, will launch more affordable broadband packages in June. (A) more largely　　(B) largeness (C) largest　　(D) largely	Merov 科技公司是俄羅斯最大的電信服務公司之一，將要在 6 月展開更實惠的寬頻服務。

■ 最高級　　　　　　　　　　　　　　　　　　　　　　　　　　　　　　　　　解答 (C)

空格應為可以修飾名詞 providers 的形容詞，因此形容詞最高級 (C) largest 為正確答案。表示「～之中最～」的 of telecommunication services 需要用到最高級，即為線索之一。副詞 (A) 和 (D) 無法修飾名詞，名詞 (B) 不是複合名詞，所以也不能修飾。

單字 affordable a.（價錢）適當的　broadband n. 寬頻網路

124

Anson Furnishings supplied all the furniture in the new office _____ for the bookshelves, which were customized by Woodworks International. (A) as　　(B) near (C) except　　(D) apart	除了由 Woodworks 國際公司客製的書櫃之外，Anson 家具公司供應所有新辦公室所需的家具。

■ 選擇介系詞 排除　　　　　　　　　　　　　　　　　　　　　　　　　　　　解答 (C)

由「供應除了書櫃之外的所有家具」的句意看來，與空格後的 for 一起搭配表示「除了～」的 (C) except 為正確答案。(A) as 搭配介系詞 for 的話會變成 as for（與～有關），(B) near 當作介系詞時，表示位置「靠近～」，當作形容詞時表示「靠近的」，當作副詞時表示「近地」。(D) apart 與介系詞 from 搭配成為 apart from，表示「～外」的意思。

單字 customize v. 客製

125

Victoria paid the enrollment fee by bank transfer this afternoon, _____ her seat for the three-day actors' workshop in July. (A) secure　　(B) security (C) securest　　(D) securing	Victoria 今天下午用銀行轉帳來繳付註冊費，以確保她能參加在 7 月為期三天的演員研習課程。

■ 分詞構句　　　　　　　　　　　　　　　　　　　　　　　　　　　　　　　　解答 (D)

主句是含 Victoria paid the enrollment fee 的完整句子，____ her seat ~ in July 為修飾語，因為修飾語沒有動詞的成分，所以可以形成分詞構句的現在分詞 (D) securing（確保）為正確答案。要注意，題目的 securing ~ in July 是「確保她能參加研習課程」的意思，從這裡可以知道為「繳報名費進而確保～」連續動作的分詞構句。形容詞及動詞 (A)、名詞 (B)、形容詞最高級 (C) 則無法形成分詞構句的修飾語。

單字 enrollment n. 註冊　fee n. 會費，索費，手續費　secure v. 確保；a. 確定的

126

The scientists are _____ analyzing the results of their experiment to make sure the data in the concluding report is accurate.	科學家們謹慎地分析他們的實驗成果，以確保結論報告上的數據是正確的。
(A) extremely (B) cautiously (C) vainly (D) firmly	

■ 副詞語彙　　　　　　　　　　　　　　　　　　　　　　　　　　　　　　　解答 (B)

句意應為「科學家們謹慎地分析他們的實驗成果」，因此副詞 (B) cautiously（謹慎地）為正確答案。(A) extremely 是「極度地」，(C) vainly 是「徒勞地」，(D) firmly 是「穩固地」的意思。

單字 analyze v. 分析　accurate a. 正確的

127

The coupon entitles the holder to a free drink or fries and is _____ until February 28.	持有優惠券的人可享有一份免費的飲料或薯條，這項優惠至 2 月 28 日截止。
(A) valid (B) validating (C) validation (D) validate	

■ 可以當作補語的詞性：名詞與形容詞　　　　　　　　　　　　　　　　　　　解答 (A)

空格接在 be 動詞 is 後面，因此形容詞 (A)、-ing 形態的 (B) 與名詞 (C) 有可能為正確答案。由「優惠至 2 月 28 日截止」的句意看來，應為說明主詞 The coupon 的形容詞 (A) valid（有效的）為正確答案。動名詞 (B) validating 後面應加受詞。填入名詞 (C) validation（確認，批准）的話，會與主詞 The coupon 形成同位語，形成「優惠券即是批准」的奇怪語意。動詞原形 (D) validate 則不能接在 be 動詞後面。要注意，應記住「entitle + 人 + to + 名詞」（給人～的資格、權力），和與其相關的慣用語「be entitled to + 動詞原形」（有～的資格）。

單字 entitle v. 賦予資格　holder n. 持有者　validate v. 確認，證實

128

After receiving two major clothing orders in a single month, Zeus Couture's manager decided to invest in several sewing machines to increase its _____.	在一個月內接到兩筆服飾大訂單後，Zeus 服裝設計公司的經理決定投資幾台縫紉機以增加產能。
(A) affordability (B) productivity (C) subjectivity (D) attainability	

■ 名詞語彙　　　　　　　　　　　　　　　　　　　　　　　　　　　　　　　解答 (B)

句意應為「決定投資幾台縫紉機以增加產能」，因此名詞 (B) productivity（產能）為正確答案。(A) affordability 是「可負擔的費用」，(C) subjectivity 是「主觀性」，(D) attainability 是「可達成」的意思。

129

As part of its promotion, Pandora Express Train offers discounts to passengers who book their tickets ------- time. (A) beside (B) through (C) ahead of (D) due to	作為促銷活動的一部分，Pandora 快車提供優惠給提早訂票的乘客。

選擇介系詞 其他   解答 (C)

句意應為「提供優惠給提早訂票的乘客」，因此 (C) ahead of（提早～）為正確答案。應記住慣用語 ahead of time（預先）。(A) beside 的意思是「～旁」，表示位置，(B) through 表示時間時是「～期間」，表示方向是「通過」，表示方法則是「透過～」的意思。介系詞 (D) due to 表示理由「因為～」。此外，應記住慣用語 on time（準時），in time（及時）。

單字 passenger n. 乘客　book v. 預約，訂購

130

Andrea Gonzaga chose to work fewer hours per day for the weekly magazine, _____ herself more time to write her first book. (A) permits (B) permitting (C) permissible (D) permission	Andrea Gonzaga 選擇減少在週刊工作的每日工時，讓她自己有更多時間來寫她的第一本書。

分詞構句   解答 (B)

主句是含有 Andrea Gonzaga chose to work 的完整句子，____ herself ~ first book 為修飾語。因為修飾語沒有動詞的成分，所以可以形成分詞構句的現在分詞 (B) permitting 為正確答案。要注意，本句中 permitting ~ book 表示「讓她自己有更多時間來寫她的第一本書」，從這裡可以知道為「減少工作時數進而使～可能」連續動作的分詞構句。可以當動詞與名詞的 (A)、形容詞 (C)、名詞 (D) 皆無法形成分詞構句的修飾語。

單字 permit v. 使～可能，允許

131

Even before the _____ had begun, Chiba Electronics employees expressed their opposition to the merger with Tsukino Industries. (A) structures (B) assortments (C) occupations (D) negotiations	甚至在談判開始之前，Chiba 電器公司的員工就表達了他們對於和 Tsukino 工業合併的反對意見。

名詞語彙   解答 (D)

句意應為「談判開始之前員工就表達他們的反對」，因此名詞 (D) negotiations（談判，協商）為正確答案。(A) structures 是「構造」，(B) assortment 是「分類，綜合」，(C) occupation 是「工作，居住」的意思。要注意，應記住慣用語「express opposition to + 名詞」（表示對～的反對）。

單字 merger n. 合併

132

Local and international news reported on the success of the archaeological excavation in Nuremberg, which _____ by Mr. Drescher, the project manager. (A) will supervise　(B) is supervising (C) has supervised　(D) was supervised	當地與國際新聞報導了由 Drescher 先生所督導，在紐倫堡考古挖掘的好成果。

■ 主動與被動語態的區分　　　　　　　　　　　　　　　　　　解答 (D)

動詞 supervise（監督）是及物動詞，但是空格後面沒有受詞，意思為「由 Drescher 先生督導」，且有表示動作者的介系詞 by，因此被動語態 (D) was supervised 為正確答案。(A) (B) (C) 都是主動，所以並非答案。

單字 archaeological a. 考古學的　excavation n. 挖掘　supervise v. 監督

133

People who travel _____ will benefit from the Platinum Miles credit card as it lets them earn airline points that may be redeemed for plane tickets. (A) regular　(B) regularly (C) regularity　(D) regularities	經常旅行的人能從白金里程信用卡得到好處，因為此卡可讓他們賺得可以折抵機票的航空公司點數。

■ 副詞的位置　　　　　　　　　　　　　　　　　　　　　　解答 (B)

空格應為修飾動詞 travel 的副詞，因此副詞 (B) regularly（定期地）為正確答案。形容詞 (A)、名詞 (C) 與 (D) 無法修飾動詞。

單字 benefit v. 受惠　redeem v. 交換，贖回

134

Numerous recreational activities are offered at Jade Panglao Resort, making it the perfect place in _____ to spend the holidays with family and friends. (A) that　(B) when (C) which　(D) where	在 Jade Panglao 渡假村裡提供多項休閒娛樂活動，讓這個地方成為家人與朋友渡假的完美地點。

■ 介系詞 + 關係代名詞　　　　　　　　　　　　　　　　　　解答 (C)

「介系詞 + 關係代名詞」後面可以接 to 不定詞取代完整子句。因此在 to 不定詞（to spend ~ friends）前以「介系詞 + 關係代名詞」的形態修飾先行詞 the perfect place 的關係代名詞 (C) which 為正確答案。關係代名詞 (A) that 不能放在介系詞後面。關係副詞 (B) when 也不能和介系詞一起使用，而且不是表示地點，是表示時間。要注意，關係副詞 (D) where 雖然可以當作介系詞的受格並帶出名詞子句，但在關係子句的構句中 in which 兩個字即等於 where，因此不能接在 in 後面，所以不是答案。要注意不要看到「疑問詞 + to 不定詞」就選 (D) where。

單字 recreational a. 娛樂的

135

Ozzo Appliances will begin an advertising campaign for its newest line of kitchen equipment _____ the license from the patent office is released.

(A) once
(B) from
(C) in spite of
(D) along with

一旦專利局核發許可證，Ozzo 家電行將為最新系列的廚房設備展開廣告活動。

■ 副詞子句連接詞 時間　　　　　　　　　　　　　　　　　　　　　　　　　解答 (A)

主句是含 Ozzo Appliances will begin an advertising campaign 的完整句子，____ the license ~ is released 則是修飾語，因為修飾語具有動詞 is released，空格應選擇可以引導副詞子句的連接詞 (A) once（一旦～的話）為正確答案。介系詞 (B) from（從～）、(C) in spite of（儘管～）、(D) along with（與～一起）皆不能引導子句。

單字 license n. 許可　patent office phr. 專利局

136

It is _____ that interior designers keep up with the latest trends in order to come up with new and interesting concepts for their clients.

(A) vital
(B) heavy
(C) punctual
(D) prohibited

室內設計師趕上潮流是很重要的，這樣才能為他們的客戶想出新奇有趣的概念。

■ 形容詞語彙　　　　　　　　　　　　　　　　　　　　　　　　　　　　　解答 (A)

句意應為「室內設計師趕上潮流是很重要的」，因此形容詞 (A) vital（很重要的）為正確答案。(B) heavy 是「重的」，(C) punctual 是「遵守時間的」，(D) prohibited 是「被禁止的」，搭配 strictly（嚴格地）的 strictly prohibited（嚴格禁止的），為常見的慣用語。要注意，應記住慣用語 keep up with（趕上～）。

單字 keep up with phr. 跟上～　come up with phr. 想出，找出

137

Tip-Toe's shoes are quite expensive, but _____ other brands, they last for a long time and come with a 12-month warranty.

(A) after
(B) therefore
(C) unlike
(D) upon

Tip-Toe 的鞋子相當昂貴，但是不像其他牌子，他們的鞋子可以穿很久，而且有十二個月的保固。

■ 填入介系詞 其他　　　　　　　　　　　　　　　　　　　　　　　　　　　解答 (C)

空格後有名詞片語 other brands，因此可以連接名詞片語的介系詞 (A) (C) (D) 可能為正確的答案。句意應為「雖然相當昂貴但是不像其他牌子，可以穿很久」，因此 (C) unlike（不像～）為正確答案。(A) after 為「～之後」，表示時間，(D) upon 是「在～上面」，意思雖與 on 相似，但比 on 更為正式。(B) therefore（因此）是連接副詞，無法連接名詞片語。

138

The advisory from the Ministry of Health listed various _____ measures that could help minimize the risk of heat-related illnesses during the summer months.

(A) protects
(B) protected
(C) protective
(D) protectively

衛生部的特報列出了許多防護措施,可以在夏季期間幫忙把炎熱引發的疾病危機減到最小。

■ 形容詞的位置　　　　　　　　　　　　　　　　　　　　　　　　　　　　解答 (C)

空格應為修飾名詞 measures 的形容詞或可當形容詞使用的分詞,因此分詞 (B)、形容詞 (C) 有可能為正確答案。句意應為「許多可以幫忙把危機降到最低的防護措施」,因此形容詞 (C) protective（防護的）為正確答案。若填入過去分詞 (B),則句意會變為「措施被保護」。動詞 (A) 無法修飾名詞。要注意,應記住慣用語 protect A from B（保護 A 遠離 B）。

單字 advisory n. 預報,警報　measure n. 對策,措施　illness n. 疾病

139

As an advocate _____ forest preservation, Steve Riddick has organized many awareness campaigns against illegal logging and farming practices.

(A) of
(B) at
(C) by
(D) into

身為森林保育的提倡者,Steve Riddick 已經組織了許多自覺運動來對抗非法的盜木、盜墾。

■ 選擇介系詞 of　　　　　　　　　　　　　　　　　　　　　　　　　　　　解答 (A)

兩個名詞 an advocate、forest preservation 中 advocate（支持者）是可視為意義上的動詞,forest preservation（森林保育）則可視為意義上的受詞,合起來表示「提倡森林保護」的意思,因此有「森林保育的提倡者」之意。所以能連接兩名詞分別表示意義上動詞與受詞關係的介系詞 (A) of（～的）為正確答案。(B) at 是「在～」,表示時間地點,(C) by 是「～旁,依～」,表示位置或行動者,(D) into 是「往～裡」,表示方向。

單字 advocate n. 支持者　preservation n. 保護　awareness n. 察覺　logging n. 伐木

140

To save time during her presentation, Ms. Madden decided to give a brief overview of each of Transpacific Translation's offerings _____ a detailed description.

(A) in case
(B) in the event
(C) rather than
(D) whether or not

為了在口頭報告時節省時間,Madden 女士決定針對每一個 Transpacific Translation 公司的服務做簡短說明,而不會詳細介紹。

■ 其他比較級用法　　　　　　　　　　　　　　　　　　　　　　　　　　　　解答 (C)

由「在口頭報告時做簡短說明,而不會詳細介紹」的句意看來,對等連接兩個名詞片語 a brief overview、a detailed description 並可表示「～而非～」意思的連接詞 (C) rather than 為正確答案。(A) in case（在～情況）,(B) in the event（結果,到頭來）,(D) whether or not（無論是～不是～）是副詞子句連接詞,後面應連接子句。

單字 overview n. 介紹,大綱　description n. 說明,敘述

PART 6

Questions 141-143 refer to the following letter. 　　141-143 根據下面信件的內容回答問題。

Darlene Amalo Unit 320, Alto Apartment St. Peter's Street, St. Albans Hertfordshire	Darlene Amalo 赫特福德郡 St. Albans 市 St. Peter 街 Alto 公寓 320 室
Dear Ms. Amalo,	親愛的 Amalo 女士，
We are pleased to inform you that you have passed the final interview for the _____ guide position in Rhodes, 141 (A) museum　　(B) leadership 　　　(C) travel　　(D) career Greece. In this regard, we would like you to visit our London office on Friday, February 5, at 9 A.M. to discuss details about your contract.	141 我們很高興通知你，你已經通過了在希臘 Rhodes 市的旅遊導覽職位的最後面試，關於這件事，我們想要你在 2 月 5 日星期五上午 9 點到訪我們在倫敦的辦公室，以討論合約的細節。
As we already discussed during your recent interview, the successful applicant _____ in charge of organizing and 142 (A) will be　　(B) has been 　　　(C) was being　　(D) will have been facilitating island tours for guests.	142 如同我們在你最近一次面試中討論到，入選的應徵者將會負責為遊客安排島上的遊覽，並使旅程順利進行。
We believe your superb _____ of European languages and 143 (A) commandable　　(B) commander 　　　(C) command　　(D) commanded broad knowledge of Greek culture make you the right person for the position.	143 我們相信你極佳的歐語和對希臘文化的廣泛知識能讓你勝任這個工作。
Please respond to this letter as soon as possible so that we can finalize the appointment and draft a contract. Congratulations, and I look forward to working with you!	請盡速回覆此信，讓我們能敲定會面時間與起草你的合約。恭喜你，我們很期待與你共事。
Sincerely,	
Catherine Flotillas Manager	Catherine Flotillas 敬上 經理

單字 be in charge of phr. 負責　facilitate v. 使容易，促進　superb a. 出色的　finalize v. 結束

141 ■ 名詞語彙 掌握全文　　　　　　　　　　　　　　　　　　　　　　　　　　解答 (C)

由「通過了＿＿導覽職位的最後面試」的句意看來，選項 (A) museum（博物館）與 (C) travel（旅行）有可能為正確答案。因為無法單就空格所在的句子選出正確答案，因此應了解上下文或全文的含意。信件的中間部分提到，入選的應徵者將會負責為遊客安排島上的遊覽，並使旅程順利進行，因此可以知道入選者為旅行導遊職缺的申請人，所以名詞 (C) travel（旅行）是正確答案。(A) museum 是「博物館」，(B) leadership 是「領導力」，(D) career 是「職業經歷」的意思。

142 ■ 未來式　　　　　　　　　　　　　　　　　　　　　　　　　　　　　　解答 (A)

句意應為「如同我們面試中討論到，入選的應徵者將會負責為遊客安排島上的遊覽」，因此表示未來式的 (A) will be 為正確答案。因為並非是要表示在未來完成的意思，所以不能選未來完成式的 (D) will have been。

143 ■ 人物名詞 vs. 抽象名詞　　　　　　　　　　　　　　　　　　　　　　　　解答 (C)

空格受所有格 your 與形容詞 superb 修飾，並可當作名詞子句 your superb ~ make you ~ the position 的主詞，應為名詞，所以名詞 (B) (C) 為可能的答案。句意應為「極佳的歐語能力能讓你勝任這個工作」，因此抽象名詞 (C) command（運用能力）為正確答案。如果填入人物名詞 (B) commander（指揮官），則會出現「歐語的出色指揮者能讓你勝任這個工作」這種不合邏輯的句意。

Questions 144-146 refer to the following article.　　　　　　144-146 根據下面文章的內容回答問題。

HIALEAH - Bolt's World will be _____ rides on its Thunder

144 (A) offering　　　(B) scheduling
　　　(C) suspending (D) managing

Roller Coaster during the anniversary celebration this

weekend. "The theme park will have to close the world-class attraction due to a mechanical malfunction discovered by maintenance workers today," Bolt's World facilities manager Nathan Johnston said.

While workers were conducting a safety check on the ride, they noticed that the train stopped running after making a left turn on a sharp curve. The workers determined _____ the problem was a result of the guide

145 (A) that　　　(B) where
　　(C) what　　(D) when

wheels, which need replacing.

"We regret that we cannot offer roller coaster rides. Nevertheless, we are thankful that the breakdown was spotted before the event and nobody was hurt," Johnston said. To ensure guests' safety, Bolt's World will make major mechanical improvements to the ride. An _____

146 (A) extended　　(B) overworked
　　　(C) upgraded　(D) agreeable

Thunder Roller Coaster will be operational again next month.

海里亞市 – 144 Bolt's World 將會在本週的周年慶祝會上停止開放閃電雲霄飛車的搭乘。Bolt's World 的設備經理 Nathan Johnston 說：「主題公園將必須關閉世界級的景點，因為今天維修工人發現了機械無法正常運作的現象。」

當工人在雲霄飛車進行一次安全檢查，他們注意到列車在一個急彎處左轉後會停止運轉。145 工人判定問題是出在導輪，需要更換。

Johnston 說：「我們很遺憾我們無法開放雲霄飛車，然而，我們慶幸這個問題在活動開始之前，且還沒有人受傷就被發現。」為了確保遊客的安全，Bolt's World 將會針對雲霄飛車進行重大的機械改善，146 升級後的閃電雲霄飛車將會在下個月重新開放。

單字 **attraction** n. 遊樂設施　**malfunction** n. 故障　**determine** v. 判定　**breakdown** n. 故障
　　spot v. 發現　**operational** a. 營運上的

144 ■ 動詞語彙 掌握上下文　　　　　　　　　　　　　　　　　　　　　　　　　　　解答 (C)

由「將會＿＿閃電雲霄飛車的搭乘」的句意看來，所有的選項皆可能是答案。不能單就空格所在的句子選出答案時，應參考上下文的文意。後面的文章提到機械故障，因此遊樂園將必須關閉世界級的景點，由此可判斷雲霄飛車將停止開放。所以動詞 suspend（中斷）的 -ing 形 (C) suspending（中斷）為正確答案。(A) 的 offer 是「提供」，(B) 的 schedule 是「排行程」，(D) 的 manage 是「經營，管理」的意思。

145 ■ 名詞子句連接詞 掌握上下文　　　　　　　　　　　　　　　　　　　　　　　　解答 (A)

空格應為可引導名詞子句 ＿＿ the problem was a result of the guide wheels，作為動詞 determined 受詞的名詞子句連接詞。名詞子句是包含主詞 the problem、動詞 was、補語 a result 的完整子句，因此可以帶出完整名詞子句的連接詞 (A) (B) (D) 皆可能是答案。無法單就空格所在的句子判斷答案時，應參考上下文意。前文提到雲霄飛車停止，所以後文應是說明停止原因「判定問題是出在導輪」，因此 (A) that 為正確答案。填入疑問副詞 (B) where 與 (D) when 會出現「判定問題的地方／的時間是出在導輪」不合邏輯的句意。要注意，與 determine（確定）用法相同的還有 say（說）、think（認為）、know（知道）等動詞，受詞皆為 that 子句且 that 可省略。選項 (C) what 應以主詞或受詞的角色，置於不完整子句之前，所以並非正確答案。

146 ■ 形容詞語彙 掌握上下文　　　　　　　　　　　　　　　　　　　　　　　　　　解答 (C)

由「＿＿雲霄飛車將會在下個月重新開放」的句意看來，(A) (C) 可能是答案。無法單就空格所在的句子判斷答案時，應參考上下文意。前面提到為了確保遊客安全，遊樂園會針對雲霄飛車進行重大的機械改善，因此可以知道將會進行升級維修，所以動詞 upgrade（升級）的過去分詞 (C) upgraded 為正確答案。(A) extended 是「延長的，增加的」，(B) overworked 是「工作過度的」，(D) agreeable 是「令人愉快的」。

Questions 147-149 refer to the following e-mail.

147-149 根據下面備忘錄的內容回答問題。

To: University of Canterblane department secretaries
From: Jefferson Lance, IT Office director
RE: Staff Training

For the entire month of November, the IT Office will hold training seminars to acquaint professors and administrative employees with the university's improved computer system. Attendance is _____ for all teaching staff

147 (A) required　　(B) optional
　　(C) unlimited　　(D) helpful

members. Since new features were added, it is necessary for our faculty to learn about these changes.

The IT Office will conduct daily sessions Mondays through Saturdays. _____ professors may attend the training

148 (A) If　　　　(B) After
　　(C) All　　　(D) Although

anytime within the month, every department is strongly advised to arrange an exclusive session for its staff. This will allow trainers to give detailed lectures on specific functions _____to each department.

149 (A) appropriately　　(B) appropriate
　　(C) appropriateness　(D) appropriation

For more information regarding training, please contact the IT Office at extension # 521 and ask for Oscar. We look forward to your full cooperation and hope that the recent modifications to the university's computer system will be helpful for everyone. Thank you.

收件人：Canterblane 大學系辦祕書
寄件人：資訊科技辦公室主任 Jefferson Lance
關於：員工訓練

11 月整個月，資訊科技辦公室將會舉辦訓練研習會，讓教授們和行政職員熟悉大學裡更新後的電腦系統。147 所有教職員工都要參加，因為增加了新的功能，所有的教職員工都必須知道這些改變。

資訊科技辦公室從週一到週六每天都有研習會。148 雖然所有教授都可以在這個月任何時間參加訓練，但強烈建議每個科系為自己的員工安排一個專門的時段，149 如此一來能讓訓練者針對每個科系適用的特定功能，做詳細的講解。

關於訓練的更多資訊，請打分機 521 聯絡資訊科技辦公室的 Oscar。我們期待你的全力配合，並希望最新修正的大學電腦系統能對每一個人都有幫助，謝謝。

單字 **secretary** n. 祕書　**acquaint** v. 使熟悉，使了解　**feature** n. 特色　**session** n. 課程，時間，會議

147　形容詞語彙 掌握全文　　　　　　　　　　　　　　　　　　　　　　　　　　　　　解答 (A)

由「所有教職員工都____參加」的句意看來，所有選項皆有可能為正確答案。因為無法單就空格所在的文句判斷答案，因此應參考上下或全文文意。後文提到因為增加了新的功能，所有的教職員工都必須知道這些改變，由此可知教職員工都被要求參加研習會。所以形容詞 (A) required（被要求的，必須的）為正確答案。應記住慣用語「be required to + 動詞原形」（要求～，應 ～）。(B) optional 是「選擇性的」，(C) unlimited 是「無限的」，(D) helpful 是「有幫助的」的意思。

148　副詞子句連接詞 讓步　　　　　　　　　　　　　　　　　　　　　　　　　　　　　解答 (D)

主句是含有 every department is strongly advised 的完整字句，professors ~ the month 為修飾的副詞子句。因有動詞 may attend，所以可以連接副詞子句，並可表示「雖然所有教授都可以在這個月任何時間參加訓練，但強烈建議每個科系為自己的員工安排一個專門的時段」之意的副詞子句連接詞 (D) Although（雖然～）為正確答案。若填入 (A) If（若是 ～的話）與 (B) After（～之後）就會出現不通順的文意。(C) All（全部）雖然可以當作數量形容詞用於複數可數名詞之前，但無法引導子句。

149　省略關係代名詞　　　　　　　　　　　　　　　　　　　　　　　　　　　　　　　　解答 (B)

____ to each department 是將修飾前面先行詞 specific functions 的關係子句，把「關係代名詞 + be 動詞（which are）」省略掉而來的。此時後面加名詞的話則與先行詞同格，接形容詞的話則用於說明先行詞。句意應為「各學系適合的～」，所以形容詞 (B) appropriate（適當的）為正確答案。名詞 (C) 與 (D) 無法與先行詞 specific functions 同格產生「特定功能即是～」的意思，因此並非答案。要注意，通常若省略「關係代名詞 + be 動詞」，後面較不會接名詞，較常接形容詞。

April 1

Dear Valued Client,

We would like to express our gratitude to you for renewing your Internet connection subscription with Magna Link. Your continued _____ is very important to us. To serve you

150 (A) patience　　(B) success
(C) observation　(D) patronage

better, we would appreciate your answering a one-page questionnaire dealing with the quality of our network. Please answer the questions and write down any problems you may have encountered with your connection. _____,

151 (A) Then　　(B) However
(C) Meanwhile　(D) Otherwise

send us back the form using the enclosed pre-paid envelope.

Rest assured that your answers will remain confidential and be used exclusively for the company's research. _____

152 (A) In charge of　　(B) On behalf of
(C) By means of　　(D) In appreciation of

your willingness to complete this survey, you will be entitled to a chance to win a new desktop computer. The lucky winner will be announced on May 25 and contacted in writing.

We look forward to receiving your feedback. Thank you.

Sincerely,

Magna Link

---

4 月 1 日

親愛的貴賓：

對於您與 Magna Link 續約網路服務，我們想要表達感謝之意。150 您持續的愛用對我們而言很重要，為了要提供您更好的服務，若您能回答一頁我們針對網路品質的問卷，我們將非常感謝您。

請回答問題並寫下您對於我們的網路連線可能遭遇到的問題。151 然後，用隨函的回郵信封將表格寄給我們。

我們保證您的回答將會保密，而且只用於公司的研究用途上。152 為了感謝您願意完成這份問卷，您將享有贏得一台桌上型電腦的機會，幸運得主會在 5 月 25 日公布，並以郵件通知。

我們很期待能收到您的寶貴意見。謝謝。

Magna Link 敬上

單字 gratitude n. 感謝　renew v. 更新　appreciate v. 感謝　questionnaire n. 問卷調查　encounter v. 遇到　envelope n. 信封　confidential a. 祕密的　exclusively ad. 專門地

150 名詞語彙 掌握上下文　　　　　　　　　　　　　　　　　　　　　　　　　解答 (D)

由「您持續的____對我們而言非常重要」的句意看來，所有的選項皆有可能為正確答案。因為無法單就空格所在的文句判斷答案，因此應參考上下文意。前文提到感謝續約網路服務，因此可知道收信人繼續使用發信者的網路服務。所以名詞 (D) patronage（愛用）為正確答案。(A) patience 是「耐心」，(B) success 是「成功」，(C) observation 是「觀察，遵守」的意思。

151 連接副詞 掌握上下文　　　　　　　　　　　　　　　　　　　　　　　　　解答 (A)

空格與逗點在句子最前面的連接副詞位置，因此掌握前文與空格所在文句的意思便可從連接副詞 (A) (B) (C) (D) 中選出正確答案。前文提到請協助問卷調查，後面提到寄回問卷，按時間的順序看來應為 (A) Then（然後）為正確答案。(B) However 是「但是」，(C) Meanwhile 是「期間」，(D) Otherwise 是「否則」的意思，皆與句意不相符。

152 搭配名詞的介系詞用法　　　　　　　　　　　　　　　　　　　　　　　　　解答 (D)

句意應為「為了感謝您願意完成這份問卷，您將享有贏得一台桌上型電腦的機會」，所以 (D) In appreciation of（為感謝～）為正確答案。(A) In charge of 是「負責～」，(B) On behalf of 是「代表～」，(C) By means of 是「以～方式」的意思。

PART 7

Questions 153-154 refer to the following invitation.　　153-154 根據下面邀請函的內容回答問題。

154-AMargaux Mall Invites you to	154-AMargaux 購物商城邀請您參加
153THE SPRING FASHION SHOW	153 春季時裝秀
On Friday, May 6, 6 P.M. to 8 P.M.	5 月 6 日星期五晚上 6 點到 8 點
154-BAt the Margaux Mall Convention Center	154-B 位於 Margaux 購物商城的會議中心
More than thirty designers will showcase their collections at the grandest fashion event of the season	超過三十位設計師將會在本季最盛大的時尚活動中展示他們的作品
154-DSponsored by: The French Fashion Association	154-D 法國時裝協會
and	與
The Closet Channel	Closet 頻道贊助

單字 □showcase v. 展示，公開　　□collection n. 蒐藏，收集品　　□grand a. 盛大的
　　□sponsor v. 贊助

153

What will take place on May 6?	在 5 月 6 日要舉辦甚麼活動？
(A) A yearly mall sale	(A) 年度的商城拍賣活動
(B) A convention for designers	(B) 設計師的會議
(C) A fashion presentation	(C) 時裝發表
(D) A modeling seminar	(D) 舞台走秀研習會

■ 六何原則 What　　　　　　　　　　　　　　　　　　　　　　解答 (C)

這是在問 5 月 6 號要舉辦什麼（What）的六何原則問題。題目關鍵字為 take place on May 6，由 THE SPRING FASHION SHOW On Friday, May 6 可知 5 月 6 號星期五將要舉辦春季時裝秀，因此 (C) A fashion presentation 為正確答案。

換句話說
FASHION SHOW 時裝秀 → A fashion presentation 時裝發表

單字 yearly a. 年度的，每年的

154

What is indicated about the event?	關於這項活動，何者正確？
(A) It will be hosted by a French designer.	(A) 由一個法國設計師負責。
(B) It will be held at a clothing store.	(B) 在一間服飾店舉行。
(C) It will be followed by a celebratory party.	(C) 結束後會有一個慶祝派對。
(D) It will be sponsored by other organizations.	(D) 由其他單位來贊助。

■ Not/True True問題　　　　　　　　　　　　　　　　　　　解答 (D)

這是尋找題目關鍵字 the event 的相關內容，再與選項互相對照的 Not/True 問題。Margaux Mall Invites you to THE SPRING FASHION SHOW 中提到「Margaux 購物商城邀請您參加春季服裝秀」，與 (A) 的敘述不符。At the Margaux Mall Convention Center 表示於 Margaux 購物商城的會議中心舉行，與 (B) 的內容不符。(C) 的內容在文中則未被提及。Sponsored by: The French Fashion Association and The Closet Channel 中提到由法國時裝協會與 Closet 頻道贊助，與 (D) 的敘述相符，因此 (D) It will be sponsored by other organizations. 為正確答案。

單字 host v. 主辦，進行　celebratory a. 慶祝的，紀念的

Questions 155-156 refer to the following letter.

155-156 根據下面信件的內容回答問題。

Red Block Department Store

923 Westland Avenue, New York City, NY

December 1

[155]Dear Shoppers,

Red Block department store will be briefly closed on Monday, December 15, for its annual inventory. This will permit management to update its accounts and arrange its stockrooms.

[156-D]The supermarket and signature boutiques within the shopping center, however, will be open during the day. For more details, please log on to www.redblock.com.

Thank you for your continued support.

Sincerely,

Management

Red Block 百貨公司

紐約州紐約市 Westland 大道 923 號

12 月 1 日

[155] 親愛的顧客：

Red Block 百貨公司因為年度的盤點，會在 12 月 15 日星期一暫時地關閉，如此能讓管理人員校正帳戶，並且安排存貨室。

[156-D] 不過，購物中心裡的超級市場和精品酒店在那一天仍會營業。更多詳情，請上官網 www.redblock.com 查看。

謝謝您持續的支持。

管理部門敬上

單字 □briefly ad. 暫時地　　□inventory n. 庫存調查　　□account n. （會計）帳戶

　　□arrange v. 整理，排列　　□stockroom n. 倉庫，貯藏室

155

Why was the letter written?	為什麼寫這封信？
(A) To promote new products available in the supermarket	(A) 宣傳超級市場裡的新產品
(B) To seek feedback from customers	(B) 尋求顧客的意見
(C) To invite shoppers to an event	(C) 邀請顧客來參加活動
(D) To inform patrons of a temporary closure	(D) 通知顧客暫時歇業

■ 找出主題 寫文章的理由　　　　　　　　　　　　　　　　　　　　　　　解答 (D)

這題是在問寫信的原因，應注意內容的前半部分。Dear Shoppers, Red Block department will be briefly closed on Monday 提到 Red Block 百貨公司會在星期一暫時地關閉，因此 (D) To inform patrons of a temporary closure 為正確答案。

換句話說

Shoppers 購物群眾 → patrons 顧客們　　briefly closed 暫時關閉 → a temporary closure 暫時關閉

單字 promote v. 宣傳　available a. 可得到的，可用的　seek v. 尋找　patron n. 顧客，常客

　　closure n. 歇業，中斷，關閉

156

What is mentioned about the supermarket?	關於超級市場，何者正確？
(A) It plans to clear out its stock.	(A) 計畫要清空存貨
(B) It needs to renovate its facilities.	(B) 需要重新整修
(C) It is being transferred to a new building.	(C) 要搬到一棟新的建築物
(D) It is located in a shopping mall.	(D) 位在購物中心裡面

■ Not/True True問題　　　　　　　　　　　　　　　　　　　　　　　　　解答 (D)

這是尋找與題目關鍵字 the supermarket 有關的內容並與選項相互對照的 Not/True 問題。(A) (B) (C) 在文中均未被提及。由 The supermarket ~ within the shopping center 可得知超級市場位於購物中心的裡面，與 (D) 的敘述一致，因此 (D) It is located in a shopping mall 為正確答案。

換句話說

within the shopping center 購物中心內 → located in a shopping mall 位於購物中心內

單字 clear v. 整理~，清理　renovate v. 整修

Metro Sports Club	Metro 運動俱樂部
188 Longview Road, Hamilton City "Your path to wellness"	Hamilton 市 Longview 路 188 號 「你通往健康的道路」
Conveniently situated near Highway 10 in scenic Hamilton City, Metro Sports Club provides health and wellness programs for people of all ages. We have state-of-the-art facilities and a staff of competent fitness trainers, sports coaches, and professional nutritionists. 157-BWe also offer programs encouraging members to get into the greatest shape of their lives.	都會運動俱樂部位在風景優美的 Hamilton 市，靠近十號公路，地點便利，提供健身課程給各年齡階層的人。我們有頂尖的設備和優秀的健身教練、運動教練及專業的營養師。157-B 我們還提供課程能鼓勵會員得到他們人生中最美好的體態。
Body Shape Up 158-BGet fit the right way with the help of a personal trainer. 158-CBody Shape Up is highly recommended for members who would like to lose weight. Enroll in this program and we will create a workout routine suitable for your needs and body type.	**塑身課程** 158-B 藉由個人健身教練的幫助，以正確方式擁有健美勻稱的體態。158-C 我們極度推薦塑身課程給想要減重的會員，參加這個課程，我們會為你建立一個符合你需求與身體形態的日常訓練課程。
Sports and Fitness Classes Enhance your athletic skills and relieve stress by taking sports and fitness classes. We currently offer badminton and swimming lessons three times a week. 158-AWe also hold aerobics and yoga classes on weekends.	**運動與健身課程** 藉由參加運動與健身課程來加強你的運動技巧並消除壓力，我們目前有羽毛球和游泳課，一週三次，158-A 我們在週末還有有氧和瑜珈課程。
159Present this advertisement at our customer service desk to get 30 percent off one-year memberships. For more information, please contact us at 555-6984. You may also e-mail your inquiries to inq@msc.com.	159 拿這個廣告單到我們的客戶服務櫃台，就可以享有一年會費的七折優惠。更多詳情，請撥打 555-6984 和我們聯絡，你也可以寄電郵到 inq@msc.com 洽詢。

單字　□wellness n. 福祉，健康　　□situate v. 使位於　　　　□scenic a. 風景好的
　　　□state-of-the-art a. 最尖端的　□competent a. 有能力的　□nutritionist n. 營養師
　　　□get into shape phr. 練出健美體態，安排妥當　　　　□enroll v. 註冊
　　　□suitable a. 適合的，適當的，適切的　　　　　　　　□enhance v. 使提升，提高
　　　□athletic a. 運動的，運動比賽的　　　　　　　　　　□relieve v. 消解，舒緩

157

What is mentioned as the goal of the Metro Sports Club? (A) Providing facilities for sporting events (B) Helping people get in shape (C) Increasing public knowledge of physical fitness (D) Getting young people to be more active	都會運動俱樂部的目的為何？ (A) 為體育活動提供設施 (B) 幫助人們得到好身材 (C) 增加大眾對於健身的知識 (D) 讓年輕人更愛動

■ **Not/True** True 問題　　　　　　　　　　　　　　　　　　　　　　　　　　解答 (B)

這是尋找與題目關鍵字 the goal of Metro Sports Club 的相關內容並與選項相互對照的 Not/True 問題。(A) 的內容在文中並未被提及。We ~ offer programs encouraging members to get into the greatest shape of their lives. 中提到提供可以讓會員保持完美身體狀態的課程，與 (B) 的內容相符。因此 (B) Helping people get in shape 為正確答案。(C) 與 (D) 的內容在文中則未被提及。

單字　get in shape phr. 維持體態、體型　physical a. 身體的，肉體的

158

What is NOT a service offered by the club?	這個俱樂部不提供什麼服務？
(A) Aerobics classes	(A) 有氧課程
(B) Sports training	(B) 運動訓練
(C) Weight-loss programs	(C) 減重課程
(D) Tennis lessons	(D) 網球課程

■ **Not/True** Not 問題　　　　　　　　　　　　　　　　　　　　　　　　　　解答 (D)

這是尋找與題目關鍵字 a service offered by the club 有關的內容並與選項相互對照的 Not/True 問題。We also hold aerobics ~ classes 提到有有氧課程，與 (A) 的內容相符。Get fit the right way with the help of a personal trainer. 提到藉由個人健身教練的幫助以擁有健美勻稱的體態，與 (B) 的內容一致。Body Shape Up is highly recommended for members who would like to lose weight. Enroll in this program and we will create a workout routine 中提到「我們極度推薦塑身課程給想要減重的會員，參加這個課程，我們會為你建立一個符合你需求與身體形態的日常訓練課程」，與 (C) 的內容一致。(D) 的內容在文中則未被提及。所以 (D) Tennis lessons 為正確答案。

單字 **weight-loss** n. 減重

159

How can customers receive a membership discount?	顧客如何得到會費的優惠？
(A) By enrolling in a program	(A) 參加課程
(B) By submitting an advertisement	(B) 拿這個廣告單給櫃檯
(C) By calling a number	(C) 打電話
(D) By sending an e-mail	(D) 寄電郵

■ **六何原則** How　　　　　　　　　　　　　　　　　　　　　　　　　　　解答 (B)

這是在問顧客要如何（How）得到會費優惠的六何原則問題。題目關鍵字為 customers receive a membership discount，文中 Present this advertisement at our customer service desk to get 30 percent off one-year memberships. 提及拿這個廣告單到客戶服務櫃台，就可以享有一年會費的七折優惠。，因此 (B) By submitting an advertisement 為正確答案。

換句話說

receive a membership discount 獲得會費優惠 → get 30 percent off ~ memberships 獲會費七折優惠

單字 **submit** v. 繳交

Questions 160-161 refer to the following e-mail.

160-161 根據下面電郵的內容回答問題。

To: Jamal Swift <j.swift@lordmail.com>
From: Vidur Chander <v_chander@hamadamotors.com>

Subject: Car Seat Covers
Date: February 9

Dear Mr. Swift,

I hope you are enjoying the new Hamada Minivan you purchased recently. If you have any problems with the vehicle, please don't hesitate to contact us. In addition, don't forget to bring your van to our automotive center every six months for a free inspection and oil change under the terms of your five-year guarantee.

160I want to apologize for the delayed delivery of the free seat covers that come with the vehicle. I was informed that the seat covers were delivered to your house earlier today. 160Our supplier, Geisler Auto Interiors, was unable to ship them to our showroom on time due to the recent holiday. They also send their apologies to you for the inconvenience.

To compensate for the trouble, 161we hope you will accept the attached coupon issued by Geisler Auto Interiors. Simply print it out and 161present it at any of their businesses anytime within the year to receive two complimentary car mats. As we also have a consignment agreement with Geisler, you may claim the mats here at Hamada Motors.

Once again, I am very sorry for the trouble this has caused you.

Respectfully yours,

Vidur Chander
Sales representative
Hamada Motors

收件人：Jamal Swift <j.swift@lordmail.com>
寄件人：Vidur Chander
　　　　 <v_chander@hamadamotors.com>
主旨：汽車座椅護套
日期：2 月 9 日

親愛的 Swift 先生：

我希望您對您剛買的全新 Hamada Minivan 樂在其中，如果您對汽車有任何問題，請不要客氣與我們聯絡。此外，不要忘了每六個月把您的車開進我們的汽車中心做免費的檢查與換油，這是我們五年保固裡的條款。

160 因為延遲將隨車附贈的免費汽車座椅護套寄送給您，我想要向您道歉，我已經被告知座椅護套在今天稍早已經送到您府上，160 我們的供應商 Geisler 汽車內裝公司因為最近的假期，所以無法如期將護套送到我們的展示中心，他們也為了這些不便向您致歉。

為了補償您的困擾，161 我們希望您能接受附件由 Geisler 汽車內裝公司所提供的兌換券。只要列印出來，在一年內隨時 161 到任何營業據點出示給他們看就可以兌換兩個免費的汽車腳踏墊。因為我們和 Geisler 有寄賣的合約，您也可以到 Hamada 汽車公司這裡來兌換。

再一次，我們很抱歉造成您的困擾。

Vidur Chander 敬上
業務代表
Hamada 汽車公司

單字 □purchase v. 購買
　　 □guarantee n. 保固；v. 保證～
　　 □showroom n. 展示場，陳列室
　　 □compensate for phr. 補償～
　　 □present v. 展示～
　　 □claim v. 索取，要求

□hesitate v. 猶豫
□delay v. 使～延遲；n. 延遲
□due to phr. 因為～
□attach v. 附加
□complimentary a. 免費的

□automotive a. 汽車的
□ship v. 運送
□inconvenience n. 不便
□issue v. 發行
□consignment n. 委託

160

What caused the delay in delivery?	什麼原因造成延遲送貨？
(A) Products needed to be altered.	(A) 產品需要被修改。
(B) A supplier was delayed because of a holiday.	(B) 供應商因假期受到延誤。
(C) Machines were malfunctioning.	(C) 機器故障。
(D) An order was changed.	(D) 訂單更改了。

■ 六何原則 What   解答 (B)

這是在問是什麼（What）原因造成延遲送貨的六何原則問題。題目關鍵字為 the delay in delivery，由 I want to apologize for the delayed delivery of the free seat covers 與 Our supplier ~ was unable to ship them to our showroom on time due to the recent holiday. 可以知道隨車附贈的免費汽車座椅護套，是因為最近的假期，所以無法如期將護套送到展示中心，所以 (B) A supplier was delayed because of a holiday. 為正確答案。

換句話說

unable to ship them ~ on time 無法準時運送 → was delayed 延遲

單字 alter v. 改造，變更，修改   malfunction v. 故障，無法正常運作

161

What is indicated about Geisler Auto Interiors?	關於 Geisler 汽車內裝公司，何者正確？
(A) It is holding a promotional offer.	(A) 正在進行一個優惠方案。
(B) It offers free delivery service.	(B) 提供免費運送服務。
(C) It has more than one branch.	(C) 有不只一家分店。
(D) It provides full refunds.	(D) 提供全額退費。

■ 推論 詳細內容   解答 (C)

這是依題目關鍵字 Geisler Auto Interiors 來進行推論的問題。從 we hope you will accept the attached coupon issued by Geisler Auto Interiors 與 present it at any of their businesses 中提到收到 Geisler Auto Interiors 發的兌換券，向 Geisler Auto Interiors 的任一間分店出示皆可使用，因此可以推論 Geisler Auto Interiors 有一間以上的分店。所以 (C) It has more than one branch. 為正確答案。

單字 promotional a. 促銷的，宣傳的   offer n. 提出的價格；v. 提供   full refund phr. 全額退費

Questions 162-164 refer to the following memo.

162-164 根據下面備忘錄的內容回答問題。

MEMO

TO: Staff
FROM: Margaret Vonnegut, administrative assistant
DATE: January 14
SUBJECT: Employee Benefits

[162]Management has decided to upgrade the medical insurance coverage of all employees. Beginning this year, [163]each permanent employee may declare two family members, who will also be entitled to full medical and hospitalization benefits. Probationary employees, on the other hand, will receive an additional $100 in coverage for two dependents. Details of the new coverage have been posted on the Web board for your convenience.

[164]A representative from Healthpath will come by tomorrow morning at 10 A.M. to gather the information necessary to modify your insurance plans. They will also answer any questions you may have about the new policies. If you are unable to attend, please contact the personnel department so that they can collect the necessary information and forward it to Healthpath. We appreciate your cooperation in this matter.

Thank you.

備忘錄

收件人：全體員工
寄件人：行政助理 Margaret Vonnegut
日期：1 月 14 日
主旨：員工福利

[162] 管理階層已經決定要對所有的員工提高醫療保險的保障。從今年開始，[163] 每位正式員工可以加保兩位家庭成員，他們同樣享有全部的醫療與住院保障。另一方面，尚未成為正職的員工，針對兩位受撫養家屬，則可獲得一百美元的追加理賠，新的保險給付範圍已經在網站上公告以便利各位參考。

[164] 一位 Healthpath 保險公司的代表明天早上十點會過來收集必要的資料以修改你們的保單。他們還會回答你關於新保單上的任何問題。假如你無法出席，請聯絡人事部門，讓他們轉交你的必要資料給 Healthpath 保險公司。我們很感謝你們在這件事情上的合作。

謝謝。

單字
- □administrative a. 行政上的
- □permanent employee phr. 正式職員
- □entitle v. 賦予資格
- □additional a. 追加的
- □come by phr. 順道來訪
- □forward v. 轉交
- □hospitalization n. 住院治療
- □dependent n. 受扶養家屬
- □gather v. 收集，集結
- □coverage n. 保險範圍，保護
- □declare v. 申報
- □probationary a. 實習中的
- □representative n. 職員
- □modify v. 修正

162

Why was the memo written?	為什麼寫這個備忘錄？
(A) To report a salary increase	(A) 報告加薪
(B) To explain the staff policies	(B) 解釋員工政策
(C) To provide a list of job opportunities	(C) 提供工作機會清單
(D) To request family health histories	(D) 要求家族健康史

■ 找出主題 寫文章的理由

解答 (B)

這題是在問寫備忘錄的理由，應注意文章的前半部分。Management has decided to upgrade the medical insurance coverage of all employees. 中提到管理階層已經決定要對所有的員工提高醫療保險的保障，後面並繼續說明員工醫療保險的相關政策，因此 (B) To explain the staff policies 為正確答案。

單字 salary n. 薪水　history n. 經歷，履歷，歷史

163

What are permanent employees entitled to receive?	正式員工可以享有什麼？
(A) Free consultations	(A) 免費諮詢
(B) Lower fees	(B) 較低的費用
(C) Personalized care	(C) 個人化的照護
(D) Extended coverage	(D) 更多的保障

六何原則 What　　　　　　　　　　　　　　　　　　　　　　　　　　　解答 (D)

這是在問正式員工可以享有什麼（What）的六何原則問題。題目關鍵字為 permanent employees entitled to receive，文章中 each permanent employee may declare two family members, who will also be entitled to full medical and hospitalization benefits 中提到每位正式員工可以加保兩位家庭成員，同樣享有全部的醫療與住院福利，因此 (D) Extended coverage 為正確答案。

單字 consultation n. 諮詢，商議　personalize v. 個人化

164

According to the memo, what will happen tomorrow?	根據這個備忘錄，明天會發生什麼事？
(A) All staff will fill out application forms.	(A) 所有的員工都要填寫申請表。
(B) New contracts will go into effect.	(B) 新的合約正式生效。
(C) A visitor will collect information.	(C) 有人來收集資料。
(D) Employment interviews will be conducted.	(D) 舉行招聘面試。

六何原則 What　　　　　　　　　　　　　　　　　　　　　　　　　　　解答 (C)

這是問明天會發生什麼（what）的六何原則問題。與題目關鍵字 tomorrow 有關的句子為 A representative from Healthpath will come by tomorrow morning ~ to gather the information necessary to modify your insurance plans.，當中提到一位 Healthpath 保險公司的代表明天早上十點會過來收集必要的資料以修改保單，因此 (C) A visitor will collect information 為正確答案。

單字 fill out phr. 填表　application n. 申請書，申請　go into effect phr. 發揮效果　conduct v. 實施～，行動

Armstrong Town Council

Armstrong will celebrate the 30th anniversary of its foundation on July 5. The council has arranged for numerous activities to mark this special occasion. As always, volunteers are appreciated. Please contact Carol Rhea at (604) 555-9334 if you would be willing to help out. [165]Citizens are invited to take part in this important moment in the town's history by participating in the following activities:

Schedule of Town Festival Activities		
Time	Activities	Venue
9 A.M.	Opening Ceremony	City Hall Grounds
10 A.M.	[167-C]Town Parade	Starts at the City Hall Grounds
11 A.M.	Inauguration of Wallace Public Library	Wallace Library Lobby
[168]2 P.M.	[167-D]Youth Sports Fest	Hilton Complex
8 P.M.	[167-A]Grand Fireworks Display	Moonlight Bay

Additional Information

Traffic Reminder:

[166]Wilson Boulevard will be shut down to traffic an hour before the town festival activities begin. Motorists are advised to take Morgan Avenue to enter and exit the town. The roadblock will be removed the following day.

[168]Youth Sports Fest Registration:

Children and teenagers are encouraged to join the sports fest. Participants who register at the Community Affairs office will receive a free pass to Wild Water Fun Park.

Wallace Library Membership:

Get a complimentary library membership card when you attend Wallace Public Library's inaugural ceremony. The card gives members free access to the library's books, journals, and media files.

Armstrong 鎮議會

Armstrong 鎮將要在 7 月 5 日慶祝成立三十周年，鎮議會已經安排了多項活動來慶祝這個特別的場合，我們一如往常的徵求志工，如果你願意幫忙，請撥打 (604)555-9334 和 Carol Rhea 聯絡。
[165]鎮民們都受邀參加以下的活動，以參與鎮史上重要的一刻：

鎮慶活動的時間表		
時間	活動	地點
上午九點	開幕典禮	市鎮廳一樓
上午十點	[167-C]市鎮遊行	從市鎮廳出發
上午十一點	Wallace 公共圖書館啟用典禮	Wallace 公共圖書館
[168]下午兩點	[167-D]青少年運動會	Hilton 綜合館
晚上八點	[167-A]煙火秀	Moonlight 海灣

更多資訊

交通提醒：

[166] Wilson 大道將會在鎮慶活動開始前一小時封閉，建議駕駛人走 Morgan 路進出鎮區，路障會在慶典結束隔天移除。

[168]青少年運動會報名：

我們鼓勵兒童與青少年們參加青少年運動會，在社區事務辦公室報名的參加者將會得到免費進入 Wild 親水遊樂公園的門票。

Wallace 圖書館的會員資格：

參加 Wallace 公共圖書館的啟用儀式就可以得到圖書館贈與的會員卡。有了這張卡就可以免費使用圖書館書籍、期刊和媒體檔案。

單字　□council n. 議會　　　　□anniversary n. 紀念日　　□foundation n. 設立
　　　□numerous a. 無數的　　　□mark v. 紀念　　　　　□volunteer n. 志工服務
　　　□take part in phr. 參與～　□venue n. 場所　　　　　□inauguration n. 開幕式，開業
　　　□fest n. 慶典，集會　　　　□firework n. 煙火　　　　□motorist n. 駕駛者
　　　□roadblock n.（道路）路障　□inaugural a. 開幕的，就職的

165

What is the purpose of the notice?	這個告示的目的為何？
(A) To announce the opening of a public building	(A) 宣布一個公共建築物的啟用
(B) To provide a schedule to volunteers	(B) 提供志工一個時間表
(C) To notify the community about some roadwork	(C) 告知社區一些道路工程
(D) To invite townspeople to an event	(D) 邀請鎮民參加一個活動

■ 找出主題 目的 　　　　　　　　　　　　　　　　　　　　　　　　　　　解答 (D)

這是尋找告示目的的問題。Citizens are invited to take part in this important moment in the town's history by participating in the following activities 中提到鎮民們都受邀參加以下的活動，以參與鎮史上重要的一刻，並繼續說明細部的事項，因此 (D) To invite townspeople to an event 為正確答案。

換句話說
Citizens 市民 → townspeople 村民

單字　notify v. 告知　roadwork n. 道路工程

166

What is suggested about Morgan Avenue?	關於 Morgan 路，何者正確？
(A) It is located near Moonlight Bay.	(A) 在 Moonlight Bay 附近。
(B) It will be opened after the festival.	(B) 會在慶典後開放。
(C) It is an alternate route to Armstrong.	(C) 到達 Armstrong 鎮的替代道路。
(D) It has parking for visitors.	(D) 遊客可在此停車。

■ 推論 詳細內容 　　　　　　　　　　　　　　　　　　　　　　　　　　　解答 (C)

這是依題目關鍵字 Morgan Avenue 來進行推論的問題。Wilson Boulevard will be shut down to traffic an hour before the town festival activities begin. Motorists are advised to take Morgan Avenue to enter and exit the town. 中提到 Wilson 大道將會在鎮慶活動開始前一小時封閉，建議駕駛人走 Morgan 路進出鎮區，因此可以推論 Morgan 路是能夠到達鎮區的替代道路，所以 (C) It is an alternate route to Armstrong. 為正確答案。

單字　alternate a. 替代的

167

What is NOT included in the activities?	哪一項沒有包含在活動中？
(A) A fireworks display	(A) 煙火秀
(B) A fundraising event	(B) 募款活動
(C) A celebratory parade	(C) 慶祝遊行
(D) An athletic event	(D) 體育活動

■ Not/True Not 問題 　　　　　　　　　　　　　　　　　　　　　　　　　解答 (B)

這是尋找題目關鍵字 the activities 的相關內容，再與選項互相對照的 Not/True 問題。由 Grand Fireworks Display 可知道有煙火秀，與 (A) 的選項相符。(B) 的內容在文中則未被提及。因此 (B) A fundraising event 為正確答案。Town Parade 提到有遊行活動，與 (C) 的內容相符。Youth Sports Fest 提到會有青少年的體育活動，與 (D) 的內容一致。

換句話說
Sports Fest 運動會 → An athletic event 運動大會

單字　fundraising a. 募款的，籌措資金的

168

What will people who attend the event at 2 P.M. receive?	參加下午兩點活動的名眾會得到什麼？
(A) Customized T-shirts	(A) 特製的汗衫
(B) Free meals from a restaurant	(B) 一家餐廳的免費餐點
(C) Membership cards	(C) 會員卡
(D) Tickets to a water park	(D) 到親水公園的門票

■ 六何原則 What   解答 (D)

這是問參加下午兩點活動的民眾會得到什麼（What）的六何原則問題。與題目關鍵字 people who attend the event at 2 P.M. receive 有關的文句為 2 P.M., Youth Sports Fest，表示兩點會有青少年體育活動，後面 Youth Sports Fest Registration 的 Participants ~ will receive a free pass to Wild Water Fun Park. 提到在社區事務辦公室報名的參加者將會得到免費進入 Wild 親水遊樂公園的門票，因此 (D) Tickets to a water park 為正確答案。

單字 customize v. 客製化　meal n. 餐點

Questions 169-172 refer to the following article.

168-171 根據下面文章的內容回答問題。

Wasorkorf Moves Ahead of Squatrust in Aircraft Industry

[169]Russian plane manufacturer Wasorkorf had a whopping 30 percent increase in sales in October through December, according to company records. The Moscow-based company took 450 orders of airplanes this quarter. [170]It has now replaced their German-based rival Squatrust as the world's top aircraft manufacturer. Production rates also climbed nearly 10 percent to 150 units in the same period.

Wasorkorf president Leticia Ivanov relates the jump in sales to the growing popularity of budget airlines. "The rising number of people traveling around the world on cheaper airlines consequently boosted demand for more aircraft," Ivanov said. Wasorkorf has been the leading supplier of passenger aircraft in Southeast Asia for more than ten years. [171-A/B/C]Among its customers are carriers from Singapore, Malaysia, Indonesia, and the Philippines, which have been gradually expanding their fleets.

"The figure indicates that Wasorkorf and the entire airline industry are gradually bouncing back from the economic downturn," Ivanov said. [172-A]The worldwide recession, which lasted for nearly three years, severely affected the tourism industry and suppressed demand for aircraft.

飛機製造業裡的 Wasorkorf 超越了 Squatrust

[169] 俄國飛機製造商 Wasorkorf 在 10 月到 12 月期間的銷售量，根據公司的紀錄，大幅上升了 30%，這家位在莫斯科的公司在本季接了 450 張飛機訂單。[170]現在已經取代了位在德國的競爭對手 Squatrust，而成為世界第一的飛機製造商，生產率在同期也上升了十個百分點，達到 150 架。

Wasorkorf 的總裁 Leticia Ivanov 把銷售量的大增歸因於廉價航空逐漸受到歡迎，Ivanov 說：「世界上乘坐廉價航空旅行的人增加了，刺激了飛機的需求量。」Wasorkorf 在過去十幾年一直是東南亞客機的主要供應商。[171-A/B/C]他的客戶群包括新加坡、馬來西亞、印尼和菲律賓等地的運輸業者，他們逐漸地擴充他們的飛機。

Ivanov 說：「數據顯示 Wasorkorf 和整個航空業都逐漸從經濟的谷底反彈。」[172-A] 持續將近三年的世界性蕭條嚴重地影響了旅遊業，抑制了飛機的需求量。

單字 □move ahead of phr. 領先～ □manufacturer n.製造業者 □whopping a. 非常巨大的 □based a. 以～為基礎的 □quarter n. 季度 □replace v. 代替，取代 □aircraft n. 航空器 □climb v. 上升 □relate v. 相關 □budget a. 低價的，便宜的 □consequently ad. 結果地 □boost v. 提高，使提升 □leading a. 領先的 □carrier n. 運輸業 □gradually ad. 漸漸地 □fleet n. 飛機 □bounce back from phr. 回復到~ □downturn n. 沉滯 □recession n. 衰退 □last v. 持續，繼續 □severely ad. 嚴重地 □suppress v. 壓制

169

What is the article mainly about?
(A) Travel destinations
(B) Popularity of budget airlines
(C) Increased sales of a company
(D) Marketing strategies

這篇文章主要是關於什麼？
(A) 旅遊地點
(B) 廉價航空的盛行
(C) 一家公司銷售量的增加
(D) 行銷策略

■ 找出主題 主題　　　解答 (C)

這題是在找文章主旨，因此應注意文章的前半部分。Russian plane manufacturer Wasorkorf had a whopping 30 percent increase in sales in October through December 中提到俄國飛機製造商 Wasorkorf 在 10 月到 12 月期間的銷售量上升了 30%，後面並繼續做詳細的說明，因此 (C) Increased sales of a company 為正確答案。

單字 destination n. 目的地　strategy n. 戰略

What is indicated about Squatrust?	關於 Squatrust，何者正確？
(A) It has lowered its fees in response to rising competition.	(A) 為因應增加的競爭而降價。
(B) It is the world's second-largest aircraft manufacturer.	(B) 是目前世界上第二大的飛機製造商。
(C) It is a popular budget airline in Southeast Asia.	(C) 是東南亞一家受歡迎的廉價航空。
(D) It developed a successful advertising campaign.	(D) 發展了一套成功的廣告活動。

■ 推論 詳細內容　　　　　　　　　　　　　　　　　　　　　　　　　　解答 (B)

這是依題目關鍵字 Squatrust 來進行推論的問題。It has now replaced their ~ rival Squatrust as the world's top aircraft manufacturer. 中提到 Wasorkorf 公司現在已經取代了位在德國的競爭對手 Squatrust 成為世界第一的飛機製造商，因此可以推測 Squatrust 公司現在為世界第二大的飛機製造商，因此 (B) It is the world's second-largest aircraft manufacturer. 為正確答案。

單字　in response to phr. 回應～　competition n. 競爭　develop v. 開發

What country does Wasorkorf NOT export aircraft to?	Wasorkorf 沒有將飛機外銷到什麼國家？
(A) Indonesia	(A) 印尼
(B) Malaysia	(B) 馬來西亞
(C) Singapore	(C) 新加坡
(D) Germany	(D) 德國

■ Not/True Not問題　　　　　　　　　　　　　　　　　　　　　　　　解答 (D)

這是找出與題目關鍵字 country ~ export aircraft to 的相關內容，再與選項互相對照的Not/True 問題。Among its customers are carriers from Singapore, Malaysia, Indonesia, and the Philippines 中提到 Wasorkorf 公司的客戶群包括新加坡、馬來西亞、印尼和菲律賓等地的航空業者，與 (A) (B) (C) 的選項相符，(D) 在文中則未被提及。所以 (D) Germany 為正確答案。

單字　export v. 出口

What did the article mention about the global recession?	文章中提到的全球性蕭條，何者正確？
(A) It reduced the number of airplane orders.	(A) 減少了飛機的訂單。
(B) It halted the operations of some airlines.	(B) 部分航空公司停止營運。
(C) It caused air carriers to lower fares.	(C) 導致航運公司降價。
(D) It forced Wasorkorf to merge with another company.	(D) 迫使 Wasorkorf 和別家公司合併。

■ Not/True True問題　　　　　　　　　　　　　　　　　　　　　　　　解答 (A)

這是尋找題目關鍵字 the global recession 的相關內容，再與選項互相對照的 Not/True 問題。The worldwide recession, which lasted for nearly three years ~ suppressed demand for aircraft. 中提到持續將近三年的世界性蕭條嚴重地影響了旅遊業，抑制了飛機的需求量，與 (A) 的敘述相符，因此 (A) It reduced the number of airplane orders. 為正確答案。(B) (C) (D) 的內容在文中則未被提及。

單字　halt v. 使中斷　lower v. 降低　fare n. 費用　merge v. 合併

Questions 173-175 refer to the following information.

173-175 根據下面資訊的內容回答問題。

[173]Experience the Thrill of the Sea by Joining the Chesapeake Yacht Club!

Members of the Chesapeake Yacht Club are entitled to numerous privileges throughout the year, including:

* [174-A]Use of all docks and mooring facilities (for those with their own boats)

* [175-A]15 percent off on all items in our sail shop and clubhouse gift shop

* [175-D]Use of clubhouse facilities including showers, changing rooms, lounge, bar, and restaurant

* [175-C]Invitations to all CYC functions, including the Annual Grand Gala

Those registering for membership before April 1 will also receive free Chesapeake Yacht Club polo shirts!

Drop by the administrative office to pick up your registration form. If you would like further information on club fees, please feel free to call Mitzi Van Boer at 555-3030.

---

[173] 加入 Chesapeake 快艇俱樂部體驗海的刺激！

Chesapeake 快艇俱樂部的會員整年能享有多項特別待遇，包括：

*[174-A] 使用所有的船塢和泊船設施（針對有自己船隻的人）

*[175-A] 我們航行商店和俱樂部禮品店所有商品皆八五折

*[175-D] 使用俱樂部設施包括淋浴間、換衣室、休閒室、酒吧和餐廳

*[175-C] 邀請參加所有 Chesapeake 快艇俱樂部的活動，包括年度的盛宴

在 4 月 1 日前加入會員還會得到 Chesapeake 快艇俱樂部的 polo 衫！

來我們的行政辦公室拿會員申請表，如果你想要關於俱樂部費用進一步的資料，請撥打 555-3030 和 Mitzi Van Boer 聯絡。

單字 □thrill n. 顫動，引起激動的事　□privilege n. 特權　□dock n. 碼頭；v. 停靠碼頭
　　 □mooring n. 停泊　□sail n. 航海　□changing room phr. 更衣室
　　 □function n. 集會活動　□gala n. 節慶，慶典　□polo shirt phr. polo 衫
　　 □drop by phr. 順道去～

173

Why was the information written?	為什麼寫這份資訊？
(A) To publicize the building of a new facility	(A) 宣傳一個新設施大樓
(B) To give directions to a tourist area	(B) 提供到一觀光區的路線
(C) To provide details about a sporting event	(C) 提供一個運動活動的詳細資料
(D) To encourage people to apply for membership	(D) 鼓勵人們申請會員

■ 找出主題 寫文章的理由　　　　　　　　　　　　　　　　　　　　　　　　　　解答 (D)

這是尋找寫此篇文章理由的問題，應注意文章的前半部分。Experience the Thrill of the Sea by Joining the Chesapeake Yacht Club! 中提到加入 Chesapeake 快艇俱樂部體驗海的刺激，後面並介紹會員可享有的優惠，因此 (D) To encourage people to apply for membership 為正確答案。

單字 publicize v. 宣傳　give directions to phr. 告知～的路線

174

What is true about the Chesapeake Yacht Club?	關於 Chesapeake 快艇俱樂部，何者正確？
(A) It provides docking areas for members.	(A) 提供停靠區域給會員。
(B) It has a high number of applicants.	(B) 有很多的申請者。
(C) It has an online registration form.	(C) 有線上申請表。
(D) It is only open during the summer.	(D) 只有在夏季才開放。

■ Not/True True問題　　　　　　　　　　　　　　　　　　　　　　　　　　　解答 (A)

這是尋找題目關鍵字 Chesapeake Yacht Club 的相關內容，再與選項互相對照的 Not/True 問題。Use of all docks and mooring facilities 中提到可使用所有的船塢和泊船設施，與 (A) 的內容相符，因此 (A) It provides docking areas for members. 為正確答案。(B) (C) (D) 的內容在文中則未被提及。

單字 applicant n. 申請者

What is NOT mentioned as a benefit for members?	哪一項不是會員的福利？
(A) Lower prices on retail items	(A) 零售商品的優惠價
(B) Complimentary meals at a restaurant	(B) 餐廳裡免費的餐點
(C) Invitations to the Grand Gala	(C) 邀請參加盛宴
(D) Access to clubhouse showers	(D) 使用俱樂部的淋浴間

Not/True Not問題　　解答 (B)

這是尋找題目關鍵字 a benefit for members 的相關內容，再與選項互相對照的 Not/True 問題。15 percent off on all items in our sail shop and clubhouse gift shop 中提到在航行商店和俱樂部禮品店所有商品皆有八五折優惠，與 (A) 的敘述相符，(B) 的內容在文中則未被提及，因此 (B) Complimentary meals at a restaurant 為正確答案。Invitations to all CYC functions, including the Annual Grand Gala 中提到邀請會員參加所有 Chesapeake 快艇俱樂部的活動，包括年度的盛宴，與 (C) 相符，Use of clubhouse facilities including showers 中提到使用包括淋浴間的俱樂部設施，與 (D) 的敘述相符。

單字 complimentary a. 免費的　access n. 進入、使用的權利

August 25

Dwight Simmons
General Manager
Victoria Cruise Line

Dear Mr. Simmons,

I want you to know that I had a wonderful time during a recent Southeast Asian cruise. I was greatly impressed by Victoria Cruise Line's accommodating and caring staff. In particular, [176]I can never forget Andrew Hudson, one of your tour guides, who helped me locate my purse when I lost it on the second day of the trip.

After a late afternoon stroll on the ship, I went to Flavors Bistro for dinner. As I was about to leave, I noticed that my purse was missing. I searched the table where I was seated, the restaurant, and other places I had gone, to no avail. Mr. Hudson saw me looking for something, so he came up to me and offered his assistance. [178-A/D]He talked to waiters and asked some people from housekeeping if they had seen my purse. [178-B]He also accompanied me to the security department to report my problem. The purse was not found that night, but Mr. Hudson called me in my room the next day to say that [179]a housekeeper had retrieved my purse inside one of the ship's restrooms.

If not for Mr. Hudson's persistence, I think I would never have recovered my purse. He is really an asset to your company. I hope you will appreciate his dedication to his job and reward him accordingly. It is because of employees and service like this that [177]I have often used your cruise line, and will continue to do so. Thank you.

Respectfully yours,

Candymae Suarez

8 月 25 日

Dwight Simmons
總經理
Victoria 郵輪

親愛的 Simmons 先生：

我想要讓你知道我在最近參加的東南亞郵輪之旅玩得很愉快，對於 Victoria 郵輪的親切而體貼的員工，我真的印象深刻，[176] 我特別無法忘記其中的一位導遊 Andrew Hudson，他幫我找到我在旅程第二天遺失的皮包。

有一個傍晚我在船上散步後，我去 Flavors Bistro 吃晚餐，當我要離開時，我發現我的皮包不見了，我在我坐的位置、餐廳，還有我去過的地方尋找，一無所獲，Hudson 先生看到我在找東西，他走上前來幫助我，[178-A/D] 他問服務生，也問一些打掃的人員是否看到我的皮包。[178-B] 他還陪我到保全單位去通報我的問題。那天晚上我的皮包並沒有找到，但是隔一天 Hudson 先生打電話到我的房間說 [179] 有一個打掃人員在船上的一間廁所裡找到我的皮包。

如果不是 Hudson 先生的堅持，我想我不會找到我的皮包，他真是你們公司寶貴的資產，我希望你們能珍視他對工作的盡心盡力，並且給予獎勵，因為有這樣的員工及服務，[177] 我才會經常搭乘你們的郵輪，之後也會繼續搭乘。感謝你們。

Candymae Suarez 敬上

單字 □accommodating a. 親切的　□impressed a. 印象深刻的　□caring a. 關心的
□in particular phr. 特別　□locate v. 找出　□purse n. 錢包
□stroll n. 散步　□to no avail phr. 徒勞地　□assistance n. 幫助
□housekeeping n. 飯店的清潔服務　□accompany v. 同行　□security n. 保安，警備
□retrieve v. 重新得到，收回　□persistence n. 堅持　□recover v. 恢復
□asset n. 資產　□dedication n. 奉獻　□accordingly ad. 照著，相應地

Why was the letter written?	為什麼寫這封信？
(A) To book a travel package	(A) 預定一個旅遊行程
(B) To discuss a security problem	(B) 討論一個安全問題
(C) To acknowledge a crew member	(C) 答謝一位船上的員工
(D) To report a complaint about housekeeping	(D) 對打掃清潔工作提出抱怨

■ **找出主題** 寫文章的理由　　　　　　　　　　　　　　　　　　　　　解答 (C)

這題是要找出寫信的目的，應注意文章的前半部分。I can never forget Andrew Hudson, one of your tour guides, who helped me locate my purse 中提到不會忘記幫忙找到皮包的導遊 Andrew Hudson，後面並詳細說明並表達感謝之意，因此 (C) To acknowledge a crew member 為正確答案。

單字 book v. 預約　acknowledge v. 表示感激

What is indicated about Ms. Suarez?	關於 Suarez 女士，何者正確？
(A) She would like compensation for her lost item.	(A) 她想要對她遺失的東西求償。
(B) She travels frequently on business trips.	(B) 她常常出差。
(C) She was not satisfied with the housekeeping staff.	(C) 她對清潔人員不滿意。
(D) She has been on trips with Victoria Cruise Line before.	(D) 她曾經搭過 Victoria 郵輪。

■ **推論** 詳細內容　　　　　　　　　　　　　　　　　　　　　　　　　解答 (D)

這是尋找題目關鍵字 Ms. Suarez 的相關內容來進行推論的問題，由 I have often used your cruise line 可以知道寫信的 Ms. Suarez 經常搭乘 Victoria Cruise Line 的郵輪，因此可以判斷她之前曾經搭過 Victoria Cruise Line，所以 (D) She has been on trips with Victoria Cruise Line before. 為正確答案。

單字 compensation n. 補償　frequently ad. 經常　be satisfied with phr. 滿足於～

What is NOT a measure that Mr. Hudson took to help retrieve Ms. Suarez's property?	哪一項不是 Hudson 先生幫助 Suarez 女士找到財物的方法？
(A) Contacting housekeepers	(A) 聯繫打掃人員
(B) Notifying the security department	(B) 通知保全單位
(C) Searching restrooms	(C) 到洗手間尋找
(D) Asking waiters	(D) 詢問服務生

■ **Not/True** Not問題　　　　　　　　　　　　　　　　　　　　　　　解答 (C)

這是尋找與題目關鍵字 a measure that Mr. Hudson took 相關的內容並與選項相互對照的 Not/True 問題。He ~ asked some people from housekeeping if they had seen my purse. 中提到 Mr. Hudson 中問了一些打掃的人員是否看到皮包，與 (A) 的內容一致。He also accompanied me to the security department to report my problem. 提到他還陪同 Ms. Suarez 到保全單位去通報，與 (B) 的敘述相符。(C) 的內容在文中則未被提及。因此 (C) Searching restrooms 為正確答案。He talked to waiters 提到 Mr. Hudson 曾與服務生交談，與 (D) 的敘述一致。

單字 measure n. 方式　property n. 所有物，財產　notify v. 告知，通知　restroom n. 化妝室

179

Who found Ms. Suarez's property?	誰找到 Suarez 女士的東西？
(A) A waiter from a restaurant	(A) 餐廳的服務生
(B) A security guard	(B) 警衛
(C) A member of the housekeeping	(C) 打掃人員
(D) A ship engineer	(D) 郵輪工程師

■ 六何原則 Who   解答 (C)

這是問誰（Who）找到 Suarez 女士的東西的六何原則問題。與題目關鍵字 found Ms. Suarez's property 相關的文句為 a housekeeper had retrieved my purse inside one of the ship's restrooms，當中提到一位打掃人員在化妝室中發現皮包，因此 (C) A member of the housekeeping 為正確答案。

180

The word "accommodating" in paragraph 1, line 2 is closest in meaning to	在第一段第二行的「accommodating」，最接近哪一個字的意思？
(A) comfortable	(A) 舒服的
(B) customary	(B) 慣常的
(C) memorable	(C) 令人難忘的
(D) hospitable	(D) 招待周到的

■ 同義詞   解答 (D)

提到 accommodating 的文句為 I was greatly impressed by Victoria Cruise Line's accommodating and caring staff.，其中的 accommodating 為親切的意思，因此同義的 (D) hospitable 為正確答案。

例文1

To: Leonard Ellis <l_ellis@soulfultravels.com>

From: Donna Hayes <donna369@pathosmail.com>

Date: February 9
Subject: Egyptian Odyssey

Dear Mr. Ellis,

I looked over the brochure you sent me last week, and I must say that I was quite impressed with the wide variety of tour packages that your travel agency offers.

182-DI became particularly interested in the Red Sea Escape, but since 182-Aone of my traveling companions has already been to the Red Sea, 181I opted for the Egyptian Odyssey, instead. However, when I looked it up on your Web site to find out more, 181I became somewhat confused since your Web site contains information that is different from what is in the brochure. 184The online advertisements stated that the visit to the Valley of the Kings and the Hatshepsut Temple takes place on the third day of the tour, not on the fifth day, as was indicated in your brochure. 181Can you let me know which is correct? 182-CThe schedule will influence whether or not my friends and I will book the tour.

Meanwhile, 183I would greatly appreciate it if you could provide me with a quotation for the Egyptian Odyssey tour for six people by tomorrow afternoon. Since we are planning to travel early next month, we would like to get all of the arrangements sorted out as soon as possible. Furthermore, I would also like to ask what the weather will be like in that area around the time of our trip. We would like to make sure to bring the right kind of clothing.

Thank you, and I hope to hear from you soon.

Donna Hayes

收件人：Leonard Ellis
　　　　<l_ellis@soulfultravels.com>
寄件人：Donna Hayes
　　　　<donna369@pathosmail.com>
日期：2 月 9 日
主旨：埃及的奧德賽

親愛的 Ellis 先生：

我看了你上週寄給我的小冊子，我必須說，我對於你們旅行社提供的多樣化旅遊行程相當印象深刻。

182-D 我特別對於 「脫出紅海」 有興趣，不過 182-A 我的一個旅遊夥伴已經去過紅海，181 我換成了 「埃及的奧賽德」。然而，當我想在你們網站上找更多的資料，181 你們網站上的資料和小冊子裡的資料有出入，令我有些困惑。184 線上的廣告說第三天的行程是參觀帝王谷和哈塞普蘇女王葬祭殿，而不是小冊子上寫的第五天，181 你能讓我知道哪一個是正確的嗎？182-C 這個行程會影響我和我的朋友是否能訂下這個旅遊。

同時，183 我很感謝你能在明天下午前提供我埃及的奧德賽行程六人團的報價，因為我們計畫在下個月初去旅行，我們希望一切都能盡早安排妥當，此外，我還想要問當地在這個時間的氣候如何，我們想要確保帶合適的衣物去。

謝謝你，希望很快得到你的回音。

Donna Hayes

例文2

To: Donna Hayes <donna369@pathosmail.com>

From: Leonard Ellis <l_ellis@soulfultravels.com>

Date: February 10
Subject: Re: Egyptian Odyssey

Dear Ms. Hayes,

184The tour schedules on the brochure are correct. The other schedules you saw were the result of an error made by our marketing staff. We sincerely apologize for the discrepancy.

I have prepared a quotation for six people for the tour you requested, but a network problem has been preventing

---

收件人：Donna Hayes
　　　　<donna369@pathosmail.com>
寄件人：Leonard Ellis
　　　　<l_ellis@soulfultravels.com>
日期：2 月 10 日
主旨：回覆：埃及的奧德賽

親愛的 Hayes 小姐，

184 在小冊子上的行程時間表是正確的，你看到的另一個時間表是我們行銷人員誤植的結果，我們誠摯地為這個矛盾致歉。

應你的要求，我已經備妥六人團的報價，但是由於網路的問題，讓我無法將

me from attaching the file to this e-mail. If you are able to read this by noon today, ¹⁸²⁻ᴮplease reply with your fax number. That way, I can send you the file this afternoon, as you asked. You can also just call me directly at 555-9617.

As for your other concerns, ¹⁸⁵you could not have picked a better time to travel to Egypt as the weather is quite ideal for sightseeing. Bringing along some cool, light clothing should suffice, unless you plan to dine out at one of the city's finer restaurants. For that purpose, one set of smart casual clothing will do.

Thank you.

Sincerely,
Leonard Ellis

檔案附加在這封電郵裡，如果你在今天中午前看到這封信，¹⁸²⁻ᴮ 請回覆給我你的傳真號碼，如此一來，我便能如你要求的在今天下午把檔案寄給你，你也可以直接打 555-9617 給我。

至於你其他的問題，¹⁸⁵ 你挑選到埃及的時間是最好的，因為現在的天氣非常適合觀光賞景，帶一些涼爽輕便的衣物應該就足夠了，除非你打算在城裡比較好的餐廳用餐，為了這個目的，帶一套半正式的衣服就足夠了。

謝謝你。

Leonard Ellis 敬上

例文 1 單字 □particularly ad. 特別，尤其　□companion n. 同伴，朋友　□opt for phr. 選擇～
□look up phr. 尋找～　□somewhat ad. 稍微　□confused a. 混亂的，困惑的
□temple n. 寺廟　□take place phr. 舉辦　□appreciate v. 感謝
□quotation n. 報價　□sort out phr. 解決

例文 2 單字 □sincerely ad. 真心地　□apologize v. 道歉　□discrepancy n. 不一致，錯誤
□request v. 要求　□directly ad. 直接地　□sightseeing n. 觀光
□suffice v. 充分　□dine out phr. 外出用餐

181

What is the purpose of the first e-mail?	第一封電郵的目的為何？
(A) To change a flight schedule	(A) 要改變飛機時間
(B) To request a new brochure	(B) 要求新的旅遊小冊
(C) To ask about a tour package	(C) 詢問一個旅遊行程
(D) To cancel travel plans	(D) 取消旅遊計畫

■ 找出主題 目的　　　　解答 (C)

題目是在問第一封電郵的目的，因此應先看第一篇的內容，尤其要注意文章中後段有提及主旨的部分。I opted for the Egyptian Odyssey 與 I became somewhat confused since your Web site contains information that is different from what is in the brochure 提到選了一個網站資料和小冊子裡的資料有出入的行程，所以感到困惑，接著並說 Can you let me know which is correct?，應是在問哪一項資訊是正確的，所以 (C) To ask about a tour package 為正確答案。

182

What is NOT indicated about Ms. Hayes?	關於 Hayes 女士，何者不正確？
(A) She is traveling with a group.	(A) 她和一個團體一起旅行。
(B) She will contact Mr. Ellis again.	(B) 她會和 Ellis 先生再次聯絡。
(C) She has not set a firm travel date.	(C) 她還沒有確定旅遊日期。
(D) She has been to the Red Sea before.	(D) 她曾經到過紅海。

■ Not/True Not問題　　　　解答 (D)

這是尋找題目關鍵字 Ms. Hayes 的相關內容，再與選項互相對照的 Not/True 問題。兩封信都有提到 Ms. Hayes，因此兩篇的內容都要注意。第一篇提到 one of my traveling companions has already been to the Red Sea，即「我的一個旅遊夥伴已經去過紅海」，可以知道她和一個團體一起旅行，與 (A) 的敘述一致。第二封信的 please reply with your fax number. That way, I can send you the file this afternoon 提到「請回覆給我你的傳真號碼，如此一來，我能在今天下午把檔案寄給你」，由此可知 Ms. Hayes 會再次與 Mr. Ellis 聯絡，與 (B) 的內容一致。第一封信的 The schedule will influence whether or not ~ I will book the tour. 提到這

個行程會影響她和她的朋友是否能訂下這個旅遊，因此可知她尚未決定旅遊日期，與 (C) 的敘述相符。第一封信的 I became particularly interested in the Red Sea Escape, but since one of my traveling companions has already been to the Red Sea, I opted for the Egyptian Odyssey, instead. 提到「我的一個旅遊夥伴已經去過紅海，因此我想選擇『埃及的奧賽德』來取代之」，可以知道 Ms. Hayes 沒有去過紅海，與 (D) 選項的敘述不符，所以 (D) She has been to the Red Sea before. 為正確答案。

單字 firm a. 確實的，堅固的

183

What does Ms. Hayes request?		Hayes 小姐要求甚麼？	
(A) A price quote	(B) A gift certificate	(A) 報價	(B) 禮券
(C) A calendar of events	(D) A reservation form	(C) 活動的行事曆	(D) 預約單

■ 六何原則 What　　　　　　　　　　　　　　　　　　　　　　　　　　　解答 (A)

這是在問 Ms. Hayes 要求什麼（What）的六何原則問題。因此應看第一封由 Ms. Hayes 所寫的信件，並確認與 request 有關的內容。I would greatly appreciate it if you could provide me with a quotation for the Egyptian Odyssey tour for six people 中提到「如果你能在明天下午前提供我埃及的奧德賽行程六人團的報價我會很感謝」，因此 (A) A price quote 為正確答案。

單字 quote n. 報價單　gift certificate phr. 商品禮券

184

On which day of the tour does the visit to the Valley of the Kings take place?		在哪一天會去帝王谷參觀？	
(A) On the second day	(B) On the third day	(A) 第二天	(B) 第三天
(C) On the fourth day	(D) On the fifth day	(C) 第四天	(D) 第五天

■ 六何原則 聯結問題　　　　　　　　　　　　　　　　　　　　　　　　　解答 (D)

這是在問哪一天（On which day）會去帝王谷參觀的六何原則問題，題目關鍵字 the visit to the Valley of the Kings 牽涉到兩篇文章，所以也是要參考兩篇文章內容才能解決的聯結問題。

先看有第一封信有提到帝王谷的部分。第一封信的 The online advertisements stated that the visit to the Valley of the Kings ~ takes place on the third day of the tour, not on the fifth day, as was indicated in your brochure. 提到線上的廣告說第三天的行程是參觀帝王谷和哈塞普蘇女王葬祭殿，而不是小冊子上寫的第五天，因為無法確認是兩天中的哪一天，因此要看第二封信。第二封信的 The tour schedules on the brochure are correct. 提到在小冊子上的內容是正確的，因此綜合這兩點可以知道 (D) On the fifth day 為正確答案。

185

What does Mr. Ellis recommend Ms. Hayes do?	Ellis 先生建議 Hayes 小姐做什麼？
(A) Reserve flight tickets by this afternoon	(A) 在今天下午預訂機票
(B) Dress appropriately for warm weather	(B) 在溫暖的天氣穿著適當的衣物
(C) Book a table at a fine dining restaurant	(C) 在一家好的餐廳訂位
(D) Pack a light suitcase for her trip	(D) 為旅行準備一個輕便的行李箱

■ 六何原則 What　　　　　　　　　　　　　　　　　　　　　　　　　　　解答 (B)

這題是問 Mr. Ellis 建議 Ms. Hayes 做什麼（What）的六何原則問題。因此應看第二篇由 Mr. Ellis 所寫的信，其中提到題目關鍵字 recommend 的相關內容。第二篇電子郵件的 you could not have picked a better time ~ as the weather is quite ideal for sightseeing. Bringing along some cool, light, clothing should suffice 提到「你挑選到埃及的時間是最好的，因為現在的天氣非常適合觀光賞景，帶一些涼爽輕便的衣物應該就足夠了」，所以 (B) Dress appropriately for warm weather 為正確答案。

單字 reserve v. 預約　appropriately ad. 適合地　suitcase n. 行李箱

Questions 186-190 refer to the following Web page and form.

186-190 根據下面網頁和表格的內容回答問題。

例文1

WALDORF SCHOOL FOR CULINARY ARTS

| Home | About Us | Courses | News and Events | FAQ |

SPECIAL COURSES

Would you like to have a fun and productive summer? Then join us and learn how to cook new dishes. [188-A]Enroll in any of our weekend classes and become an expert in Asian cuisine!

It's A Thai!
July 14 – September 1
Wisit Chadhury
Discover what makes Thai dishes special through a series of informative lectures and hands-on cooking demonstrations conducted by [186]renowned Bangkok Diner owner, Wisit Chadhury. Learn how to mix sour, sweet, salty, and spicy ingredients to make amazing Thai dishes!

[188-B]**A Taste of Japan**
July 22 – August 26
Yukio Kakutani
Ever wondered how sushi, sashimi, udon, donburi, and other traditional Japanese foods are prepared? [188-C/D] Award-winning chef Yukio Kakutani will not only teach you how to make delectable dishes, but also introduce you to some regional specialties not often served in local Japanese restaurants.

[188-B]**A Weekend in India**
August 11 – August 12
Amir Muhammad
Take a gastronomic journey to one of Asia's most culturally diverse countries. Amir Muhammad leads an intensive two-day course exploring the flavorful vegetarian dishes of India, such as biryani and malai kofta.

[190]**Viva Vietnam!**
August 18 – September 8
Anh Poc Long
Known for its use of fresh and scrumptious ingredients, Vietnamese cuisine is relatively unknown on this side of the planet. Let Chef Anh Poc Long guide you through the diverse culinary tradition of Vietnam, from making simple meals like dumplings, pancakes, and soups to cooking mouth-watering seafood, meat, and curry dishes.

[187]Interested applicants may download the form below. Just be sure to e-mail it to us at info@waldorfschool.com no later than one week before the start of the selected course. All courses are limited to 20 participants.

Application form

Waldorf 烹飪藝術學校

| 首頁 | 關於我們 | 課程 | 最新消息與活動 | 常見問題 |

特別課程
你想要有一個有趣而豐收的夏天嗎?加入我們來學習如何做新的菜餚,[188-A] 參加我們任何一個週末的課程,成為亞洲美食的專家。

就是泰國菜!
7 月 14 日～ 9 月 1 日
Wisit Chadhury
透過一系列由 [186] 著名的曼谷餐廳老闆 Wisit Chadhury 教授內容充實的講課和親自烹飪的示範,探索是什麼讓泰式料理如此特別。學習如何混合酸、甜、鹹、辣和香料,做出令人驚豔的泰式料理。

[188-B] **日本的風味**
7 月 22 日～ 8 月 26 日
Yukio Kakutani
想知道壽司、生魚片、烏龍麵、蓋飯和其他傳統日式料理是如何做出來的嗎?[188-C/D] 得獎主廚 Yukio Kakutani 不僅會教你如何做美味的料理,還會介紹一些不常在日本餐廳吃到的地區性料理。

[188-B] **在印度的週末**
8 月 11 日～ 8 月 12 日
Amir Muhammad
來一趟亞州最多元文化的國家的美食之旅,Amir Muhammad 帶領一個緊湊的兩天課程,來探索印度美味的素食料理,例如 biryani 和 malai kofta。

[190] **歡樂越南!**
8 月 18 日～ 9 月 8 日
Anh Poc Long
以採用新鮮絕妙食材著稱,越南料理在地球的這一端是相對不為人知的,讓主廚 Anh Poc Long 指導你走進越南多元烹調的傳統,從餃子、煎餅和湯餚等簡單的餐點到海鮮、肉類和咖哩等令人垂涎的佳餚。

[187] 有興趣的報名者可以下載下面的表格,只要在所選課程開課前一週用電郵寄到 info@waldorfschool.com 給我們。所有課程僅限二十名學員。

報名表

例文2

WALDORF SCHOOL FOR CULINARY ARTS	Waldorf 烹飪藝術學校
Where cooking is a journey!	在這裡烹飪就是旅行
944 Fairfield Road, West Alley, AZ 58709	58709 亞利桑那州 West Alley 市
www.waldorfculinary.com	Fairfield 路 944 號
	www.waldorfculinary.com

Name: CATHERINE PEÑAFLOR	Age: 22	Sex: Female
Address: 122 Riverside Village, Tucson, AZ 58705		
Tel. No.: 555-0099	E-mail Address: c_pena@ion.com	
190Course: Viva Vietnam!		
Payment Details:		
X Cash	Check	Credit Card
Card Name:	Card No.:	Expiry:
Total amount: $120	Signature: *C. Peñaflor*	
189-DDo you have any food allergies?		
Yes, I am allergic to most types of nuts (peanuts, almonds, walnuts...)		
Would you like to subscribe to our mailing list? Sure.		
For inquiries, please call 555-6356 and ask for Janet LeBlanc.		

姓名： CATHERINE PEÑAFLOR	年齡： 22	性別：女
地址：58705 亞利桑那州 Tucson 市 河畔村 122 號		
電話號碼： 555-0099	電子郵件： c_pena@ion.com	
190 課程：歡樂越南！		
付款細節：		
X 現金	支票	信用卡
卡名：	卡號：	到期日：
總金額：美金 120元	簽名：*C. Peñaflor*	
189-D 你對任何食物過敏嗎？		
有，我對大部分的堅果過敏（花生、杏仁、核桃…..）		
你想要加入我們的郵件名單嗎？ 好的		
欲洽詢，請撥打 555-6356 找 Janet LeBlanc		

例文 1 單字 □culinary a. 料理的　□enroll v. 註冊　□expert n. 專家
□discover v. 發現，知道　□hands-on a. 親手的　□demonstration n. 示範，示例
□conduct v. 進行，執行　□renowned a. 有名的　□ingredient n. 材料
□delectable a. 好吃的，令人愉快的　□gastronomic a. 烹飪學的，美食的
□diverse a. 多樣的　□intensive a. 集中的　□explore v. 探險，探究
□flavorful a. 有風味的　□scrumptious a. 非常好吃的，心情好的
□cuisine n. 料理，料理方法　□relatively ad. 相對地　□mouth-watering a. 令人垂涎的

例文 2 單字 □check n. 支票　□allergic a. 有過敏的　□subscribe v. 訂閱

186

Which lecturer owns a dining establishment?	哪一個講師是餐廳老闆？
(A) Wisit Chadhury	(A) Wisit Chadhury
(B) Yukio Kakutani	(B) Yukio Kakutani
(C) Amir Muhammad	(C) Amir Muhammad
(D) Anh Poc Long	(D) Anh Poc Long

■ 六何原則 Which　　　　　　　　　　　　　　　　　　　　　　　　解答 (A)

這題是在問哪一位（Which）講師是餐廳老闆的六何原則問題。應注意提及關鍵字 lecturer owns a dining establishment 的第一篇文章。文中提到 renowned Bangkok Diner owner, Wisit Chadhury，即 Wisit Chadhury 是知名 Bangkok Diner 的所有者，因此 (A) Wisit Chadhury 為正確答案。

單字 establishment n. 設施，設立

187

According to the Web page, how can applicants sign up for a class? (A) By making a telephone call (B) By dropping by the head office (C) By e-mailing a document (D) By sending a fax message	根據網頁，報名者如何報名課程？ (A) 打電話 (B) 到總部辦公室 (C) 用電子郵件寄送文件 (D) 傳送傳真

■ 六何原則 How　　　　　　　　　　　　　　　　　　　　　　　　　　　　　　解答 (C)

這題是問根據網頁，報名者如何（how）報名課程的六何原則問題。因此應看第一篇的相關內容。Interested applicants may download the form below. Just be sure to e-mail it to us ~ no later than one week before the start of the selected course. 中提到有興趣的報名者可以下載以下的表格，只要在所選課程開課前一週用電郵寄到 info@waldorfschool.com 即可，因此 (C) By e-mailing a document 為正確答案。

188

What is NOT mentioned about A Taste of Japan? (A) It will be conducted on weekends. (B) It is the shortest program at the learning center. (C) It includes lessons in cooking rare dishes. (D) It is facilitated by a prizewinning instructor.	關於日本風味，何者不正確？ (A) 在週末上課。 (B) 是學習中心裡最短的課程。 (C) 介紹不常見的料理。 (D) 由得獎的講師上課。

■ Not/True Not問題　　　　　　　　　　　　　　　　　　　　　　　　　　　　解答 (B)

這題是尋找與題目關鍵字 A Taste of Japan 有關的內容再與選項相互對照的 Not/True 問題，因此應從第一篇提到日本風味的內容確認。Enroll in any of our weekend classes 提到參加任何週末的課程，與 (A) 的敘述一致。A Taste of Japan: July 22 – August 26 與 A weekend in India: August 11 – August 12 可以知道「在印度的週末」比「日本風味」的課程內容還短，與 (B) 的內容不符，因此 (B) It is the shortest program at the learning center. 為正確答案。Award-winning chef Yukio Kakutani will ~ introduce you some regional specialties not often served in local Japanese restaurants. 中提到得獎主廚 Yukio Kakutani 不僅會教如何做美味的料理，還會介紹一些不常在日本餐廳吃到的地區性料理，和 (C) 與 (D) 的敘述相符。

單字 facilitate v. 進行，使～容易進行

189

What is true about the Waldorf School for Culinary Arts? (A) It accepts students of all ages. (B) It has recently updated its Web site. (C) It has several openings for instructors. (D) It requires information about food allergens.	關於 Waldorf 烹飪藝術學校，何者為真？ (A) 接受各年齡層的學生。 (B) 最近更新了網站。 (C) 有好幾個講師的職缺。 (D) 要求提供食物過敏源的資訊。

■ Not/True True問題　　　　　　　　　　　　　　　　　　　　　　　　　　　　解答 (D)

這是尋找題目關鍵字 the Waldorf School for Culinary Arts 的相關內容再與各選項對照的 Not/True 問題，應注意有提到 Waldorf 烹飪藝術學校的部分。(A) (B) (C) 的內容在文中並未提到。表格中的 Do you have any food allergies? 詢問是否對食物有過敏，可以推測 Waldorf 烹飪藝術學校要求提供食物過敏的資訊，因此 (D) It requires information about food allergens. 為正確答案。

單字 accept v. 接受　opening n. 開放　allergen n. 過敏源

What is indicated about Ms. Peñaflor?	關於 Peñaflor 小姐，何者正確？
(A) She missed the first few sessions of her preferred course.	(A) 她錯過了她想要上的課程的前幾堂課。
(B) She joined a class that is scheduled to last until September.	(B) 她上的課要上到 9 月。
(C) She has prior experience in preparing Vietnamese food.	(C) 她之前有烹飪越南菜的經驗。
(D) She specified her credit card information on a payment form.	(D) 她在付款單上詳列她的信用卡資料。

■ 推論 聯結問題　　　　　　　　　　　　　　　　　　　　　　　　　　　　解答 (B)

這是將兩篇文章內容相互對照後進行推測的整合推測問題。應先注意提到題目關鍵字 Ms. Peñaflor 的第二個表格。

第二個表格的 Course: Viva Vietnam! 中可知道 Ms. Peñaflor 申請了越南相關的課程，此為第一個線索。但是因為沒有提到上課的時間，因此要看網站內容的部分，在第一篇內容中的 Viva Vietnam!: August 18 – September 8 表示「越南萬歲！」的課程要上到 9 月 8 日為止，此為第二個線索。

綜合兩個線索可推論 Ms. Peñaflor 要上課上到 9 月，因此 (B) She joined a class that is scheduled to last until September. 為正確答案。

單字 miss v. 錯過，漏掉　prior a. 之前的　specify v. 詳細地記述

Questions 191-195 refer to the following letter and e-mail.

191-195 根據下面信件和電郵的內容回答問題。

例文1

192-ASeptember 13

Deborah Garret
Circulation Manager
Beryl Publishing Company
5236 Guevara Avenue
Albuquerque, NM 87120

Dear Ms. Garret,

192-CI have been a subscriber of *The Clarion Monthly* for the last two years, and 191my subscription was not supposed to end until December of this year. However, 192-B I have not received a single issue since last July, 192-Awhich prompted me to call your company's customer service hotline yesterday to relay my concern. I spoke with Mr. Ross Lawrence, who informed me that *The Clarion Monthly* is no longer in print, and that the last issue was released three months ago.

Mr. Lawrence also informed me that subscribers were sent a notice via e-mail. I never received this notice, however. Since I have received only six issues of the journal this year, 195I would like to request a 50 percent refund of the $430 annual fee that I paid.

I am hoping that you will address my concern as soon as possible. Thank you.

Yours truly,

Arthur Clayton

例文2

To: Arthur Clayton <clayart@masterson.com>

From: Deborah Garret <dgar@beryl.co.us>

Date: September 15
Subject: Subscription

I am deeply sorry for the inconvenience you experienced with your subscription to *The Clarion Monthly*. Although 193we notified our subscribers in April that the magazine would cease publication after June, it appears that there was a computer error and a few of our readers did not receive the notification. We hope that you will accept our apology.

195We have verified that there are six months remaining in your subscription, and will issue you a refund for the unfilled portion of the agreement. 194The amount will be transferred to your account unless you prefer a check, which we can mail to your home or office. In addition, 192-D we are sending you a 30 percent discount voucher, which you can use to subscribe to any of our other publications.

192-A9 月 13 日

Deborah Garret
流通部經理
Beryl 出版公司
87120 新墨西哥州 Albuquerque 市 Guevara 大道 5236 號

親愛的 Garret 女士：

192-C 我已經訂購了 *Clarion* 月刊兩年了，191 我的訂閱要到今年 12 月才到期，但是，192-B 我從 7 月以後就沒有收到任何一期刊物了，192-A 驅使我昨天打電話給你們公司的客服熱線反應此事，我和 Ross Lawrence 先生通話，他告訴我 *Clarion* 月刊已經停刊了，最後一期出刊是三個月前的事了。

Lawrence 先生還告知我，通知訂閱者的電郵寄出去了，但是我並沒有收到這封電郵，由於我今年只收到六期刊物，195 我想要要求退還我今年付的年費，430 美元的 50%。

我希望你能盡快處理我的要求，謝謝。

Arthur Clayton 敬上

收件人：Arthur Clayton
　　　　<clayart@masterson.com>
寄件人：Deborah Garret
　　　　<dgar@beryl.co.us>
日期：9 月 15 日
主旨：訂閱

我很抱歉你訂閱我們 *Clarion* 月刊經歷了如此不便，雖然 193 我們在 4 月就通知我們的訂閱者月刊在 6 月已就要停刊，但很顯然的，因為電腦的錯誤而使少數的讀者沒有收到通知。我們希望你能接受我們的道歉。

195 我們已經確認在你的訂購中還有剩餘六期，我們將會將合約中尚未執行的部分退款給你。194 這筆錢會匯給你，除非你比較偏好支票，我們可以寄到你家或辦公室。此外，192-D 我們會寄給你一張七折的折價券，可以用來訂閱我們任何其他的刊物。

Thank you, and again, my sincerest apologies.	謝謝你，且再次向你致歉。
Best regards,	
Deborah Garret	Deborah Garret 敬上

例文 1 單字　□subscriber n. 訂閱者　　□subscription n. 訂閱　　□prompt v. 驅使，刺激
　　　　　　　□relay v. 傳達　　　　　□concern n. 問題，擔憂　　□inform v. 告知
　　　　　　　□release v. 發表，出示　□notice n. 公告　　　　　□address v. 處理，解決

例文 2 單字　□inconvenience n. 不方便　□notify v. （正式）告知，通知　□cease v. 中斷
　　　　　　　□publication n. 發行，出版品　□verify v. 確認　　　　　□remain v. 剩餘
　　　　　　　□issue v. 發行，支付　　□unfilled a. 未達的，未滿的　□portion n. 部分
　　　　　　　□transfer v. 帳戶轉帳　　□prefer v. 偏好　　　　　　□voucher n. 優惠券

191

Why did Mr. Clayton send the letter to Ms. Garret?	為什麼 Clayton 先生寄了這封信給 Garret 女士？
(A) To request a membership extension	(A) 要求延長會員的期限
(B) To inquire about an unpaid balance	(B) 詢問未付款的金額
(C) To make a complaint about a subscription	(C) 對訂閱刊物提出抱怨
(D) To arrange an interview for a magazine article	(D) 安排雜誌文章的訪問

■ **找出主題** 寫文章的理由　　　　　　　　　　　　　　　　　　　　　　　　　解答 (C)

這題是在問 Mr. Clayton 寄信給 Ms. Garret 的理由，應注意第一封由 Mr. Clayton 所寫的信件前半部分。信中的 my subscription was not supposed to end until December of this year. However, I have not received a single issue since last July 提到訂閱到今年 12 月才到期，但是從 7 月以後就沒有收到任何一期刊物，因此可知道他是在抱怨這件事，所以 (C) To make a complaint about a subscription 為正確答案。

單字 extension n. 延長，擴大　balance n. 餘額，平衡　complaint n. 不滿，抱怨

192

What is NOT indicated about Mr. Clayton?	關於 Clayton 先生，何者錯誤？
(A) He contacted a customer service representative on September 12.	(A) 他在 9 月 12 日和一位客戶服務代表聯絡。
(B) He called Mr. Lawrence to inquire about a subscription extension.	(B) 他打電話給 Lawrence 先生詢問關於延長訂閱事宜。
(C) He has received *The Clarion Monthly* for more than two years.	(C) 他已經收到 *Clarion* 月刊超過兩年了。
(D) He will be offered a reduced rate for a publication.	(D) 他會得到一個出版品的折扣。

■ **Not/True** Not問題　　　　　　　　　　　　　　　　　　　　　　　　　　解答 (B)

這是尋找與題目關鍵字 Mr. Clayton 相關的內容並與選項相互對照的 Not/True 問題，因此提到 Mr. Clayton 的兩封郵件內容皆要注意。第一封信的 September 13 與 which prompted me to call your company's customer service hotline yesterday 可以知道寄信的時間為 9 月 13 日，且昨天曾打電話給客戶服務代表處聯絡，與 (A) 的敘述一致。第一封信的 I have not received a single issue since last July, which prompted me to call ~ customer service hotline ~ to relay my concern. I spoke with Mr. Ross Lawrence 提到他從七月以後就沒有收到任何一期刊物了，而他昨天打電話給公司的客服熱線反應這件事，並和 Ross Lawrence 先生通話，與 (B) 的選項不符，因此 (B) He called Mr. Lawrence to inquire about a subscription extension. 為正確答案。第一封信的 I have been a subscriber of *The Clarion Monthly* for the last two years 提到他已經訂購了 *Clarion* 月刊兩年了，與 (C) 的內容相符。第二封信的 we are sending you a 30 percent discount voucher, which you can use to subscribe to any of our other publications 提到會寄給 Clayton 先生一張七折的折價券，可以用來訂閱任何其他的刊物，與 (D) 的內容一致。

單字 representative n. 職員　inquire v. 詢問

193

What does Ms. Garret say Beryl Publishing did in April? (A) Offered discount vouchers to customers (B) Printed several revised editions (C) Informed customers of a discontinuation (D) Announced an upcoming magazine	Garret 女士説 Beryl 出版公司在 4 月時做了什麼？ (A) 提供折價券給顧客 (B) 印刷了好幾個更新版 (C) 告知顧客停刊的消息 (D) 宣布一個即將問世的雜誌

■ 六何原則 What   解答 (C)

這題是問 Garret 女士說 Beryl 出版公司在 4 月時做了什麼（What）的六何原則問題，因此要注意第二篇由 Ms. Garret 所寫的電子郵件內容。信中的 we notified our subscribers in April that the magazine would cease publication after June 提到他們在 4 月時就通知訂閱者月刊在 6 月要停刊，所以 (C) Informed customers of a discontinuation 為正確答案。

換句話說

notified ~ subscribers 告知訂閱者 → Informed customers 告知顧客

單字 discontinuation n. 中止

194

What is suggested in the second e-mail? (A) Issues of *The Clarion Monthly* will be unavailable temporarily. (B) Mr. Clayton's subscription was terminated by mistake. (C) Ms. Garret would prefer to send a check. (D) Mr. Clayton will need to provide his payment preference.	關於第二封電郵，提示了什麼？ (A) *Clarion* 月刊的出刊將會暫時停止。 (B) Clayton 先生的訂閱被誤停。 (C) Garret 女士偏好寄送支票。 (D) Clayton 先生必須要告知他想要的收款方式。

■ 推論 詳細內容   解答 (D)

這是要推論有關第二封電郵的內容，因此應注意第二篇的部分。The amount will be transferred to your account unless you prefer a check, which we can mail to your home or office. 是在說「這筆錢會匯給你，除非你比較偏好支票，我們可以寄到你家或辦公室」，因此可以推測 Mr. Clayton 應告知他想要的收款方式，所以 (D) Mr. Clayton will need to provide his payment preference. 為正確答案。

單字 unavailable a. 不可得的   temporarily ad. 暫時地   terminate v. 使結束

195

How much does Ms. Garret agree to send to Mr. Clayton? (A) $50 (B) $215 (C) $430 (D) $860	Garret 女士同意要寄多少錢給 Clayton 先生？ (A) 50 美元 (B) 215 美元 (C) 430 美元 (D) 860 美元

■ 六何原則 聯結問題   解答 (B)

這是要分析兩篇文章才能解決的聯結問題。題目是在問 Garret 女士同意要寄多少錢給 Clayton 先生，因此先從第二篇 Ms. Garret 寄的電郵看起。第二封的內容寫到 We have verified that there are six months remaining in your subscription, and will issue you a refund for the unfilled portion of the agreement.，即已經確認還有剩餘六期，將會將合約中尚未執行的部分退款，此為第一個線索。然而並不知道剩餘六期的價錢為多少，因此要繼續確認相關的內容。第一篇的信件中 I would like to request a 50 percent refund of the $430 annual fee that I paid 表示希望要求年費 430 美元 50% 的退款，因此可知道 6 個月的訂閱費用為 215 美元。由這兩個線索可以知道 (B) $215 為正確答案。

例文1

Job Positions Available:

Intima Restaurant, 18 East Second Avenue, New York, NY 10003

Intima Restaurant, *Al Dente Magazine*'s Choice Restaurant of the Year, is constantly looking for hardworking individuals to join its elite team of food service professionals. Intima recognizes that people are its most valuable asset, and this summer, it is seeking qualified individuals to fill the following positions:

[196/197]Line Cook – The ideal candidate should have a basic knowledge of food preparation. [197]The hired applicant will not only prepare food items as directed by the executive chef, but also follow recipes, portion controls, and presentation specifications set by the restaurant. [196]This position requires 20 hours per week, Mondays through Thursdays.

[196]Food Server – The successful applicant will take and serve the guests' orders, make sure that they are satisfied with their food, and efficiently handle any of their requests and concerns. [196]There are shifts available on Mondays, Tuesdays, and Wednesdays from 11 A.M. to 3 P.M.

[196/199]Host – This is the ideal position for someone with excellent communication skills and a courteous and outgoing personality. The successful candidate will manage all restaurant bookings, meet, greet, and seat guests, and ensure that the front desk area is clean and presentable at all times. [196/199]This is an evening shift position on Fridays and Saturdays.

[196]Cashier – The selected applicant will handle payment transactions, issue receipts, verify the accuracy of all items on guest checks, and be responsible for calculating the business's revenue at the end of each night. [196]This position is from 6 P.M. to 10 P.M. Tuesdays, Wednesdays, and Thursdays.

Intima offers competitive hourly rates. [198]Overtime pay of 20 percent per hour is given to staff members who work longer than their actual shift times. Staff members also receive a 50 percent discount on all menu items. Only full-time workers are eligible for the company's medical plan. Training will be given to new employees if necessary. Interested parties should contact the assistant restaurant manager, Anita Marks, at asst.manager@intima.com no later than June 10.

職缺公告：

Intima 餐廳，10003 紐約州紐約市第二大道東 18 號

Al Dente 雜誌所選的年度餐廳，Intima 餐廳，一直在找工作勤奮的人加入我們專業飲食服務的菁英團隊。Intima 餐廳認為人是我們最重要的資產，在今年夏天，我們正在尋找合適的人選來擔任以下職缺：

[196/197] 作業流程廚師 – 理想的人選應該對食物的準備有基本的知識。[197] 不僅要準備主廚所交代的每一項食物，而且還要依照餐廳訂定的食譜、分量控制、呈現方式。[196] 這個職位每週從週一到週四需要工作二十個小時。

[196] 服務員 – 成功得到這份工作的人會負責客人的點餐和送餐，確定客人滿意他們的食物，而且能夠有效率地處理客人的要求和問題。[196] 週一、週二和週三從早上十一點到下午三點可以輪班。

[196/199] 接待員 – 這個職位適合的人選要有絕佳的溝通技巧，同時要是個性有禮外向的人，錄取者要負責所有的餐廳訂位、招呼客人、帶位，並確保前台區域隨時都乾淨而合宜。[196/199] 這個職位是週五和週六晚班。

[196] 收銀員 – 成功錄取者要負責收款、開收據、確認帳單與顧客開的支票無誤。並且負責在每晚結束營業後計算收入。[196] 這個職位的工作時間是週二、週三和週四的下午六點到十點。

Intima 餐廳提供具有競爭性的時薪。[198] 員工的工作時間若超過他們所分配到的輪班時間，加班費比一般時薪多 20%。所有的員工都可享菜單上所有食物的五折優待，只有全職員工享有公司的醫療保險，新進員工會給予必要的訓練。有興趣者應在 6 月 10 日前電郵聯絡餐廳的助理經理 Anita Marks: asst.manager@intima.com。

例文2

To: Anita Marks <asst.manager@intima.com>	收件人：Anita Marks <asst.manager@intima.com>
From: April Galloway <aprilgall@contact.org>	寄件人：April Galloway <aprilgall@contact.org>
Date: June 2 Subject: Advertisement	日期：6 月 2 日 主旨：廣告
Dear Ms. Marks,	親愛的 Marks 小姐：
I am writing in response to your establishment's job advertisement and am interested in applying for either the food server or host position. I have had relevant experience with both jobs and I am certain I could make a valuable contribution to the restaurant. I have attached my résumé for your consideration.	我針對你們的職缺廣告寫這封信，我想要應徵服務員或接待員的工作，我在這兩個職位都有相關的經驗，我相信我能對你們的餐廳有所貢獻，附件是我的履歷表，供您參考。
In case it might impact your decision, I'd like to add that [199]I am presently attending classes on Monday and Wednesday afternoons, but I am otherwise free to dedicate my time to the restaurant. In addition, [200]I was wondering if the hourly pay for both positions is the same. Thank you for your time and I eagerly await your response.	也許這會影響你的決定，我想要補充一點，[199] 我目前週一和週三下午有課，但其他時間都可以來你們的餐廳工作。此外，[200] 我想知道這兩個工作的時薪是否相同？感謝您花時間看這封信，希望很快能得到你的回音。
Sincerely,	
April Galloway	April Galloway 敬上

例文 1 單字
☐constantly ad. 持續地，總是　☐recognize v. 認識到　☐seek v. 找，追求
☐ideal a. 理想的　☐specification n. 明細，說明，詳述
☐handle v. 處理　☐shift n. 輪班　☐courteous a. 有禮的
☐outgoing a. 活潑的，外向的　☐greet v. 迎接　☐seat v. 帶位
☐presentable a. 可以見人的，漂亮的　☐transaction n. 交易
☐issue v. 開立，發行　☐receipt n. 收據　☐verify v. 確認
☐accuracy n. 正確性　☐calculate v. 計算

例文 2 單字
☐relevant a. 相關的　☐certain a. 確信的　☐contribution n. 貢獻
☐impact v. 影響　☐presently ad. 現在　☐dedicate v. 奉獻
☐eagerly ad. 渴望地　☐await v. 等待

196

What can be inferred about the advertised jobs? (A) They provide fixed wages. (B) They are part-time positions. (C) They require relevant experience. (D) They involve only kitchen duties.	關於這個職缺廣告可以推論出什麼？ (A) 有固定的薪水。 (B) 是兼職的工作。 (C) 要求相關的經驗。 (D) 只做廚房的工作。

■ 推論 詳細內容　　　　　　　　　　　　　　　　　　　　　　　　　　　解答 (B)

這是依題目關鍵字 the advertised jobs 推論的問題，因此應注意第一篇廣告文章的相關內容。由廣告中 Line Cook 的 This position requires 20 hours per week, Mondays through Thursdays.、Food Server 的 There are shifts available on Mondays, Tuesdays, and Wednesdays from 11 A.M. to 3 P.M.、Host 的 This is an evening shift position on Fridays and Saturdays.、Cashier 的 This position is from 6 P.M. to 10 P.M. Tuesdays, Wednesdays, and Thursdays. 可推論此工作是依時間計算的職缺，因此 (B) They are part-time positions. 為正確答案。

197

What is a requirement for line cooks?	作業流程廚師的工作要求為何？
(A) A presentable appearance	(A) 好看的外表
(B) Willingness to work nights	(B) 願意在晚上工作
(C) Ability to follow direction	(C) 能夠遵從指示的能力
(D) A degree in culinary arts	(D) 烹調藝術方面的學位

■ 六何原則 What   解答 (C)

這是在問作業流程廚師的工作要求是什麼（What）的六何原則問題。因此應看提及題目關鍵字 a requirement for line cooks 的相關內容。第一篇廣告文中 Line Cook 的 The hired applicant will not only prepare food items as directed by the executive chef, but also follow recipes, portion controls, and presentation specifications set by the restaurant. 提到作業流程廚師應該對食物的準備有基本的知識，不僅要準備主廚所交代的每一項食物，而且還要依照餐廳訂定的食譜、分量控制、呈現方式，因此 (C) Ability to follow direction 為正確答案。

198

According to the advertisement, what benefit is offered to successful candidates?	根據這則廣告，對於成功錄取者可以得到什麼福利？
(A) Medical insurance coverage	(A) 醫療保險
(B) Higher hourly wages for extra work	(B) 加班可以得到較高的時薪
(C) Free meals during shifts	(C) 輪班時可得到免費的食物
(D) Paid vacation days	(D) 支薪假期

■ 六何原則 What   解答 (B)

這題是問錄取者可以得到什麼福利（What）的六何原則問題。因此應確認有提到題目關鍵字 benefit ~ offered to successful candidates 的相關內容。第一篇廣告中的 Overtime pay of 20 percent per hour is given to staff members who work longer than their actual shift times. 提到員工的工作時間若超過他們所分配到的輪班時間，加班費比一般時薪多 20%。因此 (B) Higher hourly wages for extra work 為正確答案。

換句話說
Overtime pay of 20 percent per hour 每一小時多百分之二十的薪水
→ Higher hourly wages for extra work 較高的加班時薪

199

What position matches April Galloway's schedule?	哪個職位能配合 April Galloway 的時間？
(A) Cashier	(A) 收銀員
(B) Line Cook	(B) 作業流程廚師
(C) Food Server	(C) 服務員
(D) Host	(D) 招待員

■ 六何原則 聯結問題   解答 (D)

這是結合兩篇文章內容的聯結問題。因為是問什麼（What）職位能配合 April Galloway 的時間，因此應先從第二封 April Galloway 所寫的電子郵件看起。第二封中的 I am presently attending classes on Monday and Wednesday afternoons, but I am otherwise free to dedicate my time to the restaurant 提到目前週一和週三下午有課，但其他時間都有空去餐廳工作，此為第一個線索，要知道符合這個時間的職缺就必須看第一篇的內容，第一篇的廣告文中 Host 的 This is an evening shift position on Fridays and Saturdays. ，表示這個職位是週五和週六晚班，此為第二個線索，綜合以上兩個線索可以知道 (D) Host 為正確答案。

單字 **match** v. （互相）適合，搭配，一致

What does Ms. Galloway ask Ms. Marks?	Galloway 小姐問 Marks 小姐什麼？
(A) What hours the restaurant is open	(A) 餐廳的營業時間
(B) Which days are usually the busiest	(B) 哪幾天通常最忙
(C) How much training will be provided	(C) 會提供多少訓練
(D) If the salary is identical for two jobs	(D) 兩個職位的薪水是否相同

■ 六何原則 What   解答 (D)

這題是問 Galloway 小姐問 Marks 小姐什麼（What）的六何原則問題。因此應先從第二篇 Ms. Galloway 寄的信件看起。I was wondering if the hourly pay for both positions is the same 中提到想知道兩個工作的時薪是否相同，因此 (D) If the salary is identical for two jobs 為正確答案。

單字 salary n. 薪水   identical a. 一樣的

TEST 07

PART 5

101

It was Governor Richards _____ who took charge of relief efforts last week in the hurricane-affected area near the coast. (A) himself (B) him (C) his (D) he	上週 Richards 州長親自到靠近沿海受到颶風影響的地區負責救災工作。

■ 反身代名詞　　　　　　　　　　　　　　　　　　　　　　　　　　　　　　　　　解答 (A)

由「Richards 州長親自～」的語意看來，應為強調補語 Governor Richards 的反身代名詞 (A) himself 為正確答案。句子中已經有主詞 It 與補語 Governor Richards，所以不能再有受詞 (B)、所有格代名詞 (C) 與主格 (D)。(C) 雖然也可以當作所有格，但後面沒有名詞可供修飾，所以仍然不是答案。

單字 governor n. 州長　take charge of phr. 負責～　relief effort phr. 救災工作　affected a. 受影響的

102

Some people who leave their homeland _____ overseas may end up living permanently outside of their native countries. (A) work (B) works (C) worked (D) to work	有些離開家鄉到國外工作的人，最後可能會永遠住在他們祖國之外的地方。

■ to 不定詞的用法　　　　　　　　　　　　　　　　　　　　　　　　　　　　　　解答 (D)

修飾名詞 Some people 的關係子句是 who ~ overseas，因為是有主詞 who、動詞 leave、受詞 homeland 的完整子句，因此 _____ overseas 為非子句的修飾語。可以做為非子句的修飾語有分詞 (C) 與 to 不定詞 (D)，其中表示目的「為了工作」的 to 不定詞 (D) to work 為正確答案。若填入過去分詞 (C) worked 的話，受修飾的名詞 homeland 與分詞會變為被動關係，形成「讓家鄉在國外被工作」這種不合邏輯的語意。可當作動詞與名詞的 (A) 與 (B) 則不能當作修飾語。

單字 overseas ad. 國外地　end up phr. 結果～　permanently ad. 永遠地　native country phr. 母國，本國

103

The new shop on Maple Street specializes in imported art _____ from China and Thailand. (A) supplier (B) to supply (C) supplies (D) supplying	在 Maple 街的那間新開的店，專賣由中國及泰國進口的美術用品。

■ 人物名詞 vs. 抽象名詞　　　　　　　　　　　　　　　　　　　　　　　　　　　解答 (C)

art _____ 是介系詞 in 的受詞，同時也是受分詞 imported 修飾的名詞，因此名詞 (A) 與 (C) 有可能為正確答案。空格前沒有冠詞，所以複數事物名詞 (C) supplies（用品）為正確答案。若填入人物名詞 (A) supplier（供應者）就會出現「進口藝術供應者」的奇怪語意。要注意，art supplies（美術用品）是「名詞＋名詞」形態的複合名詞，因此 to 不定詞 (B) 與可當作分詞和動名詞的 (D) 都無法跟 art 結合形成介系詞 in 的受詞。

單字 specialize v. 專門做～，專攻

104

Cairo-based Astarte Language School offers high-quality translation services for multinational firms _____ very reasonable prices. (A) in (B) at (C) over (D) from	以開羅為根據地的 Astarte 語言學校，以非常合理的價錢為跨國公司提供高品質的翻譯服務。

■ 介系詞 at   解答 (B)

空格與後面的 reasonable prices 一起搭配為「合理的價錢」之意，因此介系詞 (B) at（以～，在～）為正確答案。(A) in（在～）表示時間或場所，(C) over（～ 期間，～ 上）表示期間或位置。(D) from（從～）表示出發時間或出處。請記住慣用語 at a reasonable price（以合理的價格）。

單字 multinational firm phr. 跨國企業   reasonable a. 合理的

105

Harizze Condominiums' building administrator _____ circulated a memorandum on proper garbage disposal. (A) while (B) very (C) before (D) recently	Harizze 大廈的大樓管理員最近傳閱了一份有關正確丟棄垃圾的備忘錄。

■ 副詞語彙   解答 (D)

句意應為「傳閱了一份有關正確丟棄垃圾的備忘錄」，因此副詞 (D) recently（最近）為正確答案。要注意，recently 主要和過去與現在完成式一起使用。(A) while 是表示「～期間，然而」之意的副詞子句連接詞。(B) very 是表示「非常」之意的副詞，(C) before 是表示「～前」之意的介系詞，也可以當作副詞子句連接詞。

單字 administrator n. 管理員   circulate v. 傳閱，循環   memorandum n. 備忘錄，紀錄
      garbage disposal phr. 垃圾處理

106

As executive chef, Jennifer Windings is _____ to not just the owner of Lucina Ristorante, but also its customers. (A) accountable (B) accounted (C) account (D) accountably	身為行政主廚，Jennifer Windings 不僅要對 Lucina Ristorante 餐廳的老闆負責，也要對其顧客負責。

■ 形容詞相關用法   解答 (A)

空格置於 be 動詞 is 之後，因此形容詞 (A)，動詞 p.p. 形 (B) 與名詞 (C) 皆有可能為正確答案。由「Jennifer Windings 不僅要對 Lucina Ristorante 餐廳的老闆負責，也要對其顧客負責」的語意看來。空格前的 be 動詞 is 與空格後的介系詞 to 一起使用表示「負責」，因此 (A) accountable（負責的）為正確答案。若填入動詞 p.p. 形 (B) accounted 則會出現「Jennifer Windings 被負責 / 說明」的奇怪句意。若使用名詞 (C) account（說明）的話，則會與主詞 Jennifer Windings 成為同位語，形成「Jennifer Windings 即是說明」的奇怪語意。請記住對等連接詞慣用語 not just A but also B （不只 A 還有 B 也～）。

單字 customer n. 顧客   accountably ad. 可說明地，有責任地

107

The board will have a meeting next week to discuss the possibility for _____ with the expansion of the firm's operations in Europe. (A) rise　　　　(B) boost (C) growth　　　(D) climb	董事會將在下週舉行一個會議，討論在歐洲擴大公司營運帶來成長的可能性。

■ 似意義的名詞　　　　　　　　　　　　　　　　　　　　　　　　　解答 (C)

句意應為「在歐洲擴大公司營運帶來成長的可能性」，因此名詞 (C) growth（成長）為正確答案。(A) rise 是表示數量或水準的「上升」，(B) boost 是表示增加或幫助改善的「促進」，(D) climb 則表示價值或量的「上升」。

單字 board n. 董事會　operation n. 營運，事業，企業

108

By the time Paola Conti became head designer for Fiori Fashions, she _____ more than 15 collections for the company's line of sportswear. (A) had developed　　　(B) will develop (C) has developed　　　(D) develops	在 Paola Conti 成為 Fiori Fashions 的首席設計師時，她已替公司的運動服開發了 15 種以上的產品。

■ 過去完成式　　　　　　　　　　　　　　　　　　　　　　　　　解答 (A)

By the time 帶出的時間副詞子句用的是過去式動詞 became，表示過去的事，因此應使用過去完成式來表示在過去已完成的事。所以過去完成式 (A) had developed 為正確答案。(B) 是未來式，(C) 是現在完成式，(D) 是現在式，時態皆不符。應記住副詞子句連接詞 By the time（到～的時候）。

單字 head a. 首席的，龍頭的

109

Dupont Air requires that travel agencies _____ passport numbers prior to issuing travel itineraries to customers. (A) obtain　　　　(B) contact (C) fulfill　　　　(D) preside	Dupont Air 要求旅行社在發給客戶旅遊行程前先取得護照號碼。

■ 動詞語彙　　　　　　　　　　　　　　　　　　　　　　　　　解答 (A)

由「要求先取得客戶的護照號碼」的句意看來，動詞 (A) obtain（到手，取得）為正確答案。(B) contact 是「聯絡」，(C) fulfil 是「使滿足」，(D) preside 是「主導」的意思。

單字 require v. 要求　prior to phr. ～前　issue v. 發布　itinerary n. 旅行行程

110

The computer began processing data much more _____ after several large files were deleted from the hard drive. (A) quick　　　　(B) quickly (C) quickness　　　(D) quicker	從硬碟中刪除幾個大的檔案後，電腦在處理資料的速度更迅速。

■ 副詞的位置　　　　　　　　　　　　　　　　　　　　　　　　　解答 (B)

要修飾動名詞 processing 的話空格應為副詞，所以副詞 (B) quickly（快速地）為正確答案。可當作形容詞與副詞的 quick（快的，快地），其比較級不是 more quick 而是 quicker，所以 (A) quick 不是答案。名詞 (C) 不能修飾動名詞。可當作形容詞與副詞比較級的 (D) quicker，因為空格前已有表示比較級的 more，所以會與 -er 重複，因此也不是答案。要注意，動詞 begin 動名詞與 to 不定詞都可以當作受詞。

單字 process v. 處理

111

For a $25 fee, Silverbell Florist will extend its delivery _____ to cities as far north as Santa Barbara. (A) serving　　　　(B) service (C) is serving　　　(D) has served	加收 25 元美金，Silverbell 花店的運送服務將延伸到遠至 Santa Barbara 市等北方城市。

■ 名詞的位置　　　　　　　　　　　　　　　　　　　　　　　　　　　解答 (B)

its delivery~ 為及物動詞 will extend 的受詞，因此可以當作受詞的動名詞 (A) 與名詞 (B) 有可能為正確答案。空格後沒有受詞，所以名詞 (B) service（服務）為正確答案。動名詞 (A) serving 後面必須要有受詞，所以並非答案。

單字 fee n. 費用　extend v. 擴張，延伸　delivery n. 配送

112

Applicants _____ pass the first test will be contacted for a panel interview, which will be conducted by the company's executives. (A) whoever　　　　(B) whenever (C) who　　　　　(D) where	通過第一次考試的應徵者將會被通知參加一個由公司主管主導的小組面談。

■ 關係副詞　　　　　　　　　　　　　　　　　　　　　　　　　　　解答 (C)

空格帶出修飾名詞 Applicants 的關係子句，空格後面的子句 pass the first test will be contacted for a panel interview 是沒有主詞的不完整子句，因此主格關係代名詞 (C) who 為正確答案。複合關係代名詞 (A) whoever（無論是誰）帶出名詞子句，表示「代名詞 + 關係代名詞」，前面不能有先行詞。複合關係副詞 (B) whenever（無論何時）帶出的子句為副詞子句，前面也不能有先行詞。(D) where 是以地點為先行詞的關係副詞，後面無法連接完整子句。

單字 applicant n. 應徵者　panel interview phr. 小組面談　executive n. 主管

113

For an additional _____, Doyle Convention Center can provide refreshments at the upcoming corporate event. (A) value　　　　　(B) worth (C) charge　　　　(D) bill	支付額外的費用後，Doyle 會議中心可在即將展開的公司活動中提供茶點。

■ 類似意義的名詞　　　　　　　　　　　　　　　　　　　　　　　　解答 (C)

句意應為「以額外的費用提供茶點」，因此名詞 (C) charge（費用）為正確答案。(A) value 是經濟的「價值」，(B) worth 是金錢面的「價值」，(D) bill 是「帳單」的意思。要注意，應記住並區分 fare（交通費用）、fee（費用，手續費）。

單字 refreshment n. 茶點　corporate a. 公司的

114

Since its establishment, Kalywa Textiles has strived to maintain a superior _____ of quality in making its products. (A) proportion　　　(B) standard (C) period　　　　(D) estimate	從創建以來，Kalywa 紡織廠努力保持以卓越水準的品質製造產品。

■ 名詞語彙　　　　　　　　　　　　　　　　　　　　　　　　　　　解答 (B)

語意應為「卓越水準的品質」，因此名詞 (B) standard（水準，基準）為正確答案。(A) proportion 是「部分，比例」，(C) period 是「期間」，(D) estimate 是「估計，估計值」的意思。

單字 establishment n. 設立　strive to phr. 奮鬥~，致力~　superior a. 優秀的

115

_____ Mr. Harris has been a committed employee of the hotel for ten years, the supervisor recommended him for promotion. (A) As　　　　　　　(B) Previously (C) But　　　　　　(D) Therefore	由於 Harris 先生十年來是飯店的忠實員工，他的主管推薦他晉升。

■ 副詞子句連接詞 理由　　　　　　　　　　　　　　　　　　　　　　　　　　　　　　解答 (A)

主句是包含 the supervisor recommended him 的完整子句，因此 ____ Mr. Harris ~ ten years 為修飾語，空格後有動詞 has been，可知修飾語為副詞子句，因此副詞子句連接詞 (A) As（因為～）為正確答案。副詞 (B) Previously（先前）與 (D) Therefore（因此）無法連接副詞子句，如果放在文章開頭的話，後面則一定要加逗點。(C) But（但是）則為對等連接詞，必須連接文法作用相同的單字與單字、片語與片語、子句與子句。

單字 committed a. 忠實的　supervisor n. 主管　promotion n. 晉升，宣傳

116

Mr. McLeish and his colleagues _____ need to make any changes to the draft blueprint because the client thought it was excellent. (A) hardness　　　　　(B) harder (C) hardly　　　　　(D) hard	McLeish 先生及他的同事們幾乎不用對草稿藍圖做任何的修改，因為客戶覺得很好。

■ 相似形態卻意義不同的副詞　　　　　　　　　　　　　　　　　　　　　　　　　　　解答 (C)

要修飾動詞 need 的話空格應為副詞，因此副詞 (C) 與 (D) 有可能為正確答案。由「客戶覺得草稿藍圖很好，所以幾乎不用做任何修改」的句意看來，(C) hardly（幾乎不 ～）為正確答案。若填入 (D) hard（認真地，強力地）則無法有順暢的語意搭配。名詞 (A) 與形容詞比較級 (B) 無法修飾動詞。要注意，應記住並區分形態相似但意義不同的 hardly 與 hard。

單字 colleague n. 同事　blueprint n. 藍圖，計畫　hardness n. 堅固

117

Adam Bower and his team of property developers are _____ to start working on the shopping center project, as they only have one year to finish it. (A) gradual　　　　　(B) uniform (C) absolute　　　　(D) eager	Adam Bower 和他的房地產開發團隊急於開始建造購物中心的計畫，因為他們只有一年的時間來完成。

■ 形容詞語彙　　　　　　　　　　　　　　　　　　　　　　　　　　　　　　　　　　解答 (D)

由「因為只有一年的時間來完成，所以急於開始建造購物中心的計畫」的句意看來，形容詞 (D) eager（急切的）為正確答案。(A) gradual 是「逐漸的」，(B) uniform 是「一致的，一律的」，(C) absolute 是「絕對的」的意思。要注意，應記住慣用語 be eager to（渴切做～，希望做～）。

單字 property n. 房地產

118

------ attending the workshops, Emily Chassell hopes to improve her interior decorating skills and stay up-to-date on the latest industry trends.

(A) Except
(B) Whether
(C) Into
(D) By

藉由參加工作坊，Emily Chassell 希望可以增進她室內設計的技巧，並讓她可以掌握最新的產業趨勢。

■ 選擇介系詞 其他　　　　　　　　　　　　　　　　　　　　　　　解答 (D)

由「希望藉由參加工作坊可以增進技巧，並掌握最新的產業趨勢」的句意看來，空格搭配後面的動名詞 attending 為「藉由參加～」之意，因此 (D) By 為正確答案。應記住表示手段或方法的 by+ -ing（藉由～）。(A) Except 當作介系詞時常用的用法有 except for（除了～），(C) Into 是「向～內」的意思，表示方向。(B) Whether 是「無論～」的意思，可當作名詞子句與副詞子句的連接詞。要注意，應記住慣用語 stay up-to-date（掌握最新動向）。

單字 attend v. 參加　up-to-date a. 最新的，最流行的

119

Pevensey Cosmetics doubled its production capacity after ------ its goal to upgrade all of its factory equipment.

(A) consuming
(B) practicing
(C) achieving
(D) deciding

在完成將所有工廠設備升級的目標後，Pevensey 化妝品公司的生產能力增加了一倍。

■ 動詞語彙　　　　　　　　　　　　　　　　　　　　　　　　　　解答 (C)

由「完成將所有工廠設備升級的目標後，生產能力增加了一倍」的句意看來，動詞 achieve（達成）的現在分詞 (C) achieving 為正確答案。(A) consume 是「消費」，(B) practice 是「練習」，(D) decide 是「決定」的意思。

單字 double v. 使加倍　capacity n. 容量，能力

120

Next week's conference will discuss ------ aspiring entrepreneurs can open their own profitable businesses.

(A) unless
(B) during
(C) much
(D) how

下週的會議將討論有抱負的企業家們如何開創他們自己的賺錢生意。

■ 名詞子句連接詞 how　　　　　　　　　　　　　　　　　　　　　解答 (D)

名詞子句 ____ aspiring ~ businesses 為動詞 will discuss 的受詞，空格應為帶出子句的連接詞，因此疑問詞 (D) how（如何）為正確答案。副詞子句連接詞 (A) unless 無法連接名詞子句，介系詞 (B) during 與可以當作不定代名詞、形容詞與副詞的 (C) much 則無法連接子句。

單字 aspiring a. 有抱負的　entrepreneur n. 企業家　profitable a. 盈利的

121

| _____ Ms. Willows was delivering her presentation to the board, her secretary was taking minutes of the meeting.
(A) So (B) While
(C) Even (D) As if | 當 Willows 女士在對董事會作報告時，她的祕書同時在做會議記錄。 |

■ 副詞子句連接詞 時間　　　　　　　　　　　　　　　　　　　　　　　　　　　　　　　　解答 (B)

這句是包含 her secretary was taking minutes 的完整子句，因此 Ms. Willows ~ board 為修飾用的從屬子句。空格應帶出包含動詞 was delivering 的從屬子句，因此副詞子句連接詞 (B) 與 (D) 有可能為正確答案。句意應為 Willows 女士在報告時，她的祕書同時會做會議記錄，(B) While（當～）為正確答案。填入 (D) As if（就像～）的話，則無法有順暢的語意搭配。可當作副詞與對等連接詞的 (A) So（太，所以）與副詞 (C) Even 則無法連接子句。

122

| Columns published in *Weekday Quill* do not _____ reflect the views and opinions of the newspaper company.
(A) temporarily (B) visually
(C) necessarily (D) primitively | 在 *Weekday Quill* 所刊登的專欄不一定反映此報社的觀點及意見。 |

■ 副詞語彙　　　　　　　　　　　　　　　　　　　　　　　　　　　　　　　　　　　　解答 (C)

由「專欄不一定反映此報社的觀點及意見」的句意看來，副詞 (C) necessarily（一定，必須地）為正確答案。要注意，應記住 necessarily 用於強調事情的必須要件，(A) temporarily 是「一時的」，(B) visually 是「視覺上的」，(D) primitively 是「最初地，主要地」的意思。

單字 column n. 專欄，柱子　reflect v. 反映

123

| The bridge _____ the fishing village and the town underwent extensive repair work after it collapsed in last week's storm.
(A) commuting (B) traveling
(C) connecting (D) transferring | 在上週的暴風雨中倒塌後，那個連接漁村及城鎮的橋梁，進行了大量的維修工程。 |

■ 動詞語彙　　　　　　　　　　　　　　　　　　　　　　　　　　　　　　　　　　　　解答 (C)

由「連接漁村及城鎮的橋梁」的句意看來，動詞 connect（連結）的 -ing (C) connecting 為正確答案。(A) commute 是「通勤」，(B) travel 是「旅行」，(D) transfer 是「移動，轉移」的意思。

單字 extensive a. 廣泛的　collapse v. 倒塌

124

| Cepeda Food has successfully gained a solid client base on the East Coast after only two years of _____.
(A) operator (B) operative
(C) operation (D) operates | 在僅僅兩年的經營後，Cepeda Food 成功地在東岸獲得穩固的客戶群。 |

■ 人物名詞 vs. 抽象名詞　　　　　　　　　　　　　　　　　　　　　　　　　　　　　　解答 (C)

介系詞 of 的受詞應為名詞，因此名詞 (A) (B) (C) 有可能為正確答案。由「兩年的經營後獲得穩固的客戶群」的句意看來，抽象名詞 (C) operation（經營）為正確答案。人物名詞 (A) operator（經營者）和 (B) operative（工人）搭配則無法有順暢的語意。動詞 (D) 不能放在名詞的位置。要注意，operative 當作形容詞的話，表示「操作的，運行的」的意思。

單字 solid a. 堅固的，堅定的，確實的

125

| Although the dance contest is only one month away, participating performers have _____ to schedule a rehearsal.
(A) soon   (B) again
(C) later   (D) yet | 雖然距離舞蹈大賽只剩下一個月,參加的表演者卻還沒有安排彩排。 |

■ 副詞 yet   解答 (D)

語意應為「還沒有安排彩排」,因此表示「尚未」的副詞 (D) yet 為正確答案。(A) soon 是「快速地」,(B) again 是「再次」,(C) later 是「之後」,皆為副詞。

單字 performer n. 表演者　have yet to ~ phr. 尚未~

126

| _____ Kelly Denson possesses the necessary educational qualifications for the accountant position, she doesn't meet the job's work experience requirements.
(A) Provided that   (B) Although
(C) In spite of   (D) Already | 雖然 Kelly Denson 具備此會計師職缺所需的教育資格,但是她並未達到此工作所需的工作經驗要求。 |

■ 副詞子句連接詞 讓步   解答 (B)

這句是含有主詞 she、動詞 doesn't meet、受詞 requirements 的完整子句,因此 ____ Kelly Denson ~ position 為修飾語。空格後有動詞 possesses,可以知道修飾語為副詞子句,因此副詞子句連接詞 (A) 與 (B) 有可能為正確答案。由「雖然具備所需的教育資格,但是她並未達到此工作所需的工作經驗要求」的句意看來,(B) Although(雖然~)為正確答案。(A) Provided that(要是~)則無法有順暢的語意搭配。介系詞 (C) In spite of(儘管~)與副詞 (D) Already(已經)則無法連接子句。

單字 qualification n. 資格　meet v. 滿足

127

| The historical courthouse contains an _____ selection of thousands of legal documents dating back to the establishment of the city in 1840.
(A) impermissible   (B) ineligible
(C) extensive   (D) urgent | 此歷史久遠的法院中容納了廣泛的、數以千計的法律文件精選,最早可追溯至 1840 年城市建立之初。 |

■ 形容詞語彙   解答 (C)

由「數以千計的法律文件精選」的句意看來,形容詞 (C) extensive(廣泛的)為正確答案。(A) impermissible 是「不容許的」,(B) ineligible 是「沒有資格的」,(D) urgent 是「緊急的」的意思。

單字 courthouse n. 法院　date back to phr. 追溯至~

128

| When submitting their reports to the Revenue Bureau, property appraisers must attach _____ documentation to support their assessments.
(A) satisfied   (B) relevant
(C) attentive   (D) adhesive | 當繳交報告給國稅局時,財產鑑定人應附上相關的文件來支持他們的估價。 |

■ 形容詞語彙   解答 (B)

由「應附上相關的文件來支持他們的估價」的句意看來,形容詞 (B) relevant(相關的)為正確答案。(A) satisfied 是「滿足的」,(C) attentive 是「專注的」,(D) adhesive 是「黏著的,有黏性的」的意思。

單字 submit v. 繳交　appraiser n. 鑑定人　documentation n. 資料　assessment n. 估價

129

According to the National Weather Service's forecast, rainfall will be _____ distributed throughout western Scotland this year. (A) even　　　　　(B) evenly (C) evening　　　　(D) evener	根據國家氣象局的預報，今年的降雨將會均勻分佈在整個蘇格蘭西部。

■ 形態相似意義不同的副詞　　　　　　　　　　　　　　　　　　　　解答 (B)

空格應為修飾動詞 will be distributed 的副詞，所以副詞 (A) 與 (B) 有可能為正確答案。由「降雨將會均勻分佈」的句意看來，副詞 (B) evenly（均勻地）為正確答案。(A) even 當作副詞使用時表示「甚至～連，更」的意思，產生「今年的降雨甚至會遍布整個蘇格蘭西部」這種不合邏輯的語意。可當作分詞與動名詞的 (C)、名詞 (D) 皆不能當作副詞。

單字 distribute v. 分布

130

After only two years as advertising manager for Yan Beverages, Mr. Lu has already proven _____ to be a valuable asset to the company. (A) he　　　　　　(B) his (C) him　　　　　(D) himself	僅僅在 Yan 飲料公司擔任兩年的廣告經理後，Lu 先生已經證明自己是公司一項寶貴的資產。

■ 反身代名詞　　　　　　　　　　　　　　　　　　　　　　　　　　解答 (D)

可以當作動詞 has proven 受詞的有所有格代名詞 (B)、受詞人稱代名詞 (C) 與反身代名詞 (D) 都有可能為正確答案。由「Lu 先生已經證明他自己是公司一項寶貴的資產」的句意看來，動詞 has proven 的受詞應為和主詞 Mr. Lu 相同，即反身代名詞 (D) himself 為正確答案。要注意，應記住受詞和主詞相同時，則會使用反身代名詞做為受詞。主格人稱代名詞 (A) 無法當作受詞，(B) 即使當作所有格人稱代名詞，後面也不能接名詞，因此並非答案。

單字 valuable a. 貴重的　asset n. 資產

131

Travelers are required to be at the platform _____ than 15 minutes before the departure time, or they may be prohibited from boarding the train. (A) no earlier　　　(B) no more (C) no later　　　　(D) no longer	乘客最遲需要在出發時間前的十五分鐘抵達月台，否則他們可能會被禁止登上火車。

■ 比較級　　　　　　　　　　　　　　　　　　　　　　　　　　　　解答 (C)

由「最遲需要在出發時間前的十五分鐘抵達月台」的句意看來，空格與後面的 than 搭配為 no later than 成「最晚～」的意思，因此 (C) no later 為正確答案。若填入 (A) 成 no earlier than，意思為「最早」、「再快也」，填入 (B) 成 no more than（= only），意思為「只」，(D) no longer 是「再也不～」的意思，無法與 than 一起使用。要注意，應記住慣用語 prohibit A from B（禁止 A 做 B）。

單字 platform n. 月台　board v. 搭乘

132

Jazz singer Elizabeth Stanley confirmed at yesterday's press conference that she had signed an _____ five-year contract with Noril Records. (A) indifferent (B) abstract (C) exclusive (D) inconclusive	爵士歌手 Elizabeth Stanley 在昨天的記者會上證實，她已經跟 Noril 唱片簽了五年的專屬合約。

■ 形容詞語彙　　解答 (C)

由「已經跟 Noril 唱片簽了五年的專屬合約」的句意看來，形容詞 (C) exclusive（獨家的，專屬的）為正確答案。(A) indifferent 是「不感興趣的，冷漠的」，(B) abstract 是「抽象的」，(D) inconclusive 是「不確定的」的意思。

單字 press conference phr. 記者會　contract n. 契約

133

The board members of EON Incorporated will _____ review the credentials of the top three candidates for the regional director position at least two weeks before making a selection. (A) lucratively (B) memorably (C) meticulously (D) overwhelmingly	EON 公司的董事會成員至少會花兩週時間，仔細地檢閱前三名爭取區域總監職位的候選人資歷，再做出決定。

■ 副詞語彙　　解答 (C)

由「仔細地檢閱前三名爭取區域總監職位的候選人資歷」的句意看來，副詞 (C) meticulously（仔細地）為正確答案。(A) lucratively 是「有利可圖地」，(B) memorably 是「值得紀念地」，(D) overwhelmingly 是「壓倒性地」的意思。

單字 credential n. 資格　candidate n. 候選人

134

A new _____ procedure has been proposed by the company's financial consultant in order to minimize the potential for fraud. (A) auditory (B) auditing (C) will audit (D) has audited	公司的財務顧問提議了一個新的審計程序，來降低被詐騙的可能性。

■ 複合名詞　　解答 (B)

語意應為「審計程序」，因此名詞 (B) auditing（審計）為正確答案。應記住慣用語 auditing procedure（審計程序）。形容詞 (A) auditory（聽力的）雖可以放在名詞 procedure 之前，但與原本的語意不符，因此並非答案。動詞 (C) (D) 則無法修飾名詞。

單字 procedure n. 程序　consultant n. 顧問　minimize v. 最小化　fraud n. 詐欺，騙子

135

Chilean-owned firm Uriale Consulting is known for providing outstanding legal services to _____ large corporations and medium-sized enterprises. (A) each　　　　　(B) both (C) though　　　　(D) whereas	智利國營 Uriale 顧問公司以提供大型公司和中型企業優質的法律服務而聞名。

■ 相關連接詞　　　　　　　　　　　　　　　　　　　　　　　　　　　解答 (B)

和 and（和）搭配形成相關連接詞 both A and B（A 與 B 都）的 (B) both （兩者都）為正確答案。要注意，both A and B 用於連接名詞 large corporations 與名詞 medium-sized enterprises，(A) each（各個）應置於單數名詞前面，副詞子句連接詞 (C) though（雖然～）與 (D) whereas（反之）則應放在子句前面。

單字 be known for phr. 以～而知名　outstanding a. 傑出的　enterprise n. 企業

136

Organizers for the Logia Museum's Annual Gala _____ a higher turnout this year, as the fundraiser will be held in a larger venue. (A) expect　　　　　(B) contain (C) recover　　　　(D) compel	Logia 博物館年度盛會的規劃者預估今年會有比較多的出席人數，因為募捐活動將會在一個比較大的場地舉辦。

■ 動詞語彙　　　　　　　　　　　　　　　　　　　　　　　　　　　解答 (A)

由「募捐活動將會在一個比較大的場地舉辦，因此預估會有比較多的出席人數」的句意看來，動詞 (A) expect （預估）為正確答案。(B) contain 是「包含」，(C) recover 是「恢復」，(D) compel 是「強制」的意思。

單字 turnout n. 出席者　fundraiser n. 募捐活動

137

Choco Haven was able to launch a new store in Montpellier last month _____ the rising demand for its chocolate products. (A) in case　　　　(B) due to (C) except for　　　(D) so that	Choco Haven 上個月得以在 Montpellier 開一家新店，是因為它的巧克力產品的需求量大增。

■ 選擇介系詞 理由　　　　　　　　　　　　　　　　　　　　　　　　解答 (B)

主句是包含 Choco Haven was able to launch a new store 的完整子句，因此 _____ the rising demand ～ products 為修飾語。該修飾語為沒有動詞的名詞片語，選項中可以連接名詞片語的有介系詞 (B) 與 (C)。由「因為需求上升所以在 Montpellier 城市開一家新店」的句意看來，(B) due to （因為～）為正確答案。(C) except for （除了～）則會出現「除了巧克力產品的需求大增，在城市開一家新店」不合邏輯的語意。(A) in case （如果發生～）與 (D) so that （以至於～）則是連接子句。

單字 launch v. 開（店），開始　demand n. 需求

138

Ms. Reeds is waiting to hear from the supermarket _____ whether or not they can deliver the meat products to her restaurant by Wednesday.
(A) but for
(B) as to
(C) from which
(D) along with

Reeds 女士正在等待超級市場回覆關於他們是否可以在星期三將肉品送達她的餐廳。

■ 選擇介系詞 相關   解答 (B)

由「正在等待超級市場回覆關於他們是否可以在星期三將肉品送達她的餐廳」的句意看來，(B) as to（與～有關）為正確答案。(A) but for 是「假如沒有～」的意思，(D) along with 是「和～一道」的意思，「介系詞＋關係代名詞」的 (C) from which 是「從～開始」的意思，無法和名詞子句連接詞 whether 並列使用，後面必須接完整的子句。要注意，whether or not 的名詞子句 whether or not ～ Wednesday 是介系詞 as to 的受詞。

139

Chris Thomson, CEO of Remar Company Limited, said at a press conference yesterday that he is considering Tisto Corporation's proposal to _____ at least 20 percent of Remar's outstanding shares.
(A) reproduce
(B) acquire
(C) institute
(D) confirm

Remar 有限公司的執行長 Chris Thomson 昨天在記者會上表示，他正在考慮 Tisto 公司所提議的取得 Remar 公司至少百分之二十的流通股數。

■ 動詞語彙   解答 (B)

由「取得流通股數的提案」的句意看來，動詞 (B) acquire（取得，得到）為正確答案。(A) reproduce 是「複製，繁殖」，(C) institute 是「創立，開始」，(D) confirm 是「確認」的意思。

單字 outstanding share phr. 在外流通股數

140

In honor of its second anniversary, Neticroix Gym gave its members _____ gift certificates for a two-hour group training session with one of its fitness specialists.
(A) durable
(B) probable
(C) elapsed
(D) complimentary

為了慶祝第二個周年慶，Neticroix 健身房贈送它的會員一份可與一位健身教練進行兩小時的團體訓練課程的免費禮卷。

■ 形容詞語彙   解答 (D)

由「為了慶祝第二個周年慶給予會員免費禮卷」的句意看來，形容詞 (D) complimentary（免費的）為正確答案。(A) durable 是「耐用的，持久的」，(B) probable 是「有可能的」，(C) elapsed 是「經過的，過去的」的意思。

　　　　141-143 根據下面信件的內容回答問題。

Matthew Wang
National Culture Institute

Dear Mr. Wang,

I would like to apply for the position of part-time _____
141 (A) accounting　(B) research
(C) sales　(D) administrative

assistant as advertised in *The Yuan Times*. I am currently employed as a writer at Caimen Museum's cultural properties division, which conducts studies on heritage structures in the mainland. As an employee at the museum, I have written articles about the preservation of numerous historical sites in China. This experience has given me skills that I think will be useful in completing your report on the evolution of Chinese architecture. _____, I was one
142 (A) In addition　(B) Instead
(C) Nevertheless　(D) However

of the people who documented the restoration work at the Mausoleum of the First Qin Emperor.

I am very _____ in collecting and analyzing data for your
143 (A) accurate　(B) critical
(C) relaxed　(D) interested

project, as I believe doing so will provide me with a greater appreciation of the country's historical sites.

Enclosed are a copy of my résumé and a few samples of my work. Should you find that I am qualified for the position, please contact me at your most convenient time. Thank you.

Sincerely,

Thompson Lee

收信人：Matthew Wang
國家文化研究院

親愛的王先生：

141 我希望可以應徵刊登在 *Yuan Times* 報紙上的兼任研究助理一職。

我目前受雇於 Caimen 博物館，是一名文化財產部門的文字工作者，文化財產部門是進行中國古蹟結構的研究。身為博物館的職員，我撰寫了有關保存大陸眾多古蹟的文章。這方面的經驗讓我學習到一些我認為對於完成您的中國建築演變報告有幫助的技能。142 此外，我也是記錄秦始皇陵墓修復工程的一員。

143 我對於為您的計畫收集和分析資料很有興趣，因為我相信如此可以讓我對國家的歷史遺跡有更深一層的瞭解。

隨信附上的是我的履歷及我工作的幾個作品，如果您覺得我有能力勝任此職位，請在您方便的時間與我聯絡。謝謝您。

Thompson Lee 敬上

單字 **property** n. 資源，財產　**heritage** n. 遺跡　**mainland** n. 大陸　**evolution** n. 進化　**preservation** n. 保存　**restoration** n. 復原，修復

141 名詞語彙 掌握上下文　　　　　　　　　　　　　　　　　　　　　　　　　　　解答 (B)

由「希望應徵兼任____助理一職」的句意看來，所有的選項皆可能為正確答案。因為無法單就空格所在的文句判斷答案，應參考上下文意。文中提到「我撰寫了有關保存大陸眾多古蹟的文章。這方面的經驗我想將對於您的報告有幫助」，可以判斷文章與申請的職缺和研究有所相關，因此名詞 (B) research（研究）為正確答案。(A) accounting 是「會計」，(C) sales 是「販賣」(D) administrative 是「行政上的」的意思。

142 連接副詞 掌握上下文　　　　　　　　　　　　　　　　　　　　　　　　　　　解答 (A)

空格與逗點一起置於句子的最前面，應為連接副詞，應了解空格所在文句的意思來選出連接副詞 (A) (B) (C) (D) 中的正確答案。前面提到撰寫了有關保存大陸眾多古蹟的文章，後面又提到是記錄秦始皇陵墓修復工程的一員，因此表示補充說明的 (A) In addition（再加上）為正確答案。(B) Instead（取代～），(C) Nevertheless（即使）、(D) However（然而）皆與句意不相符。

143 形容詞語彙 掌握全文　　　　　　　　　　　　　　　　　　　　　　　　　　　解答 (D)

由「我對於為您的計畫收集和分析資料很____」的句意看來，所有的選項皆有可能為正確答案。因為無法單就空格所在的文句判斷答案，因此應參考上下或全文文意。前面提到古蹟的相關事項，並想申請研究助理一職，表現了對於該領域的興趣，因此形容詞 (D) interested（有興趣的）為正確答案。(A) accurate 是「精確的」，(B) critical 是「批判的，嚴重的」，(C) relaxed 是「放鬆的」的意思。

Questions 144-146 refer to the following letter.

Dear Mr. Miller,

We received your letter requesting help to _____ your access

144 (A) change   (B) recover
     (C) create   (D) remove

code so that you can gain admittance to *Chenez's* online magazine. We tried to retrieve your lost code yesterday, but unfortunately a system error is preventing us from accessing many of our users' personal information.

Our technicians are now trying to fix the problem. We plan to register new usernames and access codes for our subscribers once the repair is finished, as we _____ that

145 (A) debate   (B) negotiate
     (C) suspect   (D) doubt

others have also been lost. We will provide you with a new access code within two days. If you do not receive this information by Friday, please send us an e-mail again, and we will do our best to resolve the matter.

To compensate you for the inconvenience, we will give you a free two-month subscription to *Chenez*. This will take effect immediately after your current subscription ends and will allow you to continue _____ our stories. This means

146 (A) enjoy   (B) enjoyable
     (C) enjoys   (D) enjoying

your membership will be valid until January of next year.

We sincerely apologize for the trouble.

Respectfully yours,

Alice Efron
Chenez Magazine
Account Manager

親愛的 Miller 先生：

144 我們收到關於您要求我們幫助恢復您通行密碼的信，讓您能夠進入 *Chenez* 線上雜誌。我們昨天試著尋回您遺失的密碼，但不幸的是，一個系統錯誤使我們無法取得很多用戶的個人資料。

我們的技術人員現在正在試著解決這個問題，維修完成後，我們計畫為我們的客戶註冊新的使用者名稱跟密碼，145 因為我們懷疑其他客戶的使用者名稱與密碼也已經遺失了。

我們將會在兩天之內給予您新的通行密碼，如果您在星期五還沒有收到此資訊，請再寄一次電郵給我們，我們將盡我們最大的努力來解決此問題。

為了彌補對您造成的不便，我們將給予您兩個月免費的 *Chenez* 雜誌，會從您目前的訂閱截止日後馬上開始，146 讓您能繼續享受我們的雜誌，這意味著您的會員資格一直到明年一月都有效。

我們誠摯地為造成您的不便道歉。

Allen Efron 敬上
Chenez 雜誌
客戶經理

單字 **retrieve** v. 恢復，尋回   **access code** phr. 密碼   **subscriber** n. 訂閱者   **resolve** v. 解決   **compensate** v. 補償   **inconvenience** n. 不便

---

144 ■ 動詞語彙 掌握上下文   解答 (B)

由「要求我們幫助____您通行密碼的信」的句意看來，所有的選項皆有可能為正確答案。因為無法單就空格所在的文句判斷答案，因此應參考上下文意。後文提到「我們昨天試著尋回您遺失的密碼」，因此可以判斷應是要求恢復密碼，所以動詞 (B) recover（恢復）為正確答案。

145 ■ 相似意義的動詞   解答 (C)

由「因為我們懷疑其他的密碼也已經遺失了」的句意看來，動詞 (C) suspect（懷疑）為正確答案。(D) doubt 也有「懷疑」的意思，但是 suspect 是懷疑某件事為肯定，doubt 則較偏向懷疑某件事為否定。(A) debate 是「爭論」，(B) negotiate 是「協商」的意思。

146 ■ 用動名詞當作受詞的動詞   解答 (D)

用動名詞當作受詞的動詞 continue，在本句尚無受詞，因此動名詞 (D) enjoying 為正確答案。動詞 (A) 與 (C)，形容詞 (B) 則不能當作受詞。

The Tourism Department _____ a cultural exhibit at the

147 (A) held　　　　(B) should hold
　　(C) will hold　　(D) has held

Kosan Hall as part of Bhutan's Cultural Month celebration. The exhibit, which will showcase the country's Tibetan and Indian roots, will be open for viewing from July 2 to 5. It will be an exciting learning experience for everyone who attends.

Opening ceremonies will be _____ by tourism director Jigme

148 (A) situated　　(B) combined
　　(C) evaluated　(D) conducted

Chong on July 2 at 8 A.M.

Various public officials and artists are expected to be at the event. The exhibits will showcase a variety of traditional costumes, artifacts, and handicrafts. In addition, the _____ of

149 (A) binding　　　(B) release
　　(C) independence　(D) revision

a limited photography publication about Bhutanese culture will also occur on the opening night.

For more details about the exhibit or venue, please visit www.bhutantour.com or call the Tourism Department hotline at 555-3247.

147 觀光部將在 Kosan Hall 舉辦一個文化展覽，作為不丹文化月慶祝活動的一部分。此次展覽將展現該國的藏族及印度淵源，從 7 月 2 日到 5 日開放參觀，這將會是一個令參觀者相當振奮的學習經驗。

148 開幕式將會在 7 月 2 日早上 8 點由旅遊局長 Jigme Chong 主持。

預計將有眾多的公職人員及藝術家參加此活動，展覽將展示各種的傳統服飾、文物及手工藝品。149 此外，一份限量的不丹文化攝影集也會在開幕式的晚上公開發行。

有關展覽或地點的更多詳情，請上 www.bhutantour.com.com 或打觀光局諮詢電話 555-3247。

單字 showcase v. 展示　public official phr. 公務員　artifact n. 工藝品　handicraft n. 手工藝品
venue n.（展示、演唱會、會談等等的）地點　hotline n. 諮詢電話

---

147 ■ 未來式 掌握上下文　　　　　　　　　　　　　　　　　　　　　　　　　　　　　　　解答 (C)

由「觀光部將在 Kosan Hall 舉辦一個文化展覽」看來，無法單就空格所在的文句選出正確時態的動詞，因此應了解前後文意才能選出正確答案。後文提到從 7 月 2 日到 5 日開放參觀，因此未來式的 (C) will hold 為正確答案。

148 ■ 動詞語彙　　　　　　　　　　　　　　　　　　　　　　　　　　　　　　　　　　　　解答 (D)

由「開幕式將會在 7 月 2 日早上 8 點由旅遊局長 Jigme Chong 主持」的句意看來，空格與空格前的 be 動詞為被動語態，因此動詞 conduct（管理，主持）的 p.p. 形 (D) conducted 為正確答案。(A) situate 是「置於～，定位」，(B) combine「結合」，(C) evaluate 是「評估」的意思。

149 ■ 名詞語彙 掌握上下文　　　　　　　　　　　　　　　　　　　　　　　　　　　　　　　解答 (B)

由「攝影集也會在開幕式的晚上____」的句意看來，(A) binding（裝訂），(B) release（發行，公開，發表會，公布），(D) revision（修正，檢討）皆有可能為正確答案。因為無法單就空格所在的文句判斷答案，因此應參考上下文意。前面提到展覽將展示各種的傳統服飾、文物及手工藝品，可以知道攝影集也將會被公開發行。因此名詞 (B) release 為正確答案。(C) independence 則是「獨立」的意思。

Questions 150-152 refer to the following article.　　　　150-152 根據下面文章的內容回答問題。

People from across the country and around the world gathered at Ponda Bay last night to witness the FlyFlicks Festival. The annual _____ attracted nearly 15-thousand

　　150 (A) screening　　(B) competition
　　　　(C) reunion　　　(D) convention

spectators, mostly from the United States and Central America.

The fireworks contest featured entries from 20 countries and was judged by fireworks experts who are well established within the industry. Among _____ were Dragon

　　151 (A) yourselves　(B) us
　　　　(C) them　　　　(D) you

Gate founders Tsien Long and Kenneth Kang. The event began with a vibrant display by the US team. Following that, several European squads displayed their shows before the evening concluded with a set by the Taiwanese team that was accompanied by music. Winners will be awarded tomorrow. Although all the participants delivered unique presentations, observers expect _____ Greece

　　152 (A) that　　　　(B) thus
　　　　(C) and　　　　(D) on

will take home this year's title for its groundbreaking display.

來自全國各地及世界各國的人們，昨晚聚集在 Ponda Bay 見證 FlyFlicks 慶典。150 這一年一度的比賽吸引了將近一萬五千名的觀眾，大部分來自美國及中美洲。

這次煙火比賽以二十國的參賽作品做為號召，由業界中公認的煙火專家來評定。151 這當中有 Dragon Gate 的創辦人 Tsien Long 及 Kenneth Kang。

此活動由美國隊充滿活力的表演揭開序幕，接著，幾支歐洲的隊伍呈現他們的表演，最後，由台灣團隊搭配音樂的一套表演替這個晚上畫下句點。獲勝者將在明天接受頒獎。
152 雖然所有的參賽者都呈現了獨特的表演，觀察家預測，希臘將會以其突破性的表演抱回今年的冠軍。

單字 attract v. 吸引，誘惑　firework n. 煙火　feature v. 特別包含～　entry n. 參加作品　vibrant a. 充滿活力的
squad n. 隊伍，分隊　observer n. 觀眾　groundbreaking a. 突破性的

150 ■ 名詞語彙 掌握上下文　　　　　　　　　　　　　　　　　　　　　　　　　　　　　解答 (B)

由「一年一度的比賽吸引了觀眾」的句意看來，所有的選項皆有可能為正確答案。因為無法單就空格所在的文句判斷答案，因此應參考上下文意。後文提到煙火比賽包含了二十國參賽作品，因此可以知道名詞 (B) competition（比賽）為正確答案。(A) screening 是「上映」，(C) reunion 是「聚會，同學會」，(D) convention 是「大會，會議」的意思。

151 ■ 人稱代名詞 掌握上下文　　　　　　　　　　　　　　　　　　　　　　　　　　　　　解答 (C)

因為空格是介系詞 Among 的受詞，因此反身代名詞 (A)、受格 (B) (C) (D) 皆有可能為正確答案。因為無法單就空格所在的文句判斷答案，因此應參考上下文意。前面提到由業界中公認的煙火專家來評定，空格所在的文句羅列了人名，句意應為「這當中的」，所以第三人稱複數人稱代名詞 (C) them 為正確答案。

152 ■ 名詞子句 連接詞 that　　　　　　　　　　　　　　　　　　　　　　　　　　　　　　　解答 (A)

動詞 expect 的受詞為子句 Greece will take home ~ display，因此空格應為名詞子句連接詞，所以 (A) that 是正確答案。連接副詞 (B) thus（所以），對等連接詞 (C) and（和），介系詞 (D) on（在～上）無法連接名詞子句。

Questions 153-154 refer to the following registration details.　153-154 根據下面註冊詳情的內容回答問題。

Venus Swimming School Enrollment Information (Summer)	
Courses	[154]**Fee**
Basic Course Will teach water safety drills and basic swimming skills, including submerging, floating, moving forward, and breathing exercises	$140
[153-A/C/D]**Advanced Course 1** Will focus on freestyle, backstroke, and basic diving	$120
Advanced Course 2 Will focus on breaststroke, butterfly, and competitive freestyle	$150
[154]**Refresher** Will review basic swimming skills and strokes	$130

The deadline for enrollment is on April 1. Please visit the school's official Web site at www.venus.com for class schedules.

維納斯游泳班 註冊資訊 （夏天）	
課程	[154]**費用**
基本課程 將教導水上安全演練及基本的游泳技巧，包含潛入水中、漂浮、向前移動及呼吸練習	140 美元
[153-A/C/D]**進階課程 1** 將集中在自由式、仰式及基本的潛水	120 美元
進階課程 2 將集中在蛙式、蝶式及競技自由式	150 美元
[154]**複習課程** 將複習基本的游泳技巧及姿勢	130 美元

報名截止日期為 4 月 1 日。請上學校官網 www.venus.com 查詢課程表。

單字 □ **enrollment** n. 註冊，報名　□ **drill** n.（因應突發狀況）訓練，反覆練習　□ **submerge** v. 潛入水中
　　□ **float** v. 浮　□ **breath** v. 呼吸　□ **focus on** phr. 聚焦於～
　　□ **freestyle** n. 自由式　□ **backstroke** n. 仰式　□ **breaststroke** n. 蛙式
　　□ **butterfly** n. 蝶式　□ **competitive** a. 競爭的

153

What will NOT be taught in Advanced Course 1? (A) Freestyle (B) Butterfly (C) Diving (D) Backstroke	進階課程一中將不會教到下列哪一項？ (A) 自由式 (B) 蝶式 (C) 潛水 (D) 仰式

■ **Not/True** Not 問題　解答 (B)

這是尋找題目關鍵字 taught in Advanced Course 1 再與選項對照的 Not/True 問題。在 Advanced Course 1 Will focus on freestyle, backstroke, and basic diving 中提到「進階課程 1 將集中在自由式、仰式及基本的潛水」，與 (A)(C)(D) 相符，(B) 的內容在文中則未被提及，因此 (B) Butterfly 為正確答案。

154

How much is the fee for a swimming review course? (A) $120 (B) $150 (C) $140 (D) $130	游泳複習課程要多少錢？ (A) 120 美元 (B) 150 美元 (C) 140 美元 (D) 130 美元

■ 六何原則 How much　解答 (D)

這是在問游泳複習課程要多少錢（How much）的六何原則問題。與題目關鍵字 the fee for a swimming review course 相關的內容為 Refresher Will review basic swimming skills and strokes，提到將複習基本的游泳技巧及姿勢，後面並寫 Fee, $130，可知 (D) $130 為正確答案。

Questions 155-156 refer to the following invitation.

155-156 根據下面邀請函的內容回答問題。

¹⁵⁵Please join us
for cocktails to celebrate the publication of
Chef Melinda Waterston's
*Recipes for Rainy Days:
A Cookbook*

Myrtle Publishing is proud to present Chef Melinda Waterston's latest collection of recipes, gathered over the years from friends, family, and loved ones. This Seattle native has warmed the local residents' hearts and bellies as the owner and operator of Waterston's, a landmark restaurant in downtown Seattle for the past 15 years.

¹⁵⁵On Sunday, August 25
at 8 P.M.

Eastside Clubhouse
7 Clarinet Street, Melody Gardens
Clifford Hill, Seattle, Washington

Light refreshments will be served.

^{156-B}Please confirm your attendance by calling
Lance Fox at 555-6910 or 555-5632.

¹⁵⁵ 歡迎加入我們為了慶祝主廚
Melinda Waterston 的
《Recipes for Rainy Days：烹飪手冊》出版而舉辦的雞尾酒宴

Myrtle 出版社很榮幸為您介紹主廚 Melinda Waterston 最新的食譜集，內容是多年來從朋友、家人及親人所蒐集而來的。這位土生土長的西雅圖人，身為西雅圖市中心具指標性的 Waterston's 餐廳的老闆和經營者，在過去的 15 年間溫暖了當地居民的心和肚子。

¹⁵⁵8 月 25 日星期天
晚上 8 點

Eastside 俱樂部
Melody 花園, Clarinet 街 7 號
華盛頓州, 西雅圖市, Clifford Hill 郡

輕食招待

^{156-B} 請來電與 Lance Fox 確認您的出席
555-6910 或 555-5632

單字 □publication n. 出版　　　□native a. 土生土長的　　　□belly n. 肚子
　　 □refreshment n. 點心　　　□attendance n. 出席

155

What event will be held on August 25?	8 月 25 日將舉辦什麼活動？
(A) A company celebration	(A) 公司慶祝活動
(B) A family reunion	(B) 家庭聚會
(C) A book launch	(C) 新書發表會
(D) A restaurant opening	(D) 餐廳開幕式

六何原則 What 　　　　　　　　　　　　　　　　　　　　　　　　　　解答 (C)

這題是在問 8 月 25 日將舉辦什麼（What）活動的六何原則問題，與題目關鍵字 event ~ on August 25 相關的文句為 Please join us for cocktails to celebrate the publication of Chef Melinda Waterston's *Recipes for Rainy Days: A Cookbook*，提到請加入雞尾酒宴來慶祝主廚 Melinda Waterston 的食譜出版，後面又提到 On Sunday, August 25，即 8 月 25 日星期天，因此可知 8 月 25 日將會有新書發表會，所以 (C) A book launch 為正確答案。

156

What is stated about the event?	文中提到有關活動的什麼事？
(A) Directions may be found on a Web site.	(A) 網頁上可能可以找到指示。
(B) Attendees must contact Mr. Fox.	(B) 參加者須連絡 Fox 先生。
(C) Formal attire is required.	(C) 需穿著正式服裝。
(D) A buffet dinner will be served.	(D) 將提供自助式晚餐。

Not/True True 問題 　　　　　　　　　　　　　　　　　　　　　　　解答 (B)

這是找出題目關鍵字 the event 的相關內容，再與選項互相對照的 Not/True 問題。(A) (C) (D) 的內容在文中未被提及。(B) Please confirm your attendance by calling Lance Fox 提到「請來電與 Lance Fox 確認您的出席」，因此 (B) Attendees must contact Mr. Fox 為正確答案。

Derma House

Do you spend thousands of dollars on over-the-counter medications that fail to solve your skin problems? If you want to have that clear and youthful-looking glow, come to Derma House. [157/158-B]We specialize in customized skin treatments that match your skin type. [158-A]Our dermatologists use state-of-the-art equipment and solutions based on natural ingredients for acne, skin whitening, and anti-aging treatments.

Discover what Derma House can do for you. [158-D/159]Visit any of our clinics from May 6 to May 10 to get a free consultation and 20 percent off on any regular facial treatment.

Derma House is an affiliate of Skin Medical Center.
www.dermahouse.com
Dial 555-8471

Derma House

您是否花了成千上萬的錢在那些沒有辦法解決您皮膚問題的成藥上？如果您想要擁有潔淨並煥發出青春亮麗的皮膚，來 Derma House。[157/158-B] 我們專精於客製化符合您肌膚類型的皮膚護理。[158-A] 我們的皮膚科醫生使用最先進的儀器及以天然成分為基底的美容液來治療痘痘、美白及抗老化。

來看看 Derma House 能為您做些什麼，[158-D/159] 在 5 月 6 日至 10 日，來我們任何一家診所，您可獲得一次免費的諮詢以及任何一般臉部護理八折的折扣。

Derma House 是 Skin Medical Center 的關係企業
www.dermahouse.com
請打 555-8471

單字
- □over-the-counter a. 無處方籤的
- □medication n. 醫藥品
- □glow n. 光采
- □specialize v. 專精
- □dermatologist n. 皮膚科醫生
- □state-of-the-art a. 最先進的
- □ingredient n. 材料，組成要素
- □acne n. 痘痘
- □consultation n. 諮詢，協議
- □affiliate n. 關係企業

157

What type of business is being advertised?	廣告的是哪種生意？
(A) A fitness facility	(A) 健身設施
(B) A dermatology clinic	(B) 皮膚科診所
(C) A health food store	(C) 健康食品店
(D) A hair salon	(D) 髮廊

■ 找出主題 主題　　　　　　　　　　　　　　　　　　　　　　　　　　　　　解答 (B)

這題是在問廣告的主旨，應特別注意文章中段有提及主旨的相關內容。We specialize in customized skin treatments that match your skin type. 中提到「我們專精於客製化符合您肌膚類型的皮膚護理」，因此 (B) A dermatology clinic 為正確答案。

單字 facility n. 設施　dermatology n. 皮膚科

158

What is NOT mentioned about the Derma House?	文中沒有提到 Derma House 的哪件事？
(A) It utilizes natural ingredients.	(A) 它利用天然的成分。
(B) It offers a personalized service.	(B) 它提供個人化的服務。
(C) It provides affordable cosmetic surgery.	(C) 它提供負擔得起的美容手術。
(D) It has a number of different locations.	(D) 它有幾個不同的地點。

■ **Not/True** Not 問題   解答 (C)

這是找出題目關鍵字 the Derma House 的相關內容再與選項相互對照的 Not/True 問題。Our dermatologists use ~ solutions based on natural ingredients 中提到「我們的皮膚科醫生使用～天然成分」，與 (A) 的內容一致。We specialize in customized skin treatments that match your skin type. 提到「我們專精於客製化符合您肌膚類型的皮膚護理」，與 (B) 的內容相符。(C) 的內容在文中則未被提及。因此 (C) It provides affordable cosmetic surgery. 為正確答案。Visit any of our clinics 表示 Derma House 有許多分店，與 (D) 的敘述相符。

單字 utilize v. 利用，善用   affordable a. 負擔得起的，便宜的

159

What does Derma House offer to do?	Derma House 提供什麼？
(A) Distribute free samples	(A) 發送免費的試用品
(B) Hold makeup demonstrations	(B) 舉辦化妝示範
(C) Extend operation hours	(C) 延長營業時間
(D) Provide skin consultations	(D) 提供皮膚諮詢

■ **六何原則** What   解答 (D)

這是在問 Derma Hose 提供什麼（What）的六何原則問題。與題目關鍵字 offer to do 相關的內容有 Visit any of our clinics ~ to get a free consultation，當中提到「來我們任何一家診所，您可獲得免費的諮詢」，因此 (D) Provide skin consultations 為正確答案。

單字 distribute v. 發送，分派   demonstration n. 示範

Scaper Phones	Scaper 電話公司
January 15	日期：1 月 15 日
Diana Price 252 77th Street Aurora, IL 60504	收件人： Diana Price 地址： 60504 依利諾州 極光郡 第 77 號街 252 號
Dear Ms. Price,	親愛的 Price 小姐：
[160]The mobile phone that you shipped to us for replacement arrived this morning. The unit has been forwarded to the technical support department for a diagnostic test, and the results will be released in three days.	[160] 您寄給我們要更換的手機在今早送達。且已轉發給技術支援部門作診斷測試，結果會在三天後公布。
Our warranty guarantees replacement of mobile phones returned to us within three weeks of purchase. [161]Should we find the product you purchased defective, we will immediately send you a new unit of the same model.	我們的保固保證在購買我們手機後的三個星期內可以退回更換，[161] 如果我們發現您購買的產品有瑕疵，我們會立刻寄送一個同樣型號的新手機給您。
Thank you for your patience.	感謝您的耐心等待。
Respectfully yours,	
Ted Patel Customer service representative Scaper Phones	Ted Patel 敬上 客戶服務代表 Scaper 電話公司

單字 □replacement n. 更換，交替　□forward v. 傳達　□diagnostic a. 診斷的
　　 □warranty n. 保固　　　　　　□guarantee v. 保障，保證　□defective a. 有瑕疵的，不良的
　　 □immediately ad. 即時，即刻

160

Why did Scaper Phones write to Ms. Price? (A) To introduce a new service to a client (B) To acknowledge receipt of an item (C) To request a replacement (D) To advertise a special offer	為什麼 Scaper 電話公司要寫信給 Price 小姐？ (A) 向客戶介紹一項新的服務 (B) 確認收到物品 (C) 要求更換 (D) 宣傳一個特別的優惠

■ 找出主題 寫文章的理由　　　　　　　　　　　　　　　　　　　　　　　　　　　　　解答 (B)

這是在問 Scaper Phones 為什麼要寫信給 Ms. Price，為尋找文章主旨的問題，應注意文章的前半部分。The mobile phone that you shipped to us for replacement arrived this morning. 提到 Ms. Price 寄出欲更換的手機在今早已送達，因此可知是要確認相關事項，所以 (B) To acknowledge receipt of an item 為正確答案。

單字 introduce v. 介紹　acknowledge v. 告知，確認　receipt n. 收據

What will Scaper Phones do if a product is defective?	如果產品有瑕疵，Scaper 電話公司會怎麼做呢？
(A) Forward it to a repair center	(A) 送到維修中心
(B) Refund the customer's money	(B) 退還客戶錢
(C) Deliver a new one of the same kind	(C) 寄送一個同樣的新品
(D) Provide credit for future purchases	(D) 提供未來購買的信貸

■ 六何原則 What   解答 (C)

這題是在問如果產品有瑕疵，Scaper 電話公司會做什麼（What）的六何原則問題。與題目關鍵字 if a product is defective 相關的文句為 should we find the product you purchased defective, we will immediately send you a new unit of the same model.，提到「如果我們發現您購買的產品有瑕疵，我們會立刻寄送一個同樣型號的新手機給您」，因此 (C) Deliver a new one of the same kind 為正確答案。

單字 refund v. 退款，償還

READING TEST 1 2 3 4 5 6 7 8 9 10

Questions 162-164 refer to the following e-mail.

162-164 根據下面電郵的內容回答問題。

From: Annette Hoskins <ahoskins@zollinger-insurance.com>

To: Raymond Lewis <rlewis@makeityours.com>

[163]Date: October 15
Subject: Products

Dear Mr. Lewis,

I was referred to you by a former colleague, Alfred Newton, who now works at Reflex Media. He told me you could supply us with customized office merchandise and that you give special rates for large corporate orders. I was hoping you could answer some questions.

First, [164]I am planning to buy 225 planners, 250 t-shirts, and 200 coffee mugs, which we intend to give out as mementos to our clients beginning in December. How long will it take for these items to be made? [163]We'd prefer to have them by the end of next month. Next, the items will need to have our company logo printed on them. How do I send you an image of it? Last but not least, [162]would an order of the size we want qualify us for the discount Mr. Newton mentioned?

Please inform me as soon as possible by replying to this message. If you'd like, I can meet with you sometime this week to discuss the matter further. You may also call me at my office number, 555-9312.

Thank you.

Annette Hoskins
Marketing director, Zollinger Insurance

寄件人：Annette Hoskins <ahoskins@zollinger-insurance.com>
收件人：Raymond Lewis <rlewis@makeityours.com>
[163] 日期：10 月 15 日
主旨：產品

親愛的 Lewis 先生：

我是藉由以前的同事 Alfred Newton 介紹的，他現在在 Reflex 媒體工作，他告訴我，你可以為我們提供客製化的辦公商品，而且你會給大型企業訂單特別的優惠，我希望你可以回答我一些問題。

首先，[164] 我計畫要購買 225 本手帳、250 件 T-Shirt 及 200 個咖啡杯，這些是我們打算要在十二月開始發送給我們客戶作為紀念品的，這些物品需要製造多久呢？[163] 我們希望下個月月底前可以拿到。然後，這些物品需要印有我們公司的標誌在上面，我如何傳圖像給你呢？最後很重要的一點是，[162] 我們所要的訂單數量不曉得是否足以讓我們享有 Newton 先生所提到的折扣呢？

請儘快以回覆此信件來通知我，如果你想要，我可以在這個星期的某一天與您碰面來進一步討論此事，你也可以打我辦公室的電話：555-9312。

謝謝您。

Annette Hoskins
Zollinger 保險行銷總監

單字 □refer to phr. 提及　□former a. 以前的　□colleague n. 同事
　　 □customized a. 客製化的　□memento n. 紀念品，遺物　□qualify v. 有資格

162

What does Ms. Hoskins inquire about?	Hoskins 小姐詢問何事？
(A) Whether Mr. Newton is suited for a position	(A) Newton 先生是否適合一個職務
(B) Where to find a company's closest branch	(B) 何處找到一間公司最近的分店
(C) What it will cost to print in different colors	(C) 列印不同的顏色要多少錢
(D) Whether she is eligible to receive a special rate	(D) 她是否有資格享有特價

■ 六何原則 What

解答 (D)

這題是在問 Ms. Hoskins 詢問什麼（What）的六何原則問題，與題目關鍵字 inquire about 相關的文句為 would an order ~ qualify us for the discount ~?，是在詢問所要的訂單數量是否足以享有折扣，因此 (D) Whether she is eligible to receive a special rate 為正確答案。

換句話說

qualify ~ for the discount 有享有折扣的資格 → is eligible to receive a special rate 足以享有折扣

單字 suited a. 適合的　eligible a. 有資格的

163

When does Ms. Hoskins want the order delivered?	Hoskins 小姐希望訂貨何時送達？
(A) In September	(A) 九月
(B) In October	(B) 十月
(C) In November	(C) 十一月
(D) In December	(D) 十二月

■ 六何原則 When　　　　　　　　　　　　　　　　　　　　　　　　解答 (C)

這題是在問 Ms. Hoskins 希望訂貨何時送達（When）的六何原則問題。與題目關鍵字 the order delivered 相關的文句為 We'd prefer to have them by the end of next month.，當中提到「我們希望下個月月底前可以拿到。」，由信件上的『Date: October 15』可知下個月為十一月，因此 (C) In November 為正確答案。

164

What is suggested about Ms. Hoskins?	文中暗示 Hoskins 小姐什麼事？
(A) She wants to purchase gifts for her staff.	(A) 她希望替她的員工購買禮物。
(B) She owns an insurance corporation.	(B) 她擁有一家保險公司。
(C) She plans to organize an event in December.	(C) 她計畫在十二月舉辦一個活動。
(D) She is in charge of promotional items.	(D) 她負責宣傳品。

■ 推論 詳細內容　　　　　　　　　　　　　　　　　　　　　　　　解答 (D)

這是依題目關鍵字 Ms. Hoskins 來進行推論的問題。I am planning to buy 225 planners, 250 t-shirts, and 200 coffee mugs, which we intend to give out as mementos to our clients 當中提到計畫要購買 225 本手帳、250 件 T-Shirt 及 200 個咖啡杯，這些是打算要發送給客戶作為紀念品，所以 (D) She is in charge of promotional items. 為正確答案。

單字 insurance n. 保險

Kaleidoscope
by Emma Graham

After a stressful week at work, it is always nice to drop by the spa to relax and recharge. [165]For more than three years now, spa treatments have helped me fight fatigue. All the while, I thought I had been enjoying the greatest spa services in the area, but that notion changed when I visited the Red Sea Spa.

The newest spa in the metropolitan area offers a variety of hydrotherapy massages. [167-A]The Red Sea Spa resembles a water theme park with ten swimming pools, providing soft, moderate, and hard massages using only water pressure. Among my favorite spots in the premises is the hydro-acupuncture pool. [166-D]It squirts warm water that gives a pricking sensation similar to what is experienced during real acupuncture treatment. [166-C]The pool works well to soothe sore muscles.

[167-B]The water spa is also equipped with basic amenities, such as saunas and facial rooms. [167-D]It also has pools for children, as well as dining facilities serving American and Italian dishes. Regarding the service, the spa employs a pleasant and accommodating staff to ensure that guests enjoy their visit.

If you want a different relaxation experience with your family and friends, then the Red Sea Spa is the place to go. And from June 1 through the end of August, [168-A] the spa is giving away free gym towels with the cost of admission. The Red Sea Spa is open daily from 8 A.M. to 11 P.M.

萬花筒
作者：Emma Graham

經過一週的緊張工作後，能去水療中心放鬆和充電是件很棒的事。[165] 超過三年以來，水療護理幫我對抗疲勞。這當中，我以為我已經享受到這區域最棒的水療服務，但在我去了 Red Sea Spa 之後，我改變了這個想法。

這個位於都會區的最新水療館提供多種水療按摩，[167-A] Red Sea Spa 像一座水的主題樂園，有十座游泳池提供以純水壓式輕量、中等及強力的按摩。在這裡，我最喜歡的地點之一就是水針灸池，[166-D] 它噴出的溫水，會有一種類似真正針灸治療時的刺痛感覺，[166-C] 這池對舒緩肌肉酸痛也很有效。

[167-B] 這個水療館也配有其他基本的設施，如三溫暖及做臉室，[167-D] 它也有兒童池和提供美式及義式菜餚的餐廳，至於服務方面，水療中心聘用了一群和藹可親及樂於助人的工作人員，以確保客人享受他們的造訪。

如果您想要與您的家人和朋友有一個不同的放鬆體驗，那 Red Sea Spa 是您要去的地方，而且，從 6 月 1 日到 8 月底，[168-A] 只要入場，水療館將贈送免費的健身房毛巾。Red Sea Spa 的開放時間是每日的早上 8 點到晚上 11 點。

單字
□ drop by phr. 順道
□ notion n. 想法，概念
□ resemble v. 類似，相像
□ squirt v. 噴
□ acupuncture n. 針灸
□ accommodating a. 親切的，樂於助人的

□ recharge v. 充電
□ metropolitan a. 大都市的
□ moderate a. 適當的
□ prick v. 刺
□ soothe v. 舒緩

□ fatigue n. 疲勞
□ hydrotherapy n. 水療法
□ premises n. 用地，經營場地
□ sensation n. 感覺
□ be equipped with phr. 配備有～

165

What is suggested about Emma Graham? (A) She writes dining reviews for a publication. (B) She frequently seeks out spa services. (C) She has visited the Red Sea Spa before. (D) She was disappointed with the Red Sea Spa.	文中指出有關 Emma Graham 的什麼事？ (A) 她書寫有關於餐飲評論的出版物。 (B) 她時常尋求水療服務。 (C) 她以前曾經到過 Red Sea Spa。 (D) 她對 Red Sea Spa 很失望。

■ 推論 詳細內容　　　　　　　　　　　　　　　　　　　　　　　　　　　　　　　　　　　　解答 (B)

這是依題目關鍵字 Emma Graham 來進行推論的問題。For more than three years now, spa treatments have helped me fight fatigue. All the while, I thought I had been enjoying the greatest spa services in the area 中提到「超過三年以來，水療護理幫我對抗疲勞。這當中，我以為我已經享受到這區域最棒的水療服務」，因此可以推論 Emma Graham 經常使用水療服務，所以 (B) She frequently seeks out spa services 為正確答案。

166

What is mentioned about the hydro-acupuncture pool? (A) It is inadvisable for children. (B) It is a popular feature of the spa. (C) It relieves muscle pain. (D) It uses soft water pressure.	文中提到水針灸池的什麼事？ (A) 它是兒童不宜。 (B) 它是水療館一個受歡迎的特色。 (C) 它可緩解肌肉疼痛。 (D) 它使用柔和的水壓。

Not/True True 問題　　　　　　　　　　　　　　　　　　　　　　　　　　　　解答 (C)

這是尋找題目關鍵字 the hydro-acupuncture pool 的相關內容再與選項相互對照的 Not/True 問題。(A) 與 (B) 的內容在文中未被提及。The pool works well to soothe sore muscles. 提到這池對舒緩肌肉酸痛很有效，與 (C) 的內容相符。因此 (C) It relieves muscle pain 為正確答案。It squirts warm water that gives a pricking sensation similar to what is experienced during real acupuncture treatment. 提到它噴出的溫水，會有一種類似真正針灸治療時的刺痛感覺，與 (D) 的敘述不符。

單字 inadvisable a. 不宜的　relieve v. 舒緩

167

What is NOT a facility at the Red Sea Spa? (A) Swimming pools (B) Saunas (C) Childcare center (D) Restaurants	哪一個不是 Red Sea Spa 的設施？ (A) 游泳池 (B) 三溫暖 (C) 兒童中心 (D) 餐廳

Not/True Not 問題　　　　　　　　　　　　　　　　　　　　　　　　　　　　解答 (C)

這是尋找題目關鍵字 a facility at the Red Sea Spa 的相關內容，再與選項互相對照的 Not/True 問題。The Red Sea Spa resembles a water theme park with ten swimming pools 中提到 Red Sea Spa 像一座水的主題樂園，有十座游泳池，與 (A) 的內容相符。The water spa is also equipped with basic amenities, such as saunas 中提到這個水療館也配有其他基本的設施，如三溫暖，與 (B) 相符。(C) 的內容在文中則未被提及。因此 (C) Childcare center 為正確答案。It also has ~ dining facilities 中提到它也有餐廳，與 (D) 的敘述相符。

168

What is indicated about the Red Sea Spa? (A) It is offering a special incentive to customers. (B) It serves a variety of healthy cuisines. (C) It trains acupuncture practitioners. (D) It closes later on the weekends.	文中指出有關 Red Sea Spa 的什麼事？ (A) 它現在提供顧客一個特別的優惠。 (B) 它提供各種不同的健康料理。 (C) 它訓練針灸師。 (D) 它在週末比較晚關門。

Not/True True 問題　　　　　　　　　　　　　　　　　　　　　　　　　　　　解答 (A)

這是尋找題目關鍵字 the Red Sea Spa 的相關內容，再與選項互相對照的 Not/True 問題。the spa is giving away free gym towels with the cost of admission 中提到水療館入場即贈送免費的健身房毛巾，與 (A) 的內容一致。因此 (A) It is offering a special incentive to customers 為正確答案。(B) (C) (D) 的內容在文中則未被提及。

單字 cuisine n. 料理

Questions 169-171 refer to the following memo.

169-171 根據下面文件的內容回答問題。

MEMORANDUM

TO: Producers
FROM: Lawrence Bash, *Kitchen Hub* executive producer

SUBJECT: Partial Viewers Survey Report

[169]Below are the preliminary findings from the viewers' survey carried out by the researchers of the show in April. A total of 2,000 local respondents participated in the online survey. It has only been a week since the research team concluded data collection, so we still need to wait another month for the complete findings. In the meantime, take note of the viewers' responses as they might yield some useful insights:

[170]Question number 1: [169]How often do you watch *Kitchen Hub*?

Every week	20 percent
Once a month	50 percent
Twice a month	20 percent
Three times a month	10 percent

Question number 2: [169]How would you rate *Kitchen Hub*?

Excellent	10 percent
Good	20 percent
Satisfactory	20 percent
Needs improvement	50 percent

Question number 3: [169]Please rate the difficulty of *Kitchen Hub* recipes.

Appetizers:	Easy	80 percent
	Moderate	15 percent
	Difficult	5 percent
Main courses:	Easy	30 percent
	Moderate	10 percent
	Difficult	60 percent
Desserts :	Easy	80 percent
	Moderate	17 percent
	Difficult	3 percent

Note: [171]Most of respondents said that many of the main courses were difficult to cook because they required the use of unconventional cooking tools and equipment.

We will have a meeting tomorrow at 9 A.M. to discuss these findings.

備忘錄

受件者：製片人
寄件者：Lawrence Bash, *Kitchen Hub* 執行製片人
主題：部分觀眾調查報告

[169]下面是本節目研究人員在四月進行一項觀眾調查的的初步結果，一共有兩千名本地受訪者參與本次的網上調查，研究團隊結束數據的收集至今只有一個星期，我們仍需要再等待一個月才有完整的調查結果，在此期間，留意觀眾的回答，因為它們可能會提供一些有用的意見：

[170]問題 1：[169] 你多久看一次 *Kitchen Hub*？

每週	百分之二十
每月一次	百分之五十
每月兩次	百分之二十
每月三次	百分之十

問題 2：[169] 你對 *Kitchen Hub* 的評價如何？

優等	百分之十
良好	百分之二十
滿意	百分之二十
需要改進	百分之五十

問題 3：[169] 請評估 *Kitchen Hub* 食譜的難度。

前菜：	簡單	百分之八十
	中等	百分之十五
	困難	百分之五
主菜：	簡單	百分之三十
	中等	百分之十
	困難	百分之六十
甜點：	簡單	百分之八十
	中等	百分之十七
	困難	百分之三

註記：[171] 大部分的受訪者表示，許多主菜很難煮，因為他們需要使用非傳統的烹飪工具和設備。

我們在明天早上九點會有一個會議來討論這些調查的結果。

單字 □partial a. 一部分的，部分的　　□preliminary a. 預備的　　□respondent n. 應答者
□rate v. 評價　　□unconventional a. 不尋常的，非常規的

169

Why was the survey most likely conducted?	此調查最可能的進行原因是？
(A) To find out about product usage	(A) 了解產品的使用
(B) To compile a list of new recipes	(B) 收集新食譜的清單
(C) To research cooking methods	(C) 研究烹飪方法
(D) To get opinions on a TV program	(D) 得到關於一個電視節目的意見

推論 詳細內容　　　　　　　　　　　　　　　　　　　　　　　　　　　　　解答 (D)

這是依題目關鍵字 the survey 來進行推論的問題。Below are the preliminary findings from the viewers' survey 中提到下面是本節目研究人員進行的一項觀眾調查的初步結果，問卷中的問題有 How often do you watch *Kitchen Hub*?、How would you rate *Kitchen Hub*?、Please rate the difficulty of *Kitchen Hub* recipes.，即「你多久看一次 *Kitchen Hub*？、你對 *Kitchen Hub* 的評價如何？、請評估 *Kitchen Hub* 食譜的難度」，可知道是在蒐集觀眾對節目的意見，所以 (D) To get opinions on a TV program 為正確答案。

單字 usage n. 活用，用法　compile v. 收集，編輯

170

What do the survey results suggest about *Kitchen Hub*?	調查的結果指出 *Kitchen Hub* 的什麼事？
(A) It is popular in other countries.	(A) 它在其他國中很流行。
(B) It is broadcast once a week.	(B) 它每週播放一次。
(C) It is highly rated by viewers.	(C) 它受到觀眾高度的評價。
(D) It is replayed at the end of each month.	(D) 它每個月底會重播。

推論 詳細內容　　　　　　　　　　　　　　　　　　　　　　　　　　　　　解答 (B)

這是依題目關鍵字 *Kitchen Hub* 來進行推論的問題。Question number 1: How often do you watch *Kitchen Hub*? Every week, Once a month, Twice a month, Three times a month 中提到「你多久看一次 *Kitchen Hub*？每週？每月一次？每月兩次？每月三次？」可以推斷這個節目每個禮拜播放一次，因此 (B) It is broadcast once a week 為正確答案。

單字 broadcast v. 播映

171

According to the memo, why do viewers find featured main courses difficult to make?	根據備忘錄，為什麼觀眾覺得很難做出特色主菜？
(A) Their ingredients are rarely available at supermarkets.	(A) 它們的原料在超市很難買到。
(B) They have long preparation times.	(B) 它們須有很久的準備時間。
(C) They are prepared with uncommon cooking utensils.	(C) 它們需要以不常見的廚具來準備。
(D) Their recipe instructions require professional skills.	(D) 他們的食譜指南需要專業的技能。

六何原則 Why　　　　　　　　　　　　　　　　　　　　　　　　　　　　　解答 (C)

這題是在問為什麼（why）觀眾發現很難做出特色主菜的六何原則問題。與題目關鍵字 viewers find featured main courses difficult to make 相關的文句為 Most of respondents said that many of the main courses were difficult to cook because they required the use of unconventional cooking tools and equipment.，提到大部分的回答者認為料理需要以不常見的廚具來製作，所以有困難，因此 (C) They are prepared with uncommon cooking utensils 為正確答案。

換句話說

unconventional cooking tools 不常見的廚具 → uncommon cooking utensils 不常見的廚具

單字 ingredient n. 材料　require v. 要求，使必要

172-175 根據下面公告的內容回答問題。

National Mail Service	國家郵政局
Money Orders	匯票
172The National Mail Service has recently discovered several counterfeit money orders. These money orders are suspected to have come from other countries and have been used for purchasing goods online. A number of local online businesses have been victimized by this fraud.	172 國家郵政局最近發現有幾件偽造的匯票。這些匯票懷疑是來自其他國家,並已被使用在線上購物,已有一些本地的線上公司已成為這種詐欺行為的受害者。
Please note that 173-DUS money orders can be purchased from the National Mail Service only. No other institution is allowed to produce US money orders. Therefore, it is more likely that money orders from abroad are forged.	請注意,173-D 美國的匯票只能在國家郵政局購買,沒有其他的機構獲准生產匯票,因此,來自國外的匯票更可能是偽造的。
Money orders presented at post offices and banks are subject to validation and clearance before payment. 174To ensure payment for purchased goods, the National Mail Service advises online businesses to check the authenticity of the money orders they receive before shipping merchandise.	郵局和銀行匯票付款前需驗證和許可,174 為了確保購買貨物能確實收款,國家郵政局建議在進行線上交易時,應在出貨前檢查他們所收到匯票的真假。
The US Federal Police and the mail service have been investigating the matter.	美國國家聯邦警察及郵政局已經著手調查此事。
175Information regarding the US money order service may be viewed by logging on to www.nationalmailservice.gov. Those who would like to verify money orders or report counterfeit payments may call (405) 555-3204.	175 有關美國匯票服務的資訊可上網查看:www.nationalmailservice.gov。想要驗證匯票或舉報偽造款項者請來電:(405)555-3204。

單字 □money order phr. 郵政匯票　□counterfeit a. 偽造的,仿造的　□suspect v. 懷疑
　　 □victimize v. 受到損害,使犧牲　□forge v. 偽造,架構　□clearance n. 承認,許可
　　 □verify v. 確認　□fraud n. 欺騙　□be subject to phr. 需經～
　　 □authenticity n. 真實性　□note v. 知道,注意　□validation n. 確認,評價
　　 □investigate v. 調查

172

Why was the notice written?	為什麼寫這份公告?
(A) To introduce a form of payment	(A) 介紹一種付款方式
(B) To notify the public about a problem	(B) 告知大眾一個問題
(C) To inform customers about a new service	(C) 知會顧客一項新服務
(D) To provide details on shipping fees	(D) 提供運費的詳細資料

■ 找出主題 寫文章的理由　　　　　　　　　　　　　　　　　　　　　　　　解答 (B)

這題是在問這篇廣告的主旨,應注意文章的前半部分。The National Mail Service has recently discovered several counterfeit money orders. 中提到國家郵政局最近發現有幾件偽造的匯票,後面又提醒應注意那些事項才能不受到損害,因此 (B) To notify the public about a problem 為正確答案。

單字 notify v. 告知

173

What is indicated about the money orders?	文中指出匯票的什麼事？
(A) They are rarely accepted by banks.	(A) 它們很少被銀行接受。
(B) They are difficult to authenticate.	(B) 它們很難被鑑定。
(C) They are necessary for online transactions.	(C) 它們在線上交易是必須的。
(D) They are only available from the mail service.	(D) 只在郵政局有提供。

■ Not/True True 問題   解答 (D)

這是尋找題目關鍵字 the money orders 的相關內容，再與選項互相對照的 Not/True 問題。(A) (B) (C) 的內容在文中未被提及。US money orders can be purchased from the National Mail Service only 中提到美國的匯票只能在國家郵政局購買，因此 (D) They are only available from the mail service. 為正確答案。

單字 transaction n. 交易，買賣

174

How are online companies advised to protect their businesses?	文中建議線上公司如何保護他們的生意？
(A) By installing credit card security applications	(A) 安裝信用卡安全應用程式
(B) By discouraging the use of money orders	(B) 不鼓勵使用匯票
(C) By verifying payment before sending products	(C) 在送貨前確認款項
(D) By asking for identification documents before dispatching goods	(D) 在送出物品前要求證明文件

■ 六何原則 How   解答 (C)

這題是在問建議線上公司如何（How）保護他們的生意的六何原則問題。與題目關鍵字 online companies advised to protect their businesses 相關的文句為 To ensure payment for purchased goods, the National Mail Service advises online businesses to check the authenticity of the money orders they receive before shipping merchandise. 為了確保購買貨物能確實收款，建議在進行線上交易時應在出貨前檢查匯票的真假，所以 (C) By verifying payment before sending products 為正確答案。

單字 install v. 設置　application n.（應用）程式　discourage v. 不鼓勵，阻止　dispatch v. 派送

175

How can people learn more about money order payments?	人們如何得到更多有關匯票付款的資訊？
(A) By writing a letter	(A) 寫信
(B) By visiting a Web site	(B) 上網頁
(C) By calling a number	(C) 打電話
(D) By going to a post office	(D) 去郵局

■ 六何原則 How   解答 (B)

這題是在問人們如何（How）得到更多有關匯票付款資訊的六何原則問題。與題目關鍵字 learn more about money order payments 有關的語句為 Information regarding the US money order service may be viewed by logging on to www.nationalmailservice.gov.，提到有關美國匯票服務的資訊可上網查看，因此 (B) By visiting a Web site 為正確答案。

May 25

Setsuko Uchiyama, Boksun Fashions
Takaoka Road, Nagoya

Dear Ms. Uchiyama,

Fabric Warehouse is moving!

[176]We are pleased to announce that we are opening a new store in June on Tenmacho Street in Atsuta Ward. [177-B]We have expanded our silk, cotton, wool, linen, and polyester sections to provide you with a wider selection of materials for clothing and home decoration. In addition, [178]we have set up design assistance counters where you may seek professional advice on choosing the appropriate materials for your projects. Apart from introducing the new service, [177-A/C]we guarantee to give you greater shopping convenience with the store's spacious underground car park and nearby food vendors. For directions to our new address, please see the map printed in the enclosed catalogue.

[179]As a devoted client, [180]you are invited to our grand opening on June 5. On that day, all designer textiles will be marked down by 15 percent. We will also hold a raffle where you will have the chance to win a Konoya 525 portable sewing machine.

Thank you for your patronage, and we will see you soon!

Kuneho Tanaka
General Manager, Fabric Warehouse

日期：5 月 25 日

收件者：Setsuko Uchiyama, Boksun 服飾
地址：Takaoka 路，名古屋

親愛的 Uchiyama 小姐：

Fabric Warehouse 要開分店了！

[176] 我們很高興的宣佈我們六月要在熱田區的 Tenmacho 街上開一間新的店，[177-B] 我們擴展了我們的絲綢、棉花、羊毛、亞麻布及聚酯部門，為您提供服裝和家居裝飾材料更廣泛的選擇。除此之外，[178] 我們成立了設計協助櫃檯，在那您可以尋求專業的意見，為您的計畫來選擇合適的材料。除了引入新的服務，[177-A/C] 我們保證讓您在購物時更便利，提供寬敞的地下停車場和鄰近的飲食攤販。關於我們新的店的位置，請見隨信附上的目錄內的地圖。

[179] 因為您是我們忠實的客戶，[180] 我們邀請您參加我們 6 月 5 日隆重的開幕式，在當天，所有的紡織品設計款將打八五折。我們也會舉辦抽獎，您將有機會贏得 Konoya 牌 525 攜帶式縫紉機。

感謝您的惠顧，我們近期見！

Kuneho Tanaka
Fabric Warehouse 總經理

單字		
□expand v. 擴張	□assistance n. 支援，協助	□seek v. 找，求
□appropriate a. 適切的	□guarantee v. 保障，保證	□enclosed a. 隨信附上的
□portable a. 攜帶的	□material n. 布料，材料	□spacious a. 寬廣的
□textile n. 衣料，紡織品	□sewing machine phr. 縫紉機	□apart from phr. 再加上～，除了～
□underground n. 地下	□raffle n. 抽獎，摸彩	□patronage n. 惠顧，資助

176

Why was the letter written?	為什麼寫這封信？
(A) To provide an update on a store's operations	(A) 提供商店營運的最新消息
(B) To advertise innovations in tailoring equipment	(B) 廣告一項創新的裁縫設備
(C) To let Ms. Uchiyama know about new products	(C) 讓 Uchiyama 小姐知道新產品
(D) To report the highlights from a design workshop	(D) 報告設計工作坊上的重點

■ 找出主題 寫文章的理由　　　　　　　　　　　　　　　　　　　　　　　　　　　解答 (A)

這題是在問寫這封信的目的，應注意文章的前半部分。We are pleased to announce that we are opening a new store 提到很高興的宣佈開了一間新的店，並接著介紹新店與舊店的改善之處與特徵，因此 (A) To provide an update on a store's operations 為正確答案。

單字 operation n. 營運　tailoring n. 成衣業，裁縫技術

177

What is NOT a feature of the new store?	哪一項不是新店的特色？
(A) Large parking area	(A) 大的停車場
(B) Wider varieties of textiles	(B) 更廣泛的紡織品種類
(C) Snack bars	(C) 小吃店
(D) Fashion exhibits	(D) 時裝展

■ **Not/True** Not 問題

解答 (D)

這題是尋找與題目關鍵字 a feature of the new store 的相關內容，再與選項互相對照的 Not/True 問題。we guarantee to give you greater shopping convenience with the store's spacious underground car park and nearby food vendors 提到「我們保證讓您在購物時有更大的便利性，提供寬敞的地下停車場和鄰近的飲食攤販」，與 (A) 和 (C) 的敘述相符。We have expanded our silk, cotton, wool, linen, and polyester sections to provide you with a wider selection of materials 提到「我們擴展了我們的絲綢、棉花、羊毛、亞麻布及聚酯部門，為您提供更廣泛的選擇」，與 (B) 的內容一致。(D) 的內容在文中則未被提及。所以 (D) Fashion exhibits 為正確答案。

178

Why did the store add assistance counters?	為什麼店家增加協助櫃檯？
(A) To conduct membership registrations	(A) 進行會員註冊
(B) To deal with customer complaints	(B) 處理客戶投訴
(C) To demonstrate the latest sewing materials and equipment	(C) 展示最新的縫紉材料和設備
(D) To recommend the most suitable fabric to clients	(D) 向客戶推薦最適合的布料

■ 六何原則 Why

解答 (D)

這是在問為什麼（Why）店家增加協助櫃檯的六何原則問題。與題目關鍵字 assistance counters 相關的文句為 we have set up design assistance counters where you may seek professional advice on choosing the appropriate materials for your projects，當中提到「我們成立了設計協助櫃檯，在那您可以尋求專業的意見，為您的計畫來選擇合適的材料」，因此 (D) To recommend the most suitable fabric to clients. 為正確答案。

換句話說

the appropriate materials 適當的材料 → the most suitable fabric 適當的布料

單字 registration n. 註冊　demonstrate v. 展示，說明　suitable a. 適合的

179

What is suggested about Setsuko Uchiyama?	文中暗示有關 Setsuko Uchiyama 的什麼事？
(A) She is a newly hired employee at Boksun Fashions.	(A) 她是 Boksun 服飾新聘的員工。
(B) She needs training in interior design.	(B) 她需要在室內設計上的訓練。
(C) She is a regular customer of Fabric Warehouse.	(C) 她是 Fabric Warehouse 的常客。
(D) She makes all of her own clothing.	(D) 她自己生產她所有的服飾。

■ 推論 細節

解答 (C)

這是依題目關鍵字 Setsuko Uchiyama 進行推論的問題。As a devoted client, you are invited to our grand opening 中提到「忠實的客戶如您被邀請參加我們的開幕式」，因此可以推論 Setsuko Uchiyama 是 Fabric Warehouse 的常客，所以 (C) She is a regular customer of Fabric Warehouse.。

What will take place on June 5?	6 月 5 日將發生什麼事？
(A) New designs will be presented to the public.	(A) 會向大眾呈現新的設計。
(B) Some fabrics will be sold at a reduced price.	(B) 有些布料會以較少的價格來販售。
(C) The store will close for a holiday.	(C) 商店會因節日而休息。
(D) A new catalog will be launched.	(D) 將推出一個新的產品目錄。

■ 六何原則 What   解答 (B)

這題是在問 6 月 5 日將發生什麼事（What）的六何原則問題。與題目關鍵字 June 5 相關的文句為 you are invited to our grand opening on June 5，提到 6 月 5 號為開幕式，後面又提到 On that day, all designer textiles will be marked down by 15 percent.，即當天將會有 85 折的折扣，所以 (B) Some fabrics will be sold at a reduced price 為正確答案。

換句話說

textiles will be marked down 紡織品特價 → fabrics will be sold at a reduced price 布料折扣出售

單字 present v. 發表   launch v. 舉辦

Questions 181-185 refer to the following advertisement and e-mail.

181-185 根據下面廣告和電郵的內容回答問題。

Great Job Opportunities Await You at EMRE!

Recognized as a leading manufacturer of high-quality dairy products, EMRE PASTEURS has enjoyed profitable growth since its establishment 14 years ago. It is constantly seeking out talented and motivated professionals who can help it achieve its global expansion goals.

EMRE currently has openings in the following areas:

183-A/B/CSales Representative – 183-A/BThis job primarily entails day-to-day operational support for sales executives, driving brand awareness, and increasing market share. Superb communication and presentation skills are necessary, as is 183-Cthe ability to quickly build rapport with clients.

Quality Controller – The selected candidate will report directly to the operations director on a weekly basis. The applicant should have knowledge of general standards of hygiene, quality, and food safety and must hold a degree in food service management or its equivalent.

184Financial Analyst – Facilitation of financial reports in compliance with established accounting practices is the key role of this position. The ideal candidate must know how to use applicable software programs for financial and management reporting and business analysis. 184Four years of relevant experience is needed.

Distribution Manager – The hired applicant will manage the warehouse and ensure the smooth distribution of finished products. The chosen candidate will oversee the quality, cost, and efficiency of the movement and storage of goods while also managing the departmental budget. Previous experience in a similar role is an advantage.

181-AInterested individuals may send their résumé, together with two letters of reference, to davis@emrepasteurs.co. The deadline for all applications is September 30.

To: Evelyn Davis <davis@emrepasteurs.co>

From: Mehmet Korkmaz <mehmetkorkmaz@anatoliamail.com>
Date: September 25
Subject: Job Advertisement

Dear Ms. Davis,

I saw your company's posting on an online job site, and 184I would like to apply for the financial analyst position. I can assure you that my academic and professional background, as outlined in detail in the attached résumé, make me an excellent candidate for the job. EMRE PASTEURS has always had a notable reputation in the industry, and I would be grateful for the opportunity to work at your company.

TEST 4 PART 7 | 353

Please feel free to let me know if you need any further information. [185]You can contact me directly on my mobile phone at 555-9082 if you would like to arrange an interview. Your time and consideration is much appreciated. Yours truly, Mehmet Korkmaz	如果您需要任何進一步的資料，請隨時讓我知道，[185] 如果您想要安排面試，您可以直接撥打我的手機 555-9082。對於您所付出的時間及考慮我深表感謝。 Mehmet Korkmaz 敬上

例文 1 單字 □manufacturer n. 製造公司，製造業者

□profitable a. 有利潤的	□constantly ad. 持續地	□dairy a. 乳製品的
□expansion n. 擴張	□primarily ad. 基本地	□seek v. 找
□operational a. 經營上的	□drive v. 鼓吹，趕走	□entail v. 必須，使承擔
□superb a. 最佳的，傑出的	□rapport n.（親密的）關係	□market share phr. 市佔率
□equivalent n. 相等物	□facilitation n. 便利，容易	□hygiene n. 衛生
□analysis n. 分析	□distribution n. 流通，分布	□in compliance with phr. 依照～
□oversee v. 管理，監督	□efficiency n. 效率	□warehouse n. 倉庫，物流
□budget n. 費用，預算		□departmental a. 部門的

例文 2 單字 □outline v. 製作（概要），敘述 □notable a. 引人注目的，亮眼的 □reputation n. 名聲
□consideration n. 關心，考慮

181

What is indicated about EMRE PASTEURS? (A) It requires applicants to send several documents. (B) It is currently constructing a manufacturing plant. (C) It is looking to fill executive positions in sales. (D) It has reduced its workforce in recent years.	文中指出有關 EMRE PASTEURS 的什麼事？ (A) 它要求申請者寄送幾份文件。 (B) 它目前正在建造一間生產工廠。 (C) 它正在尋找有人來填補業務總監的職務。 (D) 它最近幾年減少了工作人員。

■ Not/True True 問題　　　　　　　　　　　　　　　　　　　　　　　　　　　　　　解答 (A)

這是尋找與題目關鍵字 EMRE PASTEURS 相關的內容，再與選項互相對照的 Not/True 問題，應從提到 EMRE PASTEURS 的第一篇文章看起。Interested individuals may send their résumé, together with two letters of reference 中提到有興趣者可寄送簡歷及兩封推薦信，與 (A) 的敘述一致。因此 (A) It requires applicants to send several documents 為正確答案。(B) (C) (D) 的內容在文中則未被提及。

換句話說
résumé ~ with two letters of reference 兩封推薦函與履歷 → several documents 一些資料

單字 construct v. 蓋，建設　manufacturing a. 生產的，製造的

182

In the advertisement, the word "oversee" in paragraph 5, line 2 is closest in meaning to (A) survey (B) examine (C) monitor (D) guide	在廣告中，第五段第二行中「oversee」一字最接近的意思是 (A) 調查 (B) 檢查 (C) 監控 (D) 引導

■ 同義詞　　　　　　　　　　　　　　　　　　　　　　　　　　　　　　　　　　解答 (C)

第一篇廣告有 oversee 的文句為 The chosen candidate will oversee the quality, cost, and efficiency of the movement and storage，當中的 oversee 為「監督」的意思，因此表示「監視」的 (C) monitor 為正確答案。

183

What is NOT stated as a responsibility of the sales representative? (A) Providing assistance to the sales manager (B) Increasing brand recognition to consumers (C) Establishing immediate ties with customers (D) Searching for additional clients	哪一項不是文中所陳述的業務代表的職責？ (A) 協助業務主管 (B) 增加消費者對品牌的辨識度 (C) 建立與客戶的直接聯繫 (D) 尋找額外的客戶

■ **Not/True** Not 問題 　　　　　　　　　　　　　　　　　　　　　　　　　　　　　　　解答 (D)

這題是尋找題目關鍵字 a responsibility of the sales representative 的相關內容，再與選項互相對照的 Not/True 問題。應從第一篇提到業務代表職責的內容看起。sales Representative 的 This job primarily entails day-to-day operational support for sales executives, driving brand awareness 當中提到這項工作主要是需要在平日提供業務主管業務上的支援、推動品牌知名度，和 (A) 與 (B) 的敘述相符。sales Representative 的 the ability to quickly build rapport with clients 當中提到快速與客戶建立融洽的關係，與 (C) 的內容相符。(D) 的內容在文中則未被提及。所以 (D) Searching for additional clients 為正確答案。

單字 recognition n. 辨識度，認識　　tie n. 關係，友誼

184

What is suggested about Mr. Korkmaz? (A) He studied food service management in college. (B) He held a job in finance for the last four years. (C) He has supervised the performance of a whole team. (D) He previously applied for a position at EMRE PASTEURS.	文中暗示有關 Korkmaz 先生的什麼事？ (A) 他在大學時學習餐飲服務管理。 (B) 他在過去四年中在金融業工作。 (C) 他監督整個團隊的表現。 (D) 他之前申請過 EMRE PASTEURS 的一個職位。

■ **推論** 聯結問題 　　　　　　　　　　　　　　　　　　　　　　　　　　　　　　　　　解答 (B)

這是將兩篇文章內容相互對照後進行推測的推論聯結問題。應先從提到題目關鍵字 Mr. Korkmaz 的第二篇文章看起。第二篇信件內容的 I would like to apply for the financial analyst position. I can assure you that my academic and professional background ~ make me an excellent candidate for the job. 提到 Mr. Korkmaz 想申請財務分析師的職務。且可以保證以其學歷和專業背景，是此工作的優秀人選，此為第一個線索。但這邊並沒有提到財務分析師需要什麼樣的學經歷，因此應從廣告的部分確認。第一篇的廣告文 Financial Analyst 的 Four years of relevant experience is needed. 提到需要四年相關的工作經驗，此為第二個線索。綜合這兩個線索可以知道 Mr. Korkmaz 在金融業有四年的工作經驗，因此 (B) He held a job in finance for the last four years 為正確答案。

單字 previously ad. 之前地

What does Mr. Korkmaz want Ms. Davis to do?	Korkmaz 先生希望 Davis 女士做什麼事？
(A) Schedule a testing date	(A) 安排一個考試的日期
(B) Offer him a salary raise	(B) 給他加薪
(C) Send him an application form	(C) 寄給他一份申請表
(D) Make arrangements to meet him	(D) 安排與他會面

■ 六何原則 What   解答 (D)

這題是在問 Korkmaz 先生希望 Davis 女士做什麼的六何原則問題。與題目關鍵字 Mr. Korkmaz want Ms. Davis to do 相關的文句在第二篇 Mr. Korkmaz 寄的信件當中。信件的 You can contact me ~ if you would like to arrange an interview. 提到 Ms. Davis 如果想要安排面試，可以直接連絡 Mr. Korkmaz，因此 (D) Make arrangements to meet him 為正確答案。

換句話說
arrange an interview 安排面試 → Make arrangements to meet 安排見面

單字 raise n. 提升　application n. 申請（書）

Questions 186-190 refer to the following e-mail and schedule.

186-190 根據下面的電郵和時刻表的內容回答問題。

例文1

To: Lauren Wulff <l.wulff@jetsetgo.com>

From: Steven Mansfield <s.mansfield@jetsetgo.com>

Date: February 15
Subject: Flight Schedules
Attachment(s): Skywing schedule

Dear Ms. Wulff,

I hope that everything in Washington is proceeding as you had hoped. [187]As instructed, I have confirmed your return flight to Paris on Friday. In addition, [187]I am finalizing your travel arrangements for the three-day seminar you will be attending in Spain next month. I tried reserving tickets with Bonjour Airlines, but unfortunately, their flights are already fully booked. It looks like Skywing Airlines is your next best option, though I'd like to consult you about the flight schedule before making a decision.

[189]Please note that the seminar will begin on Tuesday, March 24 at 1 P.M. and end on Thursday, March 26 at 5 P.M. Since your hotel is a 25-minute drive from the airport, [189]it would be good to arrive in Barcelona at least an hour before the event. Also, [188]we might need to reconsider your return flight schedule. [186]I received a call from Martha Tate, an *On Foot* magazine correspondent, and she told me that her publication is planning to feature our company's new line of luggage and travel accessories. She would like to know if she can conduct an interview with you in Paris on Friday, March 27 at 11 A.M. If you agree to the interview, you can take the second flight to Paris on that day to get back in time for the appointment.

Please let me know what you think about the matters I've discussed, so that I may immediately respond to Ms. Tate's inquiry and book your flights. Thank you.

Steven

收件人：Lauren Wulff
　　　　<l.wulff@jetsetgo.com>
寄件人：Steven Mansfield
　　　　< s.mansfield@jetsetgo.com>
日期：2 月 15 日
主旨：航班時刻表
附件：Skywing 公司時刻表

親愛的 Wulff 女士：

我希望在華盛頓的一切正按你所希望的進行。[187] 如您的指示，我已確認您週五返回巴黎的航班。此外，[187] 我正在替您下個月在西班牙要參加的三天研討會完成旅程安排。我嘗試預訂 Bonjour 航空的機票，但很不幸，他們的機票已全被訂滿。看起來您第二好的選擇是 Skywing 公司，但在做決定之前，我想要與您商量有關於飛機航班的安排。

[189] 請注意，研討會將在 3 月 24 日星期二下午 1 點開始，在 3 月 26 日星期四下午 5 點結束，由於您的飯店離機場有 25 分鐘的車程，[189] 您最好至少在活動前一個小時抵達巴塞隆納。此外，[188] 我們可能需要重新考慮您回程的航班。[186] 我接到 On Foot 雜誌特派員 Martha Tate 的電話，她告訴我，她的出版物正計畫特別介紹我們公司新生產的旅行箱及旅行用品。她想知道能否在巴黎，與您約在 3 月 27 日星期五早上 11 點進行採訪，如果您同意此訪問，您可搭乘當天第二班往巴黎的班機趕上此行程。

請讓我知道，您對於我與您所討論的事情的想法，如此一來，我可以立即回應 Tate 小姐的詢問和預訂機票。謝謝您。

Steven

例文2

Skywing Airlines

Flight Schedules CDG-BCN

[189]Paris, France (CDG) to Barcelona, Spain (BCN)

Departure	[189]Arrival	[189]Flight	Stopover	[190-D]Frequency	[190-A]Meals
7:40 A.M.	9:20 A.M.	8699AF	0	3	B
9:35 A.M.	11:15 A.M.	8392AF	0	2,3,5	S
10:55 A.M.	12:40 P.M.	8393AF	0	1,2,6	S
12:55 P.M.	2:35 P.M.	8704AF	0	Except 7	L

Skywing 航空公司

航班時刻表 CDG-BCN

[189] 從法國巴黎（CDG）到西班牙巴塞隆納（BCN）

起程	[189]抵達	[189]航班	中途停留	[190-D]頻率	[190-A]餐點
早上 7:40	早上 9:20	8699AF	0	3	B
早上 9:35	早上 11:15	8392AF	0	2,3,5	S
早上 10:55	下午 12:40	8393AF	0	1,2,6	S
下午 12:55	下午 2:35	8704AF	0	7 除外	L

Barcelona, Spain (BCN) to Paris, France (CDG)

Departure	Arrival	Flight	Stopover	190-D Frequency	190-A Meals
4:40 A.M.	6:30 A.M.	8700AF	0	1,5	B
6:50 A.M.	8:45 A.M.	8445AF	0	Except 7	B
7:35 A.M.	9:30 A.M.	8377AF	0	7	B
10:25 A.M.	12:20 P.M.	8670AF	0	Except 4,7	L

Certain flights may not be offered on holidays. Please contact a Skywing office in your area for more information.

190-D Frequency Codes:

Flights are offered daily unless otherwise designated.
1-Monday 2-Tuesday 3-Wednesday 4-Thursday
5-Friday   6-Saturday 7-Sunday

190-A Meal Codes:

B-Breakfast L-Lunch D-Dinner S-Snack

190-B Reservations and Seat Assignments:

Reservations may be made online, by phone, or by visiting any of our ticketing centers and affiliate travel agencies. Flight bookings and seat assignments may be forfeited if passengers are not present at the designated check-in counter or boarding gate as scheduled.

從西班牙巴塞隆納（BCN）到法國巴黎（CDG）

起程	抵達	航班	中途停留	190-D 頻率	190-A 餐點
早上 4:40	早上 6:30	8700AF	0	1,5	B
早上 6:50	早上 8:45	8445AF	0	7 除外	B
早上 7:35	早上 9:30	8377AF	0	7	B
早上 10:25	下午 12:20	8670AF	0	4,7 除外	S

某些航班可能在節假日沒有提供。需要更多資訊者，請聯繫您所在地區的 Skywing 辦公室。

190-D 頻率代碼

航班每天提供，除非另行指定
1-星期一 2-星期二 3-星期三 4-星期四
5-星期五 6-星期六 7-星期日

190-A 餐點代碼

B-早餐 L-中餐 D-晚餐 S-點心

190-B 預訂和座位安排

預訂可透過網路、電話，或是前往我們的票務中心和附屬旅行社。如果乘客沒有如期出現在指定的檢查櫃檯或登機口，預訂機票和座位分配可能會因此喪失。

例文 1 單字 □proceed v. 進行　　　□book v. 預約　　　□reconsider v. 再思考，再考慮
　　　□correspondent n. 駐地記者，特派員　　□feature v. 製作特輯
例文 2 單字 □designated a. 指定的，設定的　　　□forfeit v. 剝奪，失去權利

186

What is suggested about Jet Set Go?
(A) It has manufacturing facilities in several locations.
(B) It sponsors events for entrepreneurs.
(C) It creates products for travelers.
(D) It has recently established sales centers abroad.

文中指出 Jet Set Go 的什麼事？
(A) 它在幾個地區有製造設備。
(B) 它贊助企業家活動。
(C) 它為旅客創造產品。
(D) 它最近在國外設置銷售中心。

■ 推論 詳細內容　　　　　　　　　　　　　　　　　　　　　　　　　　　解答 (C)

這是依題目關鍵字 Jet Set Go 進行推論的問題，因此應先從有提到 Jet Set Go 的郵件看起。郵件的 I received a call from Martha Tate, an On Foot magazine correspondent, and she told me that her publication is planning to feature our company's new line of luggage and travel accessories. 中提到「我接到 On Foot 雜誌特派員 Martha Tate 的電話，她告訴我，她的出版物正計畫特別介紹我們公司新生產的旅行箱及旅行用品。」，因此可推論 Jet Set Go 是為旅客製作產品的公司。所以 (C) It creates products for travelers. 為正確答案。

單字 entrepreneur n. 企業家

187

What most likely is Mr. Mansfield's job? (A) A business executive secretary (B) A corporate event organizer (C) A customer representative (D) A ticketing agent	Mansfield 先生最有可能的工作是什麼? (A) 一位業務執行祕書 (B) 一位企業活動的組織者 (C) 一位客戶代表 (D) 一位票務代理商

■ 推論 詳細內容   解答 (A)

這是依題目關鍵字 Mr. Mansfield's job 進行推論的問題,因此應先從第一篇 Mr. Mansfield 寄給 Ms. Wulff 的郵件看起,確認其職業的相關內容。郵件的 As instructed, I have confirmed your return flight 中提到已按照 Ms. Wulff 的指示確認航班,後面又說 I am finalizing your travel arrangements for the ~ seminar you will be attending,即正在完成 Ms. Wulff 即將參與的研討會旅程安排,因此可以推論 Mr. Mansfield 是 Ms. Wulff 的私人祕書,所以 (A) A business executive secretary 為正確答案。

單字 secretary n. 祕書

188

What does Mr. Mansfield recommend Ms. Wulff do? (A) Allow time to prepare for a workshop (B) Reconsider her return flight options (C) Avoid missing a connecting trip in the afternoon (D) Submit a client contract as scheduled	Mansfield 先生建議 Wulff 女士做什麼? (A) 預留時間來準備工作坊 (B) 重新考慮她回程的航班選擇 (C) 避免錯過下午的轉機 (D) 如期提交一份客戶合約

■ 六何原則 What   解答 (B)

這題是在問 Mansfield 先生建議 Wulff 女士做什麼(What)的六何原則問題。因此應先從提到題目關鍵字 Mr. Mansfield recommend Ms. Wulff do 的第一篇文章相關內容看起。郵件的 we might need to reconsider your return flight schedule 提到「我們可能需要重新考慮您回程的航班」,因此 (B) Reconsider her return flight options 為正確答案。

189

Which flight should Ms. Wulff take to arrive at the seminar on time? (A) 8704AF (B) 8393AF (C) 8699AF (D) 8392AF	如果 Wulff 女士要準時到達工作坊,她應該搭哪一班飛機? (A) 8704AF (B) 8393AF (C) 8699AF (D) 8392AF

■ 六何原則 聯結問題   解答 (D)

這是要整合兩篇文章內容的聯結問題。題目關鍵字為 flight ~ Ms. Wulff take to arrive at the seminar on time,即在問要準時到達工作坊應該搭哪(Which)一班飛機,因此應先從第一篇研討會相關的內容看起。

第一篇郵件的 Please note that the seminar will begin on Tuesday, March 24 at 1 P.M. 中提到研討會將在 3 月 24 日星期二下午 1 點開始,之後又說 it would be good to arrive in Barcelona at least an hour before the event 提早一小時到是最好的,此為第一個線索。但是此處並沒有提到哪一班飛機可以讓她提早一小時到,因此要從行程表當中的機票確認。第二篇行程表 Paris, France(CDG)to Barcelona, Spain(BCN)中的 Arrival 11:15 A.M. 與 Flight 8392AF 為第二個線索,綜合這兩個線索可以知道她應該要搭 8392AF 的飛機,因此 (D) 8392AF 為正確答案。

What information is NOT included in the schedule?	時刻表中沒有包含哪一項資訊？
(A) The types of meals served to passengers	(A) 供應乘客的餐點類型
(B) A policy on seat assignments	(B) 座位安排的策略
(C) A set of guidelines for checked baggage	(C) 拖運行李的一套指導方針
(D) The number of times a flight is offered in a week	(D) 每個航班一週所提供的次數

Not/True Not 問題   解答 (C)

這是針對行程表問的 Not/True 問題。因為沒有題目關鍵字，所以必須將各選項與文中內容對照。行程表的 Meals 與 Meals code 提供了各飛機在早餐、中餐、晚餐各供應了什麼樣的餐點，與 (A) 的內容相符。Reservations and Seat Assignments 中介紹了訂位與座位安排的資訊，與 (B) 的內容相符。(C) 的內容在文中則未被提及。因此 (C) A set of guidelines for checked baggage 為正確答案。行程表的 Frequency 與 Frequency Codes 提供了航班營運的時間，由此便可知道一週所提供的次數，因此與 (D) 的內容相符。

Questions 191-195 refer to the following letter and e-mail.

191-195 根據下面信件和電郵的內容回答問題。

例文1

ASTRAL HOME CENTER 1916 Barnes Avenue, Cincinnati, OH 45214	"*The Quality You Trust*" Since 1975

September 18

Alessandro Kapranos
798 Duffy Street
South Bend, IN 46601

Dear Mr. Kapranos,

We appreciate your business and hope you enjoy the appliance you purchased from Astral Home Center. As one of the country's most trusted electronic centers, we pride ourselves in distributing the finest appliances to suit our patrons' everyday needs and providing the most efficient customer service.

194Your item is under warranty for 12 months starting from the date of purchase. During this period, you are entitled to free maintenance checkup and repair depending on the cause of the damage. In the event that your item needs to be repaired after the warranty period, you can still bring it to one of our service centers and our technicians will be happy to assist you.

194APPLIANCE TYPE	OUT OF WARRANTY REPAIR COST (STANDARD FEES)
Air-conditioner	$150
Washing machine	$200
Television	$100
DVD player	$50
Laptop and tablet computers	$250

Please take note that you might need to pay an additional fee for the cost of replacement parts. The out-of-warranty repair cost includes all brands and units that fall under the appliance type.

191For complete guidelines on our repair services, please refer to the booklet enclosed with this letter. 192It also includes a list of service centers located across the country.

Should you have any questions, you may call our 24-hour hotline at 555-9987 or e-mail us at custserv@astralhc.com.

Sincerely,

Blake Boer
Operations manager
Astral Home Center

ASTRAL HOME CENTER 45214 俄亥俄州, 辛辛那提郡, Barnes 道 1916 號	「你所信賴的品質」1975 創立

9 月 18 日

Alessandro Kapranos
Duffy 街 798 號
南本德郡, 印地安那州, 46601

親愛的 Kapranos 先生：

我們謝謝您的惠顧，並希望您能喜歡您從 Astral Home Center 所購買的家電。身為本國最值得信賴的電子中心之一，我們對於配送最好的設備以滿足我們客人的日常需求，以及提供最有效率的客戶服務而感到自豪。

194 您的產品從購買日的十二個月皆在保固期內。在此期間，你有權免費維修檢查以及根據損壞的原因進行修理，如果您的產品在過了保固期後需要修理，您仍然可以把它拿到我們的服務中心，我們的技術人員將樂意幫助您。

194 電器類型	過保固期的修理費用（標準收費）
冷氣機	$150
洗衣機	$200
電視機	$100
DVD 播放機	$50
筆電及平板電腦	$250

請注意，您可能需要支付零件成本的額外費用，過保固期之後的維修費用涵蓋所有屬於該家電類型的品牌及裝置。

191 關於我們維修服務的完整規定，請參閱隨信附上的小冊子，192 裡面亦包含了全國的服務中心清單。

如果您有任何問題，您可以撥打我們二十四小時的服務熱線 555-9987，或是寫電郵到 custserv@astralhc.com 給我們。

Blake Boer 敬上
業務經理
Astral Home Center

例文2

To: Blake Boer <custserv@astralhc.com>

From: Alessandro Kapranos
        <alessandro.kapranos@rocketmail.com>

Date: January 25
Subject: Service Center in Alabama

Dear Mr. Boer,

[194]Two years ago, I bought an Automaton LED Plasma TV from your store in Cincinnati. My wife and I were pleased with its excellent picture quality and ability to access the Internet. [194]However, during a recent move to our current residence in Alabama, the TV was damaged while in transit.

Since I no longer have the booklet that was included with my purchase, [195]I was wondering if you could refer me to the nearest service center in our area. [194]We'd like to take our unit in for repair as soon as possible, so I'd appreciate it if you called my office number at 555-5837.

I'm looking forward to your swift response. Thank you.

Sincerely,

Alessandro Kapranos

收件人：Blake Boer
        <custserv@astralhc.com>
寄件人：Alessandro Kapranos
        <alessandro.
        kapranos@rocketmail.com>
日期：1 月 25 日
主旨：阿拉巴馬州的服務中心

親愛的 Boer 先生：

194 兩年前，我在你們辛辛那提的商店購買了一台自動 LED 電漿電視，我和我的太太對於其出色的影像質量及上網的功能很滿意，194 但是，在最近一次搬到我們目前所居住的阿拉巴馬州的運送過程中，電視壞了。

因為我已經沒有購買當時所附上的小冊子，195 我在想，你是否可以告訴我本地區最近的服務中心，194 我們希望把我們的電視盡快送修，如果你可以打我辦公室的電話 555-5837，我會感激你。

我期待著你的迅速反應，謝謝你。

Alessandro Kapranos 敬上

例文 1 單字 □astral a. 星星的，星形的　　□appliance n. 家電　　□purchase v. 購買
　　　　　□distribute v. 使流通　　□efficient a. 有效率的　　□replacement n. 替代，更換
　　　　　□suit v. 滿足　　□warranty n. 保固　　□patron n. 顧客
　　　　　□maintenance n. 修理，維持

例文 2 單字 □residence n. 居住地　　□in transit phr. 在運輸中

191

What was included in the letter?	信中包含了什麼？
(A) Directions to a nearby repair center	(A) 到附近維修中心的指示
(B) Details regarding a store policy	(B) 商店政策的細節
(C) A list of prices for some new appliances	(C) 一些新的電器用品的價格清單
(D) Information on an upcoming warehouse sale	(D) 即將到來的倉庫拍賣資訊

■ 六何原則 What　　　　　　　　　　　　　　　　　　　　　　　　　解答 (B)

這是在問信中包含了什麼（What）的六何原則問題，因此應先從提到題目關鍵字 included in the letter 的第一篇相關內容看起。信中的 For complete guidelines on our repair services, please refer to the booklet enclosed with this letter. 提到「關於我們維修服務的完整規定，請參閱隨信附上的小冊子。」，因此 (B) Details regarding a store policy 為正確答案。

換句話說

guidelines on our repair services 關於維修服務的規定 → a store policy 商家政策

單字 policy n. 政策，指南

192

What is suggested about Astral Home Center?	文中指出有關 Astral Home Center 的什麼事？
(A) It conducts online transactions.	(A) 它進行線上交易。
(B) It ships merchandise internationally.	(B) 它在國際間寄送貨物。
(C) It has several outlets nationwide.	(C) 它在全國有幾間通路商店。
(D) It organizes promotional offers every month.	(D) 它每個月會舉辦促銷優惠。

■ 推論 詳細內容   解答 (C)

這是依題目關鍵字 Astral Home Center 進行推論的問題，應先從第一篇文章提及 Astral Home Center 的內容看起。信中的 It also includes a list of service centers located across the country. 提到也包含了遍布全國服務中心的清單，因此可推知 Astral Home Center 在全國都有服務中心，所以 (C) It has several outlets nationwide. 為正確答案。

換句話說

across the country 遍布全國 → nationwide 全國性地

單字 transaction n. 交易 nationwide ad. 全國性地

193

In the letter, the phrase "fall under" in paragraph 3, line 2 is closest in meaning to	在信中，在第三段的第二行中「fall under」這個片語最接近的意思是
(A) lower	(A) 低於
(B) comprise	(B) 包含
(C) drop	(C) 落下
(D) deteriorate	(D) 惡化

■ 同義詞   解答 (B)

提到 fall under 的文句為 The out-of-warranty repair cost includes all brands and units that fall under the appliance type.，當中的 fall under 為「所屬於～，～的一部分」的意思，因此表示「包含」的 (B) comprise 為正確答案。

194

What is indicated about Mr. Kapranos?	文中指出有關 Kapranos 先生的什麼事？
(A) He must pay $100 for a repair.	(A) 他一定要付 $100 的修理費。
(B) He formerly resided in Ohio.	(B) 他之前住在俄亥俄州。
(C) He recently placed a bulk order.	(C) 他最近下了一個大宗訂單。
(D) He maintains a home office.	(D) 他有一間家庭辦公室。

■ 推論 聯結問題   解答 (A)

這是將兩篇文章內容相互對照後進行推測的推論聯結問題。應從提及題目關鍵字 Mr. Kapranos 的第二篇郵件內容看起。

當中的 Two years ago, I bought ~ TV from your store 與 However, ~ the TV was damaged 提到 Mr. Kapranos 在辛辛那提的商店購買了一台自動 LED 電漿電視，但是電視壞了，後又提到 We'd like to take our unit in for repair，表示想要修理，此為第一個線索。但是此處並未提到修理電視的費用，因此應從信件中確認。第一封信中的 Your item is under warranty for 12 months starting from the date of purchases. 提到產品從購買日的十二個月皆在保固期內，但 Mr. Kapranos 已經超過保固期。後面表格的 APPLIANCE TYPE: Television, OUT OF WARRANTY REPAIR COST（STANDARD FEES）：$100 提到保固期間外的修理費用為 100 美元。綜合以上兩個線索，可知道 (A) He must pay $100 for a repair. 為正確答案。

單字 formerly ad. 之前地 reside v. 住 bulk a. 大量的

Why did Mr. Kapranos contact Mr. Boer?	為什麼 Kapranos 先生要聯絡 Boer 先生?
(A) To reschedule an appointment with a repairperson	(A) 與維修人員重新安排時間
(B) To ask for replacement of a defective electronic product	(B) 要求更換一項有瑕疵的電子產品
(C) To inquire about the services offered by a moving company	(C) 詢問一家搬家公司的服務
(D) To request information about a specific establishment	(D) 要求一個特定機構的資訊

■ 六何原則 Why　　　　　　　　　　　　　　　　　　　　　　　　　　　　　　　　解答 (D)

這題是在問為什麼（Why）Kapranos 先生要聯絡 Boer 先生的六何原則問題。應從第二封 Kapranos 先生寫的郵件看起。郵件的 I was wondering if you could refer me to the nearest service center in our area 提到 Kapranos 先生在想，Boer 先生是否可以告訴他本地區最近的服務中心，因此 (D) To request information about a specific establishment 為正確答案。

單字 defective a. 有缺陷的，受損傷的　establishment n. 設施，機關

Questions 196-200 refer to the following e-mail and schedule.

196-200 根據下面電郵和課程表的內容回答問題。

例文1

To: Curtis Freeman <cfreeman@hyperionskills.com>

From: Jodi Grant <jodi_grant@theiaristorante.net>

Date: May 30
Subject: Excellent Course

196I am responding to your request for comments and feedback on Hyperion's classes this month. 197-AI saw the advertisement on the Internet and 197-C/198signed up for the class that began on May 5. I thought it would be very useful for me, 197-Das I work in the hospitality industry and am planning to open a new restaurant this coming fall. I have to say that I was not disappointed at all with the class. I learned a lot after completing the last session a few days ago. I found the lessons taught in each session to be informative and helpful. I gained a lot of insight and ideas that I will use for my upcoming business venture. 198The instructor, Mr. Alex Hernandez, was very patient and innovative in his teaching approach. Also, I heard great things about the class on storage space taught by Laura Palmer. I was wondering if you will be offering this class again. If so, please let me know as I am very interested in attending.

Thanks again, and you can be assured that I will refer your center to my colleagues.

Sincerely,
Jodi Grant

收件人：Curtis Freeman
　　　　<cfreeman@hyperionskills.com>
寄件人：Jodi Grant <jodi_grant@
　　　　theiaristorante.net>
日期：5 月 30 日
主旨：優良的課程

196 我是來回應您所要求的關於本月 Hyperion 課程的意見和回饋，197-A 我在網路上看到廣告，並197-C/198報名了 5 月 5 日開課的課程，我想它將會對我非常有用，197-D 因為我在餐旅業工作，而且我正打算在今年秋天開一間新餐廳，我不得不說，我對此課程一點都沒有失望，在幾天前我完成了最後一堂的研習課程，我學到很多，我發現在每次課程的內容都深具教育性也很有幫助，我得到了很多的見解和想法，我將會運用在我接下來的事業。198 講師 Alex Hernandez 先生很有耐心，且教學方法新穎。此外，我聽到很多有關於 Laura Palmer 授課的儲存空間課很棒的意見。我想知道，您是否將會再次開設這個課程，如果是的話，請讓我知道，因為我很有興趣參加。

您可以放心我將會把您的中心介紹給我的同事，再次感謝您。

Jodi Grant 敬上

例文2

Hyperion Skills Development Center
Programs for May

STARTING DATE	CLASS	DESCRIPTION
200May 3, 9:30 A.M.	FPC780	Emphasizes the fundamental principles and methods of equipment use in food preparation and proper food cleaning
May 4, 8:00 A.M.	FBP415	Deals with methods for estimating bulk storage space and the quantity of food and beverages needed for running a restaurant
198May 5, 10:00 A.M.	MMR823	Teaches the creation of profitable and affordable prices for menu items, as well as the supervision and execution of marketing campaigns
May 6, 7:30 A.M.	199-A ESS609	Outlines the essential safety measures and sanitation methods kitchen staff members need to know

Hyperion 職能開發中心
5 月課程

開始日期	課程	敘述
2005 月 3 日早上 9:30	FPC780	強調在準備食物及適當食物清洗所使用的設備的基本原則和方法
5 月 4 日早上 8:00	FBP415	處理經營一家餐館估算所需大容量儲存空間及食物和飲料數量的方法
1985 月 5 日早上 10:00	MMR823	教授如何創造菜單中有利潤又實惠的菜單價格，以及行銷活動的監督和執行
5 月 6 日早上 7:30	199-A ESS609	概述廚房工作人員所需要知道的必要安全措施和衛生法

Each course consists of four weekly two-hour sessions and is taught by different instructors. For inquiries about the registration process and fees, you may send an e-mail to our registrar, Alicia Paguin at reg@hyperionskills.com.

每門課程由四週每週兩小時的研習課程所組成，且由不同的講師教授。若您要詢問有關報名程序及費用，您可以寄電郵給我們的報名組長 Alicia Paguin，電郵信箱是 reg@hyperionskills.com。

例文 1 單字
- request n. 要求
- complete v. 完成，結束
- hospitality a. 好客的
- informative a. 有益的，情報的
- disappointed a. 失望的，沮喪的
- insight n. 洞察力，遠見
- venture n. 企業，投機活動
- innovative a. 創新的
- approach n. 方式，方法

例文 2 單字
- estimate v. 估計，預測
- essential a. 必須的
- quantity n. 量
- sanitation n. 衛生
- run v. 經營
- profitable a. 有利潤的
- affordable a. 負擔得起的
- supervision n. 管理，監督
- execution n. 執行
- registrar n. 報名主任

196

Why was the e-mail written?	為什麼要寫這封電郵？
(A) To inquire about payment methods	(A) 詢問有關付款方式
(B) To provide comments on a class	(B) 提供對於一個課程的意見
(C) To request instructional materials	(C) 要求教學資料
(D) To ask for a program brochure	(D) 詢問課程手冊

■ 找出主題 寫文章的理由   解答 (B)

這題是在問寫這篇電子郵件的理由，應從第一篇郵件的內容看起。郵件中的 I am responding to your request for comments and feedback on Hyperion's classes this month. 提到是來回應關於本月 Hyperion 課程的意見和回饋，因此 (B) To provide comments on a class 為正確答案。

單字 instructional a. 教學用的

197

What is indicated about Ms. Grant in the e-mail?	在電郵中指出 Grant 小姐的什麼事？
(A) She saw Hyperion's advertisement in a newspaper.	(A) 她在報紙上看到 Hyperion 的廣告。
(B) She has registered for additional courses.	(B) 她已經登記了額外的課程。
(C) She has taken several classes at Hyperion.	(C) 她已在 Hyperion 上了幾門課。
(D) She plans to open a new business.	(D) 她計畫展開一個新的生意。

■ Not/True True 問題   解答 (D)

這是在第一篇文章尋找題目關鍵字 Ms. Grant 的相關內容，並與選項對照的 Not/True 問題。I saw the advertisement on the Internet 提到是在網路上看到廣告的，與 (A) 的內容不符。(B) 的內容在文中則未被提及。signed up for the class that began on May 5 提到報名了 5 月 5 號開始的課程，沒有提到有報名其他的課程，因此與 (C) 的敘述不符。as I work in the hospitality industry and am planning to open a new restaurant 提到因為其在餐旅業工作，而且正打算開一間新餐廳，與 (D) 的敘述相符。所以 (D) She plans to open a new business. 為正確答案。

198

Who most likely taught a class on pricing? (A) Curtis Freeman (B) Alicia Paguin (C) Laura Palmer (D) Alex Hernandez	誰最有可能教關於訂價的課？ (A) Curtis Freeman (B) Alicia Paguin (C) Laura Palmer (D) Alex Hernandez

■■ 推論 聯結問題　　　　　　　　　　　　　　　　　　　　　　　　　　　　　解答 (D)

這是將兩篇文章內容相互對照後進行推測的推論聯結問題。題目關鍵字為 taught a class on pricing，即在問.誰最有可能教關於訂價的課，因此應先從第二篇提及講座說明的相關內容看起。行程表的 May 5, 10:00 A.M. ~ Teaches the creation of profitable and affordable prices for menu items 提到 5 月 5 號的課程為教授如何創造菜單項目中有利潤及實惠的價格，此為第一個線索。但是並沒有提到是由誰來授課，因此應從電子郵件中的相關內容確認。第一封電子郵件中的 signed up for the class that began on May 5 提到 Ms. Grant 報名了 5 月 5 號的講座，The instructor, Mr. Alex Hernandez, was very patient and innovative in his teaching approach. 提到 Mr. Alex Hernandez 講師十分有耐心而且教學方式十分創新，此為第二個線索。綜合以上兩個線索可知道 Mr. Alex Hernandez 教授關於訂價的課，因此 (D) Alex Hernandez 為正確答案。

199

What is mentioned about the class on safety and sanitation? (A) It is intended for kitchen staff. (B) It has been moved to a later date. (C) It is conducted by two instructors. (D) It takes place every Wednesday.	文中提到關於安全及衛生課程的什麼事？ (A) 它是打算要給廚房工作人員上的。 (B) 它已經被移到較後面的日期。 (C) 它由兩位講師進行。 (D) 它在每週三舉行。

■■ Not/True True 問題　　　　　　　　　　　　　　　　　　　　　　　　　　解答 (A)

這是尋找題目關鍵字 the class on safety and sanitation 的相關內容再與選項對照的 Not/True 問題。應從第二篇提及講座課程的相關內容看起。ESS609 的 Outlines the essential safety measures and sanitation methods kitchen staff members need to know 提到 ESS609 課程包含概述廚房工作人員所需要知道的必要安全防範措施和衛生法，與 (A) 的內容相符。因此 (A) It is intended for kitchen staff. 為正確答案。(B) (C) (D) 的內容在文中則未被提及。

200

What time does the course on equipment use start? (A) At 7:30 A.M. (B) At 8:00 A.M. (C) At 9:30 A.M. (D) At 10:00 A.M.	設備使用課程幾點開始？ (A) 在早上 7:30 (B) 在早上 8:00 (C) 在早上 9:30 (D) 在早上 10:00

■■ 六何原則 What time　　　　　　　　　　　　　　　　　　　　　　　　　　解答 (C)

這是在問設備使用課程幾點開始（What time）的六何原則問題。應先從提及題目關鍵字 the course on equipment use start 相關內容的第二篇文章看起。行程表的 May 3, 9:30 A.M. ~ Emphasizes the fundamental principles and methods of equipment use 提到使用設備的基本原則和方法的課程在 9 點 30 分開始，因此 (C) At 9:30 A.M.為正確答案。

TEST 08

PART 5

101

| Garrison Peters will be the fashion _____ for Tate Clothiers' new line of sportswear for both men and women.
(A) designer   (B) will design
(C) designed   (D) designers | Garrison Peters 將會是 Tate Clothiers' 公司新款男女運動服飾的時尚設計師。 |

■ 可以放在補語位置的單字：名詞或形容詞   解答 (A)

因為可以放在 be 動詞的補語位置的是名詞或形容詞，所以可以和空格前的名詞 fashion 一起組成複合名詞的 (A) 和 (D) 都可能是正確答案。因為補語和成為同位語的主詞 Garrison Peters 都是單數，所以單數名詞 (A) designer 就是正確答案。動詞 (B) 和 (C) 不能放在補語位置。(C) 雖然可以看成修飾名詞 fashion 的分詞，但是翻譯成「Garrison Peters 是新款男女運動服飾設計的時尚」的話，意思很奇怪，人不能成為設計的產品，因此不是正確答案。

102

| During the staff meeting, Ms. Crabbe emphasized the importance of observing office dress codes at _____ times.
(A) all   (B) only   (C) entire   (D) whole | 在員工會議上，Crabbe 小姐強調隨時遵守公司衣著規定的重要。 |

■ 形容詞片語   解答 (A)

空格前面的介係詞 at 和空格後面的名詞 times，以及 all 一起組成的詞句 at all times，意思是「隨時」。因此，形容詞 (A) all（所有）就是正確答案。at all times（隨時）作為慣用語，一定要背起來。(B) only 的意思是「唯一的」，(C) entire 的意思是「整體的」，(D) whole 的意思是「所有的」。

單字 observe v. 遵守   dress code phr. 衣著規定

103

| It is the responsibility of agents at the airline's check-in counters to have baggage tags on hand for travelers who _____ them.
(A) requesting   (B) request   (C) requests   (D) to request | 航空公司登機辦理櫃檯的人員有責任隨時攜帶行李標籤以便供應有需求的旅客們。 |

■ 主格關係子句的先行詞和動詞的一致性   解答 (B)

主格關係子句 who ____ them 中沒有動詞，所以 (B) 和 (C) 都可能是正確答案。主格關係代名詞 who 的先行詞 travelers 是複數，所以正確答案是 (B) request。

單字 check-in n. 登機手續   baggage tag phr. 行李標籤   on hand phr. 持有的

104

| Although she _____ difficulty in the beginning, Marla Ambers learned to cope with the fast-paced work environment at Gordem Entertainment Studios.
(A) will have had   (B) is having
(C) was having   (D) to have | 雖然 Marla Ambers 剛開始遭遇困難，但是她學會應付 Gordem 娛樂影視公司裡步調快速的工作環境。 |

■ 時態一致   解答 (C)

副詞子句連接詞 Although 引出的子句 Although she ~ beginning 中沒有動詞，所以 (A) (B) (C) 都可能是正確答案。主句的動詞 learned 是過去時態，所以從屬子句，也就是 Although 引出的副詞子句也必須是過去時態或過去完成時態。因此，過去進行時態的 (C) was having 是正確答案。未來時態的 (A) 和現在時態的 (B) 都不能一起使用。to 不定詞 (D) 則無法放在動詞的位置上。還有，「have difficulty in + 名詞 / -ing」（做～有困難），一定要作為慣用詞背起來。

單字 cope with phr. 應付   fast-paced a. 步調快速的

105

| The annual performance _____ allows management to determine whether employees are doing what they are supposed to .
(A) resolution (B) interpretation
(C) evaluation (D) estimation | 年度績效評鑑能讓管理部門判斷員工們是否如被要求的執行工作。 |

■ 複合名詞 　　　　　　　　　　　　　　　　　　　　　　　　　　　解答 (C)

可以跟空格前面的名詞 performance 組成複詞名詞，意思是「績效評鑑」的 (C) evaluation（評價）是正確答案。(A) resolution 的意思是「決心，決定」，(B) interpretation 的意思是「口譯，解析」，(D) estimation 的意思則是「估算」。

單字 allow v. 允許，許可　determine v. 判斷，決定　be supposed to phr. 有義務做～，決定做～

106

| Popular with locals and tourists _____, Gaiman's jewelry store has been a treasured landmark on First Street for many years.
(A) alike (B) all
(C) every (D) same | Gaiman 珠寶店多年來是第一街上珍貴的地標，受到當地人與遊客的喜愛。 |

■ 副詞的位置 　　　　　　　　　　　　　　　　　　　　　　　　　　解答 (A)

強調空格前面的名詞片語 locals and tourists，意思是「受到當地人與遊客的喜愛」的副詞 (A) alike（都，一樣的）是正確答案。A and B alike （A 和 B 都）要作為慣用語背起來。(B) (C) (D) 如果要修飾名詞，必須位於名詞的前面。

單字 treasure v. 珍貴　landmark n. 地標

107

| Darius Spencer is the most _____ candidate to replace the retiring senior accountant because of his experience and educational background.
(A) legible (B) legal
(C) partial (D) likely | 因為他的經驗與教育背景，Darius Spencer 是最可能取代即將退休的資深會計的人選。 |

■ 形容詞語彙 　　　　　　　　　　　　　　　　　　　　　　　　　　解答 (D)

文意是「Darius Spencer 因為經驗與教育背景是最有希望的人選」，所以 (D) likely（有希望的，可能～）就是正確答案。(A) legible 的意思是「可讀的，容易讀的」，(B) legal 的意思是「法律上」，(C) partial 的意思則是「一部份的」。

單字 candidate n. 候選人　replace v. 成為接班人，代替　accountant n. 會計　background n. 學歷，背景

108

Construction companies should _____ run maintenance checks on all their equipment to ensure optimal performance. (A) modestly (B) usefully (C) regularly (D) formerly	建設公司應該要定期地對所有的設備做保養檢查，以確保最佳的性能。

■ 副詞語彙　　　　　　　　　　　　　　　　　　　　　　　　　　　　　解答 (C)

文意是「建設公司應該要定期地對所有的設備做保養檢查」，所以副詞 (C) regularly（定期地）是正確答案。(A) modestly 的意思是「謙虛地」，(B) usefully 的意思是「有用的」，(D) formerly 的意思則是「之前」。還有，run a check（檢查）要作為慣用語背起來。

單字 construction n. 建設　maintenance n. 保養　optimal a. 最好的，最佳的

109

At last week's meeting, the research team presented the _____ of next quarter's revenues to the company president. (A) estimates (B) circulations (C) engagements (D) appointments	在上週的會議中，研究團隊向公司總裁提出下一季營收的預測值。

■ 名詞語彙　　　　　　　　　　　　　　　　　　　　　　　　　　　　　解答 (A)

文意是「研究團隊提出下一季營收的預測值」，所以名詞 (A) estimates（預測值，估算單）就是正確答案。(B) circulation 的意思是「循環，流通」，(C) engagement 的意思是「合約」，(D) appointment 的意思則是「約定」。還有，price estimate（費用估算單）要作為慣用句背起來，和 estimate 意思相似的名詞還有 quotation（估價）。

單字 present v. 提出　quarter n. 季　revenue n. 營收

110

According to the Department of Transportation, the additional street lights and road signs have led to _____ safety conditions on the highway. (A) improve (B) improves (C) improvement (D) improved	根據交通部，增加的街燈與路標已經讓高速公路上的安全情況改善了。

■ 分詞的角色　　　　　　　　　　　　　　　　　　　　　　　　　　　　解答 (D)

為了在前面修飾名詞 safety conditions，一定要出現形容詞。因此，像形容詞一樣在名詞前面或後面扮演修飾角色的分詞 (D) improved（改善）就是正確答案。動詞 (A) 和 (B) 不能修飾名詞，名詞 (C) 如果不是複合名詞，是不能出現在名詞前面的。另外，lead to (have led to) 的 to 是介系詞，所以 to 後面不是接動詞原形，而是要接名詞。

單字 according to phr. 根據～　highway n. 高速公路

111

Classrooms are kept at a comfortable temperature to provide an environment that is ------- to learning.
(A) enviable   (B) proficient
(C) profitable   (D) conducive

教室裡保持舒服的溫度,提供了一個有利學習的環境。

■ 形容詞語彙   解答 (D)

文意是「有利學習的環境」,所以形容詞 (D) conducive(有幫助的)就是正確答案。(A) enviable 的意思是「羨慕的」,(B) proficient 的意思是「熟練的」,(C) profitable 的意思則是「(金錢上的)有利的」。

單字 comfortable a. 舒適的,便利的   temperature n. 溫度

112

------- lessen the risk of accidents while on the project site, Theobald Developments created new work safety policies.
(A) Moreover   (B) In addition to
(C) As though   (D) In order to

為了在工作地點減少意外的風險,Theobald Developments 公司制定了新的工作安全守則。

■ to 不定詞的形態   解答 (D)

文意是「為了減少意外的風險制定守則」,所以為了使用表示目的的 to 不定詞,動詞原形 lessen 的前面一定要出現 to。不過,選項中並沒有 to,因此可以代替 to 的 (D) In order to 就是正確答案。(A) Moreover(而且)和 (B) In addition to(除~之外)、副詞子句連接詞 (C) As though(像~一樣)都無法使用在動詞原形前面。另外,to 不定詞在表示目的時,可以用 in order to 或 so as to 來代替 to。「in order that + 子句」(為了~)也需要一起知道一下。

單字 lessen v. 減少,降下   site n. 現場

113

The La Familia residential condominium ------ opened for occupancy following six years of construction.
(A) equally   (B) occasionally
(C) finally   (D) previously

La Familia 住宅公寓大樓在施工六年後終於開放使用。

■ 副詞語彙   解答 (C)

文意是「La Familia 住宅公寓大樓在施工六年後終於開放使用」,所以副詞 (C) finally(終於)是正確答案。另外,finally 通常用於強調經過比較長時間的努力之後所達到的結論或行動。(A) equally 的意思是「相同地」,(B) occasionally 的意思是「偶爾」,(D) previously 的意思則是「之前地」。

單字 residential a. 住宅的   condominium n. 公寓,大樓   occupancy n. 居住,使用

114

The blueprints for the renovation had to be revised because the apartment's living room was ------ measured.
(A) incorrect   (B) incorrectness
(C) more incorrect   (D) incorrectly

整修的藍圖必須重新修正因為公寓的客廳測量不正確。

■ 副詞的位置   解答 (D)

為了修飾動詞 was measured,一定要出現副詞。因此,副詞 (D) incorrectly 是正確答案。形容詞 (A) 和形容詞的比較級 (C),名詞 (B) 都不能修飾動詞。

單字 blueprint n 藍圖,設計   redecoration n. 整修,重新裝飾   revise v. 修正

115

Once _____ MacDougal Boulevard, the street is undergoing repairs and will be called Cosa Boulevard after the construction is completed. (A) name (B) to name (C) named (D) naming	曾經被命名為 MacDougal 的道路要進行整修，而且在工程結束後會改名為 Cosa 大道。

■ 現在分詞 vs.過去分詞　　　　　　　　　　　　　　　　　　　　　　　　　　　　　解答 (C)

這句話是具有必要成分 the street is undergoing repairs and will be called Cosa Boulevard 的完整子句，所以要把 Once____ MacDougal Boulevard 看成是可省略的修飾語。可以成為修飾語的 to 不定詞 (B)、分詞 (C) 和 (D) 都可能是正確答案。因為文意是「曾經被命名為 MacDougal 的道路」，所以過去分詞 (C) named 是正確答案。如果使用表示目的的 to 不定詞 (B) to name 的話，意思就變成「曾經為了給 MacDougal 大道命名而修路中」，這樣整個句子的意思就會很奇怪。如果使用現在分詞 (D) naming 的話，被修飾的名詞 the street 和分詞就成為主動關係，文意就變成「曾經街道取名為 MacDougal 大道」，也很奇怪。動詞 (A) 則不能成為修飾語。

單字 boulevard n. 大道　undergo v. 經歷

116

The board members of Portia Coffee Company have _____ some administrative changes to accommodate the requests of the workers union. (A) alternated (B) refrained (C) reminded (D) instituted	Portia 咖啡公司的董事會成員已經開始一些行政上的改弦易轍，以配合勞工工會的要求。

■ 動詞語彙　　　　　　　　　　　　　　　　　　　　　　　　　　　　　　　　　　解答 (D)

文意是「為了配合勞工工會的要求，開始一些行政上的改弦易轍」，所以動詞 institute（開始）的過去式 (D) instituted 就正確答案。(A) alternate 的意思是「交替」，(B) refrain 的意思是「節制，抑制」，(C) remind 的意思是「提醒」。另外，remind 經常使用的形態是 remind A of B（使 A 想起 B）。

單字 board n. 董事會　administrative a. 行政上的　accommodate v. 符合　request n. 要求

117

_____ the Invierna Electronics compound, visitors will find a large production plant, workers' dormitories, and a modern warehouse. (A) Within (B) Between (C) Over (D) Onto	在 Invierna 電子公司的廠區內，訪客會看到一個大型的生產工廠、勞工宿舍和一個現代化倉庫。

■ 選擇介系詞 位置　　　　　　　　　　　　　　　　　　　　　　　　　　　　　　　解答 (A)

文意是「廠區內可以看到生產工廠、勞工宿舍、倉庫」，所以表示存在於某個範圍內的介系詞 (A) Within（～內）就是正確答案。(B) Between（～之間）表示兩個以上事物的關係或位置，(C) Over（～內，～期間）表示位置或期間，(D) Onto（～內）表示位置。

單字 compound n. （住宅，工廠）內部　plant n. 工廠　dormitory n. 宿舍　warehouse n. 倉庫

118

The marketing director arranged _____ with advertising and promotion advisors to obtain feedback on her newly designed advertisement campaign. (A) proposals　　　(B) consultations (C) layouts　　　(D) deliveries	行銷主任安排了和廣告與宣傳顧問的諮詢，以獲取對她的新設計廣告活動的反饋意見。

■ 名詞語彙　　　　　　　　　　　　　　　　　　　　　　　　　解答 (B)

文意是「行銷主任安排了和顧問的諮詢」，所以名詞 (B) consultations（諮詢）是正確答案。(A) proposal 的意思是「申請，提案」，(C) layout 的意思是「配置」，(D) delivery 的意思是「送達」。

單字 arrange v. 準備，安排　advisor n. 顧問　obtain v. 獲得

119

Tennyson Banks' _____ of kindness, in the form of a large monetary donation, has made it possible for the city museum to proceed with the improvements of its exhibit rooms. (A) entry　　　(B) act (C) idea　　　(D) option	Tennyson 銀行的善舉，用大筆金錢的捐助，讓市立博物館能夠進行展示廳的改善。

■ 名詞語彙　　　　　　　　　　　　　　　　　　　　　　　　　解答 (B)

文意是「Tennyson 銀行的善舉，用大筆金錢的捐助」，所以動詞 (B) act（行為）是正確答案。(A) entry 的意思是「入場」，(C) idea 的意思是「想法」，(D) option 的意思則是「選擇（權）」。另外，「of + 抽象名詞」可以作為形容詞來使用，所以 of kindness 和形容詞 kind（親切的）是一樣的意思。

單字 kindness n. 善舉，親切　in the form of phr. ～形式　monetary a. 金融的，金錢的　donation n. 捐獻
　　proceed with phr. 進行

120

On the online order form, Ms. Jung requested that she be notified _____ the packages are shipped from the manufacturing plant. (A) furthermore　　　(B) despite (C) rather than　　　(D) as soon as	在線上訂購單上，Jung 小姐要求在包裹從製造工廠運出後就要馬上通知她。

■ 副詞子句連接詞 時間　　　　　　　　　　　　　　　　　　　　解答 (D)

that 子句是具有必要成分 she be notified 的完整子句，所以可以把 __the packages ~ plant 看成可省略的修飾語。在這個修飾語中有動詞 are shipped，可知為子句形態，所以副詞子句連接詞 (C) (D) 都可能是正確答案。文意是「包裹從製造工廠運出後就要馬上通知」，所以 (D) as soon as（一～就～）是正確答案。選擇 (C) rather than（而不是～）的話，文意就是「要求通知她，而不是從製造工廠運出」不合邏輯的意思。接續副詞 (A) furthermore（而且）和介系詞 (B) despite（不管～也～）無法引出子句，所以不是正確答案。另外，如 request（請求）、suggest（提案）、demand（要求）等表示提案 / 請求 / 任務的動詞的受詞位置上出現的 that 子句中要使用動詞原形。

單字 adequately ad. 適當地　accommodate v. 使相符，容納

121

Most of the employees said that the new software program has been _____ useful in speeding up the database search process. (A) consideration (B) considering (C) considerable (D) considerably	大部分的員工表示新的軟體程式在加速資料庫搜尋的過程有顯著的助益。

■ 副詞的位置   解答 (D)

為了修飾形容詞 useful，一定要出現副詞。因此，副詞 (D) considerably（相當地）就是正確答案。名詞 (A)，動名詞或副詞 (B)，形容詞 (C) 都不能修飾形容詞。

單字 speed up phr. 加速　consideration n. 考慮，思考

122

Viewers may watch the all new season of Dining Haven for _____ recipes specially created by celebrity cook Steven Brant. (A) prompted (B) described (C) scarce (D) healthy	觀眾可以收看全新一季的 Dining Haven，有名廚 Steven Brant 特別設計的健康食譜。

■ 形容詞語彙   解答 (D)

文意是「健康食譜」，所以形容詞 (D) healthy（健康的）是正確答案。(A) prompted 的意思是「激起」，(B) described 的意思是「描述」，(C) scarce 的意思則是「不足的」。

單字 viewer n. 觀眾　recipe n. 食譜　cook n. 廚師

123

Even though Ms. Regina had been in transit for 24 hours, she still managed to give an _____ lecture at the university. (A) energizer (B) energetically (C) energetic (D) energize	儘管 Regina 女士舟車勞頓二十四小時，她仍然能精力旺盛地在大學裡講授一堂課。

■ 形容詞的位置   解答 (C)

為了修飾名詞 lecture，一定要出現形容詞，所以 (C) energetic（精力旺盛的）就是正確答案。名詞 (A)、副詞 (B)、動詞 (D) 都不能修飾名詞。另外，manage to（設法～）要作為慣用語背起來。

單字 in transit phr. 移動中，運送中　manage to phr. 設法～　lecture n. 授課

124

_____ changing your mobile phone plan, please present valid identification at the customer service counter. (A) When (B) As if (C) Therefore (D) In regards	當你要改變你的手機方案，請在客服櫃台出示有效的證件。

■ 副詞子句連接詞 時間   解答 (A)

這句是具有必要成分 present valid identification 的完整子句，所以可以把 ____changing ~ plan 看成是可省略的修飾語。在這個可省略的修飾語中出現的分詞片語，前面可出現的副詞子句連接詞 (A) (B) 都可能是正確答案。因為句子的意思是「改變你的手機方案時，請出示有效的證件」，所以 (A) When（～的時候）是正確答案。如果選擇 (B) As if（像～），句子就會變成「像改變你的手機方案一樣，出示有效的證件」，意思就會變得很奇怪。接續副詞 (C) Therefore（因此）不能引出子句。(D) In regards 後面要跟介系詞 to 一起使用，意思是「關於～」，同樣也無法引出子句，所以不是正確答案。

單字 plan n. 計畫　valid a. 有效的　identification n. 證件

125

At Mr. Kincaid's retirement party, the staff conveyed their ------- of his 20 years of committed service to the company.

(A) appreciatively   (B) appreciated
(C) appreciative   (D) appreciation

在 Kincaid 先生的退休宴上，員工們對他二十年來在公司的貢獻表達感激之意。

■ 名詞的位置   解答 (D)

除了是動詞 conveyed 的受詞，同時也是所有格 their 後面要接的名詞，所以名詞 (D) appreciation（感謝）就是正確答案。副詞 (A)、動詞或分詞 (B)、形容詞 (C) 都不可以放在名詞的位置上。

單字 convey v. 表達　　committed a. 堅定的

126

Due to a change in tomorrow's work schedule, the refined oil will need to be ------- into the tankers before the end of the day.

(A) expanded   (B) loaded
(C) translated   (D) engaged

由於明天工作時間表的改變，精煉過的油必須在明天結束前裝載到運油船裡。

■ 動詞語彙   解答 (B)

文意是「精煉過的油必須裝載到運油船裡」，所以和空格前面的 be 動詞 to be 一起製造出被動形 to 不定詞的 load（裝載）的 p.p. 形態 (B) loaded 就是正確答案。(A) expand 的意思是「擴大」，(C) translate 的意思是「翻譯」，(D) engage 的意思則是「約定」。

單字 refined a. 精煉的

127

Andromeda, which ------- Rosy Trinkets' most in-demand jewelry collection for the last six months, will soon become available in Asia.

(A) to be   (B) will be
(C) has been   (D) is being

Andromeda 是 Rosy Trinkets 在過去六個月需求最大的珠寶品牌，很快就會在亞洲銷售。

■ 現在完成時態   解答 (C)

關係子句 which ~ months 中沒有動詞，所有 (B) (C) (D) 都可能是正確答案。因為有表示現在完成的時間表達 for the last six months，所以現在完成時態的 (C) has been 是正確答案。句中沒有跟未來時態 (B) 和現在進行時態 (D) 相對應的時間表達，to 不定詞 (A) 則不能放在動詞位置上。

單字 in-demand a. 需求很大的　　available a. 可以買的，可使用的

128

------- is on duty tonight must check that all the entrances are locked and the security alarm is set before leaving the building.

(A) That   (B) Whoever
(C) Someone   (D) Whenever

不管今天晚上是誰值班，在離開建築物前，必須檢查所有的入口都上好鎖、設好警鈴。

■ 名詞子句連接詞 whoever   解答 (B)

出現在主詞位置的名詞子句 _____is ~ tonight 中的主詞是空格，所以複合關係代名詞 (B) Whoever 是正確答案。(A) That 必須引出完整的子句，所以不是正確答案。(C) Someone 的意思是「某人」，但也因為不能引出子句，所以不是答案。副詞子句連接詞 (D) Whenever 可以出現在完整的子句前面，但不能出現在沒有主詞的不完整子句前面。

單字 on duty phr. 值班中　　entrance n. 入口

129

In accordance with the new company policy, all Fuschia Travels clients will be billed for flights _____ from accommodation costs.

(A) separately　　　　(B) commonly
(C) positively　　　　(D) personally

為了配合公司的新政策，所有 Fuschia 旅行公司客戶的飛機與住宿將會分開收費。

■ 副詞語彙　　　　　　　　　　　　　　　　　　　　　　　解答 (A)

文意是「所有客戶的飛機與住宿將會分開收費」，所以副詞 (A) separately（另外，分開）是正確答案。(B) commonly 的意思是「一般地」，(C) positively 的意思是「明確地」，(D) personally 的意思是「親自」。另外，separate 跟介系詞 from 一起使用時，經常使用 separate from（分開，分離）這個形態。

單字 in accordance with phr. 根據～　bill v. 開帳單　accommodation n. 住宿費

130

Asaha Telecommunications does not require staff to participate in its community outreach programs, but many employees _____ do so.

(A) voluntarily　　　　(B) memorably
(C) divisively　　　　(D) infrequently

Asaha 電信公司沒有要求員工參加社區慈善活動，但是很多員工都自願參與。

■ 副詞語彙　　　　　　　　　　　　　　　　　　　　　　　解答 (A)

文意是「很多員工都自願參與慈善活動」，所以副詞 (A) voluntarily（自發性地）是正確答案。(B) memorably 的意思是「難忘的」，(C) divisively 的意思是「區分，不合」，(D) infrequently 的意思是「不常的」。

單字 require v. 要求　participate in phr. 參與　outreach n. 慈善活動

131

The local newspaper reported that the damaged electrical lines were the _____ cause of the four-hour power outage yesterday evening.

(A) clear　　　　(B) clears
(C) clearly　　　　(D) clearness

當地的報紙報導，損毀的電力管線很顯然是昨天晚上停電四小時的原因。

■ 形容詞的位置　　　　　　　　　　　　　　　　　　　　　解答 (A)

為了修飾名詞 cause，所以一定要出現形容詞。也就是說，形容詞 (A) clear（明白的，清晰的）就是正確答案。動詞 (B)、副詞 (C) 都不能修飾名詞，名詞 (D) 則只有在複合名詞時才可以出現在名詞的前面。

單字 report v. 報導　damaged a. 破損的　outage n. 停電，停水　clearness n. 分明的，鮮明的

132

Aqua Mouthwash repackaged its dental care products and launched an information campaign to _____ a favorable reputation. (A) pass　　　　　(B) regain (C) leave　　　　　(D) attach	Aqua 漱口水為了要重新贏回好名聲，重新包裝牙齒保健產品，並開始了一項宣傳活動。

■ 動詞語彙　　　　　　　　　　　　　　　　　　　　　　　　　　　　解答 (B)

文意是「重新贏回好名聲」，所以動詞 (B) regain（恢復）是正確答案。(A) pass 的意思是「過去」，(C) leave 的意思是「離開」，(D) attach 的意思則是「貼上」。

單字 dental a. 牙科的　launch v. 開始，發布　favorable a. 好的，好意的　reputation n. 名譽，聲望

133

Du Vin Restaurant does not provide delivery service for orders under \$50, _____ does it offer catering for groups of fewer than 20 guests. (A) also　　　　　(B) so (C) either　　　　(D) nor	Du Vin 餐廳不提供五十元以下的外送服務，也不提供二十人以下的團體外燴。

■ 倒裝句　　　　　　　　　　　　　　　　　　　　　　　　　　　　解答 (D)

在主詞和動詞倒裝的子句 does it offer ~ guests 前面，可以引出倒裝句的 (B) 和 (D) 都可能是正確答案。文意是「不提供外送服務，也不提供團體外燴」，所以否定詞 (D) nor（～也不～）是正確答案。(B) so 用於肯定句中要反覆提到前面出現的內容時，起到代替的作用，所以在這裡不是正確答案。另外，當 nor does it offer 中的否定詞出現在子句前面時，就可以知道主詞和動詞倒裝了。

單字 catering n. 團體外燴

134

_____ the fierce competition in the shipping industry, Kingfisher Express remains the most successful cargo company in the region. (A) Frequently　　　　(B) In spite of (C) As far as　　　　　(D) Otherwise	儘管在貨運業的激烈競爭，Kingfisher 快遞仍然是當地最成功的貨運公司。

■ 介系詞選擇 讓步　　　　　　　　　　　　　　　　　　　　　　　解答 (B)

這個句子是具有必要成分 Kingfisher Express remains the ~ cargo company 的完整子句，所以可以把 ____ the fierce ~ industry 看成可省略的修飾語。因為修飾語中是沒有動詞的，所以選項中可以引出片語形態修飾語的介系詞 (B) In spite of（儘管～）就是正確答案。副詞 (A) Frequently（經常），副詞子句連接詞 (C) As far as（盡～），接續副詞 (D) Otherwise（不然）是無法引出修飾語的。

單字 fierce a. 強烈的　remain v. 依然　cargo n. 貨物

135

Customers patronize the Evergreen Pharmacy because of its _____ to providing the community with high-quality, affordable medicines.

(A) commits
(B) committed
(C) commitment
(D) committable

顧客支持 Evergreen 藥局是因為它為社區提供高品質、價格實惠的藥品的承諾。

■ 名詞的位置　　　　　　　　　　　　　　　　　　　　　　　　　　　解答 (C)

除了是介系詞 because of 的受詞，同時也可以出現在所有格 its 和介系詞 to 之間的名詞 (C) commitment（承諾）是正確答案。動詞 (A)，動詞或分詞 (B)，形容詞 (D) 都不能放在名詞的位置上。另外，provide A with B（給 A 提供 B）要作為慣用語背起來。

單字 patronize v. 愛用　community n. 居民　affordable a. 價格適當的　medicine n. 藥

136

Because of his _____ superb sales presentations, Mr. Lim is always selected to represent the home appliance company at trade fairs.

(A) approximately
(B) variably
(C) impartially
(D) consistently

因為 Lim 先生一貫優秀的銷售簡報，他總是被選為貿易展中家用電器公司的代表。

■ 副詞語彙　　　　　　　　　　　　　　　　　　　　　　　　　　　解答 (D)

文意是「因為一貫優越的銷售報告」，所以副詞 (D) consistently（一貫地，固守地）是正確答案。(A) approximately 的意思是「大略」，(B) variably 的意思是「易變地，不一定」，(C) impartially 的意思則是「不偏不倚地，公平公正地」。

單字 superb a. 優越的，最棒的　sales a. 銷售的，買賣的　represent v. 代表　home appliance phr. 家用電器

137

Elven Hotel has three _____ banquet halls that are large enough to hold corporate events and social functions of any kind.

(A) spacious
(B) coherent
(C) fulfilled
(D) insatiable

Elven 飯店有三間寬敞的宴會廳，足以容納各式公司活動與社交活動。

■ 形容詞語彙　　　　　　　　　　　　　　　　　　　　　　　　　　解答 (A)

文意是「有三間寬敞的宴會廳，足以容納公司活動」，所以形容詞 (A) spacious（寬敞）是正確答案。(B) coherent 的意思是「連貫的」，(C) fulfilled 的意思是「感到成就感的」，(D) insatiable 的意思則是「永不滿足的」。

單字 banquet n. 宴會，晚餐　corporate a. 企業的　social function phr. 社交聚會，社交派對

138

A building located in the financial _____ was sold to a property developer who had offered the owner an amount that was higher than the current market price. (A) resource　　　　　(B) industry (C) system　　　　　(D) district	一棟位在金融區的大樓賣給了一個開出高於現今市場行情價格的地產開發商。

■ 名詞片語　　　　　　　　　　　　　　　　　　　　　　　　　　　　　解答 (D)

文意是「位在金融區的大樓」，所以可以跟 financial 一起組成「金融區」這一單字的 (D) district 是正確答案。（financial district：金融區）(A) resource 的意思是「資源」，(B) industry 的意思是「產業」，(C) system 的意思是「體系」。

單字 financial district phr. 金融區　property n 不動產　offer v. 提案

139

Out of the 36 applicants, Wally Brennan was _____ the research funding from Indigo Foundation for his well-defined project proposal on the study of alternative fuel sources. (A) granted　　　　　(B) assisted (C) encouraged　　　　　(D) maintained	在三十六位應徵者中，Wally Brennan 以他對替代能源研究的周詳計畫書獲得了 Indigo 基金會的研究贊助經費。

■ 動詞語彙　　　　　　　　　　　　　　　　　　　　　　　　　　　　　解答 (A)

文意是「Wally Brennan 獲得了研究贊助經費」，所以跟空格前面的 be 動詞 was 組成被動態的 grant（給與）的 p.p. 形態 (A) granted 是正確答案。(B) assist 的意思是「幫助，協助」，(C) encourage 的意思是「鼓勵，獎勵」，(D) maintain 的意思則是「持續，維持」。另外，grant 作為第 4 類動詞，可以後接兩個受詞，經常使用的形態是「grant＋人＋物」（給誰什麼、承認）。

單字 applicant n. 申請者　well-defined a. 明確的，清楚的　proposal n. 企畫案，提案　alternative a. 代替的

140

Hermaine Electronics' newly-released photo printer is _____ in price and functionality to those of the company's market rivals. (A) comparable　　　　　(B) momentous (C) operative　　　　　(D) practical	Hermaine Electronics 最新發表的相片列表機，對公司在市場上的競爭對手而言，在價格與功能上都很實惠。

■ 形容詞語彙　　　　　　　　　　　　　　　　　　　　　　　　　　　　解答 (A)

文意是「最新發表的相片影印機，對公司在市場上的競爭對手而言，在價格與功能上都很實惠」，所以形容詞 (A) comparable（可比較的，比得上的）是正確答案。(B) momentous 的意思是「重大的」，(C) operative 的意思是「有效的，作業的」，(D) practical 的意思則是「實用的」。

單字 newly-released a. 新上市的　functionality n. 機能，機能性

PART 6

Questions 141-143 refer to the following letter.　　141-143 根據下面信件的內容回答問題。

December 18	12 月 18 日
Human Resources Flavors Group 28 Wood Street, Pittston, PA 18640	人力資源部門 Flavors 集團 賓州 Pittston 市 Wood 街 28 號
Dear Madam or Sir,	敬啟者：
I am writing to apply for the franchise supervisor position advertised on your company's Web site on December 15. I believe that I possess the needed expertise for the job, and that my future in your company could be a _____ one. 141 (A) promising　　(B) distant 　　(C) shared　　(D) predictable	我寫這封信來應徵你們公司網站在 12 月 15 日刊登的特許經營主管一職，我相信我擁有這份工作需要的專業，141 而我未來在你們公司會很有發展性。
I have been an account supervisor in Blast Foods Corporation's franchising department for the last four years. As a supervisor, I am in charge of the account executives who sell the corporation's franchise permits. The job has enhanced my marketing skills and _____ me 142 (A) enabling　　(B) enabled 　　(C) to enable　　(D) will be enabled to learn how a franchise is operated.	在過去四年，我一直是 Blast 食品公司特許經營部門的財務主管，身為一個主管，我負責管理銷售公司特許經營許可證的財務專員，142 這份工作讓我的行銷技巧更上層樓，也讓我知道特許經營是如何運作。
I have included with this letter my résumé and three references. Should you need to know more about my credentials, please call me at 555-6323.	隨函附有我的履歷表和三封推薦信，如果您需要更了解我的資歷，請撥打 555-6323 與我聯絡。
Your _____ is greatly appreciated. 143 (A) donation　　(B) recommendation 　　(C) invitation　　(D) consideration	143 對於您的考慮我深表感激。
Sincerely,	
Ewan Walken	Ewan Walken 敬上

單字 human resources phr. 人事部門　apply for phr. 應徵　franchise n. 連鎖店經營權，給予連鎖店經營權
supervisor n. 監督，管理者　possess v. 具有，擁有　expertise n. 專業知識　account n. 帳戶，帳目
in charge of phr. 正在管理～，負責～　executive n. 經營主管，理事　permit n. 許可證　enhance v. 提高
operate v. 經營，工作　reference n. 推薦書　credential n. 資格，資歷　appreciate v. 感謝

141 ■ 形容詞語彙　　　　　　　　　　　　　　　　　　　　　　　　　　　　　　　　　　解答 (A)

文意是「在你們公司會很有發展性」，所以形容詞 (A) promising（有望的）是正確答案。(B) distant 的意思是「遠的，遠離的」，(C) shared 的意思是「公有的」，(D) predictable 的意思是「可預測的」。

142 ■ 倒裝句　　　　　　　　　　　　　　　　　　　　　　　　　　　　　　　　　　　　解答 (B)

文意是「這份工作讓我的行銷技巧更上層樓，也讓我知道特許經營是如何運作」，由此可以知道對等連接詞 and 連接的是動詞 has enhanced 和另外的動詞。和前面的動詞 has 一起組成現在完成時態的 p.p. 形 enhanced，所以動詞的 p.p. 形 (B) enabled 是正確答案。

143 ■ 名詞語彙 掌握全文　　　　　　　　　　　　　　　　　　　　　　　　　　　　　　解答 (D)

文意是「您的_____我深表感激」，全部選項都可能是正確答案。只看有空格的句子而無法選出正確的答案時，要先了解前後文意或整體文意。這封信是求職者為了應徵管理職務而把自已的履歷表和推薦信寄給人事部門的內容。由此可以知道發信者希望人事部門考慮自已是否適合這個職務。因此，名詞 (D) consideration 是正確答案。(A) donation 的意思是「捐獻」，(B) recommendation 的意思是「推薦」，(C) invitation 的意思是「邀請」。

Questions 144-146 refer to the following e-mail.

TO: Victoria Morgan <v.morgan@towerdevt.com>
FROM: Kate Lee <kate.lee@burnmail.com>
DATE: July 14
SUBJECT: Meeting

Dear Ms. Morgan,

We appreciate getting the information packet from you, but we would like to request that our business appointment for Thursday be rescheduled. We need some extra time to consider different _____ before meeting with you.
144 (A) properties (B) furniture (C) technology (D) instructions

My husband and I found Summersville to be a nice vacation place for the family. However, we are as yet _____
145 (A) uninformed (B) enlightened (C) undecided (D) outspoken

about the farm estate you showed us. This is because we are currently considering beachside properties recommended by other developers. Some of them are willing to provide a 20 percent discount on beachfront lots. That said, your offers are also attractive, particularly the quotations you gave us that _____ a 25 percent discount
146 (A) specifying (B) specifies (C) specification (D) specify

on properties of 400 square meters and above. I hope you can give us at least two weeks to review all the proposals. We will let you know of our decision shortly. Thank you.

Best regards,

Kate Lee

收件人：Victoria Morgan <v.morgan@towerdevt.com>
寄件人：Kate Lee <kate.lee@burnmail.com>
日期：7 月 14 日
主旨：會議

親愛的 Morgan 小姐：

我們很謝謝你寄來的資料，不過，我們想要重新安排約在週四的商務會議。在與你會面之前，144 我們需要更多的時間來考慮不同的房地產產品。

145 我丈夫和我得知 Summersville 是一個適合家庭的度假地點，但是我們還沒有決定你介紹給我們的莊園，因為我們目前在考慮其他地產商推薦的濱海地產，有一些海濱地區的地願意給我們八折的折扣。

146 也就是説，你給我們的優惠也很吸引人，特別是你在四百平方公尺以上的地產，給我們七五折的折扣，我希望你能給我們至少兩週的時間來重新考慮所有的地產，我們會很快給你答覆，謝謝。

Kate Lee 敬上

單字 packet n. 小包裹，小袋 estate n. 地產，土地 beachfront a. 靠海濱的 lot n. 空地
quotation n. 估價單 shortly ad. 馬上

144 名詞語彙掌握 全文　　　　　　　　　　　　　　　　　　　　　　　　　解答 (A)
文意是「需要更多的時間來考慮不同的____」，所以所有選項都可能是正確答案。只看有空格的句子無法選出正確的答案時，就要先了解前後文意或整體文意。後面的句子中提到正在考慮其他地產商推薦的地產，由此可以知道是請求多一點的考慮時間。因此，名詞 (A) properties（地產）是正確答案。(B) furniture 的意思是「家具」，(C) technology 的意思是「技術」，(D) instruction 的意思是「說明，指示」。

145 形容詞語彙 掌握上下文　　　　　　　　　　　　　　　　　　　　　　　解答 (C)
文意是「還____你介紹給我們的莊園」，所以 (A) uninformed（沒有知識的），(C) undecided（沒決定的）都可能是正確答案。只看有空格的句子無法選出正確的答案時，就要先了解前後文意或整體文意。後面的句子中提到「給我們至少兩週的時間來重新考慮所有的地產」，由此可以知道還沒有決定莊園。因此，形容詞 (C) undecided（沒決定的）是正確答案。如果選擇 (A) uninformed（沒有知識的），文意就會變得很奇怪。(B) enlightened 的意思是「開明的」，(D) outspoken 的意思是「直言不諱的」。

146 主格關係子句的先行詞單複數和動詞要一致　　　　　　　　　　　　　　解答 (D)
修飾先行詞 quotations 的主格關係子句 that ~ above 中沒有動詞，所以動詞 (B) (D) 可能是答案。先行詞 quotations 是複數，所以動詞 (D) specify（明確說明）是正確答案。動名詞或分詞的 (A) 和名詞 (C) 都不能放在動詞的位置。另外，you gave us 是修飾先行詞 quotations 的另一個關係子句，對選出正確答案沒有影響。

TEST 8 PART 6 | 383

READING TEST 1 2 3 4 5 6 7 8 9 10

Questions 147-149 refer to the following article.

Actor Alfred Monaco has been cast in a starring role for a television show _____ this fall.

147 (A) reviewing　(B) premiering
　　(C) hosting　　(D) subscribing

In the comedy series The Stage, Alfred will play the role of Donald Williams, an aspiring singer who does _____ it

148 (A) whenever　(B) whatever
　　(C) most　　(D) such

takes to land a career at Park Studios, a company at the center of the country's entertainment industry. In an interview with News Time, the actor said the show _____ a

149 (A) will expose　(B) exposed
　　(C) had exposed　(D) has exposed

different side of him to the public. "This will be my first time performing on television," Alfred said. "I'm very excited about the project because the script is really engaging."

The season's first episode will be broadcast on November 6 at 9 P.M.

147 男演員 Alfred Monaco 在今年秋季上演的一齣電視劇中演出。

148 在這部喜劇影集 The Stage，Alfred 將飾演 Donald Williams 這個角色，是一位激勵人心的歌手，在 Park 工作室中竭盡所能地發展他的職業生涯，這是位在該國娛樂事業中心的一家公司。在 News Time 的一次訪談中，149 這位男演員說這齣戲會讓觀眾看到他不同的一面，Alfred 說：「這是我第一次在電視上演出，我很興奮，因為這齣戲的劇本很吸引人。」

本季的第一集將會在 11 月 6 日晚間九點播出。

單字 cast v. 選角；投射　aspiring a. 有抱負的，有志氣的　perform v. 演技　engaging a. 魅力的
broadcast v. 放映

147 ■ 動詞語彙　　　　　　　　　　　　　　解答 (B)

文意是「在今年秋季上演的一齣電視劇」，所以動詞 premiere（初次上演）的 -ing 形的 (B) premiering 是正確答案。(A) review 的意思是「評論，複習」，(C) host 的意思是「主辦」，(D) subscribe 的意思是「訂閱」。

148 ■ 名詞子句連接詞 whatever　　　　　　　　解答 (B)

who 子句 who ~ Studios 的受詞位置上出現的子句 ___ it takes ~ Studios 的最前面一定要有名詞子句，所以名詞子句的連接詞 (B) whatever（不論什麼）是正確答案。複合關係副詞 (A) whenever 的意思是「不論何時」，可以跟 no matter when 交替使用，並引出副詞子句。(C) most 無法引出子句，作為限定詞來使用時，意思是「大部分的」，可用於可數和不可數名詞前面。意思是「大部分的」時，也可以作為代名詞來使用。作為副詞來使用時，意思是「最」，可以修飾動詞。(D) such 也是不能引出子句。作為限定詞來使用時，意思是「那麼」，作為代名詞來使用時，意思是「那樣的」，作為副詞來使用時，意思是「非常」，且可以修飾形容詞。

149 ■ 填入正確時態的動詞 掌握上下文　　　　　解答 (A)

文意是「這齣戲會讓觀眾看到他不同的一面」。這時候只看有空格的句子無法選出正確時態的動詞，要先了解前後文意或整體文意才能選出正確答案。後面的句子中提到這是他第一次在電視上演出，由此可以知道這事情是發生在寫「這齣戲會讓觀眾看到他不同的一面」的新聞後，未來會發生的事情。因此，未來時態 (A) will expose 是正確答案。

Questions 150-152 refer to the following memo.　　　150-152 根據下面備忘錄的內容回答問題。

TO: Staff
FROM: Dennis Buckmaster, HRD head
SUBJECT: Job Advertisements
DATE: August 5

Since Solano Marketing was established, the human resources department has counted on newspapers to advertise job openings in the company. However, we have observed that _____ to printed advertisements have

150 (A) responses　　　(B) responded
　　(C) responding　　(D) respondent

dropped since the onset of online employment agencies. To reach out to more applicants, we will use the services of Workhunter.com starting in July.

The _____ agency will post our advertisements on their
151 (A) security　　　　　(B) recruitment
　　(C) transportation　　(D) housing

Web site. And they will match the company with job seekers who might qualify for the positions.

Workhunter requests that the advertisements be submitted next week. _____, each advertisement should

152 (A) Instead　　(B) Otherwise
　　(C) At last　　(D) As always

contain a brief description of our firm and the position, as well as a list of requirements.

Please e-mail the advertisements to Tess no later than Friday. Thanks.

收件人：員工
寄件人：人力資源部主任 Dennis Buckmaster
主旨：職缺廣告
日期：8 月 5 日

自從 Solano 行銷公司建立以來，人力資源部門一直仰賴報紙來刊登公司的職缺廣告。150 不過，我們觀察到自從線上人力公司新興以來，回應報紙廣告的應徵者已經減少了。為了要接觸到更多應徵者，我們 7 月開始要使用 Workhunter.com 的服務。

151 這個徵人的仲介商會在他們網站上刊登我們的廣告，而且他們會把適合這些職位的求職者找出來。

152 Workhunter 要求下星期要交付廣告，一如往常，廣告應該要包含我們公司和職缺的簡短敘述，還有職缺的條件要求

請在星期五以前把廣告寄給 Tess，謝謝。

單字 establish v. 成立　count on phr. 依存～，相信　job openings phr. 空缺，徵人　observe v. 知道，看
onset n. 攻擊，開始　applicant n. 應徵者　job seeker phr. 求職者　submit v. 提交　contain v. 包含

---

150 ■ 單數主詞後面使用單數動詞，複數主詞後面使用複數動詞　　　解答 (A)

空格是 that 子句的主詞，所以可以當主詞的名詞 (A)，動名詞 (C) 都可能是正確答案。that 子句的動詞 have dropped 是複數，所以複數主詞 (A) responses（應答）是正確答案。主詞和動詞之間的介系詞片語 to printed advertisements 修飾空格上的名詞，意思是「報紙廣告」。這是可省略的修飾語，所以對於選擇正確答案沒有影響。

單字 respondent n. 應答者，被告

151 ■ 名詞語彙 掌握上下文　　　解答 (B)

文意是「____仲介商會在他們網站上刊登我們的廣告」，所有選項都可能是正確答案。只看有空格的句子無法選出正確的答案時，要先了解前後文意或整體文意。後面的句子中提到他們會把適合這些職位的求職者找出來，由此可以知道這是跟徵人有關的仲介商。因此，名詞 (B) recruitment（徵人）是正確答案。(A) security 的意思是「保安」，(C) transportation 的意思是「輸送，交通」，(D) housing 的意思是「住宅」。

152 ■ 填入連接副詞 掌握上下文　　　解答 (D)

空格和逗號一起出現在句首，就是連接副詞的位置。了解前面句子和有空格的句子之間的關係，就可以從四個連接副詞中選出正確答案。前面的句子中提到 Workhunter 公司要求下星期要交付廣告，而有空格的句子中則說明了提交的廣告要具備哪些條件，因此使用於說明跟過去相似情況的 (D) As always（一如往常）是正確答案。(A) Instead 的意思是「代替～」，(B) Otherwise 的意思是「否則」，(C) At last 的意思是「終於」。

PART 7

Questions 153-154 refer to the following invitation.　　　　153-154 根據下面告示的內容回答問題。

Paul's Bar and Grill	Paul 炭烤酒吧
153-A We are celebrating our 10th anniversary and you're invited!	153-A 我們歡慶十周年，歡迎你來參加！
For the entire month of November, we have great specials on our food and drinks. Also, don't miss our Saturday night events, featuring performances from up-and-coming bands in today's music industry.	11 月整個月，我們的餐點和飲品都有優惠，還有，別錯過星期六晚上的活動，有現今樂壇的明日之星帶來的表演。

November 4	– Retro (McMusic and Smart Waves)	11 月 4 日	– 復古流行風（McMusic 和 Smart Waves）
November 11	– Acoustic Night (The Pluckers and The Fireflies)	11 月 11 日	– 演奏之夜（Pluckers 樂團和螢火蟲樂團）
November 18	– Reggae Mania (South Drifters)	11 月 18 日	– 雷鬼狂熱（南方流浪人樂團）
154 November 25	– The Search for the Ultimate Rock Band (Grand Prize: $2,000)	154 11 月 25 日	– 終極搖滾樂團選拔（大獎兩千元）

單字 □celebrate v. 紀念，慶祝　　□anniversary n. 紀念日　　□feature v. 特別包含，特定
　　　□up-and-coming a. 顯露頭角的，很有前途的　　□retro n. 復古品，復古風
　　　□grand prize phr. 大獎、好對象

153

What is indicated about Paul's Bar and Grill?	關於 Paul 炭烤酒吧，何者正確？
(A) It has been operating for a decade.	(A) 已經營業十年了
(B) It features special menus on Saturdays.	(B) 週六有特別的菜單
(C) It offers complimentary beverages.	(C) 贈送免費飲料
(D) It provides special exotic dishes.	(D) 有提供異國風味的佳餚

■ **Not / True** True 問題　　　　　　　　　　　　　　　　　　　　　　　　　解答 (A)

這是找出跟問題核心詞語 Paul's Bar and Grill 相關的內容後，再跟選項作對比的 Not / True 問題。We are celebrating our 10th anniversary 中提到 Paul's Bar and Grill 要歡度 10 周年，所以跟 (A) 的內容一致。因此，(A) It has been operating for a decade. 是正確答案。(B) (C) (D) 都是文中沒提到的內容。

單字 operate v. 經營，操作　complimentary a. 免費的　beverage n. 飲料　exotic a. 異國的，外國的
　　　dish n. 食物，碟子

154

When will the music contest be held?	音樂比賽何時舉行？
(A) On November 4	(A) 11 月 4 日
(B) On November 11	(B) 11 月 11 日
(C) On November 18	(C) 11 月 18 日
(D) On November 25	(D) 11 月 25 日

■ 六何原則 When　　　　　　　　　　　　　　　　　　　　　　　　　　　　解答 (D)

這是問音樂比賽何時（When）開始的六何原則問題。跟問題的核心詞語 the music contest 相關的內容 November 25 - The Search for the Ultimate Rock Band (Grand Prize: $2,000) 中提到 11 月 25 日終極搖滾樂團選拔的大獎是 2000 美金。因此，(D) On November 25 是正確答案。

單字 contest n. 比賽　hold v. 召開（會議 / 比賽）

Questions 155-156 refer to the following letter.

155-156 根據下面廣告的內容回答問題。

Bay Shop	海灣商店
Finding the best gifts for your loved ones can sometimes be stressful and frustrating. But here at Bay Shop, [155]we sell a wide array of gift items that will surely please the people dear to you. [156-C]Our talented craftsmen make a variety of unique toys, handicrafts, and personal accessories. So if you are looking for presents for any occasion or tokens of appreciation, come and visit Bay Shop.	為了要找到最好的禮物給你所愛的人，有時令人備感壓力又沮喪，不過在海灣商店，[155] 我們販售各種樣式的禮品，一定能討好你心愛的人。[156-C]我們有才華的手藝師傅做各式各樣的獨特玩具、手工藝品和個人配件。所以假如你要找適合任何場合或表示心意的禮物，來我們店裡看看。
Our store is open every day from 9 A.M. to 7 P.M. You may also view our products online by visiting www.bayshop.com.	我們商店的營業時間從早上九點到下午七點，你也可以上官網 www.bayshop.com 來看我們的產品。

單字 □loved one phr. 愛的人　　　　□frustrating a. 失望的，有挫折感的 □dear a. 重要的
　　　□craftsman n. 工藝家　　　　□unique a. 獨特的，特別的
　　　□handicraft n. 手工藝品，手製品　□token n. 標誌　　　　□appreciation n. 感謝

155

What most likely is Bay Shop?	海灣商店最有可能是什麼？
(A) A handicraft importer	(A) 手工藝品進口商
(B) A gift retailer	(B) 禮品零售商
(C) A furniture distributor	(C) 家具批發商
(D) A fashion boutique	(D) 流行服飾店

■ 推論 整體情報　　　　　　　　　　　　　　　　　　　　　　　　　　解答 (B)

這是把句子分散開來的各種資訊綜合起來，推論 Bay Shop 是什麼的問題。we sell a wide array of gift items 中提到 Bay Shop 販售各種樣式的禮品後，接著介紹 Bay Shop 所販賣的禮品、營業時間等等。由此可以推論出 Bay Shop 是一間禮品店。因此，(B) A gift retailer 是正確答案。

單字 importer n. 進口商，進口業者　distributor n. 批發商　boutique n. 賣場，精品店

156

What is indicated about Bay Shop?	關於海灣商店，何者正確？
(A) It imports finished goods from nearby countries.	(A) 從鄰近國家進口已完工的商品
(B) Its customers can order items from a Web site.	(B) 顧客可以從網站訂購商品
(C) Its products are created by highly skilled workers.	(C) 他們的商品是手藝高超的人做出來的
(D) It gives gift certificates to clients registering online.	(D) 線上註冊的顧客可以得到禮券

■ Not / True True 問題　　　　　　　　　　　　　　　　　　　　　　解答 (C)

這是找出跟問題核心詞語 Bay Shop 相關的內容後，再跟選項作對比的 Not / True 問題。(A) 和 (B) 都是文中沒提到的內容。Our talented craftsmen make a variety of unique toys, handicrafts, and personal accessories.中提到有才華的手藝師傅做各式各樣的獨特玩具、手工藝品和個人配件，所以跟 (C) 的內容一致。因此，(C) Its products are created by highly skilled workers. 是正確答案。(D) 是文中沒提到的內容。

換句話說

talented craftsmen 有才華的手藝師傅 → skilled workers 熟練的工作者

單字 nearby a. 周圍的　gift certificate phr. 禮券

Allergy Reports Prompt Vaccine Recall	過敏通報促使疫苗回收
KUALA LUMPUR – The Health Department recalled 5,000 doses of tetanus vaccine after receiving several reports about its side effects on patients.	吉隆坡 - 衛生部在收到好幾個關於發生在病患身上的副作用報告後，回收了五千劑破傷風疫苗。
According to the department, [157]30 patients from around the capital suffered from rashes last week after receiving the shots at state hospitals, indicating a high rate of allergic reactions to the medicine. [158-B]Health Secretary Rajah Hashmid immediately recalled the vaccines and ordered public hospitals to stop using them.	根據衛生部，[157]三十個來自首都附近的病患於上週在州立醫院注射疫苗後出現紅疹，顯示對此藥物產生過敏反應的比例很高。[158-B]衛生部祕書長 Rajah Hashmid 立即回收此疫苗，並下令公立醫院禁止使用。
[158-D]Manufactured by Indian pharmaceutical company Alhira, the tetanus vaccines were imported by the government last month along with other medicines. An investigation into the patients' cases is underway.	[158-D]這個破傷風疫苗是由印度藥劑公司 Alhira 所製造，上個月隨其他藥品由政府引進。目前對這些病例正在調查中。

單字 □prompt v. 激勵　　　　□side effect phr. 副作用　　　　□underway a. 進行中的

157

Why did Rajah Hashmid suspend use of the vaccines?	為什麼 Rajah Hashmid 禁用這些疫苗？
(A) They had passed an expiration date.	(A) 因為過期了。
(B) They cause an adverse physical response.	(B) 因為對身體產生不利的反應。
(C) They were exposed to toxic materials.	(C) 因為暴露在有毒的物質中。
(D) They were not approved by the Health Department.	(D) 因為未受衛生部核准。

■ 六何原則 Why　　　　　　　　　　　　　　　　　　　　　　　　　　　　　　　解答 (B)

這是問 Rajah Hashmid 為什麼（Why）中斷使用疫苗的六何問題。跟問題的核心詞語 Rajah Hashmid suspend use of vaccines 相關的 30 patients ~ suffered from rashes ~ after receiving the shots ~ indicating a high rate of allergic reactions to the medicine. Health Secretary Rajah Hashmid ~ ordered ~ public hospitals to stop using them. 中提到三十個病患注射疫苗後出現紅疹，顯示對此藥物產生過敏反應的比例很高，接著 Rajah Hashmid 就下令公立醫院禁止使用。因此，(B) They cause an adverse physical response. 是正確答案。

換句話說
allergic reactions 過敏反應 → an adverse physical response 有害身體的反應

單字 suspend v. 中斷　expiration date phr. 有效期限　adverse a. 有害的，否定的　toxic a. 有毒性的，有害的　approve v. 認可，承認

158

What is mentioned about the shots?	關於這些疫苗，何者正確？
(A) They were provided free of charge.	(A) 免費施打。
(B) They were only available at private hospitals.	(B) 只有私立醫院才提供。
(C) They were required for government workers.	(C) 政府員工必須施打。
(D) They were shipped from a foreign country.	(D) 從國外進口的。

■ Not / True True 問題　　　　　　　　　　　　　　　　　　　　　　　　　　　解答 (D)

這是找出跟問題核心詞語 the shots 相關的內容後，再跟選項作對比的 Not / True 問題。(A) 是文中沒提到的內容。Health Secretary ~ ordered public hospitals to stop using them.中提到衛生部祕書長下令公立醫院禁止使用疫苗，所以跟 (B) 的內容不一致。(C) 是文中沒提到的內容。Manufactured by Indian pharmaceutical company ~, the tetanus vaccines were imported 中提到這個破傷風疫苗是由印度藥劑公司所製造，由政府引進。跟 (D) 的內容一致。因此，(D) They were shipped from a foreign country. 是正確答案。

換句話說
imported 進口 → shipped from a foreign country 從國外運送進來

Questions 159-161 refer to the following letter.

159-161 根據下面信件的內容回答問題。

The Kayak Resort
Kohala Coast, Hawaii

February 24

Dear Ms. Scott,

[159/161-B]We regret that you did not enjoy your island excursion yesterday. However, we must clarify that we did not intend to cut your trip short. [159]Your tour guides decided to skip some islands to allow more time for your parasailing activity, which you requested yesterday morning. [159]We sincerely apologize for not discussing the matter with you immediately upon your return.

[160]We have been informed that you are demanding a refund because of your unsatisfactory experience. Unfortunately, we are unable to provide a refund. [161-C]Our policy states that fees for water recreation and sports activities are nonrefundable. To compensate you, [161-A]we will give you two meal vouchers for any of the restaurants on the premises, which you may use during your stay with us.

Thank you for your understanding. We hope you will enjoy the rest of your holiday at the Kayak Resort.

Respectfully yours,

Luke Dunstan
Manager
The Kayak Resort

Kayak 渡假村
夏威夷 Kohala 海岸

2 月 24 日

親愛的 Scott 女士：

[159/161-B]我們很遺憾你昨天的海島之旅無法盡興。不過，我們必須澄清我們並沒有故意縮短行程，[159]你的導遊決定略過幾個島嶼，讓你有更多時間花在帆傘活動上，這是你在昨天早上所要求的。[159]我們誠摯地向你道歉沒有在你回來時立即與你討論這件事。

[160]我們得知你要求退費，因為不滿意這個行程。但是，我們無法退費。[161-C]我們規定水上娛樂與運動活動是無法退費的。為了補償你，[161-A]我們將提供你兩張餐飲券，讓你住在我們這裡時，可以到任何我們渡假村內的餐廳用餐。

謝謝你的諒解，我們希望你在 Kayak 渡假村的剩餘時間能夠愉快。

Luke Dunstan 敬上
經理
Kayak 渡假村

單字 □excursion n. 旅行 　□clarify v. 明確表明，分明地區別 　□intend v. 意圖
　　 □sincerely ad. 真心地 　□state v. 明示，陳述 　□nonrefundable a. 不可以退款的
　　 □compensate v. 賠償 　□voucher n. 禮卷，商品交換卷 　□premises n. 用地，經營場地

159

Why was the letter written?	為什麼寫這封信？
(A) To make changes in a plan	(A) 改變計畫
(B) To schedule an island tour	(B) 安排島上旅遊的時間
(C) To apologize for an incident	(C) 為一個事件道歉
(D) To introduce a new policy	(D) 介紹一個政策

■ 找出主題 寫文章的理由　　　　　　　　　　　　　　　　　　　　　　　　　　　　　解答 (C)

這是問寫信原因，需找出文章主題的問題，所以要特別注意文章的前半部份。We regret that you did not enjoy your island excursion yesterday. 中提到「我們很遺憾你昨天的海島之旅無法盡興。」之後，在 Your tour guides decided to skip some islands 和 We sincerely apologize for not discussing the matter 中又說「我們誠摯地向你道歉沒有跟你討論導遊決定略過幾個島嶼」。因此，(C) To apologize for an incident 是正確答案。

單字 incident n. 事件，事情

What did Ms. Scott want to do?	Scott 女士想做什麼？
(A) Recover her payment	(A) 退款
(B) Transfer to another resort	(B) 轉到另一個渡假村
(C) Try a different activity	(C) 試不同的活動
(D) Confirm her flight	(D) 確認她的班機

■ 六何原則 What　　　　　　　　　　　　　　　　　　　　　　　　　解答 (A)

這是問 Ms. Scott 想要什麼（What）的六何原則問題。跟問題的核心詞語 Ms. Scott want to do 相關的內容 We have been informed that you are demanding a refund 中提到我們得知你，也就是 Ms. Scott 要求退費。因此，(A) Recover her payment 是正確答案。

換句話說

a refund 退費 → Recover ~ payment 收回付出的錢

單字 transfer v. 調動　confirm v. 確定

What is NOT suggested about the Kayak Resort?	關於 Kayak 渡假村，何者錯誤？
(A) It operates more than one restaurant.	(A) 經營不只一家餐廳。
(B) It organized a tour for some guests.	(B) 為一些旅客安排旅遊。
(C) It maintains a strict refund policy.	(C) 有嚴格的退費規定。
(D) It overbooked a sports activity.	(D) 超額接受一項運動活動的預定。

■ Not / True Not 問題　　　　　　　　　　　　　　　　　　　　　　解答 (D)

這是找出跟問題的核心詞語 the Kayak Resort 相關的內容後，再跟選項作對比的 Not / True 問題。we will give you two meal vouchers for any of the restaurants on the premises 中提到「我們將給你兩張餐飲券可以到任何我們渡假村內的餐廳用餐」，由此可以知道 Kayak 渡假村的餐廳有超過一間以上。因此，和 (A) 的內容一致。We regret that you did not enjoy your island excursion yesterday. However, ~ we did not intend to cut your trip short.中提到我們很遺憾你，也就是 Ms. Scott 旅行無法盡興。不過，我們，也就是 Kayak 渡假村沒有故意縮短行程。因此，跟 (B) 的內容一致。Our policy states that fees for water recreation and sports activities are nonrefundable.中提到我們，也就是 Kayak 渡假村的政策規定水上娛樂與運動活動是無法退費的。因此，跟 (C) 的內容一致。(D) 是文中沒提到的內容。因此，(D) It overbooked a sports activity. 是正確答案。

單字 overbook v. 過量預訂

Questions 162-164 refer to the following advertisement.　　162-164 根據下面廣告的內容回答問題。

Join the Team at Pan-Global Web!	加入 Pan-Global Web 的團隊！
[162]Pan-Global Web Designs, based in Montreal, is searching for a full-time graphic artist. This job is for professional artists with at least two years of experience in a related field. [163]Applicants must have graduated with a relevant degree, and be willing to move to Montreal by November 1. Those with strong French skills are also preferred.	[162]Pan-Global 網站設計，位在蒙特婁，正在尋找一位全職的繪圖藝術家，這份工作要找在相關領域工作至少兩年的專業藝術家，[163]應徵者必須要有相關的學位，並願意在 11 月 1 日搬到蒙特婁，具有法語能力者優先。
Successful applicants will receive two weeks of training, along with a competitive salary package and a moving allowance. [164-C]The position also includes medical benefits and quarterly incentives.	成功獲得應聘的應徵者會有兩週的受訓、優渥的薪資待遇和搬遷費。[164-C]這個職位還提供醫療福利和季獎金。
Those wishing to apply should send a résumé and cover letter to hrpanglobal@global.net. Applicants who meet our criteria will be contacted for an interview. The deadline for application is September 19. For further information, contact our human resources department at (503) 555-8899.	有興趣應徵者請將履歷表、求職信寄至 hrpanglobal@global.net。條件符合我們需求的應徵者，我們會聯繫安排面試，應徵截止日期為 9 月 19 日，更多詳情，請聯絡我們的人力資源部門，電話是 (503) 555-8899。

單字　□based in phr. 總公司在～　　□relevant a. 有關聯的　　□degree n. 學位
　　　□salary package phr. 薪水，工資　□allowance n. 費用，補貼，零用錢　□quarterly a. 季度的
　　　□cover letter phr. 附信；求職信　□criteria n. 基準（criterion 的複數）

162

For whom is the advertisement most likely intended?	這個廣告最有可能是給誰看？
(A) Computer programmers	(A) 電腦程式設計師
(B) Experienced graphic artists	(B) 有經驗的繪圖藝術家
(C) Web site owners	(C) 網站站主
(D) Recruitment specialists	(D) 徵人專家

■ 推論 整體情報　　　　　　　　　　　　　　　　　　　　　　　　　　　　　　　　解答 (B)

這是推論廣告對象的問題。Pan-Global Web Designs ~ is searching for a full-time graphic artist.中提到 Pan-Global Web Designs 公司正在尋找一位全職的繪圖藝術家。接著，This job is for professional artists with at least two years of experience in a related field. 又提到這份工作要找在相關領域工作至少兩年的專業藝術家。由此可以推論出廣告對象是有經驗的繪圖藝術家。因此，(B) Experienced graphic artists 是正確答案。

單字 experienced a. 有經驗的　recruitment n. 徵人

163

What requirement is necessary for the advertised position?	廣告的職缺有什麼必要的條件？
(A) Fluency in French	(A) 流利的法語
(B) Computer programming skills	(B) 電腦程式技巧
(C) A degree in management	(C) 管理學位
(D) Willingness to relocate	(D) 願意搬遷

■ 六何原則 What　　　　　　　　　　　　　　　　　　　　　　　　　　　　　　　　解答 (D)

這是問廣告的職位中提到需要什麼（What）資格條件的六何原則問題。跟問題的核心詞語 requirement 相關的內容。Applicants must ~ be willing to move to Montreal 中提到應徵者一定要願意搬到蒙特婁。因此，(D)Willingness to relocate 是正確答案。

單字 requirement n. 資格條件　fluency n. 熟練，順暢　willingness n. 意向，意圖

164

What is indicated about Pan-Global Web?	關於 Pan-Global Web，何者正確？
(A) It has international branches.	(A) 有國際分公司。
(B) It will sponsor a graphic arts workshop.	(B) 將贊助一場繪圖藝術交流會。
(C) It provides staff with medical insurance.	(C) 提供員工醫療保險。
(D) It is moving its Montreal office.	(D) 即將遷移位在蒙特婁的辦公室。

■ **Not / True** True 問題   解答 (C)

這是找出跟問題的核心詞語 Pan-Global Web 相關的內容後，再跟選項作對比的 Not / True 問題。(A) 和 (B) 都是文中沒提到的內容。The position also includes medical benefits 中提到 Pan-Global Web 公司廣告的職位有**醫療福利**，所以跟 (C) 的內容一致。因此，(C) It provides staff with medical insurance. 是正確答案。(D) 是文中沒提到的內容。

換句話說

medical benefits 醫療福利 → medical insurance 醫療保險

單字 branch n. 分支，分店　　sponsor v. 贊助，支持

Questions 165-167 refer to the following e-mail.

165-167 根據下面電郵的內容回答問題。

From: Georgina Valencia <gina_valencia@aceconcrete.com>

To: Reagan Tan <r.tan@digconstruct.com>

Subject: Re: Xinjiang Cement Factory inquiry
Date: August 19

Dear Mr. Tan,

Thank you for your interest in purchasing our cement factory in Xinjiang. As one of Ace Concrete's largest cement factories, the plant has the capacity to produce 200,000 metric tons of cement annually and supply the needs of major construction firms such as yours.

167-A/B/C We would be happy to show you our equipment, production line, and warehouse. 165/166 If you want to stop by, we recommend that you make arrangements for Friday so that the factory's operations manager, Mr. Gerald Ong, will be available to give you a tour of the plant. Mr. Ong is currently setting up our new factory in Beijing, which will become the base of our operations over the next five years. He will be back in Xinjiang on Thursday.

165 Please let us know your decision before the end of the week. Feel free to contact us at 555-1478, and we would be happy to address any inquiries you may have.

We look forward to meeting you.

Sincerely,

Georgina Valencia

寄件人：Georgina Valencia
<gina_valencia@aceconcrete.com>

收件人：Reagan Tan
<r.tan@digconstruct.com>

主旨：Re：詢問新疆水泥工廠
日期：8月19日

親愛的 Tan 先生：

謝謝你對購買我們在新疆的水泥工廠有興趣，身為 Ace 混凝土集團最大的水泥工廠之一，這裡每年可以生產二十萬公噸的水泥，可符合像你們公司這種大型建築公司的需求。

167-A/B/C 我們很樂意讓你參觀我們的設備、生產線和倉庫，165/166 如果你想要來看看，我們建議安排在星期五，工廠的營運經理 Gerald Ong 先生能為你導覽。Ong 先生目前正在設立我們在北京的新工廠，新工廠在未來五年會成為我們營運的基地，他在星期四會回到新疆。

165 請在本週讓我們知道你的決定，歡迎撥打 555-1478 與我們聯絡，我們會很樂意回答你的問題。

很期待與你會面。

Georgina Valencia 敬上

單字 □purchase v. 買入，購買   □plant n. 工廠   □capacity n. 能力，承受力
□metric ton phr. 公噸（1,000kg）   □annually ad. 年度，每年   □equipment n. 裝備
□warehouse n. 倉庫   □set up phr. 成立～，安置

165

Why was the e-mail written?
(A) To arrange a factory tour
(B) To propose a merger
(C) To introduce an executive
(D) To evaluate an inspection

為什麼寫這封信？
(A) 要安排一個工廠導覽
(B) 要提出合併計畫
(C) 要介紹一位主管
(D) 要評估一項檢驗

■ **找出主題** 寫文章的理由   解答 (A)

這是問寫信原因，需找出文章主題的問題，所以要特別注意文章的前半部份是否提到相關內容。If you want to stop by, we recommend that you make arrangements for Friday so that the factory's operations manager ~ will be able to give you a tour of the plant.中提到「如果你想要來看看，工廠的營運經理能為你導覽」。接著，Please let us know your decision before the end of the week.中又提到「請在本週讓我們知道你的決定」。因此，(A) To arrange a factory tour 是正確答案。

單字 arrange v. 計畫，安排   executive n. 職員，經營主管   evaluate v. 評價   inspection n. 檢察，檢討

Why is Mr. Tan advised to visit on Friday?	為什麼要建議 Tan 先生星期五來參觀？
(A) The factory is undergoing renovation.	(A) 工廠目前正在整修。
(B) The operations manager will be available.	(B) 工廠的營運經理那天有空。
(C) The company needs time to prepare a presentation.	(C) 該公司需要時間準備簡報。
(D) The plant's selling price has yet to be finalized.	(D) 工廠銷售的價格還沒有確定。

六何原則 Why　　　　　　　　　　　　　　　　　　　　　　　　　　　　　　　　　　解答 (B)

這是問 Mr. Tan 為什麼（Why）星期五可以參觀的六何原則問題。跟問題的核心詞語 advised to visit on Friday 相關的內容。If you want to stop by, we recommend that you make arrangements for Friday so that the factory's operations manager ~ will be available to give you a tour of the plant.中提到「如果你想要來看看，我們建議你安排在星期五，工廠的營運經理能為你導覽」。因此，(B) The operations manager will be available. 是正確答案。

單字 undergo v. 進行，遭遇～　renovation n. 維修工程　finalize v. 確定，結尾

According to the e-mail, what will Mr. Tan NOT see during his visit?	根據電郵，Tan 先生在參觀時不會看到什麼？
(A) Machines	(A) 機器
(B) Production line	(B) 生產線
(C) Warehouse	(C) 倉庫
(D) Merchandise samples	(D) 商品樣本

Not / True Not 問題　　　　　　　　　　　　　　　　　　　　　　　　　　　　　　解答 (D)

這是找出跟問題核心詞語 Mr. Tan ~ see during his visit 相關的內容後，再跟選項作對比的 Not / True 問題。We would be happy to show you our equipment, production line, and warehouse. 中提到我們很樂意讓你，也就是 Mr. Tan 參觀我們的設備、生產線和倉庫，所以跟 (A) (B) (C) 的內容一致。(D) 是文中沒提到的內容。因此，(D) Merchandise samples 是正確答案。

單字 merchandise n. 製品，商品

Questions 168-171 refer to the following letter.

168-171 根據下面信件的內容回答問題。

Brosnan Lawyers Association
75 North Drive, Burbank, CA 9985

December 1

Dear colleagues,

171-CBrosnan Lawyers Association (BLA) will hold a talk on corporate law on February 20 at the Lincoln Plenary Hall from 9 A.M. to 5 P.M. 168-CExperienced business attorneys will discuss key legal issues concerning companies. The talk is free of charge and is exclusive to BLA members only. The schedule is as follows:

Time	Topic	Speaker
9:00 A.M. - 10:30 A.M.	169Corporate Policies	Francis Adams
10:30 A.M. - 12:00 P.M.	Financial Management	Jeffrey McMahon, Jr.
12:00 A.M. - 1:30 P.M.	BREAK	
1:30 P.M. - 3:00 P.M.	Mergers and Acquisitions	Philip Kaimo
3:00 P.M. - 5:00 P.M.	Intellectual Property Protection	Nathan Combs

Moreover, 170the association's newly elected officials will be introduced at a banquet to be held immediately following the talk. All members are requested to attend this celebration. 171-DTo register for the talk and confirm your attendance to the banquet, 171-Aplease call the BLA office or e-mail events@bla.com by December 15.

Best regards,

Sarah Ludwig
Chairperson
Brosnan Lawyers Association

Brosnan 律師協會
9985 加州 Burbank 市北方路 75 號

12 月 1 日

親愛的同事們，

171-CBrosnan 律師協會（BLA）將於 2 月 20 日上午九點至五點在 Lincoln 大會堂舉辦一場公司法的演講，168-C資深商業律師將討論關於公司的核心法律議題。這場演講完全免費，而且僅限 BLA 的會員參加，時間表如下：

時間	主題	講員
上午九點～上午十點三十分	公司政策	Francis Adams
上午十點三十分～中午十二點	財務管理	Jeffrey McMahon, Jr.
中午十二點～下午一點三十分	休息時間	
下午一點三十分～下午三點	合併與收購	Philip Kaimo
下午三點～下午五點	智慧財產權保護	Nathan Combs

此外，170協會新選出的幹事將會在演講結束後舉辦的晚宴上介紹給大家，所有的會員都要參加這個慶祝活動。171-D要報名參加演講以及確認參加晚宴的人，171-A請在 12 月 15 日前致電 BLA 辦公室，或寄電子郵件至 events@bla.com

Sarah Ludwig 敬上
主席
Brosnan 律師協會

單字 □corporate a. 企業的，法人的 □attorney n. 律師 □key a. 主要的，核心的
□legal a. 法規的，法律的 □issue n. 爭論點，問題
□exclusive a. 限定的～，專用的，獨佔的 □merger n. 合併
□acquisition n. 收穫 □intellectual property phr. 智慧產權
□elect v. 選出 □official n. 幹事 □banquet n. 晚宴

168

What does the letter mention about the speakers? | 關於演講者，這封信提到什麼？
(A) They are partners in a law office. | (A) 他們是律師事務所的合夥人。
(B) They work for large firms. | (B) 他們在大型事務所工作。
(C) They are accomplished legal professionals. | (C) 他們是學識淵博的法律專業人士。
(D) They are university professors. | (D) 他們是大學教授。

■ **Not / True** True 問題　　　　　　　　　　　　　　　　　　　　　　　　　　解答 (C)

這是找出跟問題核心詞語 the speakers 相關的內容後，再跟選項作對比的 Not / True 問題。(A) 和 (B) 都是文中沒提到的內容。Experienced business attorneys will discuss key legal issues concerning companies.中提到資深商業律師將討論關於公司的核心法律議題，所以跟 (C) 的內容一致。因此，(C) They are accomplished legal professionals. 是正確答案。(D) 是文中沒提到的內容。

換句話說

experienced ~ attorneys 資深律師 → accomplished legal professionals 出色的法律專家

單字 firm n. 公司

169

Who will deliver a lecture on company regulations? | 誰會演講公司的政策規定？
(A) Jeffrey McMahon, Jr. | (A) Jeffrey McMahon, Jr.
(B) Francis Adams | (B) Francis Adams
(C) Nathan Combs | (C) Nathan combs
(D) Philip Kaimo | (D) Philip Kaimo

■ **六何原則** Who　　　　　　　　　　　　　　　　　　　　　　　　　　　　解答 (B)

這是問演講公司的政策規定的是誰（Who）的六何原則問題。跟問題的核心詞語 deliver a lecture on company regulations 相關的表格中 Corporate Policies, Francis Adams 提到 Francis Adams 將演說公司政策，因此 (B) Francis Adams 是正確答案。

換句話說

company regulations 公司規定→ corporate policies 公司政策

單字 deliver a lecture phr. 演說，演講

170

What is suggested about the BLA? | 關於 BLA，何者正確？
(A) It has appointed new leaders. | (A) 已任命的新領導人。
(B) It is recruiting staff members. | (B) 正在招募新的員工。
(C) It is celebrating an anniversary. | (C) 正在慶祝周年。
(D) It has changed its regulations. | (D) 已改變了政策規定。

■ **推論** 詳細內容　　　　　　　　　　　　　　　　　　　　　　　　　　　解答 (A)

這是跟問題核心詞語 the BLA 有關的推理問題。the association's newly elected officials will be introduced at a banquet 中提到新選出的幹事將在晚宴上介紹給大家，所以可以推斷出 BLA 有任命新的領導者。因此，(A) It has appointed new leaders. 是正確答案。

單字 appoint v. 任命　recruit v. 募集　regulation n. 法規，規定

What information is NOT provided in the letter?	這封信沒有提供什麼資訊？
(A) An e-mail address	(A) 電郵信箱
(B) A telephone number	(B) 電話號碼
(C) A seminar venue	(C) 研習會地點
(D) A cutoff date for registration	(D) 報名截止日期

■ **Not / True** Not 問題　　　　　　　　　　　　　　　　　　　　　　　　　　　　解答 (B)

這是找出跟問題核心詞語 information ~ provided 相關的內容後，再跟選項作對比的 Not / True 問題。please ~ e-mail events@bla.com 中提供了電郵地址，所以跟 (A) 的內容一致。(B) 是文中沒提到的內容。因此，(B) A telephone number 是正確答案。Brosnan Lawyers Association (BLA) will hold a talk ~ at the Lincoln Plenary Hall 提到 Brosnan 律師協會（BLA）在 Lincoln 大會堂舉辦演講，所以跟 (C) 的內容一致。To register for the talk ~ please call ~ or e-mail ~ by December 15. 中提到要報名的人，請在 12 月 15 日前打電話或發電郵，所以跟 (D) 的內容一致。

單字　venue n. 場所　　cutoff date phr. 截止日　　registration n. 報名

[172]Raul Vargas Reveals Retirement Plans
By Donny Chu

Despite his flourishing career in the English League, Stallions player Raul Vargas wants to become more than a sports star. At the Soccer Federation Awards on Saturday, [172]the newly hailed Goalie of the Year revealed his plan to quit sports and pursue another profession.

"Lately, I have been thinking of giving up soccer," Vargas said during his acceptance speech. "Receiving this award is a sign that it's time for me to retire."

Such words were never expected to come from the Brazilian, who is the most treasured goalkeeper in the league. During *Stopwatch Magazine*'s exclusive interview with the player, however, Vargas explained that he made the decision because he has responsibilities that have forced him to retire from soccer.

"I have reached the point where I have fully achieved my dreams as an athlete," Vargas said. "More importantly, [174]I need to become more involved with my family's corporation, an obligation I have put aside since I began my career."

Being the sole heir of the Biobras Corporation, Vargas was originally groomed to lead the company. His parents sent him to Brasilia University to study industrial engineering, with the expectation that he would take up a master's degree in the United States later on. While preparing to lead [175-B]the top biofuel company in Brazil, however, Vargas was making a name for himself as one of the best goalkeepers in college.

Because of his impressive talent, [173]Vargas was offered a spot on the national team immediately after graduation. Thus, he set aside plans of obtaining a graduate degree and entering Biobras Corporation, choosing rather to accept the team's offer upon receiving the blessing of his parents.

Soccer fanatics witnessed how the career of the 29-year-old boomed. Apart from playing for the national team, Vargas joined English clubs East Hampton, Armorshire, and Hemel Finstead before he was signed by the Stallions.

"I have enjoyed putting on exciting matches with my teams. It's rewarding to bring joy to football fans," Vargas said.

However, Vargas has made the choice to take off his uniform and venture into the corporate world.

"[176-B]Nothing is permanent in the sports industry. I have to establish a more stable career, and I hope this decision will allow me to do it. Nevertheless, soccer will always be my first love," Vargas said.

[172]Raul Vargas 透露了退休計畫
Donny Chu 報導

儘管在英國球壇的豐功偉業，公馬隊的球員 Raul Vargas 想成為的不只是一位運動明星。在星期六的足球聯邦獎的典禮上，[172]這位新任的年度守門員透露了他想告別體壇，去追求另一個專業。

Vargas 在他得獎感言中說：「最近我一直想要放棄足球，得到這個獎項是我該退休的一個徵兆。」

沒有人想到這樣的話是出自一個球壇中最優秀的巴西守門員口中。在 *Stopwatch* 雜誌的球員獨家訪談中，Vargas 卻解釋這樣的決定是因為他擔負著促使他從足球體壇中退休的責任。

Vargas 說：「我已經完全達成了我作為一位運動員的夢想，更重要的是，[174]我想要更深入我的家族企業，這是我本該擔負的義務，卻因足球生涯而置於一旁。」

作為 Biobras 集團的唯一繼承人，Vargas 原本被培養來領導這家公司，他的父母送他到 Brasilia 大學去學習工業工程，期望他之後能在美國取得碩士學位。當準備著要領導[175-B]這家巴西最大的生物燃油公司之際，Vargas 成為了大學裡最佳的守門員之一。

因為他的天賦異稟，[173]Vargas 在畢業後立即被延攬進入國家代表隊，因此，他把進修碩士學位和進入 Biobras 公司的計畫擱置一旁，在父母的祝福下，選擇接受球隊的延攬。

球迷們目睹這位二十九歲球員在職業生涯上的大放異彩，除了為國家代表隊效力，Vargas 在為公馬隊效力前，曾參加和 Hemel Finstead 等球隊。

Vargas 說：「我和我的球隊有過精彩的戰役，把歡樂帶給球迷讓我得償所願。」

不過，Vargas 決定要脫下隊服，要走進企業的世界。

Vargas 說：「[176-B]在體壇上沒有什麼是永恆的。我必須要建立更穩固的事業生涯，我希望我這個決定能讓我做到這一點，然而，足球永遠都是我的最愛。」

單字　□retirement n. 退休　　□flourishing a. 興旺的，茂盛的　　□hail v. 被承認，歡呼，描寫
　　　□goalie n. 守門員　　　　□reveal v. 展現，顯露　　　　　□profession n. 職業
　　　□acceptance speech phr. 得獎演說，受獎演說　　　　　　　　　□obligation n. 義務
　　　□put aside phr. 擱在一邊，延後　□sole a. 單獨的，唯一的　　□heir n. 繼承人，嗣子
　　　□groom v. 訓練，使準備　　□industrial engineering phr. 工業工程
　　　□master's degree phr. 碩士學位　□make a name phr. 揚名，變有名　□set aside phr. 延後，擱放一邊
　　　□blessing n. 許可，承認，祝福　□fanatic n. 粉絲，愛好者　　□witness v. 目擊；n. 證人
　　　□boom v. 成功，蓬勃發展　　□apart from phr. 除～之外，和～分別　□rewarding a. 有報酬的，有益的
　　　□venture v. 冒險　　　　　□permanent a. 永遠的，安定的　□stable a. 穩固的

172

What is the main purpose of the article?	這篇文章的主要目的為何？
(A) To report about a soccer match	(A) 報導一場足球比賽
(B) To publicize a sports magazine	(B) 宣傳一本體育雜誌
(C) To provide information about an athlete	(C) 提供關於一位運動員的資訊
(D) To introduce a new type of fuel	(D) 介紹一種新的能源

■ 找出主題 目的　　　　　　　　　　　　　　　　　　　　　　　　　解答 (C)

這是問寫這篇新聞的目的的找主題問題，所以要特別注意文章的前半部份。報導的開頭 Raul Vargas Reveals Retirement Plans 中提到 Raul Vargas 透露了退休計畫，the newly hailed Goalie of the Year revealed his plan to quit sports and pursue another profession 中又提到 Raul Vargas 這位新任的年度守門員透露了他想告別體壇，去追求另一個專業。由此可以知道這篇報導是介紹他到目前為此的選手生活及未來計畫。因此，(C) To provide information about an athlete 是正確答案。

173

What is suggested about Mr. Vargas?	關於 Vargas 先生，何者正確？
(A) He did not attend graduate school.	(A) 他沒有上研究所。
(B) He played soccer in high school.	(B) 他在高中踢足球。
(C) He is a young entrepreneur.	(C) 他是一位年輕的企業家。
(D) He will transfer to a new team.	(D) 他將會轉到一個新的球隊。

■ 推論 詳細內容　　　　　　　　　　　　　　　　　　　　　　　　解答 (A)

這是跟問題核心詞語 Mr. Vargas 有關的推理問題。Vargas was offered a spot on the national team immediately after graduation. Thus, he set aside plans of obtaining a graduate degree 中提到 Mr. Vargas 在畢業後被延攬進入國家代表隊，所以他把進修碩士學位擱置一旁。由此可以知道 Mr. Vargas 沒有讀碩士。因此，(A) He did not attend graduate school. 是正確答案。

單字 attend v. 上（學），參加　graduate school phr. 研究所　entrepreneur n. 企業家　transfer v. 調動，移動

174

Why is Mr. Vargas retiring from soccer?	Vargas 先生為什麼要從足球退休？
(A) He will continue his studies.	(A) 他要繼續讀書。
(B) He will play another sport.	(B) 他要從事另一種運動。
(C) He wants to move to another location.	(C) 他想要搬到另一個地方。
(D) He wants to enter the family business.	(D) 他想要進入家族企業。

■ 六何原則 Why　　　　　　　　　　　　　　　　　　　　　　　　解答 (D)

這是問 Mr. Vargas 為什麼（Why）要放棄足球的六何原則問題。跟問題的核心詞語 Mr. Vargas retiring from soccer 相關的內容。I need to become more involved with my family's corporation, an obligation I have put aside since I began my career 中提到 Mr. Vargas 想要更深入自己的家族企業，這是他本該擔負的義務，卻因足球生涯而置於一旁。因此，(D) He wants to enter the family business. 是正確答案。

換句話說

become ~ involved with ~ family's corporation 深入家庭企業 → enter the family business 進入家庭企業

單字 location n. 地區，場所

175

What is indicated about Biobras?	關於 Biobras，何者正確？
(A) It recently laid off some employees.	(A) 最近資遣了一些員工。
(B) It is involved in the fuel industry.	(B) 是從事能源產業。
(C) It maintains a branch office in England.	(C) 在英格蘭有一分公司。
(D) It sponsors a Brazilian soccer team.	(D) 贊助一個巴西足球隊。

■ **Not / True** True 問題　　　　　　　　　　　　　　　　　　　　　　　　解答 (B)

這是找出跟問題核心詞語 Biobras 相關的內容後，再跟選項作對比的 Not / True 問題。(A) 是文中沒提到的內容。the top biofuel company in Brazil 中提到巴西最大的生物燃油公司，所以跟 (B) 的內容一致。因此，(B) It is involved in the fuel industry. 是正確答案。(C) 和 (D) 都是文中沒提到的內容。

單字 lay off phr. 解雇

176

What does Mr. Vargas mention about his current career?	關於 Vargas 先生目前的職業生涯，他提到了什麼？
(A) It is a well-paying job.	(A) 是一份待遇很好的工作。
(B) It is not very predictable.	(B) 前景難以預測。
(C) It inspires him to play other sports.	(C) 啟發他去從事另一項運動。
(D) It does not develop his skills.	(D) 無法發揮他的技能。

■ **Not / True** True 問題　　　　　　　　　　　　　　　　　　　　　　　　解答 (B)

這是找出跟問題核心詞語 his current career 相關的內容後，再跟選項作對比的 Not / True 問題。(A) 是文中沒提到的內容。Nothing is permanent in the sports industry. 中提到在體壇上沒有什麼是永恆的，所以 (B) It is not very predictable. 是正確答案。(C) 和 (D) 都是文中沒提到的內容。

單字 well-paying a. 待遇很好的　predictable a. 可預測的　inspire v. 啟發，激勵

Questions 177-180 refer to the following letter.

177-180 根據下面廣告的內容回答問題。

MJA Cleaning Services
250 Grocer Drive, Salt Lake City, UT
www.mja.com

Imagine the relief of coming home to a spotless house after a busy day at work. [177]Whether you have a studio apartment or a two-story house, MJA Cleaning Services can tidy it up for you. Spend your leisure hours enjoying the things that are important to you, and let us worry about your housework.

MJA has been serving the Salt Lake City area for the past 15 years and is well-known for its efficiency, professionalism, and speed. [178-A/C]We offer weekly and biweekly cleaning, window washing, carpet cleaning, and floor stripping and waxing services. [178-B]We also move furniture and clean up after parties. In addition, we use environmentally-friendly housekeeping materials and equipment.

[179]Visit our Web site, check out our rates, and think about the money you will save by using our services. We supply professional-quality cleaning at a low cost.

As part of a special offer, [180]we will give you a 50 percent discount on our carpet cleaning service for every biweekly cleaning. Contact us now at 555-2524, and we will set up a consultation.

MJA 清潔服務公司
猶他州鹽湖城 Grocer 路 250 號
www.mja.com

想像在忙碌工作一天後回到一塵不染的家有多輕鬆，[177]不管你有一間小套房，或者是兩層樓的房子，MJA 清潔公司能為你打掃，把你的休閒時間花在對你重要的事情上，把你的家事交給我們來操心。

MJA 在過去十五年來在鹽湖城地區提供服務，以效率、專業和速度聞名，[178-A/C]我們提供每週或隔週的打掃、洗窗、地毯清理、地板清潔和打蠟服務，[178-B]我們還提供派對後家具搬動和清潔的工作，此外，我們使用的是環保的清潔劑和設備。

[179]來我們的網站看看我們的收費標準，想想用我們的服務你能省下的錢，我們以低價提供專業品質的清潔工作。

[180]我們的優惠方案之一是隔週一次的地毯清理服務，你能享有五折的價格，現在就撥打 555-2524 和我們聯絡，我們會為你提供諮詢。

單字 □relief n. 舒適，消遣　　□spotless a. 一塵不染的　　□studio apartment phr. 小套房
　　□tidy v. 整理，收拾　　□biweekly a. 隔週的　　□efficiency n. 效率
　　□strip v. 拆掉　　□environmentally-friendly a. 環保的
　　□housekeeping n. 家事，家務活

177

What is implied about MJA services?	關於 MJA 服務，何者正確？
(A) It is affiliated with an environmental organization.	(A) 和一家環保機構有關。
(B) It provides discounts for long-term customers.	(B) 給長期客戶提供折扣。
(C) It offers round-the-clock assistance.	(C) 提供一天二十四小時的服務。
(D) It mainly does work in residential buildings.	(D) 主要提供服務給住宅建築。

■ 推論 詳細內容　　　　　　　　　　　　　　　　　　　　　　　　　　　解答 (D)

這是跟問題核心詞語 MJA services 有關的推理問題。Whether you have a studio apartment or a two-story house, MJA Cleaning Services can tidy it up for you. 中提到「不管你有一間小套房，或者是兩層樓的房子，MJA 清潔公司能為你打掃」。由此可以推斷出 MJA 主要為住宅服務。因此，(D) It mainly does work in residential buildings. 是正確答案。

換句話說

studio apartment or a two-story house 小套房，或者兩層樓的房子 → residential buildings 住宅建築

單字 affiliate v. 發生聯繫，合併　round-the-clock a. 24 小時的　residential a. 住宅的，居住的

What is NOT a service offered by MJA?	哪一項不是 MJA 提供的服務？
(A) Carpet cleaning	(A) 地毯清理
(B) Event cleanup	(B) 活動的清理工作
(C) Floor waxing	(C) 地板打蠟
(D) Furniture cleaning	(D) 家具清潔

■ **Not / True** Not 問題   解答 (D)

這是找出跟問題核心詞語 a service offered by MJA 相關的內容後，再跟選項作對比的 Not / True 問題。We offer ~ carpet cleaning, and floor ~ waxing services. 中提到 MJA 提供地板清潔和打蠟服務。所以跟 (A)(C) 的內容一致。We ~ clean up after parties. 中提到「我們可以提供派對後的清潔」，所以跟 (B) 的內容一致。(D) 是文中沒提到的內容。因此，(D) Furniture cleaning 是正確答案。

What does the advertisement suggest about the company?	這個廣告提到關於這家公司的甚麼？
(A) It opened very recently.	(A) 最近才開張。
(B) It publishes rates online.	(B) 網站上公告收費標準。
(C) It charges more than its competitors.	(C) 比同業競爭者收費較高。
(D) It is looking to hire more staff.	(D) 要雇用更多員工。

■ **推論** 詳細內容   解答 (B)

這是跟問題核心詞語 the company 有關的推理問題。Visit our Web site, check out our rates 中提到來網站看收費標準。由此可以推斷出公司在網站上公告費用。因此，(B) It publishes rates online. 是正確答案。

單字 **charge** v. 收取（費用）

What will be given to customers who have their house cleaned every two weeks?	對於每兩周清掃一次的客人，會給予什麼？
(A) Gift certificates	(A) 禮券
(B) Housekeeping guidebooks	(B) 居家清潔手冊
(C) A store coupon	(C) 商店折價券
(D) A discount on a service	(D) 服務上的折扣

■ **六何原則** What   解答 (D)

這是問對於每兩周清掃一次的客人，會給予什麼（What）的六何原則問題。跟問題的核心詞語 given to customers who have their house cleaned every two weeks 相關的內容。we will give you a 50 percent discount on our carpet cleaning service for every biweekly cleaning 中提到所有隔週一次地毯清理的顧客能享有五折的價格。因此，(D) A discount on a service 是正確答案。

換句話說
every two weeks 每兩週 → biweekly 隔週

單字 **guidebook** n. 手冊

Questions 181-185 refer to the following e-mail and brochure.

例文1

To: Pauline Sotto <psotto@pyrosbiz.com>

From: Joey Clarete <joclare@comptav.org>

Date: June 26
Subject: Product Inquiry

182-A I am one of the owners of CompTavern Internet Café, and 185we are set to open an additional branch in Rhode Island in September. 181TechSavvy Magazine recently came out with an excellent review of your newest merchandise, which was how I found out about your business.

183/185We are currently looking to buy 32 web cameras for the desktop computers at our new branch. In addition, we are looking at the possibility of obtaining three color laser printers and a photocopier which has the capacity to produce a minimum of 60 pages per minute. Can you mail us a copy of your brochure describing all of your merchandise in detail? Please also include some information regarding your shipping. I hope to hear from you as soon as possible so that I can place an order.

Thank you.

例文2

185Pyros Biz Summer Brochure
22 Cunningham Square, Providence, Rhode Island 02918

183LASER PRINTER - Black and white printer **ideal for small- to medium-size offices** - Capable of double-sided printing	$289.99
183/184-BPHOTOCOPIER - User-friendly LCD control panel - Capacity: 40 pages per minute	$576.16
184-CFAX MACHINE - Transmits at 14,400 bits per second (bps) - Has an energy-efficient sleep mode function	$195.44
SCANNER - Fast precision scanning in black-and-white, 24-bit-color, and grayscale - Full-featured photo software solution	$118.37
183/184-DWEB CAMERA - Superior image quality (two-megapixel sensor) - Comes with software **and a sturdy stand**	$59.50

S H I P P I N G   P O L I C Y
Please allow three to five business days for national delivery (within the United States). For foreign orders, a handling fee of $25 will be charged in addition to the regular shipping costs. Products can take two to five

---

181-185 根據下面電郵和型錄的內容回答問題。

收件人：Pauline Sotto
<psotto@pyrosbiz.com>
寄件人：Joey Clarete
<joclare@comptav.org>
日期：6 月 26 日
主旨：產品詢問

182-A 我是 CompTavern 網咖的老闆之一，185我們計畫於 9 月在羅德島開一家分店，181 TechSavvy 雜誌最近對你們最新的商品有一篇很不錯的評論，這也是我為什麼知道你們公司的原因。

183/185我們目前正要為我們新的分店買三十二台安裝在桌上型電腦的網路照相機，此外，我們可能要買三台彩色雷射印表機和一台每分鐘最少能夠印出六十頁的影印機。你能寄給我你們有所有商品詳細敘述的型錄嗎？也請提供關於商品運送的資訊，我希望能盡快得到回音，讓我能夠早日下單。

謝謝。

185Pyros Biz 夏季型錄
02918 羅德島 Providence 市 Cunningham 廣場 22 號

183雷射印表機 -黑白印表機，適合小型至中型的辦公室 -能夠雙面列印	$289.99
183/184-B影印機 -使用便利的 LCD 控制面板 -每分鐘 40 頁	$576.16
184-C傳真機 -每秒傳輸 14400 bits（bps） -具備省電睡眠模式功能	$195.44
掃描機 -黑白快速準確掃描，24 bit 彩色、灰階 -全功能相片軟體	$118.37
183/184-D網路攝影機 -優質影像畫質（2 mega 畫素感應器） -附軟體與支撐架	$59.50

運送規定
國內運送（美國境內）需三到五個工作天。國外訂單要加收 25 元處理費，在下訂單後，會花上三至五週運送貨物。185提供運

weeks to ship after an order is placed. [185]Reduced shipping fees are available for both national and foreign bulk orders (20 pieces minimum). For more information, please call 555-8497 or log on to www.pyrosbiz.com.

費優惠的國內外大宗訂單（至少二十件）。更多詳情，請撥打 555-8497，或上網站 www.pyrosbiz.com

例文 1 單字 □inquiry n. 詢問　　　　□currently ad. 現在　　　　□possibility n. 可能性
　　　　　□obtain v. 購買，獲得　　□photocopier n. 影印機　　□place an order phr. 下訂單

例文 2 單字 □user-friendly a. 方便使用的，考慮使用者需求的　　　　□transmit v. 轉送
　　　　　□energy-efficient a. 節能的　□sleep mode phr. 睡眠模式　　□precision n. 準確
　　　　　□superior a. 厲害的，優秀的　□sturdy a. 堅固的，牢固的　　□stand n. 支架
　　　　　□domestic a. 國內的，家庭的　□bulk n. 大量，大規模

181

How did Mr. Clarete learn about Pyros Biz products?	Clarete 先生如何得知 Pyros Biz 的產品？
(A) Through a friend's recommendation	(A) 透過朋友的介紹
(B) Through an online advertisement	(B) 透過線上的廣告
(C) Through a phone directory	(C) 透過電話簿
(D) Through a published article	(D) 透過一篇刊登的文章

■ 六何原則 How 　　　　　　　　　　　　　　　　　　　　　　　　　　　解答 (D)

這是問 Mr. Clarete 如何（How）知道 Pyros Biz 公司商品的六何原則問題。因此，要先確認第一篇文章，也就是 Mr. Clarete 所寫的電郵中跟問題的核心詞語 Pyros Biz products 相關的內容。電郵中的 *TechSavvy Magazine recently came out with an excellent review of your newest merchandise, which was how I found out about your business.* 提到 *TechSavvy* 雜誌最近對 Pyros Biz 公司最新的商品有一篇很不錯的評論，這也是 Mr. Clarete 知道 Pyros Biz 公司公司的原因。因此，(D) Through a published article 是正確答案。

單字 recommendation n. 推薦　phone directory phr. 電話簿

182

What is stated about CompTavern Internet Café?	關於 CompTavern 網咖，何者正確？
(A) It will open a new branch.	(A) 將開一家新分店。
(B) Its computers are outdated.	(B) 他們的電腦都落伍了。
(C) It recently hired employees.	(C) 最近新聘了員工。
(D) Its number of customers has risen.	(D) 顧客數量增加了。

■ Not / True True 問題 　　　　　　　　　　　　　　　　　　　　　　　　解答 (A)

這是找出跟問題核心詞語 CompTavern Internet Café 相關的內容後，再跟選項作對比的 Not / True 問題。因此，要先確認第一篇文章中跟問題的核心詞 CompTavern 網咖相關的內容。I am one of the owners of CompTavern Internet Café, and we are set to open an additional branch ~ in September.中提到 Mr. Clarete 自己是 CompTavern 網咖的老闆之一，他們計畫於 9 月在羅德島開一家分店。因此，跟 (A) 的內容一致。所以，(A) It will open a new branch. 是正確答案。(B) (C) (D) 都是文中沒提到的內容。

單字 outdated a. 老的，舊的　recently ad. 最近　hire v. 雇用

183

What items will Mr. Clarete probably order?	Clarete 先生可能訂購什麼產品？
(A) Scanners	(A) 掃描機
(B) Laser printers	(B) 雷射印表機
(C) Web cameras	(C) 網路攝影機
(D) Photocopiers	(D) 影印機

■ 推論 聯結問題　　　　　　　　　　　　　　　　　　　　　　　　　解答 (C)

這是要把兩篇文章的內容綜合起來才能解開的聯結問題。問題核心詞語 items ~ Mr. Clarete probably order 中問到 Mr. Clarete 可能訂購什麼產品，所以要先確認 Mr. Clarete 所寫的電郵。

第一篇文章中 We are currently looking to buy 32 web cameras ~ . In addition, we are looking at the possibility of obtaining three color laser printers and a photocopier which has the capacity to produce a minimum of 60 pages per minute. 中提到我們，也就是 Mr. Clarete 買三十二台網路照相機之後，可能要買三台彩色雷射印表機和一台每分鐘最少能印出六十頁的影印機。不過，並沒有提到 Pyros Biz 公司是否有 Mr. Clarete 想買的所有商品。因此，要確認型錄中 Pyros Biz 公司的產品。第二篇文章中的型錄上 LASER PRINTER, Black and white printer, PHOTOCOPIER, Capacity: 40 pages per minute, WEB CAMERA 提到有在賣「雷射印表機，黑白印表機」，「影印機，每分鐘 40 頁」，「網路攝影機」。

把 Mr. Clarete 打算買網路相機和彩色雷射印表機，以及每分鐘最少印出六十頁的影印機的內容和 Pyros Biz 公司有在賣黑白印表機、每分鐘印 40 頁的影印機和網路攝影機的內容綜合起來，就可以知道符合購買條件的只有網路攝影機。因此，可以推斷出 Mr. Clarete 會買網路攝影機。因此，(C) Web cameras 是正確答案。

184

What is NOT mentioned as a characteristic of any Pyros Biz products?	哪一項 Pyros Biz 的產品特色沒有被提及？
(A) Stylish design	(A) 具有風格的設計。
(B) User friendliness	(B) 方便使用
(C) Energy efficiency	(C) 節能
(D) Free software	(D) 免費軟體

■ Not / True Not 問題　　　　　　　　　　　　　　　　　　　　　　解答 (A)

這是找出跟問題核心詞語 a characteristic of any Pyros Biz products 相關的內容後，再跟選項作對比的 Not / True 問題。因此，要確認第二篇文章中提到跟 Pyros Biz 公司商品的相關內容。(A) 是文中沒提到的內容。因此，(A) Stylish design 是正確答案。PHOTOCOPIER, User-friendly LCD control panel 中提到影印機使用便利的 LCD 控制面板，所以跟 (B) 的內容一致。FAX MACHINE, Has an energy-efficient sleep mode function 中提到傳真機具備節能睡眠模式功能，所以跟 (C) 的內容一致。WEBCAMERA, Comes with software 中提到網路攝影機附軟體與支撐架，所以跟 (D) 的內容一致。

185

| What kind of shipping fees will Mr. Clarete probably be charged?
(A) Regular national fees
(B) Bulk national fees
(C) Regular foreign fees
(D) Bulk foreign fees | 哪種運費 Clarete 先生最有可能支付？
(A) 一般的國內運費
(B) 大宗的國內運費
(C) 一般的國外運費
(D) 大宗的國外運費 |

■ 推論 聯結問題   解答 (B)

這是要把兩篇文章的內容綜合起來才能解開的聯結問題。問題核心詞語 kind of shipping fees ~ Mr. Clarete ~ be charged 中問哪種運費 Mr. Clarete 先生最有可能支付。因此，要先確定第二篇文章中提到有關運費的內容。

第二篇文章的型錄中 Pyros Biz Summer Brochure ~ Rhode Island 提到 Pyros Biz 公司位於羅德島。Reduced shipping fees are available for both national and foreign bulk orders (20 pieces minimum). 中又提到運費優惠的國內外大宗訂單（至少二十件）。不過，Mr. Clarete 要送的地區和要下訂單的商品是多少都沒有明確寫出來。這時候，需要確定第一篇文章電郵的內容。電郵中 we are set to open an additional branch in Rhode Island 提到 Mr. Clarete 計畫在羅德島開一家分店，還有，We are currently looking to buy 32 web cameras 又提到 Mr. Clarete 要買三十二台網路照相機。

把位於羅德島的 Pyros Biz 公司針對國內外大宗訂單（至少二十件）提供費用打折的內容和 Mr. Clarete 要在羅德島開新分店，打算買三十二台網路照相機的內容綜合起來時，就可以推論出 Mr. Clarete 是要支付大宗的國內運費。因此，(B) Bulk national fees 是正確答案。

Questions 186-190 refer to the following advertisement and e-mail. 186-190 根據下面廣告和電郵的內容回答問題。

例文1

NexusWire
Your Ultimate Link to the World

POSITIONS AVAILABLE:

To uphold our reputation as one of the most widely read news magazine in Europe, we are constantly seeking out talented staff writers to join our dynamic editorial team. At present, [187]four full-time jobs are available at our main headquarters in Prague, where the selected candidates will start work on April 1. From time to time, they will also be assigned to cover events in Amsterdam, Copenhagen, Berlin, and other European cities.

Application forms are available for download on our Web site at www.nexuswire.com. Our section editors will personally review the applications, so please e-mail them directly with your form, references, and samples of your work.

SECTION	EDITOR	E-MAILADDRESS
Health and Lifestyle	Dwayne Perez	d.perez@nexuswire.com
Science and Technology	Roger Stanley	r.stanley@nexuswire.com
Travel and Leisure	Eleanor Hansen	e.hansen@nexuswire.com
[190]Business and Finance	Claudia Young	c.young@nexuswire.com

[186]The deadline for all applications is February 28. Qualified candidates will be invited for interviews which will take place at the Prague office on March 10.

NexusWire
你與世界的終極連結

職缺：

為了維持我們是歐洲最被廣泛閱讀的新聞雜誌的風評，我們持續地尋找優秀的執筆者加入我們有活力的編輯團隊。目前，[187]在布拉格的總部有四個全職的職缺，受聘者會在 4 月 1 日開始工作，偶爾他們也會被派去寫關於阿姆斯特丹、哥本哈根、柏林和其他歐洲城市的重要事件。

應徵表格可以在我們的官網 www.nexuswire.com 下載，我們的部門編輯會親自評選應徵者，所以請把你的申請表、推薦信和過去的作品直接寄電郵給他們。

部門	編輯	電郵
健康與生活形態	Dwayne Perez	d.perez@nexuswire.com
科學與技術	Roger Stanley	r.stanley@nexuswire.com
旅行與休閒	Eleanor Hansen	e.hansen@nexuswire.com
[190]商業與金融	Claudia Young	c.young@nexuswire.com

[186]應徵截止日期為 2 月 28 日，符合資格的應徵者，我們會邀請你在 3 月 10 日來面試，地點在布拉格辦公室。

例文2

To: c.young@nexuswire.com
From: jacob_v0918@zircmail.com
Date: February 18
Subject: Job Advertisement

[190]Dear Ms. Young,

I am writing in response to *NexusWire's* posting for staff writers. Because of my knowledge and considerable experience in the field, I believe I am fully qualified for the position.

[188-D/190]As a reporter for *The Liberic Business Daily* for two years, I was assigned to write a minimum of three articles per day. While writing full-time at the newspaper, [190]I also did some freelance writing for several business journals. [188-C]I obtained my university diploma from the Liberic School of Journalism and am [188-B]fluent in English, Dutch, and German.

[190]Attached to this e-mail are some of my published works,

收件人：c.young@nexuswire.com
寄件人：jacob_v0918@zircmail.com
日期：2 月 18 日
主旨：職缺廣告

[190]親愛的 Young 小姐：

這封信是為了回應 *NexusWire* 雜誌徵求執筆作家的徵人啟事。基於我對這個領域的知識和豐富的經驗，我認為我符合這個職位的資格。

[188-D/190]作為 *The Liberic Business Daily* 的記者兩年，我的工作每天要寫至少三篇的文章，除了在報社全職的寫作，[190]我還為數家商業雜誌兼職撰稿。[188-C]我在 Liberic 新聞學院取得學位，[188-B]英文、荷蘭文和德文都很流暢。

[190]附件是我過去出版的一些作品，我希望

which I hope meet the standards of *NexusWire*. Thank you for your time and I look forward to your positive reply.	能達到 *NexusWire* 的標準，謝謝你的時間，期待你的正面回應。
Respectfully,	
Jacob Vaughn	Jacob Vaughn 敬上

例文 1 單字 □**uphold** v. 維持　□**reputation** n. 名聲　□**constantly** ad. 不中斷地
　　　　　□**dynamic** a. 動態的　□**editorial** a. 編輯的　□**headquarters** n. 總部
　　　　　□**from time to time** phr. 有時候　□**assign** v. 指派
　　　　　□**cover** v. 刊載　□**deadline** n. 截止日　□**candidate** n. 候選者，支援者
例文 2 單字 □**considerable** a. 相當的　□**field** n. 領域　□**diploma** n. 畢業證書
　　　　　□**fluent** a. 精通的，流暢的　□**meet** v. 符合～,使滿足

186

What will most likely take place after February 28?	在 2 月 28 日以後，最有可能發生什麼事？
(A) A new magazine issue will be released.	(A) 新一期的雜誌出刊。
(B) Applications for jobs will no longer be accepted.	(B) 不再接受此職缺的應徵。
(C) Candidates will be sent job application forms.	(C) 應徵者會收到應徵申請表格。
(D) Editorial staff will convene for a meeting.	(D) 編輯群會召開一個會議。

■ 推論 詳細內容　　　　　　　　　　　　　　　　　　　　　　　　　　解答 (B)

這是跟問題核心詞語 take place after February 28 有關的推理問題。首先要確認第一篇文章中提到跟 2 月 28 日有關內容。廣告中的 The deadline for all applications is February 28. 提到應徵截止日期為 2 月 28 日，由此可以推斷出 2 月 28 日之後就不會再收履歷表。因此，(B) Applications for jobs will no longer be accepted. 是正確答案。

單字 **submit** v. 提交　**convene** v. 聚集，聚會

187

Where will the successful applicants be based?	受到聘僱的人會在哪裡工作？
(A) In Copenhagen	(A) 哥本哈根
(B) In Amsterdam	(B) 阿姆斯特丹
(C) In Prague	(C) 布拉格
(D) In Berlin	(D) 柏林

■ 六何原則 Where　　　　　　　　　　　　　　　　　　　　　　　　解答 (C)

這是問受到聘僱的人會在哪裡（Where）工作的六何原則問題。首先確認第一篇文章中跟問題的核心詞語 the successful applicants be based 相關的內容。第一篇廣告中 four full-time jobs are available at our main headquarters in Prague, where the selected candidates will start work 中提到在布拉格的總部有四個全職的職缺，受聘者會那裡開始工作。因此，(C) In Prague 是正確答案。

換句話說

the successful applicants 受到聘僱的應徵者 → the selected candidates 被選出來的應徵者

188

Which qualification does Mr. Vaughn NOT mention?	Vaughn 先生沒有提到哪項資格？
(A) An internship at a media company	(A) 在媒體公司的實習
(B) Proficiency in foreign languages	(B) 熟練的外語
(C) A degree from a journalism school	(C) 從新聞學院取得的學位
(D) Previous work as a business reporter	(D) 過去做商業記者的工作

■ **Not / True** Not 問題 　　　　　　　　　　　　　　　　　　　　　　　解答 (A)

這是問有關問題核心詞語 qualification，Mr. Vaughn 沒有提到哪項資格的 Not / True 問題。要確認第二篇文章，也就是 Mr. Vaughn 寫的電郵中跟 qualification 相關聯的內容。(A) 是文中沒提到的內容。因此，(A) An internship at a media company 是正確答案。fluent in English, Dutch, and German 中提到英文、荷蘭文和德文都很流暢，所以跟 (B) 的內容一致。I obtained my university diploma from the Liberic School of Journalism 中提到「我在 Liberic 新聞學院取得學位」，所以跟 (C) 的內容一致。As a reporter for The Liberic Business Daily for two years 中提到作為 The Liberic Business Daily 的記者兩年，所以跟 (D) 的內容一致。

單字 qualification n. 資格，能力　media company phr. 媒體公司　proficiency n. 熟練　journalism n. 新聞學

189

In the advertisement, the word "cover" in paragraph 1, line 4 is closest in meaning to	廣告中，第一段第四行「cover」這個字最接近哪的字的意思？
(A) conceal	(A) 隱匿
(B) speak about	(B) 談論
(C) protect	(C) 保護
(D) report on	(D) 報導

■ 同義詞 　　　　　　　　　　　　　　　　　　　　　　　　　　　　　解答 (D)

第一篇文章包含廣告的 cover 的詞句 they will also be assigned to cover events in Amsterdam 中的 cover 的意思是「採訪」。因此，意思是「報導」的 (D) report on 是正確答案。

190

Which section of NexusWire is Mr. Vaughn most likely interested in?	NexusWire 的哪個部門是 Vaughn 先生最有可能感興趣的？
(A) Travel and Leisure	(A) 旅行與休閒
(B) Health and Lifestyle	(B) 健康與生活形態
(C) Business and Finance	(C) 商業與金融
(D) Science and Technology	(D) 科學與科技

■ 推論 聯結問題 　　　　　　　　　　　　　　　　　　　　　　　　　解答 (C)

這是要把兩篇文章的內容綜合起來才能解開的聯結問題。問題核心詞語 section of NexusWire ~ Mr. Vaughn ~ interested in 中問到 Mr. Vaughn 對 NexusWire 雜誌的哪個部門最可能感興趣，所以要確認第二篇文章，也就是 Mr. Vaughn 也寫的電郵內容。

第二篇文章的 Dear Ms. Young, I am writing in response to NexusWire's posting for staff writers. 中提到 Mr. Vaughn 給 Ms. Young 寫這封信來回應 NexusWire 雜誌尋求執筆作家的廣告刊登。接著，As a reporter for The Liberic Business Daily for two years 和 I also did some freelance writing for several business journals 提到 Mr. Vaughn 作為 The Liberic Business Daily 的記者兩年，且為數家商業雜誌兼職撰稿。不過，並沒有提到 Ms. Young 是 NexusWire 雜誌哪個部門的負責人。因此，就需要去確定廣告的內容。第一篇文章的 Business and Finance, Claudia Young 中提到 Claudia Young 是商業與金融的編輯。

把 Mr. Vaughn 給 Ms. Young 寫信提到的商業經歷和第一篇文章中 Claudia Young 是商業與金融的編輯的內容綜合起來後，就可以推論出 Mr. Vaughn 對 NexusWire 雜誌的商業與金融感興趣。因此，(C) Business and Finance 是正確答案。

例文1

Xyther Software Unlimited
Please use the form below to contact us.

Name	Caleb Guillory
191-AE-mail	cguillory@bwmail.com
191-APhone	555-6074
191-BSubject	Software Problem
Message	191-CI purchased a software program at your shop on September 3, but I've been having some problems using it. I was able to install it successfully on my desktop computer. However, 194every time I use the program for more than five minutes, the operating system automatically shuts down and then restarts. The same thing happened when I tried using the application a second time, and it has continued to happen since. I cannot seem to figure out what the problem is. 191-BI would be extremely grateful if you could help me with this issue before the 90-day warranty ends. Thank you, and I hope to hear from you soon.

Xyther 軟體公司
請使用以下的表格與我們聯繫

姓名：	Caleb Guillory
191-A電郵：	cguillory@bwmail.com
191-A電話：	555-6074
191-B主旨：	軟體問題
訊息：	191-C我於 9 月 3 日在你們店裡買了一套軟體程式，可是我在使用上遭遇到問題，我能夠在我的桌上型電腦安裝，但是194每次我使用該軟體超過五分鐘，作業系統就會自動關機並重新啟動。同樣的情況在我第二次使用時再度發生，且持續發生，我沒辦法找出問題所在。 191-B若你能在九十天的保固期結束前幫我解決這個問題，我會非常感激你。非常感謝，希望能很快得到你的回音。

例文2

To: cguillory@bwmail.com
From: custserv@xythersoftware.com
Date: September 28
193Subject: Inquiry Form No. 95204 - Received September 27, 4:58 P.M.

Dear Mr. Guillory,

Thank you for your e-mail. 192We are so sorry for the troubles you have experienced in using our software. In the past three months, we have received inquiries from other customers who also had difficulties with their purchases, so we decided to conduct a series of tests. The results suggest that defective source codes caused the various programs to malfunction: Web Browser is unable to load pages completely; error messages appear upon the start-up of Database Organizer; certain files cannot be opened using Document Manager; and 194Image Editor shuts down computer systems after operating for about five minutes.

Rest assured, 192we have fixed the errors and would be more than happy to replace your software. 195Please do not forget to submit your official receipt when you return the item to our shop. And to make up for the trouble this incident has caused, we have attached a printable coupon that you can use on your next purchase.

收件者：cguillory@bwmail.com
寄件者：custserv@xythersoftware.com
日期：9 月 28 日
193主旨：詢問表 No. 95204 –於 9 月 27 日下午四點五十八分收到

親愛的 Guillory 先生：

謝謝你的電郵，192很抱歉你在使用我們的軟體上所遭遇到的問題。在過去三個月裡，我們也收到其他顧客的詢問，他們也反應對購買的軟體遭遇的使用上的困難，所以我們決定進行一系列的測試，結果顯示瑕疵的原始碼造成好幾個程式無法正常運作：Web Browser 網頁瀏覽器無法完全打開網頁；Database Organizer 在啟動時會出現錯誤訊息；某些檔案無法以 Document Manager 打開、194Image Editor 影像編輯器會在運作約五分鐘後關閉電腦系統。

別擔心，192我們會修復這些錯誤，並且很樂意更換你購買的軟體。在你來店退貨時，請不要忘了交給我們你的正式收據，為了彌補這件事造成你的麻煩，我們附上可列印的折價券，讓你下次購物時使用。

| Sincerely,

Customer Service Team
Xyther Software Unlimited | Xyther 軟體公司客戶服務團隊敬上 |

例文 1 單字 □install v. 安裝　　　　　　　　　　□automatically ad. 自動地
　　　　　□shut down phr. 終止，停止　　　　　□grateful a. 感謝的
　　　　　□warranty n. （品質）保證，保證書

例文 2 單字 □a series of phr. 一系列的　　　　　　□defective a. 有缺陷的
　　　　　□malfunction v. 機器故障　　　　　　□run v. 運作
　　　　　□receipt n. 收據　　　　　　　　　　□make up for phr. 賠償
　　　　　□incident n. （特別或不愉快的）事情　　□attach v. 添附　　□printable a. 可印出的

191

| What did Mr. Guillory NOT include on the form?
(A) Contact information
(B) Purpose for writing
(C) Date of purchase
(D) Shipping address | Guillory 先生沒有在表格上寫什麼？
(A) 聯絡方式
(B) 填寫表格的目的
(C) 購買日期
(D) 收貨地址 |

■ **Not / True** Not 問題　　　　　　　　　　　　　　　　　　　　　　　　　　　解答 (D)

這是找出跟問題核心詞語 Mr. Guillory ~ include on the form 相關的內容後，再跟選項作對比的 Not / True 問題。確認第一篇文章中 Mr. Guillory 所寫的跟連絡表格有關的內容。E-mail, cguillory@bwmail.com 和 Phone, 555-6074 中提到電郵地址和電話，所以跟 (A) 的內容一致。subject, Software Problem 中提到主旨是軟體問題。接著 I would be extremely grateful if you could help me with this issue 中提到「我會非常感激你，如果你能幫我解決這個問題」。因此，跟 (B) 的內容一致。I purchased a software program ~ on September 3 中提到「我於 9 月 3 日買了軟體程式」，所以跟 (C) 的內容一致。(D) 都是文中沒提到的內容。因此，(D) Shipping address 是正確答案。

192

| Why was the e-mail written?
(A) To offer a solution to Mr. Guillory
(B) To request a warranty extension
(C) To conduct a customer survey
(D) To explain a reimbursement policy | 為什麼寫這封電郵？
(A) 給 Guillory 先生提供一個解決方案
(B) 要求延長保固
(C) 進行一次顧客調查
(D) 解釋退費規定 |

■ **找出主題** 寫文章的理由　　　　　　　　　　　　　　　　　　　　　　　　　解答 (A)

這是問寫信原因，需找出文章主題的問題，所以要先確認第二篇電郵的內容。電郵中 We are so sorry for the troubles you have experienced in using our software. 中提到很抱歉顧客在使用軟體上所遭遇到的問題。接著，we have fixed the errors and would be more than happy to replace your software 中提到「我們會修復這些錯誤，並且很樂意更換你購買的軟體」，也就是 Mr. Guillory 購買的軟體。因此，(A) To offer a solution to Mr. Guillory 是正確答案。

單字 solution n. 解決方法　　extension n. 延長，擴大　　reimbursement n. 補償，退款

193

What is indicated about Mr. Guillory?	關於 Guillory 先生，何者正確？
(A) He will receive a full refund for the product.	(A) 可以得到全額退費。
(B) He has not yet received the software he purchased.	(B) 還沒有收到他買的軟體。
(C) He sent an inquiry on September 27.	(C) 他在 9 月 27 日寄出詢問表。
(D) He does not agree with the research.	(D) 他不同意這個研究。

■ 推論 詳細內容　　　　　　　　　　　　　　　　　　　　　　　　　解答 (C)

這是跟問題核心詞語 Mr. Guillory 有關的推理問題。首先確認第二篇文章，也就是寄給 Mr. Guillory 的電郵中的內容。電郵的 subject: Inquiry Form ~ Received September 27 中 Mr. Guillory 詢問的表格已經在 9 月 27 日收到。由此可以推論出 Mr. Guillory 是在 9 月 27 日寄出詢問表格。因此，(C) He sent an inquiry on September 27. 是正確答案。

194

Which program did Mr. Guillory most likely use?	哪個程式是 Guillory 最有可能使用的？
(A) Database Organizer	(A) Database Organizer
(B) Image Editor	(B) Image Editor
(C) Document Manager	(C) Document Manager
(D) Web Browser	(D) Web Browser

■ 推論 聯結問題　　　　　　　　　　　　　　　　　　　　　　　　　解答 (B)

這是要把兩篇文章的內容綜合起來才能解開的聯結問題。問題核心詞語 program ~ Mr. Guillory ~ use 中問 Mr. Guillory 最有可能使用哪個（Which）程式。因此，要先確認第一篇文章，也就是 Mr. Guillory 寫的電郵。

第一篇文章的 every time I use the program for more than five minutes, the operating system automatically shuts down 中提到 Mr. Guillory 每次使用該軟體超過五分鐘，作業系統就會自動關機。不過，這裡並沒有提到是使用哪個程式五分鐘以上，作業系統就會自動關機。因此，要確認第二篇文章中相關的內容。第二篇文章的 Image Editor shuts down computer systems after operating for about five minutes 中提到影像編輯器會在運作約五分鐘後關閉電腦系統。

把 Mr. Guillory 每此使用該軟體超過五分鐘，作業系統就會自動關機的內容和影像編輯器會在運作約五分鐘後關閉電腦系統的內容綜合起來，就可以推論出 Mr. Guillory 使用的是影像編輯器。因此，(B) Image Editor 是正確答案。

195

What does Xyther Software Unlimited ask Mr. Guillory to do?	Xyther 軟體公司要求 Guillory 先生做什麼？
(A) Hand in a receipt	(A) 交出收據
(B) Return an item by mail	(B) 以郵寄退貨
(C) Reinstall a program	(C) 重新安裝程式
(D) Submit a payment	(D) 付款

■ 六何原則 What　　　　　　　　　　　　　　　　　　　　　　　　解答 (A)

這是問 Xyther 軟體公司要求 Mr. Guillory 做什麼（What）的六何原則問題。首先要確認 Xyther 軟體公司寫給 Mr. Guillory 的電郵內容。電郵的 Please do not forget to submit your official receipt when you return the item to our shop. 中提到「在你來店退貨時，請不要忘了交給我們你的正式收據」。因此，(A) Hand in a receipt 是正確答案。

Questions 196-200 refer to the following e-mail and announcement. 196-200 根據下面電郵和告示的內容回答問題。

例文1

To: Parvati Malik <parvatim@fastmail.com>

From: Chandrika Rao <ChanRao@allmail.com>

Date: October 2
Subject: GPD Seminar

Dear Parvati,

I enjoyed talking with you at the Singapore convention last month. 197-DIt was unfortunate that there wasn't enough time to speak about the several projects you are going to oversee in January. 196I completely understand your anxiety about working on all those projects, since I went through the same thing last year. 196I found that listening and talking to industry experts was very beneficial, which is why 199I strongly suggest that you participate in the three-day seminar my company is sponsoring next month. 199One of the speakers, Omar Pillai of Lakshman Developers, will go over the challenges of project management and provide corresponding solutions.

Attached are some seminar details. I would be happy to personally answer any questions you might have, so please contact me directly at (+9122) 555-1308.

Best regards,

Chandrika

收件人：Parvati Malik
　　　　<parvatim@fastmail.com>
寄件人：Chandrika Rao
　　　　<ChanRao@allmail.com>
日期：10 月 2 日
主旨：GPD 研習會

親愛的 Parvati，

上個月在新加坡會議和你談話談得很愉快，197-D 但是很可惜沒有足夠的時間和你談論你在 1 月要監督的幾個專案，196 我完全了解你對做這些專案會感到焦慮，因為我去年也經歷了同樣的事情，196 我發現聆聽和與業界專家交談很有幫助，199 因此我強烈建議你參加我們公司在下個月贊助的三天研習會，199 其中一位講員是 Lakshman 地產開發公司的 Omar Pillai，將會談論專案管理的挑戰，並提供對應的解決方案。

附件是一些研習會的詳細資料，我很樂意親自回答你的問題，所以請撥打 (+9122) 555-1308 直接與我聯絡。

Chandrika 敬上

例文2

9th GLOBAL PROPERTY AND REAL ESTATE SEMINAR
Satya Yuga Convention Center
November 7 to 9
198Below are the presentations that were recently added to the seminar.
On October 31, the final timetable will be forwarded by e-mail to each participant who has signed up.

DATE/TIME	PRESENTATION	PRESENTER
November 6 10 A.M.	200Investing in your First Property: For Beginners	200Balram Jhadav Strategic Consultant VGS Consultancy
November 7 4 P.M.	Understanding Commercial Property Investment	Vineeta Das Corporate Finance Head Gandhari Property Incorporated
199November 8 1 P.M.	Effective Building Project Management: Handling Various Projects All at Once	199Omar Pillai Operations Director Lakshman Developers
November 9 9 A.M.	Moving Toward Sustainable Property Development Menaka Sarin	Menake Sarin Chief Executive Officer Kaurava Enterprises

第九屆全球房地產研習會
Satya Yuga 會議中心
11 月 7～9 日
198以下是最近新增至研習會的演説
10 月 31 日，定案後的時間表會以電郵寄送到所有報名參加的人

日期 / 時間	演説	講員
11 月 6 日 上午十點	200投資你的第一份房地產： 新手入門	200Balram Jhadav 策略顧問 VGS 顧問公司
11 月 7 日 下午四點	了解商業房地產投資	Vineeta Das 公司財務主任 Gandhari 地產公司
19911 月 8 日 下午一點	有效的專案管理：同時處理多項專案	199Omar Pillai 營運主任 Lakshman 地產開發公司
11 月 9 日 上午九點	轉向穩定的房地產發展	Menaka Sarin 營運長 Kaurava 企業公司

Registration has been extended to October 20. For more information, please log on to www.gpdseminars.com.	報名日期延至 10 月 20 日 更多詳情，請上官網 www.gpdseminars.com

例文 1 單字 □oversee v. 監督　　　　□anxiety n. 擔心，顧慮，不安　　□go through phr. 經驗，經歷
　　　　　　□expert n. 專家　　　　　□beneficial a. 有幫助的　　　　□corresponding a. 相對應的
例文 2 單字 □property n. 土地，資產，財產　□participant n. 參加者　　　　□invest v. 投資
　　　　　　□effective a. 有效的　　　　□sustainable a. 支撐得住的; 能承受的

196

What is the main purpose of the e-mail?	這封電郵的主要目的為何？
(A) To invite a speaker to a seminar	(A) 邀請演講者參加研習會
(B) To suggest participation in an event	(B) 建議參加一個活動
(C) To request an opinion about a service	(C) 對一項服務徵求意見
(D) To provide an update on a project	(D) 提供一項專案計畫的更新資料

■ 找出主題 目的　　　　　　　　　　　　　　　　　　　　　　　　　　　　　　　解答 (B)

這是問寫電郵目的的找主題問題，因此先確認第一篇文章，也就是電郵的內容。電郵的 I completely understand your anxiety about working on all those projects 中提到「我完全了解你對做這些專案會感到焦慮」。接著，I found that listening and talking to industry experts was very beneficial, which is why I strongly suggest that you participate in the three-day seminar 中提到「我發現聆聽和與業界專家交談很有助益，因此我強烈建議你參加三天研習會」。因此，(B) To suggest participation in an event 是正確答案。

197

What is indicated about Ms. Malik?	關於 Malik 小姐，何者正確？
(A) She has to recruit more staff for her department.	(A) 她必須聘更多人到她的部門。
(B) She has been offered a higher position with a competitor.	(B) 競爭對手延聘她擔任更高的職位。
(C) She is having difficulty finding major property investors.	(C) 她在找主要不動產投資者這件事上有困難。
(D) She will be managing multiple tasks at the same time.	(D) 她要在同時管理多項專案。

■ Not / True True 問題　　　　　　　　　　　　　　　　　　　　　　　　　　　解答 (D)

這是找出跟問題核心詞語 Ms. Malik 相關的內容後，再跟選項作對比的 Not / True 問題。首先確認第一篇文章中給 Ms. Malik 的電郵中的相關內容。(A) (B) (C)都是文中沒提到的內容。It was unfortunate that there wasn't enough time to speak about the several projects you are going to oversee in January. 中提到很遺憾沒有足夠的時間和 Ms. Malik 談論其 1 月要監督的幾個專案。因此，(D) She will be managing multiple tasks at the same time. 是正確答案。

單字 recruit v. 雇用，聚集　department n. 部門　multiple a. 多數的，很多的　task n. 工作，課題

198

What is suggested about the presentations described in the announcement? (A) They will be held in different venues. (B) They were recently added to the timetable. (C) They are the only talks taking place at the seminar. (D) They will be led by people from the same company.	關於公告中所提到的演說，何者正確？ (A) 會在不同的地方舉行。 (B) 最近才加進時間表裡。 (C) 這些是在研習會裡僅有的演説。 (D) 這些演説由同一家公司的人來主導。

■ 推論 詳細內容　　　　　　　　　　　　　　　　　　　　　　　　　　　　　解答 (B)

這是問公告中提到的問題核心詞語 the presentations 有關的推理問題。因此，先確認第二篇文章中公告的相關內容。公告的 Below are the presentations that were recently added to the seminar. 中提到以下是最近新增至研習會的演說，還用表格整理出來。由此可以推斷出公告中刊出的演說者是最近才加進時間表的。因此，(B) They were recently added to the timetable. 是正確答案。

單字 talk n. 演説，演講

199

Which date's presentation does Ms. Rao think will benefit Ms. Malik? (A) November 6 (B) November 7 (C) November 8 (D) November 9	哪一天的演説是 Rao 女士認為對 Malik 小姐有幫助的？ (A) 11 月 6 日 (B) 11 月 7 日 (C) 11 月 8 日 (D) 11 月 9 日

■ 六何原則 聯結問題　　　　　　　　　　　　　　　　　　　　　　　　　　　解答 (C)

這是要把兩篇文章的內容綜合起來才能解開的聯結問題。問題核心詞語 presentation ～ Ms. Rao think will benefit Ms. Malik 中問到哪（Which）一天的演説是 Ms. Rao 認為對 Ms. Malik 有幫助的。因此，要先確認第一篇文章，也就是 Ms. Rao 寄出的電郵內容。

第一篇文章的 I strongly suggest that you participate in the three-day seminar 中提到「我強烈建議你參加三天研習會」。接著，在 One of the speakers, Omar Pillai ～ will go over the challenges of project management and provide corresponding solutions. 中提到其中一位講員 Omar Pillai 將會談論專案管理的挑戰，並提供對應的解決方案。因此，可以確定的是 Ms. Rao 是推薦 Ms. Malik 參加 Omar Pillai 的演說。不過，這裡並沒有說明 Omar Pillai 是在哪一天演說，所以要確定公告的相關內容。第二篇文章上的表格的 November 8, Omar Pillai 中提到 Omar Pillai 是 11 月 8 日發表。

把 Ms. Rao 推薦 Ms. Malik 參加 Omar Pillai 的演說的內容和 Omar Pillai 是 11 月 8 日發表的內容綜合起來，就可以知道 Ms. Rao 認為對 Ms. Malik 有幫助的演說日期是 11 月 8 日。因此，(C) November 8 是正確答案。

200

Who would most likely be interested in Mr. Jhadav's presentation? (A) First-time property buyers (B) Business consultants (C) Recent college graduates (D) Financial investors	誰最有可能對 Jhadav 先生的演説感興趣？ (A) 第一次買房地產的人 (B) 企業顧問 (C) 大學剛畢業的人 (D) 金融投資者

■ 推論 詳細內容　　　　　　　　　　　　　　　　　　　　　　　　　　　　　解答 (A)

這是跟問題核心詞語 Mr. Jhadav's presentation 有關的推理問題。因此，先確認第二篇文章中提到 Mr. Jhadav 的相關內容。公告中的表格的 Investing in your First Property: For Beginners, Balram Jhadav 中提到 Mr. Jhadav 的演說內容室是「投資你的第一分房地產：新手入門」。因此，可以推斷出對 Mr. Jhadav 演說感興趣的對象是第一次買房子的人。因此，(A) First-time property buyers 是正確答案。

單字 graduate n. 畢業生，研究生

TEST 09

PART 5

101

The foreign delegates are expected to arrive at the hotel _____ noon on Friday at the latest. (A) by (B) above (C) within (D) of	外國代表預計最晚在週五的中午抵達飯店。

■ 選擇介系詞 時間和期間 　　　　　　　　　　　　　　　　　　　　　　　　　　　　解答 (A)

文意是「預計最晚中午抵達飯店」，所以和時間單字 noon 一起表達時間點的介系詞 (A) by（到～為止）是正確答案。(C) within 的意思是「～之內」，跟文意不合，不是正確答案。(B) above（比～上面）是表示位置的介系詞。(D) of（～的）則是表示所有或同位語的介系詞。另外，be expected to（預計～）要作為慣用語背起來。

單字　delegate n. 代表，使節　at the latest phr. 最晚

102

Dr. Clark notified _____ patients that he would be out of town this week to attend a medical convention. (A) its (B) his (C) him (D) they	Clark 醫生通知他的病人，他這週將出城參加一個醫療會議。

■ 名詞-代名詞一致 　　　　　　　　　　　　　　　　　　　　　　　　　　　　　　　解答 (B)

文意是「Dr. Clark 通知他的病人」，所以空格上的代名詞指的就是 Dr. Clark。因此，除了可以指示單數人稱名詞 Dr. Clark 之外，還可以像形容詞一樣用於名詞 patients 前面的所有格 (B) his 就是正確答案。指示事物名詞的所有格人稱代名詞 (A)、受格人稱代名詞 (C)、主格人稱代名詞 (D) 都不是正確答案。另外，「notify＋人＋that 子句」和「notify＋人＋of」的意思都是「通知某人某事」。

單字　notify v. 通知　patient n. 病人　be out of town phr.（因出差等）出城　convention n. 協會，會議，風俗

103

Mr. Barnett reserved his flight to Hanoi directly with the airline company because it was _____ than booking with a travel agent. (A) simply (B) simpler (C) simplest (D) simplicity	Barnett 先生直接跟航空公司預訂他前往河內的班機，因為這樣比跟旅行社預訂還簡單。

■ 比較級 　　　　　　　　　　　　　　　　　　　　　　　　　　　　　　　　　　　解答 (B)

be 動詞 was 後面接的是補語，又可以跟空格後面的 than 組成比較級的形容詞比較級 (B) simpler 就是正確答案。副詞 (A) 只能放在補語的位置。最高級 (C) 不能和 than 一起使用。名詞 (D) 如果要使用比較級，其用法必須是「more / fewer / less＋名詞＋than」（比～多 / 少）。

單字　reserve v. 預訂　directly ad. 直接　travel agency phr. 旅行社

104

Because of his knowledge of foreign markets, Alex is a valuable ------- of the advertising and promotion department. (A) resident　　　　　(B) applicant (C) member　　　　　(D) tenant	因為 Alex 對海外市場的了解，他是廣告宣傳部中重要的成員。

■ 名詞語彙　　　　　　　　　　　　　　　　　　　　　　　　　解答 (C)

文意是「廣告宣傳部中重要的成員」，所以名詞 (C) member（成員）是正確答案。(A) resident 的意思是「居住者，居民」，(B) applicant 的意思是「應徵者」，(D) tenant 的意思則是「房客」。

單字　knowledge n. 見識　valuable adj. 珍貴的　promotion n. 促銷

105

According to his professor at Becker University, Arlen Thornton has earned adequate _____ to pursue a career in industrial engineering. (A) quality　　　　　(B) qualifications (C) qualifying　　　　(D) qualified	根據他在 Becker 大學的教授指出，Arlen Thornton 已經取得足夠的資格，他可以朝工業工程上發展事業。

■ 名詞位置　　　　　　　　　　　　　　　　　　　　　　　　　解答 (B)

可以扮演動詞 has earned 的受詞，還可以被形容詞 adequate 修飾的就是名詞了。因此，名詞 (A) 和 (B) 都可能是正確答案。文意是「已經取得足夠的資格，他可以朝工業工程上發展事業」，所以名詞 (B) qualifications（資格）是正確答案。如果使用 (A) quality（質量，品質），文意就變成「取得恰當的品質」，跟上下文都說不通。分詞 (C) 和 (D) 不能位於名詞的位置。雖然 (C) 也可以當成動名詞，但是動名詞也不能被形容詞 adequate 修飾，所以也不可能是正確答案。

單字　adequate a. 足夠的

106

The consumer survey conducted in the Eastern European region revealed a _____ decline in the residents' preference for online shopping. (A) notes　　　　　(B) notably (C) noting　　　　　(D) notable	在東歐地區進行的消費者調查顯示，當地居民上網購物的偏好明顯下降。

■ 形容詞位置　　　　　　　　　　　　　　　　　　　　　　　　解答 (D)

位於不定冠詞 a 和名詞 decline 之間，又可以修飾名詞的就是形容詞了。因此，扮演形容詞的分詞 (C) 和形容詞 (D) 都可能是正確答案。文意是「居民偏好明顯下降」，所以形容詞 (D) notable（值得注意的，顯著的）是正確答案。如果使用分詞 (C) noting，文意就會變成「居民偏好的注意下降」，句子就變得很奇怪。動詞或名詞的 (A) 和副詞 (B) 都不能修飾名詞。

單字　consumer n. 消費者　survey n. 調查　conduct v. 實行　reveal v. 顯示　decline n. 下降

107

Museum guests are not allowed to touch the sculptures on display, _____ are they permitted to take pictures of the art pieces.

(A) nor   (B) so

(C) until   (D) during

博物館的來賓不允許觸摸展示的雕刻品，也不允許對藝術作品拍照。

■ 倒裝句   解答 (A)

可以在前面引出主詞和動詞倒裝的子句 are they permitted ~ pieces 的否定詞 (A) nor 就是正確答案。 (B) so 雖然可以引出倒裝句，但是只能用於「～果然也～」的肯定句中，不能用於否定句。 (C) until 的意思是「～為止」，是介系詞也是連接詞。 (D) during 的意思是「～期間」，是介系詞。 (C) 和 (D) 都無法引出倒裝句。

單字 sculpture n. 雕刻品   permit v. 允許

108

Once all the applications are received, Wei Foundation's scholarship committee _____ only 40 individuals to send to China for a year of study.

(A) to select   (B) will select

(C) have selected   (D) were selecting

當收到所有的申請書後，Wei 基金會的獎學金委員會將只選擇 40 個人到中國進行為期一年的研習。

■ 未來時態   解答 (B)

主子句中沒有動詞，所以動詞 (B) (C) (D) 都可能是正確答案。當主子句是未來時態時，表示時間或條件的從屬句中為了體現未來時態，就必須用現在時態來代替未來時態。這句話中的從屬句 Once ~ received 也使用現在時態 are received 來表達「收到的申請書後」的未來的事情。主子句中的動詞也必須使用未來時態。因此，(B) will select 就是正確答案。 (C) 是現在完成式，(D) 是過去進行式，兩者的時態都不正確。to 不定詞 (A) 則無法放在動詞的位置上。

單字 application n. 申請書，適用   scholarship n. 獎學金

109

Candidates who receive notifications to attend a second interview must _____ their intentions to proceed with the application process.

(A) confirmed   (B) confirm

(C) confirmation   (D) confirming

收到參加第二次面試通知的候選人，必須確認他們的意願，以繼續進行申請的流程。

■ 助動詞 + 動詞原形   解答 (B)

助動詞 must 後面一定要接動詞原形。因此，(B) confirm 就是正確答案。過去動詞 (A)、名詞 (C)、現在分詞或動名詞的 (D) 都不能位於助動詞後面。

單字 candidate n. 候選人   notification n. 通知   intention n. 意圖   proceed with phr. 繼續～
      application n. 申請

110

| The workplace safety regulations _____ helped to prevent serious accidents from occurring at the construction site.
(A) define　　　　　(B) definitely
(C) definite　　　　(D) definitions | 工作場所安全法規明顯地幫助了防止工地發生嚴重的事故。 |

■ 副詞位置　　　　　　　　　　　　　　　　　　　　　　　　　　　　　解答 (B)

為了修飾動詞 helped，一定要出現副詞。因此，副詞 (B) definitely（明顯地）就是正確答案。動詞 (A)、形容詞 (C)、名詞 (D) 都無法修飾動詞。

單字　workplace n. 工作場所，作業現場　regulation n. 規定　occur v. 發生　definite a. 明顯的
　　　definition n. 定義，清晰

111

| The plumber conducted a thorough ------- of how much it would probably cost to replace the old water pipes in Ms. Kent's apartment.
(A) inspection　　　　(B) inspects
(C) inspect　　　　　(D) inspecting | 水電工對 Kent 女士的公寓進行徹底的檢查，用來評估替換舊的水管可能所需的花費。 |

■ 名詞位置　　　　　　　　　　　　　　　　　　　　　　　　　　　　　解答 (A)

除了可以位於動詞 conducted 的受詞的位置，還可以和不定冠詞 a 一起使用，又可以被形容詞 thorough 修飾的就是名詞了。因此，名詞 (A) inspection（檢查）是正確答案。動名詞 (D) inspecting 不能和不定冠詞 a 一起使用，且要以副詞修飾。動詞 (B) 和 (C) 則都不能位於名詞位置。

單字　replace v. 取代

112

| ------- to providing reliable electrical services to households and commercial establishments in Denver, Voltworks hires only highly skilled electricians.
(A) Consisted　　　　(B) Regarded
(C) Reconstructed　　(D) Committed | Voltworks 致力在提供丹佛家庭和商業機構可靠的電力供應，因此他們只僱用技術精湛的電工。 |

■ 動詞語彙　　　　　　　　　　　　　　　　　　　　　　　　　　　　　解答 (D)

文意是「致力在提供電力供應」，所以動詞 commit（獻身）的 p.p. 形 (D) Committed 就是正確答案。 (A) consist 的意思是「～組成」，(B) regard 的意思是「看作～」，(C) reconstruct 的意思則是「重建，修復」。另外，這句話的分詞句 Committed ~ Denver 前面省略了 being。

單字　reliable a. 可靠的　highly ad. 非常　electrician n. 電工，電力技術者　connect v. 連接
　　　reconstruct v. 重建

113

The new admissions standards that were implemented last year by Columna University made it _____ than before for graduating high school students to apply to the institution.

(A) easily
(B) easy
(C) ease
(D) easier

■ 比較級

解答 (D)

去年 Columna 大學所實施的新入學標準，使得高中畢業生比以前更容易申請進入此大學。

受詞 it 後面要接受格補語，又可以跟空格後面的 than 組成比較級表達的形容詞比較級 (D) easier 就是正確答案。副詞 (A) 不能位於補語位置，形容詞 (B) 不能和 than 一起使用。名詞 (C) 的比較級用法是「more / fewer / less + 名詞 + than」（比～多 / 少），所以也不是正確答案。

單字 admission n. 入學　standard n. 標準　implement v. 實施　institution n. 學校，機構

114

Many citizens across the state are having difficulty finding _____ these days due to the economic crisis.

(A) employable
(B) employing
(C) employed
(D) employment

■ 動名詞 vs.名詞

解答 (D)

這些日子以來，全國各州有許多公民因為經濟危機而就業困難。

可以扮演動名詞 finding 的受詞的是名詞，所以動名詞 (B) 或名詞 (D) 可能是正確答案。因為空格後面沒有受詞，所以動名詞 (B) employing 不是正確答案，名詞 (D) employment 才是正確答案。形容詞 (A)，分詞或動詞 (C) 不能位於動名詞的受詞的位置。另外，「have difficulty + -ing」（做～有困難）要作為慣用語背起來。

單字 state n. 國家，狀態

115

The famous director found Rachel Burns to be sufficiently _____ to play almost any role, no matter how challenging.

(A) variable
(B) essential
(C) comprehensive
(D) versatile

■ 形容詞語彙

解答 (D)

著名導演發現 Rachel Burns 相當多才多藝，幾乎可以飾演任何角色，無論角色多麼的有挑戰性。

文意是「多才多藝，幾乎可以飾演任何角色」，所以形容詞 (D) versatile（多才多藝的）是正確答案。(A) variable 的意思是「變動的」，(B) essential 的意思是「必要性的」，(C) comprehensive 的意思則是「廣泛的，理解力高的」。

單字 sufficiently ad. 充分地　role n. 角色

116

The event organizer said that the annual organic products expo will be held _____ the Ivory Cultural Center next year.

(A) at
(B) beneath
(C) about
(D) through

■ 介系詞 at

解答 (A)

本次活動的主辦單位表示，年度有機產品博覽會明年將於象牙文化中心舉行。

文意是「博覽會於象牙文化中心舉行」，所以表示場所的介系詞 (A) at（在～）就是正確答案。(B) beneath 的意思是「在～下面」，表示位置，(C) about 的意思是「關於～」，(D) through 的意思是「～期間，通過～」，表示期間或方向、手段、方法等。

單字 annual a. 年度的，年間的

117

The board gave Mr. Liebnitz a week to decide whether or not he would accept the _____ to the advertising department.
(A) vote
(B) report
(C) transfer
(D) advance

董事會給了 Liebnitz 先生一個星期的時間來決定他是否接受調動到廣告部門。

■ 名詞語彙　　　　　　　　　　　　　　　　　　　　　　　解答 (C)

文意是「調動到廣告部門」，所以名詞 (C) transfer（調動）是正確答案。 (A) vote 的意思是「票，投票」，(B) report 的意思是「報告」，(D) advance 的意思則是「推進，促進」。

單字 accept v. 接受

118

Upon _____ of the registration forms, scholarship applicants are advised to submit them to the registrar's office.
(A) computation
(B) completion
(C) declaration
(D) adaptation

獎學金申請者完成登記表格後，建議將表格送到註冊組辦公室。

■ 名詞語彙　　　　　　　　　　　　　　　　　　　　　　　解答 (B)

文意是「完成登記表格後，將表格送到註冊組辦公室」，所以 (B) completion（完成，結束）是正確答案。(A) computation 的意思是「計算」，(C) declaration 的意思是「宣告」，(D) adaptation 的意思是「適應」。

單字 registration form phr. 登記表格　applicant n. 申請者

119

Test results showed _____ some soaps and shampoos contain chemicals which may cause skin dryness and irritation.
(A) that
(B) this
(C) whenever
(D) what

試驗結果表明，一些肥皂和洗髮精含有化學物質，可能會導致皮膚乾燥和刺激。

■ what 和 that 的區分　　　　　　　　　　　　　　　　　　解答 (A)

動詞 showed 的受詞位置上出現的子句 ____ some soaps ~ irritation 的最前面一定要有名詞子句的連接詞。因此，名詞子句的連接詞 (A) 和 (D) 都可能是正確答案。因為空格後面是完整子句，所以 (A) that 是正確答案。 (D) what 後面要接不完整子句，因此不是正確答案。 (B) this 作為指示代名詞、代名詞、副詞來使用，是無法引出子句的。而作為副詞子句連接詞來使用的複合關係副詞 (C) whenever 無法引出名詞子句。

單字 contain v. 含有　chemicals n. 化學物質　skin irritation phr. 皮膚發炎，皮膚刺激

120

The new restaurant on Oak Grove Avenue is _____ by food critics for people who enjoy Mediterranean cuisine.
(A) recommended
(B) specialized
(C) delivered
(D) consumed

美食評論家推薦在 Oak Grove 大道的那間新餐廳給喜愛享受地中海料理的人。

■ 動詞語彙　　　　　　　　　　　　　　　　　　　　　　　解答 (A)

文意是「美食評論家推薦在 Oak Grove 大道的新餐廳給喜愛享受地中海料理的人」，所以和空格前面的 be 動詞 is 一起組成被動態的動詞 recommend（推薦）的 p.p. 形 (A) recommended 就是正確答案。 (B) specialize 的意思是「專精」，(C) deliver 的意思是「運送」，(D) consume 的意思則是「花費、消耗」。

單字 critics n. 評論家，批評家　Mediterranean a. 地中海的　cuisine n. 食物，料理

121

All passenger vessels are required by law to make _____ for people with physical disabilities.
(A) perceptions　　　　(B) directions
(C) provisions　　　　(D) restrictions

法律規定所有的客機,需要向身體殘障者提供其所需的服務。

■ 名詞語彙　　　　　　　　　　　　　　　　　　　　　　　解答 (C)

文意是「法律規定所有的客機,需要向身體殘障者提供其所需的服務」,所以名詞 (C) provisions（準備）是正確答案。make provision for（為～作準備）要作為慣用語背起來。 (A) perception 的意思是「感知,理解」, (B) direction 的意思是「指示」, (D) restriction 的意思是「限制」。

單字 passenger vessel phr. 客機　physical a. 身體的　disability n. 障礙

122

Mr. Hall visits the project site _____ to make sure that the renovation is going according to schedule.
(A) any　　　　　　　(B) soon
(C) hardly　　　　　　(D) frequently

Hall 先生經常去裝修現場,以確保裝修按照預定計畫進行。

■ 副詞語彙　　　　　　　　　　　　　　　　　　　　　　　解答 (D)

文意是「經常去裝修現場,以確保裝修按照預定計畫進行」,所以副詞 (D) frequently（經常）是正確答案。 (A) any 的意思是「任何,一點」, (B) soon 的意思是「馬上」, (C) hardly 的意思是「幾乎不～」。

單字 site n. 現場　renovation n. 修理,翻新　according to phr. 根據～,按照～

123

_____ returning a defective item to the store for replacement, please do not forget to bring the official receipt.
(A) Into　　　　　　　(B) When
(C) Whoever　　　　　(D) Following

當回到商店裡退換有缺陷的品項時,請不要忘記帶正式的收據。

■ 副詞子句連接詞 時間　　　　　　　　　　　　　　　　　解答 (B)

這句話是具有必要成分 please do not forget ~ the official receipt 的完整子句,所以要把 ____ returning ~ for replacement 看成是可省略的修飾語。這個修飾語是表現「當回到商店裡退換有缺陷的品項時」這個時間的分詞片語,為了更明確地表達,可以出現在分詞片語前面的副詞子句連接詞 (B) When（～的時候）就是正確答案。介系詞 (A) Into（往～裡面）和 (D) Following（～之後）都不能放在分詞片語前面。可以引出名詞子句或副詞子句的複合關係代名詞 (C) Whoever 也不能位於分詞片語前面。 (D) Following 雖然可以當作是 returning 的受詞的分詞,但是文意就會變成很怪的「為了更換有缺陷的品項,根據商店來交換」。另外,「forget to + 動詞原形（忘記去做～）」和「forget + -ing「（忘了做過～）」要記得區分開來。

單字 defective a. 有缺陷的　replacement n. 更換　receipt n. 收據

124

| For the past eight years, Vincent Silva has _____ supported organizations which protect endangered animals.
(A) nearly　　　(B) delicately
(C) convincingly　　(D) consistently | 在過去的八年裡，Vincent Silva 一直在支持保護瀕臨絕種動物的組織。 |

■ 副詞語彙　　　　　　　　　　　　　　　　　　　解答 (D)

文意是「在過去的八年裡，一直在支持保護瀕臨絕動物的組織」，所以副詞 (D) consistently（持續地）是正確答案。另外，要注意的是 consistently 用於強調其他事物或人一直用相同態度和方式在行動的時候。(A) nearly 的意思是「幾乎」，(B) delicately 的意思是「微妙地」，(C) convincingly 的意思是「有說服力地」。

單字 endangered a. 瀕臨絕種的，處於危險的

125

| The Cerea Hub is an online specialty shop _____ ceramic figurines crafted by people from around the world.
(A) offer　　　(B) offering
(C) will offer　　(D) has offered | Cerea Hub 是一個線上專賣店，提供來自世界各地的人所製作的陶瓷雕像。 |

■ 分詞的角色　　　　　　　　　　　　　　　　　　解答 (B)

這個句子是具有主詞 The Cerea Hub、動詞 is、補語 an online specialty shop 的完整子句，所以可以把 ____ ceramic figurines ~ world 看成是可省略的修飾語。在選項中，可以成為修飾語的分詞 (B) offering 是正確答案。offering ~ world 是分詞片語，修飾前面的名詞 shop。動詞或名詞 (A)，動詞 (C) 和 (D) 都不能放在修飾語上。

單字 figurine n. 小雕刻像　craft v. 精心製作

126

| Dr. Munoz _____ experimental methods for obtaining energy from natural sources long before GDS Incorporated developed its own.
(A) is devising　　(B) had devised
(C) was devised　　(D) has devised | 在 GDS 公司開發出自己的方法前，Munoz 博士早已設計出從天然資源獲得能源的實驗方法。 |

■ 過去完成時態　　　　　　　　　　　　　　　　　解答 (B)

從屬句 long before ~ own 中使用了副詞連接詞 before（~之前），所以可以知道主子句比從屬句提早發生。為了表達過去特定時間點（GDS 公司開發出自己方法的時間點）之前，就發生了事情（Munoz 博士設計出獲得能源的方法），一定要使用過去完成時態。因此，過去完成時態 (B) had devised 就是正確答案。空格後面有動詞受詞 experimental methods，所以被動式 (C) 不是答案。

單字 experimental a. 實驗性的　obtain v. 獲得

127

| The job in the warehouse is best suited to someone who is physically strong as it will _____ involve lifting heavy objects.
(A) vividly　(B) mainly　(C) rarely　(D) summarily | 倉庫的工作最適合身體強壯的人來做，因為大部分的工作內容都需要抬舉重物。 |

■ 副詞語彙　　　　　　　　　　　　　　　　　　　解答 (B)

文意是「倉庫的工作最適合身體強壯的人來做，因為大部分的工作內容都需要抬舉重物」，所以副詞 (B) mainly（主要，大部分）是正確答案。(A) vividly 的意思是「鮮明的」，(C) rarely 的意思是「難得」，(D) summarily 的意思是「概要地，立刻」。

單字 warehouse n. 倉庫

128

The Orlando Bolts baseball team _____ a proposal to endorse the athletic shoes manufactured by Armor Basics. (A) concentrated　　(B) accepted (C) originated　　(D) assigned	Orlando Bolts 棒球隊接受了一項提案，為 Armor Basics 所製造的運動鞋背書。

■ 動詞詞辨　　　　　　　　　　　　　　　　　　　　　　　　　　　　　　解答 (B)

文意是「接受了一項提案，為 Armor 所製造的運動鞋背書」，所以動詞 accept（接受）的過去式 (B) accepted 是正確答案。 (A) concentrate 的意思是「集中」，(C) originate 的意思是「來自，引起」，(D) assign 的意思是「指定，分配」。

單字 offer n. 提案　endorse v. 背書，認可　manufacture v. 製造，生產

129

Stage director Delfin Matthews _____ with Saguijo Theater Company's public relations team to promote the opening of his new play, *Nebuchadnezzar's Bane*. (A) collaborated　　(B) distributed (C) drafted　　(D) granted	舞台劇導演 Delfin Matthews 與 Saguijo 劇團公司的公關團隊合作，來宣傳他的新戲，Nebuchadnezzar 之禍。

■ 動詞語彙　　　　　　　　　　　　　　　　　　　　　　　　　　　　　　解答 (A)

文意是「舞台劇導演與 Saguijo 劇團公司的公關團隊合作，來宣傳他的新戲」，所以動詞 collaborate（共同工作，合作）的過去式 (A) collaborated 是正確答案。 (B) distribute 的意思是「分配」，(C) draft 的意思是「起草，設計，選派」，(D) grant 的意思是「給，認可」。

單字 public relation phr. 公關　promote v. 廣告，促進，晉升　opening n. 開幕

130

Scientists believe that either volcanic activity or large meteor impacts _____ what led to the extinction of the dinosaurs. (A) is　　(B) has been (C) are being　　(D) are	科學家們認為，不是火山活動就是大的流星撞擊，導致恐龍的絕種。

■ 和用連接詞連接一起的主詞單複數一致化　　　　　　　　　　　　　　　　解答 (D)

that 子句 that ~ dinosaurs 的動詞位置是空著的。當空格前面的主詞是 either A or B（A 或 B 中之一）的時候，動詞要跟 B（large meteor impacts）保持單複數一致化。因此，複數動詞 (C) 和 (D) 都可能是正確答案。文意是「不是火山活動就是大的流星撞擊，導致恐龍的絕種」，所以表示一般事實時所使用的 (D) are 是正確答案。 (C) are being 是現在進行時態，表示當下這一瞬間正在進行的動作，跟文意不符。另外，what 子句 what ~ dinosaurs 是扮演 be 動詞 are 的補語角色的名詞子句。

單字 volcanic activity phr. 火山活動　meteor n. 流星　impact n. 撞擊　extinction n. 絕種

131

Investors remain hopeful of a positive outcome despite only a _____ agreement being reached in the last round of negotiations between the two trading partners.

(A) vigilant   (B) tentative
(C) diligent   (D) reliant

投資者對於取得一個正面的結果仍抱持希望，儘管兩個貿易夥伴在最後一輪的談判中只達成了暫時性的協議。

■ 形容詞語彙   解答 (B)

文意是「投資者對於取得一個正面的結果仍抱持希望，儘管只達成了暫時性的協議」，所以形容詞 (B) tentative（暫時性的）是正確答案。 (A) vigilant 的意思是「警惕的」，(C) diligent 的意思是「勤勞的，勤奮的」，(D) reliant 的意思則是「依靠的」。

單字 investor n. 投資者　outcome n. 結果　agreement n. 協議　reach v. 達成　negotiation n. 協商　tentative a. 暫時性的

132

The newly recruited junior data analysts at Adeco Technologies may begin working on actual projects _____ following the mandatory two-week training period.

(A) suddenly   (B) importantly
(C) immediately   (D) recurrently

剛進入 Adeco 技術公司的新進數據分析師，可在強制為期兩週的培訓後，馬上開始參與實際專案的工作。

■ 副詞語彙   解答 (C)

文意是「培訓後，馬上開始參與實際專案的工作」，所以副詞 (C) immediately（馬上）是正確答案。 (A) suddenly 的意思是「突然」，(B) importantly 的意思是「慎重地」，(D) recurrently 的意思是「一再發生的，週期的」。

單字 recruit v. 聘用　following prep. ～後　mandatory a. 強制性的　immediately ad. 馬上

133

Prior to the start of the leadership seminar, participants _____ to spend five minutes preparing a list of goals, which they later shared with the group.

(A) to be asked   (B) were asked
(C) would ask   (D) have been asking

在領導力研討會開始前，參與者被要求花五分鐘準備一個目標清單，之後與小組分享。

■ 被動態動詞的俗語   解答 (B)

句中沒有動詞，所以動詞 (B) (C) (D) 都可能是正確答案。文意是「參與者被要求花五分鐘」，具有被動意義，加上空格沒有受詞，所以被動態動詞 (B) were asked 是正確答案。另外，be asked to（被要求～）要作為慣用語來使用。

單字 participant n. 參與者　prepare v. 準備　goal n. 目標

134

The Silvanus Museum staff is organizing a retirement party in honor of its _____ director, Mr. Alvaro, who has served there for 25 years.
(A) definite
(B) total
(C) outgoing
(D) withdrawn

Silvanus 博物館的工作人員正在籌劃一場退休派對，來表示對在此已服務 25 年即將離職的主管 Alvaro 先生的敬意。

■ 形容詞語彙

解答 (C)

文意是「籌劃一場退休派對，來表示對在此已服務 25 年即將離職的人的敬意」，所以形容詞 (C) outgoing（離職）是正確答案。(A) definite 的意思是「確實的，確定的」，(B) total 的意思是「總，整體的」，(D) withdrawn 的意思是「內向的」。另外，in honor of（向～表敬意）要作為慣用語背起來。

單字 organize v. 策畫　in honor of phr. 跟～表示敬意，恭喜　serve v. 工作，服務

135

Staff members are required to obtain authorization from their supervisors before gaining access to _____ customer information in the firm's database.
(A) familiar
(B) secluded
(C) confidential
(D) formative

在他們從公司的數據庫中獲得機密的客戶資料前，工作人員必須取得他們上司的授權。

■ 形容詞語彙

解答 (C)

文意是「獲得機密的客戶資料前，工作人員必須取得他們上司的授權」，所以形容詞 (C) confidential（機密的，祕密的）是正確答案。(A) familiar 的意思是「熟悉的」，(B) secluded 的意思是「與世隔絕的，隱退的，隱居的」，(D) formative 的意思是「形成的，造成的」。

單字 authorization n. 授權　supervisor n. 上司　gain v. 獲得　access n. 取得的權利

136

Esham Pharmaceuticals has adopted various preventive _____ to protect its employees from possible accidents in its laboratories.
(A) benefits
(B) strengths
(C) measures
(D) amounts

Esham 製藥公司已經採取了各種的預防措施，以避免其員工在實驗室中可能發生的意外。

■ 名詞語彙

解答 (C)

文意是「採取了各種的預防措施，以避免其員工在實驗室中可能發生的意外」，所以名詞 (C) measures（設施，措施）是正確答案。(A) benefit 的意思是「利益，好處」，(B) strength 的意思是「力量，長處」，(D) amount 的意思是「量，總金額」。

單字 adopt v. 採用　preventive a. 預防的　laboratory n. 實驗室

137

Instead of closing just the stations experiencing technical difficulties, the Transit Authority chose to shut down the subway system _____.
(A) differently　(B) altogether　(C) usefully　(D) halfway

與其只關閉遭受技術困難的車站，交通當局選擇將地下鐵系統完全關閉。

■ 副詞語彙

解答 (B)

文意是「與其只關閉遭受技術困難的車站，交通當局選擇將地下鐵系統完全關閉」，所以副詞 (B) altogether（完全地）是正確答案。(A) differently 的意思是「不同地」，(C) usefully 的意思是「有用地」，(D) halfway 的意思是「中途」。

單字 technical a. 技術的　shut down phr. 關閉

138

At last month's conference, keynote speaker Dana Stewart identified the essential _____ that make a successful Web hosting business.

(A) varieties
(B) components
(C) exhibits
(D) lectures

主講人 Dana Stewart 在上個月的會議上，指出了成為一個成功的網路託管公司的重要元素。

■ 名詞語彙 　　　　　　　　　　　　　　　　　　　　　解答 (B)

文意是「成功的網路託管公司的重要元素」，所以名詞 (B) components（成分）是正確答案。(A) variety 的意思是「多樣化，種類」，(C) exhibit 的意思是「展示，展示品」，(D) lecture 的意思是「演講」。

單字 conference n. 會議　keynote speaker phr. 主要演講者　identify v. 表明，確定　component n. 成分

139

_____ Mr. Ware departs for Belgium next week, he will present his cost-cutting proposal to the logistics department at the company-wide meeting this Friday.

(A) However
(B) Once
(C) Before
(D) Prior

在 Ware 先生下禮拜前往比利時前，他將在這個星期五的全體公司同仁會議中，向物流部門提出削減成本的提案。

■ 副詞子句連接詞 時間 　　　　　　　　　　　　　　　　解答 (C)

這句話是具有必要成分 he will present ~ proposal 的完整子句，所以可以把 ____ Mr. Ware ~ next week 看成可省略的修飾語。這個修飾語是有動詞 departs 的子句形態，所以可以引出子句的副詞子句連接詞 (B) 和 (C) 都可能是正確答案。主句是未來時態，子句是現在時態，所以可以知道一定要出現的是可以用現在時態表現未來的時間的副詞子句。因此，(C) before（～之前）是正確答案。(B) Once 也可以引出時間的副詞子句，但是文意就會變成很怪的「一旦 Ware 先生下禮拜前往比利時，他將在這個星期五提出提案」。連接副詞 (A) However（不過）和形容詞 (D) Prior（之前的）都無法引出修飾語。

單字 proposal n. 提案（書）　logistics n. 物流管理，細部計畫　company-wide a. 整體的，公司全部的

140

_____ new employees found the weeklong orientation valuable and the assigned instructors both knowledgeable and professional.

(A) Most
(B) Any
(C) None
(D) Each

大多數的新員工發現為期一週的新訓很有用，且指派的指導者博學又專業。

■ 數量表達 　　　　　　　　　　　　　　　　　　　　　解答 (A)

複數名詞 new employees 前面有空格，所以可以出現在複數名詞前面的數量形容詞 (A) 和 (B) 都可能是正確答案。文意是「大多數的新員工發現為期一週的新訓有用」，所以 (A) Most（大多數）是正確答案。(B) Any 在肯定句中的意思是「任何～也」，這時候文意就會變成很怪的「任何新員工也發現了為期一週的新訓有用」。(C) None 通常作為代名詞來使用，當作形容詞來使用時，意思是「一點也～不」，跟文意不符。(D) Each 要跟單數可數名詞一起使用，所以也不是正確答案。

單字 weeklong a. 歷經一週的，一週時間的　valuable a. 有價值的，有用的　assigned a. 指派的
　　　instructor n. 指導者　knowledgeable a. 博學的

PART 6

Questions 141-143 refer to the following article.

141-143 根據下面文章的內容回答問題。

The Department of Culture has announced plans to _____

    141 (A) demolish   (B) modernize
       (C) construct   (D) repair

a cultural complex adjacent to the Widmark Sports Center on Anders Avenue over the next 12 months. The structure, which will tentatively be named the Coleman Cultural Complex, will house a theater, a musical performance facility and a library. Funded by the city's local government office in conjunction with Coleman-Winters Transnational Corporation, the _____ is expected to be completed by

    142 (A) projected   (B) project
       (C) projectile   (D) to project

September of next year.

The huge theater will seat 2,000 persons, and several performances, including the Pembroke Orchestra and the opera La Bohème, are scheduled to take place at the complex. Preparations for the library are _____ and will

    143 (A) in progress (B) progress
       (C) progression (D) progressively

soon be finalized. Updates on the date of the actual opening and schedule of events will be provided via press release in the future.

141 文化廳已宣布，將計畫在未來的十二個月內，在與 Widmark 體育中心相鄰的 Anders 大道上，構建一個文化中心。此建築物，將暫定命名為 Coleman 文化中心，將設有一個劇場，一個音樂表演設施和一座圖書館。

142 此專案由當地政府部門與 Coleman-Winters 跨國公司一起合資，預計將於明年 9 月完成。

此巨大的劇場將可容納 2000 人，且有幾場表演預定在此中心上演，包括 Pembroke 管弦樂團和歌劇「波希米亞人」。

143 圖書館的籌備工作正在進行中，且將很快定案。未來，關於實際開放日期及活動時間表的更新將透過新聞稿來提供。

單字 complex n. 綜合設施　adjacent a. 相鄰的　tentatively ad. 暫時性地　in conjunction with phr. 和～一起

141 ■ 動詞語彙 掌握全文　　　　　　　　　　　　　　　　　　　　　　　　　　　　　　解答 (C)

文意是「文化廳已宣布將計畫____一個文化中心」，所以全部的選項都可能是正確答案。當從有空格的句子中無法選擇答案時，就要先了解前後文或整篇文章的內容。在後面的句子中，提到此建築物暫定命名為 Coleman 文化中心，且未來會提供實際開放日期。由此就可以知道有個建構文化中心的計畫。因此，動詞 (C) construct（建築）是正確答案。(A) demolish 的意思是「拆除」，(B) modernize 的意思是「現代化」，(D) repair 的意思是「修理」。

142 ■ 名詞位置　　　　　　　　　　　　　　　　　　　　　　　　　　　　　　　　解答 (B)

空格是句子的主詞位置，空格前面又有定冠詞 the，所以名詞 (B) 和 (C) 都可能是正確答案。因為文意是「此專案預計將於明年 9 月完成」，所以名詞 (B) project（專案）是正確答案。如果使用 (C) projectile（發射體），文意就會變得很奇怪。因為空格前面有定冠詞 the，所以不定冠詞 to (D) to project 不會是正確答案。分詞或動詞的 (A) 不能放在主詞的位置。

143 ■ 補語位置　　　　　　　　　　　　　　　　　　　　　　　　　　　　　　　　解答 (A)

因為 be 動詞 are 後面有空格，所以可扮演形容詞的介系詞 (A)、名詞 (B) 和 (C) 都可能是正確答案。文意是「圖書館的籌備工作正在進行中，且將很快會定案」，所以 (A) in progress（進行中）是正確答案。如果使用 (B) progress（前進，進行）或 (C) progression（進行，進展）的話，主詞 Preparations 和動詞一起使用，就會讓文意變成很怪的「準備是進行」或「準備是進展」。(D) progressively（持續地）後面所修飾的是形容詞或動詞，所以不會是答案。另外，「介系詞 + 名詞」在句中可以扮演形容詞或副詞的角色。

Questions 144-146 refer to the following letter. 　　144-146 根據下面信件的內容回答問題。

Norman King Unit 502, Maze Central Albert Road, Bristol	寄件人：Norman King 地址：502 室，Maze Central，Albert 路，布里斯托爾
Dear Mr. King,	親愛的 King 先生：
You have made the right decision to lead a _____ lifestyle.	144 你已經做了過健康生活方式的正確決定。

144   (A) relaxed   (B) prosperous
            (C) healthy   (D) green

We at Bud's Gym are happy to assist you in achieving this goal. To get started, we will see you on Saturday for orientation. Please keep the enclosed membership card and present it at _____ reception counter upon your arrival.

145 (A) our   (B) your
       (C) his   (D) their

A premium membership gives you unlimited access to gym facilities and fitness classes. The card is valid at all Bud's Gym branches across the country, allowing you to work out wherever you are. As you can see, membership with Bud's Gym is an ideal way to help _____ your fitness

146 (A) fulfilling   (B) fulfill
       (C) fulfillment   (D) has fulfilled

goals.
We look forward to seeing you on your first day at the gym.

Sincerely,
Alison Hanson
Manager
Bud's Gym

在 Bud's 健身房，我們樂意協助您實現這一個目標。首先，我們將在這週六的新成員說明會上與您見面。145 請保管隨函附上的會員卡，並在您到來時出示給我們的接待櫃檯。

超值的會員身分讓您可以無限制地使用健身房的設施及健身課程。該卡適用於全國各地所有 Bud's 健身房分店，讓您無論在哪裡都可以鍛鍊身體。146 正如您可以看到的，Bud's 健身房的會員是幫助您實現健身目標的一種理想方式。

我們期待著看到您在健身房的第一天。

Alison Hanson 敬上
經理
Bud's 健身房

單字 assist v. 幫助　enclosed a. 隨函附上的　present v. 出示　unlimited a. 無限制的

144 ■ 形容詞詞彙 掌握全文 　　　　　　　　　　　　　　　　　　　　　　解答 (C)

文意是「做了過 ____ 生活方式的正確決定」，所以全部選項都可能是正確答案。當從有空格的句子中無法選擇答案時，就要先了解前後文或整篇文章的內容。後面的句子中提到 Bud's 健身房很樂意協助您，且您可以無限制地使用健身房的設施及健身課程，由此可以知道跟建康的生活有關。因此，(C) healthy（健康的）是正確答案。 (A) relaxed 的意思是「悠閒的」，(B) prosperous 的意思是「繁榮的」，(D) green 的意思則是「環保的」。

145 ■ 名詞-代名詞一致 掌握全文 　　　　　　　　　　　　　　　　　　　　解答 (A)

文意是「請保管隨函附上的會員卡，並在您到來時將它出示給 ____ 的接待櫃檯」，單從這句話來看，所有選項都可能是正確答案。當從有空格的句子中無法選擇答案時，就要先了解前後文或整篇文章的內容。寫信的人 Bud's 健身房的管理者，整篇文章都是在說明 Bud's 健身房的設施等，所以位於空格的代名詞 manager 指的也是寫信的人。因此，指示寫信人的第一人稱代名詞 (A) our 就是正確答案。

146 ■ 把原形不定詞作為受格補語的動詞 　　　　　　　　　　　　　　　　　解答 (B)

準使役動詞 help (to help) 的受格補語是原形不定詞或 to 不定詞。因此，原形不定詞 (B) fulfill（達成）就是正確答案。

SNA Summer Block Party

Southdale Neighborhood Association (SNA) invites all residents to a daylong block party on Marigold Street on the last Saturday of the month. This will be a great opportunity to _____ know your neighbors better and meet

147 (A) stick to　　(B) get to
　　(C) look up to　(D) turn to

new people in the community. A solo performance from country musician Andrea McCain will start the event and will be followed by a dance number from the Elizabeth School of the Arts students. _____, SNA chairperson Garry

148 (A) Nevertheless　　(B) For instance
　　(C) Afterward　　　(D) However

Moss will host games and other activities for adults and children. Tickets to the party cost $24 each and are _____

149 (A) inclusive　　(B) included
　　(C) including　　(D) inclusion

of dinner and drinks.
Residents who would like to attend may contact SNA secretary Lucy Lee at 555-3557 for ticket reservations and other inquiries.

SNA 夏日街區舞會

Southdale 鄰里協會（SNA）邀請所有的居民，在這月份的最後一個星期六，來參加在 Marigold 街舉行一整天的街區舞會，147 這將是一個很好的機會，讓你可以更了解你的鄰居，並遇見這社區上新的人。

本活動將由鄉村音樂家 Andrea McCain 的獨奏表演揭開序幕，接著將由伊麗莎白藝術學校的學生表演舞蹈節目，148 之後，SNA 主席 Garry Moss 將主持適合大人和小孩的遊戲和其他活動。

舞會的門票是 24 塊美金，149 包括晚餐和飲料。

想參加的居民可致電 SNA 祕書 Lucky Lee 來訂票或是查詢其他相關資訊，電話是 555-3557。

單字 daylong a. 一整天的　opportunity n. 機會　chairperson n. 主席

147 ■ 動詞語彙　　　　　　　　　　　　　　　　　　　　　　　　解答 (B)

文意是「這將是一個很好的機會，讓你可以更了解你的鄰居」，所以可以跟空格後的 know 組成 get to know（使知道～）的 (B) get to 是正確答案。(A) stick to 的意思是「堅守～」，(C) look up to 的意思是「尊敬～」，(D) turn to 的意思是「依靠～」。

148 ■ 填連接副詞 掌握上下文　　　　　　　　　　　　　　　　　　解答 (C)

空格和逗號一起出現在句首，由此可得知是連接副詞的位置。這時候需要先了解前面的句子和有空格的句子的關係，才能選出正確的答案。前面的句子中提到將由 Andrea McCain 的獨奏表演揭開序幕，有空格的句子則提到接著將由伊麗莎白藝術學校的學生表演舞蹈節目。因此，表示時間前後順序，連接兩件事情的連接副詞 (C) Afterward（那之後）是正確答案。(A) Nevertheless 的意思是「不過」，(B) For instance 的意思是「例如」，(D) However 的意思是「然而」。

149 ■ 形容詞位置　　　　　　　　　　　　　　　　　　　　　　　　解答 (A)

be 動詞 are 後面就有空格，所以形容詞 (A)、p.p. 形 (B)、-ing 形 (C)、名詞 (D) 都可能是正確答案。文意是「門票包括晚餐和飲料」，所以可以和空格前面的 be 動詞 are 和空格後面的介系詞 of 一起組成 inclusive of（包含～）的形容詞 (A) inclusive（包含）是正確答案。和空格前面的 be 動詞 are 組成被動態的 p.p. 形 (B) included 以及 -ing 形 (C) including 都無法把後面的介系詞 of dinner and drinks 當成受詞。如果使用名詞 (D)，會和主詞 Tickets 同位語化，文意就變成很怪的「票是包含」。

Questions 150-152 refer to the following memo.　　　　150-152 根據下面電郵的內容回答問題。

From: Daryl Craig <d.craig@fma.com> To: Vernice Newmark <vn@firemail.com> Subject: Auto Fair Date: May 6 Dear Ms. Newmark, Thank you for giving me an update on the final preparations for the Florida Motors Association's auto fair on Monday. I am _____ with the way you designed the booths for the car **150** (A) hesitant　　(B) concerned 　　(C) anxious　　(D) satisfied companies. I think your method of arranging them alphabetically will make them more accessible to guests. I would also like to inform you that the association's _____ 　　　　**151** (A) officials　　(B) official 　　　　　　(C) officially　　(D) offices are looking forward to the special presentations that will be given in the opening day's activities. Because of the great work you have done, the association has decided to hire your company again for its silver anniversary. The celebration _____ in July. We will talk 　　**152** (A) will be held　　(B) was held 　　　　(C) has been held　　(D) could have been held about the details of this event after the fair. In the meantime, we hope that everything runs smoothly next week. Thank you for your hard work and have a nice weekend. Sincerely, Daryl Craig Vice President Florida Motors Association	寄件人：Daryl Craig <d.craig@fma.com> 收件人：Vernice Newmark 　　　　　<vn@firemail.com> 主旨：汽車博覽會 日期：5 月 6 日 親愛的 Newmark 小姐： 謝謝妳讓我知道星期一佛羅里達州汽車協會汽車博覽會最後準備的最新狀況。**150** 我很滿意妳設計各家汽車公司展位的方式。我覺得妳按字母順序排列的方法，會讓客人更容易找到他們。 我還想告訴妳，**151** 該協會的高層都期待著開幕當天的活動將有特別的呈現方式。 因為妳做的很好，所以該協會已決定在他們二十五週年慶時繼續聘請妳的公司。**152** 慶祝活動將在 7 月舉行。我們將在博覽會後再討論此活動的細節。於此同時，我們希望下週一切順利。 謝謝你們的辛勤工作，並希望你們有一個愉快的週末。 Daryl Craig 敬上 副總裁 佛羅里達州汽車協會

單字 update n. 最新情報　association n. 協會　alphabetically ad. 照字母順序排列地　smoothly ad. 平滑地

150 ■ 形容詞語彙 掌握上下文　　　　　　　　　　　　　　　　　　　　　　　　　　　　解答 (D)

文意是「很＿＿你設計各家汽車公司展位的方式」，所有選項都可能是正確答案。當從有空格的句子中無法選擇答案時，就要先了解前後文。後面的句子中提到按字母順序排列的方法，會讓客人更容易找到他們，由此可以得知寫信的人很滿意安排展位的方式。因此，形容詞 (D) satisfied（滿意）是正確答案。(A) hesitant 的意思是「遲疑的」，(B) concerned 的意思是「擔心的」，(C) anxious 的意思是「不安的」。

151 ■ 人物名詞 vs. 事物名詞　　　　　　　　　　　　　　　　　　　　　　　　　　　　解答 (A)

that 子句中沒有主詞，動詞 are 又是複數動詞，所以名詞 (A) 和 (D) 都可能是正確答案。文意是「高層都期待特別的呈現方式」，所以人物名詞 (A) officials（高層）是正確答案。如果使用事物名詞 (D) offices（辦公室），文意就會變成很怪的「辦公室都期待特別的呈現方式」。單數名詞 (B) 不能和複數名詞 are 一起使用，副詞 (C) 則不能放在名詞的位置。

152 ■ 未來時態 掌握上下文　　　　　　　　　　　　　　　　　　　　　　　　　　　　　解答 (A)

文意是「慶祝活動將在 7 月舉行」。這時候只看有空格的句子無法選出正確時態的動詞，要先了解前後文意或整體文意才能選出正確答案。後面的句子提到在博覽會後再討論此活動的細節，由此可以知道活動是還沒發生的未來的事情。因此，未來時態 (A) will be held 是正確答案。

PART 7

Questions 153-154 refer to the following invitation.

153-154 根據下面廣告的內容回答問題。

Felicity Salon		幸福沙龍	
Where beauty is an art!		在此美容是一門藝術！	
153 Open daily:		153 每日營業時間：	
Weekdays	10 A.M. - 8 P.M.	平日	早上 10 點到晚上 8 點
Weekends	9 A.M. - 6 P.M.	週末	早上 9 點到晚上 6 點
National Holidays	11 A.M. - 5 P.M.	國定假日	早上 11 點到下午 5 點
Basic Services Offered:		**基本服務：**	
Haircut		理髮	
154-C Ladies' precision cut (starts at*)	$30	154-C 女士精緻剪髮（起價*）	$30
Men's precision cut	$20	男士精緻剪髮	$20
Blow-dry and style	$25	吹髮及造型	$25
Permanent waves (starts at*)		燙捲（起價*）	
or straightening	$100	或燙直	$100
Semi-permanent color	$30	半永久染髮	$30
European hair coloring	$60	歐洲染髮	$60
154-C *Different rates apply depending on hair length		154-C *不同的頭髮長度將有不同的收費	
More information is available on our Web site:		更多的資訊請上我們的官網：	
www.felicitysalon.com		www.felicitysalon.com	

單字 □blow-dry n. 吹乾   □straighten v. 弄直，挺直   □semi-permanent a. 半永久性的
□rate n. 價格，費用

153

When does Felicity Salon close on Mondays?	幸福沙龍星期一幾點關門？
(A) At 6 P.M.	(A) 晚上六點
(B) At 5 P.M.	(B) 下午五點
(C) At 9 P.M.	(C) 晚上九點
(D) At 8 P.M.	(D) 晚上八點

■■ 六何原則 when   解答 (D)

這是問 Felicity Salon 星期一何時（When）關門的六何問題。跟問題的核心詞語 Felicity Salon close on Mondays 相關的內容 Open Daily: Weekdays 10 A.M. - 8 P.M. 中提到平日從早上 10 點開始營業到晚上 8 點。因此，(D) At 8 P.M.是正確答案。

154

What is indicated about the ladies' precision cut?
(A) Its price includes washing.
(B) It is currently on special promotion.
(C) Its rate varies with a client's hair length.
(D) It comes free with a coloring service.

文中指出有關女士精緻剪髮的什麼事？
(A) 它的價錢包含洗髮。
(B) 它目前正在做特別的促銷。
(C) 它的價格依顧客頭髮長短變化。
(D) 若有染髮服務，則此項免費。

Not / True True 問題   解答 (C)

這是找出跟問題核心詞語 the ladies' precision cut 相關的內容後，再跟選項作對比的 Not / True 問題。 (A) 和 (B) 都是文中沒提到的內容。Ladies' precision cut (starts at*) $30 和 *Different rates apply depending on hair length 的意思是女士剪髮的價格是 30 美金起以及不同的頭髮長度將有不同的收費，跟 (C) 的內容是相同的。因此，(C) Its rate varies with a client's hair length. 是正確答案。 (D) 是文中沒提到過的內容。

換句話說

Different rates apply depending on hair length 不同的頭髮長度將有不同的收費
→ rate varies with ~ hair length 價格根據頭髮長度而不同

單字 vary v. 不同

Children to Pose as Future Selves at Little Rock Party

Charleston, October 25 – [155]In an effort to inspire children to start thinking about their future careers, the Little Rock Community Center will be holding a different kind of costume party at the end of the month.

With the theme of "My Future Self," [156-D]children between the ages of seven and nine will come dressed in costumes that show what they want to be when they grow up. Each child will also be given a chance to speak in front of an audience about their chosen profession and what they hope to achieve in their field.

Catherine Knox, the director of the community center, believes that young children should already have an idea of what they want to do later in life. "They may not fully understand the demands of a career yet, but becoming aware of it at an early age may help them establish a clear path to follow as they study in school," says Ms. Knox.

[156-A]The costume party will be held at the community center from 6 P.M. to 8 P.M. on October 30.

在小石城派對讓兒童展現自己未來的姿態

查爾斯頓，10 月 25 日 – [155]為了激發孩子們開始思考他們未來的職業生涯，小石城社區中心將在月底舉辦一場不一樣的化妝舞會。

以「未來的自己」為主題，[156-D]七歲到九歲的孩子，穿著可以展示他們長大想要成為的樣子的服飾，每個孩子也將被給予在觀眾面前談論自己所選擇的職業的機會，以及他們希望在自己的領域實現什麼。

社區中心主任 Catherine Knox 認為，年幼的孩子應該已經有他們在以後的生活想要做什麼的想法。Knox 女士說：「他們可能還沒有辦法完全理解一個職業的要求，但在幼年意識到這一點，可以幫助他們在學校學習時，建立清晰的路徑去追尋。」

[156-A]化妝舞會將於 10 月 30 日下午 6 點至晚上 8 點在社區中心舉行。

單字 □in an effort to phr. 為～努力　□inspire v. 激發，鼓舞　□costume party phr. 化妝舞會　□audience n. 觀眾　□profession n. 職業　□achieve v. 成就，達成　□establish v. 建立，設定

155

Why is the Little Rock Community Center hosting an event?
(A) To encourage children to consider possible occupations
(B) To mark the beginning of a school program
(C) To introduce a new method of teaching
(D) To celebrate the opening of a public facility

為什麼小石城社區中心要舉辦這項活動？
(A) 鼓勵兒童思考可能的職業
(B) 標明一項學校計畫的開始
(C) 引入一項新的教學方法
(D) 慶祝一項公共設施的開幕

六何原則 Why　　解答 (A)

這是問 Little Rock 社區中心為何（Why）辦活動的六何原則問題。和問題核心詞語 the Little Rock Community Center hosting an event 相關的內容是 In an effort to inspire children to start thinking about their future careers, the Little Rock Community Center will be holding a different kind of costume party。在這裡提到為了激發孩子們開始思考他們未來的職業生涯，Little Rock 社區中心將舉辦化妝舞會。因此，(A) To encourage children to consider possible occupations 是正確答案。

單字 host v. 舉辦　mark v. 紀念

What is stated about the costume party?	文中提到化妝舞會的什麼事？
(A) It will be held for an entire day.	(A) 將舉行一整天。
(B) It is sponsored by an academic institution.	(B) 它是由一個學術機構所贊助的。
(C) It will give a chance for participants to show their talents.	(C) 它會給參與者一個展示他們才華的機會。
(D) It is exclusively for a particular age group.	(D) 它針對一個特定的年齡族群。

■ **Not / True** True 問題   解答 (D)

這是找出跟問題核心詞語 the costume party 相關的內容後，再跟選項作對比的 Not / True 問題。the costume party will be held ~ from 6 P.M. to 8 P.M.中提到變裝派對是從下午 6 點開到晚上 8 點，所以 (A) 跟文意不符。 (B) 和 (C) 是文中沒有提到的內容。children between the ages of seven and nine will come dressed in costumes 中提到 7 歲到 9 歲的小孩穿著特定服裝前來，所以 (D) 跟文意相符。因此，(D) It is exclusively for a particular age group 是正確答案。

單字 exclusively ad. 專有地

Mr. Enriquez Lobbies Child Health Care Bill	Enriquez 先生遊説兒童健保法案
[157]Regional State Representative Fernando Enriquez has proposed a law aimed at mandating health insurance for the state's youth population. "Our youth are the future of this nation. This bill will provide additional protection not only for our children, but the future prosperity of our country," Enriquez said in a press release. [158-B]According to the Health Care for Young Bill, all children ages 18 and under will have free access to medical services in both private and public hospitals. Funding for the insurance will be derived from the Health Department and public assistance allowances of some legislators. [157]The bill will undergo its first reading tomorrow in the nation's capital. If signed into law, the Healthcare for Young Bill will benefit more than two million children in the country.	[157]地方州議員 Fernando Enriquez 提出了一項法案，是針對強制要求國家少年兒童人口需有健康保險。Enriquez 在一個新聞稿內説到：「我們的青年是這個國家的未來，該法案將不僅為我們的孩子提供額外的保障，而且也保障了我們國家的未來繁榮」。[158-B]根據青年健保草案，18 歲以下的所有兒童將在私立和公立醫院獲得免費的醫療服務。保險的經費將來自衛生署和一些立法委員的政府補助津貼。[157]該草案明天將在國家的首都進行一讀。如果簽署成為法律，青年健保法案將會讓全國超過兩百萬名的兒童受益。

單字 □representative n. 代表　　□mandate v. 授權　　□prosperity n. 繁榮
　　□derive v. 衍生，引出　　□public assistance phr. 政府補助　□allowance n. 補貼
　　□legislator n. 國會議員　　□reading n. （議會法案審議）讀

157

What is suggested about Fernando Enriquez? (A) He made a recent legislative proposal. (B) He is a representative of a firm. (C) He works in the medical industry. (D) He is campaigning for a government position.	文中指出 Fernando Enriquez 的什麼事？ (A) 他最近提了一個立法案。 (B) 他是一間公司的代表。 (C) 他從事醫療行業。 (D) 他正在競選一項公職。

■ 推論 詳細內容　　　　　　　　　　　　　　　　　　　　　　　　解答 (A)

這是跟問題核心詞語 Fernando Enriquez 有關的推理問題。Regional State Representative Fernando Enriquez has proposed a law 提到地方州議員 Fernando Enriquez 提出了一項法案，the bill will undergo its first reading tomorrow 又提到該法案明天將進行一讀。由此，可以推斷出 Fernando Enriquez 最近提出了法律制定案。因此，(A) He made a recent legislative proposal. 是正確答案。

換句話說

has proposed a law 提出法案 → made a ~ legislative proposal 提出法律制定案

單字 legislative a. 立法的，法律上的

158

What is mentioned about the bill? (A) It will assign more doctors to states. (B) It will grant free medical checkups. (C) It will promote disease prevention. (D) It will privatize public hospitals.	文中提到草案的什麼事？ (A) 它會分配更多的醫生到各州。 (B) 它將給予免費的體檢。 (C) 它將促進疾病的預防。 (D) 它將會民營化公立醫院。

■ Not / True True 問題　　　　　　　　　　　　　　　　　　　　　解答 (B)

這是找出跟問題核心詞語 the bill 相關的內容後，再跟選項作對比的 Not / True 問題。(A) 是文中沒有提過的內容。According to the Health Care for Young Bill, all children ages 18 and under will have free access to medical services 中提到根據青年健保草案，18 歲以下的所有兒童將獲得免費的醫療服務，跟 (B) 文意相符。因此，(B) It will grant free medical checkups. 是正確答案。(C) 和 (D) 都是文中沒提過的內容。

單字 assign v. 分配，指派　grant v. 給予，認可　prevention n. 預防　privatize v. 民營化，私營化

Questions 159-161 refer to the following notice.

159-161 根據下面公告的內容回答問題。

NOTICE: Alison Grand to Visit Pageturners

Award-winning novelist, [159-A/160-A/D/161-A]Alison Grand, will visit the Missoula branch of Pageturners on April 19 at 3 P.M. to promote her newest book, A Laugh in the Dark. She will read an excerpt from the novel which is part of her Daughters of the Summer series. Following the reading, [160-C]Ms. Grand will answer questions from the audience. [161-A]Copies of her book will be available for sale and Ms. Grand will be on hand to sign autographs at the conclusion of the event.

Ms. Grand has written more than 15 novels during her career, with many topping international bestsellers lists. [161-C]Three of her works have been made into feature films, which have also experienced financial and critical success.

For information on other events scheduled at Pageturners, visit www.pageturners.com or check out the calendar posted at our service counter.

公告：
Alison Grand 將參觀 Pageturners 書店

得獎小說家[159-A/160-A/D/161-A] Alison Grand 將在 4 月 19 日下午 3 點，訪問位於 Missoula 的 Pageturners 分店，以宣傳她的最新著作，《黑暗中的笑》。她將朗讀小說中的一段摘錄，這是她《夏季的女兒》系列的一部分。朗讀之後，[160-C]她會回答聽眾的提問。[161-A]現場將發售她的書，且 Grand 女士將在活動結束時在現場替大家親筆簽名。

Grand 女士在她的寫作生涯中寫了超過 15 本的小說，其中有許多登上國際暢銷書名單。[161-C]她的三項作品已被製作成電影，且均叫好又叫座。

若需要 Pageturners 書店其它的活動訊息，請上 www.pageturners.com 或是查看張貼在我們服務檯的行事曆。

單字 □award-winning a. 得獎的　　□novelist n. 小說家　　□excerpt n. 摘錄
　　□financial success phr. 票房的成功 □critical success phr. 好評，評論家的稱讚

159

What is stated about Ms. Grand?
(A) She will be promoting her recent work.
(B) She recently performed in a movie.
(C) She is employed at a bookstore.
(D) She will visit several Pageturners branches.

文中說明 Grand 女士的什麼事？
(A) 她將宣傳她最近的作品。
(B) 她最近在一部電影中演出。
(C) 她受雇於一家書店。
(D) 她將參訪幾家 Pageturners 書店的分店。

■ **Not / True** True 問題

解答 (A)

這是找出跟問題核心詞語 Ms. Grand 相關的內容後，再跟選項作對比的 Not / True 問題。 (A) 跟 Alison Grand, will ~ promote her newest book 中提到 Alison Grand 將宣傳她的最新著作的內容一致，所以 (A) She will be promoting her recent work. 是正確答案。 (B) (C) (D) 都是文中沒提過的內容。

換句話說
newest book 最新的書 → recent work 最近作品

單字 employ v. 雇用，使用

160

What is NOT indicated about the upcoming event?
(A) It will be held in the afternoon.
(B) It will charge a small admission fee.
(C) It will include a question and answer period.
(D) It will be held at a retail outlet.

文中沒有指出即將舉辦的活動的什麼事？
(A) 它將在下午舉行。
(B) 它將收取小額的入場費。
(C) 它將包含問答時間。
(D) 它將在一個零售店舉行。

■ **Not / True** Not 問題　　　　　　　　　　　　　　　　　　　　　　解答 (B)

這是找出跟問題核心詞語 the upcoming event 相關的內容後，再跟選項作對比的 Not / True 問題。Alison Grand will visit ~ at 3 P.M. 中提到 Alison Grand 將在下午 3 點訪問，跟 (A) 的內容相符。 (B) 是文中沒提過的內容。因此，(B) It will charge a small admission fee. 是正確答案。Ms. Grand will answer questions from the audience 中提到的 Ms. Grand 將回答聽眾的提問，跟 (C) 的內容相符。Alison Grand, will visit the Missoula branch of Pageturners ~ to promote her newest book 中提到 Alison Grand 訪問位於 Missoula 的 Pageturners 分店，以宣傳她的最新著作，跟 (D) 的內容一致。

單字 admission n. 入場　retail outlet phr. 零售店

161

What is mentioned about some of Ms. Grand's books?
(A) They are unavailable at Pageturners.
(B) They were recently revised.
(C) They were developed into films.
(D) They will be given away at the event.

文中提到 Grand 女士一些書的什麼事？
(A) 它們在 Pageturners 書店並沒有販售。
(B) 它們最近被修改。
(C) 它們被改編成電影。
(D) 它們們將在活動中被送出。

■ **Not / True** True 問題　　　　　　　　　　　　　　　　　　　　　　解答 (C)

這是找出跟問題核心詞語 Ms. Grand's books 相關的內容後，再跟選項作對比的 Not / True 問題。Alison Grand, will visit the Missoula branch of Pageturners 中提到 Alison Grand 訪問位於 Missoula 的 Pageturners 分店，Copies of her book will be available for sale 中指出將發售她的書。這些內容跟 (A) 不相符合。 (B) 是文中沒提到的內容。three of her works have been made into feature films 提到 Ms. Grand 的三項作品已被製作成電影，跟 (C) 的內容一致。因此，(C) 是正確答案。 (D) 是文中沒提到的內容。

單字 give away phr. 分發

Questions 162-164 refer to the following letter.　　　　162-164 根據下面信件的內容回答問題。

High Pitch Unit 901, Ellis Tower, Brighton, Massachusetts September 25 Dorothy Taylor Sales Director Soundbits Dear Ms. Taylor, [162]Thank you for your interest in consigning your company's products with us. [164-C]We understand you wish to supply us with violins and guitars. [162/164-C]Unfortunately, we must respectfully decline as we have just signed contracts with three other manufacturers of stringed instruments. However, [164-A/B/D]we are interested in the possibility of selling your flutes, drum kits, and keyboards. We are impressed with the quality of your products, and we believe displaying them in [163-D]our shops across the state would increase your brand's popularity in Massachusetts. We hope to discuss the matter with you sometime this week. When you are available, please call me at 555-9632. We eagerly await your response. Truly yours, Hubert Night High Pitch, Massachusetts Regional Manager	**High Pitch 公司** 901 室，埃利斯塔 布萊頓郡，麻薩諸塞州 日期：9 月 25 日 收件者：Dorothy Taylor 銷售主任 Soundbits 公司 親愛的 Taylor 女士： [162]感謝您有興趣將貴公司的產品委託給我們販賣。[164-C]我們知道您希望向我們提供小提琴和吉他。[162/164-C]不幸的是，我們必須鄭重地婉拒，因為我們剛剛才和三家弦樂器廠商簽訂合約。 然而，[164-A/B/D]我們對於出售您們的笛子、鼓組和鍵盤有興趣。我們對於您們產品的品質印象深刻，我們相信在[163-D]我們全州的商店中展示它們，將會增加您們在麻薩諸塞州的品牌知名度。 我們希望在本週能與您討論此事。當您有空時，請聯絡我 555-9632。 我們很期待您的回音。 Hubert Night 敬上 High Pitch 公司，麻薩諸塞州 區域經理

單字 □consign v. 委託　　　　□decline v. 拒絕　　　　□sign v. 簽合約
　　　□contract n. 合約　　　　□stringed instruments phr. 弦樂器 □kit v. 成套（工具或物件）
　　　□popularity n. 普及，流行　□discuss v. 討論，商議

162

Why was the letter written? (A) To end a contract (B) To turn down a proposal (C) To introduce a service (D) To cancel an order	為什麼寫這封信？ (A) 為了結束一個合約 (B) 為了拒絕一個提案 (C) 為了介紹一項服務 (D) 為了取消一個訂單

■ **找出主題** 寫文章的理由　　　　　　　　　　　　　　　　　　　　　　　　　　　　解答 (B)

這是問寫信原因，需找出文章主題的問題，所以要特別注意文章的前半部份。thank you for your interest in consigning your company's products with us. 中提到「感謝您有興趣將產品委託給我們」，接著 Unfortunately, we must respectfully decline 中又說「不幸的是，我們必須鄭重地婉拒」。因此，(B) To turn down a proposal 是正確答案。

換句話說
decline 拒絕 → turn down 拒絕

單字 introduce v. 介紹　cancel v. 取消

163

What is indicated about High Pitch?	文中指出 High Pitch 公司的什麼事？
(A) It imports musical instruments.	(A) 它進口樂器。
(B) It runs its own factory.	(B) 它有自己的工廠。
(C) It offers voice lessons.	(C) 它有提供聲樂課。
(D) It operates multiple branches.	(D) 它有多個分店在經營。

■ **Not / True** True 問題   解答 (D)

這是找出跟問題核心詞語 High Pitch 相關的內容後，再跟選項作對比的 Not / True 問題。 (A) (B) (C) 都是文中沒提過的內容。our shops across the state 提到州裡的 High Pitch 公司，跟 (D) 的內容相符。因此，(D) It operates multiple branches. 是正確答案。

單字 import v. 進口

164

What is NOT a Soundbits product that High Pitch wants to sell in its store?	下列哪一個 Soundbits 公司的產品，不是 High Pitch 公司想要在它的商店販售的？
(A) Drums	(A) 鼓
(B) Keyboards	(B) 鍵盤
(C) Guitars	(C) 吉他
(D) Flutes	(D) 笛子

■ **Not / True** Not 問題   解答 (C)

這是找出跟問題核心詞語 a Soundbits product that High Pitch wants to sell 相關的內容後，再跟選項作對比的 Not / True 問題。we are interested in the possibility of selling your flutes, drum kits, and keyboards 中提到 High Pitch 公司對出售 Soundbits 公司的笛子、鼓組和鍵盤的可能性有興趣，所以跟 (A) (B) (D) 的內容相符。We understand you wish to supply us with ~ guitars. 中雖然提到寫信者知道 Soundbits 公司希望向他們提供吉他，但是 Unfortunately, we must respectfully decline as we have just signed contracts with three other manufacturers of stringed instruments. 中指出「不幸的是，我們必須鄭重地婉拒，因為我們才剛剛和三家弦樂器廠商簽訂合約。」由此可以得知跟 (C) 的內容不相同。因此，(C) Guitars 是正確答案。

165-167 根據下面廣告的內容回答問題。

1 2 3 4 5 6 7 8 9 10

Career Specialist

(Jobs 1 out of 5) [next] [edit online profile] [home]

Application period: June 1 - October 30

[165]PetroLine Corporation

[167-A/C]Other Vacancies	[165/167-D]Credit Representative
[167-A]PR Specialists (3) Accountants (2) [167-C]Finance Analysts (4) Marketing Assistants(2)	[165]Duties • Follow up on unpaid fuel deliveries • Arrange payment terms for clients • Participate in planning debt collection measures • Document and report overdue debts that must be reported to the collection department [166-A/B/C]Qualifications • [166-A]A bachelor's degree in accounting, finance, business management, or equivalent. • [166-B]At least three years' work experience in a related industry • [166-C]Proficiency in basic computer applications • Good command of English language, both oral and written Applicants may apply by clicking the button below or by sending their résumés and references to hr@petroline.com. Previous applicants need not apply. send résumé

職涯專家

（工作 1，共 5 個）〔下一個〕
〔編輯線上個人資料〕〔首頁〕

申請日期：6 月 1 日到 10 月 30 日

[165]PetroLine 公司

[167-A/C]其他職缺	[165/167-D]信用代表
[167-A]公關專家(3) 會計(2) [167-C]財務分析師(4) 行銷助理(2)	[165]職責 • 追蹤未付款的已送燃料 • 為客戶安排付款方式 • 參與規劃收債對策 • 提供有關必須報告給收款部門的逾期債務的文件和報告 [166-A/B/C]資格 • [166-A]具有會計、金融、企業管理或同等學歷之學士學位 • [166-B]至少有三年在相關產業的工作經驗 • [166-C]熟練基礎的電腦應用程式 • 良好的英文口語及寫作能力 申請人可以通過點擊下面的按鈕或發送自己的履歷及推薦函到 hr@petroline.com。之前的申請者無需申請。 送履歷

單字
- □ specialist n. 專家
- □ accountant n. 會計師
- □ credit representative phr. 信用代表
- □ arrange v. 處理
- □ measure n. 措施
- □ equivalent n. 等值的
- □ command n. （語言）能力，應用力
- □ previous a. 之前的

- □ vacancy n. 空間，空缺
- □ analyst n. 分析師

- □ terms n. 條件
- □ overdue a. 超過期限的
- □ proficiency n. 精通，熟練

- □ PR (public relations) phr. 公關

- □ follow up phr. 採取後續措施
- □ debt n. 負債
- □ bachelor's degree phr. 學士學位
- □ application n. 使用，應用程式
- □ reference n. 推薦書

165

What is suggested about PetroLine?	文中指出有關 PetroLine 的什麼事？
(A) It provides loans to clients.	(A) 它提供貸款給客戶。
(B) It delivers fuel to customers.	(B) 它運送燃料給客戶。
(C) It recently underwent expansion.	(C) 它最近進行了擴展。
(D) It provides training to new staff.	(D) 它提供新員工的培訓。

■ **推論** 詳細內容
解答 (B)

這是跟問題核心詞語 PetroLine 有關的推理問題。「PetroLine Corporation」，「Credit Representative」，「Duties, Follow up on unpaid fuel deliveries」中提到 PetroLine 公司的信用代表的職責中有一項是追蹤未付款的已送燃料，由此可以推理出 PetroLine 公司有在運送燃料。因此，(B) It delivers fuel to customers. 是正確答案。

單字 loan n. 借貸

166

What is NOT a requirement for the job?	什麼不是這份工作的要求？
(A) A college diploma	(A) 大學文憑。
(B) A degree of experience	(B) 一定的經驗。
(C) A familiarity with computers	(C) 熟悉電腦。
(D) A willingness to travel	(D) 願意出差。

■ **Not / True** Not 問題
解答 (D)

這是找出跟問題核心詞語 a requirement for the job 相關的內容後，再跟選項作對比的 Not / True 問題。Qualifications 的 A bachelor's degree 提到需要學士學位，跟 (A) 的內容一致。Qualifications 的 At least three years' work experience 中提到至少有三年的工作經驗，跟 (B) 的內容一致。Qualifications 的 Proficiency in basic computer applications 中提到熟練基礎的電腦應用程式，跟 (C) 的內容一致。 (D) 是文中沒提到的內容，所以 (D) A willingness to travel 是正確答案。

單字 diploma n. 學位   familiarity n. 熟悉，親近

167

According to the advertisement, what is NOT a position that needs to be filled?	根據廣告，哪一個不是需要徵人的職缺？
(A) PR Specialist	(A) 公關專家
(B) Account Manager	(B) 會計經理
(C) Finance Analyst	(C) 財務分析師
(D) Credit Representative	(D) 信用代表

■ **Not / True** Not 問題
解答 (B)

這是找出跟問題核心詞語 a position that needs to be filled 相關的內容後，再跟選項作對比的 Not / True 問題。Other Vacancies 的 PR Specialists (3) 和 Finance Analysts (4) 中的其他空缺有公關專家和財務分析師，跟 (A) 及 (C) 的內容相符。 (B) 是文中沒提到的內容，所以 (B) Account Manager 是正確答案。Credit Representative 中說明信用代表的職務和所需要的條件、申請方法，所以和 (D) 的內容相同。

換句話說
a position that needs to be filled 需要徵人的位置 → Vacancies 空缺

單字 account n. 會計

Questions 168-172 refer to the following article.

168-172 根據下面文章的內容回答問題。

Local Hospital to Have Better Facilities

AKRON, Ohio, August 14 – [168]The Margaret Labonte Memorial Hospital will soon have improved facilities, as its board of directors finally approved a proposal to expand the 150-bed hospital in order to treat and accommodate more patients.

[170]A groundbreaking ceremony and press conference will be held behind the main building of the hospital along Rickshaw Avenue on Wednesday, August 20, at 10 A.M.

Patricia Mellencamp, the hospital administrator, believes that the additional 30,000 square feet of space will bring more success and growth not only for their health professionals and staff but also to their medical programs.

"[171]Our hospital is known for its wide range of surgical treatments for various conditions. In addition, our team of well-respected doctors attracts patients who seek quality health care," says Ms. Mellencamp. "Patients will no longer need to go to other hospitals across or outside the state to seek medical treatment."

[172-A/D]The project will provide the hospital eight new operating rooms with state-of-the-art medical equipment, 30 additional patient rooms, and an outpatient surgery waiting area. All these facilities will be housed in a new building designated as the Outpatient Surgery Center. The construction of the surgery center will start in September and is estimated to last a year and half. [172-B]A new parking lot will also be completed within the same timeframe.

The Margaret Labonte Memorial Hospital was established 30 years ago and now has about 600 employees. It has been providing medical care to the residents of Akron and surrounding communities of Cuyahoga Falls, Tallmadge, Portage Lakes, and Hudson. The hospital is also affiliated with the Ohio Health Foundation, a non-profit organization dedicated to giving free medical health care to low-income families several times a year.

當地的醫院有更好的設施

俄亥俄州阿克倫城，8 月 14 日 – [168] 瑪格麗特拉布隆特紀念醫院將很快擁有更好的設施，為了要治療與容納更多病患，董事會終於通過擴大這間有 150 張病床的醫院的提案。

[170]開工儀式暨記者會將在 8 月 20 日星期三上午 10 點在醫院主樓後面的 Rickshaw 街舉行。

醫院管理者 Patricia Mellencamp 認為，額外 30000 平方英尺的空間，不僅將為他們的醫療專業人員和工作人員帶來更多的成功和成長，他們的醫療計畫亦是如此。

Mellencamp 女士說到：「[171]我們醫院以廣泛的手術治療各種疾病而聞名。此外，我們的團隊有備受推崇的醫生來吸引追求高品質的醫療服務的病人。且病人將不再需要在其他州內或是跨州的醫院來尋求醫療服務。」

[172-A/D]該計畫將提供醫院八間新的配有最先進醫療設備的手術室，30 間額外的病房以及門診手術等候區。所有的這些設施將安置於一棟作為門診外科中心的新大樓。外科中心的建設將在 9 月開始，預計持續一年半，[172-B]一個新的停車場也將在同一時限內完成。

瑪格麗特拉布隆特紀念醫院建於三十年前，且現在約有六百名員工，它提供了阿克倫城居民和周邊社區的醫療保健，周邊社區包含 Cuyahoga Falls、Tallmadge、Portage Lakes 以及 Hudson，該醫院也隸屬於俄亥俄州健康基金會，此非營利性組織的基金會致力於為低收入家庭每年提供數次的免費醫療保健服務。

單字 □memorial a. 紀念的　□improve v. 改善　□board n. 董事會
　　 □accommodate v. 容納　□groundbreaking ceremony phr. 動土典禮
　　 □press conference phr. 記者會　□administrator n. 管理者　□surgical a. 外科的
　　 □seek v. 探索　□state-of-the-art a. 最先進的　□outpatient n. 門診病人
　　 □house v. 搬進去，容納　□timeframe n. 時間表　□affiliate v. 隸屬，聯繫
　　 □foundation n. 基金會　□non-profit a. 非營利的

What is suggested about the hospital?	文中指出有關醫院的什麼事？
(A) It concluded a construction project.	(A) 它完成了一項建案。
(B) It is transferring to another location.	(B) 它將轉移到另一個位置。
(C) It is taking steps to improve its services.	(C) 它正採取措施以改善其服務。
(D) Its clinic plans to hire additional employees.	(D) 其門診計畫增聘員工。

■ 推論 詳細內容　　　　　　　　　　　　　　　　　　　　　　　　　　　　解答 (C)

這是跟問題核心詞語 the hospital 有關的推理問題。the Margaret Labonte Memorial Hospital will soon have improved facilities ~ in order to treat and accommodate more patients. 中提到 Margaret Labonte 紀念醫院將很快擁有更好的設施，以治療和容納更多的患者。由此可以推斷出醫院目前為了改善服務準備中。因此，(C) It is taking steps to improve its services. 是正確答案。

單字 take step phr. 採取措施

The word "conditions" in paragraph 3, line 7, is closest in meaning to	在第三段的第七行中「conditions」一字的意思最接近
(A) terms	(A) 用語
(B) factors	(B) 因素
(C) environments	(C) 環境
(D) ailments	(D) 疾病

■ 同義詞　　　　　　　　　　　　　　　　　　　　　　　　　　　　　　　解答 (D)

包含 conditions 的句子 Our hospital is known for its wide range of surgical treatments for various conditions. 中 conditions 是使用「疾病」這個意思。因此，同樣具有「疾病」這個意思的 (D) ailments 是正確答案。

What will happen on August 20?	8 月 20 日將發生什麼事？
(A) An event will take place in a nearby city.	(A) 附近的城市將舉行一個活動。
(B) The beginning of a project will be celebrated.	(B) 將慶祝一個計畫的開始。
(C) A series of medical training programs will begin.	(C) 將展開一系列的醫療培訓課程。
(D) A new hospital building will be opened.	(D) 將開放一棟新的醫院建築。

■ 六何原則 What　　　　　　　　　　　　　　　　　　　　　　　　　　　解答 (B)

這是問 8 月 20 日發生什麼（What）的六何原則問題。跟問題核心詞語 August 20 有關的 A groundbreaking ceremony and press conference will be held ~ on Wednesday, August 20 中提到開工儀式暨記者會將在 8 月 20 日舉行。因此，(B) The beginning of a project will be celebrated. 是正確答案。

單字 take place phr. 發生　　nearby a. 附近的

171

According to the article, what is the hospital known for?	根據文章，此醫院以什麼聞名？
(A) Advanced medical equipment	(A) 先進的醫療儀器
(B) Quality outpatient care	(B) 優質的門診服務
(C) Diverse health departments	(C) 多樣化的醫療部門
(D) Treatments involving surgery	(D) 包括手術的治療

■ 六何原則 What　　　　　　　　　　　　　　　　　　　　　　　　　　　解答 (D)

這是問醫院以什麼（what）聞名的六何原則問題。跟問題核心詞語 the hospital known for 相關的 Our hospital is known for its wide range of surgical treatments for various conditions. 中提到「我們醫院以廣泛的手術治療各種疾病而聞名。」因此，(D) Treatments involving surgery 是正確答案。

單字 advanced a. 先進的　diverse a. 多樣的

172

What is NOT being added to the hospital?	醫院將不會加入哪一項？
(A) Surgery rooms	(A) 手術房
(B) Parking spaces	(B) 停車位
(C) A pharmacy counter	(C) 領藥櫃台
(D) A waiting area	(D) 等候區

■ Not / True Not 問題　　　　　　　　　　　　　　　　　　　　　　　　解答 (C)

這是找出跟問題核心詞語 added to the hospital 相關的內容後，再跟選項作對比的 Not / True 問題。the project will provide the hospital eight new operating rooms ~ and an outpatient surgery waiting area. 中提到該計畫將提供醫院八間新手術室和門診手術等候區，跟 (A) 和 (B) 的內容相同。A new parking lot will also be completed 中提到新的停車場將完成，跟 (B) 的內容一致。 (C) 是文中沒提過的內容。因此，(C) A pharmacy counter 是正確答案。

單字 pharmacy n. 藥局

NOTICE TO ALL RESIDENTS
May 6

In an effort to conserve resources and ensure a steady supply of drinking water for residents, [173]the Helena City Government will replace old water lines on Queensville Boulevard. [174]The three-week project will start on Thursday, June 20. The outer lanes of the boulevard will be closed, as the excavation and replacement of water pipes will be done on both sides of the road.

In this regard, [175-A/C/D/176]motorists regularly passing along Queensville are requested to take detours during this time. Signs to Canine Lane, Jostein Road, and Amerbliss Avenue will be put up on June 19. [176]Those who still wish to take Queensville should expect heavy congestion from Mondays to Fridays between 8 A.M. and 5 P.M. Officers will be assigned to the area and the surrounding roadways to ensure smooth traffic flow.

Additional details about the project may be found by logging on to www.helenapublicworks.com.

Thank you for your cooperation.

Sincerely,

Carmen Boyle
Director of the Department of Transit
Helena City Government

致全體居民
5 月 6 日

為了節約資源以及確保穩定供應居民飲用水，[173]Helena 市政府將更換 Queensville 大道的舊水管，[174]為期三週的工程將在 6 月 20 日星期四開始，大道的外側車道將被關閉，因為水管的開挖和更換將在道路的兩側進行。

在這方面，[175-A/C/D/176]經常路過 Queensville 的汽車駕駛請在此期間繞道而行，Canine 巷、Jostein 路和 Amerbliss 大道的標誌將在 6 月 19 日張貼出來。[176]仍然想要走 Queensville 的人應預料到星期一至星期五上午 8 點及下午 5 點，會有嚴重的交通堵塞，警察會被分配到該區域及周邊道路，以確保交通暢順。

關於該工程更多的詳情，可透過登錄下列網址得知：www.helenapublicworks.com。

謝謝您的合作

Carmen Boyle 敬上
交通部主任
Helena 市政府

單字　□in an effort to phr. 為～努力　□conserve v. 保護　□steady a. 持續的，平穩的
　　　□replace v. 更換　□water line phr. 水管　□outer a. 外廓的，外部的
　　　□lane n. 車道　□excavation n. 開挖　□in this regard phr. 關於這一點
　　　□motorist n. 開車的人　□regularly ad. 有規律地　□detour n. 繞道
　　　□still ad. 依舊　□heavy congestion phr. 交通堵塞　□assign v. 分配

173

What is the purpose of the notice?
(A) To request drainage system maintenance
(B) To announce an upcoming repair project
(C) To order road safety equipment
(D) To propose a construction plan

通知的目的為何？
(A) 要求維修排水系統
(B) 宣布即將到來的維修工程
(C) 訂購道路安全設備
(D) 提出一個建設方案

■ 找出主題 目的　　　　　　　　　　　　　　　　　　　　　　　　　　　　解答 (B)

這是問公告目的，找主題的問題，所以要特別留意文章的前面部分。the Helena City Government will replace old water lines on Queensville Boulevard 中提到 Helena 市政府將更換 Queensville 大道的舊水管，之後公告跟工程相關的詳細資訊。因此，(B) To announce an upcoming repair project 是正確答案。

單字 drainage n. 排水　upcoming a. 即將到來的

174

When is the project scheduled to begin?	工程計畫什麼時候開始？
(A) On a Monday	(A) 星期一
(B) On a Tuesday	(B) 星期二
(C) On a Thursday	(C) 星期四
(D) On a Friday	(D) 星期五

■ 六何原則 When　　　　　　　　　　　　　　　　　　　　　　　　　　　　　解答 (C)

這是問工程預計何時（When）開始的六何原則問題。跟問題核心詞語 the project scheduled to begin 相關的 the three-week project will start on Thursday 中提到為期三週的工程將在星期四開始。因此，(C) On a Thursday 是正確答案。

單字 be scheduled to phr. 預計

175

What is NOT an alternate route mentioned in the letter?	何者不是信中提到的替代道路？
(A) Amerbliss Avenue	(A) Amerbliss 大道
(B) Bellbay Avenue	(B) Bellbay 大道
(C) Jostein Road	(C) Jostein 路
(D) Canine Lane	(D) Canine 巷

■ Not / True Not 問題　　　　　　　　　　　　　　　　　　　　　　　　　　解答 (B)

這是找出跟問題核心詞語 an alternate route 相關的內容後，再跟選項作對比的 Not / True 問題。motorists ~ are requested to take detours ~. Signs to Canine Lane, Jostein Road, and Amerbliss Avenue will be put up 中提到請開車的人繞路而行，且到 Canine 巷、Jostein 路和 Amerbliss 大道的標誌將張貼出來。這些跟 (A) (C) (D) 的內容一致。(B) 是文中沒提過的內容。因此，(B) Bellbay Avenue 是正確答案。

單字 alternate route phr. 替代道路

176

What is indicated about Queensville Boulevard?	文中指出有關 Queensville 大道的什麼事？
(A) It is connected to a major highway.	(A) 它連接到一個主要的高速公路。
(B) It is often flooded.	(B) 它經常淹水。
(C) It will remain open to drivers.	(C) 它會繼續開放給開車的人。
(D) It needs new road signs.	(D) 它需要新的路標。

■ 推論 詳細內容　　　　　　　　　　　　　　　　　　　　　　　　　　　　　解答 (C)

這是跟問題核心詞語 Queensville Boulevard 有關的推理問題。motorists regularly passing along Queensville are requested to take detours 中要求經常路過 Queensville 的開車的人繞道而行，之後 those who still wish to take Queensville should expect heavy congestion 中又說仍然想走 Queensville 的人應預期會有嚴重的交通堵塞。由此可以推斷出 Queensville 持續開放給開車的人行駛。因此，(C) It will remain open to drivers. 是正確答案。

單字 flood v. 淹沒　remain v. 維持　road sign phr. 道路號誌

Questions 177-180 refer to the following letter.

177-180 根據下面報告的內容回答問題。

BOARD MEETING SUMMARY REPORT:

Since [177-B]the Rowers Foundation was established in 1960, we have accepted financial support for our scholarship programs. However, [178]donations to the foundation have been diminishing over the past months due to economic constraints affecting our corporate benefactors. If this continues, the foundation will be incapable of going ahead with our scheduled projects for next year.

During the foundation's quarterly board meeting on Friday September 30, the chairperson proposed to temporarily stop accepting new scholars and funding overseas study programs. However, a majority of the board members disagreed with the proposal, saying it would not be the best solution to the problem. Thus, instead of limiting grants, the board has decided to seek aid from private individuals. [179]The board plans to encourage executives and young professionals to sponsor a scholar's education by donating a portion of their monthly earnings. This campaign would be carried out in major business districts across the country. Apart from this, the board is considering accepting contributions and selling items on the Rowers Foundation Web site to generate additional funds.

Rowers will continue to solicit funding from corporate bodies, but is hopeful about the proposed funding methods. Public relations director Michelle Depuis says "We are counting on these solutions to generate enough money to bring the level of scholarships up to where it was previously."

董事會會議摘要報告

[177-B]自從 Rowers 基金會於 1960 年成立，我們一直在財政上資助獎學金計畫，然而，[178]在過去的幾個月內，由於經濟緊縮而影響我們的企業捐贈者，對基金會的捐款逐漸減少。如果這種情況持續下去，基金會將無法進行我們明年預定的計畫。

在上週五 9 月 30 日的基金會每季會議中，主席建議暫時停止接受新的獎學金獲得者和停止資助留學計畫，然而，大多數的董事會成員不同意這項提案，表明這不會是問題的最佳解決方案，所以，與其限制獎學金，董事會已決定向私人尋求協助，[179]董事會研擬鼓勵高階主管和年輕專業人士透過捐贈每月其收入的一部分，來贊助獎學金獲得者的教育，該活動將在全國各主要商業區進行，除此之外，董事會正在考慮接受捐款和在 Rowers 基金會的網頁上販賣物品來募集額外的資金。

Rowers 基金會將繼續從公司機構徵求資金，但對於所提出的募集資金的方法滿懷希望，公關部主任 Michelle Depuis 說：「我們期望這些解決方案，能夠募集足夠的資金，將獎學金計畫維持在之前的水平」。

單字
- □support n. 支援
- □diminish v. 減少
- □incapable of phr. 不能～
- □propose v. 提案
- □solution n. 解決對策
- □encourage v. 鼓勵
- □district n. 地區，區域

- □scholarship n. 獎學金
- □constraint n. 限制
- □board meeting phr. 董事會會議
- □temporarily ad. 暫時地
- □grant n. 補貼
- □portion n. 一部分
- □generate v. 產生

- □donation n. 捐獻
- □benefactor n. 支援者
- □chairperson n. 主席
- □a majority of phr. 多數
- □aid n. 幫助，救助
- □carry out phr. 進行
- □solicit v. 要求

177

What is mentioned about Rowers Foundation?
(A) It owns a university.
(B) It was founded in 1960.
(C) It has been raising funds through a store.
(D) It employs young executives.

文中提到 Rowers 基金會的什麼事？
(A) 它擁有一間大學。
(B) 它成立於 1960 年。
(C) 它透過一個商店來募集資金。
(D) 它聘用年輕的主管。

■ **Not / True** True 問題　　　　　　　　　　　　　　　　　　　　　　　　　　　　　　解答 (B)

這是找出跟問題核心詞語 Rowers 基金會相關的內容後，再跟選項作對比的 Not / True 問題。(A) 是文中沒提到的內容。the Rowers Foundation was established in 1960 中提到 Rowers 基金會成立於 1960 年，和 (B) 的內容一致。因此，(B) It was founded in 1960. 是正確答案。(C) (D) 都是文中沒提到的內容。

換句話說
established 成立 → founded 成立

178

What issue does the foundation face?	基金會所面臨的問題是什麼？
(A) It does not have sufficient funds.	(A) 它沒有足夠的資金。
(B) It has too many applicants.	(B) 它有太多的申請者。
(C) Its Web site is under repair.	(C) 它的網頁正在維修。
(D) Its chairperson resigned.	(D) 它的主席辭職了。

■ 六何原則 What　　　　　　　　　　　　　　　　　　　　　　　　　　　　　　　　解答 (A)

這是問基金會面臨什麼（What）問題的六何原則問題。跟問題核心詞語 issue ~ the foundation face 相關的內容 donations to the foundation have been diminishing over the past months 中在過去的幾個月內，對基金會的捐款減少。接著，If this continues, the foundation will be incapable of going ahead with our scheduled projects for next year. 中又說如果這種情況持續下去，基金會將無法進行明年的計畫。因此，(A) It does not have sufficient funds. 是正確答案。

單字 face v. 面臨　　sufficient a. 充分的　　applicant n. 申請者　　resign v. 辭職

179

How does the board plan to solve the problem?	董事會計畫如何解決這個問題？
(A) By seeking help from executives	(A) 向主管尋求協助
(B) By decreasing scholarship grants	(B) 減少獎學金
(C) By advertising programs online	(C) 在線上打廣告
(D) By reorganizing the board of directors	(D) 重新組織董事會

■ 六何原則 How　　　　　　　　　　　　　　　　　　　　　　　　　　　　　　　　解答 (A)

這是問董事會怎樣（How）解決問題的六何原則問題。跟問題核心詞語 the board plan to solve the problem 相關的 the board plans to encourage executives ~ to sponsor a scholar's education by donating a portion of their monthly earnings. 中提到董事會研擬鼓勵公司主管透過捐贈每月其收入的一部分，來贊助獎學金得主的教育。因此，(A) By seeking help from executives 是正確答案。

單字 reorganize v. 重新組織，再編組　　board of directors phr. 董事會

180

The phrase "carried out" in paragraph 2, line 7 is closest in meaning to	在第二段的第七行中「carried out」這個片語的意思最接近：
(A) moved away	(A) 搬走
(B) conducted	(B) 進行
(C) held over	(C) 暫緩
(D) illustrated	(D) 說明

■ 同義詞　　　　　　　　　　　　　　　　　　　　　　　　　　　　　　　　　　　解答 (B)

包含 carried out 的句子 this campaign would be carried out in major business districts across the country. 中的 carried out 是「施行」的意思。因此，意思也是「施行」的 (B) conducted 是正確答案。

例文1

Zoon Health and Fitness Club

185-APamposh Deewani　　　　　　　　　　November 4
Unit 507, Jadwali Apartments
Langu Road, 185-AMumbai 400 001

Dear Ms. Deewani,

We hope that over the past 12 months you have found your membership at Zoon Health and Fitness Club to be a worthwhile investment. In the future, you can rest assured that we will continue with our commitment to providing excellent services to help our valued members stay fit and healthy.

Consequently, 181we are providing reduced rates to those who renew their memberships on or before December 31.

MEMBERSHIP TYPE	SPECIAL RATE
Student	$433.50
183Individual	$493.00
Couple	$943.50
Corporate(seven or more)	$454.75/person

Enclosed you will find a membership renewal form. We strongly encourage you to renew now so that you are eligible for this limited time offer to continue enjoying the advantages provided to Zoon members. You can send the completed form to our office either by fax or mail, or you can submit it at the front desk of our center.

If you have questions or concerns, please do not hesitate to contact us at +91-22-555-6801 or at custserv@zoonclub.com.

Sincerely yours,

182Norman Misri
Membership Coordinator

例文2

To: <custserv@zoonclub.com>
From: Pamposh Deewani <pdeewani@ganjumail.com>

184Date: January 28
Subject: Member ID 91211

To whom it may concern,

184I called your office on January 21 to ask for a temporary suspension of my membership because 185-AI'm leaving for Copenhagen next week and won't be back until February 25. I was told then that my request would be processed in three business days, but it has already been a week and I still haven't heard back from anyone.

185-CI have been a Zoon member for the past two years and have always been happy with your center. You have

---

Zoon 健身俱樂部

185-APamposh Deewani　　　　　　11 月 4 日
507 室，Jadwali 公寓，
Langu 路，185-A孟買 400001

親愛的 Deewani 女士：

我們希望在過去的十二個月中，您已發現您成為 Zoon 健身俱樂部的會員是一項值得的投資。在未來，您可以放心，我們將繼續致力於提供卓越服務的承諾，幫助我們尊貴的會員保持體態和健康。

因此，181我們現在正提供較優惠的價格給那些在 12 月 31 日前續約的會員。

會員身分種類	特價
學生	$433.50
183個人	$493.00
夫妻	$943.50
公司（七人以上）	$454.75 / 每人

隨函附上會員續約表格，我們強烈建議您現在就續約，讓您有資格獲得這個限時優惠，讓您繼續享受提供給 Zoon 會員的好處，您可以通過傳真或郵寄填妥的表格到我們的辦公室，或者您也可以在我們中心臨櫃繳交。

如果您有問題或疑慮，請隨時與我們聯繫，電話是 + 91-22-555-6801，或是電子郵件：custserv@zoonclub.com。

182Norman Misri 上
會員服務專員

收件者：<custserv@zoonclub.com>
寄件者：Pamposh Deewani
　　　　　<pedeewani@ganjumail.com>
184日期：1 月 28 日
主題：會員編號 91211

給相關負責人：

184我在 1 月 21 日打電話到您的辦公室，要求暫停我的會員資格，因為185-A我下週要去哥本哈根，直到 2 月 25 日才會回來。當時有人告訴我，我的要求會在三個工作日內處理，但已經一個星期了，我還沒有接到任何的回應。

185-C 在過去兩年中，我一直是 Zoon 的成員，並一直很滿意您們中心，你們有

competent fitness instructors and state-of-the-art equipment and facilities. That was why ^{185-D}I decided to renew my membership. If you check your records, you will see that ^{183/185-B/D}I faxed the form to your office in December and transferred $493 through my bank. So, I would really appreciate it if you could attend to my concern as quickly as possible and notify me regarding the status of my request before my departure. Thank you.

Pamposh Deewani

稱職的健身教練和最先進的設備和環境，這就是為什麼^{185-D}我決定續約我的會員資格，如果您檢查您的記錄，^{183/185-B/D}您就會看到我在 12 月就將表格傳真到您的辦公室，並透過我的銀行轉了$493。如果您能盡快處理我的要求，我將會很感激您，並請在我離開前通知我處理的狀態。謝謝您。

Pamposh Deewani

例文 1 單字 □worthwhile a. 有價值的　　□investment n. 投資
　　　　　　□rest assured phr. 可以相信的，可以放心的　　　　　　□commitment n. 承諾
　　　　　　□valued a. 重要的，貴重的　□rate n. 費用　　　　　□renewal n. 更新
　　　　　　□submit v. 提出　　　　□hesitate v. 猶豫　　　　　□contact v. 聯絡

例文 2 單字 □temporary a. 暫時的　□suspension n. 停止，中止　□request n. 要求（事項）
　　　　　　□process v. 處理　　　□competent a. 有能力的，有競爭力的
　　　　　　□state-of-the-art a. 最尖端的 □transfer v. 轉帳，調動　□attend to phr. 處理～
　　　　　　□notify v. 告知　　　□status n. 狀態，（進行中的）情況 □departure n. 出發，離開

181

Why was the letter written?	為什麼要寫這封信？
(A) To publicize new operating hours	(A) 宣傳新的營業時間
(B) To announce special renewal rates	(B) 宣布特別的續約費用
(C) To follow up on some unpaid bills	(C) 追蹤一些未付的賬單
(D) To promote a new facility	(D) 宣傳一項新的設施

■ **找出主題** 寫文章的理由　　　　　　　　　　　　　　　　　　　　　　　解答 (B)

這是問寫信原因的找主題問題，所以要了解第一封信的內容。特別要注意的是信的中間部分提到跟主題相關的內容。we are providing reduced rates to those who renew their memberships on or before December 31 中提到「我們現在正提供較低的價格給那些在 12 月 31 日前續約的會員」，接著又說明了會員身分種類和與之對應的價錢。因此，(B) To announce special renewal rates 是正確答案。

單字 publicize v. 公告　operating hours phr. 營業時間　follow up on phr. 後續處理　unpaid a. 未付的
　　　promote v. 宣傳

182

What is indicated about Mr. Misri?	文中指出 Misri 先生的什麼事？
(A) His business license has expired.	(A) 他的營業執照已經過期。
(B) He is an athletic trainer.	(B) 他是一位運動教練。
(C) He lives in Jadwali Apartments.	(C) 他住在 Jadwali 公寓。
(D) He works for a fitness center.	(D) 他在一家健身中心工作。

■ **推論** 詳細內容　　　　　　　　　　　　　　　　　　　　　　　　　　　解答 (D)

這是跟問題核心詞語 Mr. Misri 有關的推理問題。因此，要確定的是 Mr. Misri 所寫的第一封信的內容。從信中的 Norman Misri, Membership Coordinator 可以知道 Norman Misri 是會員服務專員，整封信的內容都是在說明的健身俱樂部會員續約的內容。由此可以推斷出 Mr. Misri 是健身俱樂部會員續約的負責人。因此，(D) He works for a fitness center. 是正確答案。

單字 license n. 營業執照

183

| Which type of membership did Ms. Deewani request?
(A) Individual
(B) Corporate
(C) Student
(D) Couple | Deewani 女士申請的是哪一種類型的會員？
(A) 個人
(B) 公司
(C) 學生
(D) 夫妻 |

■ 六何原則 聯結問題　　　　　　　　　　　　　　　　　　　　　　　　　解答 (A)

這是要把兩封信的內容綜合起來才能找出答案的問題。問題核心 type of membership ~ Ms. Deewani request 中提到 Ms. Deewani 問哪種（Which）類型的會員，由此可先知道第二封信是 Ms. Deewani 所寫的。

第二封信中的 I faxed the form to your office in December and transferred $493 through my bank 中提到「我將表格傳真到您的辦公室，並透過我的銀行轉了 $493」。可是這裡並沒有說明 $493 的會員類型是哪一種。不過，第一封信中的「Individual, $493.00」中指出個人會員是 $493.00。

把「Ms. Deewani 將表格傳真到辦公室，並透過銀行轉了$493」和「個人會員是 $493.00」這兩個內容綜合起來，就可以知道 Ms. Deewani 是申請了個人會員。因此，(A) Individual 是正確答案。

184

| How did Ms. Deewani contact Zoon about her suspension request?
(A) By fax
(B) By mail
(C) By phone
(D) By e-mail | 關於資格暫停的要求，Deewani 女士以什麼方式連絡 Zoon？
(A) 傳真
(B) 信件
(C) 電話
(D) 電郵 |

■ 六何原則 How　　　　　　　　　　　　　　　　　　　　　　　　　　解答 (C)

這是問 Ms. Deewani 的暫停要求是怎樣（How）跟 Zoon 的六何原則問題。跟問題核心詞語 Ms. Deewani contact Zoon about her suspension request 相關的內容是 Ms. Deewani 所寫的第二封信。這封信中的 I called your office ~ to ask for a temporary suspension of my membership 中提到 Ms. Deewani 打電話到辦公室要求暫停會員資格。因此，(C) By phone 是正確答案。

185

| What is NOT stated about Ms. Deewani?
(A) She is going on an overseas trip.
(B) She submitted her renewal form in person.
(C) She has been satisfied with Zoon's services.
(D) She updated her membership before December 31. | 文中沒有提到有關 Deewani 女士的哪件事？
(A) 她打算到國外旅行
(B) 她親自繳交續約的表格。
(C) 她一直對於 Zoon 的服務感到滿意。
(D) 她在 12 月 31 日前更新了她的會員。 |

■ Not / True Not 問題　　　　　　　　　　　　　　　　　　　　　　　解答 (B)

這是找出跟問題核心詞語 Ms. Deewani 相關的內容後，再跟選項作對比的 Not / True 問題。因此，Ms. Deewani 收到的信和 Ms. Deewani 寄出的信都要確認。第二封信中的 I'm leaving for Copenhagen next week 提到 Ms. Deewani 下週要去哥本哈根。而由第一封信中的「Pamposh Deewani」、「Mumbai」可以知道 Ms. Deewani 目前正在孟買。由此可以判斷 Ms. Deewani 將要去國外。因此，跟 (A) 的內容是相符的。第二封信中 I faxed the form 提到 Ms. Deewani 將表格傳真了，所以跟 (B) 的內容不一樣。因此，(B) She submitted her renewal form in person 是正確答案。第二封信中的 I have been a Zoon member ~ and have always been happy with your center. 提到 Ms. Deewani 一直是 Zoon 的成員，並總是感到很滿意。因此，跟 (C) 的內容相符。第二封信中的 I decided to renew my membership 中提到「我決定續約我的會員資格」，接著 I faxed the form to your office in December and transferred $493 through my bank 中又說 Ms. Deewani 在 12 月就將表格傳真了，且通過銀行轉了 $493。因此，跟 (D) 的內容相符。

單字 overseas a. 國外的　in person phr. 親自　satisfy v. 使滿意　update v. 更新

Questions 186-190 refer to the following e-mails.

例文1

To: Soledad Vasquez
    <manager@confianzacatering.com>
From: Javier Rivera
    <jay.rivera@virtuosoengineering.com>
Date: November 18
Subject: Annual Company Gala

Dear Ms. Vasquez,

186We are interested in hiring Confianza Catering for our annual company gala. The event is set for December 21, from 6 P.M. to 10 P.M., in our building's conference room. All of Virtuoso Engineering's 45 employees will attend, plus 12 of our most important clients.

I have met with the other managers, and we all agreed that your Prudentia buffet package has the best selection of dishes. 190Could you give me a price quote for the number of attendees I have indicated above? Please also indicate the rental costs for tables, chairs, serving dishes, and utensils, as well as the fees for the wait staff.

Thank you, and I hope to hear from you soon.

Javier Rivera

例文2

To: Javier Rivera <jay.rivera@virtuosoengineering.com>

From: Soledad Vasquez <manager@confianzacatering.com>

Date: November 19
Subject: Re: Annual Company Gala

Dear Mr. Rivera,

187We would be more than happy to once again be of service to Virtuoso Engineering. You have become one of our most valuable clients, and we thank you for recommending us to your affiliates. 188-BThe number of our clients has increased in the past months due to your efforts.

189Prudentia is one of our most popular buffet packages, but may I offer a recommendation? Our Veritas package might give you greater value for your money. The two have nearly the same food selections, but Veritas has a wider assortment of beverages, including coffee and tea, whereas you will be billed separately for those two if you order the Prudentia package.

To make your decision easier, 190I have attached the file you asked for, and another which provides all of the relevant details on the Veritas package. Once you have made your choice, you can contact me directly at 555-4218, and we will start making the necessary preparations.

TEST 9 PART 7 | 455

Sincerely,	
Soledad Vasquez Manager Confianza Catering	Soledad Vasquez 經理 Confianza 外燴

例文 1 單字　□annual a. 年度的　　　□gala n. 活動，晚會　　□hire v. 雇用
　　　　　　□attend v. 參加　　　　□plus prep. 加上　　　□dish n. 料理
　　　　　　□price quote phr. 報價單　□rental n. 租借　　　□utensil n. 餐具，用具
　　　　　　□wait staff phr. 服務人員，服務生

例文 2 單字　□be of service to phr. 對～提供服務
　　　　　　□affiliate n. 分支機構，分社　□nearly ad. 幾乎　　□recommend v. 推薦
　　　　　　□beverage n. 飲料　　　　□whereas conj. 反之～　□assortment n. 種類，分類
　　　　　　□separately ad. 另外，個別地　　　　　　　　　□bill v. 開帳單
　　　　　　□once conj. 一旦～就　　□necessary a. 需要的　□relevant a. 相關聯的
　　　　　　　　　　　　　　　　　　　　　　　　　　　　□preparation n. 準備

186

Why was the first e-mail written? (A) To confirm attendance to a meeting (B) To ask for details about a convention (C) To inquire about hiring services (D) To answer questions about order processing	為什麼要寫第一封電郵？ (A) 確認會議的出席狀況 (B) 詢問有關一個會議的細節 (C) 詢問有關聘用的服務 (D) 回答有關訂單處理的問題

■■ 找出主題 寫文章的理由　　　　　　　　　　　　　　　　　　　　　　　　　　解答 (C)

這是問寫第一封信原因的問主題問題，所以要確認的是第一封信的內容。We are interested in hiring Confianza Catering for our annual company gala. 中提到「我們對於聘請 Confianza Catering 公司來辦年度晚會很感興趣」，之後又問服務相關的報價。因此，(C) To inquire about hiring services 是正確答案。

單字 confirm v. 確認，使確定　convention n. 會議，集會　inquire v. 諮詢　process v. 處理

187

What is suggested about Virtuoso Engineering? (A) It has done business with Confianza Catering before. (B) It underwent a management reorganization last month. (C) It is negotiating a merger with one of its affiliate companies. (D) It will host a banquet exclusively for its clients in December.	文中指出 Virtuoso 工程公司的什麼事？ (A) 它以前和 Confianza 外燴做過生意。 (B) 它上個月進行了一次管理層級的重組。 (C) 它正在與它的一個附屬公司談合併。 (D) 它在 12 月將專門為客戶設宴。

■■ 推論 詳細內容　　　　　　　　　　　　　　　　　　　　　　　　　　　　　解答 (A)

這是跟問題核心詞語 Virtuoso Engineering 有關的推理問題。因此，要確認的是有提到 Virtuoso Engineering 公司的第二封信的內容。We would be more than happy to once again be of service to Virtuoso Engineering. 中 Confianza Catering 公司非常樂意再次為 Virtuoso Engineering 公司服務，由此可以推斷出 Virtuoso Engineering 公司之前就跟 Confianza Catering 公司做過生意。因此，(A) It has done business with Confianza Catering before. 是正確答案。

單字 do business with phr. 做生意　undergo v. 經歷　management n. 管理階層　reorganization n. 組織重組
　　 negotiate v. 協商　merger n. 合併　host v. 主辦　banquet n. 宴會　exclusively ad. 專門地

188

What does Ms. Vasquez indicate in the second e-mail?	Vasquez 女士在第二封電郵中指出什麼？
(A) The buffet packages are discounted for a limited time.	(A) 自助餐組合在限定的時間內有特價。
(B) The customer base of Confianza Catering has grown.	(B) Confianza 外燴的客源有所增長。
(C) A whole week is needed to finalize the preparations.	(C) 完成準備工作需要一整個星期的時間。
(D) A deposit is required upon confirmation of a booking.	(D) 預訂確認後需付訂金。

■ **Not / True** True 問題   解答 (B)

這是在第二封信中 Ms. Vasquez 提到的內容跟選項作對比的 Not / True 問題。這個問題沒有核心詞語，所以要找出跟各個選項中的核心詞語相關的內容再來作答。 (A) 是文中沒提到過的內容。the number of our clients has increased in the past months 提到 Confianza Catering 公司的客戶量在過去幾個月有所增加，所以跟 (B) 的內容一致。因此，(B) The customer base of Confianza Catering has grown. 是正確答案。 (C) 和 (D) 是文中沒提到過的內容。

單字 limited a. 限定的，有限的　finalize v. 完成，結束　deposit n. 訂金

189

What does Ms. Vasquez recommend?	Vasquez 女士推薦什麼？
(A) Developing a dinner menu	(A) 開發一個晚餐菜單
(B) Choosing another package	(B) 選擇另一個組合
(C) Moving the gala to a later date	(C) 移動晚會到較晚的日期
(D) Reducing the number of guests	(D) 降低客人的數量

■ 六何原則 What   解答 (B)

這是問 Ms. Vasquez 推薦什麼（What）的六何原則問題。因此，要確認跟問題核心詞語 Ms. Vasquez recommend 相關的 Ms. Vasquez 所寫的第二封信的內容。第二封信的 Prudentia is one of our most popular buffet package, but may I offer a recommendation? Our Veritas package might give you greater value for your money. 中提到「雖然 Prudentia 是我們最受歡迎的自助餐組合之一，但是 Veritas 組合可能會讓您的錢花得更有價值。」所以推薦用 Veritas 代替 Prudentia。因此，(B) Choosing another package 是正確答案。

單字 develop v. 開發　reduce v. 降低

190

What did Ms. Vasquez send to Mr. Rivera?	Vasquez 女士寄給 Rivera 先生什麼？
(A) A revised schedule for a corporate gathering	(A) 企業聚會的修訂時間表
(B) Price quotes for a catering service	(B) 外燴服務的報價
(C) An updated list of buffet packages	(C) 自助餐組合最新表單
(D) A product catalog for an establishment	(D) 公司的產品目錄

■ 六何原則 聯結問題   解答 (B)

這是要把兩篇文章的內容綜合起來才能解開的聯結問題。問題核心詞語 Ms. Vasquez send to Mr. Rivera 中問 Ms. Vasquez 寄給 Mr. Rivera 什麼（What），所以要先確認 Ms. Vasquez 所寫的第二封信的內容。

第二封信的 I have attached the file you asked for 中提到 Ms. Vasquez 附上 Mr. Rivera 詢問的文件。不過，並沒有說明 Mr. Rivera 詢問了哪種文件。這時候，就需要確認第一封信的內容。第一封信的 Could you give me a price quote 中 Mr. Rivera 要求 Ms. Vasquez 寄報價單。

綜合 Ms. Vasquez 寄給 Mr. Rivera 詢問的文件和 Mr. Rivera 要求 Ms. Vasquez 寄報價單這兩個內容，就可以知道 Ms. Vasquez 寄給 Mr. Rivera 的是報價單。因此，(B) Price quotes for a catering service 是正確答案。

單字 revise v. 變更，修正　gathering n. 聚會　establishment n. 公司

例文1

GRAND AUTO JOURNAL
The First Fedfire Auto Racing Competition

Published quarterly by Aardvark Publishing, *Grand Auto Journal* is one of the country's most widely read car magazines. It offers comprehensive reviews of new and vintage automobiles as well as features on celebrities and their driving preferences. *Grand Auto Journal* is popular with car enthusiasts and those who enjoy motorbikes, recreational vehicles, or SUVs.

On its 10th anniversary, the magazine is organizing the First Fedfire Auto Racing Competition. It is open to both amateur and professional race car drivers.

CATEGORY	PRIZES
Adult (Professional)	$30,000
Adult (Amateur)	$20,000
194-DTeens (Professional)	$25,000
Teens (Amateur)	$15,000

192Interested parties can read the contest regulations in the latest issue of *Grand Auto Journal* or visit www.fedfirerace.com. 191You can download the registration form on the Web site and you must submit all the requirements before October 15. The one-day competition, which will be attended by some of the country's most esteemed sports celebrities, will be held at the Schoonmaker Field in Austin, Texas on November 17.

例文2

AUSTIN SENTINEL   Volume X Issue 4
MOTORING NEWS

The First Fedfire Auto Racing Competition: A Success

AUSTIN – Over 5,000 people attended the First Fedfire Auto Racing Competition at the Schoonmaker Field on November 17. The event, organized by *Grand Auto Journal* in partnership with Raikonen Motors, is the first of its kind in the city, attracting numerous car enthusiasts from all over the country.

194-B/CHunter Harrington and 194-DRandy Wilson emerged as winners in the professional categories, for adults and teens respectively, beating 40 other participants in a competition that lasted for more than five hours. 194-CIn the amateur categories, their counterparts were Louella Anderson and Dwight Morgan. City mayor Fred Gellar was the special guest at the awards ceremony that took place right after the competition. There he delivered a speech congratulating everyone involved in the day's events.

193-BEli Thomson, chief editor of *Grand Auto Journal*, thanked everyone who attended the event.

Grand 汽車雜誌
第一屆 Fedfire 賽車比賽

由 Aardvark 出版的季刊《Grand 汽車雜誌》是全國最被廣泛閱讀的汽車雜誌之一，它提供新型和古董汽車全面性的評論，以及名人和他們駕駛偏好的特別報導。Grand 汽車雜誌很受汽車愛好者和那些喜歡摩托車、休閒車或 SUV 者的歡迎。

在其 10 週年紀念，該雜誌正在籌劃第一屆的 Fedfire 賽車比賽，比賽開放給業餘和職業賽車手。

種類	獎金
成人（職業）	$30,000
成人（業餘）	$20,000
194-D青少年（職業）	$25,000
青少年（業餘）	$15,000

192有興趣者可在最新一期的 Grand 汽車雜誌閱讀比賽規則或上網 www.fedfirerace.com。191你可以在網站下載報名表，你必須在 10 月 15 日前繳交所有的必要資料。為期一天的比賽中將會有國內一些最受人尊敬的體育界名人出席，比賽將會在 11 月 17 日德州奧斯汀的 Schoonmaker 運動場舉行。

AUSTIN SENTINEL 報 第 10 卷第 4 期
汽車新聞

第一屆 Fedfire 汽車比賽：成功！

奧斯汀 - 超過 5000 人參加了於 11 月 17 日在 Schoonmaker 運動場的賽車比賽，本次活動由 Grand 汽車雜誌主辦，Raikonen 汽車公司協辦，是本市此類活動的首創，吸引了全國各地眾多的汽車愛好者。

194-B/CHunter Harrington 和 194-DRandy Wilson 分別為成人職業和青少年職業選手類別的贏家，在比賽中擊敗了四十位其他的參賽者，這場比賽持續了五個多小時，194-C在業餘組，成人業餘及青少年業餘的贏家分別是 Louella Anderson 和 Dwight Morgan，市長 Fred Gellar 是比賽後的頒獎儀式中的特別嘉賓，他在儀式中發表了演講，祝賀每個當天參與活動的人。

193-BGrand 汽車雜誌的編輯 Eli Thomson 感謝大家參加此次的活動，

"It fills me with satisfaction to know that [195]we have turned our dream of organizing a community sports event into a reality," Thomson said. "It's unbelievable. [195]We're already excited for next year!"

Along with cash prizes, winners were also given trophies and certificates, as well as free annual subscriptions to *Grand Auto Journal*. The auto racing competition was the culmination of the magazine's month-long celebration of its 10th anniversary.

Thomson 說：「我心滿意足地知道，[195]我們已經把組織社區運動活動的夢想化為現實，真是不可思議，[195]我們已為明年而興奮！」

除了獎金，獲勝者還獲得了獎杯和證書，以及一年 *Grand* 汽車雜誌的免費訂閱。這場賽車比賽是該雜誌長達一個月的慶祝成立 10 周年活動的高潮。

例文 1 單字　□competition n. 大會，比賽　□publish v. 發行，出版　□quarterly ad. 每季
　　　　　□widely ad. 廣泛　□comprehensive a. 無所不包的，全面的
　　　　　□review n. 評論，複審　□feature v. 特徵，特色，報導　□celebrity n. 名人
　　　　　□preference n. 偏愛　□enthusiast n. 愛好者，熱衷　□recreational a. 消遣的，娛樂的
　　　　　□party n. 當事人，集會　□regulation n. 規定　□issue n. 發行
　　　　　□esteemed a. 受尊敬的，高評價的

例文 2 單字　□in partnership with phr. 和～合作　　　　　　　□attract v. 吸引，引起
　　　　　□numerous a. 很多的　□respectively ad. 各自地　□beat v. 打擊，打敗
　　　　　□participant n. 參加者　□last v. 持續，繼續　□counterpart n. 有對應關係的人，對方
　　　　　□involved a. 有關聯的，包含的　□satisfaction n. 滿足　□community n. 共同體，社區
　　　　　□reality n. 現實　□subscription n. 訂閱　□culmination n. 高潮，頂點

191

According to the advertisement, when is the deadline to sign up for the competition? (A) October 4 (B) November 10 (C) October 15 (D) November 17	根據廣告，報名參加比賽的最後期限是什麼時候？ (A) 10 月 4 日 (B) 11 月 10 日 (C) 10 月 15 日 (D) 11 月 17 日

■ 六何原則 When　　　　　　　　　　　　　　　　　　　　　　　　　解答 (C)

這是問根據廣告，報名比賽的最後期限是何時（when）的六何原則問題。首先確定第一篇文章中跟問題核心詞語 the deadline to sign up for the competition 相關聯的內容。 You can download the registration form on the Web site and you must submit all the requirements before October 15. 中提到「你可以在網站下載報名表，你必須在 10 月 15 日前繳交所有的必要資料」。因此，(C) October 15 是正確答案。

單字　deadline n. 期限　sign up phr. 報告；簽名

192

Why are readers asked to visit a Web site? (A) To view the tentative schedule for an upcoming automobile show (B) To learn more about the details of a sporting event (C) To participate in a discussion on an online forum (D) To register for membership with an athletic organization	為什麼會邀請讀者上一個網站？ (A) 查看即將到來的汽車展的暫定時間表 (B) 了解更多有關於一件體育賽事的詳情 (C) 參加一個線上論壇的討論 (D) 註冊成為一個運動組織的會員

■ 六何原則 Why　　　　　　　　　　　　　　　　　　　　　　　　　解答 (B)

這是問為何（Why）邀請讀者上網站的六何原則問題。跟問題核心詞語 readers ~ visit a Web site 相關的內容可以在第一篇文章中找出來。廣告的 Interested parties can read the contest regulations ~ visit www. fedfirerace.com. 中提到有興趣者可上網閱讀比賽規則。因此，(B) To learn more about the details of a sporting event 是正確答案。

單字　tentative a. 暫時的，一時的，不確定的

What is mentioned about Eli Thomson?	文中提到有關 Eli Thomson 的什麼事？
(A) He spoke on behalf of the mayor of Austin.	(A) 他代表奧斯汀市長發言。
(B) He is responsible for overseeing a magazine.	(B) 他負責監督一本雜誌。
(C) He was asked to write an article about the event.	(C) 他被要求寫有關該活動的文章。
(D) He was one of the participants at a competition.	(D) 他是比賽的參賽者之一。

■ **Not / True** True 問題　　　　　　　　　　　　　　　　　　　解答 (B)

這是找出跟問題核心詞語 Eli Thomson 相關的內容後，再跟選項作對比的 Not / True 問題。第二篇文章中提到 Eli Thomson 的內容。 (A) 是文中沒提到的內容。Eli Thompson, chief editor of Grand Auto Journal 中提到 Eli Thompson 是 Grand Auto 雜誌的編輯，所以跟 (B) 的內容一致。 (C) 和 (D) 都是文中沒提到的內容。

單字 **on behalf of** phr. 代替，代表　　**responsible** a. 有責任的　　**oversee** v. 監督，管理

What is NOT indicated about the contestants?	文中沒有指出有關參賽者的哪件事？
(A) Dwight Morgan was personally congratulated by Fred Gellar.	(A) Fred Gellar 親自向 Dwight Morgan 表示祝賀。
(B) Hunter Harrington raced as a professional adult.	(B) Hunter Harrington 以成人職業組出賽。
(C) Louella Anderson placed first in the amateur adult category.	(C) Louella Anderson 在成人業餘組排名第一。
(D) Randy Wilson received a $25,000 cash prize.	(D) Randy Wilson 獲得 25000 美元的獎金。

■ **Not / True** Not 問題　　　　　　　　　　　　　　　　　　　解答 (A)

這是找出跟問題核心詞語 the contestants 相關的內容後，再跟選項作對比的 Not / True 問題。因此，提到參賽者的廣告和報導都需要確認。 (A) 是文中沒提到的內容。第二篇文章的 Hunter Harrington and Randy Wilson emerged as winners in the professional categories, for adults and teens respectively 中提到 Hunter Harrington 和 Randy Wilson 為成人職業和青少年職業選手類別的贏家，In the amateur categories, their counterparts were Louella Anderson and Dwight Morgan. 中提到在業餘組，贏家是 Louella Anderson 和 Dwight Morgan。因此，跟 (B) 和 (C) 的內容相符。第二篇文章的 Randy Wilson emerged as winners in the professional categories, for ~ teens 中 Randy Wilson 是青少年職業選手類別的贏家，而由第一篇文章中的廣告 teens (Professional), $25,000 中可以知道青少年職業選手類別的獎金是$25,000。因此，跟 (D) 的內容一致。

單字 **contestant** n. （大會、比賽等的）參加者　　**race** v. 出賽　　**personally** ad. 個人地

What is suggested about the Fedfire Auto Racing Competition?	文中指出有關 Fedfire 賽車比賽的什麼事？
(A) It honored past winners during the awards ceremony.	(A) 在頒獎典禮中，它向過去的獲獎者表達敬意。
(B) It will be broadcast on national television.	(B) 它將在全國的電視上播出。
(C) It was a project of the local government.	(C) 它是當地政府的一個計畫。
(D) It is going to be held again in the coming year.	(D) 它將在明年再次舉辦。

■ 推論 詳細內容　　　　　　　　　　　　　　　　　　　解答 (D)

這是跟問題核心詞語 the Fedfire Auto Racing Competition 有關的推理問題，所以要確認的是第二篇文章中提到 Fedfire 賽車比賽的相關內容。we have turned our dream of organizing a community sports event into a reality 中提到「我們已經把組織社區運動活動的夢想化為現實」。接著，在 We're already excited for next year! 中又說「我們已為明年而興奮」。由此可以推斷出明年會再次舉辦活動。因此，(D) It is going to be held again in the coming year. 是正確答案。

換句話說

Auto Racing Competition 賽車大會 → sports event 運動賽事

單字 **honor** v. 榮譽，頒獎　　**broadcast** v. 廣播，播送

Questions 196-200 refer to the following invitation and e-mail.

196-200 根據下面邀請函和電郵的內容回答問題。

例文1

[197]The Musen Academy of Motion Pictures
requests the pleasure of your company at the
23rd Liberaz Film Honors
to recognize remarkable accomplishments
in the film industry this year.
[198]The black-tie affair will start at 6 P.M. on February 8
at the Fracasso Exhibition Facility.

PROGRAM

6:00	Introductory Speech	Violet Tyler - Director, Musen Academy of Motion Pictures
6:20	Keynote Address	Joseph Roscoe - Liberaz Film Honors Hall of Fame Honoree
7:00	[196/197]TROPHY PRESENTATION	[197]*Surviving Millicent,* Best Picture — Zoren Graham, Best Director — Carlo Sutter, Best Actor / [197]*Surviving Millicent,* Best Script — The Alley, Best Cinematography — [196]Lisette Hamilton, Best Actress
8:00	Closing Remarks	Penelope Daly - Board Member, Musen Academy of Motion Pictures

Please confirm your attendance by contacting Jacqueline Finney at jfinney@musen.org or Kirby Velasco at kvelasco@musen.org on or before January 20.

---

[197]Musen 電影協會
邀請您蒞臨參加
第 23 屆 Liberaz 電影獎
以表揚今年在電影界的卓越成就。
[198]正式活動將在 2 月 8 日晚上 6 點在
Fracasso 展覽會場展開。

節目表

6:00	開場演講	Violet Tyler - Musen 電影協會導演
6:20	主題演講	Joseph Roscoe – Liberaz 電影獎名人堂受勳人
7:00	[196/197]頒獎典禮	[197]*Surviving Millicent*：最佳影片獎 — Zoren Graham：最佳導演獎 — Carlo Sutter：最佳男演員獎 / [197]*Surviving Millicent*：最佳劇本獎 — The Alley：最佳攝影獎 — [196]Lisette Hamilton：最佳女演員獎
8:00	閉幕詞	Penelope Daly - Musen 電影協會理事會委員

請在 1 月 20 日前用聯繫 Jacqueline Finney 或 Kirby Velasco 確認您的出席，電郵地址各為：jfinney@musen.org 和 kvelasco@musen.org。

例文2

To: Jacqueline Finney <jfinney@musen.org>

From: Kirby Velasco <kvelasco@musen.org>

[200-B/D]Date: January 15

Subject: Mr. Laughlin

Jacqueline,

[198/200-C/D]I got a call from acclaimed director Alexander Laughlin this morning. He agreed to deliver the keynote address at the Liberaz Film Honors ceremony in place of Joseph Roscoe, who is out of town until February 12 for the shooting of his new film. Mr. Laughlin only asks that we give him enough time to prepare his speech before he sends it to us for review. As co-organizer of the event, [200-B]I took the liberty of telling him that it's OK and that we'll give him until January 22 to write his draft.

Anyway, most of the people we invited have already confirmed their attendance. If you'd like, [199]I can write them a group e-mail to let them know about Mr. Laughlin

---

收件人：Jacqueline Finney <jfinney@musen.org>
寄件人：Kirby Velasco <jfinney@musen.org>
[200-B/D]日期：1 月 15 日
主旨：Laughlin 先生

Jacqueline：

[198/200-C/D]我今天早上接到了名導演 Alexander Laughlin 的電話，他同意代替 Joseph Roscoe 在 Liberaz 電影獎頒獎典禮上發表主題演講，因為 Joseph 去外地拍攝他的新電影，直到 2 月 12 日才會回來。他只要求在他把演講稿發送給我們審查前，我們給他足夠的時間來準備他的演講稿，身為活動協辦者的我，[200-B]冒昧地答應了他，我們會給他到 1 月 22 日來寫草稿。

至少，大部分我們邀請的人已經確認過他們的出席狀況，如果你想，[199]我可以寫群組電子郵件給他們，讓他們知道 Laughlin 先生是新的主題演講的主講

being the new keynote speaker **so there won't be any confusion on February 8.**	人，這樣就不會在 2 月 8 日時引起任何騷動。
Kirby	Kirby

例文 1 單字 □company n. 同伴，同行　□recognize v. 認可　□remarkable a. 卓越的
　　　　　□accomplishment n. 成果　□industry n. 產業，業界　□black-tie a. 穿著正式的
　　　　　□affair n. 活動，聚會，業務　□keynote address phr. 主題演講　□honoree n. 得獎人
　　　　　□cinematography n. 電影拍攝
例文 2 單字 □acclaim v. 稱讚　□deliver v. 發表（演講，報告等）　□in place of phr. 代替～
　　　　　□shooting n. 拍攝　□review n. 檢討
　　　　　□take the liberty of -ing phr. 冒昧地，不顧禮節地　□draft n. 草案
　　　　　□confusion n. 疑惑，騷動

196

Who will be given a trophy for acting?	誰會得到最佳演員獎？
(A) Violet Tyler	(A) Violet Tyler
(B) Lisette Hamilton	(B) Lisette Hamilton
(C) Penelope Daly	(C) Penelope Daly
(D) Jacqueline Finney	(D) Jacqueline Finney

■ 六何原則 Who　　　　　　　　　　　　　　　　　　　　　　　　解答 (B)

這是問誰（Who）會拿到最佳演員獎的六何原則問題，所以要確認邀請函中跟問題核心詞語 given a trophy for acting 相關的內容。第一篇文章的邀請函中 TROPHY PRESENTATION 的 Lisette Hamilton, Best Actress 中寫到最佳女演員獎是 Lisette Hamilton。因此，(B) Lisette Hamilton 是正確答案。

197

What is suggested about *Surviving Millicent*?	文中指出 *Surviving Millicent* 的什麼事？
(A) It will be shown in theaters on February 8.	(A) 它會在 2 月 8 日在電影院演出。
(B) It gained recognition from other prize-giving institutions.	(B) 它獲得其他頒獎機構的認可。
(C) It will receive two awards from the Musen Academy of Motion Pictures.	(C) 它會從 Musen 電影協會得到兩個獎項。
(D) It has been scheduled for a special preview at the Fracasso Exhibition Facility.	(D) 它被安排在 Fracasso 展覽會場有一個特別的試映會。

■ 推論 詳細內容　　　　　　　　　　　　　　　　　　　　　　　　解答 (C)

這是跟問題核心詞語 *Surviving Millicent* 有關的推理問題，所以要確認有提到 *Surviving Millicent* 的第一篇文章的內容。the Musen Academy of Motion Pictures requests the pleasure of your company at the 23rd Liberaz Film Honors 中提到 Musen Academy of Motion Pictures（邀請您蒞臨參與第 23 屆 Liberaz 電影獎）。接著，由 TROPHY PRESENTATION 的 *Surviving Millicent*, Best Picture 和 *Surviving Millicent*, Best Script 可以知道 *Surviving Millicent* 得到了最佳影片獎和最佳劇本獎。由此可以推斷出 *Surviving Millicent* 在 Musen Academy of Motion Pictures 拿到了兩個獎。因此，(C) It will receive two awards from the Musen Academy of Motion Pictures. 是正確答案。

單字 institution n. 機關　preview n. 試映會

198

What will Mr. Laughlin most likely do on February 8? (A) Send a draft of his speech (B) Deliver a talk (C) Help organize the event (D) Meet with Joseph Roscoe	Laughlin 先生在 2 月 8 日最有可能做什麼？ (A) 寄出他演講的草稿 (B) 發表演講 (C) 協助策劃這個活動 (D) 與 Joseph Roscoe 見面

🔲 **推論** 聯結問題　　　　　　　　　　　　　　　　　　　　　　　　　　　　　　解答 (B)

這是要把兩篇文章的內容綜合起來才能解開的聯結問題。問題核心詞語 Mr. Laughlin ~ do on February 8 中問 Mr. Laughlin 在 2 月 8 日可能將做什麼，所以先確認第二篇文章中提到 Mr. Laughlin 的信件內容。

第二篇文章的 I got a call from ~ Alexander Laughlin this morning. He agreed to deliver the keynote address at the Liberaz Film Honors ceremony 中提到 Alexander Laughlin 將在 Liberaz 電影獎頒獎典禮上發表主題演講。而第一篇文章的 the black-tie affair will start at 6 P.M. on February 8 中提到正式活動將在 2 月 8 日下午 6 點展開，也就可以確定 Liberaz 電影獎頒獎典禮也是 2 月 8 日舉辦。

把 Mr. Laughlin 將在 Liberaz 電影獎頒獎典禮上發表主題演講和 Liberaz 電影獎頒獎典禮在 2 月 8 日下午展開綜合起來，就可以推斷出 Mr. Laughlin 將在 2 月 8 日發表主題演講。因此，(B) Deliver a talk 是正確答案。

199

What does Mr. Velasco say he can do? (A) Help Mr. Laughlin edit his speech (B) Notify attendees about a change in the program (C) Follow up on the attendance of invited guests (D) Give updates on the status of event preparations	Velasco 先生說他可以做什麼？ (A) 幫助 Laughlin 先生編輯他的演講稿 (B) 通知出席者節目的改變 (C) 追蹤受邀嘉賓的出席狀況 (D) 提供活動準備情況的最新消息

🔲 **六何原則** What　　　　　　　　　　　　　　　　　　　　　　　　　　　　　　解答 (B)

這是問 Mr. Velasco 將做什麼（What）的六何原則問題，所以可以在問題核心詞語 Mr. Velasco 所寫的第二篇文章中找答案。信中 I can write them a group e-mail to let them know about Mr. Laughlin being the new keynote speaker 中提到 Mr. Velasco 可以寫群組電子郵件給他們，讓他們知道 Mr. Laughlin 是新的主題演講的主講人，所以 (B) Notify attendees about a change in the program 是正確答案。

單字 edit v. 修改，修正，編輯　　notify v. 通知

200

What is NOT indicated about Mr. Laughlin in the e-mail? (A) He is shooting a new movie. (B) He was given a week to write his speech. (C) He is well known in the film industry. (D) He spoke to Kirby Velasco on January 15.	電郵中沒有指出有關 Laughlin 先生的什麼事？ (A) 他正在拍攝一部新電影。 (B) 他有一個星期來寫他的演講稿。 (C) 他在電影界很有名。 (D) 他在 1 月 15 日跟 Kirby Velasco 講過話。

🔲 **Not / True** Not 問題　　　　　　　　　　　　　　　　　　　　　　　　　　　解答 (A)

這是在信中找出 Mr. Laughlin 跟相關內容，再跟選項作對比的 Not / True 問題。因此，要先確認第二篇文章的相關內容。(A) 是文中沒提到的內容。因此，(A) He is shooting a new movie. 是正確答案。由 Date: January 15 和 I took the liberty of telling him that it's OK and that we'll give him until January 22 to write his draft 可以知道在 1 月 15 日寄出的信中說會給 Mr. Laughlin 到 1 月 22 日來寫講稿。因此，跟 (B) 的內容一致。I got a call from acclaimed director Alexander Laughlin 中提到著名導演 Alexander Laughlin，所以跟 (C) 的內容一致。由 Date: January 15 和 I got a call from ~ Alexander Laughlin this morning 可以知道 Kirby Velasco 在 1 月 15 日早上接到 Alexander Laughlin 的電話，所以跟 (D) 的內容相符。

TEST 10

PART 5

101

Glencore International would like to request _____ guests to present their invitation cards upon entering the ballroom. (A) our (B) every (C) ours (D) theirs	Glencore 國際公司要求他們的客人在進入舞廳時要出示邀請函。

■ 人稱代名詞的格   解答 (A)

可以在名詞 guests 前面像形容詞一樣修飾名詞的人稱代名詞是所有格。因此，所有格人稱代名詞 (A) our 是正確答案。空格後面是複數名詞 guests，所以修飾單數名詞的 (B) every 不是正確答案。所有代名詞的 (C) 和 (D) 則不能修飾名詞。另外，要把「would like to + 動詞原形」（想做～）和「upon + -ing」（做～的時候，一～就）背起來。

單字 present v. 出示，給　ballroom n. 宴會場，舞會場

102

Please note that the application period for the credit manager position _____ tomorrow and conclude on September 15. (A) will start (B) starting (C) had started (D) started	請注意信用部經理一職的應徵日期從明天開始到 9 月 15 日為止。

■ 未來時態動詞   解答 (A)

因為 that 子句中沒有動詞，所以 (A) (C) (D) 都可能是正確答案。因為有未來時間的表達 tomorrow，所以未來式 (A) will start 是正確答案。過去完成式 (C) 和過去式 (D) 都不能和未來式一起使用。分詞或動名詞 (B) 都不能放在動詞的位置。

單字 application n. 應徵，採用　conclude v. 結束，有結論

103

Dukebox has been one of the most profitable recording companies in the music industry for _____ three decades. (A) other (B) over (C) throughout (D) much	Dukebox 公司超過三十年來是音樂界最賺錢的唱片公司之一。

■ 選擇介系詞 期間   解答 (B)

文意是「超過三十年」，又有表示期間的表達 three decades，所以介系詞 (B) over（超過～期間）是正確答案。(C) throughout（～期間內一直）雖然也是表示期間的介系詞，但是通常會使用 for three decades 或 throughout three decades 這樣的表達。不能重複使用介系詞 for，所以 (C) 不會是正確答案。如果使用形容詞 (A) other（其他）和副詞 (D) much（非常）的話，文意就會變得很奇怪，所以也不會是正確答案。

單字 profitable a. 有賺錢的　decade n. 十年

104

Flight service _____ New York to Chicago will be unavailable until weather conditions improve. (A) from (B) in (C) at (D) between	從紐約飛往芝加哥的班機在天氣狀況改善前都停止服務。

■ 選擇介系詞 方向　　　　　　　　　　　　　　　　　　　　　　　　　　　　　　　解答 (A)

文意是「從紐約飛往芝加哥的班機」，所以表示出發地的介系詞 (A) from（從～）是正確答案。另外，介系詞 from 主要跟 to（到～）一起組成 from A to B（從 A 到 B）來使用。(B) in（在～裡面）和 (C) at（在～）都是表示時間或場所。不過，in 用於月、年、季節或大空間內的場所，而 at 用於時刻、時點或比較小的空間。(D) between（～之間）表示兩個以上的對象之間的關係或位置，經常使用的方式是 between A and B（A 和 B 之間）。

單字 unavailable a. 無法使用的，不可使用的

105

| Ms. Zaragoza was _____ notified of her reassignment to the Dublin office in a letter from the human resources director.
(A) officially　　　　(B) official
(C) officials　　　　(D) officiate | Zaragoza 小姐收到人力資源部門主任的一封信，正式通知她被派往都柏林辦公室。 |

■ 副詞的位置　　　　　　　　　　　　　　　　　　　　　　　　　　　　　　　　　解答 (A)

為了修飾動詞 was notified，所以一定要用副詞。因此，(A) officially（正式地）是正確答案。名詞或形容詞 (B) 和 (C)，動詞 (D) 都不能修飾動詞。

單字 official n. 公務員，職員；a. 公務上的，正式的　officiate v. 執行職務

106

| To receive online billing service, clients should _____ a request by e-mail including their name, e-mail address, and account number.
(A) submits　　　　(B) submitted
(C) submit　　　　(D) submitting | 要收到線上帳單服務，客戶應該要用電郵寄出申請，包括名字、電子郵件帳號和帳戶號碼。 |

■ 助動詞 + 動詞原形　　　　　　　　　　　　　　　　　　　　　　　　　　　　　解答 (C)

助動詞 should 後面一定要接動詞原形。因此，(C) submit（提出）是正確答案。第三人稱單數動詞 (A)，過去式動詞或過去分詞 (B)，動名詞或現在分詞 (D) 都不能位於助動詞後面。

單字 billing n. 開帳單　account number phr. 帳戶號碼

107

| The main agenda of the board of directors' meeting was a _____ of the issues that would arise once the purchase of an affiliate pushed through.
(A) deliberate　　　　(B) deliberately
(C) deliberated　　　　(D) deliberation | 董事會會議的主要議程是商議買下一家公司時所會產生的問題。 |

■ 名詞的位置　　　　　　　　　　　　　　　　　　　　　　　　　　　　　　　　　解答 (D)

因為空格前面有不定冠詞 a，所以名詞 (D) deliberation（商討，深思熟慮）是正確答案。動詞 (A)、副詞 (B)、動詞或分詞 (C) 都不能位於名詞的位置。

單字 main a. 主要的　agenda n. 議題，議程　affiliate n. 成員組織，分會　push through phr. 使完成，促成
　　　deliberately ad. 故意地

108

| A couple of trucks and three cranes are scheduled to arrive at the construction site no later than the _____ week.
 (A) principal (B) random
 (C) following (D) partial | 兩輛卡車和三輛起重機預計在下週前抵達工地。 |

■ 形容詞語彙　　　　　　　　　　　　　　　　　　　　　　解答 (C)

文意是「預計在下週前抵達」，所以形容詞 (C) following（接下來的）是正確答案。(A) principal 的意思是「主要的」，(B) random 的意思是「任意的」，(D) partial 的意思是「局部的」。

單字 no later than phr. 最晚到～

109

| Customers can inquire about the status of their orders by _____ calling our hotline or visiting one of the store branches.
 (A) every (B) either
 (C) just as (D) next | 顧客可藉由撥打我們的熱線或親臨我們的分店來詢問訂單的狀況。 |

■ 相關連接詞　　　　　　　　　　　　　　　　　　　　　　解答 (B)

正好可以跟相關連接詞 or 配對的 (B) either 是正確答案。（either A or B：A 或 B 其中一個）另外，either A or B 可以連接動名詞片語 calling our hotline 和動名詞片語 visiting ~ branches。

單字 inquire v. 詢問　status n. 狀態，地位　order n. 訂單，順序

110

| The accountant needs to finalize the expense report before noon tomorrow no matter _____ difficult the paperwork is.
 (A) since (B) how
 (C) what (D) now | 不管文書工作有多困難，會計需要在明天中午前總結開銷報告。 |

■ 副詞子句連接詞 however　　　　　　　　　　　　　　　　解答 (B)

文意是「不管有多困難，需要在明天中午前總結報告」，所以跟空格前面的 no matter 組成 no matter how（不管～也）的 (B) how 是正確答案。另外，也可以用複合關係副詞 however 來代替 no matter how。常使用的用法是「however + 形容詞 / 副詞 + 主詞 + 動詞」。(A) since 的意思是「自從～」，作為連接詞也可以引出子句，不過不能跟 no matter 一起使用。(C) what 跟 no matter 組成的 no matter what（什麼～也）可以引出副詞子句。不過，跟 whatever 一樣作為複合關係代名詞的時候，可以扮演副詞子句的主詞或受詞；但作為複合關係形容詞的時候，後面要接名詞，因此不能放在形容詞 difficult 的前面。 (D) now 的意思是「現在」，作為副詞時，不能跟 no matter 一起使用。

單字 finalize v. 完成　expense n. 支出，費用　paperwork n. 文書工作

111

Vielle Software releases free trial versions of its products ------- potential customers can try out the programs for a limited time. (A) despite (B) so that (C) or (D) though	Vielle 軟體公司發表他們產品的免費試用版本，以便潛在的客戶可以在期限內試用軟體。

■ 副詞子句連接詞 目的 　　　　　　　　　　　　　　　　　　　　　　　　　　　解答 (B)

這句話是具有必要成分 Vielle Software releases free trial versions 的完整子句，所以要把 ____ potential ~ time 看成是可省略的修飾語。這個修飾語中是有動詞的子句形態，所以可以引出子句的副詞子句連接詞 (B) 和 (D) 都可能是正確答案。文意是「提供潛在的客戶在期限內試用軟體」，所以表示目的的 (B) so that（以便）就是正確答案。如果使用表示讓步的副詞子句連接詞 (D) though（儘管）的話，文意就會變成很怪的「儘管潛在的客戶可以在期限內試用，但是提供免費版」。介系詞 (A) 和對等連接詞 (C) 都不能引出修飾語。

單字 release v. 發表　trial n. 試用　potential a. 潛在的

112

Registration is required for all _____ of the Chamber of Commerce's workshop on marketing for small businesses. (A) participants (B) participation (C) participated (D) participate	所有參加商會針對小型企業舉辦的行銷研討會的人都要報名。

■ 人物名詞 vs.抽象名詞 　　　　　　　　　　　　　　　　　　　　　　　　　　　解答 (A)

可以位於形容詞 all 和介系詞 of 之間的就是名詞。因此，名詞 (A) 和 (B) 都可能是正確答案。文意是「所有參加研討會的人都要報名」，所以人物名詞 (A) participants（參加者）是正確答案。如果使用抽象名詞 (B) participation（參加），文意就會變成很怪的「所有的參加活動本身都要報名」。動詞或分詞 (C)，動詞 (D) 不能位於名詞的位置。

單字 Chamber of Commerce phr. 商會

113

The campaign sponsored by Green World Society is _____ focused on saving a huge area of land affected by rampant deforestation in Tanzania. (A) satisfactorily (B) promptly (C) primarily (D) successively	由 Green World Society 所贊助的活動主要針對保育大片在坦尚尼亞被猖獗濫伐的土地。

■ 副詞語彙 　　　　　　　　　　　　　　　　　　　　　　　　　　　　　　　　解答 (C)

文意是「活動主要針對保育大片土地」，所以副詞 (C) primarily（主要）是正確答案。(A) satisfactorily 的意思是「令人滿意，令人滿足」，(B) promptly 的意思是「馬上」，(D) successively 的意思是「相繼地」。

單字 sponsor v. 贊助　rampant a. 猖獗的　deforestation n. 砍伐森林

114

AirWheel _____ a Globetech International Certificate for its new line of industrial fans and will now start selling them in retail outlets.

(A) has attained   (B) attains

(C) is attained   (D) attaining

AirWheel 的工業用風扇新產品已經獲得 Globetech 國際認證，而且將會在零售店開始銷售。

■ 現在完成式   解答 (A)

因為句子中沒有動詞，所以動詞 (A) (B) (C) 都可能是正確答案。文意是「已經獲得國際認證，將開始銷售」。由此可以知道過去拿到國際認證這件事情對現在產生了影響。因此，現在完成式 (A) has attained 是正確答案。現在式 (B) 主要用於反覆的動作或習慣。被動語態 (C) 用於表達「主詞被～，受到～」。分詞或動名詞 (D) 則不能位於動詞的位置。

單字 certificate n. 證明書   retail outlet phr. 零售店   attain v. 取得

115

Only when the restaurant opened _____ the owner realize that she needed more kitchen help to complete the numerous cooking tasks.

(A) do   (B) is doing

(C) did   (D) has done

當餐廳開張時，老闆才發現到她需要更多廚房助手來做繁多的烹飪工作。

■ 倒裝句填充   解答 (C)

「Only + 副詞子句」Only when the restaurant opened 位於句首，這就是主詞和動詞倒裝的句子。因為有主詞 the owner 和動詞原形 realize，所以 do 助動詞要出現在主詞的前面。從屬子句 she needed ~ tasks 的動詞是過去時態。因為主子句的時態要與其相對應，所以主子句的時態也必須是過去時態。因此，do 助動詞的過去式 (C) did 是正確答案。另外，當「Only + 副詞子句（片語）」出現在句首時，就要知道是倒裝句。

單字 numerous a. 繁多的   task n. 工作，任務

116

As this is a self-service laundry with coin-operated machines, all washing, drying and folding must be done on _____.

(A) yours   (B) your

(C) your own   (D) yourselves

因為這是投幣式的自助洗衣，所有清洗、烘乾和摺衣服都要自己做。

■ 反身代名詞   解答 (C)

(C) your own 可以和介系詞 on 一起組成跟反身代名詞相關的表達 on one's own，意思是「自己地，獨自地」，所以 (C) 是正確答案。所有代名詞 (A) 代替「所有格 + 名詞」用，所有格 (B) 則像形容詞一樣用到名詞前面。反身代名詞 (D) 用於指示受詞跟主詞一樣是人或事物的時候，或者強調主詞或受詞的時候。另外，on one's own 的意思跟 by oneself 一樣。

單字 coin-operated a. 投幣式的   fold v. 摺

117

As soon as he assumed his new position, sales director Carl Reynolds set an _____ target for the team for the next quarter. (A) eligible　　　　　(B) affluent (C) ambitious　　　　(D) influential	銷售主任 Carl Reynolds 一接任新職位，便為團隊設定一個有企圖心的下一季目標。

■ 形容詞語彙　　　　　　　　　　　　　　　　　　　　　　　　　　　　解答 (C)

文意是「設定一個有企圖心的下一季目標」，所以形容詞 (C) ambitious（有企圖心的）是正確答案。 (A) eligible 意思是「有資格～」，(B) affluent 的意思是「富裕的」，(D) influential 的意思是「有影響力的」。

單字 as soon as phr. 一～就～　assume v. 擔當，認為　quarter n. 季度，四分之一

118

Keeping clients happy by providing a variety of banking services in an efficient manner is the _____ of Midelson Savings Bank. (A) condition　　　　(B) structure (C) priority　　　　　(D) range	以有效率的方法提供多種銀行服務使顧客高興是 Midelson 儲蓄銀行的首要工作。

■ 名詞語彙　　　　　　　　　　　　　　　　　　　　　　　　　　　　　解答 (C)

文意是「使顧客高興是銀行的首要工作」，所以位於空格的名詞 (C) priority（首要工作）是正確答案。(A) condition 的意思是「條件」，(B) structure 的意思是「構造」，(D) range 的意思是「範圍」。另外，priority 和形容詞 top 組成 top priority 的意思是「最優先事項」。Range 經常使用的片語是 a wide range of（廣大範圍的）。

單字 a variety of phr. 多樣的，各式各樣的　manner n. 方法，態度

119

To confirm the _____ with the marketing director, please coordinate with his assistant, Ms. White, before Tuesday, June 6. (A) interview　　　　(B) interviewer (C) interviewing　　　(D) interviewed	要確定和行銷主任的面談，請在 6 月 6 日星期二前和他的助理 White 小姐協調。

■ 人物名詞 vs 抽象名詞　　　　　　　　　　　　　　　　　　　　　　　解答 (A)

可以放在動詞 confirm (To confirm) 的受詞的位置，又可以用於定冠詞 the 和介系詞 with 之間的就是名詞。因此，名詞 (A) 和 (B) 都可能是正確答案。文意是「確定和行銷主任的面談」，所以抽象名詞 (A) interview 是正確答案。如果使用人物名詞 (B) interviewer（面試官），文意就會變成很怪的「確定和行銷主任的面試官」。分詞 (C) 和 (D) 無法位於名詞位置。(C) interviewing 雖然可以當成是動名詞，但還是無法位於定冠詞 the 的後面，所以也不會是正確答案。

單字 confirm v. 確定　coordinate v. 協調，適合　assistant n. 祕書，助理

| On April 3, the collections department will be _____ to a larger space on the third floor from its current office in the basement.
(A) declining　　　　(B) transferring
(C) disappearing　　　(D) estimating | 在 4 月 3 日，收帳部門將會從目前在地下室的辦公室移到三樓較大的空間。 |

■ 動詞語彙　　　　　　　　　　　　　　　　　　　　　　　　　　　解答 (B)

文意是「收帳部門移到三樓較大的空間」，所以可以和空格前面的 be 動詞一起組成進行式的動詞 transfer（移動）的 -ing 形 (B) transferring 就是正確答案。(A) decline 的意思是「減少，拒絕」，(C) disappear 的意思是「消失」，(D) estimate 的意思是「估算」。

單字 basement n. 地下室

| Health club members who are unable to pay their outstanding balance _____ the due date will be charged a late fee as penalty.
(A) by　　　　　　　(B) from
(C) inside　　　　　(D) toward | 無法在期限內付清欠款的健康俱樂部會員會被收取滯納金。 |

■ 介系詞選擇 時間點　　　　　　　　　　　　　　　　　　　　　　解答 (A)

文意是「無法在期限內付清欠款的會員」，所以表示時間點的介系詞 (A) by（到～為此）是正確答案。另外，until（直到～）是表示到狀況或狀態持續的時間點，而 by（到～為此）是表示到動作發生的時間點。(B) from 的意思是「從～開始」，表示出發點或出處。(C) inside 的意思是「在～裡面」，表示位置。(D) toward 的意思是「往～」，表示方向。

單字 unable a. 無法的　outstanding balance phr. 未支付的金額　charge v. 收取，繳納　penalty n. 罰金

| For further _____ precautions on installing the air conditioner, customers can refer to the product manual.
(A) safety　　　　　(B) most safely
(C) safes　　　　　(D) safeties | 有關安裝冷氣機的更多安全預防措施，顧客可以參考產品手冊。 |

■ 複合名詞　　　　　　　　　　　　　　　　　　　　　　　　　　　解答 (A)

_____ precautions 是介系詞 For 的受詞，也是被形容詞 further 修飾的名詞。因此，可以跟 precautions（預防措施）一起組成複合名詞的 (A) safety（安全）是正確答案。另外，跟複合名詞 safety precautions（安全預防措施）相類似的名詞還有 safety measures（安全措施）, safety regulations（安全規定）。

單字 precaution n. 預防措施　refer to v. 參考　manual n. 手冊　safety n. 安全

123

Parsons Financial Group _____ a new work schedule policy for contract workers in their regional branch offices. (A) acted (B) persuaded (C) implemented (D) informed	Parsons 金融集團針對他們地區分公司的約聘員工實施了一個新的工作進度政策。

■ 動詞語彙 　　　　　　　　　　　　　　　　　　　　　　　　　解答 (C)

文意是「實施了新的工作進度政策」，所以動詞 implement（實施）的過去式 (C) implemented 是正確答案。(A) act 的意思是「行動」，(B) persuade 的意思是「說服」，(D) inform 的意思是「通知～」，以人作為受詞。

單字 regional a. 地區的　branch n. 分公司，分枝

124

As explained in the company manual, employees may work overtime _____ their supervisor's written authorization. (A) without (B) unless (C) among (D) about	如同公司手冊中所說明的，員工可以沒有主管的書面授權就加班。

■ 副詞子句連接詞 vs.介系詞 　　　　　　　　　　　　　　　　　　　解答 (A)

這句話是具有主詞 employees 和動詞 may work 的完整子句，所以要把 _____ their supervisor's written authorization 看成是可省略的修飾語。這個修飾語是沒有動詞的片語形態，所以選項中可以引出修飾語的介系詞 (A) (C) (D) 都可能是正確答案。文意是「員工可以沒有主管的書面授權就加班」，因此 (A) without（沒有～）就是正確答案。(C) among 的意思是「～之間」，用於三個以上的事物或人之間。(D) about 的意思是「有關於～」。副詞子句連接詞 (B) unless（除非）不能引出修飾語。

單字 manual n. 手冊　supervisor n. 上司，主管　authorization n. 許可，授權

125

The staff member _____ current assignment is to arrange for applicant interviews is Joyce Moore of the personnel department. (A) whoever (B) whose (C) whom (D) who	目前負責安排應徵者面試的員工是人事部門的 Joyce Moore。

■ 關係代名詞的格和選擇 　　　　　　　　　　　　　　　　　　　　解答 (B)

這句話是具有主詞 The staff member，動詞（第二個 is）和補語 Joyce Moore 的完整子句，所以要把 _____ current ~ interviews 看成是可省略的修飾語。這個修飾語中包含了動詞（第一個 is）的子句形態，也是主詞 The staff member 作為先行詞的關係子句。要可以修飾關係子句 _____ current assignment ~ interviews 內的名詞 current assignment，又要構成意思是「目前負責的員工」的話，需要所有格的關係代名詞。因此，(B) whose 是正確答案。(A) whoever 是引出名詞子句的名詞子句的連接詞，所以不能引出扮演形容詞角色的關係子句。這個關係子句中不需要受詞，所以受格關係代名詞 (C) whom 也不能使用。主格關係代名詞 (D) who 後面接的不是名詞，而是動詞。

單字 applicant n. 應徵者　personnel department phr. 人事部門

126

All corporate giveaways made by Gorkis Creations may be _____ customized for an extra fee to fit the client's needs. (A) cautiously　　　　(B) enormously (C) individually　　　　(D) normally	所有 Gorkis Creation 公司做的免費樣品都可以多花一點費用來針對客戶的需求個別訂製。

■ 副詞語彙 　　　　　　　　　　　　　　　　　　　　　　　　　　　　　　　　　　　　解答 (C)

文意是「所有公司做的免費樣品可以個別訂製」，所以副詞 (C) individually（個別地）是正確答案。 (A) cautiously 的意思是「小心地」，(B) enormously 的意思是「相當地，巨大地」，(D) normally 的意思是「一般地」。另外，for an extra fee（付額外費用）要作為慣用語背起來。

單字 giveaway n. 贈品　customize v. 訂製

127

On her daily morning show, Rachael Burns gives her viewers practical _____ on home decorating and maintenance. (A) recommending　　　　(B) recommendations (C) recommended　　　　(D) recommend	在 Rachael Burns 早上的節目裡，她給觀眾們實用的居家裝潢維護建議。

■ 名詞的位置 　　　　　　　　　　　　　　　　　　　　　　　　　　　　　　　　　　解答 (B)

可以加兩個受詞的第四類動詞 give 的間接受詞 her viewers 後面接直接受詞，所以可以被形容詞 practical 修飾的名詞 (B) recommendations（提案，建議）是正確答案。動名詞或現在分詞 (A)，動詞或過去分詞 (C)，動詞 (D) 都不能放在受詞的位置。(A) recommending 雖然可以作為動名詞，但是無法被形容詞 practical 修飾，所以也不是正確答案。

單字 practical a. 實用的　maintenance n. 管理維護　recommendatory a. 推薦的

128

The _____ brochure includes additional information on some tiles and bricks that will be showcased at the construction fair. (A) revision　　　　(B) revises (C) revised　　　　(D) revise	修訂過的宣傳小冊子包含了一些在建築展中會展示的磁磚和磚塊等更多的資訊。

■ 形容詞的位置 　　　　　　　　　　　　　　　　　　　　　　　　　　　　　　　　　解答 (C)

可以在名詞前面扮演修飾作用的形容詞角色的是分詞。因此，動詞 revise（修訂）的過去分詞 (C) revised 是正確答案。另外，像 revised brochure（修訂過的小冊子）這樣分詞和名詞是被動關係時，要使用過去分詞。名詞 (A)，動詞 (B) 和 (D) 都不能修飾名詞。

單字 showcase v. 展示

129

| Zaykov Enterprises is planning to hold another trade show next year given that the feedback from this year's participants was so _____.
(A) enthuse   (B) enthusiastic
(C) enthusiastically   (D) enthusiasm | 因為今年參加者的熱烈反應，Zaykov 企業計畫在明年舉行另一個貿易展。 |

■ 可以放在補語位置的單字：名詞或形容詞   解答 (B)

be 動詞 was 有空格，所以形容詞 (B) 和名詞 (D) 都可能是正確答案。文意是「熱烈反應」，所以說明主詞 feedback 的形容詞 (B) enthusiastic（熱烈的）是正確答案。如果使用名詞 (D) enthusiasm（熱烈）的話，跟主詞 feedback 變成同位語關係，意思就變成很怪的「反應是熱烈」了。動詞 (A) 和副詞 (C) 不能放在補語的位置。

單字 **given that** phr. 考慮～的話   **enthusiastic** a. 熱烈的

130

| Front row tickets to the final round of the Wilbur Tennis Championship are sold out as the event is fast _____.
(A) commenting   (B) admitting
(C) approaching   (D) happening | Wilbur 網球賽決賽的前排座位票在活動即將開始前就已經銷售一空了。 |

■ 動詞語彙   解答 (C)

文意是「活動即將開始」，所以和 be 動詞 is 一起組成現在進行式的動詞 approach（即將）的 -ing 式 (C) approaching 是正確答案。另外，approach 除了表示時間、行程等等即將到來，也表示物理上的距離很短，意思是「接近，靠近」。(A) comment 的意思是「評論」，(B) admit 的意思是「認可」，(D) happen 的意思是「發生」。

131

| Jaydee Construction's management decided to transfer Cindy Lee to an _____ role because of her leadership experience.
(A) interested   (B) understood
(C) administrative   (D) unintended | Jaydee 建設公司的管理階層決定因為 Cindy Lee 的領導經驗，而將她轉任行政職。 |

■ 形容詞語彙   解答 (C)

文意是「Jaydee 建設公司的管理階層決定要將 Cindy Lee 轉任行政職」，所以形容詞 (C) administrative（管理的）是正確答案。(A) interested 是「感興趣的」，(B) understood 的意思是「理解」，(D) unintended 的意思是「不是故意的」。

單字 **management** n. 主管，管理階層   **transfer** v. 搬動，移動

132

| Many tourists like to attend the annual cultural festival, which is usually held at the public park _____ the post office.
(A) upon   (B) near
(C) between   (D) toward | 很多遊客喜歡參加通常都在郵局附近的公園裡舉辦的年度文化慶典。 |

■ 選擇介系詞 位置   解答 (B)

文意是「文化慶典通常都在郵局附近的公園舉辦」，所以表示距離上很近的位置的介系詞 (B) near（附近的，旁邊）是正確答案。(A) upon 的意思是「有關於～」，(C) between 的意思是「～之間」，這兩個都是表示兩個以上對象的關係或位置。(D) toward 的意思是「往～」，表示方向。

單字 **annual** a. 年度的   **cultural** a. 文化的

133

Most countries in Southeast Asia are undergoing gradual _____ from developing economies to industrialized nations.

(A) ignitions (B) transitions
(C) exchanges (D) corrections

大多數在東南亞的國家都正經歷從發展中經濟體到工業化國家的轉型期。

■ 名詞語彙　　　　　　　　　　　　　　　　　　　　　　　　　　　　　解答 (B)

文意是「正經歷從發展中經濟體到工業化國家的轉型變化中」，所以名詞 (B) transitions（轉變）是正確答案。另外，gradual（漸進的）和 improvement（改善）都是經常表示轉變的的單字。 (A) ignition 的意思是「著火」，(C) exchange 的意思是「交換」，(D) correction 的意思是「修訂」。

單字 undergo v. 遭遇　gradual a. 漸進的

134

In fulfillment of the Education Ministry's order, multimedia equipment will be _____ in public school classrooms nationwide.

(A) called back (B) picked out
(C) set up (D) counted on

為了要配合教育部的規定，全國公立學校教室將會裝上多媒體設備。

■ 動詞片語　　　　　　　　　　　　　　　　　　　　　　　　　　　　　解答 (C)

文意是「全國公立學校教室將會裝上多媒體設備」，所以具有「安裝」意思的動詞片語 (C) set up 是正確答案。 (A) call back 的意思是「回電」，(B) pick out 的意思是「選擇」，(D) count on 的意思是「相信～」。

單字 fulfillment n. 達成，實踐　equipment n. 裝備　nationwide ad. 全國地

135

Centuries ago, people in the mountain community developed effective techniques for farming on _____ slopes.

(A) steep (B) concrete
(C) loaded (D) temporary

幾個世紀以前，在山區的人發展出在陡峭山坡農耕的有效技術。

■ 形容詞語彙　　　　　　　　　　　　　　　　　　　　　　　　　　　　解答 (A)

文意是「發展出在陡峭山坡農耕的技術」，所以形容詞 (A) steep（陡峭的）是正確答案。 (B) concrete 的意思是「具體的」，(C) loaded 的意思是「滿滿的」，(D) temporary 的意思是「暫時的」。

單字 effective a. 有效的　slope n. 山坡

136

In relation to the other projects currently being implemented, the proposal writing task recently given by the supervisor is of _____ importance.

(A) higher (B) less highly
(C) highly (D) most highly

就其他目前正在執行的專案而言，主管最近給的計畫書撰寫的任務是比較重要的。

■ 形容詞的位置　　　　　　　　　　　　　　　　　　　　　　　　　　　解答 (A)

可以修飾位於介系詞 of 的受詞位置的名詞 importance 必須是形容詞，所以形容詞比較級 (A) higher 是正確答案。副詞的比較級 (B)，副詞 (C)，副詞的最高級 (D) 都不能修飾名詞。

單字 in relation to phr. 和～比較，跟～有關　implement v. 執行，實行

137

Every six months, Filigre Insurance asks clients for their updated personal information and organizes its customer database _____. (A) distinctly (B) markedly (C) accordingly (D) exceptionally	Filigre 保險公司要求客戶每六個月更新個人資料，並據此整理顧客資料庫。

■ 副詞語彙　　　　　　　　　　　　　　　　　　　　　　　　　解答 (C)

文意是「要求客戶更新個人資料，以據此整理顧客資料庫」，所以副詞 (C) accordingly（根據）是正確答案。(A) distinctly 的意思是「清晰地」，(B) markedly 的意思是「顯著地」，(D) exceptionally 的意思是「例外地，異常地」。

單字 insurance n. 保險　organize v. 整理，組織

138

The president has much _____ in his newly hired accountant, who has significant experience in the field. (A) confidence (B) confidently (C) confide (D) confident	總裁對於他新聘的會計師很有信心，這個會計師在這個領域有相當的經驗。

■ 名詞的位置　　　　　　　　　　　　　　　　　　　　　　　　解答 (A)

是動詞 has 的受詞，又可以被形容詞 much 修飾的就是名詞。因此，名詞 (A) confidence（信賴，信心）是正確答案。另外，have confidence in（信賴～）要作為慣用語背起來。副詞 (B)，動詞 (C)，形容詞 (D) 都不能位於名詞位置。還有，much 作為形容詞來使用的時候，意思是「相當的，很多的」；作為副詞來使用的時候，意思是「非常，很」。

單字 accountant n. 會計師　significant a. 重要的　confide v. 透露（祕密等）

139

Foreign nationals who would like to apply for work permits in the UAE must present substantial _____ that they are being hired by companies based in the country. (A) evidence (B) trust (C) motivation (D) perception	想要在 UAE 申請到工作證的外國國民，必須出示充分的證據以證明他們是被當地公司所雇用。

■ 名詞語彙　　　　　　　　　　　　　　　　　　　　　　　　　解答 (A)

文意是「必須提供充分的證據，證明被當地公司雇用」，所有名詞 (A) evidence（證據）是正確答案。(B) trust 的意思是「信賴」，(C) motivation 的意思是「刺激，動機」，(D) perception 的意思是「認知，感覺」。

單字 apply for phr. 申請～，請求　hire v. 雇用

140

The Yarikh Art Gallery is known for its _____ collections of paintings and sculptures from the 17th century. (A) various (B) variety (C) variously (D) varies	Yarikh 藝廊以其十七世紀各式各樣的畫作與雕像作品收藏而聞名。

■ 形容詞的位置　　　　　　　　　　　　　　　　　　　　　　　解答 (A)

為了修飾名詞 collections，一定需要出現形容詞，所以 (A) various（多樣的）是正確答案。副詞 (C)，動詞 (D) 都不能修飾名詞，名詞 (B) 如果不是要組成複合名詞，也不能修飾名詞。另外，be known for（因～聞名）要作為慣用語背起來。

單字 collection n. 收集品，收藏　sculpture n. 雕刻品

PART 6

Questions 141-143 refer to the following instruction.　　　141-143 根據下面說明的內容回答問題。

To streamline the leave application and approval process, the management has made new guidelines for vacation leave requests. First, personnel who would like to take a day off must fill out the new forms supplied to their respective offices. The forms should be submitted to the human resources department at least two days before the date of _____.

141 (A) employment　(B) absence
　　　(C) separation　(D) completion

Second, staff members who want to apply for long vacations should inform their superiors and the department at least two weeks in advance.

Since the department is currently busy recruiting new personnel for the company's satellite office, _____ will be

142 (A) someone　　(B) everyone
　　　(C) nobody　　(D) anybody

assigned to receive leave forms until next month. In the meantime, all forms must be left in the receptacle near the department's entrance. A clerk _____ your office

143 (A) has contacted　(B) was contacting
　　　(C) is contacting　(D) will contact

to confirm receipt of your form. You should receive a response to your request within a week.

為了要簡化請假申請與核准程序，管理階層針對特別休假申請制定了新的規定。首先，要請一天假的人必須填寫提供給個別部門的新的表格，這個表格應該至少在 141 請假前兩天繳交給人力資源部門。

其次，想要請長假的員工應該在至少兩週前事先告知主管和其所屬部門。

因為目前部門忙於為分處的辦公室招募新員工，所以在下個月之前，142 沒有人會負責受理請假單。

在此同時，所有的表格必須投遞在部門入口的收件匣中，143 職員會和你的辦公室聯絡，確認收到你的假單，你會在一週內收到關於你請假申請的回音。

單字 **streamline** v. 使有效率，簡化　**respective** a. 各自的　**satellite office** phr. 分社，分局
in the meantime phr. 在此同時　**receptacle** n. 貯藏所，存放的地方　**receipt** n. 收到，接到

141 ■ 名詞語彙 掌握全文　　　　　　　　　　　　　　　　　　　　　　　　　　　　　　　　解答 (B)

文意是「表格應該至少在 ＿＿ 前兩天繳交給人力資源部門」，所以所有選項都可能是正確答案。只看有空格的句子無法選出正確的答案時，就要先了解前後文意或整體文意。前面的句子中提到要請一天假的人必須填寫新的表格，由此可以知道請假前一定要交表格。因此，(B) absence（不在，缺席）是正確答案。(A) employment 的意思是「雇用」，(C) separation 的意思是「分離」，(D) completion 的意思是「完成」。

142 ■ 不定代名詞　　　　　　　　　　　　　　　　　　　　　　　　　　　　　　　　　　　　解答 (C)

文意是「部門很忙，沒有人會負責受理請假單」，所以不定代名詞 (C) nobody（誰也不～）是正確答案。(A) someone 的意思是「某人」，(B) everyone 的意思是「每一個人」，(D) anybody 的意思是「任何人」。

143 ■ 未來時態 掌握上下文　　　　　　　　　　　　　　　　　　　　　　　　　　　　　　　解答 (D)

文意是「職員會和你的辦公室聯絡，確認收到你的假單」。這時候只看有空格的句子是無法選出正確時態的動詞，要先了解前後文意或整體文意才能選出正確答案。前面的句子中提到所有的表格投遞在收件匣中，因此可以知道職員和你的辦公室聯絡是在表格投遞之後發生的事情。因此，未來時態 (D) will contact 是正確答案。

Questions 144-146 refer to the following memo.   144-146 根據下面説明的備忘錄回答問題。

To: Sales Staff
From: Edward House, Solepad Assistant Manager

Subject: Silvercup Gift Certificate

To encourage everyone to sell more shoes, management has decided to reward staff members who meet their weekly quotas with gift certificates for Silvercup Mall. This new _____ program will be effective throughout the year.

144 (A) incentive   (B) elaborate
    (C) legislative   (D) economic

We have obtained the certificates and the first sales team to be awarded will be announced tomorrow.

The certificates, which are worth $50, expire at the end of _____ year. In addition, they may be accumulated and used

145 (A) many   (B) both
    (C) neither   (D) each

for larger purchases. Simply _____ the certificates at any

146 (A) copy   (B) prepare
    (C) present   (D) exhibit

store in the Silvercup Mall. Any amount in excess of the certificates' total value, however, must be paid for by the holder.

收件人：銷售部門員工
寄件人：Solepad 公司助理經理
         Edward House
主旨：Silvercup 禮券

為了要鼓勵大家多賣些鞋子，管理階層已經決定要以 Silvercup 購物中心的禮券來獎勵達成每週銷售額度的員工，144 這個新的獎勵辦法整年都會執行，我們已經備妥禮券，第一個獲獎的團隊將會在明天宣布。

145 這些五十元的禮券在每年年底到期，此外，這些禮券可以累積使用在較大金額的消費上。

只要在 Silvercup 購物中心的任何商店 146 出示禮券就可以了，不過，超出禮券總額的部分，必須自行負擔。

單字 **reward** v. 給予報酬　**quota** n. 配額　**throughout** prep. ～期間　**award** v. 授予，給予　**expire** v. 過期　**accumulate** v. 累積　**holder** n. 持有者

144 ■ 形容詞語彙 掌握上下文　　　　　　　　　　　　　　　　　　　　　　　　　　解答 (A)

文意是「這個新的 ＿＿＿ 辦法整年都會執行」，所以所有選項都可能是正確答案。只看有空格的句子無法選出正確的答案時，就要先了解前後文意或整體文意。前面的句子中提到為了多賣些鞋子，以禮券來獎勵員工，所以形容詞 (A) incentive（有獎金的，獎勵）是正確答案。(B) elaborate 的意思是「精緻的」，(C) legislative 的意思是「立法的」，(D) economic 的意思是「經濟上的」。

145 ■ 數量表達　　　　　　　　　　　　　　　　　　　　　　　　　　　　　　解答 (D)

空格是介系詞 of 的受詞，空格後面又有單數名詞 year，所以可以修飾名詞的數量形容詞 (D) each（各自的）是正確答案。用於複數名詞前面的數量形容詞 (A) many 不是正確答案。(B) both 和 and 一起組成 both A and B（A 和 B 都），(C) neither 和 nor 一起組成 neither A nor B（A 和 B 兩者皆非～）使用。(B) 和 (C) 都是相關連接詞。

146 ■ 動詞語彙 掌握全文　　　　　　　　　　　　　　　　　　　　　　　　　　解答 (C)

文意是「任何商店 ＿＿＿ 禮券就可以了」，所以所有選項都可能是正確答案。只看有空格的句子無法選出正確的答案時，就要先了解前後文意或整體文意。前面的內容中提到發禮券和可使用於消費，所以可以知道禮券使用時，要跟店家出示禮券。因此，(C) present（出示，給）是正確答案。(A) copy 的意思是「影印」，(B) prepare 的意思是「準備」，(D) exhibit 的意思是「展示」。

April 14	4月14日
Celeste Padilla, Admissions Director Zuidema Business School Calle La Guerta 96 Chuao, Caracas 1060A	招生入學部主任 Celeste Padilla Zuidema 商學院 Calle La Guerta 96 號 Caracas 省 Chuao 市，郵遞區號 1060A
Dear Ms. Padilla,	親愛的 Padilla 小姐
I would like to _____ Adela Ugarte's admission to your 147 (A) postpone　　(B) recommend 　　(C) evaluate　　(D) disapprove	147 我想要推薦 Adela Ugarte 進入貴校的商業管理碩士班就讀，我和 Ugarte 小姐在工作上密切合作，而且深信她應該進入 Zuidema 商學院就讀。
school's Master of Business Administration program. I have worked closely with Ms. Ugarte and strongly believe that she deserves to be accepted to the Zuidema Business School.	
Since Ms. Ugarte joined our firm as a financial analyst four years ago, she has always displayed a strong initiative and work ethic. Moreover, Ms. Ugarte functions well within a group setting but at the same time is capable of achieving results _____. She worked on her own to form 148 (A) cooperatively　　(B) routinely 　　(C) exclusively　　(D) independently	自從 Ugarte 小姐在四年前加入我們的公司擔任財務分析師，她總是自動自發，而且極具工作倫理，此外，Ugarte 小姐在團隊中互動良好，148 同時也能獨立勝任達成目標，她獨自做出來預測發展的明確說明書，最後成為我們新員工有用的工具。
a definitive manual on forecast development, which eventually became a useful tool for our new employees.	
I hope that my brief outline of Ms. Ugarte's skills will _____ 149 (A) benefit　　(B) enable 　　(C) convince　　(D) demonstrate	149 我希望我對 Ugarte 小姐的專業的簡介能夠讓你們認為她應該進入 Zuidema 商學院的商業管理碩士班就讀。如果你想要更詳細地討論她的資歷，請撥打 555-8321 給我，謝謝你的時間。
all concerned that she deserves to be admitted to Zuidema Business School's MBA program. If you would like to discuss her qualifications in more detail, please feel free to give me a call at 555-8321. Thank you for your time.	
Yours truly,	
Oswaldo Medina, Head, International Accounts Frechilla Enterprises	Oswaldo Medina Frechilla 企業國際帳戶主任

單字 admission n. 入學　deserve v. 有資格做～　analyst n. 分析家　initiative n. 倡議　forecast n. 預測

147 ■ 動詞語彙 掌握上下文　　　　　　　　　　　　　　　　　　　　　　　　　　　　　解答 (B)

文意是「我想要 ____ Adela Ugarte 入學貴校」，所有選項都可能是正確答案。只看有空格的句子無法選出正確的答案時，要先了解前後文意或整體文意。後面的內容中提到「我相信她具有入學資格」，所以可以知道發信者是對入學管理者推薦 Adela Ugarte。因此，動詞 (B) recommend（推薦）是正確答案。(A) postpone 的意思是「延後，推遲」，(C) evaluate 的意思是「評價」，(D) disapprove 的意思是「不贊成」。

148 ■ 副詞語彙　　　　　　　　　　　　　　　　　　　　　　　　　　　　　　　　　　解答 (D)

文意是「在團隊中互動良好，同時能獨立勝任達成目標」，所以副詞 (D) independently（獨立地）是正確答案。(A) cooperatively 是「協力」，(B) routinely 是「日常地」，(C) exclusively 是「排他地」。

149 ■ 動詞語彙　　　　　　　　　　　　　　　　　　　　　　　　　　　　　　　　　　解答 (C)

文意是「讓你們認為她有入學資格」，所以動詞 (C) convince（使確信，說服）是正確答案。(A) benefit 的意思是「有優勢」，(B) enable 的意思是「使可以」，(D) demonstrate 的意思是「出示，論證」。

Questions 150-152 refer to the following e-mail.

150-152 根據下面電郵的內容回答問題。

To: Elizabeth Marquez <emarquez@mayardbar.com>

From: Gladys Cross <melcross@pinnaclemedia.com>

Subject: Band Information
Date: December 10

Dear Beth,

I was wondering whether or not you received the package I mailed to your office earlier this week. It contains a profile and a CD of the band that I am suggesting you hire for the grand _____ of your restaurant next month.

150 (A) open   (B) opening
(C) openly   (D) opened

Velvet Jazz Band is a rising band in the local music industry. The group is composed of talented and _____

151 (A) global   (B) selective
(C) versatile   (D) acceptable

musicians. They can play jazz, rock, and other genres of music. In addition, the group's vocalist comes from a pop group that topped the Asian charts three years ago.

I guarantee you that Velvet Jazz Band will _____ many

152 (A) engage   (B) attract
(C) invite   (D) persuade

customers to your restaurant and create a lasting impression of your establishment. Just let me know if you want to personally meet the members of the band so that I can schedule an appointment with them. Thanks!

Best regards,

Gladys

收件人：Elizabeth Marquez
<emarquez@mayardbar.com>
寄件人：Gladys Cross
<melcross@pinnaclemedia.com>

主旨：樂團資訊
日期：12 月 10 日

親愛的 Beth：

我想知道你是否收到了我稍早於本週寄到你辦公室的包裹，150 裡面有我建議你為下個月餐廳開幕可以請來表演的樂團資料和 CD。

Velvet 爵士樂團是當地樂壇崛起中的一個樂團，151 這個團體由才華洋溢、多才多藝的音樂家所組成。他們可以演奏爵士、搖滾和其他種類的音樂。此外，這個團體的主唱來自一個三年前在亞洲排行頂尖的流行樂樂團。

152 我向你保證 Velvet 爵士樂團將會吸引很多客人到你的餐廳，且對你的餐廳留下難以忘懷的印象。讓我知道你是否想親自與樂團成員們會面，我可以替你安排，謝謝！

Gladys 敬上

單字 package n. 包裹　local a. 當地的　talented a. 有才能的　guarantee v. 保證

150 ■ 名詞的位置   解答 (B)

在介系詞 for 的受詞位置上，可以被「冠詞 + 形容詞」the grand 修飾的是名詞。因此，名詞 (A) 和 (B) 都可能是答案。文意是「下個月餐廳開幕」，可以跟空格前面的 grand 一起組成「開幕」的名詞 (B) opening（開幕，開張）是正確答案。如果使用名詞 (A) open（室外，打開）的話，文意就會變得很奇怪。副詞 (C)，動詞或分詞 (D) 都不能放在名詞的位置上。

151 ■ 形容詞語彙 掌握上下文   解答 (C)

文意是「由才華洋溢、＿＿＿ 的音樂家所組成」，形容詞 (A) (C) (D) 都可能是答案。只看有空格的句子無法選出答案時，要先了解前後文意或整體文意。後面的句子中提到可以演奏爵士、搖滾和其他種類的音樂。由此可知 Velvet 爵士樂團由多才多藝的音樂家組成。因此，(C) versatile（多才多藝）是正確答案。(A) global 是「世界的」，(B) selective 是「選擇的」，(D) acceptable 的意思是「可以接受的，令人滿意的」。

152 ■ 動詞語彙 掌握全文   解答 (B)

文意是「Velvet 爵士樂團將會 ＿＿＿ 很多客人到你的餐廳，且對你的餐廳留下印象」，動詞 (B) 和 (C) 都可能是答案。只看有空格的句子無法選出正確答案時，要先了解前後文意或整體文意。文章前面是為了讓餐廳雇用樂團而進行介紹，所以可以知道發信者保證推薦的樂團可以吸引顧客。因此，(B) attract（吸引）是正確答案。(A) engage 是「雇用」，(C) invite 是「邀請」，(D) persuade 是「說服」。

PART 7

Questions 153-154 refer to the following schedule.　153-154 根據下面時間表的內容回答問題。

Carpentry Association of Vermont			

Presents woodworking courses, June 2 to July 6 at the Evergreen Community Center

Time	Course	Description	Instructor
Mon/Wed 9 A.M. to 12 A.M.	Woodworking 101	Recommended for beginners. Covers the basics of woodworking.	Jonathan Smith
Fri/Sat 1 to 4 P.M.	Simple Woodworking	Make objects such as picture frames, jewelry boxes, and pen holders.	Garrett Turner
Tue/Thu 3 to 6 P.M.	Great Wooden Things	Designed for home improvement enthusiasts with advanced skills.	Sean Langley
Tue/Fri 10 A.M. to 1 P.M.	153Wood Imagination	Skills for those interested in using wood to make sculptures or fine art.	Frederick Burch

A certificate of completion will be given at the end of each course. Course materials will be provided. Sign up at www.woodcourses.org. 154Registration runs from May 10 to 25 only.

佛蒙特州木匠協會			

6 月 2 日到 7 月 6 日在 Evergreen 社區中心舉辦木工課程

時間	課程	說明	講師
星期一 / 星期三 上午 9 點到中午 12 點	木工 101	適合初學者，涵蓋基本的木工	Jonathan Smith
星期五 / 星期六 下午 1 點到 4 點	簡易木工	製造木製品，例如相框、珠寶盒和筆架	Garrett Turner
星期二 / 星期四 下午 3 點到 6 點	美哉木器	專為有進階技術的居家修繕熱衷者設計	Sean Langley
星期二 / 星期五 上午 10 點到下午 1 點	153木之想像	給那些有興趣用木頭做雕刻或藝術品的人的技巧	Frederick Burch

在課程結束後會發給結業證書，會提供上課材料，在網站 www.woodcourses.org 上報名，154報名時間為 5 月 10 日至 25 日。

單字 □carpentry n. 木匠　　　　□woodworking n. 木工
　　□home improvement phr. 居家修繕，住宅維修　　□enthusiast n. 熱衷者，粉絲
　　□advanced a. 高級的　□sculpture n. 雕刻品　　□fine art phr. 美術品
　　□run v.（在多長期間內）持續

153

Who most likely will teach a class for artists?	誰最有可能為藝術家們授課？
(A) Garrett Turner	(A) Garrett Turner
(B) Sean Langley	(B) Sean Langley
(C) Frederick Burch	(C) Frederick Burch
(D) Jonathan Smith	(D) Jonathan Smith

■ 推論 詳細內容　　　　　　　　　　　　　　　　　　　　　　　解答 (C)

這是問誰最有可能為藝術家授課的推理問題。跟問題核心詞語 teach a class for artists 相關的 Wood Imagination, Skills for those interested in using wood to make sculptures or fine art., Frederick Burch 中提到名為木之想像的這堂課中會說明用木頭做雕刻或藝術品的技巧，講師是 Frederick Burch。因此，可以推斷出 Frederick Burch 是為了藝術家們而上課的。因此，(C) Frederick Burch 是正確答案。

What will happen after May 25?	在 5 月 25 日會發生什麼事？
(A) Registration for classes will be closed.	(A) 課程報名截止。
(B) An association will be accepting members.	(B) 協會會接受會員。
(C) A Web site will be inaccessible.	(C) 網站會無法使用。
(D) Course materials will be distributed.	(D) 會發下上課材料。

■ 六何原則 What   解答 (A)

這是問 5 月 25 日會發生什麼（What）事的六何原則問題。跟問題的核心詞語 happen after May 25 相關聯的 Registration runs from May 10 to 25 only. 中提到報名時間為 5 月 10 日至 25 日。因此，(A) Registration for classes will be closed. 是正確答案。

單字 inaccessible a. 無法使用的　distribute v. 分發

Questions 155-156 refer to the following advertisement.

155-156 根據下面廣告的內容回答問題。

Marigold Spa

■Theaterbelt ■Silvertown ■Bakerville ■Wesley

For 10 years now, Marigold Spa has been promoting personal well-being through natural methods of revitalization. 155-CTo celebrate a decade of service, 156-A/C/DMarigold Spa is reducing prices by up to 30 percent on basic personal care treatments, including body massages, facials, and nail care for the entire month of June. In addition, Marigold Spa Club members will receive a free foot spa package when they visit any Marigold Spa branch this month. Celebrate with us and take advantage of this limited-time offer. For more information, log on to www.marigoldspa.com.

Marigold 水療館
分店：■ Theaterbelt
■Silvertown ■Bakerville ■Wesley

十年了，Marigold 水療館透過天然療癒的方法來促進個人的健康，155-C為了要慶祝服務十週年，156-A/C/DMarigold 水療館在 6 月一整個月裡，讓您享有基礎個人療程高達七折的優惠，包括身體按摩、做臉、指甲照護。此外，Marigold 水療俱樂部的會員在這個月到任何 Marigold 水療館分店都可以得到一次免費的足部水療課程。和我們一起慶祝，並充分利用這個限時優惠，更多詳情，請上官網 www.marigoldspa.com

單字 □revitalization n. 復興，給予活力　□decade n. 十年　□branch n. 分店
□celebrate v. 紀念，慶祝　□take advantage of phr. 利用～

155

What is indicated about Marigold Spa? (A) It is launching a new service. (B) It is introducing a membership club. (C) It is celebrating its anniversary. (D) It is opening another branch.	關於 Marigold 水療館，何者正確？ (A) 開始一項新的服務。 (B) 推出會員俱樂部。 (C) 正在慶祝周年。 (D) 分店開張。

■ **Not / True** True 問題　　　　解答 (C)

這是找出跟問題核心詞語 Marigold Spa 相關的內容後，再跟選項作對比的 Not / True 問題。 (A) 和 (B) 都是文中沒提到的內容。To celebrate a decade of service 中提到為了要慶祝服務十週年，所以跟 (C) 的內容一致。因此，(C) It is celebrating its anniversary. 是正確答案。 (D) 是文中沒提到的內容。

單字 launch v. 提示，開始　introduce v. 導入，介紹

156

What is NOT included in the discount promotion? (A) Massages (B) Spa packages (C) Facials (D) Manicure services	什麼不包含在折扣優惠中？ (A) 按摩 (B) 水療課程 (C) 做臉 (D) 修指甲

■ **Not / True** Not 問題　　　　解答 (B)

這是找出跟問題核心詞語 the discount promotion 相關的內容後，再跟選項作對比的 Not / True 問題。Marigold Spa is reducing prices ~ on basic personal care treatments, including body massages, facials, and nail care 中提到「讓您享有基礎個人療程的優惠，包括身體按摩、做臉、指甲照護」。因此，跟 (A) (C) (D) 的內容一致。 (B) 是文中沒提到的內容。因此，(B) Spa packages 是正確答案。

Questions 157-158 refer to the following notice.

157-158 根據下面告示的內容回答問題。

Notice to All Marketing Staff Members

To provide everyone with an organized record of discussions about our projects, 157members will take turns in preparing minutes of every meeting and posting them on the Intranet. This should take place immediately after each team meeting or client appointment. In addition, everyone is expected to follow a uniform format when presenting information online.

158-DSince we cannot access the Intranet right now due to ongoing network maintenance work, 158-Cthe format will be posted on the bulletin board later today. A schedule for taking minutes will be provided at our next meeting. If you have any questions, let me know.

From Justine Tuckfield
Marketing Department Head

通知所有行銷部門人員

為了要讓每個人都能獲得關於我們專案的整理過的討論紀錄，157我們要輪流做每個會議的紀錄，並公開在內部網路上。在每個團隊會議或與客戶會面後，應該立即執行，此外，每個人都要遵照統一的格式把資料放在網路上。

158-D由於目前正在進行的網路維護使我們無法連上內部網路，158-C格式會在今天稍晚公布在布告欄上，寫會議紀錄的輪班表會在我們下次的會議裡提供給各位，如果有任何問題，請讓我知道。

行銷部門主管
Justine Tuckfield

單字 □minutes n. 會議記錄　　□post v. 送上，出示　　□uniform a. 統一的
　　□format n. 表格　　　　　□ongoing a. 進行中的　　□maintenance n. 維持，保持
　　□bulletin board phr. 佈告欄

157

What is the notice mainly about? (A) Posting messages on the Intranet site (B) Keeping online information secure (C) Implementing a new office procedure (D) Making schedule changes for monthly meetings	這個通知主要是關於什麼？ (A) 在內部網路上張貼訊息 (B) 確保線上的資訊安全 (C) 執行一項新的辦公室措施 (D) 改變每月會議的時間表

■ 找出主題 主題　　　　　　　　　　　　　　　　　　　　　　　　　解答 (C)

這是問通知中主要是關於什麼的找主題問題，所以要特別注意文章的前半部份。members will take turns in preparing minutes of every meeting and posting them on the Intranet 中提到成員輪流做每個會議的紀錄，並公開在內部網路上。接著，又說明了做會議紀錄的程序及之後計畫。因此，(C) Implementing a new office procedure 是正確答案。

單字 secure a. 安全的　implement v. 實行

158

What does Ms. Tuckfield mention about the format? (A) It will remain the same as before. (B) It has been simplified. (C) It was posted for staff yesterday. (D) It is not yet accessible.	Tuckfield 女士提到關於格式，何者正確？ (A) 維持和以往一樣。 (B) 已經簡化了。 (C) 昨天已經張貼出來給員工了。 (D) 尚無法獲得。

■ Not / True True 問題　　　　　　　　　　　　　　　　　　　　　解答 (D)

這是找出跟問題核心詞語 the format 相關的內容後，再跟選項作對比的 Not / True 問題。(A) 和 (B) 都是文中沒提到的內容。the format will be posted ~ later today 中提到格式會在今天稍晚公布，所以跟 (C) 的內容不一致。since we cannot access the Intranet right now ~ the format will be posted ~ later today 中提到由於目前無法連上內部網路，格式會在今天稍晚公布，所以 (D) It is not yet accessible. 是正確答案。

單字 simplify v. 簡單化

Questions 159-161 refer to the following notice.

159-161 根據下面告示的內容回答問題。

Kensington's Wants to Serve you Better!

[159]Kensington's family restaurant is pleased to announce that we will be extending our hours of operation at all branches across the nation! This change will provide you with additional hours in the morning for breakfast service and extra time in the evening on weekends.

In line with this, [160-C/161-A/D]Kensington's will also be introducing a new breakfast buffet on weekends including such favorites as omelets, pancakes, and waffles. The new offerings will be introduced starting this weekend on May 4.

Our new hours of operation are as follows:

Monday	
Tuesday	7 A.M. to 10 P.M.
Wednesday	
Thursday	
Friday	7 A.M. to 11:30 P.M.
Saturday *	8 A.M. to 11:30 P.M.
Sunday *	

*[161-B]Breakfast buffet service is available from 9 A.M. through 12 P.M. [161-C]Reservations are recommended. To book a table, please call (504) 555-6677.

For further information on our menu, locations, and promotions, visit www.kensingtons.co.ca.

Kensington's 要提供你更好的服務！

[159]Kensington 家庭餐廳很高興地宣布我們全國各地的分店都會延長營業時間！這項改變讓你在早晨的早餐和週末晚間有更多時間。

為了配合這項改變，[160-C/161-A/D]Kensington 還會在週末推出自助早餐，包括最受歡迎的煎蛋捲、薄烤餅和鬆餅，將從 5 月 4 日這個週末開始供應。

我們新的營業時間如下：

星期一	
星期二	早上 7 點到晚上 10 點
星期三	
星期四	
星期五	早上 7 點到晚上 11 點 30 分
星期六*	早上 8 點到晚上 11 點 30 分
星期日*	

*[161-B]自助早餐供應時間為上午 9 點到中午 12 點。[161-C]建議提前預約。預約請撥打 (504)555-6677。

更多關於我們的菜單、地點和優惠活動等資訊，請上官網 www.kensingtons.co.ca

單字 □extend v. 延長，伸長　　　□in line with phr. 和～一起，根據～　　□reservation n. 預約

159

Why was the notice written?	為什麼寫這個告示？
(A) To announce business hour changes	(A) 宣布營業時間改變
(B) To inform diners of menu items	(B) 告知用餐者菜單上的食物
(C) To promote a new restaurant	(C) 宣傳新的餐廳
(D) To publicize a special discount offer	(D) 宣傳一項特別優惠方案

■ 找出主題 寫文章的理由　　　　　　　　　　　　　　　　　　　　　　　　　　　　　解答 (A)

這是問告示的原因的找主題問題，所以要特別注意文章的前半部份。Kensington's family restaurant is pleased to announce that we will be extending our hours of operation 中提到 Kensington 家庭餐廳很高興地宣布延長營業時間。接著，又說明了新的營業時間。因此，(A) To announce business hour changes 是正確答案。

換句話說

extending ~ hours of operation 延長營業時間 → business hour changes 變更營業時間

單字 promote v. 宣傳　publicize v. 公告，通知

160

What is indicated about Kensington's family restaurant?	關於 Kensington 家庭餐廳，何者正確？
(A) It only has breakfast and lunch menus.	(A) 只有早餐和午餐的菜單。
(B) It has numerous branches around the world.	(B) 全球有很多家分店。
(C) It offers a special dining option on weekends.	(C) 在週末有特別的用餐選擇。
(D) It does not accept weekday reservations	(D) 不接受週一至週五的預約。

■ **Not / True** True 問題   解答 (C)

這是找出跟問題核心詞語 Kensington's family restaurant 相關的內容後，再跟選項作對比的 Not / True 問題。 (A) 和 (B) 都是文中沒提到的內容。Kensington's will also be introducing a new breakfast buffet on weekends including such favorites 中提到 Kensington 還會在週末推出自助早餐，包括最受歡迎的菜，所以跟 (C) 的內容一致。因此，(C) It offers a special dining option on weekends. 是正確答案。 (D) 是文中沒提到的內容。

161

What is mentioned about the buffet?	關於自助餐，何者正確？
(A) It is offered Monday through Friday.	(A) 週一至週五供應。
(B) It is only available at a particular time.	(B) 只有在特定的時間供應。
(C) It requires advance bookings.	(C) 必須事先預約。
(D) It will no longer be provided on weekends.	(D) 週末將不再供應。

■ **Not / True** True 問題   解答 (B)

這是找出跟問題核心詞語 the buffet 相關的內容後，再跟選項作對比的 Not / True 問題。Kensington's will also be introducing a new breakfast buffet on weekends 中提到 Kensington 還會在週末推出早餐自助餐，所以跟 (A) 和 (D) 的內容不一致。Breakfast buffet service is available from 9 A.M. through 12 P.M. 中提到早餐自助餐供應時間為上午 9 點到中午 12 點，所以跟 (B) 的內容一致。因此，(B) It is only available at a particular time. 是正確答案。Reservations are recommended. 提到建議提前預約，所以跟 (C) 的內容不一致。

單字 require v. 需要，要求 advance a. 事前的

School Aims to Meet Demand for Foreign Languages
[164]by Vanna Tan

Proficiency in English and other foreign languages has become a major requirement for Chinese professionals with career aspirations. Given the increasing number of foreign companies operating in the country and fierce competition in the job market, people who speak many languages have a distinct advantage. This trend made [163-A]linguist Kenny Mayer realize the need to establish a language school that would help citizens improve their performance.

"Since impressive language skills are essential in the corporate world, I decided to build a school for those who wish to enhance their abilities," [164]Mayer said in an interview.

[162/163-A]Mayer opened Fluency Masters Academy on Friday at the Collinsway Tower. All programs offered at the academy are tailored to students who are beginners and have never studied a foreign language. [163-C]Among the courses currently available are English, Japanese, and French. [163-B/C]Native speakers in each language will conduct lessons on weekday nights. Mayer says that the academy will allow professionals to learn a language without travelling abroad.

"If everything goes well during the year, I might consider offering Spanish and other European languages. But for now, the academy will continue to focus on its current three languages," Mayer said.

學校打算滿足學生對外語的需求
[164]Vanna Tan 報導

英語與其他外國語言的精通已經成為中國專業人士想要在職場一展長才的必要條件。考慮到越來越多外國公司在中國營運，以及就業市場的激烈競爭，能說多種語言的人佔有特別的優勢，這樣的趨勢讓[163-A]語言學家 Kenny Mayer 體認到建立一間語言學校的需求，能夠幫助中國人改善他們的能力。

[164]Mayer 在一次訪談中說：「因為優秀的語言技巧在企業界是很重要的，所以我決定建立一所學校給那些想要加強自己能力的人。」

[162/163-A]Mayer 創辦的 Fluency Masters Academy 於週五在 Collinsway 大樓開幕了。學校裡所有課程都是為從未學習過外語的初學者學生量身訂做，[163-C]目前開課的課程有英語、日語和法語。[163-B/C]週一到週五晚間由這些語言的母語老師授課，Mayer 表示這間學校讓想學語言的專業人士不用遠渡重洋。

Mayer 說：「假如今年一切都很順利，我會考慮開西班牙語和其他歐洲語言的課程，但是現在學校會繼續著重於目前這三種語言。」

單字　□proficiency n. 精通；熟練　　□aspiration n. 展望，抱負　　□fierce a. 狂熱的，激烈的
　　　□competition n. 競爭　　　　　□distinct a. 明確的，分明的　□trend n. 傾向，趨勢
　　　□linguist n. 語言學家　　　　　□citizen n. 市民
　　　□impressive a. 突出的，給人留下印象的　　　　　　　　　□essential a. 必須的，極為重要的
　　　□enhance v. 使成長　　　　　□tailor v. 使合適；n. (男裝) 裁縫師　□abroad ad. 國外地，海外地

162

What is the article mainly about?	這篇文章主要關於什麼？
(A) A university activity	(A) 一項大學活動
(B) The launch of a business	(B) 開始一項事業
(C) Commonly used languages	(C) 常用的語言
(D) Communication techniques	(D) 溝通技術

■ 找出主題 主題　　　　　　　　　　　　　　　　　　　　　　　　　　　　　　解答 (B)

這是問報導主要關於什麼的找主題問題，需要特別注意文章中半段中提到的相關內容。Mayer opened Fluency Masters Academy on Friday at the Collinsway Tower. 中提到 Mayer 創辦的 Fluency Masters Academy 於週五在 Collinsway 大樓開幕。接著，又說明了 Academy 提供的課程和之後的營運計畫。因此，(B) The launch of a business 是正確答案。

163

What is NOT indicated about Fluency Masters?	關於 Fluency Masters，何者不正確？
(A) It was founded by a language expert.	(A) 由一位語言專家所建立。
(B) It offers classes on weekdays.	(B) 週一至週五提供課程。
(C) It employs native English speakers.	(C) 雇用母語為英語的老師。
(D) It is affiliated with a foreign company.	(D) 附屬於一家外國公司。

■ **Not / True** Not 問題   解答 (D)

這是找出跟問題核心詞語 Fluency Masters 相關的內容後，再跟選項作對比的 Not / True 問題。linguist Kenny Mayer 中提到 Kenny Mayer 是語言學家。接著，Mayer opened Fluency Masters Academy 中提到 Mayer 開辦了 Fluency Masters Academy。因此，跟 (A) 的內容一致。Native speakers ~ will conduct lessons on weekday nights.中提到平日晚間由語言的母語老師授課，所以跟 (B) 的內容一致。Among the courses currently available are English 中提到目前開課的課程有英語。接著，Native speakers in each language will conduct lessons 中又提到由每個語言的母語老師授課。因此，跟 (C) 的內容一致。(D) 是文中沒提到的內容。因此，(D) It is affiliated with a foreign company. 是正確答案。

單字 found v. 成立　expert n. 專家　employ v. 雇用　affiliate v. 合作，連接

164

What does the article suggest?	關於這篇文章，何者正確？
(A) Ms. Tan speaks many languages.	(A) Tan 小姐會説很多種語言。
(B) The school is in a business district.	(B) 這間學校位在商業區。
(C) Ms. Tan interviewed Mr. Mayer.	(C) Tan 小姐訪問 Mayer 先生。
(D) The academy will open on Friday.	(D) 這家學校將在週五開幕。

■ **推論** 詳細內容   解答 (C)

這是問報導內容的推理問題。因為問題中沒有核心詞語，所以跟全部選項的核心詞語相關的內容都要一一確定。by Vanna Tan 中提到報導是由 Vanna Tan 所寫。Mayer said in an interview 中提到 Mayer 在一次訪談中說。由此可以推斷出 Vanna Tan 採訪了 Mayer。因此，(C) Ms. Tan interviewed Mr. Mayer. 是正確答案。

單字 district n. 地區，地帶

Questions 165-167 refer to the following letter.

165-167 根據下面信件的內容回答問題。

FOREMOST EMPLOYMENT AGENCY	**Foremost 職業介紹所**
August 14	8 月 14 日
Dear Mr. Nehru,	親愛的 Nehru 先生：
¹⁶⁵I am sorry to inform you that your application for the position of senior technical director at Goldbear Technologies was turned down. The company was recently forced to reduce its managerial workforce due to the ongoing economic crisis. ¹⁶⁵However, I plan to submit your application to another company in western India, Pioneer Plastics Manufacturing. This is a growing company in Maharashtra that is looking for someone with your specific qualifications. Please see the attachment for more details.	¹⁶⁵我很遺憾的通知你，你沒有應徵上 Goldbear 科技公司資深技術主任一職。這家公司因為持續的經濟危機，近來被迫減少管理職位。¹⁶⁵不過，我打算幫你投遞申請表到另一家在西印度的 Pioneer 塑膠製造公司。這家成長中的公司位在 Maharashtra 正在尋找有像你這種資歷的人，請參見附件的詳細資料。
¹⁶⁷If you are interested in pursuing the application, I would urge you to phone Chynna Dara in our Indian branch at 555-1433 as soon as possible. She is familiar with Pioneer Plastics and has a good relationship with its human resources manager. In the meantime, ¹⁶⁶I will go ahead and forward her your résumé and reference letters. I will also continue to scout for other opportunities, and let you know if I receive any news.	¹⁶⁷如果你有興趣應徵，我希望你趕快打電話給我們在印度分公司的 Chynna Dara，電話是 555-1433，她對 Pioneer 塑膠公司很熟悉，而且和他們人力資源部門的經理關係很好。在此同時，¹⁶⁶我會把你履歷表和介紹信轉寄給她，我也會繼續注意其他機會，如果我有任何消息，我會讓你知道。
Good luck!	祝你好運！
Sincerely,	
Henry Tang Director of Human Resources Foremost Employment Agency	Henry Tang 人力資源部門主任 Foremost 職業介紹所

單字 □application n. 申請，應用　□turn down phr. 拒絕，回絕　□managerial a. 管理的
　　□workforce n. 勞動人員　□due to phr. 因為～　□ongoing a. 持續的
　　□economic crisis phr. 經濟危機　□look for phr. 尋找　□specific a. 特定的
　　□qualification n. 資格，能力　□attachment n. 附加文件　□pursue v. 追求，從事
　　□urge v. 勸告，忠告　□be familiar with phr. 和～很熟知，和～很親近
　　□in the meantime phr. 在那期間　□forward v. 發送，傳送　□scout v. 找，發掘

165

What is the main purpose of the letter?	這封信的主要目的為何？
(A) To apologize for a misunderstanding	(A) 為一個誤解道歉
(B) To terminate a manager's contract	(B) 結束一位經理的合約
(C) To discuss a client's application status	(C) 討論一位客戶的應徵情況
(D) To report on a company's economic crisis	(D) 報告一家公司的經濟危機

■ 找出主題 目的

解答 (C)

這是問寫信目的的找主題問題，所以要特別注意文章的前半部份。I am sorry to inform you that your application for the position ~ was turned down. 中提到「我很遺憾通知你，你沒有應徵上。」接著，However, I plan to submit your application to another company 中又提到「不過，我打算幫你投遞申請表到其他公司」。由此可以推斷出寫信目的是為了討論顧客的應徵狀態。因此，(C) To discuss a client's application status 是正確答案。

單字 apologize v. 道歉　misunderstanding n. 誤會，誤解　terminate v. 終了，結束　contract n. 合約，約定
　　status n. 狀態，地位，身分

166

What does Mr. Tang say he will do?	Tang 先生說他會做什麼？
(A) Revise an application process	(A) 修訂應徵程序
(B) Send some documentation	(B) 寄一些文件
(C) Call another branch associate	(C) 打電話給分公司同事
(D) Forward information to Goldbear Technologies	(D) 轉寄資料給 Goldbear 科技公司

■ 六何原則 What   解答 (B)

這是問 Mr. Tang 說他會做什麼的六何原則問題。跟問題的核心詞語 Mr. Tang ~ will do 相關的內容 I will ~ forward ~ your résumé and reference letters 中提到 Mr. Tang 會把 Mr. Nehru 的履歷表和介紹信轉寄，所以 (B) Send some documentation 是正確答案。

換句話說

forward ~ résumé and reference letters 轉寄履歷表和介紹信 → Send some documentation 寄一些文件

單字 revise v. 修正，改正   associate n. 同事

167

Who most likely is Ms. Dara?	Dara 小姐最有可能是誰？
(A) An employment agent	(A) 一位職業仲介人員
(B) A technical director	(B) 技術主任
(C) A factory inspector	(C) 工廠檢驗員
(D) A business owner	(D) 公司老闆

■ 推論 詳細內容   解答 (A)

這是跟問題核心詞語 Ms. Dara 有關的推理問題。If you are interested in pursuing the application, I would urge you to phone Chynna Dara in our Indian branch 中提到「如果你有興趣應徵，我希望你趕快打電話給我們在印度分公司的 Chynna Dara」。由此可以推斷出 Ms. Dara 是在 Foremost 職業介紹所工作的職業仲介人員。因此，(A) An employment agent 是正確答案。

單字 agent n. 代理人   inspector n. 督察員，檢察員

If you're employed in the field of business, there is something you have likely experienced before: the feeling of helplessness and stress as deadlines pass and work piles up. For many, it seems like an endless battle. After all, there are only so many hours in a day. Thankfully, there is a way to make the most out of your time. [168]Here are some tips from successful executives who have learned to manage their schedules and be more productive.

[169-D]**1. Plan ahead**

Time management is less about managing time and more about managing activities. Assign "things to do" to specific times of the day, days of the week, months of the year, and so on. In addition, assign deadlines to each task or project, but set them at least two days ahead of the actual due dates so you will always be on time.

[170]**2. Prioritize tasks**

If you have too much work, try to complete the most important tasks and projects early in the morning to avoid being overwhelmed with work later in the day. Too often throughout a day, other obligations and responsibilities creep in and distract you from your work.

[169-B]**3. Take notes**

Keep a notebook handy to record something you have neglected to include in your schedule, or to write down ideas. Otherwise, it becomes increasingly difficult to stay focused on the tasks before you.

[169-A]**4. Put everything in its place**

At home, in the car, and especially at work, minimize distractions by maintaining orderly surroundings. Keep frequently used items within reach, but store everything else in drawers and cabinets.

5. Reward yourself

[172]Motivate yourself to finish tasks by rewarding major accomplishments. Depending on the nature of a completed task, your reward can be as simple as giving yourself a break to enjoy a leisurely activity.

假如你在商業界工作，你可能曾經遇過這種事：因為期限已過但工作做不完而感到無助、壓力。對於很多人而言，這像是一場永無止境的戰鬥，畢竟，一天就是這麼多個小時。很慶幸地，有辦法可以讓你的時間發揮最大的效用，[168]這裡有一些來自成功學習時間管理的主管的祕訣，他們透過時間管理來讓自己更具有生產力。

[169-D]**1. 事先計畫**

時間管理其實不在管理時間，而在管理事情。把「要做的事」分配在一天的特定時段、一週的特定日子、一年的某個月分，依此類推。此外，給每件任務或專案設定一個期限，但是要比實際上的截止日期早個兩天，所以你永遠都不會來不及。

[170]**2.決定事情的優先順序**

如果你有太多工作，試著在早上完成最重要的工作，以避免稍晚趕到焦頭爛額。而一天當中，常常會有其他該做的事情會出現，讓你從工作中分心。

[169-B]**3. 作筆記**

準備一本筆記本可隨時記錄你行程表中忽略的事情，或者寫下你的想法，否則，會越來越難專注於你眼前的工作。

[169-A]**4. 讓每樣東西各就各位**

在家、在車裡，特別在工作上，維持周遭環境的井然有序，將讓你分心的因子減至最低。常用的東西放在伸手可及的地方，而把其他東西放置在抽屜或櫃子裡。

5. 獎勵你自己

[172]藉著獎勵重大的成就來激勵自己完成工作。視完成工作的本質而定，你的獎勵可以只是讓自己休息一番去做點休閒活動。

單字
□helplessness n. 無能為力	□deadline n. 截止日	□pile up phr. 累積，變多
□after all phr. 畢竟	□executive n. 經理人，經營主管	□productive a. 生產的
□assign v. 分配	□ahead of phr. 在～之前，領先	□actual a. 實際的
□due date phr. 截止日	□prioritize v. 決定優先順序	□avoid v. 避開
□overwhelm v. 征服，淹沒	□obligation n. 義務	□creep in phr. 擠進去
□distract v. 分散	□handy a. 方便的，有用的	□minimize v. 使最少化
□distraction n. 分心	□neglect v. 忽略	□orderly a. 整齊的
□motivate v. 給予～動機	□accomplishment n. 成就	□nature n. 性格，本質
□leisurely a. 從容不迫的，悠閒的		

168

What is the information mainly about?	這段訊息主要關於什麼？
(A) Becoming your own boss	(A) 做自己的老闆
(B) Being more productive	(B) 變得更有生產力
(C) Motivating coworkers	(C) 激勵同事
(D) Managing employees	(D) 管理職員

■ 找出主題 主題　　　　　　　　　　　　　　　　　　　　　　　　　　　　解答 (B)

這是問訊息主要關於什麼的找主題問題，所以要特別注意文章的前半部份。Here are some tips from successful executives who have learned to ~ be more productive. 中提到這裡有一些來自成功主管的祕訣。接著，介紹了幫助提高生產力的方法。因此，(B) Being more productive 是正確答案。

單字 coworker n. 同事，一起工作的人

169

Which method is NOT included in the information?	哪個方法沒有被提及？
(A) Organizing personal belongings	(A) 整理個人的東西
(B) Keeping a notebook	(B) 作筆記
(C) Turning off your phone	(C) 關掉電話
(D) Scheduling activities	(D) 安排活動的時間

■ Not / True Not 問題　　　　　　　　　　　　　　　　　　　　　　　　解答 (C)

這是找出跟問題核心詞語 method 相關的內容後，再跟選項作對比的 Not / True 問題。4. Put everything in its place 中提到讓每樣東西各就各位，所以跟 (A) 的內容一致。3. Take notes 中提到作筆記，所以跟 (B) 的內容一致。(C) 是文中沒提到的內容。因此，(C) Turning off your phone 是正確答案。1. Plan ahead 中提到事先計畫，所以跟 (D) 的內容一致。

單字 organize v. 整理　belongings n. 物品，所有品

170

What does the information suggest people with excessive workloads do?	這段訊息對工作量過多的人建議了什麼？
(A) Outsource some of the workload	(A) 把一些工作外包出去
(B) Hire a professional assistant	(B) 雇用專業助理
(C) Go to the workplace early	(C) 早一點上班
(D) Rate the importance of tasks	(D) 決定工作的優先順序

■ 六何原則 What　　　　　　　　　　　　　　　　　　　　　　　　　　解答 (D)

這是問什麼（What）方法是用來建議工作量過多的人的六何原則問題。跟問題的核心詞語 people with excessive workloads 相關的內容 2. Prioritize tasks, If you have too much work, try to complete the most important tasks and projects early in the morning 中提到「決定事情的優先順序後，如果你有太多工作，試著在早上完成最重要的工作」。因此，(D) Rate the importance of tasks 是正確答案。

換句話說

Prioritize tasks 決定工作的優先順序 → Rate the importance of tasks 訂出工作重要性的順序

單字 excessive a. 過量的　workload n. 工作量　outsource v. 外包　rate v. 訂出順序，評價

171

| The word "reach" in paragraph 5, line 2 is closest in meaning to
(A) proximity
(B) extension
(C) area
(D) category | 第五段第二行的「reach」最接近哪個字的意思？
(A) 接近
(B) 延伸
(C) 地區
(D) 分類 |

■ 同義詞   解答 (A)

含 reach 的詞句 Keep frequently used items within reach 中的 reach 的意思是「（伸手可及）的距離，範圍」。因此，意思是「接近」的 (A) proximity 是正確答案。

172

| According to the information, how can people motivate themselves?
(A) By scheduling their time carefully
(B) By giving themselves a reward
(C) By setting reasonable goals
(D) By writing down their successes | 根據這則資訊，人們可以如何激勵自己？
(A) 仔細地安排自己的時間
(B) 給自己獎勵
(C) 設定合理的目標
(D) 寫下自己的成功事蹟 |

■ 六何原則 How   解答 (B)

這是問人們可以如何（how）激勵自己的六何原則問題。跟問題的核心詞語 people motivate themselves 相關的內容 Motivate yourself ～ by rewarding major accomplishments.中提到藉著獎勵重大的成就來激勵自己完成工作。因此，(B) By giving themselves a reward 是正確答案。

單字 reasonable a. 合理的，適當的　write down phr. 寫下～，記載

Questions 173-176 refer to the following e-mail.　　　　　173-176 根據下面通知的內容回答問題。

[173]From:　Liza Singer <accounting@pencilstudios.com>

To:　　　Lisa Chang <lchang@pencilstudios.com>,
　　　　　Kevin Olsen <kolsen@pencilstudios.com>,
　　　　　William Kane <wkane@pencilstudios.com>
Date:　　September 3
Subject:　Reimbursements

As we have discussed, [173]/[176-A/C]all project leaders will be in charge of turning in [176-D]monthly reimbursement requests to the accounting department beginning this month. [174]To file a refund, fill out a reimbursement request form. [175]/[176-A/C] Attach all original receipts for project expenses to the form and hand it in to Ms. Ricks. After that, she will forward the documents to Mr. Scott for evaluation and refund all valid expenses after three days.

Refunds may be claimed in cash or deposited into your payroll accounts. Please inform Ms. Ricks of the option you prefer.

In addition, [176-B]please take note that expenses without official receipts will not be reimbursed. Therefore, you need to remind your team members to give you the receipts for all work-related expenditures.

Lastly, [176-D]I request that you submit a summary of your team's expenses at least two weeks before the end of each quarter. This will hasten the process of preparing the company's quarterly income statement. If you have questions, send an e-mail to the accounting department.

Liza Singer

[173]寄件者：Liza Singer
　　　　　<accounting@pencilstudios.com>
收件者：Lisa Chang <lchang@pencilstudios.com>,
　　　　　Kevin Olsen <kolsen@pencilstudios.com>,
　　　　　William Kane <wkane@pencilstudios.com>
日期：9 月 3 日
主旨：墊款付還

如同我們所討論的，[173]/[176-A/C]所有專案負責人將要負責在[176-D]本月初繳交月墊款付還的申請給會計部門，[174]凡申請退款，都要填寫墊款付還申請表，[175]/[176-A/C]把所有專案開銷的收據正本附在申請表上，交給 Ricks 小姐。在這之後，她會將文件轉給 Scott 先生評估，並在三天後付還所有核准的費用。

可以要求現金退款或存到你的薪資帳戶裡，請讓 Ricks 小姐知道你要退還的方式。

此外，[176-B]請注意沒有正式收據的開銷無法報帳，所以，你們必須提醒你們的團隊成員交給你們所有工作相關的收據。

最後，[176-D]我要求你們在每季結束前至少兩個星期繳交你們團隊的開銷費用，如此能加速準備公司的季損益表，如果你們有任何問題，請寄電郵給會計部門。

Liza Singer

單字　□reimbursement n. 償還，退款　□in charge of phr. 負責　□turn in phr. 提交
　　　□attach v. 添加，附上　□expense n. 費用　□hand in phr. 繳交
　　　□forward v. 寄出，發送　□evaluation n. 審查，評價　□valid a. 有效的
　　　□deposit v. 存錢，儲蓄　□payroll n. 發薪，發薪對象名單　□remind v. 使想起，提醒
　　　□expenditure n. 支出，經費　□hasten v. 催促，趕快　□quarterly a. 季度別的
　　　□income n. 收入

173

Who most likely is Ms. Singer?
(A) A company investor
(B) A member of accounting staff
(C) A public relations officer
(D) A company sales agent

Singer 小姐最有可能是誰？
(A) 公司投資者
(B) 會計部門的員工
(C) 公關主管
(D) 公司的銷售人員

推論 詳細內容　　　　　　　　　　　　　　　　　　　　　　　　　　　　解答 (B)

這是跟問題核心詞語 Ms. Singer 有關的推理問題。電郵前端的 From: Liza Singer accounting@pencilstudios. com 中顯示發信人 Liza Singer 的電郵地址屬於 accounting（會計）。接著，all project leaders will be in charge of turning in monthly reimbursement requests to the accounting department 中提到所有專案負責人將要負責在本月初繳交月墊款付還的申請給會計部門。由此可以推斷出她是會計部門的員工。因此，(B) A member of accounting staff 是正確答案。

單字　investor n. 投資者　　sales agent phr. 銷售員

174

According to the e-mail, what must be included with the request form?	根據這封電郵，什麼必須包含在申請表中？
(A) Account numbers	(A) 帳號
(B) An expense report	(B) 開銷報告
(C) Proof of payment	(C) 付款證明
(D) A project outline	(D) 專案大綱

六何原則 What   解答 (C)

這是問申請表中必須包含（What）的六何原則問題。跟問題的核心詞語 included with the request form 相關的內容 To file a refund, fill out a reimbursement request form. Attach all original receipts ~ to the form 中提到凡申請退款，都要填寫墊款付還申請表，把所有專案開銷的收據正本附在申請表上。因此，(C) Proof of payment 是正確答案。

換句話說

original receipts 收據正本 → Proof of payment 付款證明

單字 outline n. 大綱

175

What most likely is Ms. Ricks responsible for?	Ricks 小姐最有可能負責什麼？
(A) Organizing reimbursement documents	(A) 整理退款文件
(B) Evaluating the results of projects	(B) 評估專案成果
(C) Managing customer accounts	(C) 管理客戶帳戶
(D) Sending out billing statements	(D) 寄出帳單

推論 詳細內容   解答 (A)

這是問 Ms. Ricks 最有可能負責什麼的推理問題。跟問題的核心詞語 Ms. Ricks responsible 相關的內容 Attach all original receipts ~ to the form and hand it in to Ms. Ricks.中所有專案開銷的收據正本附在申請表上，並交給 Ms. Ricks。由此可以推斷出 Ms. Ricks 是負責整理退款文件的人。因此，(A) Organizing reimbursement documents 是正確答案。

單字 billing statement phr. 請款單

176

What is NOT indicated about the receipts?	關於收據，何者不正確？
(A) They should be sent to the accounting office.	(A) 應該要送到會計部門。
(B) They serve as records of official expenses.	(B) 作為公務開銷的紀錄。
(C) They should be collected on a recurring basis.	(C) 要經常性地收集收據。
(D) They are turned in at the end of every quarter.	(D) 要在每季結束前繳交。

Not / True Not 問題   解答 (D)

這是找出跟問題核心詞語 the receipts 相關的內容後，再跟選項作對比的 Not / True 問題。all project leaders will be in charge of turning in monthly reimbursement requests to the accounting department 和 Attach all original receipts ~ to the form 中提到所有專案負責人將要負責在本月初繳交月墊款付還的申請給會計部門，凡申請退款，都要填寫墊款付還申請表，把所有專案開銷的收據正本附在申請表上。由此可以推斷出每個月都要收集收據。因此，跟 (A) 和 (C) 的內容一致。please take note that expenses without official receipts will not be reimbursed 中提到請注意沒有正式收據的開銷無法報帳。由此可知道收據扮演公務開銷紀錄的角色，所以跟 (B) 的內容一致。monthly reimbursement 中提到按月別退款申請書，由此可以知道退款申請書是每個月都要提交的。接著，I request that you submit a summary of your team's expenses at least two weeks before the end of each quarter 中又提到「我會要求你們在每季結束前至少兩個星期繳交你們團隊的開銷費用」，由此可以知道每季結束之前要提交的不是收據，而是團隊開銷費用，所以跟 (D) 的內容不符。因此，(D) They are turned in at the end of every quarter. 是正確答案。

單字 turn in phr. 提交   quarter n. 季度

Merrick Foods, Incorporated

To: Factory personnel
From: Doug Leavesley, Chief Operations Officer
Re: Food Handling

[178]The Consumer Safety Board (CSB) has issued a new set of policies for the proper handling of food. [178]To conform to these new policies, [177]we have revised some of our own internal regulations. Copies of the relevant sections have been posted in the employee lunchroom. The personnel department will issue a comprehensive document in a few weeks that includes our own changes.

Prior to ordering
Effective immediately, [179]the purchasing control department must log on weekly to the CSB Web site at www.csb.gov to verify information provided about our farm sources' crop conditions and insect infestations. In addition, beginning in May, the company will no longer accept shipments of potatoes that are more than 30 days old.

Upon arrival
Unsorted potatoes must be washed and stored immediately. The temperature setting within storage containers can be no more than 40 degrees Fahrenheit. Following the initial inspection for blemishes, shipments whose rejected portions are more than 25 percent of the total gross weight must be returned in their entirety.

Processing stage
Potatoes must be washed a second time after slicing in order to reduce the vegetable's starch content. In addition, we will be applying a different chemical agent for color treatment that has already been approved by the CSB.

Lastly, [180-D]all food handlers and machine operators are required to put on gloves, rubber aprons, and face masks. These items are to be deposited each day at the laundry department for sterilization.

Thank you for your cooperation in these matters.

Merrick 食品公司

收件人：工廠員工
寄件人：總營運主管 Doug Leavesley
主旨：食品處理

[178]消費者安全委員會發布了一套關於妥善處理食品的新政策，[178]為了要遵守這些新政策，[177]我們已修訂了一些我們內部的規定。相關的修訂內容已公布在員工午餐室，人事部門將會在幾週後公布一份全面的資料，包含我們所做的修正。

在訂購之前
[179]採購控制部門必須每週登入消費者安全委員會的網站 www.csb.gov 去確認我們農場來源所提供的農作物情況與病蟲害資訊，此規定立即生效。此外，從5月開始，公司將不再接受超過三十天的馬鈴薯。

運送抵達
沒有整理過的馬鈴薯必須馬上清洗和儲存起來，在儲存容器裡的溫度設定不能超過華氏四十度，在對瑕疵的初步檢驗之後，不合格的比例超過總重百分之二十五的貨，將全數退回。

處理階段
馬鈴薯必須在切片以後再次清洗，以減少蔬菜的澱粉含量，此外，我們將會使用一種經過消費者安全委員會所核准的不同的化學品做顏色處理。

最後，[180-D]所有處理食物的人和機器操作者都必須戴上手套，塑膠圍裙和面罩。這些護具每天都要被收集到洗衣部門來消毒。

謝謝您對於這些措施的配合。

單字
□ issue v. 發表，公布
□ conform v. 遵守
□ regulation n. 規定
□ effective a. 實行的，有效的
□ infestation n. （害蟲 / 昆蟲）大批出沒、繁殖
□ shipment n. 運送，輸送
□ blemish n. 不良，缺點，疤痕
□ entirety n. 全部
□ agent n. 藥品，物質
□ sterilization n. 消毒，殺菌

□ proper a. 適當的，恰當的
□ revise v. 修訂，變更
□ comprehensive a. 綜合的，包含的
□ verify v. 確認，查證
□ storage n. 儲存倉庫，儲藏所
□ portion n. 部分，一部分
□ starch n. 澱粉，太白粉
□ apron n. 圍裙
□ cooperation n. 協力，協助，合力

□ handling n. 處理
□ internal a. 內部的
□ crop n. 農產品
□ no longer phr. 不再～
□ Fahrenheit a. 華氏的
□ gross a. 毛額的，總額的
□ chemical a. 化學的
□ deposit v. 放置，儲存

177

What is the memo mainly about?	這個備忘錄是關於什麼？
(A) Training for new employees	(A) 訓練新進員工
(B) Changes to a facility's practices	(B) 改變工廠的處理作業
(C) Procedures for preparing a dish	(C) 準備一道菜的程序
(D) Advances in storage equipment	(D) 儲存設備的先進技術

■ 找出主題 主題　　　　　　　　　　　　　　　　　　　　　　　　　　　　　　　解答 (B)

這是備忘錄是關於什麼的找主題問題，所以要特別注意文章的前半部份。we have revised some of our own internal regulations 中提到「我們已修訂了一些我們內部的規定」。接著，又說明了修訂的細部事項。因此，(B) Changes to a facility's practices 是正確答案。

換句話說

revised ~ internal regulations 修訂內部規定 → Changes to a facility's practices 改變工廠作業

單字 practice n. 業務，實踐

178

What is suggested about Merrick Foods?	關於 Merrick 食品公司，何者正確？
(A) It is required to follow CSB guidelines.	(A) 必須遵守消費者安全委員會的規定。
(B) It is closing its factory in May.	(B) 在 5 月時工廠要關閉。
(C) It uses outdated machinery.	(C) 使用老舊的機器設備。
(D) It had an issue related to food handling.	(D) 關於食品處理方面有問題。

■ 推論 詳細內容　　　　　　　　　　　　　　　　　　　　　　　　　　　　　　解答 (A)

這是跟問題核心詞語 Merrick Foods 有關的推理問題。The Consumer Safety Board (CSB) has issued a new set of policies 中提到消費者安全委員會發布了一套新政策。接著，To conform to these new policies, we have revised some of our own internal regulations. 中提到為了要遵守這些政策，我們，也就是 Merrick 食品公司已修訂了一些內部的規定。由此可以推斷出 Merrick 食品公司是跟隨 CSB 的方針。因此，(A) It is required to follow CSB guidelines. 是正確答案。

換句話說

conform to ~ policies 跟隨政策 → follow ~ guidelines 跟隨方針

單字 outdated a. 舊式的　machinery n. 機器

179

What is the purchasing control department required to do?	採購控制部門被要求做什麼？
(A) Inspect for defects	(A) 查驗不良品
(B) Limit their weekly budget	(B) 限制他們每週的預算
(C) Check a Web site regularly	(C) 定期上網確認
(D) Count rejected items	(D) 清點不合格物件

■ 六何原則 What　　　　　　　　　　　　　　　　　　　　　　　　　　　　　　解答 (C)

這是問採購控制部門被要求做什麼（What）的六何原則問題。跟問題的核心詞語 the purchasing control department required to do 相關的內容 the purchasing control department must log on weekly to the CSB Web site 中提到採購控制部門必須每週登入 CSB 的網站，所以 (C) Check a Web site regularly 是正確答案。

換句話說

log on weekly to the ~ Web site 每週登入網站 → Check a Web site regularly 定期上網確認

單字 inspect v. 檢查　defect n. 缺陷　regularly ad. 定期地

What is mentioned in the memo? (A) Shipments must be sterilized prior to delivery. (B) Items must be sorted in the order they arrive. (C) Chemicals must be refrigerated when not in use. (D) Specific types of clothing must be worn.	在備忘錄中提到什麼？ (A) 貨物在運送之前必須消毒。 (B) 物品必須按照到達的順序分類整理。 (C) 化學物品在不使用時要冷藏。 (D) 必須穿戴特定種類的衣物。

■ **Not / True** True 問題　　　　　　　　　　　　　　　　　　　　　　　　　　　　　解答 (D)

這是在備忘錄中提到什麼，並跟選項作對比的 Not / True 問題。因為這個問題中沒有核心詞語，所以每個跟選項核心詞語相關的內容都要一一確認。 (A) (B) (C) 都是文中沒提到的內容。all food handlers and machine operators are required to put on gloves, rubber aprons, and face masks 中提到「最後，所有處理食物的人和機器操作者都必須戴上手套，塑膠圍裙和面罩」，所以跟 (D) 的內容一致。因此，(D) Specific types of clothing must be worn. 是正確答案。

換句話說
required to put on gloves, rubber aprons, and face masks 必須戴上手套，塑膠圍裙和面罩
→ Specific types of clothing must be worn 必須穿特定種類的衣物

單字 shipment n. 出貨，運送品　sterilize v. 殺菌　sort v. 分類　refrigerate v. 冷藏

Questions 181-185 refer to the following e-mails.

例文1

To: Neil Grossman
    <neil.grossman@brooksconstruction.com>
From: Audrey Stanford <a.stanford@mckinleytiles.com>

Date: August 8
Subject: Order of tiles

Dear Mr. Grossman,

This is concerning your recent order of floor tiles from our Web site. I am pleased to inform you that 600 pieces of Iklimler Ceramics (floral beige) and 400 pieces of Oakland Terrazzo (reddish brown) will be delivered to your office tomorrow at 8 A.M. [181]Brian, my personal assistant, will supervise the delivery to make sure that the items are not mishandled. Please let him know if you encounter any problems.

With regard to your inquiry about customized tiles, I believe we have enough time to accommodate your order, but it would depend on the design and quantity. Could you give us a rough idea of what you're looking for by sending a draft of your design? Also, please specify the number of pieces you need so we can provide you with a price estimate. Then we will let you know when the order can be completed. [185]Orders of 300 or more customized tiles usually take at least two weeks to manufacture. But in case you need the tiles sooner, we offer rush services for an additional fee of $150.

Please do not hesitate to contact me if you have any questions. You can call me at 555-9696. My extension number is 104.

Thank you.

Sincerely yours,

Audrey Stanford
Manager
McKinley Tiles Incorporated

例文2

To: Audrey Stanford <a.stanford@mckinleytiles.com>
From: Neil Grossman <neil.grossman@brooksconstruction.com>
[184]Date: August 9
Subject: Re: Order of Tiles
Attachment: Tile Design

Dear Ms. Stanford,

I'd like to thank you for the timely delivery of the two orders of tiles. They arrived this morning in good condition. I really appreciate that you had Brian supervise the delivery. He was very kind and helpful.

181-185 根據下面電郵的內容回答問題。

收件人：Neil Grossman
    <neil.grossman@brooksconstruction.com>
寄件人：Audrey Stanford
    <a.stanford@mckinleytiles.com>
日期：8 月 8 日
主旨：磁磚訂購

親愛的 Grossman 先生：

這是關於你最近在我們的網站訂購地板磁磚，我很高興地通知你六百片 Iklimler Ceramics（淺褐花色）和四百片 Oakland Terrazzo（紅褐色）將會在明天上午八點送到你的辦公室。[181]我的個人助理 Brian 會監督運送過程，確定所有商品都被妥善處理。如果你有任何問題，請讓他知道。

關於你詢問的客製磁磚，我相信我們有足夠的時間來配合你的訂單，但是要視設計與數量而定，你能寄來你設計的草稿，讓我們大概知道你要找的東西嗎？此外，請確切告知你要的數量，我們才能為你預估價錢，然後我們會讓你知道什麼時候可以完成產品，[185]三百片以上的客製磁磚通常要花至少兩週來製作。不過你如果比較急著要，我們加收美金一百五十元，可以為你趕工。

請不要客氣向我們詢問任何問題，你可以打電話給我，我的電話是 555-9696，分機 104。

謝謝你。

Audrey Stanford
經理
McKinley 磁磚公司

收件人：Audrey Stanford
    <a.stanford@mckinleytiles.com>
寄件人：Neil Grossman
    <neil.grossman@brooksconstruction.com>
[184]日期：8 月 9 日
主旨：回覆：磁磚訂購
附件：磁磚設計
親愛的 Stanford 小姐：
我想要謝謝妳準時地將兩批磁磚送到，它們在今天早上狀態良好的送達。我真的很感激妳讓 Brian 監督運送過程，他人很好，而且幫了很多忙。

[185]I'm also grateful for your prompt response about the customized tiles. As I told you, they will not be for our clients but for our office. We're planning to renovate our customer service area, and we thought it would be a good idea to use tiles that better reflect our brand identity. I attached a copy of the design to this e-mail. [184]The tentative schedule for the renovation project is in the third week of September. [185]Do you think you can make 500 pieces by then?

By the way, as I mentioned in my previous e-mail, [183-B]the company is organizing an event for the launch of our newly designed Web site, which will allow our customers to make online purchases. Since you are a trusted supplier, you might be interested in attending this activity. I will ask my secretary to send you a formal invitation once it's finalized.

Sincerely,

Neil Grossman
Supervisor
Brooks Construction Supplies

[185]我也很謝謝妳快速地回應了客製磁磚的問題。如同我告訴妳的，這不是給我們客戶的，而是我們辦公室要的。我們打算重新裝潢我們的顧客服務區，我們認為使用能更加表現我們品牌特性的磁磚是不錯的點子，我在這封電郵附上設計稿，[184]目前暫定重新裝修的時間是 9 月的第三個禮拜。[185]妳認為有可能在那之前做出五百片嗎？

順便一提，在我之前的電郵中說到，[183-B]我們公司正為我們新設計的網站籌備一個活動，讓我們的客戶能在網上購物。因為你們是一個有信譽的供應商，你們可能有興趣參加這個活動，一旦正式的邀請函準備好了，我會請我的祕書寄一份給妳。

Neil Grossman
主管
Brooks 建築材料供應商

例文 1 單字 □concerning prep. 跟～有關　□inform v. 通知　□supervise v. 監督
□mishandle v. 錯誤地處理　□encounter v. 面臨　□customized a. 訂做的，客製的
□accommodate v. 容納　□depend on phr. 根據～，取決於～　□quantity n. 數量
□rough a. 大概的，粗略的　□draft n. 草案　□specify v. 明示
□estimate n. 估價，估價單　□hesitate v. 猶豫　□extension number phr. 分機號碼

例文 2 單字 □appreciate v. 感激　□grateful a. 感恩的　□prompt a. 立即的
□renovate v. 翻修　□brand identity phr. 品牌特性　□tentative a. 嘗試的，不確實的
□launch n. 上市，開工　□allow v. 使可行，許可　□secretary n. 祕書
□formal a. 正式的，正規的　□finalize v. 完成，結束

181

According to the first e-mail, why is Ms. Stanford sending her personal assistant?
(A) To install a set of floor tiles
(B) To collect payment for an order
(C) To ensure the safety of merchandise
(D) To take measurements of a room

根據第一封電郵，為什麼 Stanford 小姐派出她的個人助理？
(A) 去安裝一套磁磚
(B) 去收一筆訂單的款項
(C) 去確保商品的安全
(D) 去測量一間房間

六何原則 Why　　　　　　　　　　　解答 (C)

這是根據第一封電郵，為什麼（why）Ms. Stanford 派出她的個人助理的六何原則問題。和第一封電郵的核心詞語 Ms. Stanford sending her personal assistant 相關聯的內容 Brian, my personal assistant, will supervise the delivery to make sure that the items are not mishandled. 中提到「我的個人助理 Brian 會監督運送過程，確定所有商品都被妥善處理」。因此，(C) To ensure the safety of merchandise 是正確答案。

換句話說
make sure that the items are not mishandled 確定商品沒有被亂處理
→ ensure the safety of merchandise 確保商品的安全

單字 install v. 安置　ensure v. 確保　measurement n. 大小，測量

182

| In the first e-mail, the word "rough" in paragraph 2, line 3 is closest in meaning to
(A) coarse
(B) approximate
(C) difficult
(D) uneven | 在 第 一 封 電 郵 中 , 第 二 段 第 三 行 的 「rough」最接近哪一個字的意思?
(A) 粗糙的
(B) 大約的
(C) 困難的
(D) 不均勻的 |

■ 同義詞 解答 (B)

第一封電郵中包含 rough 的詞句 Could you give us a rough idea of what you're looking for 中的 rough 的意思是「大略的」。因此,意思也是「大略的」的 (B) approximate 是正確答案。

183

| What is indicated about Brooks Construction Supplies?
(A) Its clients have recently given positive feedback about its services.
(B) It is providing customers with additional shopping options.
(C) It is extending its contract with McKinley Tiles Incorporated.
(D) Its sales of building materials increased in the previous quarter. | 關於 Brooks 建築材料供應商,何者正確?
(A) 他們的顧客最近針對他們的服務給了正面的回應。
(B) 提供顧客更多的購物選擇。
(C) 延長與 McKinley 磁磚公司的合約。
(D) 在前一季的建築材料銷售成長了。 |

■ **Not / True** True 問題 解答 (B)

這是找出跟問題核心詞語 Brooks Construction Supplies 相關的內容後,再跟選項作對比的 Not / True 問題。因此,要確定的是 Brooks Construction Supplies 公司職員所寫的第二電郵中的相關內容。 (A) 是文中沒提到的內容。the company is organizing an event for the launch of our newly designed Web site, which will allow our customers to make online purchases 中提到「我們公司正為我們新設計的網站籌備一個活動,讓我們的客戶能在網上購物」,所以跟 (B) 的內容一致。因此,(B) It is providing customers with additional shopping options. 是正確答案。(C) (D) 都是文中沒提到的內容。

單字 extend v. 延長　contract n. 合約　previous a. 之前的,以前的　quarter n. 季度

184

| According to the second e-mail, what will happen next month?
(A) A merger agreement will be signed.
(B) An office space will be renovated.
(C) A company will transfer to a new location.
(D) A department will release the budget. | 根據第二封電郵,下個月會發生什麼事?
(A) 會簽訂一個併購的合約。
(B) 辦公室的空間要重新裝修。
(C) 公司要搬到一個新的地點。
(D) 一個部門會釋出預算。 |

■ 六何原則 What 解答 (B)

這是問根據第二封電郵,下個月會發生什麼(what)事的六何原則問題,所以要確認的是在第二封電郵中跟問題核心詞語 next month 相關的內容。第二封電郵前端的 Date: August 9 中顯示電郵是 8 月寫的。接著,The tentative schedule for the renovation project is in the third week of September. 中提到目前暫定重新裝修的時間是 9 月的第三個禮拜。因此,(B) An office space will be renovated. 是正確答案。

單字 merger n. 合併　agreement n. 合約,契約　transfer v. 移轉,調動　release v. 發表,公開　budget n. 預算

What is suggested about the items Mr. Grossman wants to order?	關於 Grossman 先生想要訂購的商品，何者正確？
(A) They will require at least two weeks to be produced.	(A) 至少要花兩週來製造。
(B) They were delivered on schedule.	(B) 按照計畫送到。
(C) They are being offered at a discounted price.	(C) 獲得折扣價格。
(D) They will be used in a new building.	(D) 會用在新的大樓。

■ 推論 聯結問題 　　　　　　　　　　　　　　　　　　　　　　　　　　　　　解答 (A)

這是要把兩篇文章的內容綜合起來才能解開的聯結問題。問題核心詞語 the items Mr. Grossman wants to order 中問到 Mr. Grossman 想要訂購的商品，所以要先確認第二封電郵，也就是 Mr. Grossman 寫的電郵內容。

第二封電郵的 I'm ~ grateful for your prompt response about the customized tiles. 和 they will ~ be ~ for our office 中提到「我也很謝謝你快速地回應了客製磁磚的問題，這是我們辦公室要的」。接著，又問是否有可能做出 500 片。由此可以推斷出 Mr. Grossman 要下訂客製磁磚 500 片。不過，卻沒有提到 500 片客製磁磚的訂單內容。因此，要確認 McKinley Tiles 公司寄出的電郵內容。第一封電郵的 Orders of 300 or more customized tiles usually take at least two weeks to manufacture. 中提到 300 片以上客製磁磚至少要花至少兩週來製作。

把 Mr. Grossman 訂購 500 片客製磁磚的內容和 300 片以上客製磁磚至少要花至少兩週的內容綜合起來，就可以推論出 Mr. Grossman 訂購的商品生產至少需要兩週。因此，(A) They will require at least two weeks to be produced. 是正確答案。

單字 at least phr. 至少，最好　discounted a. 打折的

例文1

To: All supervisors <supervisors@haydenboutique.com>
From: Julien Hirsch <julien.hirsch@haydenboutique.com>
Subject: Fashion Show
Attachment: One file
Date: February 15

Dear supervisors,

Over the past nine years, the Annual Hayden Couture Fashion Show has become one of the most highly anticipated events in the industry. [187-A]Now in its 10th year, we plan to make it bigger and better. The event will not only showcase our latest collection of clothes but also introduce a selection of work from some of the country's young fashion designers. [186]As supervisors, you will be responsible for receiving entries, so please make sure you are well informed about the details of the competition.

For this year, [187-D]we will be accepting entries from university students for several categories in the show. Interested applicants are required to complete and submit a copy of the registration form attached with this e-mail. We have invited a panel of renowned fashion designers to screen the entries and serve as judges for each category. Once the final entries are chosen, applicants will be given time to execute their designs in time for the fashion show. Complete information about these categories is now available on our Web site.

CATEGORY	SCREENING COMMITTEE HEAD
Ready-to-Wear	Mr. Amir Salood
Specialty Hats	Ms. Marga Silverio
[189]Athletic Wear	Mr. Vittorio Bellucci
Haute Couture	Ms. Shalani San Pedro

All entries should be submitted to the Hayden Boutique main office before March 20. We are still finalizing the arrangements for the venue, but if everything goes well, the show will be held on May 18 at Preminger Trade Center. That will give the short-listed applicants enough time to complete their designs. All inquiries should be sent irectly to Ms. Vicki Bergamo at vicki.bergamo@haydenboutique.com. She is responsible for the organization of the entire event.

We look forward to your cooperation. Thank you.

Sincerely yours,

Julien Hirsch
Regional director
Hayden Boutique Incorporated

收件人：所有主管 <supervisors@haydenboutique.com>
寄件人；Julien Hirsch <Julien.hirsch@haydenboutique.com>
主旨：服裝展示會
附件：一個檔案
日期：2 月 15 日

親愛的主管們：

在過去 9 年，年度 Hayden 服裝設計展示會已經成為業界最受期待的活動之一，[187-A]現在已經是第十年了，我們打算辦得更大更好，這個活動不僅展示我們最新的服裝設計，而且還會介紹我們國家一些年輕設計師的作品。[186]身為主管，你們要負責收件作業，所以請確定你們對於比賽的細節相當清楚。

今年[187-D]我們會接受大學生針對展示會的數個主題所做的設計，有興趣的參加者要填寫並繳交一份附件中的報名表，我們已經邀請一群著名的服裝設計師來檢視參加者的作品，並擔任各個主題的裁判，一旦成為最後被選上的作品，參賽者會有時間來完成他們的作品以參加服裝展示會。在我們的網站上有這些主題的完整資料。

主題	評選委員會主席
馬上可穿戴	Amir Salood 先生
特別的帽子	Marga Silverio 女士
[189]運動衣著	Vittorio Bellucci 先生
高級時裝	Shalani San Pedro 女士

所有作品應該在 3 月 20 日前寄到 Hayden 流行專賣店總部，我們還在最後確認地點的安排，如果一切順利，展示會會在 5 月 18 日在 Preminger 貿易中心舉行，通過初選的參賽者會有足夠的時間完成他們的設計作品。有任何問題請直接寄電郵到 vicki.bergamo@hayden-boutique.com 給 Vicki Bergamo 小姐，她負責籌備這整個活動。

我們期待你的合作，謝謝。

Julien Hirsch
地區主任
Hayden 流行專賣店公司

例文2

From: Vicki Bergamo <vicki.bergamo@haydencouture.com>
To: Antoine Rohmer <antoine.rohmer@ohlala.fr>
Subject: Hayden Couture Fashion Show
Date: April 2

Dear Mr. Rohmer,

I'm pleased to inform you that your entry was selected to be part of the 10th Annual Hayden Couture Fashion Show. [189]The panel of judges liked the stylishness of your swimwear design. It combines fashion and convenience while demonstrating your individuality as a designer. Congratulations!

[190]As one of the finalists, you are required to attend the orientation on Friday April 5, at the Hayden Boutique head office. [187-B]You will be provided with the materials you need to complete your design, as well as detailed instructions about the fashion show in May. In addition to having your design presented at the event, [188-C]your work will be included in our upcoming summer collection that will be launched in June.

If you have any questions, please call my assistant, Nicole, at 555-9009 local 125. I'm looking forward to see you on Friday.

Sincerely,

Vicki Bergamo
Operations manager
Hayden Boutique Incorporated

寄件人： Vicki Bergamo
<vicki.bergamo@haydenboutique.com>
收件人：Antoine Rohmer
<antoine.rohmer@ohlala.fr>
主旨： Hayden 服裝設計展示會
日期：4 月 2 日

親愛的 Rohmer 先生：

我很高興通知你的作品入選第十屆年度 Hayden 服裝設計展示會，[189]裁判群很喜歡你泳衣的時尚設計。結合時尚與便利的同時，也展現了你身為設計師的個人風格，恭喜你！

[190]身為決選參賽者，你必須參加 4 月 5 日星期五在 Hayden 流行專賣店總部舉辦的座談會。[187-B]我們會提供你完成設計作品所需要的材料，還有 5 月服裝展示會的詳細規定。[188-C]你的作品除了會在我們這個活動上展示，還會被收錄在我們即將在 6 月推出的夏季設計。

如果你有任何問題，請打電話給我的助理 Nicole，電話是 555-9009，分機 125。我很期待在星期五見到你。

Vicki Bergamo 敬上
營運經理
Hayden 流行專賣店公司

例文 1 單字 □supervisor n. 管理者　□annual a. 每年的　□highly ad. 非常
□anticipate v. 期待，預想　□industry n. 業界　□entry n. 參賽品
□accept v. 收到　□registration form phr. 報名表
□renowned a. 有名的　□screen v. 遮擋，審查　□execute v. 製作，創造
□venue n. 場所

例文 2 單字 □swimwear n. 泳裝　□convenience n. 便利　□individuality n. 個性，特徵
□head office phr. 總公司　□launch v. 上市

186

What does Julien Hirsch ask the supervisors to do?
(A) Organize individual store events
(B) Select applicants from a list of entries
(C) Attend a meeting with committee heads
(D) Become familiar with a contest's guidelines

Julien Hirsch 要求主管們做什麼？
(A) 籌備個別商店的活動
(B) 從作品名單中選出參賽者
(C) 和委員會主席參加一個會議
(D) 熟悉比賽規則

📖 六何原則 What　　　　　　　　　　　　　　　　　　　　解答 (D)

這是問 Julien Hirsch 要求主管們做什麼（What）的六何原則問題，所以先確認跟問題核心詞語 Julien Hirsch ask the supervisors to do 相關的第一封電郵。第一封電郵的 As supervisors, ~ please make sure you are well informed about the details of the competition. 中提到「身為主管，請確定你們對於比賽的細節相當清楚。」因此，(D) Become familiar with a contest's guidelines 是正確答案。

換句話說
well informed about the details of the competition 了解比賽的詳細資料
→ Become familiar with a contest's guidelines 熟知比賽方針

單字 familiar with phr. 熟知～　guideline n. 方針

What is NOT mentioned about the fashion show?	關於服裝展示會，何者錯誤？
(A) It is celebrating its tenth anniversary.	(A) 慶祝十周年。
(B) It is supplying production materials to participants.	(B) 會提供作品材料給參賽者。
(C) It is presenting an award to an esteemed artist.	(C) 頒獎給一位備受尊崇的藝術家。
(D) It is opening categories for young people.	(D) 開放主題給年輕人參加。

■ **Not / True** Not 問題　　　　　　　　　　　　　　　　　　　　　　　　　　　　　　　　　　解答 (C)

這是找出跟服裝展示相關的內容後，再跟選項作對比的 Not / True 問題。跟問題核心詞語 the fashion show 相關的第一封電郵和第二封電郵的內容都要確認。第一封電郵的 Now in its 10th year 中提到現在已經是第十年了，所以跟 (A) 的內容一致。第二封電郵的 You will be provided with the materials you need 中提到「我們會提供你所需要的材料」，所以跟 (B) 的內容一致。 (C) 是文中沒提到的內容。因此，(C) It is presenting an award to an esteemed artist. 是正確答案。第一封電郵的 we will be accepting entries from university students for several categories in the show 中提到「我們會接受大學生針對展示會數個主題所做的設計」，所以跟 (D) 的內容一致。

單字 celebrate v. 慶祝　present v. 授予　esteemed a. 受人尊敬的

What is indicated about Hayden Boutique?	關於 Hayden 流行專賣店，何者正確？
(A) It has several branches outside the country.	(A) 在國外有幾個分店。
(B) It designs clothes for renowned personalities.	(B) 為名人設計衣服。
(C) It is planning to launch some new merchandise.	(C) 計畫要推出新的商品。
(D) It is offering positions to new university graduates.	(D) 提供職缺給大學畢業生。

■ **Not / True** True 問題　　　　　　　　　　　　　　　　　　　　　　　　　　　　　　　　　　解答 (C)

這是找出跟問題核心詞語 Hayden Boutique 相關的內容後，再跟選項作對比的 Not / True 問題。 (A) 和 (B) 都是文中沒提到的內容。your work will be included in our upcoming summer collection that will be launched in June 中提到「你的作品還會被收錄在我們即將在 6 月推出的夏季設計」，所以跟 (C) 的內容一致。因此，(C) It is planning to launch some new merchandise. 是正確答案。 (D) 是文中沒提到的內容。

單字 personality n. 名人，性格

Who most likely screened Antoine Rohmer's entry?	Antoine Rohmer 的作品最有可能是誰選出來的？
(A) Vittorio Bellucci	(A) Vittorio Bellucci
(B) Marga Silverio	(B) Marga Silverio
(C) Amir Salood	(C) Amir Salood
(D) Shalani San Pedro	(D) Shalani San Pedro

■ **推論** 聯結問題　　　　　　　　　　　　　　　　　　　　　　　　　　　　　　　　　　　　解答 (A)

這是要把兩篇文章的內容綜合起來才能解開的聯結問題。問題核心詞語 screened Antoine Rohmer's entry 中問 Antoine Rohmer 的作品最有可能是誰選出來，所以要先確認寄給 Antoine Rohmer 的第二封電郵。

第二封電郵的 The panel of judges liked the stylishness of your swimwear design. 中提到裁判群很喜歡 Antoine Rohmer 的泳衣的時尚設計，由此可以知道 Antoine Rohmer 的作品是泳衣。不過，這裡並沒有說明是誰評選泳衣的設計。第一封電郵的表格的 Athletic Wear, Mr. Vittorio Bellucci 中提到運動衣著評選人是 Mr. Vittorio Bellucci。

把 Antoine Rohmer 的作品是泳衣的內容和運動衣著評選人是 Mr. Vittorio Bellucci 的內容綜合起來，可以推斷出 Antoine Rohmer 的作品是 Mr. Vittorio Bellucci 選出來的。因此，(A) Vittorio Bellucci 是正確答案。

190

What did Ms. Bergamo say will happen on Friday?	Bergamo 小姐說星期五會發生什麼事？
(A) Additional staff members will be hired.	(A) 會聘僱更多的員工。
(B) A new clothing store will open to the public.	(B) 一家新的服飾店要開張。
(C) Some celebrities will be asked to participate in a fashion show.	(C) 有些名人會被請來參加服裝展示會。
(D) Some people will be given information about an event.	(D) 會把一個活動的資訊告知一些人。

■ 六何原則 What　　　　　　　　　　　　　　　　　　　　　　　　　　　解答 (D)

這是問 Ms. Bergamo 說星期五會發生什麼（What）事的六何原則問題，所以跟問題的核心詞語 Ms. Bergamo say will happen on Friday 相關的 Ms. Bergamo 所寫的第二封電郵。第二封電郵的 As one of the finalists, you are required to attend the orientation on Friday ~. You will be provided with ~ detailed instructions about the fashion show in May. 中提到「身為決選參賽者，你必須參加星期五舉辦的座談會，我們會提供 5 月服裝展示會的詳細規則。」因此，(D) Some people will be given information about an event. 是正確答案。

換句話說

be provided with ~ detailed instructions about the fashion show 提供服裝展詳細規則
→ be given information about an event 接受活動相關情報

單字 celebrity n. 名人

例文1

191Saggezza Historical Institute
cordially invites you
to 192-Bthe opening of a new exhibition

Alba Longa:
Demystifying the Legend
of the Ancient City

192-Bon Saturday, October 10
from 6 P.M. to 9 P.M.
191Run date: October 11 to November 30

For further information, please read through the enclosed brochure.
Also 192-A/195please attend the special premiere of
192-Dthe documentary film:
The Dionysius Chronicles
on October 23
at the Halicarnassus Auditorium
on the third floor of the Institute.

Audience members are welcome to stay
for a question and answer session with the director
after the screening.

191Saggezza 歷史館
誠摯地邀請你參加192-B一個新展覽的開幕

Alba Longa：
揭開古城傳奇的神祕面紗

192-B10 月 10 日星期六晚上 6 點到 9 點
191展覽期間：10 月 11 日至 11 月 30 日

更多詳情，請詳讀隨函小冊子
另 192-A/195請於 10 月 23 日參加在本館
3 樓 Halicarnassus 講堂的192-D紀錄片特別首映：
Dionysius 記事

觀眾歡迎於放映後留下參加與導演的對話時刻。

例文2

The Dionysius Chronicles Wins ADF Prize

Amateur film director Giannina Balducci was awarded the coveted Amateur Documentary Filmmaker (ADF) prize for her movie *The Dionysius Chronicles*. The prize is presented annually to an amateur film director who shows promise and talent. Balducci's film explores historical sites and areas related to the ancient stories of Greek teacher and historian Dionysius. Balducci spent two years travelling and filming in various locations in the Mediterranean area and interviewed numerous history scholars and experts.

Balducci was born in Italy and expressed an interest in film since a young age. 193-BBy the time she was 28, she had already filmed three documentaries. "195I am so grateful for this honor and look forward to attending the movie's premiere on October 23. I hope others will also enjoy the film," said Balducci in a telephone interview.

194A panel of six judges selected Balducci as best director among more than 300 entrants. 194Selection of the recipient was based on directorial technique, originality, editing, sound, and visual appeal. The winners receive a certificate along with a cash prize of $20,000. The ADF prize is awarded by the European Documentary Filmmakers Society. To learn more about this year's winner and past recipients of the ADF prize, visit www.adfprize.org.

Dionysius 記事贏得業餘紀錄片製作人獎

業餘影片導演 Giannina Balducci 以她的電影 *Dionysius 記事*榮獲令人欽羨的業餘紀錄片製作人獎，這個獎項每年頒發給一名展現天分與前景的業餘影片導演。Balducci 的影片探討了與希臘導師和歷史學家 Dionysius 這個遠古故事相關的歷史遺跡與地區。Balducci 花了兩年的時間旅行，並拍攝地中海地區許多地方，還訪問了好多個歷史學者與專家。

Balducci 生於義大利，從很年輕的時候就對電影感興趣，193-B在她二十八歲時，她已經拍了三部紀錄片。Balducci 在一次電話訪問中説到：「195我很感激能獲得這項殊榮，而且很期待能參加 10 月 23 日的電影首映會。我希望其他人也會喜歡這部電影。」

194由六位評審組成的評審團在三百多個參賽者中選出 Balducci 為最佳導演，194這是根據導演的技巧、原創性、編輯、音效與視覺傳達。獲獎者能得到獎狀和兩萬元的獎金。業餘紀錄片製作人獎是由歐洲紀錄片製作人學會所頒發的。想多了解業餘紀錄片製作人獎今年得獎者和過去的得獎者，請上官網 www.adfprize.org

例文 1 單字 ☐cordially ad. 真心地　　　　　　☐demystify v. 解出謎題，讓人簡單理解地說明
　　　　　☐legend n. 傳說　　　　　　　　　☐premiere n. 首映會
　　　　　☐auditorium n. 講堂
例文 2 單字 ☐award v. 給予，賦予　　　　　　☐coveted a. 渴望的，渴求的
　　　　　☐present v. 給，呈獻　　　　　　　☐promise n. 指望，前途
　　　　　☐explore v. 探險　　　　　　　　　☐historian n. 歷史學者
　　　　　☐scholar n. 學者　　　　　　　　　☐grateful a. 感謝的
　　　　　☐entrant n. 參加者　　　　　　　　☐originality n. 獨創性

191

What will most likely happen on November 30?	11 月 30 日最有可能發生什麼事？
(A) An exhibition will conclude.	(A) 展覽結束。
(B) A movie will be screened.	(B) 會播放一部電影。
(C) A presentation ceremony will be held.	(C) 舉行頒獎儀式。
(D) An auditorium will be reopened.	(D) 講堂會重新開幕。

■ 推論 詳細內容　　　　　　　　　　　　　　　　　　　　　　　　　　　　解答 (A)

這是跟問題核心詞語 happen on November 30 有關的推理問題，所以要先確認第一篇文章中提到 11 月 30 日的相關內容。邀請函的 Saggezza Historical Institute cordially invites you to the opening of a new exhibition 中「提到 Saggezza 歷史館誠摯地邀請你參加一個新展覽的開幕」。接著，Run Date: October 11 to November 30 中提到展覽期間是 10 月 11 日至 11 月 30 日。由此可以推斷出 11 月 30 日是展覽結束的時間。因此，(A) An exhibition will conclude. 是正確答案。

單字 conclude v. 結束　screen v. 上映

192

Which information is NOT included in the invitation?	哪一項資訊沒有包含在邀請函裡？
(A) The location of the event	(A) 活動地點
(B) The date of an opening	(B) 開幕日期
(C) The cost of admission	(C) 門票費用
(D) The name of a film	(D) 影片的名稱

■ Not / True Not 問題　　　　　　　　　　　　　　　　　　　　　　　　解答 (C)

這是找出邀請函中的內容後，再跟選項作對比的 Not / True 問題。因為這個問題沒有核心詞語，所以跟每個選項核心詞語相關的內容都要在第一篇文章中確認。please attend the special premiere ~ at the Halicarnassus Auditorium on the third floor of the Institute 中提到「10 月 23 日參加在本館 3 樓 Halicarnassus 講堂的紀錄片特別首映」，所以跟 (A) 的內容一致。the opening of a new exhibition 和 on Saturday, October 10 中提到新展覽的開幕是在 10 月 10 日星期六晚上，所以跟 (B) 的內容一致。 (C) 是文中沒提到的內容。the documentary film: *The Dionysius Chronicles* 中提到紀錄片的名稱是 *Dionysius 記事*，所以跟 (D) 的內容一致。

單字 admission n. 入場

What is mentioned about Ms. Balducci?	關於 Balducci 小姐，何者正確？
(A) She is a member of a filmmakers' society.	(A) 她是製片人學會的會員。
(B) She has made several documentary films.	(B) 她拍了幾部紀錄片。
(C) She is an expert on Greek history.	(C) 她是希臘歷史的專家。
(D) She has lived in Italy since she was born	(D) 她從出生以後就住在義大利。

■ **Not / True** True 問題　　　　　　　　　　　　　　　　　　　　　　　　　　解答 (B)

這是找出跟問題核心詞語 Ms. Balducci 相關的內容後，再跟選項作對比的 Not / True 問題。因此，先確認的是第二篇文章中提到 Ms. Balducci 的相關內容。 (A) 是文中沒提到的內容。By the time she was 28, she had already filmed three documentaries. 中提到在她，也就是 Ms. Balducci 28 歲時，她已經拍了三部紀錄片，所以跟 (B) 的內容一致。因此，(B) She has made several documentary films. 是正確答案。(C) 和 (D) 都是文中沒提到的內容。

單字 society n. 協會

Why did Ms. Balducci win a prize?	為什麼 Balducci 小姐得獎？
(A) For acting in a film production	(A) 在一部影片中表演。
(B) For receiving high grades in film school	(B) 在電影學校得到很好的成績。
(C) For producing a series of documentaries	(C) 製作一系列的紀錄片。
(D) For showing talent as a director	(D) 展現導演的天分。

■ **六何原則** Why　　　　　　　　　　　　　　　　　　　　　　　　　　　　解答 (D)

這是問 Ms. Balducci 為什麼（Why）得獎的六何原則問題，所以要確認第二篇文章中跟問題核心詞語 Ms. Balducci win a prize 相關的內容。報導上的 A panel of six judges selected Balducci as best director 中提到由六位評審組成的評審團選出 Balducci 為最佳導演。接著，selection of the recipient was based on directorial technique, originality, editing, sound, and visual appeal.中提到這是根據導演的技巧、原創性、編輯、音效與視覺傳達。因此，(D) For showing talent as a director 是正確答案。

What will Ms. Balducci do on October 23?	Balducci 小姐在 10 月 23 日會做什麼？
(A) Give a talk at an exhibit opening	(A) 在展覽開幕會演講
(B) Register to participate in a competition	(B) 報名參加一個競賽
(C) Attend an event at the Halicarnassus Auditorium	(C) 參加在 Halicarnassus 講堂的一個活動
(D) Begin work on a new movie production	(D) 從事一部新電影的製作

■ **六何原則** 聯結問題　　　　　　　　　　　　　　　　　　　　　　　　　　解答 (C)

這是要把兩篇文章的內容綜合起來才能解開的聯結問題。問題核心詞語 Ms. Balducci do on October 23 中問 Ms. Balducci 在 10 月 23 日會做什麼（What），所以要先確認提到 Ms. Balducci 和 10 月 23 日的內容。

第二篇文章的 I ~ look forward to attending the movie's premiere on October 23.中提到 Ms. Balducci 很期待參加 10 月 23 日電影首映會。不過，這裡並沒有說明電影首映會的場所，所以要在邀請函中確認。第一篇文章的 please attend the ~ premiere of the ~ film ~ on October 23 at the Halicarnassus Auditorium 中提到紀錄片於 10 月 23 日在 Halicarnassus 講堂首映。

把 Ms. Balducci 會參加 10 月 23 日電影首映會的內容和紀錄片於 10 月 23 日 Halicarnassus 講堂首映的內容綜合起來，就可以知道 Ms. Balducci 會參加 10 月 23 日在 Halicarnassus 講堂舉辦的活動。因此，(C) Attend an event at the Halicarnassus Auditorium 是正確答案。

Questions 196-200 refer to the following invitation and e-mail.

196-200 根據下面電郵的內容回答問題

例文1

To: Hector Quintero <quintero@isiscoffeecompany.com>
From: Zelda Corbin <corbin@isiscoffeecompany.com>
Date: August 15
Subject: Kenyan Fresh Blend
Hector,

I was reading some food magazines this morning, and
196/198-Bthere were negative reviews of one of our new
coffee blends set to launch next quarter. 199According to a
critic who was present during our coffee tasting last week,
the acidity level in the Kenyan Fresh Blend was too weak.
198-DYou might want to check out *Subway Magazine* and
The *Prime Food Journal* to see the comments he and
other critics have made.

Taking this into consideration, 196I'd be really grateful if
your research team could look into this matter more
closely. As you know, 198-Cwe're hoping that the Kenyan
Fresh Blend will become one of our main export products,
so if the acidity level is not high enough, as the critics say,
then 198-Bit would be best to address this problem before
we go into production. 197I'm having a meeting with my
other product development team members next week, so
please send me a report as soon as you finish your
research. Thanks in advance.

Zelda

收件人：Hector Quintero
<quintero@isiscoffeecompany.com>
寄件人：Zelda Corbin
<corbin@isiscoffeecompany.com>
日期：8 月 15 日
主旨：肯亞新鮮混合咖啡
Hector：

我今天早上在閱讀一些食品雜誌，
196/198-B讀到一些針對我們預計下一季要
上市的一種新混合咖啡的負面評論。199
根據上週出現在我們咖啡試飲的評論家
的意見，肯亞新鮮混合咖啡的酸度太
弱。198-D你也許會想要看看《地鐵雜
誌》和《最佳食品期刊》裡他和其他評
論家所作的評論。

考慮到這點，196如果你的研究團隊能更深
入地探討一下這件事，我會很感激你。如
同你知道的，198-C我們希望肯亞新鮮混合
咖啡能成為我們外銷主力之一，因此，假
如如評論所說的酸度不夠高，198-B在我們
生產之前，最好能好好地重視這個問題。
197我下星期會和我另一個產品發展團隊成
員開會，在你完成研究後，請盡快將報告
寄給我，先謝謝你了。

Zelda

例文2

To: Zelda Corbin <corbin@isiscoffeecompany.com>
From: Hector Quintero <quintero@isiscoffeecompany.com>
Date: August 22
Subject: Re: Kenyan Fresh Blend
Attachment: Two documents

Zelda,

199My staff and I just finished the research you requested
and our findings confirm what you mentioned in your last
e-mail. As it turns out, the lab test conducted on the blend
indicates that its acidity level is 5.0, which lacks that
sharp, clean taste that coffee lovers look for. A report
submitted by the staff who conducted the coffee tasting
stated that most of the participants said the coffee was dull.

I have attached a copy of the lab test as well as the report
on the coffee tasting held last week. Our research team
recommends changing the blend. 200It is ready to produce
several samples for your consideration, but will wait for
your instructions. Please let me know if there is anything
else you would like me to do to facilitate the development
of this coffee as an export product. I will be out of the office
today to procure some coffee bean samples from a new

收件人：Zelda Corbin
<corbin@isiscoffeecompany.com>
寄件人：Hector Quintero
<quintero@isiscoffeecompany.com>
日期：8 月 22 日
主旨：回覆：肯亞新鮮混合咖啡
附件：兩份文件

Zelda：

199我的員工和我已經完成了你要求的研
究，而且我們的結論確認了你在上一封
電郵中所提到的事。結果是這樣的，實
驗室所作的實驗顯示酸度是 5.0，的確
缺少了咖啡愛好者所要的那種純淨、強
烈的火候，由我們員工上繳的一份報告
指出，大部分參與咖啡試喝的人都說咖
啡很平淡無味。

我附上了一份實驗室的檢驗報告還有上
週咖啡試喝的報告。我們研究團隊建議
更換咖啡豆的混和比例，200我們已經提
出了一些樣本供你參考，並等待你之後
的指示。如果有任何關於幫助研發這款

supplier, so please call my mobile phone if there is anything you would like to discuss.

Hector

外銷咖啡的事情需要我做的，請你通知我。我今天不在辦公室，我要去一個新的供應商那裡採購一些咖啡豆樣品，如果你有事要找我討論，請打我的手機

Hector

例文 1 單字 □critic n. 評論家　□present a. 參加的，現在的　□tasting n. 試飲會
　　　　　 □acidity n. 酸性　□look into phr. 調查　□closely ad. 詳細地
例文 2 單字 □turn out phr. 表明，呈現　□lack v. 不足～，沒有～　□dull a. 枯燥無味的
　　　　　 □consideration n. 考慮，檢討　□facilitate v. 使容易使用　□procure v. 採購，獲得

196

What is the purpose of the first e-mail?	第一封電郵的目的為何？
(A) To ask a colleague to conduct a study	(A) 要求一位同事作一項研究
(B) To request a coworker to reschedule a meeting	(B) 要求一位同事重新安排會議時間
(C) To cancel subscriptions to several food magazines	(C) 取消數本食品雜誌的訂閱
(D) To notify staff about a change in production schedules	(D) 通知員工生產時程的改變

■ 找出主題 目的　　　　　　　　　　　　　　　　　　　　　　　　　　　　　　解答 (A)

這是問第一封電郵的目的為何的找主題問題，所以要確認第一封電郵的內容。第一封電郵的 there were negative reviews of one of our new coffee blends 中提到「一些針對我們預計下一季要上市的一種新混合咖啡的負面評論」。接著，I'd be really grateful if your research team could look into this matter more closely 中提到「如果你的研究團隊能更深入地探討一下這件事，我會很感激」。因此，(A) To ask a colleague to conduct a study 是正確答案。

單字 colleague n. 同事　coworker n. 同事，協力者　subscription n. 訂閱，訂閱費

197

What does Ms. Corbin most likely do?	Corbin 小姐最有可能做什麼的？
(A) Writes critiques for a publication	(A) 為一出版品寫評論
(B) Leads a research team	(B) 領導一個研究團隊
(C) Manages a factory	(C) 管理一間工廠
(D) Develops new products	(D) 發展新產品

■ 推論 詳細內容　　　　　　　　　　　　　　　　　　　　　　　　　　　　　解答 (D)

這是跟問題核心詞語 Ms. Corbin 可能做什麼的推理問題。第一封電郵的 I'm having a meeting with my other product development team members 中提到我，也就是 Ms. Corbin 會和另一個產品發展團隊成員開會。由此可以推斷出 Ms. Corbin 在做產品開發的工作。因此，(D) Develops new products 是正確答案。

單字 critique n. 評價　manage v. 管理

198

What is NOT indicated about the Isis Coffee Company?	關於 Isis 咖啡公司，何者不正確？
(A) It purchases its merchandise from a supplier.	(A) 從供應商那裡購買商品。
(B) Its Kenyan Fresh Blend is not yet on the market.	(B) 他們的肯亞新鮮混合咖啡尚未上市。
(C) It distributes its goods internationally.	(C) 他們的產品經銷世界各地。
(D) Its products were reviewed in two publications.	(D) 他們的產品在兩本出版品中被評論。

Not / True Not 問題   解答 (A)

這是找出跟 Isis Coffee 公司相關的內容後，再跟選項作對比的 Not / True 問題。 (A) 是文中沒提到的內容。因此，(A) It purchases its merchandise from a supplier. 是正確答案。there were negative reviews of one of our new coffee blends set to launch next quarter 中提到「針對我們預計下一季要上市的一種新混合咖啡的負面評論」。接著，it would be best to address this problem before we go into production 中提到「在我們生產之前，最好能好好地重視這個問題」。因此，跟 (B) 的內容一致。We're hoping that the Kenyan Fresh Blend will become one of our main export products 中提到「我們希望肯亞新鮮混合咖啡能成為我們外銷主力之一」，所以跟 (C) 的內容一致。You might want to check out *Subway Magazine* and *The Prime Food Journal* to see the comments 中提到「你也許想要看看《地鐵雜誌》和《最佳食品期刊》的評論」，所以跟 (D) 的內容一致。

199

What does Mr. Quintero report about the Kenyan Fresh Blend? (A) It was taken off the market temporarily. (B) It is an expensive product. (C) It has a very low acidity level. (D) It has an unpleasant taste.	Quintero 先生對於肯亞新鮮混合咖啡提出什麼報告？ (A) 要暫時從市場上下架。 (B) 是很貴的產品。 (C) 酸度很低。 (D) 口味不好。

六何原則 聯結問題   解答 (C)

這是要把兩篇文章的內容綜合起來才能解開的聯結問題。問題核心詞語 Mr. Quintero report about the Kenyan Fresh Blend 中問到 Mr. Quintero 對於肯亞新鮮混合咖啡提出什麼（What）報告，所以要先確認 Mr. Quintero 寫的第二封電郵。

第二封電郵的 My staff and I just finished the research you requested and our findings confirm what you mentioned in your last e-mail. 中提到 Mr. Quintero 和他的員工已經完成 Ms. Corbin 要求的研究，而且結論確認了 Ms. Corbin 在上一封電郵中所提到的事。接著，the lab test conducted on the blend indicates that its acidity level is 5.0 中提到實驗室所作的實驗顯示酸度是 5.0。不過，這裡並無說明 Ms. Corbin 在上一封電郵中所提到的事是哪一事。因此，要確認第一封電郵的內容。第一封電郵的 According to a critic ~, the acidity level in the Kenyan Fresh Blend was too week. 中提到根據這個出現在上週咖啡試飲的評論家的意見，肯亞新鮮混合咖啡的酸度太弱。

把實驗顯示酸度是 5.0，確認了 Ms. Corbin 在上一封電郵中所提到的事的內容和第一封電郵中 Ms. Corbin 提到肯亞新鮮混合咖啡的酸度太弱的內容綜合起來，就可以知道 Mr. Quintero 是在報告肯亞新鮮混合咖啡的酸度太弱。因此，(C) It has a very low acidity level 是正確答案。

單字 take off phr. 退出，中斷　temporarily ad. 一時地，暫時地　unpleasant a. 不愉快的

200

What does Mr. Quintero ask Ms. Corbin to do? (A) Plan a marketing campaign (B) Provide further instruction (C) Arrange a meeting with critics (D) Attend a magazine interview	Quintero 先生要求 Corbin 小姐做什麼？ (A) 計畫一個行銷活動 (B) 提出進一步的指示 (C) 安排和評論家會面 (D) 參加一家雜誌的訪問

六何原則 What   解答 (B)

這是問 Mr. Quintero 要求 Ms. Corbin 做什麼（What）的六何原則問題，所以要確認 Mr. Quintero 所寫的第二封電郵的內容。第二封電郵的 It is ready to produce several samples for your consideration, but will wait for your instructions. 中提到研究團隊已經做了一些樣品讓 Ms. Corbin 可以參考，但是正在等 Ms. Corbin 的指示。因此，(B) Provide further instruction 是正確答案。

🎧 RC_Test01-A.mp3

1	keynote speaker	phr. 特邀演講者	26	organize	v. 規畫，安排
2	toll-free	a. 免費的	27	consider	v. 考慮
3	enclosed	a. 附上的	28	human resources director	phr. 人力資源主任
4	offering	n. 商品；供奉；貢獻	29	inquire	v. 提問
5	negotiate	v. 商議，洽談	30	laboratory test	phr. 臨床病理檢查，實驗室實驗
6	employment	n. 雇用	31	unforeseen	a. 無法預測的
7	arrangeable	a. 可準備的	32	circumstance	n. 情況
8	proceed to	phr. 繼續下去，往	33	until further notice	phr. 直到另行通知為止
9	routine	n. 日常，例行事務	34	innovative	a. 創新的
10	maintenance	n. 維修，維持	35	proficient	a. 熟練的
11	inspection	n. 檢測，調查	36	line	n. 系列產品
12	confectioner	n. 糕餅，做糕餅的人	37	hardware	n. 硬體
13	fundraiser	n. 資金籌集人，募款活動	38	surveillance	n. 監視
14	representative	n. 職員，代表	39	partnership	n. 合作關係，合力，聯手
15	impress	v. 給予深刻的印象	40	visibility	n. 能見度
16	manner	n. 方式	41	imaginative	a. 虛構的；幻想的
17	promptly	ad. 迅速地，即時地	42	make certain	phr. 確認
18	noticeably	ad. 顯眼地，顯著地	43	explicitly	ad. 明確地
19	indirectly	ad. 間接性地	44	outlet	n. 特賣店，排出口
20	mistaken	a. 判斷錯誤的，做錯的	45	secretary	n. 祕書
21	gift certificate	phr. 禮券	46	stay in touch	phr. 保持聯繫
22	instructive	a. 有教育意義的，有啟發性的	47	pass	n. 搭乘券，通行證
23	diplomatic	a. 外交的	48	compliance	n. 遵守
24	mention	v. 言及	49	authorization	n. 權限
25	personnel	n. 人事部	50	determination	n. 決定，決心

🎧 RC_Test01-B.mp3

1	allocation	n. 配置	26	lengthy	a. 長的
2	merchandise	n. 商品	27	observe	v. 遵守，注意
3	firework	n. 煙火	28	orderly	a. 有秩序的，整頓的
4	showcase	v. 展示	29	give way to	phr. 讓路給～
5	fulfill	v. 實行義務、約定、職務	30	pedestrian	n. 行人
6	branch	n. 分店	31	honk	v. 按喇叭
7	cooperation	n. 協助	32	windshield	n. 擋風玻璃
8	business	n. 交易，惠顧	33	motorist	n. 駕駛
9	questionable	a. 可疑的，懷疑的	34	register	v. 登記，註冊
10	solely	ad. 只有，惟	35	sign up for	phr. 申請，登記
11	relocation	n. 搬家，轉移	36	identification card	phr. 身分證件
12	retrieve	v. 找到～並帶來，回收	37	a wide range of	phr. 大範圍的，多樣的
13	belonging	n. 物件，私人物品，攜帶品	38	carry	v. 陳列販售
14	occupancy	n. 居住，佔領	39	mutually	ad. 相互，彼此
15	operation	n. 營運，手術	40	consignment	n. 代售
16	certification	n. 資格證	41	charge account	phr. 記帳戶頭
17	precaution	n. 預防措施	42	range from A to B	phr. 範圍從A 至B
18	guarantee	v. 確保	43	commission	n. 佣金
19	gear	n. 裝備	44	fill out	phr. 填寫
20	working order	phr. 正常的運作	45	commit	v. 專精，致力
21	glove	n. 手套	46	compromise	v. 連累，妥協
22	coral	n. 珊瑚	47	efficiency	n. 效能，效率
23	deal with	phr. 解決	48	enable	v. 讓～能夠
24	score	v. 得分	49	evenly	ad. 均勻，平等地
25	moderate	a. 適當的	50	dual-direction	a. 雙向的

🎧 RC_Test01-C.mp3

1	be equipped with	phr. 配備，具有	26	break down	phr. 瓦解
2	patent	v. 取得專利權；n. 專利	27	radio wave	phr. 無線電波
3	rating	n. 等級，排名	28	abdominal	a. 腹部的
4	alternative	a. 替代的	29	physician	n. 醫師，內科醫生
5	durable	a. 耐久的	30	desired	a. 渴望的，希望的
6	equalization	n. 均等化	31	on a regular basis	phr. 定期地
7	calculate	v. 測量，計算	32	improve	v. 改善
8	tricky	a. 麻煩的，辛苦的	33	amplifier	n. 擴音器
9	manufacturer	n. 製造商	34	loudspeaker	n. 揚聲器，擴音喇叭
10	hue	n. 顏色，色相	35	microphone	n. 麥克風
11	extensive	a. 大範圍的	36	seasoned	a. 老練的，有經驗的
12	establishment	n. 店鋪，賣場	37	province	n. 州，省
13	chart	v. 設立計畫，規畫	38	launch	n. 商品發表
14	in store	phr. 準備，儲藏	39	musical recording	phr. 唱片
15	exceptional	a. 超群的，例外的	40	meet a requirement	phr. 滿足需求
16	competitive	a. 有競爭力的	41	stock exchange	phr. 股票交易市場
17	interactive	a. 互動的	42	float	v. 發行股票、公債
18	commemorate	v. 慶祝，紀念	43	apiece	a. 各個，每個
19	breakthrough	n. 革新，突破	44	equity capital	phr. 主權資本
20	exploration	n. 探查，探險	45	venture into	phr. 冒險進入，投注事業
21	upcoming	a. 即將到來的，接近的	46	renovate	v. 更新，修繕
22	fascinating	a. 迷人的	47	retailer	n. 零售業者，零售業
23	treatment	n. 手術，治療	48	real estate	phr. 不動產
24	convince	v. 說服	49	alleged	a. 聲稱的，被斷言的
25	radio frequency	phr. 無線電頻率	50	press release	phr. 新聞稿

🎧 RC_Test01-D.mp3

1	custom-made	a. 客製的	26	donate	v. 捐贈
2	loan	n. 貸款，借出的東西	27	closing remarks	phr. 閉幕致詞
3	broaden	v. 擴大	28	executive	n. 主管，執行長
4	board	v. 用木板覆蓋，供膳宿	29	veterinary	a. 獸醫的；n. 獸醫師
5	groom	v. 清潔寵物	30	accredited	a. 認可的，公認的
6	trim	v. 修剪	31	domesticated	a. 馴化的
7	voucher	n. 折價券	32	comprehensive	a. 綜合性的，包括性的
8	breed	n. 品種	33	compensation package	phr. 福利，津貼
9	exclusively	ad. 只為了～，獨家地	34	retirement	n. 退休
10	abandoned	a. 被遺棄的	35	liability	n. 責任
11	frequent customer	phr. 常客	36	interpersonal	a. 待人處事的
12	industry	n. 產業	37	preventive	a. 預防的
13	commencement exercise	phr. 畢業典禮	38	reference letter	phr. 推薦信
14	accompany	v. 陪同，伴隨	39	submission	n. 提交
15	faculty	n. 教職員，學系	40	profession	n. 職業，專業
16	in charge of	phr. 負責	41	significant	a. 相當的，重要的
17	processional	n. 列隊行進時唱的聖歌	42	financial	a. 財政上的，財務上的
18	pledge	n. 誓言；v. 發誓	43	insufficient	a. 不充分的
19	national anthem	phr. 國歌	44	be unwilling to	phr. 不想做～
20	intermission	n. 中場休息時間	45	enroll	v. 登錄，入學
21	choir	n. 合唱團	46	shipment	n. 配送，輸送
22	diploma	n. 畢業證書，學位	47	specify	v. 具體指明
23	recessional	n. 退場讚美詩	48	be forced to	phr. 被迫做～
24	alter	v. 變更	49	substantially	ad. 相當大地
25	top honor	phr. 首席，最高榮耀	50	reimburse	v. 賠償，歸還

🎧 RC_Test02-A.mp3

1	obtain	v. 可取得的，可獲得的	26	crisis	n. 危機
2	pay in full	phr. 支付全額	27	incident	n. 事情，事件
3	booking	n. 預約	28	agenda	n. 議程，案件
4	strategy	n. 策略	29	shut down	phr. 關門，停止
5	tenant	n. 承租人，房客	30	manage to	phr. 設法應付～
6	productive	a. 有生產力的	31	imitate	v. 模仿
7	fixed	a. 固定的	32	dispatch	v. 派遣
8	deliver	v. 配送，運送	33	feasible	a. 可實行的
9	inaugurate	v. 舉行開幕式，使正式就任	34	extent	n. 程度，大小
10	driving range	phr. 高爾夫練習場	35	closely	ad. 嚴密地，接近地
11	resident	n. 居住者	36	swiftly	ad. 迅速地，快速
12	provable	a. 可以認證的	37	marginally	ad. 微小地，微不足道
13	categorize	v. 分類，分類為～	38	ballroom	n. 宴會廳，跳舞大廳
14	supervisor	n. 監督員，管理者，主管	39	unanimous	a. 一致同意的
15	implement	v. 實行	40	concise	a. 簡潔的
16	individual	n. 個人	41	clear	a. 分明的；v. 使乾淨
17	seasonal	a. 季節性的	42	work out	phr. 想出～，找出～
18	composer	n. 作曲家	43	undeniably	ad. 不可否認地
19	stunning	a. 驚豔的	44	arguably	ad. 可以認為，可以說是
20	score	n. 樂譜	45	oversee	v. 監督
21	enforce	v. 執行，強制	46	publication	n. 出版
22	on leave	phr. 休假中	47	throughout	ad. 遍布，從頭到尾
23	headquarters	n. 總部	48	virtually	ad. 實際上，差不多
24	overseas	a. 海外的	49	availability	n. 可利用性
25	not only A but also B	phr. 不只A還有B	50	prohibition	n. 禁止

🎧 RC_Test02-B.mp3

1	contingency	n. 突發狀況	26	obligate	v. 使遵行義務
2	ensure	v. 保障，一定要～	27	suspension	n. 停職
3	accomplishment	n. 成就，才藝	28	get in touch with	phr. 與～聯絡
4	landscaper	n. 園藝師，造景師	29	tardiness	n. 遲到
5	acquisition	n. 獲得	30	confidentiality	n. 祕密
6	anticipate	v. 預測	31	security	n. 安全
7	surpass	v. 優於	32	so that	phr. 所以～，因此可以～
8	speed limit	phr. 速限	33	no later than	phr. 不要晚於～
9	violation	n. 違反	34	be involved in	phr. 參與～
10	boulevard	n. 大路，寬廣的林蔭道	35	outreach	n. 到家關懷服務
11	perform	v. 實施	36	incorporate	v. 統整
12	offer	v. 提供，提案	37	prior to	phr. 在～之前
13	infuse	v. 注入	38	whereas	conj. ～的相反
14	council	n. 議會	39	unavailable	a. 無法配合的，無法取得的
15	bid	n. 投標	40	neurologist	n. 精神科醫師
16	restoration	n. 整修，復原	41	informative	a. 資訊豐富的
17	streamlined	a. 有效率的	42	nutrition	n. 營養
18	assembly	n. 組裝，協會，集會	43	come as no surprise	phr. 發生得並不意外
19	attribute	v. 歸因於～	44	take over	phr. 接管, 繼任
20	state	v. 說，明示	45	resignation	n. 辭職
21	renewal	n. 更新，重開	46	investigation	n. 調查
22	consent	n. 同意	47	doubtfully	ad. 疑惑地
23	treaty	n. 條約，協定	48	actively	ad. 主動地，積極地
24	permit	n. 許可證	49	association	n. 協會，團體
25	engage in	phr. 從事於～	50	occasion	n. 活動，盛典

🎧 RC_Test02-C.mp3

1	amusement park	phr. 遊樂園	26	warehouse	n. 倉庫
2	advertisement	n. 廣告	27	fragile	a. 易碎的
3	worth	a. 有～的價值	28	inspector	n. 督導
4	settle	v. 定居，安頓，安於	29	bureau	n. 政府部門
5	recipient	n. 獲獎者，受頒者	30	state-wide	a. 整州的，全國的
6	prominent	a. 有名的	31	proper	a. 正確的，適切的
7	discontinue	v. 中斷	32	handling	n. 處理
8	promotional	a. 促銷的	33	administrative	a. 行政上的，管理上的
9	at a glance	phr. 一眼認出，馬上	34	assistant	n. 助理，祕書
10	attachment	n. 附件	35	compile	v. 編輯，彙編，統計
11	comparable	a. 比得上的，可比較的	36	enchanting	a. 魅惑的，使人著迷的
12	sign in	phr. 登入	37	formal	a. 官方的，正式的
13	clarify	v. 澄清，闡明	38	affiliate	v. 使隸屬於，使緊密聯繫
14	terms and conditions	phr. 條款與條件	39	catering	a. 承辦宴會的，提供外燴的
15	niche	n. 合適的位置、空間	40	vegetarian	a. 素食主義者的，吃素的
16	furnishing	n. 家具	41	exotic	a. 異國情調的，外來的
17	decorative	a. 裝飾的	42	peak rate	phr. 旺季費用
18	antique	n. 骨董	43	airport transfer	phr. 機場接送
19	feature	v. 以～為特徵	44	cottage	n. 小屋，農舍
20	according to	phr. 根據～	45	apply	v. 適用
21	composition	n. 構成，作曲	46	usage	n. 使用
22	attraction	n. 景點	47	nearby	a. 鄰近的
23	proprietor	n. 經營者	48	excursion	n. 旅行
24	appraise	v. 鑑賞，評價	49	standard	n. 標準
25	inherit	v. 遺傳，繼承	50	accommodate	v. 協助，配合

🎧 RC_Test02-D.mp3

1	subscription	n. 訂閱	26	analyze	v. 分析
2	mailing list	phr. 郵寄名單	27	budget	n. 預算；a. 低廉的
3	former	a. 以前的	28	forecast	v. 預測，預想
4	understaffed	a. 人員不足的	29	socialize	v. 參與交際，社交
5	entry	n. 參加作品	30	archaeological	a. 考古學的
6	serve	v. 提供	31	crew	n. 成員，工作人員
7	adjust	v. 調整	32	excavation	n. 開挖
8	distribution	n. 分配	33	expedition	n. 考察，考察團
9	broker	n. 仲介	34	tentative	a. 暫定的
10	firm	n. 公司；企業；a. 牢固的	35	promising	a. 有希望的
11	benefit	v. 獲得幫助，獲利	36	on-site	a. 工作現場的
12	exhibition	n. 展覽	37	shelter	n. 休憩場所
13	attendee	n. 參加者	38	generator	n. 發電機
14	make arrangement for	phr. 準備～	39	allot	v. 分配
15	rebate	n. 折現，折扣	40	objective	n. 目標
16	tight	a. 緊的	41	align	v. 排成一列
17	take advantage of	phr. 利用～	42	access	n. 使用
18	input	v. 輸入，提供	43	sanitation	n. 衛生
19	second-hand	a. 二手的，間接的	44	charter	n. 交通工具的租賃
20	account	n. 帳戶	45	reputable	a. 有名望的
21	acknowledge	v. 承認	46	reliable	a. 可信賴的
22	rewarding	a. 有益的，有報酬的	47	qualification	n. 資格認證
23	transition	n. 變化，轉移	48	driver's license	phr. 駕照
24	senior-level	a. 高層的，固有的	49	expire	v. 期滿
25	medical examination	phr. 醫療檢查	50	employ	v. 雇用

🎧 RC_Test03-A.mp3

1	finals	n. 決賽	26	licensed	a. 獲得許可的
2	sustain	v. 忍受（傷害），使～維持	27	ingredient	n. 材料
3	diminutive	a. 非常小的	28	property	n. 財產，所有權
4	instructor	n. 講師，指導員	29	prepare	v. 準備
5	momentum	n. 動力，動量	30	district	n. 區
6	momentary	a. 瞬間的，短暫的	31	typical	a. 典型的
7	unattended	a. 沒人照料的	32	convention	n. 會議
8	pay a fine	phr. 支付罰金	33	charge	v. 收費
9	risk	v. 冒～的風險	34	charity	n. 慈善
10	tow	v. 牽引，拖	35	institution	n. 機關
11	removal	n. 移動，去除	36	nonprofit	a. 非營利性的
12	transit	n. 運送，變化	37	contented	a. 滿足的
13	location	n. 場所，位置	38	be exempt from	phr. 免除～
14	distribute	v. 分配	39	isolated	a. 孤立的
15	attentive	a. 留意的	40	permissive	a. 寬容的，自由放任式的
16	deadline	n. 截止日，期限	41	encourage	v. 鼓勵，慫恿
17	limit	n. 限制，界線	42	reachable	a. 可觸及的
18	grade	n. 品質，成績	43	household	a. 家用的
19	trainee	n. 受訓者	44	rather	ad. 還不如，寧願
20	permanent	a. 正職的，永遠的	45	summit	n. 高峰會
21	inconsistency	n. 不一致，前後矛盾	46	sizable	a. 具相當規模的
22	double-check	v. 再次檢查	47	collaboration	n. 協作的，聯名的
23	crucial	a. 重要的	48	participant	n. 參加者
24	comply with	phr. 依據，遵守	49	switch off	phr. 關閉～
25	unified	a. 統一的	50	automatic	a. 自動的

🎧 RC_Test03-B.mp3

1	precise	a. 精確的	26	advisor	n. 顧問
2	venture	n. 投機活動，冒險	27	dispose	v. 丟棄，處理
3	generous	a. 慷慨的	28	throw away	phr. 丟掉
4	incur	v. 使發生，招惹	29	drop off at	phr. 把～帶來交給～
5	outing	n. 短途旅遊	30	brand new	phr. 全新的
6	hire	v. 雇用	31	biodegradable	a. 可生物分解的
7	server	n. 侍者，員工	32	trivial	a. 微小的
8	authorize	v. 授權	33	region	n. 區域
9	mark	v. 紀念，標記	34	shareholder	n. 股東
10	first-ever	a. 史上最初的	35	in this regard	phr. 關於這一點
11	intention	n. 意圖，目的	36	decade	n. 十年
12	initiation	n. 加入，創始	37	finance	n. 財務，財經
13	document	n. 文件；v. 提供文件	38	instance	n. 情況，實例；v. 引證
14	recurring	a. 再發的，循環的	39	vulnerable	a. 易受傷害的
15	equipment	n. 裝備	40	burglary	n. 竊盜
16	output	n. 生產量	41	night shift	phr. 夜班
17	designation	n. 指定，指名	42	fluorescent	a. 螢光的
18	regarding	prep. 關於～	43	recommendation	n. 推薦
19	projector	n. 設計者，投影機	44	be made up of	phr. 以～而組成
20	in addition	phr. 此外	45	news conference	phr. 記者會
21	nevertheless	ad. 然而	46	annual	a. 年度的
22	avail	v. 有幫助，有用處	47	adjustment	n. 調整
23	courier	n. 信差，嚮導	48	update	v. 告知最近的情報
24	vendor	n. 賣家	49	savor	v. 享受，感受
25	developer	n. 開發者	50	brew	v. 泡、煮茶或咖啡

🎧 RC_Test03-C.mp3

1	ground	a. 磨碎的，磨平的	26	put into action	phr. 付諸行動
2	proportion	n. 份量	27	loyalty	n. 信賴，忠誠
3	stir	v. 攪拌	28	particular	a. 特定的，挑剔的
4	steep	v. 浸泡	29	valuables	n. 貴重物品
5	decode	v. 解讀，解碼	30	alternative route	phr. 替代路線
6	formula	n. 方程式	31	defensive	a. 防禦性的
7	psychiatrist	n. 精神科醫師	32	reservation	n. 預約
8	unravel	v. 解開	33	arena	n. 競技場
9	status	n. 地位，身分	34	operate	v. 營業，營運
10	passively	ad. 被動地	35	alumnus	n. 校友
11	outlook	n. 視野，觀點	36	reunite	v. 再次相遇
12	motivate	v. 給予動機，激發	37	alma mater	phr. 母校
13	stimulate	v. 刺激	38	sponsor	v. 贊助，支援
14	author	v. 開創，編寫	39	startup	a. 著手的，開始的
15	enhancement	n. 提升	40	donor	n. 捐款人
16	department	n. 系，科	41	contest	v. 對～提出質疑
17	stable	a. 穩定的	42	notice	v. 提醒
18	go by	phr. 送走～，經過	43	soft drink	phr. 無酒精飲料
19	improvement	n. 改善，進步	44	bottomless	a. 無限制的
20	enlarged	a. 擴大的	45	running total	phr. 合計
21	athletic	a. 運動的	46	deduct	v. 扣除
22	transportation	n. 交通方式	47	reference	n. 參考，參照
23	utmost	a. 最大的	48	immediate	a. 即時的
24	destination	n. 目的地	49	withhold	v. 保留，不給～
25	choosy	a. 挑剔的，挑三揀四的	50	demand	v. 要求

🎧 RC_Test03-D.mp3

1	complaint	n. 申訴，抱怨	26	contain	v. 包含
2	appoint	v. 指名，任命	27	two-way	a. 來回的，雙方的
3	recently	ad. 最近	28	overnight	a. 一夜的，一夜之間的
4	name	v. 指名，任命	29	reduce	v. 減少
5	post	n. 職位，職責	30	travel agency	phr. 旅行社
6	key	a. 關鍵的	31	modification	n. 變更
7	role	n. 角色	32	confirmation	n. 確認
8	strategic	a. 策略性的	33	utility pipe	phr. 水管
9	flexibility	n. 柔軟性，靈活性	34	stainless	a. 無瑕疵的，不銹的
10	constantly	ad. 無止盡地	35	outstanding	a. 未償付的
11	join	v. 參加，加入	36	balance	n. 餘額
12	instrumental	a. 有幫助的	37	concern	n. 關心，問題
13	secure	v. 把～弄牢，確保	38	provide	v. 提供，給
14	premier	a. 最好的	39	feedback	n. 回饋
15	portrait	n. 人物照，肖像畫	40	highland	n. 高地
16	temporarily	ad. 短暫地	41	ideal	a. 適切的，理想的
17	station	v. 配置，部署	42	animated	a. 有活力的，活潑的
18	stopover	n. 滯留，中途停留	43	ongoing	a. 進行中的
19	present	v. 出示	44	transaction	n. 交易，處理
20	check in	phr. 辦理搭乘手續	45	inconvenience	n. 不方便
21	no later than	phr. 不能夠晚於～	46	round-trip	a. 往返的
22	luggage	n. 行李	47	scenery	n. 風景，背景
23	flat rate	phr. 固定費率	48	lodging	n. 食宿，投宿
24	contrary to	phr. 與～不同	49	geography	n. 地理
25	agent	n. 職員	50	reschedule	v. 更改日程

🎧 RC_Test04-A.mp3

1	accountant	n. 會計師	26	postpone	v. 使～延期
2	key chain	phr. 鑰匙圈	27	laundry	n. 洗衣房；洗好的衣服
3	purchase	n. 購買	28	method	n. 方法
4	pleased	a. 高興的，喜歡的	29	effect	n. 效果
5	chemist	n. 化學家	30	authorized	a. 授權的
6	funding	n. 資金	31	showroom	n. 展示間
7	herbal	a. 草本的	32	lead to	phr. 導致
8	blood pressure	phr. 血壓	33	complicated	a. 複雜的
9	local	a. 國內的；地區的；n. 地區居民	34	intervene	v. 介入
10	negotiation	n. 協商	35	adequate	a. 足夠的
11	private	a. 私人的；個人持有的	36	committee	n. 委員會
12	administration	n. 行政部門	37	on sale	phr. 促銷中的
13	interruption	n. 妨礙	38	adept	a. 熟練的
14	carry out	phr. 執行	39	prosecutor	n. 檢察官
15	wiring	n. 配線	40	acclaim	n. 歡呼
16	contrary	a. 反面的	41	feasibility	n. 可行性
17	absent	a. 不在的，缺席的	42	rural	a. 鄉村的
18	stockholder	n. 股東	43	blueprint	n. 藍圖，計畫
19	plant	n. 工廠	44	restoration	n. 修復
20	species	n. 種類	45	management	n. 管理階層
21	accidentally	ad. 偶然地	46	publishing	a. 出版的；n. 出版
22	editorial board	phr. 編輯委員會	47	manuscript	n. 手稿
23	process	v. 處理	48	influx	n. 湧入
24	include	v. 包含	49	comment	n. 意見
25	vehicle	n. 汽車	50	advanced	a. 進階的

RC_Test04-B.mp3

1	corporation	n. 企業	26	overdue	a. 過期的
2	endorse	v. 推薦，背書	27	suspend	v. 中斷
3	transport	v. 輸送	28	reactivation	n. 再啟動
4	aspiration	n. 志向	29	installation	n. 設置
5	in response to	phr. 回覆～	30	curriculum	n. 課程，教程
6	reflection	n. 深思	31	educational trip	phr. 校外教學
7	pass up	phr. 放棄	32	purpose	n. 目的
8	adjust to	phr. 去適應～	33	expose	v. 使露出
9	optimistic	a. 肯定性的，樂觀的	34	conservation	n. 保存
10	collaborate	v. 合作	35	complete	v. 完成，使完整；a. 完整的
11	petition	v. 請願	36	express	v. 表現
12	relocate	v. 搬家，移動	37	support	n. 支持
13	follow-up letter	phr. 追蹤進度的信件	38	extra	a. 增加的，額外的
14	main branch	phr. 總店	39	hospitality	n. 旅館，接待，款待
15	convert	v. 轉換，換	40	complex	n. 社區，複合住宅
16	empty lot	phr. 空地	41	adversely	ad. 不利地
17	adjacent	a. 鄰接的	42	affect	v. 影響
18	pave	v. 鋪設	43	spokesperson	n. 發言人
19	commence	v. 開始	44	suffer	v. 承受，受苦
20	usable	a. 可使用的	45	loss	n. 損失
21	passage	n. 通過	46	tumble	v. 暴跌，大幅度下滑
22	convenient	a. 方便的	47	resume	v. 繼續
23	as of	phr. 以～	48	dismiss	v. 解散，否認
24	exceed	v. 超過	49	workforce	n. 人力
25	disconnection	n. 中斷	50	mix up	phr. 混合

🎧 RC_Test04-C.mp3

1	participate	v. 參加	26	hazard	n. 危險源
2	merge	v. 合併	27	adhere to	phr. 根據～，遵守
3	figure out	phr. 發現，想出	28	hidden	a. 隱藏的
4	field	n. 領域，現場	29	unfortunately	ad. 可惜地，不幸地
5	commercial	a. 商業的	30	productivity	n. 生產率，生產力
6	duplication	n. 複製，影印	31	raise	v. 舉起；n. 加薪
7	provision	n. 提供	32	wage	n. 工資，薪水
8	surveillance	n. 監視，監督	33	high performance	phr. 高性能
9	replication	n. 複製	34	protective	a. 保護的
10	multiple	a. 多樣的	35	broad array of	phr. 廣泛地
11	fire drill	phr. 火災演習	36	garment	n. 衣服
12	in accordance with	phr. 根據～	37	fireproof clothing	phr. 防火衣
13	familiarize	v. 使熟悉	38	disposable	a. 拋棄式的
14	aim	v. 目標	39	multinational	a. 多國籍的
15	evacuate	v. 逃出，躲避	40	boost	v. 強化，使增加
16	in case of	phr. 萬一～	41	logistics	n. 物流
17	instruction	n. 指導，說明	42	hotline	n. 諮詢專線
18	unit	n. 單位	43	outline	v. 講述～的概要
19	procedure	n. 程序	44	division	n. 部門
20	thoroughly	ad. 仔細地，有步驟地	45	allow	v. 同意
21	signal	v. 通知	46	wholesale	a. 批發的，大量販賣的
22	note	v. 注意	47	board	n. 董事會
23	vacate	v. 使變空，離開	48	distributor	n. 物流業者，批發商
24	knowledgeable	a. 有知識的，廣博的	49	intensify	v. 強化
25	designated	a. 指定的	50	in connection with	phr. 與～有關連

🎧 RC_Test04-D.mp3

1	client	n. 客戶	26	industrial	a. 工業用的
2	identify	v. 確認，認證	27	setup	n. 設置，組成
3	criterion	n. 基準	28	cleanup	n. 拆除，清掃
4	quotation	n. 報價	29	directly	ad. 直接
5	endorsement	n. 背書	30	ordinance	n. 規定，法令，條例
6	probable	a. 很可能發生的，可信的	31	working day	phr. 工作日，平日
7	compromise	v. 妥協，危及	32	assistance	n. 幫助，支援
8	profitability	n. 獲利性	33	sponsorship	n. 贊助
9	awareness	n. 認知度，認知	34	pick up	phr. 拿來
10	prospective	a. 將來的，有希望的	35	confectionery	a. 糖果類的
11	primarily	ad. 主要地	36	individualize	v. 賦予個性
12	rearrange	v. 重新配置	37	diversity	n. 多樣性
13	respective	a. 各自的，分別的	38	domestic	a. 國內的
14	termination	n. 終了	39	hand-finished	a. 手製的，以手工收尾的
15	insurance plan	phr. 保險計畫	40	customized	a. 客製化的
16	assignment	n. 業務，任務	41	subsidiary	n. 子公司
17	personal property	phr. 個人財產	42	limited	a. 有限制的，限定的
18	shipping	n. 海運，船舶	43	ineligible	a. 沒有資格的
19	downsize	v. 減少	44	long-term	a. 長期的
20	reorganize	v. 重新編制，重新組織	45	vouch	v. 保障，斷言
21	structure	n. 構造，體制	46	specifically	ad. 具體地
22	revise	v. 修正	47	business trip	phr. 出差
23	forward	v. 傳送	48	steadily	ad. 平穩地
24	direct	v. 指示	49	surcharge	n. 額外金額
25	attend to	phr. 處理～，實行	50	come under	phr. 被包括在～之下

🎧 RC_Test05-A.mp3

1	celebrate	v. 慶祝	26	provided that	phr. 若是～
2	exhibitor	n. 展覽者	27	deadline	n. 期限
3	gala	n. 節日；慶祝	28	put off	phr. 延期
4	direct to	phr. 將～指向～	29	announce	v. 宣布
5	manager	n. 經理	30	petroleum	n. 石油
6	policy	n. 保險單；政策	31	joint	a. 共同的
7	extract	v. 抽出	32	accounting	n. 會計
8	cardholder	n. 卡片持有人	33	solitary	a. 僅有的，單獨的
9	overcome	v. 克服	34	remote	a. 偏僻的，遙遠的
10	a variety of	phr. 各式各樣的	35	calling plan	phr. 通話方案
11	neglect	v. 疏忽，無視	36	intensive	a. 集中的
12	effectiveness	n. 有效果	37	raw material	phr. 原料
13	modify	v. 修改	38	timely	a. 及時的，適時的
14	sale	n. 銷售	39	efficient	a. 有效率的
15	census	n. 人口調查	40	obligatory	a. 有義務的
16	suburban	a. 郊外的	41	booked	a. 已預約的
17	remarkably	ad. 引人注目地，明顯地	42	suggestion	n. 建議
18	lease	n. 租賃契約	43	suitable	a. 適合的
19	utility	a. 公共的，實用的	44	urgently	ad. 緊急地
20	ensure	v. 確保	45	rotating shift	phr. 輪班
21	attendant	n. 交通運輸服務員	46	fuel	v. 以～為燃料
22	court	v. 追求	47	renewable	a. 可再生的
23	go off	phr.（警報器等）響起	48	drop	v. 丟入，扔下
24	disturb	v. 妨礙	49	job seeker	phr. 求職者
25	highlight	n. 精華，最重要的部分	50	fair	n. 博覽會

🎧 RC_Test05-B.mp3

1	dispute	n. 紛爭	26	coverage	n. 新聞報導；補償範圍
2	modest	n. 適度的，謙虛的	27	line-up	n. 行程，流程
3	journalism	n. 新聞業，新聞工作	28	souvenir	n. 紀念品
4	tableware	n. 餐具	29	signing	n. 簽署
5	expand	v. 擴張	30	overall	ad. 全面地，全部
6	charitable	a. 慈善的	31	projection	n. 計畫，預想，推測
7	broadband	a. 寬頻的	32	discuss	v. 討論，商談
8	unemployment rate	phr. 失業率	33	due	n. 期限；a. 應支付的
9	cashier	n. 出納員	34	invoice	n. 發票，請款單
10	candidate	n. 應試者，候選員	35	turn over	phr. 移交，翻轉
11	priority	n. 優先權	36	collection agency	phr. 討債公司
12	only if	phr. 唯有在～情況下	37	ignore	v. 忽略
13	admission	n. 進入許可，入場券	38	billing statement	phr. 帳單
14	payment	n. 支付的款項	39	overcharge	v. 索價過高
15	fund	v. 資助；n. 資金	40	place an order	phr. 下訂單
16	administrator	n. 管理人	41	exhibit	n. 展示，展覽
17	given	a. 指定的	42	natural wonder	phr. 驚奇的自然景觀
18	recap	v. 重述要點	43	marine life	phr. 海洋生物
19	personnel department	phr. 人事部	44	underwater	a. 水中的
20	separate	a. 各別的	45	guided	a. 導覽的
21	research	n. 研究，調查	46	lecture	n. 講座，演講
22	trial	n. 審判，試驗	47	fold	v. 停刊；摺疊
23	delayed	a. 延遲的，晚的	48	cease	v. 中斷，停止
24	inauguration	n. 開幕式	49	leading	a. 領導的，很重要的
25	invitation	n. 邀請函	50	excessively	ad. 超過地，過度地

🎧 RC_Test05-C.mp3

1	propose	v. 提案，提議	26	assemble	v. 組織，組成
2	subscriber	n. 訂戶，贊助者	27	stop by	phr. 暫停
3	title	n. 出版品，書籍	28	associate	n. 同事，職員
4	newsstand	n. 書報亭	29	facility	n. 設施
5	emerge	v. 浮現，顯露	30	nonabrasive	a. 非侵蝕的
6	successor	n. 後人，繼承者	31	conscious	a. 思考的，有意識的
7	readership	n. 讀者們	32	polish	n. 光澤，擦亮
8	retire	v. 退休	33	vacuum	n. 用吸塵器清潔
9	competitor	n. 競爭公司，競爭者	34	ultimate	a. 最終的，究極的
10	obsolete	a. 已淘汰的	35	exterior	n. 外部
11	introductory remarks	phr. 開場介紹	36	try out	phr. 嘗試
12	closed-door	a. 非公開的	37	capital	n. 資本額，資產
13	inductee	n. 入會者	38	stock offering	phr. 股票發行
14	raffle draw	phr. 摸彩	39	gloomy	a. 停滯的，沉悶的
15	autographed	a. 親筆簽名的	40	gymnasium	n. 健身房
16	memorabilia	n. 紀念品，收藏品	41	bowling alley	phr. 保齡球道；保齡球館
17	banquet	n. 宴會	42	derive from	phr. 由～產生
18	in person	phr. 直接	43	bond	n. 債券
19	career	n. 職業生涯	44	amount to	phr. 達～
20	social gathering	phr. 社交聚會	45	foreign loan	phr. 外債
21	put together	phr. 組織，安排	46	proceeds	n. 收益
22	visibly	ad. 醒目地	47	auction off	phr. 拍賣掉
23	be impressed with	phr. 對～印象深刻	48	share	n. 股份
24	stand out	phr. 突出	49	investment	n. 投資
25	incredible	a. 驚人的	50	corporate	a. 企業的，公司的

🎧 RC_Test05-D.mp3

1	approval	n. 批准	26	quality	n. 品質；a. 品質好的
2	e-commerce	n. 電子商務	27	substandard	a. 水準以下的，低於標準的
3	post	v. 公告	28	intricate	a. 精細的，巧妙的
4	in return for	phr. 作為～回禮	29	terrestrial	a. 地上的，地球的
5	executive	n. 執行部門，業務主管	30	considering	prep. 考慮到～
6	craft	n. 工藝品； v. 精巧地製作	31	confident	a. 確信的，有自信的
7	solicitation	n. 誘惑，懇請	32	average	a. 平均的；n. 平均
8	directory	n. 名單，工商名錄	33	inferior	a. 次級的
9	business	n. 企業	34	relatively	ad. 相對地，比較地
10	inclusive	a. 包含的	35	family-run	a. 家族經營的
11	specified	a. 具體的	36	completely	ad. 完美地，完全地
12	stem	n. 杯腳；莖	37	take steps	phr. 採取行動
13	along with	phr. 連同	38	rely upon	phr. 出於～，依靠～
14	replace	v. 替代	39	commitment	n. 承諾，奉獻
15	necessary	a. 必要的，必需的	40	response	n. 回答
16	exclusive	a. 除了～，獨佔的	41	professionalism	n. 專業性
17	fitness	n. 健康；適當	42	courtesy	n. 有禮
18	affiliate	n. 同盟，關係企業	43	thoroughness	n. 徹底
19	lastly	ad. 最後	44	expertise	n. 專業技術
20	complimentary	a. 免費的	45	punctuality	n. 嚴守時間
21	accommodating	a. 親切的，樂於助人的	46	satisfaction	n. 滿意度
22	the other day	phr. 之前某一天	47	patient	a. 有耐心的
23	enticement	n. 誘因	48	apply	v. 申請
24	partner	v. 合作，聯合	49	concern	v. 與～有關
25	refer	v. 歸因於～，參考～	50	contact	v. 聯絡

🎧 RC_Test06-A.mp3

1	affiliation	n. 加入，聯合	26	applicable	a. 適用的，合適的
2	concentration	n. 密集	27	reminder	n. 催單，提醒物
3	alteration	n. 變化，改造	28	urge	v. 力勸，慫恿
4	formation	n. 形成	29	stock	n. 股票，庫存品
5	make sure	phr. 確認，確保	30	delegate	v. 委任
6	replenish	v. 補充，再填滿	31	demonstrate	v. 說明，示範
7	lounge	n. 休息室	32	earthquake	n. 地震
8	progressively	ad. 日益增加地	33	press	v. 按；n. 報紙媒體
9	clerk	n. 店員，職員	34	emergency	n. 緊急事項
10	passenger	n. 乘客	35	as soon as possible	phr. 盡快
11	departure	n. 出發	36	even	ad. 更，就連～
12	be subject to	phr. 易遭～影響	37	since	conj. 自從～，因為～
13	audio-visual	a. 視聽的	38	minimal	a. 最小的
14	be known for	phr. 以～知名	39	itinerary	n. 旅行行程
15	still	ad. 仍然	40	shift	n. 輪班制的一個班
16	performance	n. 表演	41	alternate	a. 交替的
17	cast	n. 卡司	42	primetime	n. 黃金時段
18	greet	v. 致意	43	mature	a. 成熟的
19	discount	n. 折扣	44	fraction	n. 片段，一部份
20	fee	n. 費用	45	provider	n. 供應商，提供者
21	president	n. 總裁，總統	46	permissible	a. 可允許的
22	request	n. 要求事項；v. 要求	47	entitle	v. 賦予資格
23	conference	n. 會議	48	holder	n. 持有者
24	entrance	n. 出入口	49	valid	a. 有效的
25	applicant	n. 申請者	50	validate	v. 確認，證實

🎧 RC_Test06-B.mp3

1	sewing machine	phr. 縫紉機	26	facilitate	v. 使容易，促進
2	affordability	n. 可負擔的費用	27	superb	a. 出色的
3	productivity	phr. 產能	28	commander	n. 指揮官
4	subjectivity	n. 主觀性	29	ride	n. 搭乘；乘坐的東西
5	attainability	n. 可達成	30	anniversary	n. 周年紀念
6	ahead of	phr. 提早～	31	world-class	a. 世界級的
7	concluding	a. 結束的，最後的	32	mechanical	a. 機械的
8	extremely	ad. 極度地	33	determine	v. 判定
9	cautiously	ad. 謹慎地	34	thankful	a. 慶幸的，感謝的
10	vainly	ad. 徒勞地	35	spot	v. 發現
11	occupation	n. 工作，居住	36	operational	a. 營運上的
12	supervise	v. 監督	37	manage	v. 經營，管理
13	redeem	v. 交換，贖回	38	overworked	a. 工作過度的
14	regularly	ad. 定期地	39	agreeable	a. 令人愉快的
15	recreational	a. 消遣的，娛樂的	40	acquaint	v. 使熟悉，使了解
16	once	conj. 一旦～的話	41	session	n. 課程，時間，會議
17	come up with	phr. 想出，找出	42	optional	a. 選擇性的
18	vital	a. 很重要的	43	gratitude	n. 感謝
19	punctual	a. 遵守時間的	44	appreciate	v. 感謝
20	come with	phr. 伴隨提供	45	questionnaire	n. 問卷調查
21	advisory	n. 預報，警報	46	pre-paid	a. 預付的
22	advocate	n. 支持者；v. 擁護	47	confidential	a. 祕密的
23	logging	n. 伐木	48	be entitled to	phr. 得到～，獲得～資格
24	overview	n. 介紹，大綱	49	on behalf of	phr. 代表～
25	description	n. 說明，敘述	50	by means of	phr. 以～方式

🎧 RC_Test06-C.mp3

#	單字	解釋	#	單字	解釋
1	in appreciation of	phr. 為感謝～	26	salary	n. 薪水
2	sponsor	v. 贊助	27	job opportunity	phr. 工作機會
3	host	v. 主辦，進行	28	consultation	n. 諮詢，商議
4	inventory	n. 庫存調查	29	personalize	v. 個人化
5	arrange	v. 整理，排列	30	go into effect	phr. 發揮效果
6	closure	n. 歇業，中斷，關閉	31	foundation	n. 設立
7	situate	v. 使位於	32	take part in	phr. 參與～
8	scenic	a. 風景好的	33	fest	n. 慶典，集會
9	wellness	n. 福祉，健康	34	inaugural	a. 開幕的，就職的
10	competent	a. 有能力的	35	manufacturer	n. 製造業者
11	nutritionist	n. 營養師	36	whopping	a. 非常巨大的
12	get into shape	phr. 練出健美體態，安排妥當	37	quarter	n. 季度
13	submit	v. 繳交	38	aircraft	n. 航空器
14	automotive	a. 汽車的	39	consequently	ad. 結果地
15	ship	v. 運送；n. 船	40	carrier	n. 運輸業
16	attach	v. 附加	41	bounce back from	phr. 回復到～
17	issue	v. 發行	42	downturn	n. 沉滯
18	claim	v. 索取，要求	43	recession	n. 衰退
19	delivery	n. 交貨	44	severely	ad. 嚴重地
20	full refund	phr. 全額退費	45	suppress	v. 壓制
21	declare	v. 申報	46	competition	n. 競爭
22	hospitalization	n. 住院治療	47	export	v. 出口
23	probationary	a. 實習中的	48	halt	v. 使中斷
24	dependent	n. 受扶養家屬	49	fare	n. 費用
25	come by	phr. 順道來訪	50	privilege	n. 特權

🎧 RC_Test06-D.mp3

1	dock	n. 碼頭；v. 停靠碼頭	26	hands-on	a. 親手的
2	changing room	phr. 更衣室	27	renowned	a. 有名的
3	drop by	phr. 順道去～	28	delectable	a. 好吃的，令人愉快的
4	give directions to	phr. 告知～的路線	29	gastronomic	a. 烹飪學的，美食的
5	stroll	n. 散步	30	scrumptious	a. 非常好吃的，心情好的
6	to no avail	phr. 徒勞地	31	accept	v. 接受
7	persistence	n. 堅持	32	opening	n. 開放
8	recover	v. 恢復	33	release	v. 發表，出示
9	dedication	n. 奉獻	34	address	v. 處理，解決
10	accordingly	ad. 照著，相應地	35	transfer	v. 帳戶轉帳
11	compensation	n. 補償	36	prefer	v. 偏好
12	impressed	a. 印象深刻的	37	recognize	v. 認識到
13	particularly	ad. 特別，尤其	38	specification	n. 明細，說明，詳述
14	confused	a. 混亂的，困惑的	39	courteous	a. 有禮的
15	temple	n. 寺廟	40	outgoing	a. 活潑的，外向的
16	sort out	phr. 解決	41	presentable	a. 可以見人的，漂亮的
17	sincerely	ad. 真心地	42	accuracy	n. 正確性
18	apologize	v. 道歉	43	relevant	a. 相關的
19	discrepancy	n. 不一致，錯誤	44	contribution	n. 貢獻
20	sightseeing	n. 觀光	45	impact	v. 影響；n. 衝擊
21	suffice	v. 充分	46	eagerly	ad. 渴望地
22	dine out	phr. 外出用餐	47	await	v. 等待
23	culinary	a. 料理的	48	appearance	n. 外表，外觀
24	cuisine	n. 料理，料理方法	49	match	v. 搭配，一致
25	discover	v. 發現，知道	50	identical	a. 一樣的

🎧 RC_Test07-A.mp3

1	governor	n. 州長	26	aspiring	a. 有抱負的
2	take charge of	phr. 負責～	27	entrepreneur	n. 企業家
3	relief effort	phr. 救災工作	28	column	n. 專欄，柱子
4	hurricane-affected	a. 受到颶風影響的	29	collapse	v. 倒塌
5	end up	phr. 結果～	30	solid	a. 堅固的，堅定的，確實的
6	permanently	ad. 永遠地	31	operator	n. 經營者
7	specialize	v. 專門做～，專攻	32	performer	n. 表演者
8	supply	n. 用品，補給品	33	have yet to	phr. 尚未～
9	reasonable	a. 合理的	34	possess	v. 擁有，持有
10	circulate	v. 傳閱，循環	35	meet	v. 滿足
11	memorandum	n. 備忘錄，紀錄	36	if so	phr. 倘若如此
12	customer	n. 顧客	37	courthouse	n. 法院
13	accountable	a. 負責的	38	appraiser	n. 鑑定人
14	accounted	a. 被負責的，被說明的	39	documentation	n. 資料
15	climb	n. 上升	40	assessment	n. 估價
16	head	a. 首席的；v. 率領	41	prove	v. 證明
17	preside	v. 主導	42	valuable	a. 貴重的
18	quickness	n. 快速	43	asset	n. 資產
19	extend	v. 擴張，延伸	44	platform	n. 月台
20	refreshment	n. 茶點，輕食	45	prohibit	v. 禁止
21	strive to	phr. 奮鬥～，致力～	46	confirm	v. 確認
22	committed	a. 忠實的	47	press conference	phr. 記者會
23	promotion	n. 晉升，宣傳	48	credential	n. 資格
24	colleague	n. 同事	49	meticulously	ad. 仔細地
25	hardly	ad. 幾乎不～	50	minimize	v. 最小化

🎧 RC_Test07-B.mp3

1	fraud	n. 詐欺，騙子	26	binding	n. 裝訂
2	outstanding	a. 傑出的	27	independence	n. 獨立
3	enterprise	n. 企業	28	revision	n. 修正，檢討
4	turnout	n. 出席者	29	gather	v. 聚集
4	compel	v. 強制	30	spectator	n. 觀眾
6	proposal	n. 提案，提議	31	vibrant	a. 充滿活力的
7	outstanding share	phr. 在外流通股數	32	observer	n. 觀眾
8	acquire	v. 取得，得到	33	groundbreaking	a. 突破性的
9	in honor of	phr. 慶祝～，紀念～	34	screening	n. 上映
10	part-time	a. 非正職的，算鐘點的	35	enrollment	n. 註冊，報名
11	heritage	n. 遺跡	36	drill	n. 訓練，反覆練習
12	article	n. 文章	37	submerge	v. 潛入水中
13	preservation	n. 保存	38	focus on	phr. 聚焦於～
14	evolution	n. 進化，發展	39	freestyle	n. 自由式
15	architecture	n. 建築	40	backstroke	n. 仰式
16	appreciation	n. 了解某物的價值	41	breaststroke	n. 蛙式
17	sales	a. 販賣的	42	butterfly	n. 蝶式
18	accurate	a. 精確的	43	attendance	n. 出席
19	critical	a. 批判的，嚴重的	44	reunion	n. 聚會
20	access code	phr. 密碼	45	attire	n. 衣著，盛裝
21	admittance	n. 進入	46	over-the-counter	a. 無處方籤的
22	retrieve	v. 恢復，尋回	47	medication	n. 醫藥品
23	technician	n. 技術人員	48	glow	n. 光采
24	resolve	v. 解決	49	state-of-the-art	a. 最先進的
25	compensate	v. 補償	50	acne	n. 痘痘

🎧 RC_Test07-C.mp3

1	utilize	v. 利用，善用	26	relieve	v. 舒緩
2	affordable	a. 負擔得起的，便宜的	27	partial	a, 一部分的，部分的
3	demonstration	n. 示範	28	preliminary	a. 預備的
4	diagnostic	a. 診斷的	29	respondent	n. 應答者
5	immediately	ad. 即時，即刻	30	collection	n. 收集
6	acknowledge	v. 告知，確認	31	yield	v. 結出（果實）；產生（效果）
7	receipt	n. 收據	32	insight	n. 洞察力，眼光
8	refer to	phr. 提及	33	require	v. 要求，需要
9	customized	a. 客製化的	34	unconventional	a. 不尋常的，非常規的
10	memento	n.紀念品，遺物	35	counterfeit	a. 偽造的，仿造的
11	qualify	v. 有資格	36	suspect	v. 懷疑
12	eligible	a. 有資格的	37	victimize	v. 受到損害，使犧牲
13	recharge	v. 充電	38	forge	v. 偽造，架構
14	fatigue	n. 疲勞	39	subject	a. 受支配的，須經～的
15	all the while	phr. 這當中	40	validation	n. 確認，評價
16	notion	n. 想法，概念	41	clearance	n. 承認，許可
17	metropolitan	a. 大都市的	42	authenticity	n. 真實性
18	hydrotherapy	n. 水療法	43	investigate	v. 調查
19	resemble	v. 類似，相像	44	verify	v. 確認
20	premises	n. 用地，經營場地	45	install	v. 設置
21	acupuncture	n. 針灸	46	application	n. （應用）程式
22	squirt	v. 噴	47	discourage	v. 不鼓勵，阻止
23	prick	v. 刺	48	material	n. 布料，材料
24	sensation	n. 感覺	49	appropriate	a. 適切的
25	inadvisable	a. 不宜的	50	apart from	phr. 加上～，除了～

🎧 RC_Test07-D.mp3

1	spacious	a. 寬廣的	26	book	v. 預約
2	enclose	v. 隨信附上	27	correspondent	n. 駐地記者，特派員
3	textile	n. 衣料，紡織品	28	forfeit	v. 剝奪，失去權利
4	raffle	n. 抽獎，摸彩	29	astral	a. 星星的，星形的
5	portable	a. 攜帶的	30	appliance	n. 家電
6	patronage	n. 惠顧，資助	31	suit	v. 滿足
7	dairy	a. 乳製品	32	patron	n. 顧客
8	primarily	ad. 基本地	33	fall under	phr. 所屬於～，～的一部分
9	entail	v. 必須，使承擔	34	residence	n. 居住地
10	drive	v. 鼓吹，趕走	35	in transit	phr. 在運輸中
11	market share	phr. 市佔率	36	nationwide	ad. 全國性的
12	rapport	n. （親密的）關係	37	comprise	v. 包含
13	hygiene	n. 衛生	38	drop	v. 落下
14	equivalent	n. 相等物	39	deteriorate	v. 惡化
15	facilitation	n. 便利，容易	40	bulk	a. 大量的；n. 大量
16	in compliance with	phr. 依照～	41	disappointed	a. 失望的，沮喪的
17	analysis	n. 分析	42	approach	n. 方式，方法
18	notable	a. 引人注目的，亮眼的	43	fundamental	a. 基本的
19	reputation	n. 名聲	44	principle	n. 原則，原理
20	examine	v. 檢查	45	quantity	n. 量
21	monitor	v. 監控	46	supervision	n. 管理，監督
22	recognition	n. 辨識度，認識	47	execution	n. 執行
23	tie	n. 關係，友誼	48	consist of	phr. 由～所構成
24	hold a job	phr. 擁有工作	49	registrar	n. 報名主任
25	proceed	v. 進行	50	instructional	a. 教學用的

🎧 RC_Test08-A.mp3

1	waterfall	n. 瀑布	26	institute	v. 開始
2	botanical	a. 植物的	27	compound	n. 住宅、工廠的內部
3	dress code	phr. 衣著規定	28	dormitory	n. 宿舍
4	baggage tag	phr. 行李標籤	29	layout	n. 配置
5	on hand	phr. 持有的	30	in the form of	phr. ～形式
6	cope with	phr. 應付	31	monetary	a. 金融的，金錢的
7	fast-paced	a. 步調快速的	32	option	n. 選擇（權）
8	sensitive	a. 敏感的	33	furthermore	ad. 而且
9	landmark	n. 地標	34	in spite of	phr. 儘管～
10	A and B alike	phr. A 和 B 都	35	rather than	phr. 而不是～
11	optimal	a. 最好的，最佳的	36	as soon as	phr. 一～就～
12	revenue	n. 營收	37	speed up	phr. 加速
13	circulation	n. 循環，流通	38	consideration	n. 考慮，思考
14	appointment	n. 約定	39	celebrity	n. 名人
15	highway	n. 高速公路	40	cook	n. 廚師
16	comfortable	a. 舒適的，便利的	41	scarce	a. 不足的
17	enviable	a. 羨慕的	42	convey	v. 表達
18	profitable	a. 有利的	43	refined	a. 精煉的
19	conducive	a. 有幫助的	44	load	v. 裝載
20	lessen	v. 減少，降下	45	in-demand	a. 需求很大的
21	residential	a. 住宅的	46	on duty	phr. 值班中
22	condominium	n. 公寓，大樓	47	bill	v. 開帳單
23	occasionally	ad. 偶爾	48	accommodation	n. 住宿費
24	previously	ad. 之前地	49	outreach	n. 慈善活動
25	refrain	v. 節制，抑制	50	damaged	a. 破損的

RC_Test08-B.mp3

#	單字	解釋	#	單字	解釋
1	outage	n. 停電，停水	26	packet	n. 小包裹，小袋
2	clearness	n. 分明的，鮮明的	27	estate	n. 地產，土地
3	favorable	a. 好的，好意的	28	beachfront	a. 靠海濱的
4	catering	n. 團體外燴	29	lot	n. 空地
5	fierce	a. 強烈的	30	shortly	ad. 馬上
6	cargo	n. 貨物	31	enlightened	a. 開明的
7	patronize	v. 愛用	32	outspoken	a. 直言不諱的
8	community	n. 居民	33	cast	v. 選角；投射
9	represent	v. 代表	34	starring role	phr. 主角
10	social function	phr. 社交聚會，社交派對	35	engaging	a. 魅力的
11	well-defined	a. 明確的，清楚的	36	subscribe	v. 訂閱
12	grant	v. 給與；n. 補助金	37	job openings	phr. 空缺，徵人
13	maintain	v. 持續，維持	38	onset	n. 攻擊，開始
14	newly-released	a. 新上市的	39	housing	n. 住宅
15	functionality	n. 機能，機能性	40	otherwise	ad. 否則
16	comparable	a. 可比較的，比得上的	41	as always	phr. 一如往常
17	momentous	a. 重大的	42	up-and-coming	a. 顯露頭角的，很有前途的
18	operative	a. 有效的，作業的；n. 技工，諜報員	43	retro	n. 復古品，復古風
19	practical	a. 實用的	44	beverage	n. 飲料
20	apply for	phr. 應徵	45	frustrating	a. 失望的，有挫折感的
21	franchise	n. 連鎖店經營權	46	craftsman	n. 工藝家
22	enhance	v. 向上提高	47	token	n. 標誌
23	reference	n. 推薦書	48	handicraft	n. 手工藝品，手製品
24	distant	a. 遠的，遠離的	49	importer	n. 進口商，進口業者
25	predictable	a. 可預測的	50	boutique	n. 賣場，精品店

🎧 RC_Test08-C.mp3

1	prompt	v. 激勵	26	capacity	n. 能力，承受力
2	dose	n. 藥物等的一劑	27	set up	phr. 成立～，安置
3	side effect	phr. 副作用	28	arrange	v. 計畫，安排
4	rash	n. 疹子	29	evaluate	v. 評價
5	shot	n. 注射	30	legal	a. 法規的，法律的
6	indicate	v. 指示，暗示	31	intellectual property	phr. 智慧產權
7	pharmaceutical	a. 製藥的	32	elect	v. 選出
8	underway	a. 進行中的	33	attorney	n. 律師
9	expiration date	phr. 有效期限	34	deliver a lecture	phr. 演説，演講
10	adverse	a. 有害的，否定的	35	venue	n. 場所
11	toxic	a. 有毒性的，有害的	36	cutoff date	phr. 截止日
12	approve	v. 認可，承認	37	flourishing	a. 興旺的，茂盛的
13	free-of-charge	a. 免費	38	hail	v. 被承認，歡呼，描寫
14	intend	v. 意圖	39	reveal	v. 展現，顯露
15	overbook	v. 過量預訂	40	athlete	n. 運動員
16	based in	phr. 總公司在～	41	obligation	n. 義務
17	degree	n. 學位	42	put aside	phr. 擱在一邊，延後
18	salary package	phr. 薪水，工資	43	sole	a. 單獨的，唯一的
19	allowance	n. 費用，補貼，零用錢	44	heir	n. 繼承人，嗣子
20	cover letter	phr. 附信，求職信	45	groom	v. 訓練，使準備
21	experienced	a. 有經驗的	46	witness	v. 目擊；n. 證人
22	recruitment	n. 徵人	47	boom	v. 成功，蓬勃發展
23	requirement	n. 資格條件	48	venture	v. 冒險
24	fluency	n. 熟練，順暢	49	lay off	phr. 解雇
25	willingness	n. 意向，意圖	50	well-paying	a. 待遇很好的

RC_Test08-D.mp3

#	單字	詞性釋義	#	單字	詞性釋義
1	inspire	v. 啟發，激勵	26	dynamic	a. 動態的
2	imagine	v. 想像	27	editorial	a. 編輯的；n. 社論
3	relief	n. 舒適，消遣	28	headquarters	n. 總部
4	spotless	a. 一塵不染的	29	from time to time	phr. 有時候
5	studio apartment	phr. 小套房	30	assign	v. 指派
6	tidy	v. 整理，收拾	31	conceal	v. 隱匿
7	leisure	a. 休閒的	32	report on	phr. 報導
8	biweekly	a. 隔週的	33	shut down	phr. 終止，停止
9	strip	v. 拆掉	34	grateful	a. 感謝的
10	housekeeping	n. 家事，家務活	35	warranty	n.（品質）保證，保證書
11	round-the-clock	a. 24 小時的	36	a series of	phr. 一系列的
12	inquiry	n. 詢問	37	malfunction	v. 機器故障
13	additional	a. 追加的	38	make up for	phr. 賠償
14	currently	ad. 現在	39	extension	n. 延長，擴大
15	possibility	n. 可能性	40	reimbursement	n. 補償，退款
16	photocopier	n. 影印機	41	anxiety	n. 擔心，顧慮，不安
17	user-friendly	a. 方便使用的，考慮使用者需求的	42	go through	phr. 經驗，經歷
18	transmit	v. 轉送	43	beneficial	a. 有幫助的
19	energy-efficient	a. 節能的	44	corresponding	a. 相對應的
20	sleep mode	phr. 睡眠模式	45	effective	a. 有效的
21	precision	a. 準確	46	handle	v. 處理
22	sturdy	a. 堅固的，牢固的	47	sustainable	a. 撐得住的; 能承受的
23	phone directory	phr. 電話簿	48	task	n. 工作，課題
24	outdated	a. 老的，舊的	49	take place	phr. 舉行，發生
25	uphold	v. 維持	50	graduate	n. 畢業生，研究生

🎧 RC_Test09-A.mp3

1	delegate	n. 代表，使節	26	declaration	n. 宣告
2	at the latest	phr. 最晚	27	adaptation	n. 適應
3	notify	v. 通知	28	chemicals	n. 化學物質
4	be out of town	phr.（因出差等）出城	29	skin irritation	phr. 皮膚發炎，皮膚刺激
5	pursue a career in	phr. 朝著～發展事業	30	Mediterranean	a. 地中海的
6	survey	n. 調查	31	passenger vessel	phr. 客機
7	sculpture	n. 雕刻品	32	perception	n. 感知，理解
8	scholarship	n. 獎學金	33	direction	n. 指示
9	notification	n. 通知	34	provision	n. 準備
10	proceed with	phr. 繼續～	35	restriction	n. 限制
11	occur	v. 發生	36	renovation	n. 修理，翻新
12	construction	n. 建設，工事	37	defective	a. 有缺陷的
13	definite	a. 明顯的	38	replacement	n. 更換
14	definition	n. 定義，清晰	39	endangered	a. 瀕臨絕種的，處於危險的
15	plumber	n. 水管工人	40	experimental	a. 實驗性的
16	highly	ad. 非常	41	summarily	ad. 概要地；立刻
17	electrician	n. 電工，電力技術者	42	concentrate	v. 集中
18	reconstruct	v. 重建，修復	43	originate	v. 來自，引起
19	state	n. 國家，狀態	44	public relation	phr. 公關
20	sufficiently	ad. 充分地	45	promote	v. 廣告；促進；晉升
21	variable	a. 變動的	46	volcanic activity	phr. 火山活動
22	essential	a. 必要性的	47	meteor	n. 流星
23	versatile	a. 多才多藝的	48	extinction	n. 絕種
24	organizer	n. 準備者，主辦單位	49	investor	n. 投資者
25	computation	n. 計算	50	outcome	n. 結果

🎧 RC_Test09-B.mp3

1	agreement	n. 協議	26	accessible	a. 易接近的；可使用的
2	recruit	v. 聘用	27	look forward to	phr. 期待～
3	mandatory	a. 強制性的	28	celebration	n. 慶祝活動
4	authorization	n. 授權	29	in the meantime	phr. 於此同時
5	gain	v. 獲得	30	hesitant	a. 遲疑的
6	secluded	a. 與世隔絕的，隱退的，隱居的	31	concerned	a. 擔心的
7	formative	a. 形成的，造成的	32	anxious	a. 不安的
8	adopt	v. 採用	33	officially	ad. 正式地
9	laboratory	n. 實驗室	34	straighten	v. 弄直，挺直
10	substantial	a. 充分的，實在的	35	semi-permanent	a. 半永久性的
11	altogether	ad. 完全地	36	depending on	phr. 取決於～
12	halfway	ad. 中途	37	vary	v. 不同
13	variety	n. 多樣化，種類	38	in an effort to	phr. 為～努力
14	component	n. 成分	39	costume party	phr. 化妝舞會
15	tentatively	ad. 暫時性地	40	audience	n. 觀眾
16	house	v. 收容，給與房屋	41	achieve	v. 成就，達成
17	in conjunction with	phr. 和～一起	42	establish	v. 建立，設定
18	finalize	v. 完成，結束	43	lobby	v. 對議員遊說
19	repair	v. 修理	44	mandate	v. 授權
20	assist	v. 幫助	45	prosperity	n. 繁榮
21	orientation	n. 新成員說明會	46	legislator	n. 國會議員
22	number	n. 演奏樂曲；上演節目	47	prevention	n. 預防
23	chairperson	n. 主席	48	privatize	v. 民營化，私營化
24	get to know	phr. 使知道～	49	excerpt	n. 摘錄
25	update	n. 最新情報	50	give away	phr. 分發

🎧 RC_Test09-C.mp3

1	consign	v. 委託	26	lane	n. 車道
2	respectfully	ad. 恭敬地	27	detour	n. 繞道
3	sign	v. 簽合約	28	still	ad. 依舊
4	stringed instrument	phr. 弦樂器	29	heavy congestion	phr. 交通堵塞
5	kit	n. 成套（工具或物件）	30	drainage	n. 排水
6	popularity	n. 普及，流行	31	flood	v. 淹沒
7	vacancy	n. 空間，空缺	32	remain	v. 維持
8	analyst	n. 分析師	33	donation	n. 捐獻
9	credit representative	phr. 信用代表	34	diminish	v. 減少
10	terms	n. 條件	35	benefactor	n. 支援者
11	debt	n. 負債	36	incapable of	phr. 不能～
12	measure	n. 措施	37	board meeting	phr. 董事會
13	bachelor's degree	phr. 學士學位	38	scholar	n. 獎學金獲得者；學者
14	command	n.（語言）能力，應用力	39	a majority of	phr. 多數
15	undergo	v. 經歷	40	solution	n. 解決對策
16	memorial	a. 紀念的	41	aid	n. 幫助，救助
17	groundbreaking ceremony	phr. 動土典禮	42	portion	n. 一部分
18	surgical	a. 外科的	43	carry out	phr. 進行
19	outpatient	n. 門診病人	44	generate	v. 產生
20	timeframe	n. 時間表	45	solicit	v. 要求
21	diverse	a. 多樣的	46	own	v. 擁有
22	pharmacy	n. 藥局	47	face	v. 面臨
23	conserve	v. 保護	48	resign	v. 辭職
24	steady	a. 持續的，平穩的	49	worthwhile	a. 有價值的
25	outer	a. 外廓的，外部的	50	rest assured	phr. 可以相信的，可以放心的

🎧 RC_Test09-D.mp3

1	valued	a. 重要的，貴重的	26	numerous	a. 很多的
2	operating hours	phr. 營業時間	27	respectively	ad. 各自地
3	follow up on	phr. 後續處理	28	beat	v. 打擊，打敗
4	plus	prep. 加上	29	last	v. 持續，繼續
5	quote	n. 報價單	30	counterpart	n. 有對應關係的人，對方
6	rental	n. 租借；a. 供出租的	31	involved	a. 有關聯的，包含的
7	utensil	n. 餐具，用具	32	culmination	n. 高潮，頂點
8	wait staff	phr. 服務人員，服務生	33	discussion	n. 討論
9	be of service to	phr. 對～提供服務	34	responsible	a. 有責任的
10	nearly	ad. 幾乎	35	contestant	n.（大會、比賽等的）參加者
11	assortment	n. 種類，分類	36	broadcast	v. 廣播，播送
12	whereas	conj. 反之～	37	remarkable	a. 卓越的
13	separately	ad. 另外，個別地	38	affair	n. 活動，聚會，業務
14	preparation	n. 準備	39	keynote address	phr. 主題演講
15	do business with	phr. 做生意	40	honoree	n. 得獎人
16	reorganization	n. 組織重組	41	trophy presentation	phr. 頒獎典禮
17	deposit	n. 訂金；v. 付（保證金）	42	acclaim	v. 稱讚
18	develop	v. 開發	43	in place of	phr. 代替～
19	quarterly	ad. 每季	44	shooting	n. 拍攝
20	preference	n. 偏愛	45	review	n. 檢討
21	enthusiast	n. 愛好者，熱衷	46	take the liberty of	phr. 冒昧地，不顧禮節地
22	party	n. 當事人，集會	47	draft	n. 草案
23	issue	n. 發行	48	confusion	n. 疑惑，騷動
24	in partnership with	phr. 和～合作	49	preview	n. 試映會
25	attract	v. 吸引，引起	50	edit	v. 修改，修正，編輯

🎧 RC_Test10-A.mp3

1	conclude	v. 結束，有結論	26	range	n. 範圍
2	reassignment	n. 再指派，再分配	27	coordinate	v. 協調，適合
3	official	n. 公務員，職員； a. 公務上的，正式的	28	basement	n. 地下室
4	push through	phr. 使完成，促成	29	decline	v. 減少，拒絕；n. 減少
5	deliberately	ad. 故意地	30	estimate	v. 估算；n. 推估值
6	deliberation	n. 商討，深思熟慮	31	outstanding balance	phr. 未支付的金額
7	a couple of	phr. 兩個的，數個的	32	manual	n. 手冊
8	no later than	phr. 最晚到～	33	giveaway	n. 贈品
9	principal	a. 主要的	34	enormously	ad. 相當地，巨大地
10	order	n. 訂單，順序；v. 下訂單	35	revised	a. 修訂的
11	expense	n. 支出，費用	36	given that	phr. 考慮～的話
12	paperwork	n. 文書工作	37	enthusiastic	a. 熱烈的
13	potential	a. 潛在的	38	row	n. 排，列
14	participation	n. 參加	39	admit	v. 認可
15	Chamber of Commerce	phr. 商會	40	transfer	v. 搬動，移動
16	rampant	a. 猖獗的	41	attend	v. 參加
17	deforestation	n. 砍伐森林	42	be held	phr. 被舉辦
18	successively	ad. 相繼地	43	industrialized nation	phr. 工業化國家
19	certificate	n. 證明書	44	ignition	n. 著火
20	retail outlet	phr. 零售店	45	fulfillment	n. 達成，實踐
21	attain	v. 取得	46	pick out	phr. 選擇
22	coin-operated	a. 投幣式的	47	count on	phr. 相信～
23	assume	v. 擔當，認為	48	steep	a. 陡峭的
24	affluent	a. 富裕的	49	concrete	a. 具體的
25	influential	a. 有影響力的	50	loaded	a. 滿滿的

🎧 RC_Test10-B.mp3

1	temporary	a. 暫時的	26	initiative	n. 倡議
2	in relation to	phr. 和～比較，跟～有關	27	work ethic	phr. 工作倫理
3	markedly	ad. 顯著地	28	function	v. 起作用，行使職責
4	exceptionally	ad. 例外地，異常地	29	definitive	a. 決定性的，最後的
5	confide	v. 透露（祕密等）	30	in detail	phr. 詳細地
6	motivation	n. 刺激，動機	31	feel free to	phr. 隨意
7	perception	n. 認知，感覺	32	disapprove	v. 不贊成
8	streamline	v. 使有效率，簡化	33	benefit	v. 有優勢
9	superior	n. 上司；a. 優秀的	34	be composed of	phr. 由～組成
10	at least	phr. 至少	35	vocalist	n. 歌手，歌唱家
11	in advance	phr. 事先	36	top	v. 登上高峰
12	satellite office	phr. 分社，分局	37	lasting	a. 持續的
13	receptacle	n. 貯藏所，存放的地方	38	establishment	n. 設立
14	reward	v. 給予報酬	39	selective	a. 選擇的
15	quota	n. 配額	40	persuade	v. 說服
16	throughout	prep. ～期間	41	carpentry	n. 木匠
17	award	v. 授予，給予	42	home improvement	phr. 居家修繕，住宅維修
18	accumulate	v. 累積	43	fine art	phr. 美術品
19	incentive	n. 獎勵；a. 有獎金的	44	completion	n. 完成，完了
20	elaborate	a. 精緻的	45	run	v.（在多長期間內）持續
21	legislative	a. 立法的	46	inaccessible	a. 無法使用的
22	work closely	phr. 密切合作	47	revitalization	n. 復興，給予活力
23	deserve	v. 有資格做～	48	minutes	n. 會議記錄
24	financial analyst	phr. 財務分析師	49	uniform	a. 統一的
25	display	v. 展現	50	bulletin board	phr. 佈告欄

🎧 RC_Test10-C.mp3

1	simplify	v. 簡單化	26	creep in	phr. 擠進去
2	in line with	phr. 和～一起，根據～	27	handy	a. 方便的，有用的
3	publicize	v. 公告，通知	28	distraction	n. 分心
4	proficiency	n. 精通；熟練	29	surrounding	n. 周遭環境
5	distinct	a. 明確的，分明的	30	within reach	phr. 伸手可及的地方
6	linguist	n. 語言學家	31	nature	n. 性格，本質
7	impressive	a. 突出的，給人留下印象的	32	coworker	n. 同事，一起工作的人
8	tailor	v. 使合適；n.（男裝）裁縫師	33	workload	n. 工作量
9	abroad	ad. 國外地，海外地	34	outsource	v. 外包
10	commonly	ad. 一般地，通常地	35	rate	v. 訂出順序，評價
11	found	v. 成立	36	proximity	n. 接近
12	turn down	phr. 拒絕，回絕	37	turn in	phr. 提交
13	managerial	a. 管理的	38	hand in	phr. 繳交
14	look for	phr. 尋找	39	evaluation	n. 審查，評價
15	pursue	v. 追求，從事	40	payroll	n. 發薪，發薪對象名單
16	be familiar with	phr. 和～很熟知，和～很親近	41	expenditure	n. 支出，經費
17	scout	v. 找，發掘	42	hasten	v. 催促，趕快
18	misunderstanding	n. 誤會，誤解	43	sales agent	phr. 銷售員
19	terminate	v. 終了，結束	44	conform	v. 遵守
20	contract	n. 合約，約定	45	regulation	n. 規定
21	helplessness	n. 無能為力	46	crop	n. 農產品
22	pile up	phr. 累積，變多	47	infestation	n.（害蟲/昆蟲）大批出沒、繁殖
23	due date	phr. 截止日	48	no longer	phr. 不再～
24	prioritize	v. 決定優先順序	49	storage	n. 儲存倉庫，儲藏所
25	overwhelm	v. 征服，淹沒	50	Fahrenheit	a. 華氏的

RC_Test10-D.mp3

1	initial	a. 初步的	26	registration form	phr. 報名表
2	blemish	n. 不良，缺點，疤痕	27	screen	v. 遮擋，審查
3	gross	a. 毛額的，總額的	28	head office	phr. 總公司
4	entirety	n. 全部	29	familiar with	phr. 熟知～
5	starch	n. 澱粉，太白粉	30	guideline	n. 方針
6	agent	n. 藥品，物質	31	esteemed	a. 受人尊敬的
7	apron	n. 圍裙	32	personality	n. 名人，性格
8	sterilization	n. 消毒，殺菌	33	cordially	ad. 真心地
9	practice	n. 業務，實踐	34	demystify	v. 解出謎題，讓人簡單理解地說明
10	machinery	n. 機器	35	premiere	n. 首映會
11	inspect	v. 檢查	36	coveted	a. 渴望的，渴求的
12	sort	v. 分類	37	explore	v. 探險
13	refrigerate	v. 冷藏	38	historian	n. 歷史學者
14	encounter	v. 面臨	39	entrant	n. 參加者
15	accommodate	v. 容納	40	critic	n. 評論家
16	rough	a. 大概的，粗略的	41	tasting	n. 試飲會
17	hesitate	v. 猶豫	42	acidity	n. 酸性
18	extension number	phr. 分機號碼	43	look into	phr. 調查
19	brand identity	phr. 品牌特性	44	turn out	phr. 表明，呈現
20	measurement	n. 大小，測量	45	conduct	v. 實施，實行
21	coarse	a. 粗糙的	46	lack	v. 不足～，沒有～
22	approximate	a. 大約的	47	dull	a. 枯燥無味的
23	uneven	a. 不均勻的	48	procure	v. 採購，獲得
24	merger	n. 合併	49	supplier	n. 供應商
25	latest	a. 最新的	50	take off	phr. 退出，中斷

別擔心多益考題更新

多益參考書唯一經典，首度改版！
品質不變，分析更詳細！

題・庫・大・全

附單字記憶
MP3

附 2 MP3 ＋
獨創互動聽力
答題訓練光碟

全新！NEW TOEIC 新多益閱讀題庫大全
作者／David Cho 定價／880 元
雙書裝訂／832 頁／21x29.7 CM

全新！NEW TOEIC 新多益聽力題庫大全
作者／David Cho 定價／880 元
雙書裝訂／568 頁／21x29.7 CM

台灣、韓國幫助最多考生大幅進步的
TOP.1 暢銷閱讀、聽力題庫

1. 系統化分析多益題型，學習、實測一本到位。

2. 根據能力診斷測驗，量身訂做最適合自己的學習計畫。

3. 每月實際入場調查，全面更新超過 1000 道試題。

4. 配合眾多考生需求，增加題目份量，練習更充足。

，我翻新，你放心！

多益模考書唯一經典，首度改版！
品質不變，猜題更準確！

題·庫·解·析

1000 題 10 回飽足模擬測驗！
保證獲得多益黃金認證！

1. 新多益測驗全真模擬試題 10 回完整收錄！做完等於參加過 10 次多益考試。

2. 考題由每月實際派員入場調查後統計分析而出，有如現場直擊多益命題老師出題！

3. 根據能力診斷測驗，量身訂做最適合自己的學習計畫。

4. 超級詳細明瞭的解題分析，清楚了解自己對錯的原因。

題目根據近5年考題方向全面翻新
猜題更準，分數更高！

NEW TOEIC 新多益單字大全【實戰測驗更新版】
作者／David Cho 定價／ 499 元
雙書裝訂／ 560 頁／ 17x23 CM

【實戰測驗更新版】改了甚麼？
我們將所有的多益模擬測驗全部換新！
多益考題方向並非一成不變，
能跟著考題方向翻新題目，才是負責的單字書。

第一本，能跟著考試題目進化，
題目同時更新的多益單字書！

第一本，能針對個人不同需求，
個別強化弱點的多益單字書！

國家圖書館出版品預行編目資料

全新NEW TOEIC新多益閱讀題庫解析／
Hackers Academia 著. --初版.-- 新北市中和區：
國際學村, 2014.05
　　面；　　公分

ISBN 978-986-6077-75-3（平裝附光碟片）

1. 多益測驗

805.1895

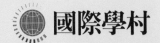

臺灣廣廈出版集團　　國際學村

全新！NEW TOEIC新多益閱讀題庫解析

作者	Hackers Academia
譯者	蘇慧容、賴維妤、李聖婷、Lora Liu
出版者	台灣廣廈出版集團
	國際學村出版社
發行人／社長	江媛珍
地址	235新北市中和區中山路二段359巷7號2樓
電話	886-2-2225-5777
傳真	886-2-2225-8052
電子信箱	TaiwanMansion@booknews.com.tw
網址	http://www.booknews.com.tw
總編輯	伍峻宏
執行編輯	徐淳輔
美術編輯	許芳莉
排版／製版／印刷／裝訂／壓片	菩薩蠻／詠富／皇甫／明和／超群
法律顧問	第一國際法律事務所　余淑杏律師
	北辰著作權事務所　蕭雄淋律師
代理印務及圖書總經銷	知遠文化事業有限公司
地址	222新北市深坑區北深路三段155巷25號5樓
訂書電話	886-2-2664-8800
訂書傳真	886-2-2664-8801
港澳地區經銷	和平圖書有限公司
地址	香港柴灣嘉業街12號百樂門大廈17樓
電話	852-2804-6687
傳真	852-2804-6409
出版日期	2015年5月4刷
郵撥帳號	18788328
郵撥戶名	台灣廣廈有聲圖書有限公司

（購書未滿300元需外加30元郵資，滿300元（含）以上免郵資）

郵票黏貼處

台灣廣廈出版集團

235 新北市中和區中山路二段359巷7號2樓
2F, NO. 7, LANE 359, SEC. 2, CHUNG-SHAN RD., CHUNG-HO DIST.,
NEW TAIPEI CITY, TAIWAN, R.O.C.

 國際學村　編輯部　收

請沿虛線剪下

全新！NEW
TOEIC
新多益閱讀題庫解析

All Fresh
新鮮直送
不添加
無效題

國際學村 讀者資料服務回函

感謝您購買這本書！
為使我們對讀者的服務能夠更加完善，
請您詳細填寫本卡各欄，
寄回本公司或傳真至（02）2225-8052，
我們將不定期寄給您我們的出版訊息。

● 您購買的書 全新！NEW TOEIC新多益閱讀題庫解析 _____
● 您 的 大 名 _____
● 購 買 書 店 _____
● 您 的 性 別 □男 □女
● 婚　　　姻 □已婚 □單身
● 出 生 日 期 _____年 _____ 月 _____ 日
● 您 的 職 業 □製造業 □銷售業 □金融業 □資訊業 □學生 □大眾傳播 □自由業
　　　　　　　□服務業 □軍警 □公 □教 □其他
● 職　　　位 □負責人 □高階主管 □中級主管 □一般職員 □專業人員 □其他
● 教 育 程 度 □高中以下（含高中）□大專 □研究所 □其他
● 您通常以何種方式購書？
　□逛書店 □劃撥郵購 □電話訂購 □傳真訂購 □網路訂購 □銷售人員推薦 □其他
● 您從何得知本書消息？
　□逛書店 □報紙廣告 □親友介紹 □廣告信函 □廣播節目 □網路 □書評
　□銷售人員推薦 □其他
● 您想增加哪方面的知識？或對哪種類別的書籍有興趣？
　_____
　_____
● 通訊地址 □□□ _____
　_____
● E-Mail _____
● 本公司恪守個資保護法，請問您給的 E-Mail 帳號是否願意收到本集團出版物相關
　資料 □願意 □不願意
● 聯絡電話 _____
● 您對本書封面及內文設計的意見
　_____

● 您是否有興趣接受敝社新書資訊？　□沒有 □有
● 給我們的建議/請列出本書的錯別字
　_____
　_____

請沿虛線剪下